FEVERS AND CHILLS

jon manchip white

FEVERS AND CHILLS/three extravagant tales

nightclimber
the game of troy
the garden game

A Foul Play Press Book
The Countryman Press
Woodstock, Vermont

This edition published in 1983 by Foul Play Press, a division of The Countryman Press,
Inc., Woodstock, Vermont 05091

introduction

"I wants to make your flesh creep", says the fat boy to the old lady in *The Pickwick Papers*: and the three tales that follow can certainly be viewed as "Creepers"—or as what Robert Louis Stevenson used to refer to as his "Crawlers".

I had written a number of "straight" realistic novels before beginning to toy with the thriller and adventure story, and it was a natural urge to stretch and enlarge the genre that prompted me to cast around for a title that would embody what these books were trying to do, and distinguish them from my other types of fiction. "Extravagant Tales" conveys, I think, something of their bizarre, melodramatic and baroque quality.

They are not, of course, novels at all, but belong to the ancient and primitive tradition of the romance. That is to say, they do not concern themselves with the social preoccupations of a George Eliot, a Trollope, or a James, but stem from the older Gothic line of a Mary Shelley, an Emily Brontë, a Poe, a Hawthorne, a Stevenson. Below the modern surface the reader will encounter much of the familiar furnishings of Gothic and High Romantic stories: strange castles, secret gardens, dungeons, battlements, drawbridges, inaccessible towers and hidden passageways. These overlay, in turn, a wealth of the archetypal paraphernalia—caverns, mazes, oceans, forests and the like—that are the basic ingredients of romance.

There is another influence at work that will be apparent to many readers: Surrealism, as evidenced in the fantastic fictions of such writers as André Dhôtel and Julien Gracq. In fact a later novel of mine, *Death By Dreaming* (1981), goes far beyond the present trio and is much more "Surrealistic" and oneiric in texture and format. But for a number of reasons Surrealism has not managed to acclimatize itself to English and American literature, as it has to French and Spanish literature, and it is unwise if not almost impossible for the writer in English to go the whole Surrealist hog. In any event, as a Welshman brought up in England, I find that in my case Celtic nature has been subjected to Anglo-Saxon nurture, with the result that the wilder imagination of the Celt has been schooled by the order and discipline of the Englishman. It is therefore not really feasible for me to experiment too radically with such Surrealist procedures as automatism and the unimpeded exploration of the unconscious. For me, the unconscious must come to terms with a good prose style, and with an abiding concern with the conduct of a shapely and well-directed narrative. Like André Pieyre de Mandiargues, with his concept of the story as " a guided dream", I remain, at least for the present, on the fringe of Surrealism.

Here, then, I offer for the reader's enjoyment some examples of my "Creepies" and "Crawlies". Though they fall into the class of literary diversions, written with the *main gauche*, they are nonetheless the product of a certain feeling of sustained compulsion and mysterious anguish. They are bad dreams, executed with the crystalline strokes that characterize our nightmares and make them memorable.

I hope the ominous and disturbing atmosphere of my "Extravagant Tales" will communicate itself to the reader, inducing a corresponding sense of uneasy pleasure.

—Jon Manchip White

nightclimber

¿Qué es la vida? Un frenesí.
¿Qué es la vida? Un ilusión,
una sombra, una ficción,
y el mejor bien es pequeño;
que toda la vida es sueño,
y los sueños sueños son.

Calderón: La Vida es Sueño

I

It is always night.

There is so little traffic that it seems to be as late as four or five o'clock in the morning. It is foggy. The cold is so piercing that it must be the dead of winter. To judge from the style of the street and the buildings, I am near the center of a big city. I cannot tell what city it is. For some reason I always feel it might be London. It could be somewhere in Bloomsbury. It has the feel and atmosphere of somewhere in the neighbourhood of the British Museum.

The city is a great metropolis. The banks of fog rolling towards me are stained with sulphurous yellow dirt and suffused by the glow of the invisible sodium lamps. When it closes around me I feel as though I am being wrapped in a mound of pus-stained cotton wool.

The street strikes me as being enormously wide. I am glad there is almost no traffic. I have lost my bearings in the fog and am weaving from one side of the road to the other. I have no idea in which direction I am walking—but I have no feeling of being lost. I am not frightened or panic-stricken. This is a very unpleasant dream, but it is not a nightmare. At least, not yet. My principal sensation is more like a numbness or a sadness, a sense of loss or desperation. There is no obvious cause for this depressed state of mind. It could be produced by the bitter weather, the vacancy of the streets, or the emptiness of the hour.

From time to time I catch the muffled rattle of a taxi or the smoother murmur of a limousine. The wheels hiss past within a few feet of me. Although I never catch sight of them I am not alarmed. I know by instinct that this is not a dream connected with being knocked down or killed by a vehicle. I know from the beginning that it must eventually become something more special and more bizarre.

In spite of my feeling of having lost or mislaid something I am also aware that I am moving towards the performance of a particular task. I have no notion of what it is. Now and again the fog thins a little, and through a ragged opening I catch a glimpse of a soaring lamppost or the face of a newly built office building. The buildings in the street are all high ones.

It is now that I catch sight of the tallest building in the street. It looms up directly in front of me. At this moment the fog always shreds away into an icy mist, a veil no thicker than a grimy lace curtain. I can see the entire bulk of the building as it stands sideways to me.

The building is huge. It looks as though it can only recently have been completed. The contractors' signboard still stands outside the entrance, and the name of the main contractor stands out boldly among the names of the smaller fry. I can make out the Gothic letters of the main contractor's name while I am still more than a hundred yards away: M. P. MIDDLEMASS AND COMPANY.

The edges of the building are as straight as the edges of a metal ruler. It is not an attractive building. It has no charm or frivolity, no individuality. It is a steel-framed box, an enormous chicken coop. As soon as I catch sight of that building I know I hate and dread it.

I also know that I am compelled to climb it.

I stop in the center of the road and survey it carefully. Slowly I crane my head back and try to count the number of stories. Twenty-seven? Twenty-eight? Thirty? The darkened windows are spaced with the regularity of the banks of switches on a mammoth computer.

At the thought of the computer my mind suffers a curious moment of confusion. Am I staring at an office building or staring in fact at some mist-shrouded piece of machinery?

Through the widening gap in the fog I can see the summit of the building and count the number of floors for the second time. Thirty. Beyond the sharp rim of the distant parapet I can see the serene blackness of the sky, studded with majestic stars. It gives me a fleeting sensation of certainty and peace. Otherwise the horror of what I must now do is flooding quickly over me.

Now I can make out a single square of pale orange in the topmost tier of windows. Someone is still in the building, at this abandoned hour. As I look up at the window I am conscious of a feeling of hopelessness. I must climb up there, but how am I to do it? I am out of condition these days—out of practice. I know perfectly well that when I wake I will call myself a fool for not having had enough sense to run away; but during the dream this obvious solution never once occurs to me. All I know is that I have been wandering for many hours (days? months? years?) in order to reach this particular building and climb into that pale-orange window. There is no moral or social pressure on me to do this. Nobody stands in the street urging me to do it, or calling me a coward if I don't. There is no one to stop me if I turn on my heel and walk in the other direction. It is simply that my destination is inevitable. I have no choice.

In spite of the cold I am sweating beneath my clothes. Fear is trickling through my limbs as I walk towards the main entrance, which is my obvious starting point. The slablike portico gives access to a pair of narrow vertical slots traversing the entire front of the building. Between each story runs a stringcourse bisecting each slot and producing an awkward overhang. Fortunately the stringcourses are shallow and negotiable. They will provide a ledge to crawl along when I reach the top window.

It never crosses my mind that what I am going to do could be illegal or even impossible. Who is there to interfere? The street is deserted.

The fog swirls up and catches at my lungs. I flex my fingers and begin the climb. There are plenty of handholds in spite of the apparent smoothness of the surface. My arms and legs move rapidly and with an easy regularity. I am not conscious of my unusual sense of strain. I ascend one of the slots, using the normal technique for climbing a rock chimney.

I reach the halfway stage without a trace of fatigue. Apart from a tightness in my chest (forty-one next birthday!) I am actually enjoying myself. The load of dread is lightening. I grow more confident. None of this is as hard as I thought it would be. I lean back and take a rest whenever a wisp of fog curls round my mouth and makes me cough. The orange glow from the window is closer. Wedged in my concrete chimney, I even risk a brief glance downwards.

A mistake. A bad one. My stomach turns over. The terror rises inside me with such violence that I am almost jerked off my perch and sent cartwheeling over and over onto the asphalt below. This is the ancient terror that has been locked inside me for years. One glance down—and it jumps out like the genie from the bottle. I close my eyes. The nausea that overwhelms me is like a cold iron wedge hammered into the pit of my stomach. It is a thousand years before I can summon the courage to move upwards.

I fasten my eyes on the surface of the concrete and drag myself up one hand after another. With my inner eye I can still see the hundred-foot drop to the street. The crazy receding diagonals of the building are spiders' webs tied to my limbs, centered on the spot in the road where my body will smash and split open. One twitch of the fine-spun filaments and I will be sent whirling into space. The trembling in my limbs becomes so extreme it takes me years of my life to inch around the overhang that looked so innocuous when viewed from the ground.

I crawl past the successive lines of windows. When I began the climb I assumed that the building was deserted except for that one room on the top floor, and when I peer through the windows into one or other of the darkened rooms at first I can make out nothing. All I can see is the edge of a desk or the outline of a filing cabinet. But suddenly I am convinced that those night-shrouded rooms are filled with living creatures. Not with men or women—but with birds. I visualize them as small birds, huddled together, on perches around the walls. They doze fitfully, twittering a little, shaking their soft wings. They are imprisoned inside the building like birds in a blacked-out aviary.

Another sensation steals over me as I haul myself upwards. It concerns the texture of the stone. During my painful progress I have been wondering about it increasingly. It has taken on a soapy, soft, yielding quality. It gives off a mild warmth. It no longer feels in the least like concrete or stone. It feels more like human skin.

There is no time left in which to indulge such speculations. My hands are gripping the sill of the lighted room. The sill is sharp and cuts into the pads of my fingers. The glow from inside the room is still orange, but now I can see that it is swelling and fading, oscillating from white to deep orange and back to white with a slow regularity. It flickers like the controlled light given off by some intricate scientific device. It stabs the fog like the beam of a lighthouse and sheds a cold radiance over the foggy street below.

This is the room which I must enter. Here I must perform my mysterious task.

11

Millimeter by millimeter I pull myself upwards. I look cautiously over the sill. Although I have dreamed the dream at least twenty times I never know until I reach the sill what the room contains or what I expect to see.

I manage to put one leg over the sill. I pause there, panting. I dare not look down. My mind still pictures the unyielding pavement beneath. I hang there, looking into the room.

At first it is impossible to distinguish any solid object. The orange light is beautiful but sinister. I must not stare into it too long or I shall become hypnotized. I shall succumb. Then either I shall topple into the street or become the prisoner of some immense and wicked power. A prisoner for eternity. Shut up with the hopeless birds in one of the rooms on the twenty-nine floors below.

I force myself to climb into the room. The orange light seems to emanate as a beam or cone from a small round machine like an electric fan set in the middle of the far wall. The whir of the fan can be heard as it swings from one side to the other. I am not convinced that the source of light is the fan. It could be the soft and burning head of some indoor plant or flower. It could emanate from the pupil of a huge eye, human or animal; the eye of an ogre or a lion.

If I had expected to see captive birds in this room, I am wrong. It takes only a moment to realize that the fauna here are not birds but fish. The walls of the room are made of a thick transparent substance like quartz, with a ribbed, pebbled surface. Behind the quartz panels can be seen the blurred ovals of fish. Their scales and fins glitter with a somber sheen, copper, bronze and pewter. Their movements are so lethargic that it occurs to me that they are not suspended in water but in some form of oil of glycerine. Alternatively they are sick and dying. As I lower my feet to the floor of the room it strikes me that all the birds below me could be ailing and dying too.

There is a desk against the right-hand wall. It is heavy and ornate, not carved from wood, but with a mottled sheen like weathered bone. In shape it resembles the base of a classical sarcophagus, bulbous and tasteless, adorned with acanthus leaves and with miniature columns ending in clawed feet. Behind it I can discern the seated figure of a man. Or, rather, not a man. A creature.

When I try to describe him, in my waking moments, my first impulse is to wonder from what primitive cranny of the brain such a monster can have crept. His torso is like the torso of a man, but the hands that lie inert on the desk end in hooked talons. As I circle the desk I see that the head bears only a superficial relationship to a human face. The contours of skull and jaw are recognizable enough, but the skin is drawn tight across the bones in a manner that gives it the appearance of a dead ape.

The figure gives no sign of emotion or recognition. The little winking eyes pay me no attention. I am able to move closer for a more intense scrutiny. Now I can see clearly that there is no skin on the face at all. The head consists of horn or cartilage: a tough, scaly material like the chitin or exterior skeleton of an insect.

Below the eyes rises a curved beak. The beak is gently grinding and masticating, like the beak of a parrot munching seed. There is a raised bony ridge on top of the skull, which in turn is crowned with a floppy, leathery crest.

My impression is that the creature is for the moment seated and immobile. It would be stupid to take its passivity for granted. The fish rise and fall in the quartz tanks behind its bulky black outline. It is impressive in its complete self-absorption. To my surprise I also feel that it is in some way pitiable. It must be very, very old. As I watch it I can see thick strings of mucus, like tears of liquid gum, dripping from its old, old eyes. Its ancient jaws champ away without pause; its ancient claws scrape with a dry sound on the ivoried top of the desk.

On the wall behind the creature is an angular black shadow. I can see now that it is a door. As soon as I catch sight of it I know that this is the point towards which the entire logic of the dream has led me.

It is just a door. An ordinary door. Painted a matte black, and with a slim silver handle.

To reach it, I must sidle around the far edge of the desk. I move forward one slow step at a time, placing one foot in front of the other across the deep, springy pile of the carpet. The creature at the desk continues to ignore me. The orange light pumps like a heartbeat, caressing the naked surface of the skull. The slimy ropes of tears that fall from its eyes shine like ropes of spun gold.

The tips of my fingers steal towards the silver handle. Then I see that there is a lock on the door. In the lock a key. The key is made of gleaming silver. I reach for it. I turn it.

The door yields and begins to open. It swings wide.

I hear a sound behind me. A clicking, slithering kind of sound.

Glancing over my shoulder, I see that the creature has risen from behind the desk and is bearing down on me. Its saurian eyes are a red-flecked amber in the light from the fan. Its curved claws are hooking out towards my face.

Then I wake.

II

————•◆•·————

It began in early May, when the gutters of Madrid are filled with the drifting, papery white blossoms of the acacias.

My mind always returns to the afternoon which was the starting point of the whole business. My point of departure is always the Prado. To be more precise, the bench in the Velázquez gallery, opposite "The Surrender of Breda." My eyes rove among the blood, the plumes, the thicket of lances. I study the figure of the defeated Justin of Nassau as, with the gesture of a man who has fought honourably and now can fight no longer, he surrenders the key of the city to the courtly and compassionate Spinola. I am fascinated by that key: a key on a long, silken ribbon with a tassel, heavy and ornate, the focus of the composition, unlocking its meaning.

I have been sitting in front of the great canvas for many hours, immersed in it, rising at intervals to examine some section of it at close quarters. I am unaware that in little more than an hour my peaceful pursuits are about to be shattered in a totally unforeseen way. I am as unaware of it as the warhorse stamping its huge hoof in the picture up there knows it is present at a historic event. Nor, looking at me as the bell rings for the Prado to close, and I yawn, rub my eyes, rise from my seat and nod to the nearby attendant, would you take me for the sort of man who is likely to become involved in a desperate enterprise. You would notice nothing very remarkable about me—a tall and rather thin Englishman of forty-odd, wearing a light-grey flannel suit. I appear ordinary enough; though, mind you, there is plenty of spring in my step as, still smothering a little yawn, I run down the short staircase of the side entrance of the Prado into the courtyard opposite the Calle de Felipe IV.

I can remember how the heat of the late afternoon strikes me like a blow in the face as I emerge from the cool interior. As usual, I stroll across to glance at Benlliure's exuberant statue of Goya, its base a stone fantasy patterned after the nightmare figures of "Los Caprichos" and "Los Sueños." They have always held some special significance for me, those nightmare shapes. The Beethoven-like head frowns down at me as I pay the old hero of my youth, the subject of my first piece of critical writing, a moment of silent tribute. From the enclosure at the back of the statue, where the poor of the city doss down at night, comes the familiar stink of urine.

Madrid is a city filled with odours. As I roam along the Paseo del Prado towards the roar of the Plaza de Cibeles my nostrils catch the smell of horses. Madrid is the last capital of the West where you can smell the scent of sweaty hides and dung, where you can see a cavalry regiment in field order cantering over the granite setts of a main street. There is the smell of dripping trees and bushes, as men with hoses fixed to hydrants give them a regular soaking. And there is the characteristic sweet perfume of the Madrid girls as they saunter through the five o'clock heat.

It is painful, at the street corners, to leave the shadow of the acacias and emerge into the glare of the sun. The sunshine enhances my feeling of drowsiness. The lozenge-patterned pavements are hot beneath the soles of my shoes. I mop at my neck and wrists with my handkerchief as I wander past the white-and-golden façade of the Palace Hotel. At the Ministry of Marine the bluejackets on duty have retired into the cool shelter of the hallway. The climate is hard on an Englishman, even an Englishman spending his third successive summer in Madrid.

I am glad to reach the Plaza de Cibeles and seat myself beneath the awning of my favourite café, between the Post Office and the brown bulk of the Banco de España. Here I can relax, easing my shirt away from my damp skin. I debate whether to order a *horchata* or a *zumo de limón,* and when the waiter arrives I ask for the latter. My mind is in a pleasant daze. I sip a little of my ice-cold drink, then take my notebook out of my pocket and begin to jot down a line or two concerning the impressions that have occurred to me while I was studying "The Surrender of Breda."

During the past months my book on Velázquez has been moving along very nicely—a further reason for the false sense of security I am enjoying at this moment. It is true that in my characteristic way I have long ago spent my publisher's generous advance on journeys to Rome, Vienna, Boston and New York to see canvases by the subject of my book. At the moment I am more or less subsidizing the work out of my own pocket. Moreover my publisher, angry with me because the delivery of the book is a year overdue, has not yet sent me the next half of the advance I have asked for. But if I am a little pressed for money at this juncture, what of that? It is a situation I am familiar with and which I have coped with before. *Diego Velázquez and His Circle* is turning out to be a fine work—a worthy companion, as the critics will say, to my *Masters of the Siglo de Oro.* That is all that matters. And perhaps the check from the publishers will be lying on the doormat when I reach home. Too many books have been ruined by their final pages, either because the writer was exhausted or because he was hurried. That was not going to be the fate of my history of the court painters of Philip IV. Howver, I must admit I felt a certain anxiety about my financial

17

situation. I would have settled down to the last four chapters of my book in a far more promising frame of mind if I could have relied on that check from London reaching me in the near future. I had long ago mulcted my German and American publishers, bless them, to the decent limit and far beyond.

I ordered another *zumo de limón* and went on with my notes about the picture I had spent the afternoon examining. That was my self-imposed target: one picture a day. Yesterday I sat for three hours in the darkened room designed to house a single painting: "Las Meninas." A plaque on the wall described it as the supreme work of the art of painting, and such was my reverence for its creator that I was inclined to agree. Tomorrow I would return to the Prado and sit in front of . . . what? "The Drunkards"? "The Weavers"? "The Forge of Vulcan"? It is extraordinary to reflect that at that moment I had nothing more serious on my mind than this unassuming choice.

I closed my notebook and let the sights and sounds of my favourite city take possession of me. Lazily I watched the shot-silk dabs of colour, like brush strokes, made by the pigeons fluttering against the ocher cliff of the Post Office. The Post Office dominated the enormous square, dwarfing the Banco de España and the Ministry of the Army on the opposite corner, where the armed sentries paced in and out of the thick shrubbery. The pigeons roosted on the ledges or flapped their wings against the massive sandstone blocks, still pitted with the shrapnel of the Civil War. In the halls of that ugly building, of which the Madrileños are so fond, a bloody battle had taken place not so many years ago.

Automatically I counted the number of stories in the building. Something about the birds and the mountain of stone stirred an obscure emotion in the bottom of my mind; but I was too drowsy to pursue it. I was still deliberating which picture I would make the subject of my researches tomorrow. Perhaps a portrait, to provide a contrast to "Las Meninas" and "The Surrender of Breda"? . . .

I paid the bill and rose. I had the whole evening to make up my mind. And a pleasant evening I (then) expected it to be. I was dining with Professor Obregón, and looked forward to an interesting discussion of his new biography of the Conde-Duque de Olivares, a personage at the center of my own studies.

Slowly I sauntered towards the Puerta de Alcalá and the Calle de Serrano. I often walked home along this busy, pretty street instead of along the grander but gloomier Paseo de la Castellana. The walk to my home was a long one, but in a sedentary profession like mine I liked to take as much exercise as possible. And I loved Madrid. Often, to help myself fall asleep, I would pick a different route through the city each night and take an imaginary walk. One night I might make my way from the Puente de Segovia to the Plaza de Toros at Las Ventas, while the following night I might start at the Atocha Station and finish at the Football Stadium. Ah! those warm soft nights, filled with the sound of the cicadas. I would try to prolong my imaginary excursions as long as I could, until I felt myself overcome by the physical torpor that would overtake me at the end of a real walk like that. Because—if I didn't—when I finally fell asleep the chances were I would encounter that damned dream again . . . find my feet walking, not on the checkered pavements of Madrid, but on the asphalt carriageway of a street I would never be able to identify—a street in Bloomsbury, near the British Museum—on a foggy night in winter. . . .

Wandering down the Calle de Serrano, how could I have known that the precious if precarious balance of my life was about to be upset? I had won through, over the years, to a plateau of professional achievement. I felt that I had only to hold a steady course for the rewards which I had earned by my industry to accrue to me. But life, of course, is not as simple as that. I forgot, as I glanced at the bright shopwindows, that I had not always been the conventional, respectable figure that the passers-by would have taken me to be. I was about to be reminded that we are the product of our past, chained to selves that we mistakenly assume are dead and done with. . . .

It seems hard that even a self-effacing art historian should be summoned to relive the follies of his youth. An artist, yes. Let artists endure the incurable untidinesses, the endless passions and mistakes. I had long ago renounced the life of a painter and thought I could reasonably expect to live secure. My God, what hope is there for any of us if even a modest historian must pay so bitterly for his errors? Mind you, I am also convinced that what was about to happen to me was the result of my vanity, of a stupid desire to cling to my vanishing youth. Didn't I mention the spring in my step as I ran down the staircase? . . .

Oh, I remember now. The picture I decided to study next day was "The Weavers." You know it, I am sure. A product of the artist's last and most majestic period. The barefoot women in the foreground laugh and gossip as they weave their tapestry. And in a tiny illuminated room at the back—like a miniature theater—a completely unnoticed drama is taking place. A scene from classical mythology is being played out. The goddess Athena is cursing Arachne. And the moral? The moral of the picture is that vanity—even innocent vanity—can arouse the jealous anger of the gods. . . .

The little *chicas*, secretaries and shopgirls trotting down the Calle de Serrano were the weavers. The messenger of the gods was already waiting, unknown to me, in my apartment.

You know what I think? I think that an Englishman of forty-one should reflect very, very carefully before he allows his emotions to run away with him.

III

————•◦•————

I took my time—why not?—walking along Serrano, and crossed over to the Avenida del Generalísimo. The feeling of sleepiness which had come over me in the Prado had evaporated now. I paused to buy an evening paper and stopped to glance through it at a pavement café, and in anticipation of the check from London I also ate a dish of *gambas* and drank two glasses of montilla. Madrid is a splendid city for loitering. Munching the *gambas*, I gazed for a long time at the sunset through the branches of the fine chestnuts that adorn the Calle de Serrano. The sky had the burnished steel-and-silver glow which is characteristic of Castile. Unless you have seen that evening glitter it is difficult to appreciate the paintings of Diego Velázquez.

Dusk was falling when at length I reached the Calle Doctor Pedrell. Now, I must explain that the balconies of my own apartment house, Number 46, face towards the rear. My balcony was on the fifth floor, sixty feet from the ground. The apartments in Doctor Pedrell are all new, part of an entire suburb which has sprung up in the past two years as the great Avenida del Generalísimo pushes out northwards mile by mile towards the slopes of the distant Guadarramas. The road is not yet topped and consists of dried yellow clay; the ground at the back of the buildings is a wasteland, an expanse of weeds and scrubby grass littered with trash and builders' rubble. I stepped through the passageway that led to the back of the building as unobtrusively as I could. As I expected, no one was about. I was unobserved. No children were playing with the broken bricks on the empty wasteland. No one was leaning over any of the balconies. I had the place to myself.

Why, you will ask, did I ignore the glass double doors of the main entrance? Why didn't I walk through the front door and take the elevator to my apartment, like a gentleman and a Christian? I wish I had. The answer is that I was sneaking around to the rear of the house because I intended to enter my apartment by a more unorthodox method. I intended to climb the exterior of the building to my balcony on the fifth floor.

Had I no key, then? Yes, I had a key. I wasn't locked out? No, I wasn't locked out. The truth is, I intended to climb up to that balcony because I have a taste for climbing. In fact, a passion for it. I am, I am afraid, a compulsive climber. Possibly you will be surprised and even a little shocked by this confession. You would never have imagined for a single moment, when you were looking at me in the Prado, that I possessed this secret compulsion. But glancing casually at a man in an art gallery, how can you tell whether or not he is a kleptomaniac, a pyromaniac, a sleepwalker, a foot-fetishist, or a man who grows orchids or collects brass door knockers? After all, a mania for climbing is only a few degrees more eccentric than most of these things.

Having confessed so much to you, I may as well confess more. I had climbed the outer wall to my apartment twice before. It was not a difficult climb; on the other hand, it was not a particularly easy one. Why did I climb it in the first place? And having climbed it, why did I want to do it again? I cannot tell you. I suppose I was a victim of that common human impulse which makes a man want to win a motor race, or kill a bull, or scale a giant peak. You would think that once the impulse has been satisfied—when the race has been won, the bull killed, the peak scaled—the compulsion would wither away. It is not so. There is always another race to run, another bull to kill, another peak to scale. Some obscure process of what the psychologists call perseveration appears to be at work. The malady is incurable.

I have thought about the matter for many years. It isn't a simple question of competitiveness, of possessing a fierce urge to succeed or to beat your rivals. Indeed, in many respects I am the most solitary and least competitive of men. No, the enemy isn't the other competitor, or the bull, or the mountain. The enemy is yourself. It is yourself you are wrestling with. It is yourself you are trying to assuage and overcome. I was devoured by this strange compulsion to climb because of something hidden in the depths of my personality. I was unable to rid myself of it. I didn't want to. We grow fond of our diseases. As a boy I liked to climb trees; and one of my earliest memories is of crashing through the branches of a huge fir and landing miraculously on a pile of sugar beet. Later I graduated to buildings. I was a devil at it, in our town, and once they had to fetch the fire brigade. If I see a good tall tree, even today I will have a crack at it, if the park keeper isn't about.

I had first climbed into Number 46 three months before. Having climbed it once, I climbed it again, just to prove that I had really conquered it and hadn't been frightened the first time. And having already climbed it twice, I suppose there wasn't any reason why I shouldn't climb it again, to show my contempt for this particular ascent.

As I have said, there was not much risk of my being spotted. It was just as well. The Spaniards are a very understanding race, but even they are apt to show curiosity if they see a man shinning up a drainpipe. The only danger, apart from the danger of the actual climb, would come when I was within ten feet of my goal. At that point I would be in full view of the nearby barracks of the Guardia Civil, situated on the corner of Doctor Pedrell and the Avenida del Generalísimo. There was always a pair of sentries in shiny black patent-leather hats patrolling the entrance of the massive windowless granite building. The notion of them catching sight of me as I hung on the outside of the building did not appeal to me. Their short-barrelled carbines looked extremely businesslike. I was glad the steely hues of the Castilian dusk were hardening into night. From the far-off buildings across the broad patch of wasteland the wan and watery electric lights were beginning to shine.

I stationed myself beneath a scraggy old eucalyptus, growing beside a mound of rubbish half as tall as itself. I had been wearing my jacket slung over my shoulders, and now I slipped my arms into the sleeves and carefully fastened all three buttons. As I did so, I considered the route which I would take to reach my balcony. This time I meant to try a different one. My mind was already three-quarters made up, and it did not take me long to reach a decision. A hundred times, sitting at my wicker table on the balcony, or leaning over the railing with a drink in my hand, I had idly studied the face of the building below me. I was working out the possible routes to the fifth floor. This kind of *coup d'oeil* is habitual with me. I can never look at the outside of any building, old or new, without making a judgment about the best way to climb it. An hour ago, in the Plaza de Cibeles, I had been indulging in this habit as I stared at the façades of the Banco de España and the Post Office. It doesn't matter if the building is a cathedral or a council house, I immediately begin to picture the route to the summit. My reaction is instinctive and automatic. I register certain features of that building in the way that a painter or an architect would.

You could say that I look at a building as a mountaineer looks at a mountain. At one time or another I have done a

24

good deal of mountaineering, but my own personal form of climbing dates from a dozen years before I had ever set eyes on a mountain, let alone set foot on one. Let the mountaineers keep their Karakorams and Himalayas; I'll stick to my man-made alps and ranges. I find them just as mysterious and exciting. For me, in fact, mountaineering was always an extension of climbing buildings, and not the other way around. To tell you the truth, my record as an orthodox mountaineer is mediocre. I have always been a lone wolf. My ability to cooperate with other people can be described as limited, to say the least. I detest the discipline which is essential for highgrade mountaineering. I dislike the roping-up, the clutter of crampons, pitons, wedges, snap links, and the rest of it. At one time I tried hard to accustom myself to the restrictions of regular climbing, but in the end I had to face the fact that I was temperamentally unsuited to it. On the other hand, I should like to see how some of those orthodox climbers would cope with the special problems of my kind of climbing. I could have given them a couple of points, I can tell you. There are very few of them who could have taken me on successfully at my own game.

Reaching the balcony ought not to present any outstanding difficulties. The question was whether I had the nerve and physical resources to do it quickly enough. I couldn't allow myself more than two and a half to three minutes, and I had to speed up over the last few yards, when I was in full view of the keen eyes of the Guardia Civil. Once I had started I would have to move fast, and at forty-one I couldn't expect to move as fast as I used to. Yet I suppose that it was the very fact that I was forty-one, and wanted to prove that I could still shift like a mountain goat, that spurred me on to this curious exercise.

My heart was pounding as I stepped from the shelter of the eucalyptus and headed for a point to the left of the multiple tiers of balconies. I was by no means as cool as I would have liked. How many times had I sworn to myself—over and over—that I would give up these unbecoming and injudicious antics? . . .

The stones and parched, brittle grass crunched under my shoes. I took out my handkerchief, scrubbed at my palms with it and pushed it back in my pocket. Then, before I could give myself a chance to change my mind, I came close under the first balcony, crouched down, then threw myself upwards to catch hold of an iron stanchion.

At the side of each balcony was a diaper pattern formed by every alternate brick sticking out an inch further than the one below; these gave me footholds. The balconies themselves were made of crisscrossed bricks with space between; these gave me my handholds. Between each balcony I would have to wriggle and swing a little on the ornamental stanchions which supported it.

In my three previous climbs I had made use principally of the piping and guttering, and I was not sure if an ascent by means of brickwork and stanchions was feasible. I soon found out that it was. My spirits rose. My judgment was vindicated. And I was elated to discover that the physical demands of the climb were being overcome as easily as the mental ones. I mounted higher and higher with a complete sense of security. I don't believe I recalled for a single second my terrible fall fifteen years before in Copenhagen. I felt nothing but the strange pleasure that rises in me during the progress of a successful climb. My brain and limbs were moving in harmony. I wasn't as middle-aged as I had begun to fear I was. I flew up those last vital ten feet of the climb more swiftly than I would have believed possible.

All the same, by the time I hauled myself over the rail of my balcony I was badly out of breath. I remember lurching over to the far wall and leaning against it, gasping. I took out my handkerchief and wiped my wrists and forehead. There were big cold patches of sweat under my arms, soaking

26

through my suit. The drawback of my odd pastime, whether in warm climates or cold, is that is is cruelly destructive of clothes. If you don't get them torn, you get them stained with sweat, or even blood. This evening's impromptu performance would certainly cost me the toecaps of a good pair of shoes.

I had more than earned my bath and my brandy and soda. Beyond the roof of a little Moorish-style villa, already half demolished to make way for another apartment building, I could see the new fountain in the Avenida del Generalísimo. The purple and emerald spotlights sealed into the basins lit up the cascades with exuberant effect. I walked forward and leaned on the rail and stared at the coloured lights as I waited to get my breath back. They looked very gay and cheerful. They gave me the last moment of unalloyed pleasure I was to know for many days to come.

I straightened up and went to the french windows, turned the handle and stepped into my bedroom. I crossed to the bathroom and switched on the light, then went back into the darkened bedroom to peel off my jacket and throw it on the bed. I started to unfasten the knot of my tie, as a preliminary to pouring my drink, running my bath and undressing. Then I stopped still. From under the door that led to the drawing room a line of bright light was shining.

I am sometimes careless and leave a light on. But this afternoon my cleaning woman, the admirable Conchita, would have been there. She would have been sure to turn it off.

Someone was in my drawing room. I gripped the doorknob and swung the door wide open.

A man was seated in one of the armchairs. His back was turned towards me, and he was facing the door to the hall. When he heard the door open behind him he swung around.

IV

We stared at each other without speaking. Then I moved slowly around the room until I was standing between the armchair in which he was sitting and the door to the hall. If he wanted to climb down the balcony, he was welcome to try.

It was a little disappointing to feel the tingle at the base of my skull begin to fade almost as soon as I set eyes on him. I had been ready to deal with a burglar or a desperate intruder. Whatever else he was, this man was plainly not desperate.

He was no Madrileño. His complexion was pasty, pointing to a northern European or American origin. But it was the clothes on his short, froglike figure that revealed him as a fellow countryman of mine. Who but an Englishman would wear a chalk-stripe suit and a double-breasted waistcoat in Madrid, in May? And on the floor beside him rested his dark topcoat with its velvet collar. True, he did not go so far as to carry an umbrella; but the black felt hat he twisted in his pudgy fingers had an unmistakable look of Lincoln Bennett. And, of course, it was his hair that finally gave him away. The Englishman abroad always appears to need a haircut. His hair is an inch longer than the natives', with a curly fuzz around the nape of the neck. The long locks on the Englishman's collar are characteristic, even if, like my visitor, his domed skull gleams under the lamp because of a distinct absence of hair.

His voice settled any doubts about his origin. The flatness of the accent suggested that he came from the Midlands, although I had been an exile from England for too long to consider myself an authority on local speech. He cleared his throat and huffed a little, as though he were perched on a lily pad instead of a chair. His small eyes disappeared among the fatty tissue as he smiled. He showed no trace whatever of nervousness.

"I must apologize," he began, "for breaking in on you like this. I realize it must seem a little odd. Naturally, if there weren't—er—special circumstances, I shouldn't have dared to do so."

"May I ask how you got in here?"

"I rang you seven or eight times during the course of the day. I couldn't get any reply. So eventually I thought I might as well take the bull by the horns, so to speak. I decided to come around here and wait until you returned. As I said, there were rather special circumstances."

"Yes, but how did you get in?"

"I persuaded your concierge to admit me." Another froglike smile. "I gave him a tip."

Rafael was an honest man, but a poor one. Nevertheless, it would have required a very substantial *propina* before he would have unlocked my door to a stranger.

"I hope you don't mind," he went on. "I convinced him that I had to see you on a very urgent matter. I also pointed out that I happen to be a very old friend of yours."

"I hope you don't think it rude," I said, "if I ask you what the hell you're doing here?"

"Of course, it's been a great many years since we last met. Still, I had hoped that by some chance you might have recognized me . . . ?"

The little eyes opened wide. The pupils were a muddy green

colour, like the bottom of a stagnant pond. The dewlaps wobbled anxiously.

"No," I said. "I've got no recollection of ever seeing you in my life. In Spain or England or anywhere else. So what exactly are you doing here?"

He said brightly: "Ridgeling? Norman Ridgeling?"

I shook my head. "I've never set eyes on you."

He grew slightly roguish. "Oh, come, surely you remember Norman Ridgeling?" And he called me by my Christian name.

I looked at him more closely. He could easily have found out my Christian name and the number of my apartment from the Madrid phone book. The name Ridgeling meant nothing to me. What was he after? He looked too prosperous to be asking for money. Anyway, if he knew so much about me, he probably knew that at the moment I was short of cash. Was he in some sort of trouble with the authorities? Madrid had its share of dubious birds of passage. I was inclined to think he was some sort of confidence trickster. He had the manner.

I walked across to the hall door and opened it. Beyond it was the front door. On the doormat lay half a dozen letters. Keeping my visitor in view through the hall doorway, I stooped down and picked them up. Rapidly I sorted through them. Where was my check? Three personal letters. Two bills. An invitation. That's all. Nothing else. Bad. Bloody awkward.

I returned to the drawing room and threw the letters on my desk. My visitor was still, watching me with unwinking eyes. Then he spoke two words. He spoke them with a confident inflection that brought my head up with a jerk.

"Conderton Building?" he said.

And immediately there flashed into my mind the image of a building of rich old plum-coloured brick, standing near the cold, slow-flowing waters of the river Cam.

Here in Madrid, in my new functional apartment, I suddenly felt a stab of longing for that crumbling building. The thought of it brought back the quiet colours of the north. I had been happy in the drafty courts of Conderton Building. I had lived there for two full years of my youth, when I was a student at the university.

"We were on the same staircase," he said. "I was on the top floor."

And his words brought back to me the oaken staircase with its shaky Jacobean balusters. The winds from The Fens bounced off the flagstones in the courtyard and scoured the cavernous hallway from floor to attic. Painted on one of the sandstone blocks of the doorway was a black panel, with the names of the dons and students and the numbers of their rooms inscribed on it in old-fashioned letters. Each name and number had been painted over so many times that the panel was a veritable palimpsest, worthy of the scrutiny of one of the university's medievalists. The presence of your name on that panel was a precious symbol. After the miserable anonymity of school it gave you a personality, an individuality. It confirmed your escape from the servitude of boyhood into the independence of manhood. I can still remember the flash of pride that went through me when, coming back from a lecture at Mill Lane, I saw the elderly, white-smocked college handyman, brush and mahlstick in hand, completing the last letters of my name. At that moment I tasted liberty. I have since tried not to lose it.

Now, in this southern capital, it all seemed a very long time ago. I closed my eyes and tried to conjure up the list of names on the black panel. They would have been obliterated and renewed many times since I had occupied a suite of rooms on that staircase. I could picture no trace of my own name there —and certainly no trace of any Norman Ridgeling. In fact, I could picture no name at all. They had all vanished. All gone. Phil Shannon. Tom Daneway. Jack Boughspring. Bill Inglatt. Even that cocky devil Bay Russell, who had lived in the rooms above mine. Many were the chairs and glasses Bay and I had smashed in our time! And as I stood there with my eyes closed I seemed to catch some of the sounds of that old staircase. Shouts. Jeers. Laughter. The smack of a mortarboard being booted across a landing. And softer noises too. The swish of a skirt as a girl ran up the stairs. The tap of her shoes . . . Yes, it was all a long, long time ago. . . . And although I was only forty-one I had that hateful sensation of ageing . . . undeniably ageing. . . .

I opened my eyes. My visitor's porky smile was still fixed in place. He had settled himself comfortably in his armchair.

"It was into my room," he said, "that you used to climb when you came back after midnight. After they'd locked the gates of the college."

"Is that so?"

"You used to wake me up in the small hours. You'd bang up my window and tramp across the floor of my bedroom." He gave a little shiver. "I'd have to crawl out of bed and shut the window after you."

That sounded authentic. In those days I wasn't famous for either tact or consideration. Barging across somebody's bedroom in the small hours sounded characteristic of me at that period.

"You used to climb onto the roof of Bollow's, the baker's shop in Brass Street," he went on. "You'd walk across the parapet until you reached the point opposite our staircase. Then you'd take a flying leap across Fox Lane. I'd hear the thump of your shoes as your body hit the guttering above my window, followed by a thud as you let yourself fall forward onto the slates. Then you'd lower yourself down onto my window sill. If by some chance I'd fastened the catch, you never had any hesitation about hammering on the glass until I got out of bed and opened it."

His words put me back on the wind-swept roof of the bakery in Brass Street. I doubt if I had ever thought of that particular escapade since I had left Cambridge. Yet I suppose I used to perform it eight or nine times a term.

"If you didn't know it at the time," he said, "I may as well tell you that you frightened me to death. When I heard you land, I knew you must be safe, but there was always the chance that the slates would crack or the guttering would give way. I used to sit bolt upright in the darkness with my heart in my mouth."

Thinking about that crazy stunt, I felt frightened to death myself. What could have induced me to take a flying leap like that? A standing jump of eight or nine feet? If I'd fallen—well, it would have been worse than Copenhagen. I wouldn't merely have dropped forty feet and cracked my bones on the paving slabs of Fox Lane. I would have been impaled on the row of spikes that garnished the sooty wall that ran beneath the windows at the back of Conderton Building. Those were no ordinary spikes. They would have spitted a rhinoceros. They must have been invented by some Cromwellian divine who believed that to be out of college after statutory hours was not only a misdemeanour but a sin. A rotating crosspiece, bristling with needles of iron, waited to tear the flesh of the fallen miscreant. Yet this fiendish mechanism had held such little terror for me, when I was only twenty, that I must have soared over it scores of times. Many times I must have done it when I was drunk. The thought of those rusty spikes made my mind shrink with nausea. Had I really stood on the flaking stonework of the bakery, gauged the distance across the dark gap, then gathered all my force and launched myself blithely into mid-air? *Horrible!* It made me see my recent feat of climbing into my apartment in the Calle Doctor Pedrell in an entirely new light. I had been unbelievably reckless and stupid.

I went across to my desk and moved aside the sheaf of notes that littered it. I reached for the bottle of Lepanto and the siphon that stood on the silver tray, poured out two brandy and sodas, and carried one of them over to Ridgeling.

"You'd better tell me what this is all about," I said. "I've got to change and go out to dinner."

33

He sighed as he raised his tumbler. "I'm sorry you don't remember me. I admired you very much, although of course you were far too grand to notice I even existed. And now here you are offering me a drink! In those days you were expected to become a great painter. Did you ever follow it up?"

I sipped some of my brandy. "Yes," I said, "but I stopped painting a few years after leaving Cambridge."

"Oh, what a pity! And your heart was so set on it."

"I think you'd better tell me what you've come for."

But he was embarked on a flood of reminiscence. "Naturally, as I was reading a dull subject like mathematics, and you and your friends were doing romantic things like philosophy or anthropology, we didn't have much in common. I hadn't many friends, as a matter of fact. I was rather shy—and rather poor."

I made an impatient gesture with my glass. Bay Russell and the rest of us weren't exactly rolling in wealth ourselves; we were mostly scholarship boys. We had the intellectual arrogance of extreme youth, but I don't recall that we had any inclination to be either social snobs or money snobs. Not that there was any point in arguing about it with my visitor; though his last remark made me see why I had avoided him during our time at Conderton Building . . . if he had ever really been there.

He was stroking the band of his hat with a pink finger. If he had ever suffered from shyness, he had certainly got over it many years ago. He was enjoying himself.

"I wonder if you can guess," he said with a smile, "how pleasant it is for me to find myself in a position to come here and be able to make you a very advantageous offer?"

"What sort of offer?"

"Won't you call me Norman?"

"What sort of offer?"

"An offer of money. What else?"

Money. That's certainly the kind of offer one always feels

bound to take seriously. I studied him more carefully. His body seemed to swell beneath his black waistcoat as he settled his elbows on the arms of his chair. His expression was arch.

"Aren't you going to ask me how much it is?"

I looked at him woodenly. In his own peculiar way he was having the time of his life.

He said, "Perhaps I ought to explain that I am an associate of Mr. Basil Merganser. In fact, I help to direct the section of the Merganser organization which is based in Western Europe. I'm sure you're familiar with the name of Mr. Merganser?"

His smile had broadened into a self-satisfied smirk. He knew I would recognize that as an associate of Basil Merganser he was someone to be reckoned with. The self-pitying little mathematician with the Midlands accent had really made good. In the eyes of society he had completely outdistanced the obscure art historian and *soi-disant* great painter who used to rap imperiously at his bedroom window.

Merganser stood in the same relation to his fellow millionaires as Epstein or Sickert once stood to their fellow Academicians. The very syllables of his name, as Ridgeling pronounced them, carried an overtone of magic; their upper partials lingered sonorously in the air. Originally of Eastern European origin, he was a naturalized Briton and had made England his international headquarters. As a reader of the air-mail editions of English newspapers I was used to reading about his benefactions and business dealings. Only a week or two ago I had read in a Madrid magazine that the Spanish government had bestowed on him the Grand Cross of the Order of Isabella the Catholic, in recognition of his services to Spanish industry. His investments in Italy had gained him the Grand Cross of the Republican Order of Merit. Greece, not to be outdone, had weighed in with the Order of the Redeemer. His influence extended all around the Mediterranean seaboard, not excluding the Communist countries of the

Balkans. It was an open secret that British policy in the Levant was heavily mortgaged to his petroleum interests; and when his name had failed to figure in last year's Honours Lists there was a crisis in the House and the Trucial Oman. According to one columnist, he had already picked his title: Baron Merganser of Geddingley, in the County of Berkshire.

I would dearly have loved to have been given permission to visit Geddingley Park. It was the former home of one of England's greatest eighteenth-century statesmen, and now housed Merganser's magnificent collection of paintings. Merganser possessed the finest group of Rembrandts outside the Rijksmuseum, the finest group of El Grecos outside the Prado, the finest Turners outside the Tate. To his paintings should be added his library of incunables and royal bindings, and also his rare china and porcelain, in which China and Japan were strongly represented. Unfortunately, permission to view these treasures was virtually unobtainable. Merganser kept them jealously to himself. Even art historians and fellow collectors were held at arm's length. Geddingley Park was guarded by teams of dogs and handlers, and surrounded by a high wire fence that was reputed to be electrified. Merganser had never lost so much as an apostle spoon, although one burglar had lost a leg and another had his throat ripped open and had bled to death before they got him to Geddingley Cottage Hospital. A formidable man, Merganser. Not to be taken lightly. But if Ridgeling was conveying a genuine offer from Merganser, it would certainly be a substantial one.

"Since you left Cambridge," Ridgeling was saying, "I have followed your career very closely."

I laughed. "What, for nearly twenty years?"

"You were one of the most colourful people at the university. You've been one of the most colourful people since."

I hardly relished being described as colourful.

"And why should you want to follow my career, Mr. Ridgeling?"

"At first, because I'd been so proud to have been associated with you, even in such a humble way. To a poor student from a small town in Cheshire you were a sort of inspiration. You were so vigorous and independent."

"All the same, I don't suppose you've come here this evening to discuss my career at Cambridge?"

"Well, I must admit that recently my interest has become a little more, shall we say, professional?"

"Why? Have you taken up painting?"

He placed the tips of his fingers together and crossed the points of his little shiny patent-leather shoes.

"A project has come up in connection with Mr. Merganser's business activities. The person who was assigned to deal with it asked for my advice. It calls for the services of a specialist. It is a task for which you happen to be very well equipped. I might almost say, uniquely equipped."

"Well, if Mr. Merganser wants me to catalogue his pictures for him, I assure you it would be a pleasure. I'd do it for a very modest fee, almost as a labour of love."

He let the carrot dangle. "We could certainly see about that later. At the moment, however, we're considering something much shorter and less elaborate."

"Like what?"

"I don't quite know how to put this. It's rather—delicate . . ."

I pointed at his glass. "Ridgeling—er—Norman . . . drink up, will you?" I was convinced now that he was trying to play some sort of confidence trick. "I'm afraid we seem to be talking at cross purposes."

"Not at all," he said blandly. "Was there anyone else who used to climb up from Brass Street and jump across to Conderton Building?"

I didn't see the point. I frowned. "Oh, I'm sure dozens of people used to do that."

He shook his head. "They used to climb into college, but

they didn't climb up from Brass Street. They made the easier climb from Fish Street and scrambled in across the roof of the chapel."

I looked at him curiously. "I didn't realize you were interested in nightclimbing, Ridgeling?"

"I made a special trip to England last week and inspected those climbs for myself . . . from the ground, of course! No, the Fish Street route was the normal one for undergraduates climbing into Conderton Building. It must have taken four or five times as long as the Brass Street route, but it was safe. Nonetheless you used to take the dangerous shortcut and make that colossal leap across Fox Lane. I tried to find someone who would demonstrate it for me. I made a lot of inquiries, offered a lot of money. Nobody came forward. Nobody believed it could be done—or that it ever had been done."

Once more I felt a sense of nausea at the idea of that wild leap. Sheer exuberance. Youthful idiocy. Are young men simply unable to visualize danger, or do they recognize it and actually go out of their way to court it?

He said, "At least I established, certainly to my own satisfaction, that no one else at the university ever made that particular jump. Neither in our time there nor afterwards."

I made a deprecating gesture. "I'm sure you're wrong. I bet Bay Russell did it at least once or twice."

He laughed. "Bay Russell? No, never."

Again I was curious. "How do you know that?"

"Because I know Bay Russell."

There was a touch of indulgent familiarity in his voice. It made me look at him sharply.

"Take it from me," he said, "when Bay Russell used to climb into Conderton Building he climbed in from Fish Street, across the chapel roof."

Now I came to think of it, I never remembered Bay actually accompanying me on the shorter climb over the roof of Bollow's. Nevertheless I felt it necessary to defend him.

"Well, Bay had more common sense than I had. He'd learned more from the war. And he'd already got a great future planned out for himself. He'd got everything cut and dried. Why risk it all for a stupid prank? I gather he went abroad almost as soon as he left Cambridge. Anyway, although we were such close friends, I'm sorry to say I soon lost touch with him."

To my annoyance, after my long walk home the brandy was making me more talkative than I wanted to be.

"Look here," I said abruptly, "what's the point of talking about things that happened so long ago? In another country, another dimension, another planet almost?"

I picked up a sheet of paper from the desk, took it across to Ridgeling and pushed it into his hands. There was something about the conversation which I found depressing and distasteful. It reminded me of a time of hope, a time that was dead.

"Write down the name and phone number of your hotel. If you're at a loose end in Madrid and feel like a chat sometime, I'll try and fit you in. But not tonight. Tonight I'm busy."

He laid the sheet of paper on his knee. "Would you be very surprised if I told you that I had made a special trip from Geneva to Madrid today simply in order to see you?"

"Just write down the name of the hotel, Norman, there's a good chap."

He picked up the sheet of paper and turned it deliberately between his fingers. "Naturally, you belonged to a later generation than the original Nightclimbers of Cambridge. But I'm told you set yourself the task of carrying out all the climbs that the Nightclimbers had done before you. Alone and unaided. Isn't that so? You achieved all the classic climbs?"

I don't know how he could have learned that, but it was true. I had repeated the whole series of safaris among the tiles and chimney pots pioneered by the Nightclimbers. Starting with the nursery slopes of the Old Schools and the Seeley Library, I had graduated to the specialist ascents. While worthier souls were debating the future of humanity at the Union, I was straddling the Doric columns of Downing; when they were sipping their late-night cocoa, I was preparing to jump across Senate House Passage to the roof of Caius; and when they were recruiting their powers in slumber for next day's lectures, I was negotiating the *chevaux de frise* bolted around the spire of King's College Chapel. The police, the proctors and the esteemed Professor Pigou had all solemnly declared that King's College Chapel was not scalable. So purely for my own satisfaction, quite privately and anonymously, I had set out to prove them wrong. I succeeded. I climbed King's College Chapel. It was a hollow, irrational sort of feat, I suppose; a triumph of pointless acrobatics. All the same, it had been difficult, and I had done it.

Ridgeling leaned forward in his chair, his dumpy body suddenly betraying an inner tension. He spoke with an anxiety he could not entirely conceal.

"Tell me, you could still do those classic climbs, couldn't you? If you had to, you could jump across Fox Lane again?"

I failed to see where this was leading. I was at a loss.

"Well?" he demanded. "You could, couldn't you?"

For some reason I was reluctant to admit to this complacent and subtly impertinent little man that I probably couldn't. I should have remembered Minerva and Arachne on the stage in the back room . . .

I reddened slightly. "Yes," I answered. "I suppose I could still manage most of them, if it was a matter of life and death."

He leaned back again, smiling, relieved.

"Not a matter of life and death, my dear fellow. Merely a matter of pounds, shillings and pence."

"I don't follow you."

His round face was tilted up at me, beaming with confidence.

"My organization does not wish to employ you in your capacity as historian. It wishes to employ you in your capacity as a climber. And we are prepared to pay you handsomely."

I stared at him. So he was going to bribe me, just as twenty minutes ago he had bribed poor Rafael, my concierge. The only difference would lie in the size of the *propina*.

Every man has his price. I was about to find out mine.

V

—————•◦•—————

"I think you had better explain."

He nodded. "That's right. There is a building we want you to climb."

The bright note was back in his voice.

For a moment I forgot all about my sweaty body, my crumpled clothes, my dinner with Professor Obregón. The proposal was startling enough to drive everything else out of my mind. I began to laugh.

"You flew all the way from Switzerland today just to ask me that?"

"I did, yes."

"And you're seriously asking me to believe you?"

"I am."

"Even if your story were true, wouldn't it strike you as a ridiculous thing to do?"

"Not in the least."

"I suppose it's the kind of thing the associates of Basil Merganser do every day?"

"It is."

His glance was as quick and cunning as an adder's.

"As soon as your name came up," he said, "I knew at once that we'd hit on the right man."

I stopped laughing and simmered down. I had disliked Ridgeling from the moment I set eyes on him, and with every minute that passed I liked him less. Somewhere, concealed in that soft carcass, I detected the seed of something like hatred for me. I couldn't imagine why or what for. I was positive that I had done him no active injury when—and if —we were at college together.

I straightened my shoulders and gazed around my comfortable living room as though to reassure myself. Yet somehow—well, it was flattering to be reminded of my flamboyant deeds of twenty years ago. Mind you, it would have been vastly more flattering to be remembered as an artist, or even an art historian; but the world often decrees that fame, if we achieve it, is thrust upon us for a minor attribute that we rather despise. For example, there was Ingres, who much preferred to play his violin—badly—to visitors to his studio instead of showing them his pictures. Nightclimbing was my *violin d'Ingres*.

I can now see that Ridgeling had begun to play, very skillfully, on my vanity—that fatal vanity! At this point I even started to make an effort to humour him. I told myself that after all the poor chap hadn't actually been offensive; and there was surely no need to end this quaint interview with a probable member of my old college on a note of peevishness.

"It seems a pity to disappoint you," I said, "especially if you've made such a long journey to see me. But you'll have to forgive me if I happen to find your proposition rather fantastic. In any case, I'm afraid I'm extremely busy at the moment."

"Yes, I was aware of that. I gather that the draft of your book should be finished in a month or two?"

I stared at him. "Now how could you have learned that?"

"Oh, we have our sources of information."

His manner was still ingratiating, but I could sense beneath it a hint of a condescension he would not have dared to show at the university.

He said, "We wouldn't ask you to break off your work for more than a few days. And you would come back to it refreshed in spirit and sounder in pocket."

I hesitated. For the first time I had the sensation of a huge intangible, external force impinging on me . . . leaning its heavy bulk against me. I shook my shoulders.

"As it happens," I said, "I have already made arrangements to drive down to Orihuela next week. I am due to examine a painting in the cathedral there."

This was a painting called "The Temptation of St. Thomas Aquinas," reportedly very fine, which I had never seen. It was discovered by Tormo sixty years ago, and first attributed by him to Nicolás de Villacis, then jointly to Alonso Cano and Velázquez; later Allende-Salazar and Ferrari had attributed it solely to Velázquez. I preened myself that I was now enough of an authority on the latter to make a definitive judgment of my own.

Ridgeling fingered his cheek. "I appreciate your position," he said, "but may I suggest—respectfully—that it might be wiser to postpone your visit to the cathedral for a short while? That is, if by postponing it you can obtain the financial security to complete the remainder of your work at perfect leisure, without worry?"

"How do you know," I said, "that I don't enjoy financial security already?"

He giggled. A rotund, fruity sound that caused a sting of irritation to run through me.

I said, "Am I to take it that you've been systematically prying into my affairs?"

Another giggle.

"Let's just say, shall we," he said softly, "that we have been making a few polite inquiries?"

My skin crawled faintly, as if an industrious little spider had

44

drawn a filament across it. I indicated the tumbler which he had put down on the carpet beside his chair.

"Well, my friend, you've finished your drink. I'm sorry, but I think it's time for you to go."

He puffed a little as he levered his body more upright in the chair.

"I assure you, the job is very brief. You would find it absurdly simple. From start to finish it will take you three days, travelling included. Naturally, we shall pay all your out-of-pocket expenses."

"Then it isn't even in Madrid?"

"No, in Paris."

I shrugged. "I spent five years of my life in Paris. I'm very fond of it. But at the moment I've got no inclination whatever to go back there."

I was moving towards the door to open it for him. I was becoming impatient. I hoped for his sake that he was a man who could take a hint.

He sat where he was and said quickly:

"It isn't even as though it was all that risky."

I seemed to detect a hint of veiled mockery in his voice. It prompted me to sarcasm.

"Oh, no! I suppose you only want me to climb the Arc de Triomphe, or the Madeleine?"

"We only want you to climb the outside of a villa."

"And what do I have to do when I've climbed it? Pinch the family portraits? Shoot somebody?"

He rubbed a fleshy hand over his mouth, as though concealing a smile.

"If I didn't know you better," he said, "that remark would make me think you might be—well, a little bit afraid."

"Afraid? You sneak your way into my apartment, with a suggestion that I should break the law!"

His tone was emollient. "I didn't say you *were* afraid. I

45

only said you might have seemed so . . . to someone who doesn't know you as I do."

"Look, Ridgeling, you haven't convinced me yet that you ever knew me at all."

I turned the handle of the door that led into the hallway, looking at my watch.

He said, "Who would ever dream of calling you a coward, after the way you climbed into this apartment a few minutes ago?"

"That isn't something I do every evening. I don't make a habit of it."

"All the same, it does prove you still possess the old ability, doesn't it?"

"I'm not in the market for undergraduate exploits any longer." Again that little stab of nostalgia. "I suggest you make another journey to Cambridge or hire someone twenty years younger."

"Won't you close that door?" he said. "You haven't heard me out yet."

"Norman, your yearly income is obviously much larger than mine. Let me congratulate you. You've done well, Norman. You've got ahead. You're a big man now. However, one of the few advantages of my lonely occupation is that I don't have to work for people I dislike."

He said easily, "Oh, you don't have to like us to do this little job for us. I promise you, it will be greatly to your advantage."

"Please—put your hat on, my dear chap. Pick up your coat. The interview is over."

Now, for the first time, a small crease of anxiety appeared on his features.

He held up a hand. "My dear fellow, don't be hasty. I'm not going to deny that we're urgently in need of your services. I assure you, you would be doing yourself and several of your old Cambridge friends a great favour."

I shook my head. "Norman, you know the saying: If you don't tell me your troubles, then I won't tell you mine. . . ."

I walked down the hall and laid my hand on the lock of the front door. Rafael had used his key to lock it behind him when he left Ridgeling in the apartment.

Behind me, Ridgeling still held aloft a well-manicured hand.

"Wait! Aren't you even going to ask me how much money we are prepared to pay you?"

I hesitated. After a moment I let my hand drop from the doorknob and leaned against the doorpost.

"Well?" I said.

The hint of derision crept back into his expression.

"The amount"—his voice was gentle—"is five thousand, eight hundred and eighty-five pounds."

I blinked. The sheer size of the sum was enough to stagger me. But there was more. The figure was somehow familiar. I racked my brain. £5-8-8-5 . . . Where had I heard it before . . . ?

"Mr. Merganser," he went on, "would make certain legal arrangements for the sum to be paid to you free of tax . . ."

Tax. At once it struck a chord. That was it! The significance of the figure registered like the ball clicking into the slot of a roulette wheel. Five thousand, eight hundred and eighty-five pounds was the exact amount I owed the Commissioners of Inland Revenue. I had owed it for four years. Only my prolonged absence abroad had enabled me to fight a long and moderately successful rearguard action with H.M.'s Commissioners. The Commissioners had really been very good about it. They accepted the fact that I was temporarily domiciled abroad, and that the sales of my latest books had been disappointing. But when I eventually returned to England I would be able to postpone payment no longer. It was alarming to be faced with a bill for over five thousand pounds. Paying it off in installments would mean two years of grind: a series of talks and lectures, articles and reviews. Of course, I could always pay it off in a single lump by selling one or two of my pictures or pieces of sculpture; but to part with any of these would be like losing a limb. I made up my mind that I would have to remain on the Continent—no great hardship, after all—until some splendid windfall enabled me to discharge my debt at a single blow. In fact, of course, my finances had been shaky for several years, particularly during the time when I supported Margaret and the boy after we split up, before she decided to marry her New York businessman. (I wondered if Ridgeling was well-informed about that wretched business, too . . . ?)

Nonetheless, my enforced residence abroad was sometimes painful, a source of sadness and humiliation. Among the harsh, baked landscape of Castile I often forgot the tediousness of English life and the meanness of its politics and longed for its physical lushness, its greenness, its rain, the alternations of its leaden skies with skies of a rinsed and dazzling blue. And all the time I was oppressed, in spite of myself, with the nagging worry of that very large debt. . . .

Ridgeling was offering me my ticket home. He was offering me the freedom to go on working in my own way. He was offering me relief from a crushing financial burden.

It was a weighty offer.

He was staring across the room at me with an eagerness that was no longer concealed. He was anxious to know whether I would capitulate. He was greedy for it. He passed his tongue, lizard-like, over his soft, slightly parted lips.

"Well?" he asked.

I grimaced. "Yes, you've certainly been doing your homework. Have you been reading my correspondence with the income tax people by any chance?"

"As I said, we have our sources of information."

"My God! You don't mean you *have*?"

48

Again I felt the clinging touch of a cobweb on the back of my neck.

"What's your answer?" he said.

His eyes glinted in their pads of fat. Another flick of the tongue across the lips; another smile.

"Well?" he demanded. "Are you willing?"

He took out his pocketbook from the inside pocket of his coat and carefully extracted a long strip of paper.

"Reckoning at two dollars and forty cents to the pound, five thousand, eight hundred and eighty-five pounds is equal to fourteen thousand, one hundred and twenty-four dollars. I have here a check for one-third of that amount. We'll regard it as a binder."

He held it out to me.

"Four thousand, seven hundred and eight dollars."

I stared at the oblong piece of paper for a long time. Ridgeling was making it clear to me that, if I wanted it, I would have to walk over to him and take it. He wore a look of supreme satisfaction and superiority. His old score with me, whatever it was, was settled.

It had taken him twenty years, but he had done it.

V I

———•◦•———

The Cadillac went down the four-lane highway that links Madrid with Barajas Airport at a steady seventy miles an hour.

There was something vulpine about the lean profile of the chauffeur, illuminated from below by the dim light of the dashboard. Flecks of light from the lamps outside distant buildings slid like snowflakes across the patent-leather peak of his cap. He held his head stiffly, without glancing around; but even if he had looked back he would have heard nothing of the strange conversation taking place behind him. Ridgeling had pressed a button that brought a glass division sliding down smoothly into place as soon as I stepped into the limousine. I call it a limousine because it seems inadequate to call a machine the size of a frigate just a car or an automobile.

Ridgeling reclined in his corner, wrapped, in spite of the heat, in his dark topcoat. His face beneath the brim of his felt hat was an indistinct half-moon. His small white hands showed as a pale circle where he held them folded in his lap. He seemed almost as far away, in the cavernous interior of the Cadillac, as if he were on the far side of a ballroom. I shifted about on the deep cushions. When I spoke into the darkness, my voice was incredulous.

"A key? You want me to bring you a key?"

His voice was muted, silky. "A key, yes."

"A key from a glass case?"

"Correct. The key is in a glass case, in the front room on the third floor."

"What does this key unlock? The safe at Cartier's? The vaults of the Banque de France?"

"That is a question that need not trouble you."

"Yes, but don't you think it would give me a lot more confidence if I knew?"

"Your only concern is simply to secure that key."

"Oh, yes? And you really expect me to believe that I won't be bothered by guards, or watchdogs, or spring traps, or burglar alarms, or anything else like that?"

"I can absolutely guarantee that you won't be."

"Forgive me if I find that very difficult to swallow."

"I assure you that there are no dangers of that sort at all."

"Then why not just put a ladder against the wall of the house and climb up to the third floor? Why use *me?*"

"You'll understand why when you get there."

I grunted. "It sounds as if I could be in for a very nasty shock."

He made no response. I tried again.

"That must be some key," I said.

Again no reply. He was not to be drawn. There was a lofty air about his silence that made me think he was giving me a taste of a relationship familiar to him but not so far familiar to me: the relationship between employer and employee. I didn't relish it. I pushed back resentfully into the thick upholstery. In spite of myself, I was rather impressed that Ridgeling had been able to whistle up a luxurious limousine for his own use on a fleeting visit to Madrid. This was no musty, clapped-out hired car: this was a spanking new model; and José-Luis, as Ridgeling had called the driver, handled it with a very un-Spanish expertise.

"Yes," I repeated sourly, "that must be a very important key . . ."

He said nothing, letting me stew in my failure to elicit an answer. I sat and glowered at the sinewy outline of José-Luis's neck and shoulders.

Ridgeling said nothing further until we reached the roundabout where the road to the airport intersects the road to Guadalajara. Then he pressed one of his battery of buttons and the inside of the Cadillac was bathed in a mellow glow.

He was holding out a long brown envelope. As soon as I took it he snapped off the light. The pasty blur of his face remained vivid in the darkness.

"That is your air ticket from Barajas to Orly and return," came his voice. "First class."

"Thank you."

"You will receive the balance of your fee when the key from the glass case is delivered to our representative at the Hotel Torcy."

"At the Hotel Torcy. As arranged."

I tried to sound brisk and businesslike—less for his sake than for mine. If I was going to take on this curious assignment, I meant to keep on my toes.

"The remainder of the fee will be in the form of a check for nine thousand, four hundred and sixteen dollars. Like the check you received last night, it will be signed by me and drawn on the Chase Manhattan Bank. If you send both checks to your London bank manager—Lloyds, isn't it? Thirty-nine Piccadilly?—he will negotiate them for you in the usual way. Our man at the Torcy will also give you a paper to certify that the entire fee was earned working wholly abroad in the employ of a foreign company. This will enable your accountant to claim tax exemption for the gross sum."

I noticed that when Ridgeling talked about money he tended to be ceremonious. It was not displeasing to me.

I tucked the air ticket in my jacket pocket as the Cadillac

began to wallow over the dirt road that led to the unfinished international air terminal. It drew up in the forecourt, and as I stepped out a porter in blue denims came forward to take my single suitcase from José-Luis, who had stowed it on the front seat beside him.

José-Luis closed the door of the Cadillac and stepped back. Ridgeling sidled his way across the back seat. A push of a button and the window slid down. His round pale face peered up at me from the shadowed interior.

"I won't leave the car, if you don't mind."

A small white paw came through the window. It felt boneless.

"It was very interesting to meet you again," he said. "It was a very great pleasure."

The porter was waiting at the entrance of the terminal.

"Good luck!" murmured Ridgeling. I wondered if I heard a giggle in his voice.

The segment of pudgy flesh with the round green eyes stared at me from the lower corner of the glass like something in the bottom of a fish tank . . . or in a dream, was it? A dream? I wondered . . . dismissed it from my mind.

The car was already driving out of the forecourt by the time I was following the porter down the steps of the escalator.

Standing on the escalator, I pulled out the Iberian Airlines ticket to check the flight number and time of arrival. Clipped to it was a strip of green-tinted paper with two lines of writing on it, neatly typed on an electric machine with an italic type face.

The writing said:

TIME: 11 p.m.–5 a.m., May 17th–18th.
PLACE: 12, Av. Fustel-de-Coulanges, Puteaux.

VII

———•━•———

I had lived in Paris for five years, but I had only a very hazy
idea concerning the whereabouts of the district called Puteaux.
I seemed to remember that it was situated somewhere to the
northwest of the Étoile.

This was confirmed next morning by Madame Martissot,
who owned the little hotel near the Luxembourg where I always stayed when I was in Paris. The short sweep of her hand
indicated that Puteaux was a place of little importance, that
one showed a strange taste to wish to visit it, but that if I did
so, then that was my own affair. Puteaux was not in the metro-
politan area; it was beyond the pale, in the *banlieu,* beyond
the farthest terminus of the metro. Its one virtue, Madame indicated, was that it was easy to find. One walked from the
Étoile straight up the Avenue de la Grande Armée and its continuation, the Avenue de Neuilly. The route, she declared,
was scenically barbarous and hideously noisy, as the Avenue
de la Grande Armée is the starting point of the autoroute to
Cherbourg.

She was amazed when I expressed the intention of walking
there. It was three kilometers from the Étoile. It would take
me over an hour. When she saw that I was serious, and that
this was not another manifestation of my English sense of

humour, she ceased trying to dissuade me. Admirable and perceptive woman that she was, she had divined that I had come to Paris in a confused and troubled frame of mind.

I walked to Puteaux because I wanted to think. The long trudge took even longer than Madame Martissot had supposed, for I went first to Lloyds Bank in the Rue des Capucines to put my dollar check into safekeeping. Then I turned my face westwards and set out for distant Puteaux.

I hoped that as I walked I would shake off some of the uneasy, what-have-I-let-myself-in-for feeling that was strengthening its grip on me. Pretend as I would, I had to admit that the entire business unnerved me. My mind was still attuned to the Prado and Velázquez.

On the way up the Avenue de la Grande Armée, which was as noisy and featureless as Madame Martissot warned me it would be, I stopped at a café to fortify myself with a pernod. Although the sun shone down, and being in Paris, even in the Avenue de la Grande Armée, is always a pleasure, I did not sip my drink in the carefree way in which I had sipped my *zumo de limón* in the Plaza de Cibeles. Was it only forty-eight hours before?

However, by the time I reached the northern stretch of the Seine, loitering for a moment on the Pont de Neuilly and gazing down at the Île de la Grande Jatte, I had regained a good deal of my self-confidence. I steeled myself to go through with this thing as rapidly and energetically as possible. It seemed the safest course.

There was a fair amount of the old spring in my step as I went on up the Avenue de Général de Gaulle to the Place de la Défense. A few more minutes and I was in the Avenue Fustel-de-Coulanges.

This was a scouting trip. I meant to keep out of sight while I was spying out the land—to mingle, as it were, with the crowd. But in the Avenue Fustel-de-Coulanges there were no crowds to mingle with.

Although it was called an avenue, and looked broad and prosperous enough, it was actually a cul-de-sac. There was a twenty-foot wall blocking off the far end of it. The purpose of the wall was unknown to me until I heard the rattle and thunder of a main-line express. It was probably a cutting of the line that ran into the Gare St. Lazare. Number Twelve was up by the wall, the last house on the right-hand side. I strolled slowly beneath the fresh emerald leaves of a row of plane trees, keeping as much under cover as possible. But if anyone was watching me from an upstairs window they would have heard my footsteps ringing on the pavement or on the round metal grilles around the base of the plane trees. The avenue was deserted. I realized that concealment was out of the question. I would have to carry out my reconnaissance for tonight's climb in full view of any observer.

My first sight of Number Twelve gave me a shock. Staring at it, my back propped against the last of the plane trees, I saw that it was empty. I took out the pair of opera glasses that I had borrowed from Madame Martissot, and with that rather limited help I scanned the front of the building carefully. Shutters with peeling grey paint were fastened across every window. I guessed that they were bolted securely from inside. The villa stood back inside its own garden, the beds and bushes untended, the drive overgrown with tussocks of weed. The ten-foot-high ornamental gates set in their massive railings were fastened with a big padlock and a thick rusty chain. Neither the gates nor the railings had known a fresh coat of paint for a good many years, and certainly not since the end of the war. The flight of steps leading up to the front door were cracked and out of joint, the bricks of the risers loose, the cement decayed. The plaster was weeping in patches of the walls. The whole picture was one of utter neglect.

What was the mystery of this place, once obviously resplendent and commodious? Property in Paris is as scarce and sought after as in every other capital city. Who could afford to keep a once-fine house, obviously the biggest in the avenue, tenantless for so many years? Puteaux was not a fashionable suburb, and the proximity of the railway line was no selling point; but the villa could even now be put back into excellent order. As it was, with the chickweed and pearlwort pushing up through the ground, and the steps invaded by stonecrop, it looked brooding and sinister.

The railings blocked me out from any close examination of the house; and the wall of the railway cutting and the wall on the other side, which shut off the house from the neighbouring property, prevented me from approaching it from the side. What I was able to see was not reassuring. I could negotiate the railings all right, but reaching the third floor of the villa would be another matter. I realized with dismay that the walls of the villa were completely smooth. They offered no handholds. The spots where the plaster had flaked off revealed only another, whiter layer of plaster beneath. There were no bricks to provide the roughened surface to which I might have clung. The outsides of French houses usually have shallow recesses at intervals of two or three feet that make them as easy to climb as a stepladder. Here this feature was lacking. There were none of the usual mouldings around the windows and over the top of them. Furthermore, the windows on each floor were arranged diagonally, and even if I could get some kind of toehold on the tight-fitting shutters, the distance between the floors was too great to attempt an upward diagonal leap.

Hadn't Ridgeling, or Merganser, or whoever wanted me to reach the third floor, seen Number Twelve, Avenue Fustel-de-Coulanges, for himself? One intelligent glance at it would have shown that I was being paid to attempt something that was impossible. Not even the most experienced of nightclimbers can scale a sheer wall. We need drainpipes, guttering, balconies, window sills, stanchions, porches, pergolas, conservatories—anything that projects and overhangs. Here there was —nothing . . .

Was this the meaning of it? Was Merganser indulging in a bet of some kind—a wager that this particular building could not be climbed? If so, his money appeared to be safe. It was possible that if, later that night, I managed to get around the back of the house, I would discover what I needed. I doubted it. I had evidently been chosen as a so-called expert for this job because the building concerned was considered virtually impregnable.

Well, as Ridgeling had told me, my only concern was to lay hands on that key. What the mighty Mr. Merganser, whose name shook thrones and rocked republics, needed it for was none of my business. All the same, my former mood of gloom came stealing back over me. If I couldn't reach the top floor and get the key, then I had no doubt that I would forfeit the promised two-thirds of my fee—almost four thousand pounds. No, somehow I had to solve the problem. Somehow I had to scramble my way up to that front room on the third floor.

The only person who had appeared in the avenue since my arrival had been a middle-aged woman in a nurse's uniform, pushing a pram. She vanished into a house a hundred yards away without glancing in my direction. Anyway, if anyone was watching me, they would already have seen me sauntering down the avenue towards the house. I needed a closer look at that villa.

I left the shade of the plane tree and stepped across to the high metal gates. I gripped the scaly surface of the iron rails and pushed my face against the railings. My eyes raked the outside of the villa with a kind of desperation that betrayed the intensity of my desire to imprint every detail on my memory. To my nostrils was wafted the evil stink of the clumps of fool's parsley dotted between the laurustinus bushes.

My grip on the railings tightened as I saw it. My eyes detected the gap in the defenses for which they were probing. But even as I saw it, my spirits sank, my mouth went dry. The chance which my eyes offered me was so problematical . . . so very slender . . .

Beside the villa, between it and the wall of the railway cutting, was an old coach house, which had probably served as a garage in the later years of this maltreated property. Its pitched roof was surmounted at one end by a small square stone platform on which stood a blackened weathercock. The platform, a slab of stone no more than eighteen inches square, was almost on a level with the side window on the third floor. And the far shutter of that window hung ajar. Could I . . . ? Was it possible . . . ? The slates of the coach-house roof were soft and friable. But it was neither of these things that troubled me. What made my mouth even drier, bringing back a sour aftertaste of pernod, was the sight of the gap between the coach-house roof and the top floor of the villa.

That gap looked enormous . . . Yet I was sure it was my one chance to get the key and earn the rest of my fee. If I could leap that gap and seize hold of the shutter . . .

My throat was tight. I gazed at the gap as if I was hypnotized. I was trying to gauge it. All at once I realized why Ridgeling had kept harping about Bollow's, and about Brass Street. The gap in front of me was about the same distance as that old leap of mine across Fox Lane. . . .

I remember thinking: If only I was the same man now that I was then . . . But *am* I? . . .

I don't know how long I stood there. I kept swallowing. My tongue seemed to have grown too big for my mouth. No doubt about it, I was horribly frightened.

My eyes travelled downwards, past the clenched white knuckles of my hands. They fell on the corroded length of chain that held the gates fast shut.

I gave the gates a half-hearted shake, knowing as I did so that they wouldn't budge. There was a loud metallic rattle, but the chain did its job. It was then I noticed that the padlock which secured the rusted links was not old and tarnished like the chain itself. It gleamed bright. Brand-new. Around the key-hole glistened a clear light smear of oil. It could only have been applied within the last day or two.

The best place to buy the supplies I needed was an out-fitter's I knew in the Boulevard des Italiens. I had an omelette and a piece of *tarte aux cérises* in a café near the Madeleine; I was anxious not to eat a heavy meal until this evening's ex-ploit was over. Then I made my way to the Boulevard des Italiens. I bought a black woollen jersey, a pair of dark woollen slacks, and a pair of the special soft suede boots made by a firm in Angoulême called Arco Frères. They laced up high in front and had a thin composition sole. The leather was of ex-traordinary suppleness. I had owned a pair of Arco boots be-fore; they fitted my feet and ankles as if moulded to them. I also bought a pair of light pigskin gloves which clung to my fingers like an extra skin, although they were only intended for emergencies and I doubted if I would use them. Then I went into Aux Trois Quartiers and bought a small torch. I was equipped.

It was only three o'clock, but I hailed a taxi and went straight back to my hotel, took a bath and slipped into bed. The hotel was in a side street, and when I pulled the curtains the room was comparatively peaceful. For a while I tried to read, in order to calm my nerves. I had packed a copy of Ortega y Gasset's *Sobre El Amor*, and I remember being amused by an essay about a boatload of English spinsters descending on Barcelona. "Always marvellous, that English nation, com-pounded equally of the Bible and *Snobisme* . . ." But I found it impossible to concentrate. I put the book down and tried to sleep. I could only doze. I turned fitfully this way and that. I don't know if the prospect of the coming ordeal kept me awake, or if I was actually afraid of sinking into sleep.

Perhaps if I drifted into a deep sleep the old dream might take hold of me, fill me with unendurable dread . . . the signboard with the Gothic letters . . . the birds twittering in the darkened office . . . the orange light palpitating on the horny skull of the creature with the gummy strands oozing from its eyes . . .

I forced myself to sit up and switch on the light. After a while I realized that staying in bed was going to make me more tired than walking about. I got up and pulled back the curtains, dashed cold water over my face and body, and dressed myself in the black jersey and dark slacks. I fastened the Arco boots carefully, neither too tight nor too slack, and made sure that the knots were doubly tied. Then I stowed my gloves and flashlight in my pockets and put on a lightweight jacket.

Killing the next four hours was an intolerable business. I must have drunk at least a pint of black coffee at various cafés before I found myself, in a somewhat somber and fatalistic frame of mind, flicking my flashlight on the dial of my wrist watch as I stood once more beneath the plane tree outside the gates of Number Twelve. Eleven-fifteen. There seemed little point in waiting until the middle of the night. My instructions said any time after eleven. I might as well get it over. I had taken the metro from the Palais Royal to the terminus at the Pont de Neuilly and the Avenue de Madrid, then walked across the Seine to the Place de la Défense as I had done twelve hours earlier.

I took off my jacket and laid it on the iron grille at the base of the tree. A few cars passed along the distant Avenue Président Wilson at the top of the cul-de-sac and changed gear to drone around the Place de la Défense. There was no traffic in the avenue itself. The cars appeared to be parked a little more densely beneath the plane trees; that was all. There were no pedestrians. This was a very lonely part of Paris. There was scarcely any light from the houses, set far back in their old-fashioned gardens. The sky was clear and the stars shone, but there was no moon. The only illumination was the bluish-crimson glow of the far-off neon signs of the Champs Elysées in the sky beyond the roof of the villa.

It was a matter of thirty seconds to reach the top of the wall that blanked off the avenue from the railway cutting. I went up easily at the point where the iron railings of Number Twelve met the wall at right angles. The brickwork and the angle irons made the climb an elementary one. There were no spikes or broken glass on top of the wall, and the upper layer of bricks was firm and solid. The layer was only one brick wide—and if it had been daytime I would simply have walked straight along it. However, I didn't want to attract attention by shining my flashlight, and as I sensed that there might be an unexpectedly sheer drop to the railway line below, I considered that my best plan was to cover the distance to the stables on my hands and knees. The wall was the same height as the roof of the stables and would bring me onto it; so it was pointless to descend into the garden unless I wanted the bother of climbing back again onto the stables afterwards.

I was standing on the wall, thinking this over, when I got a fright that almost ended the whole enterprise on the spot. Stupidly I had forgotten about the trains. I had been so busy working out my moves that I didn't hear the approach of the express. It let off its tremendous two-tone horn when it was right beneath me. Its huge headlamp scraped the wall like a searchlight. What the driver thought, if he caught sight of a black-clad figure teetering on the wall, mouth open, clawing for balance, I don't know. The train ran on, horn screaming, thumping me with a great wash of wind that nearly knocked me off the wall, then almost sucked me into the cutting. I flopped on my knees, clutched the bricks and stayed hunched down until the express had bucketed around the distant end of the cutting.

I felt sick and shivery. I was more determined than ever to

get this thing finished. I had no thought now of scouting around the garden or the back of the house, looking for a handy tree, or an outhouse with a ladder, or the latticework of an old wisteria or clematis. I knew instinctively that the walls of that house were unscalable from ground level and that my one chance was that half-opened shutter on the third floor. I crawled inelegantly but swiftly along the wall and dropped onto the coping of the stable. My heart was already beating faster than I liked. I was ominously short of breath.

I allowed myself the shortest possible time for a breather —not more than the few seconds it took to give the route up the stable roof a quick inspection with the flashlight. I knew I was forcing the pace, but I was eager to establish myself on that little stone platform with the weathercock as quickly as possible. Once I was there, I would have presented myself with a *fait accompli*. There would be no turning back. Besides, there was always the chance that some stray passer-by would catch the brief gleam of my flashlight. Nor was it out of the question that that engine driver had really spotted me and would tell the police when he reached the Gare St. Lazare that he had seen a cat burglar.

As I went hand over hand up the short ridge of the roof my feet kicked away two or three loose tiles. They fell with only a slight noise into the matted flowerbeds at the side of the stables. In no time at all I was grasping the base of the weather vane and hauling myself onto the stone platform. I guessed that it consisted of a few slabs of masonry placed on top of a bricked-in chimney. Powdery grains of mortar hissed onto the slates as I put my weight on the slabs. They wobbled and shifted unpleasantly as I slowly pulled myself upright, wondering if the weather vane would buckle or snap off and pitch me thirty feet to the ground.

Finally I stood with my back to the vane, my hands behind me, locked mistrustfully around it. From the platform I could turn my head to peer down into the black gulf of the railway cutting. The lights of central Paris were clearly visible, and from my vantage point I could see the headlights running in rows of dots along the Avenue Président Wilson and around the Place de la Défense. I had half expected that a breeze would nibble at me as I stood aloft; on the contrary, it felt even more close and clammy. Mind you, already my woollen shirt was clinging to my body, damp with sweat. The sad truth was that after less than ten minutes I was blowing hard, out of condition, regretting that I had ever taken on this bizarre assignment.

There was bitterness in my heart as I stood on those insecure slabs and strained my eyes across the gulf at the dark bulk of the house. Part of the bitterness was directed at Ridgeling and the faceless Merganser, but most of it was directed at myself. I felt that I was behaving like a mindless idiot, betrayed by my senseless pride and vanity.

The beam of the flashlight wavered as it traversed the surface of the wall, whose pitted plaster had the texture of eczema. The light travelled upwards until it came to rest on the window with the unfastened shutter. And the shutter, hanging wide, disclosed a narrow window ledge, no thicker than the shutter itself. Beyond it was the smeared gleam of a sheet of glass.

Yes, that leap, upwards though it was, was perfectly feasible: to a man of twenty—supremely fit—with his confidence in his own powers still intact. But the man who was staring across that gap tonight was over forty . . . and the wood of the window ledge might be rotten . . . and there were no flower beds but only hard-packed gravel beneath the windows of the villa . . . and the memory of what happened at Copenhagen came cutting into my brain . . .

Copenhagen. A shiver went through me. That insane adventure! And for what? An attempt to impress a woman I scarcely knew and did not particularly like. More vanity! I had not even been able to reap any reward for having beaten

Paul and Martin. You can't make love with a cracked pelvis and two broken legs. I shuddered as I recalled that lunatic scramble. I remembered the shout of triumph I had sent booming across the river towards the darkened walls of the Palace of Amalienborg. It was a shout that turned suddenly to a yell of despair as I slid off the pinnacle and went bumping and crashing down and down and down . . .

For a second my flesh felt again the final crunch and the first instant of blinding pain. I held more tightly to the weather vane, fighting off the sense of vertigo. My present situation merged with the moment when I lost my footing on that other little platform on top of the huge, ornate green copper roof . . .

Thinking back, it strikes me as fantastic that I finally got up the nerve to hurl myself upwards into the void.

I believe I jumped at the very second that I opened my eyes again. I knew by instinct that it was now or never and realized that the longer I looked at it, the less I'd like it.

I thrust hard with my heels and flung myself across the void between the stable and the villa. As I rocked forward on my toes and took off, my leg muscles went as taut as piano wires. I felt the stones of the platform crumble.

It was the collapse of the platform that made me miss my objective—the window sill.

My right hand grabbed for it . . . and missed. My legs were flailing in empty air. My brain became water.

It was a fluke that saved me. For some reason the shutters of that particular window were cut in two and hinged in the middle. My threshing left hand knocked the top half backwards, and I found myself hanging with my left arm crooked over the lower half of the shutter.

That second of grace gave me just enough leverage to make another attempt to gain the window sill. I clawed sideways, clutched the sill, heaved myself bodily right in through the window. I went through it head first in a welter of glass. The window exploded with a bang that must have been heard all down the Avenue Fustel-de-Coulanges. I hit the floor on my hands and knees among ringing stars of glass. For half a minute I was too weak to get up. I seem to remember that I was shouting with laughter like a lunatic.

When I got to my feet I stood swaying for a moment. There was a horrible smell in that room—a wet smell like rot or toadstools, or as if the room had been a cave festooned with dead seaweed. I groped for my flashlight in my trousers pocket and fumbled with the button. By its light I could see that the room was much smaller than I had supposed. It was quite empty, except for two chairs. There was something unusual about them. I went across to take a closer look. They were dentist's chairs. They were of an obsolescent pattern and very dusty, and on the neck rests, the backs and the arms there was a curious tangled-up arrangment of leather straps. I touched one. It had a soapy feel to it. On the floor nearby were two dusty coils of thick cord, like clothesline. I stirred them with my foot.

Then I remembered what I had come for. The key. There was no time to loiter. I must find the key and make that horrible jump again in reverse. And now the platform with the weather vane had gone, and I would have to leap for the base of the roof and the coping. This was bound to prove less simple than it sounds. I could break a leg and lie there on top of the stable until my shouts attracted the attention of the neighbours or the police. Or I might have to drag myself back along the top of the wall overhanging the railway cutting with a fractured arm or dislocated ankle . . .

The beam of the flashlight revealed a single door. I crossed to it. I turned the handle and found it was locked. It didn't look too formidable and I got ready to charge it. Actually, I had no alternative. I had deliberately arrived at the villa without weapons and without anything which could later be interpreted by the police as a housebreaking implement. Being caught with implements of that kind always carries a stiffer penalty. If I had encountered nothing more than a simple Yale lock, I could always have pressed its rounded tongue back with the strip of toughened plastic that covered the identification tag in my wallet. But the lock on this door was a heavy old-fashioned brass affair, with a square ward, and a thin strip of plastic would be of no use. I would have to use my shoulder.

I was not going to earn my fee, after all, without acquiring a bruise or two. . . .

I put pressure on the door with my knee and shoulder. No good. So in my usual impulsive and rather dotty way I retreated a few paces, laid the flashlight on the bare boards with its beam pointing forwards, and took a run at the door. I hit it crouching, my point of impact just above the level of the lock. There was a rending noise from the mechanism on the far side of the door. The ward had smashed through the catch. It was only then that it occurred to me what a bloody fool I should have looked if the door had opened inwards instead of outwards. I would have sustained a very sore shoulder.

I gave my upper arm a vigorous rub as I went back to recover the flashlight. I walked into the other room. Same fetid, musty smell. The beam struck directly on a small ornamental table with a glass top a few feet in front of the door. It was what is called a specimen table, standing on delicate spindle legs. The design was popular in the nineteenth century for exhibiting bibelots—coins, patch boxes, scarabs, flint arrowheads, seals, pieces of semiprecious stone. This one, I recall, was fashioned in the shape of a heart.

I stood above it, shining my light through the glass. The heart-shaped interior was lined with tattered and discoloured scarlet satin.

It held only one object: a large, dark-toned iron key,

mottled with rust. It looked clumsy, not at all distinctive or elegant. Foolishly, I felt disappointed.

Then I gave the glass a sharp tap with the blunt end of the flashlight. The glass broke with a sad little tinkle. I hate damaging anything, even mouldering specimen tables in forgotten rooms, but it had to be done. With a series of shorter blows I dabbed around the jagged hole in the center. Then I put on one of my pigskin gloves and lifted out the iron key.

At that moment the naked bulb high up on the ceiling was snapped on. I whirled around. A man in a dark uniform was standing beside a door at the far end of the room. His hand was on the tarnished light switch. Another man was seated on a kitchen chair, a few feet away from the man in the uniform.

It took me a few seconds to realize who the seated man was. After all, as I had told Norman Ridgeling, I had long ago lost touch with him. It was a dozen years since I had last seen him.

It was Bay Russell.

VIII

The man in black uniform switched off the electric light inside the room and switched on the lights on the staircase. He went ahead of me down the stairs with Bay bringing up the rear. Our steps rang hollow on the boards. At the top of the landing and in the hallway were a few forlorn chairs and tables, their surfaces coated with an inch of dust. Cobwebs drooped from the *torchères*; strips of faded silk sagged from the walls. At the foot of the stairs I passed an ormulu sofa with the stained yellow satin hanging off it in tatters. Life-sized statues of Muses or Graces held aloft lightless flambeaux, their bronze flesh ringwormed with verdigris. It was evident that this had once been a great and noble house, but it was now a shell from which the soul had departed. The stale air lent it the atmosphere of a tomb.

As the man in uniform unlocked the front door, I noted the gleam of fresh oil around the keyhole. He stood aside to let me go through, switched off all the lights and stepped out after us, closing the door and relocking it. The door was plain, solid and smooth-fitting, and on second glance I saw with surprise that it was made of grey-painted metal. It was obviously of more recent date than the rest of the house. I realized that there had never been any question of my getting into the house through that metal front door.

Bay and I stood side by side in silence at the top of the steps while the chauffeur (if that was what he was) entered the stables by a side door. A few seconds later the double doors swung open and a dark-coloured Mercedes drove out. The chauffeur brought the car to the foot of the steps, then got out and ushered us very correctly into the back seat. After much unlocking and relocking of doors and gates we drove into the Avenue Fustel-de-Coulanges towards the Place de la Défense.

Bay and I sat together without saying a word. We had said nothing to each other after my first astonished greeting, and even then his handshake had felt oddly limp. The surprise of the meeting had knocked the wind out of my sails; but I was not sorry to sit quietly for a minute or two while the Mercedes moved downhill towards the river and began to climb the hill in the direction of the distant Arc de Triomphe. I leaned back in my corner with my whole body shaking, my legs throbbing and feeling like balloons. The back of the car smelled of the sweat that soaked my woollen shirt, while my heart pumped like an engine, and I had some difficulty in controlling my thoughts. They flickered through my head like the passing lights of the Avenue de la Grande Armée. Strangely enough, it was not my jump twenty minutes ago at the villa that filled my mind; it was the jump eleven years ago in Copenhagen. Again and again my mind took me slithering down the green copper roof of the Bourse onto the moonlit cobbles, my imagination hauling up my shattered limbs like a puppet and dashing them down over and over again . . .

By the time we reached the Étoile the gloom which the villa had cast over Bay seemed to lighten. As we joined in the Catherine-wheel of cars spraying out around the arch we began to chat in a desultory way; but even then I still sensed in him that curious restraint. I wonder why we were both so ill at ease? Not that I would have expected us to behave, of course, as we would have done in the old days at Cambridge —meeting in our rooms at Conderton Building at the beginning of a fresh term, say, or at Oddenino's during the vacation for a bust-up in town. We were too middle-aged for all that youthful punching and slapping and high spirits. All the same, our mutual reticence was strange and rather sad. For an instant, when I had first spun around and blinked at him in the light of the upper room, I felt a flare-up of the old eager warmth. But then it subsided quickly, as soon as I had detected no answering enthusiasm in Bay's eyes.

The Mercedes swung left-handed down the Boulevard Pereire, then along the Boulevard Malesherbes. Bay leaned sideways and put a hand on my knee.

"Hungry?"

"Very. I feel I've lost about a stone in weight."

"You deserve something special. I've already arranged it."

The car stopped outside the Restaurant Reilhac, off the Place Malesherbes. The sight of its neat façade with the bay trees in the tubs outside the door had an agreeable effect on my gastric juices. I knew Reilhac's well; I used to dine there often when I lived in Paris . . . whenever I was in funds, that is. As we left the car I looked at my watch and saw that it was five to twelve. I raised my eyebrows at Bay, but he only smiled and motioned me to enter. The Mercedes coasted twenty yards down the street and parked under a lamp. I glanced at it as I went inside, impressed once more by the trappings in the shape of liveried chauffeurs and glittering limousines with which Mr. Merganser furnished his lieutenants.

The name of Basil Merganser was never actually uttered by either of us during the course of the subsequent meal. Yet his presence hovered almost tangibly around us; he was the invisible host at the table with the two special covers that awaited us in the corner of the empty restaurant. What but the money and prestige of the Merganser organization could have kept the Restaurant Reilhac open at midnight? Two waiters settled us into our places as briskly as though they had only just arrived on duty; the headwaiter stepped forward with the menu. I knew him and greeted him. He made no answer, although I was sure he recognized me. He looked at me obliquely out of the corner of his eye, as though seeing me in Bay's company intimidated him.

Bay ordered sparingly, but I studied the list of dishes at some length. I felt like a schoolboy being treated to a blowout after hitting the winning six. I realized that the feeling of elation which I always felt after these nocturnal adventures was stupid and dangerous; but it was undeniably exciting, nonetheless.

Bay watched me as I ate my *moules farcies*, and we talked about the old days at Cambridge. He reminisced about the dons, the girls, the trips on the river—everything. We delved conscientiously into the details of our past. But it was somehow a forced performance, and our nostalgia was perfunctory. I examined Bay over the rim of my glass and wondered what had gone wrong. Of course, in one sense the circumstances of our meeting again were unnatural; and we had also been placed in a false position by the suggestion of the employer-employee relationship. But it was more than that. In some fundamental way Bay had changed. Had I changed too? Was that why he was looking at me in the same wary manner in which I looked at him? Was he, too, saddened by the knowledge that the past was dead? The hopeful young men who had set out from Conderton Building to conquer the world had vanished. Their places had been stolen by a failed painter and the subordinate of a financial bully.

The main lights of the restaurant had been turned off, and Bay's head was outlined against the soft glow of the illuminated fish tank on the other side of the room. The shoal of trout inside it waved their fins in the tepid water in lazy contentment, unaware that they had only been reprieved until tomorrow's lunch. Bay was a lot heavier than he used to be, almost as solid-looking as the chauffeur waiting in the Mercedes outside; but unlike the chauffeur, he looked puffy and out of condition. He was the same age as I, but already had a noticeable paunch and a double chin. He looked office-bound, though nowhere near as gross in appearance, of course, as his colleague Norman Ridgeling. All the same, I was dismayed to see similarities between two men who had once been so utterly dissimilar. It had something to do with the pallor of the skin and with the cut of the expensive suit. And in spite of all their apparent prosperity, they both seemed shifty and ill-at-ease.

Our attempt at carrying on a light-hearted conversation was beginning to depress me, and when my *ris de veau* arrived I switched the talk to a more neutral topic. I was curious about the villa in the Avenue Fustel-de-Coulanges, and I asked him about it. I wanted to know about that steel front door with the flaky grey paint and the dentist's chairs with the crumbling leather straps.

He was picking slowly at the flesh in the severed claw of a cold lobster. He put the shred of pale meat between his lips and let the gutted red claw clatter back on the plate. He picked up the articulated tail portion of the lobster and placed it between the jaws of the silver cracking tool. He stared at me thoughtfully, then decided that it would do no harm to tell me. Since we had last met his voice had taken on a faint mid-Atlantic accent.

"The villa belonged to the Clairvaux family. The last of them was killed at Bir Hakeim, in the Western Desert. During the war the villa was taken over by the German army."

"The German army?"

"By Amt Two of the R.S.H.A., to be exact. It then stood empty for twenty years. Does that answer your question?"

It did. R.S.H.A.—Reichssicherheitshauptamt. I felt a little shudder of repulsion.

73

"And the place belongs to Mr. Merganser now?" I said.

"That's right."

I put down my knife and fork, took a sip of Sancerre, and felt in my trousers pocket. I brought out the iron key and placed it on the table in front of him.

"I was going to take this around to the Hotel Torcy in the morning. I may as well give it to you now and save myself a journey."

He looked at it without interest and went on scooping at his lobster. I said:

"Why did you want me to do this stunt? Was it for a bet?"

He waved his napkin towards the key.

"Keep it," he said. "A souvenir."

I stared at him. "You mean it's useless?"

"Completely. If you don't want it for a souvenir, throw it in the ash can, or the river, or somewhere."

He dipped his fingers in the finger bowl and wiped them. He took a folded square of blue-tinted paper from a top pocket of his waistcoat and threw it on the table. I picked it up and opened it. It was a check for nine thousand, four hundred and sixteen dollars. It was signed by B. R. St. J. Russell and dated that same day.

I had not been expecting any difficulty in collecting the rest of my fee; Basil Merganser was not exactly broke. But this was cash on the barrelhead. I picked up the check.

"You must have felt very sure," I said, "that I could climb into that house?"

"Oh, I was. I never had any doubts about it. One or two of my colleagues weren't so sure, but Norman saw the force of my suggestion as soon as your name was out of my mouth. That's why I sent him to Cambridge to check up. The Seeley Library, the Old Schools, the jump from Caius to the Senate House, the gatehouse at St. John's—and, of course, your *pièce de résistance*, the flying leap across Fox Lane."

"That was small stuff. You should have seen some of the buildings I've climbed since then!"

"Then it only shows that we picked exactly the right man."

I stared down at the tablecloth.

"Bay, you are Ridgeling's superior, aren't you? It isn't the other way around?"

He was nettled. "Of course I'm his superior. I gave him his job with the organization. I happen to control the entire activities of the group in Europe."

I raised my head and gave him a little smile. I would have hated it if my old friend had turned out to be Norman Ridgeling's office boy.

"I'm sorry," I said. "I haven't got my bearings in this business yet. I'm still a new boy."

After a moment he smiled back. If we were no longer close to one another, at least he didn't try to patronize me, like the egregious Ridgeling. He pushed himself back in his chair and laughed.

"My God, when you came bursting through that window . . . barged through the door . . . It was like old times! . . ."

"Well, Bay, we've certainly broken a good deal of glass in our day, you and I."

"Yes, we have—though I was never a nightclimbing type like you."

"No, you had too much common sense."

We were both laughing now. We seemed to be generating some genuine warmth at last. He took a small share of the superb soufflé pràliné I had ordered and we chattered away with increasing animation.

Then, over the coffee, I saw the cautious expression creeping back into his eyes.

"Frankly," he said, "we only picked that villa in Puteaux to . . . well . . . test you."

"And why the hell should you want to do that?" Then, before he could say anything, I went on: "Anyway, it hardly matters now. It's all over. Thank heaven I'll never have to do anything like that again. I'm cured. Tonight I cleared that particular bug right out of my system. Tonight I made my last climb. Positively. Would you like to order some of Monsieur Reilhac's special calvados, so we can celebrate?"

I ought to have foreseen what would happen next. Perhaps unconsciously I had already guessed it. He gave a kind of sigh and reached into the inside pocket of his jacket. He drew out a checkbook, placed it on the table and opened it. It contained the same type of blue-coloured checks as the one he had just given me. He produced a gold pen and laid it beside the checkbook.

"We gave you a very generous fee for climbing into the house at Puteaux. That was just the dress rehearsal. Now we want to hire you for the real performance. How much do you think we ought to pay you?"

My mouth was dry. I was suddenly aware of the fact that it was almost one o'clock in the morning; that the restaurant was silent and full of shadows; that the streets outside were hushed. The fish flapped somnolently in their brightly illuminated condemned cell. The headwaiter stood near the kitchen door, his face grey with fatigue. I shook my head.

"No. What you witnessed tonight was definitely my farewell appearance. I've entered upon a well-deserved retirement."

"If you could climb into that villa tonight, you shouldn't find the next climb too difficult. Not you, not with your nerve. And you've kept yourself wonderfully fit."

I shook my head again.

"I'm sorry. No."

"It's a challenge. When we were students I never knew you to refuse a challenge."

"Two hours ago, while you and your friend were sitting in that upper room, I nearly fell and broke my neck. Isn't that enough for you?"

"In the old days it would have been enough just to have

mentioned it to you. This time I'm not only offering you a challenge, but also a very large sum of money."

"No, Bay. No sale."

I saw, to my surprise, that he was beginning to perspire. Could the proposition really mean so much to him? He signalled to the headwaiter and told him to bring a bottle of calvados. The best. Then he continued to argue with me. My refusals became more stubborn. His fingers toyed in an agitated way with the little silver box containing the saccharin tablets which he put in his coffee. He went on insisting that the climb he wanted me to attempt was a simple one. At Cambridge I could have done it standing on my head. I would find it, he promised me, as easy as falling off a log—a phrase that he immediately realized was badly chosen.

I watched the well-manicured fingers turning the silver box over and over.

"If it's that simple," I asked, "why don't you get a professional climber to do it?"

"Oh, we tried. Professionals don't somehow seem to have the flair."

"I suppose you mean that they aren't stupid enough to jump off a garage roof onto a worm-eaten shutter?"

He sat up straight and looked me straight in the eye.

"We're very old friends, you and I. Do you imagine I'd ask you to do this if I thought there was any risk of you harming yourself? What sort of swine do you think I am?"

"Look," I said, "there's no point in us quarelling about it. My seat is already booked on the return flight to Madrid. I'm busy with a book and I want to get back to it."

"You mean *Diego Velázquez and His Circle?*"

"That's right."

I suppose Norman Ridgeling had told him about it. They were thorough, these people. I had the same creepy feeling I had had when I was with Ridgeling, of a spider's web brushing across my face. It made me doubly determined to travel

77

straight back to the Calle Pedrell. In less than forty-eight hours I would have recovered my typescript from the vaults of the Banco de Vizcaya, where I took it the morning before I came to Paris, and started work again.

Bay said, "You've already earned enough to pay off your income tax. Are you going to turn down a chance to set yourself up in comfort for the rest of your life? You could devote your entire energies to a history of art in twenty volumes, if that's what you want."

For the tenth time I shook my head.

"No. No more entanglements. I've got to finish my book. No wine, no women, and no song. Just the business of writing those last six chapters."

"We'll throw all our resources behind you. You'll have whatever help you need."

I opened my mouth to tell him for the last time to go to hell. I was going to blast him to bits. But suddenly he held up his hand and started speaking. He spoke quietly, urgently. He was pleading with me. His fist was clenched around the small silver box so hard I thought it would burst and scatter little white tablets all over the table. All at once I realized that he was afraid. Bay was frightened.

He appealed to my vanity. He appealed to my cupidity. He even appealed to our old friendship.

It was a complete reversal of our roles. Until now it had been taken for granted that as far as the Merganser organization was concerned I was the low man on the totem pole. Now it appeared that I was not only important, I was indispensable. Well, well! I leaned back and drank my calvados, letting it run through me with a malicious satisfaction. Bay was telling me how grieved he was that after he left Cambridge for Colombo as an apprentice in the oil business he had lost touch with me. Soon he was literally begging me to do this job for him. He obviously had a great deal at stake. Perhaps the order had come down personally from Mr. Merganser himself? Maybe Bay had received the royal command? Why else was he so nervous?

His voice rose higher. I glanced towards the kitchen door, but the headwaiter was leaning back discreetly against the wall, his head lowered.

Bay went on talking, obviously afraid that if he stopped I would cut in with the ultimate rejection. I am a fool, I know —but the skillful way in which he conjured up our past friendship finally made an impression on me. The years when we had been at the university together had been such buoyant ones. I hated to think of Bay in trouble.

He pushed the key from the Avenue Fustel-de-Coulanges to one side of the table.

Then he took another key from his pocket and set it down deliberately between us. It was of quite different and very unusual design.

He drew his checkbook towards him. He opened it and smoothed it with his palm.

IX

———•◆•———

They say that Venice is as much an Eastern city as a Western one; and certainly when it rains in Venice the water comes crashing down like a monsoon in Burma. Whenever I go to Venice it always seems to be raining.

The Venetians know their weather. They are a gay people, but are also well provided with raincoats and umbrellas. That evening the lights glistened on wet silk and gleaming oilskin as the rubber boots went splashing cheerfully through the downpour. The coloured umbrellas bobbed past the café where I was sitting like a shoal of jellyfish in an underwater ballet. The footlights were the weaving orange lamps of the gondolas moored to the quay, a dozen yards to my right; the backdrop was the great Basilica di San Marco, looming through the rain like an enormous coral reef.

The dusk was falling across the Canale di San Marco. The islands of Giudecca and San Giorgio were fading in the indeterminate mist of rain and sea. A curtain of moisture wreathed the Palazzo Ducale and went driving along the promenade past the pillar of the famous lion. It was a miserable night. Nonetheless I would have been happy enough in Venice under ordinary circumstances. Here I had lived for over five months when I was completing my study of the transition from the Baroque to the Rococo. This was an early piece of work, but it still has its value. I wrote it soon after my decision to abandon painting, and I shall always be grateful to Venice—rain and all—for smoothing away some of the hurt of that difficult period of my life.

Tonight I was very tense and very tired. After less than thirty-six hours in France I had found myself on a plane for Italy. I was already sorry that I had let Bay talk me into a further installment of this unusual enterprise. During the flight, and now, seated at the yellow table under the colonnade at the corner of the Libreria Vecchia, I felt an increasing desire to get back to the world of Velázquez, Coello and Zurbarán. More important writers than I have found that the forced interruption of a book can sometimes induce a sense of frustration almost akin to hysteria. My fingers trembled as I drank my third glass of Pinot; I glanced for the fiftieth time at my watch. My instructions were to sit in this particular café from nine o'clock onwards, when someone would contact me.

It was chilly in the colonnade. I thought of the genial atmosphere of Quadri's, a minute's walk away in the Piazza, and of Harry's Bar, a few steps along the quay behind me. I looked at my suitcase, propped against one of the thick pillars. The smell of damp humanity jostling all around me was oppressive; the squawking from the ubiquitous transistor radios was giving me a headache. I was tempted to pick up my suitcase and walk away. A *vaporetto* would ferry me quickly to a snug little hotel I knew near the Cà d'Oro.

What restrained me was the thought of the two checks that I had posted off that morning to my bank in the Rue de Capcines, coupled with the thought of the third and bigger one that was to come. But it was not, as I have tried to show, uniquely a matter of money. Bay had juggled with my curiosity and my pride.

All the same, I was nervous. Climbing into Number 12 Avenue Fustel-de-Coulanges had turned out to be a mad enough exploit. How much madder, therefore, was the next one likely to be? As Bay was settling the bill and giving the headwaiter an enormous tip, he had remarked that I was capable of a standing jump that would have brought me a gold medal at the Olympics, if they had awarded a medal for the standing jump. He was so pleased with the remark that he repeated it several times, slapping me on the back as we left the restaurant. *"Gold medal! . . . Gold medal! . . ."* From which I gathered that I was being paid to perform a jump that was at least as dangerous as the jump across Fox Lane, or the one from the stables to the shutter.

I found myself taking in the details of the Palazzo Ducale across the square. Automatically I made a *coup d'oeil* of its exuberant façade. I could have shinned up it in three to four minutes. I even worked out the route, having nothing better to do. I could have climbed the cream-and-buff surface of the Basilica, too, if it came to that. It presented no outstanding problems. Its bulbous contours offered innumerable hand- and toe-holds. I could travel from stylobate to pediment in one continuous movement without pausing to take a breath. In no time at all I could be perched on the tympanum, with its mosaic of gold stars, reading the inscription on the book in the paw of the winged lion.

I always used technical terms like *stylobate, pediment* and *tympanum* when thinking out my climbs. When I was climbing classical buildings I memorized their features and mentally ticked them off as I mounted higher and higher. *Entasis, echinus, abacus, architrave, triglyph, pediment, acroterion.* With buildings of the classical revival, of course, the terms were different. *Dado, entasis, impost, archivolt, extrados, spandrel, abacus, architrave. . . .*

What kind of building was I going to be faced with in the near future? Would it be a nightclimber's nightmare, like the villa in Puteaux—smooth and featureless? My travel-weary brain kept repeating the words: *"Gold medal . . . Gold medal . . . Gold medal . . .*" I remembered my most impulsive jump of all—Copenhagen—heard my nails squealing on the metal roof as I slithered towards the eaves . . . faster . . . faster . . . into the wheeling darkness beneath. . . .

My spirits sank lower as my eyes dropped on the copy of the *Corriere della Sera* that lay on the table in front of me, its pages softened by the rain. Half an hour ago, on an inner page, underneath a paragraph about a missing opera singer, I came across a news item that disturbed and saddened me. Mauro Petrel, the peerless and brave, was dead. The veteran torero, who fought under the name of *El Albaceteño*, had received a *cornada* in the groin with a trajectory of twenty centimeters and died three hours later in the bullring hospital. The item was headed Madrid, but if he actually died at the bullring it seemed more likely that the goring happened at some little town in the provinces, where the bullring hospital was primitive and the local doctor probably drunk and dirty. . . .

So a bull had finally done for Mauro Petrel. It was some years since I had followed the *fiesta brava* with my early fanaticism; but I had often heard him boast, when we were dining in company at Casa Paco or Valentín's, that the bull would never be born that could kill him. That was just the way I used to feel about the buildings I was going to climb . . . None of them would ever kill *me*. . . .

I drained my Pinot and stared at my suitcase. I reached down and took hold of the handle.

A voice called my name.

I looked up.

A young man in a white duck uniform was leaning over my table. His fingers touched the peak of his white cap, spangled with silver braid and bearing the monogram BM between crossed anchors. His hair was a straw-coloured yellow, the face square and open, skin pink and glowing, cheekbones prominent. As he smiled I noticed that his teeth were large and even; one of them on the left side was artificial and made of some metal like platinum or stainless steel.

"If you will kindly follow me, sir? The ship is ready."

His English was good. He was about to reach up and put something away in the breast pocket of his tunic when curiosity made me put out my hand and catch his wrist. He was holding a snapshot of me. It showed me sitting at the café table in the Plaza de Cibeles, a glass of *zumo de limón* beside me, writing in a notebook. He tucked it in his pocket and fastened the crested silver button.

A little stiffly I rose to my feet. Politely he took my raincoat from a chair and helped me on with it. I had not expected to be met by someone from a ship—at least, not a Merchant Navy officer. The only ship I thought might possibly become involved was a gondola or a motorboat. At that stage I thought I had come to Venice to break into a local house or palazzo. I had already pictured myself straddling some narrow ledge above a stagnant canal, nerving myself to jump for the building opposite.

I was soon to find out that I was several hundred miles wide of the mark. Venice was only the jumping-off point, as it were, in a very much wider scheme. . . .

I was cold; I was resigned. As I prepared to follow him he made a signal and another man in white uniform, without the braid and elaborate insignia on his cap, hurried forward and picked up my suitcase.

It was hard to be sure, after the fast-moving events of the past thirty-six hours, but I was almost certain that I recognized him as the chauffeur who drove me to Barajas in Norman Ridgeling's Cadillac.

X

The motor launch was large and powerful. It could have accommodated a score of passengers with ease. It was moored only a few hundred yards from the Piazzetta, and I followed my white-clad guide along the promenade of the Riva degli Schiavoni as far as the bridge leading to the Riva Cà di Dio. The boat was tied to a gold-topped pole opposite the Gabrielli Sandwirth Hotel. As soon as the hawser was cast off I left the saloon and went up on deck. The young officer was in the enclosed wheelhouse with the helmsman. He turned around and smiled.

I went to the rail and watched the elegant triple lampposts of the Venice waterfront dissolving in the mist and rain. We bore away to port, leaving the Isola di San Giorgio on our left. We were not going south towards Sottomarina or Chioggia. Was I being taken to one of the big hotels on the Lido? Again my guess was to be proved wrong by several hundred miles. . . .

I turned up the collar of my raincoat and dug my hands deep in my pockets. There was a slit in each pocket so that I could put my hands through into the pockets of my trousers. There the fingers of my right hand felt the scrap of paper in which I had wrapped the key which Bay Russell gave me at

Reilhac's. It was like no key that I had ever seen before. It was beautifully made, the shank and ward of copper, the head carved from bone or ivory. I estimated that it was between two and three hundred years old, but this was merely a rough guess. I could not even tell for certain which continent, let alone which country, it might have come from.

The launch arrowed its way into the bank of rain. It closed over us like a tunnel. The string of lights was swallowed up. The rain was all around us, almost like a fog, the soft swathes glowing in the strong headlights of the launch. I hunched my shoulders against the needles of spray. The deck rose and fell steadily beneath my feet.

The man who had carried my case stood at my elbow with a china mug of black coffee. I took it and nodded. He went back down the companion ladder without a word. I stared at the mist and sipped the scalding liquid. It was very good coffee; an unusual, pungent blend. African? Caribbean? As I drank it I reminded myself of the vow I had made on the plane from Paris. In executing this job I would allow nothing to deter me. Nothing. I was ashamed that Ridgeling and Bay Russell found it so easy to tempt me. Twice in quick succession I had let myself be bribed; perhaps *bought* was the proper word. It was true I needed the money, but where was the process which Ridgeling had set in motion to stop? Did Merganser's people only have to wave a piece of blue-tinted paper for me to drop whatever I was doing and come running? No, this time was the last. I would have salvaged my finances and earned the respite Merganser's money would give me. Therefore I would concentrate all my attention on the task ahead. I would keep my eyes wide open and my lips tight shut.

Overhead I could hear sea birds flying and calling. I wondered which way they were travelling. Their sad cries drifted down to me, muffled by the mist. Listening to them, I felt isolated, preyed upon by my fears. . . .

Then the bows of the launch swung sharply and I saw the

cheerful lights of the Lido. Soon we were sliding past it in the mist and heading out through the gap in the islands into the choppy waters of the Adriatic. The whole enterprise seemed to keep widening out into more mysterious horizons. Where on earth were they taking me?

The cold current of uncertainty flowed faster inside me, like a stream threatening to burst its bounds. Then I made up my mind to tackle the young officer in the wheelhouse. If his explanations were evasive, I would insist on him turning back. I had the irrational feeling that if I failed to act the launch would simply go on and on, swaying farther and farther across the darkening sea.

I was walking forwards towards the wheelhouse when my uncertainty was suddenly resolved. We were moving northwards, with the Punta Sabbioni abeam of us, when all at once the grey vapours appeared to shred away. There lay the ship. She was a slender, medium-sized cargo vessel; she looked fast and newly built. Her sides and superstructure were an immaculate white, glistening in the murk. She had a single yellow funnel at the stern, concealed by a swept-back cowling. On the funnel the letters BM were painted in blood-red inside a black circle. From her short tripod mast drooped a house flag which I had no doubt carried the same device.

The launch drove in towards the Jacob's ladder hanging amidships. The young officer in the wheelhouse gave a quiet order to the helmsman, carefully adjusted his cap, then turned and smiled at me.

The engine stopped. A handful of dim figures lined the rail and watched as the launch sidled up to the vessel. A name swam by in neatly blocked letters as we passed the bow.

She was called *Marmoset*.

XI

No sooner had I been shown to my cabin and my suitcase placed on the tubular stand at the foot of the bed than there was a soft concussion from the engine room beneath my feet. I could feel the steel plates tingling beneath the deep carpeting that stretched from one wood-panelled bulkhead to the other. We were on our way to sea.

My first glimpse of the *Marmoset* had given me the impression that she was a cargo carrier; but the passenger quarters were as luxurious, if not more so, than those of any of the great passenger liners. I had been given a double cabin with a wide bed, elaborately flounced and valanced, which by no means filled it; there was room to spare for a built-in wardrobe and a long dressing table. To the right of the bed a door led into a small dressing room with an ample chest of drawers; a door to the left led to the bathroom. Here, illuminated by subtly concealed pinkish lights, were the shower-bath and two washbasins. Around the big mirror was a frieze of ornamental fish—goldfish, Hi-Goi and shubunkins—embedded with shells and coloured stones and bits of red and green seaweed in glittering strips of transparent plastic. Between the lavatory and the bidet was a narrow white-painted metal door. Unlike the other doors, it had not been disguised with panelling. Its surface was studded with rivets. I tried the handle. It was locked.

I think it was when the engines started up that I first began to feel the full weight of the fear that never afterwards really left me. As long as I was in that ship I carried it around with me like a looseness of the bowels. In fact, I was already suffering from a fairly severe attack of diarrhea, brought on, I suppose, by a mixture of high-pressure travelling, my exploits at Puteaux, and wolfing too much rich food too late at night at Reilhac's. The condition wasn't improved by my present uncertainty. I hadn't bargained for a sea voyage of unstated duration towards an unspecified destination. As I fiddled in the bathroom with the new razor, new facecloth, fresh tube of shaving cream and the other toilet articles that had been placed ready for me, I remembered Ridgeling and Bay Russell. At certain moments they, too, had betrayed the presence of fear; the assured surface had cracked and revealed the funk beneath.

I lay down on the bed without bothering about the coverlet of peach-coloured satin. It was very hot down here. I felt as if I were enclosed in an iron tomb. My feeling of being in a coffin was enhanced by the low mahogany rail that ran around the edges of the bed, to stop the sleeper tumbling out in a heavy sea. I was too exhausted, too busy fighting down my rising mood of panic, to get up to look for a lever to lower the heating, or the switch to turn off the light in the pink-tinted bowl on the ceiling. I felt like a prisoner.

Someone tapped on the main door of the cabin. I crawled off the bed to open it. A steward, his jacket as white as a hospital uniform, stood in the corridor. He had the same fair hair and high cheekbones as the young officer who collected me at the Piazzetta. He spoke to me in bad French.

Captain So-and-So's compliments (I didn't catch the name). Would I care to present myself in the dining room, where a meal was awaiting me?

No. I sent the captain my thanks, but I wasn't hungry.

Could he bring me something on a tray, then? The cook would be glad to prepare anything I fancied.

I repeated that I wasn't hungry, and he bowed and went away and left me alone. I shut the door and leaned against it. I had not eaten since the plane landed at the Venice airport. I felt weak but had no appetite. I went to the bathroom and sucked down some water, tepid and tainted with chlorine, from the tap. Then I opened my suitcase and began to put my clothes away. My movements were slow and clumsy; I felt old, discouraged, out of my depth.

I remember I was fumbling my lightweight suit onto a hanger when the music first started. At first none of it registered. It was a blurred, buzzing sound, distorted somehow, as if a record or a radio were being played by someone several cabins away. It was mixed up with the general wash of noise from the ship's engines.

I had more pressing matters on my mind. Just as I had felt impelled to speak to the officer on the launch, so now I felt impelled to speak to the captain of the ship. Bay Russell had told me that my instructions would be passed on to me within twenty-four hours, and it seemed likely that the captain—who else?—would be the man to do this. At least he would be able to give me some information about what was happening. Glad to leave the cabin, I went out into the corridor.

It was wide and brightly lit. There were three doors on one side, three on the other. The passenger deck had the dead atmosphere of an empty railway carriage or an empty bus, and I felt instinctively that most if not all of the other cabins were unoccupied. Then the door of the cabin two doors along from mine suddenly opened and a woman came out.

The music flared up briefly until she shut the door behind her with a firm hand. She was a tall, solid woman, with short, thick yellow hair cut in a stiff fringe on her broad forehead. She was about thirty-two or thirty-three, handsome in a muscular kind of way. She wore a white overall in which I could actually hear the starch creaking as she moved down the corridor towards me. She advanced with an unnerving silent tread, the rubber soles of her white canvas shoes making no sound on the carpeted companionway. She looked like a masseuse, or a hospital matron, or perhaps a woman doctor. The overall was sleeveless, and around one strong wrist was a wrist watch on a thick strap of dull gold. I stood to one side as she went past. She didn't greet me or smile. Her bright blue eyes gave me a hard, deliberate stare. Then she turned the corner and was gone.

On my way towards the stairs I paused outside the cabin she had left. Now I could hear the music distinctly. A woman's voice sang a light operatic aria to an orchestral accompaniment. Softly I pressed down the spring-loaded handle and pushed.

The door was locked fast. I was becoming used to that by now. I shrugged and moved on.

I felt better as soon as I breathed the clean air on the upper deck. I made my way to the white-painted rail and gripped it, sucking down mouthfuls of the salt breeze. The shuddering and shaking of the engines had exaggerated my fears; up here the beat of the engines was almost imperceptible. As I shed the feeling of being enclosed and trapped, my confidence began to flood back.

The night was still overcast and there were no stars, but the blanket of cloud had lifted from the surface of the sea. No coastline or distant lights were visible. Apart from a certain humidity in the mild gusts that blew off the water, I might easily have been sailing across the North Sea or the Atlantic. As it was, I was bound . . . where? Never mind. At this particular moment I felt less oppressed than I had for many hours. I had a false sense that everything might turn out painlessly after all.

For some time I stood there, my legs planted apart, the cold, moist metal soothing to my fingers, alternately watching the play of the ship's lights on the bubbling wake and shutting my eyes and gulping down more lungfuls of air. At last I braced my shoulders. I felt ready.

First, though, before confronting the captain, I would take a look at the ship. I started to stroll around the main deck, half expecting a member of the crew to touch me politely on the shoulder and ask me to return below. I don't know why I was so suspicious—at least at this opening stage. I suppose ships naturally encourage my tendency to claustrophobia. There had been absolutely nothing in anyone's behaviour so far to make me think that my status was other than that of a privileged guest, except perhaps for the blond woman's failure to greet me (but perhaps she didn't speak English or French?) and the fact that the man who had carried my case may have driven me to the Madrid airport.

A very brief inspection was enough to show me that the *Marmoset* was kept in perfect order. The decks were spotless, the paintwork immaculate, the brasswork highly polished. She was a credit to the captain with the unpronounceable name. There wasn't a speck of rust or an untidy corner in any part of the ship. Every item of gear was oiled and bright. I was impressed. Even the house flag with Mr. Merganser's initials on it which flapped on the jack staff had the appearance of being brand-new.

No one spoke to me or interfered with me. Members of the crew, dressed in a neat, identical blue serge uniform, padded past me, intent on their duties. They took no notice when I showed a close interest in the cargo which was stowed on the afterdeck. It struck me as curious that a number of large canvas-covered crates were lashed down on the upper deck instead of being stowed down in the hold. I went and had a good look at them.

Three or four of them were nearly seven feet high, the remainder only a little smaller. At first I had assumed that they were wooden boxes; but when I prodded the canvas it yielded under my fingers. The canvas was stretched over what felt like a row of metal struts. It was several seconds before I realized that the so-called boxes were actually cages and that the smaller ones appeared to have some sort of wire reinforcement tensioned between the struts. As I poked at one of them the wire scraped and there was a sudden rustling and squeaking from inside the cage. There was livestock in there, birds or poultry of some kind. I pulled my hand away as if I had been stung. Those creatures penned up in there . . . perched side by side in the dark, on a rocking, swaying ship . . . And what of the bigger cages? . . . As I walked past them I caught the acrid tang of sawdust and urine.

It took me a little time to locate the captain's quarters. They were right aft, in a corridor of the same length and proportion as the passenger corridor, but without its carpeting and mellow lighting. Nonetheless the officers' quarters were quietly luxurious in comparison with those in other cargo ships.

The captain's cabin was identified by an engraved plate that gave his title in French, German and some Cyrillic script that I took for Russian or Bulgarian. I knocked. There was no reply. I waited, then knocked again. No answer.

I was lifting my hand to knock a third time when I heard a step behind me. Swinging around, I saw the young officer who had brought me aboard the *Marmoset*. The silver tooth gleamed as he smiled at me, courteous as ever.

Was the captain available? I asked. I would like to speak to him.

The captain was on the bridge.

The matter was important. Would he kindly fetch him for me?

He was sorry, but it was impossible to disturb the captain at the present moment.

All the same, I would have to insist.

Deepest regrets. The captain had given strict orders. But it was late at night, and no doubt the matter could wait until breakfast time? The captain would be delighted to welcome me to his table.

No, I wished to see him tonight. At once.

The smile stayed in place. The more I argued, the wider it became. I began to hate that pink-faced young man. I got no change whatever out of him. He was immovable.

There was nothing for it but to trail back to my cabin in a very sulky frame of mind. Who was more important to the Merganser organization, I asked myself, the captain of a tramp steamer, or a man especially employed for a very large sum of money because he possessed a unique skill? For a moment I almost caught myself playing the organization game, ranking myself in the Merganser hierarchy alongside Ridgeling and Bay Russell. The thought restored my sense of proportion, almost my sense of humour.

As I came down the companion ladder the blond woman in the white overall was taking her key out of the lock of my door. She looked in no way embarrassed as she caught sight of me and moved up the corridor to the same door that she had left earlier. She carried a small white enamelled tray covered with a white cloth. It seemed to me that she held it on the far side of her body in order to hide it from me. Nevertheless I glimpsed beneath the cloth what I took to be the blue rim of an enamelled bowl and the shining shank of a surgical instrument. She selected another key on the slender ring in her hand and disappeared into the other cabin. All her movements were remarkably quick and economical for such a big woman.

The peach-coloured cover of my bed had been removed and neatly folded over the back of a chair. The sheets had been turned down and an extra pillow put at the foot of the bed. None of my belongings appeared to have been tampered with. I checked through the drawers and cupboards. It was possible that my Arco suede boots had been arranged with the heels turned outwards instead of inwards on the shoe rack, but I couldn't swear to it.

The faint sound of the radio or record player was audible again. Far from finding it distracting, I found it restful, comforting. It seemed to emanate from the wall beyond the bathroom. I went in and pressed my ear against the cold white-painted metal. Now I could hear it distinctly. The same soprano voice was singing an operatic air.

It was only ten o'clock at night, but I was dog-tired. I slid down onto the rim of the bidet and listened to the music. Didn't I know that tune? *Je t'adore, brigand* . . . A sweet, seductive lilt . . . Offenbach's *La Périchole*, wasn't it? . . . given most winters at the Opéra Comique. I closed my eyes . . . huddled forward . . . leaned my forehead against the door . . .

The soft voice soared and dipped · . . *Je t'adore, brigand, j'ai honte à l'avouer* . . .

It took an effort to shake myself awake and get to my feet. Somehow I had to stay awake long enough to take off my clothes and crawl into bed. But first I took my keys out of my pocket and looked at them, wondering if one of them would fit the lock in the white door. There was no need to try them; they were all too small. I brought out Bay Russell's ivory-and-copper key and unwrapped it from the scrap of paper and tried that too. It failed to turn.

I went into the bedroom and put the keys on top of the dressing table. The scrap of paper caught my eye. I must have torn it from a sheet of an old Madrid newspaper left in my suitcase. There was a corner of a cartoon showing a bull's horn—hooking against a fluttering scrap of cloth—the splintered tip, smeared with blood and sand and slivers of wood, one inch from an outthrust leg encased in its thin silk and flimsy sequins . . . a sharp white crescent against the matte black bulky hide . . . And as I emptied my pockets and let their contents clatter on the dressing table beside the keys, it struck me that until now I had not fully taken in that little piece of news in the *Corriere della Sera*. I would never see *El Albaceteño* fight again.

It was a very sad thought to take to bed with me. I was too tired to read, and in any case I had decided to get as much rest and sleep as I could in the period which lay ahead, before I had to make the final climb. At forty-one I needed as much rest as I could obtain to replenish the physical batteries, to lessen the niggling worry of those mental doubts. . . .

I took a last look around the cabin, my finger on the light switch. The flounces and silken bows on the bedhead intrigued me. Evidently I had been put in the cabin usually reserved for married couples or lovers . . . maybe it was even the ship's bridal suite. This special treatment made me feel as if I were some kind of sacrificial victim. It reminded me a little, too, of the actual bridal suite I had once occupied, with a real bride, in a village inn in the Bregenzerwald. . . . But all that was in happier times, a long time ago, a lost age. . . . And all that was another story . . . or had Ridgeling and Bay Russell really known about Maggie as well?

I turned on my side and made my body relax, glad of the music from the other cabin. I settled my head on the pillows and lay staring into the darkness, listening to it. I could tell now that it was a record, not the radio, for whoever was playing the music had put the same song on all over again. There was a curious and rather haunting effect, as if two women were singing the melody at once, synchronizing almost but not quite accurately on the notes, with a rather marked disparity on the topmost notes. It was as if two high sopranos were singing simultaneously, one of them with a finer voice than the other. Too sleepy to bother about it, I attributed this effect to an echo, or to a trick played by my own tired brain. . . .

The dual voice lifted and fell like the calm waves across which the *Marmoset* carried me to my unknown encounter. The words were facile, amiable, meaningless to me then . . . *I adore you, you ruffian . . . I'm ashamed to admit it . . . I adore you and can't exist without you.* . . . Ironically, the gentle complaint of that lovesick girl made me smile into the dark as I sank into sleep. . . .

Sleep . . . to sleep sound . . . without dreams . . .

I hadn't opened the porthole of the cabin . . . no matter . . . but it was hot down here . . . like a box. . . . The sound of the orchestra sccmcd to melt into a lost sound like the twittering of captive birds in a cage . . . a rustle of imprisoned wings . . .

XII

———•—•—•———

Captain Gheorgheniu was a very imposing man, with the air and appearance of a banker rather than a seaman. He did not rise as I entered the dining room at breakfast time, but indicated a chair on the other side of the table. A steward sprang forward to draw it back for me.

Behind the captain's head, with its smoothly brushed wings of silvery hair, I could see through the porthole the sparkling sky and dancing sea. We had left the mist and rain of Venice far behind, and there was a bright, bristling feel to the morning. I had slept well and meant to eat heartily, though I regarded the captain with a cautious eye as he introduced himself and the only other occupant of the table.

The captain sat very upright in his cane-backed chair. He was exceptionally tall and slender. Around his neck he wore a cream-coloured scarf tucked into his silk shirt; his jacket was of fine dark barathea. Around the sleeves were the four thick gold rings of his rank, and it was with something of a shock that I realized that his cuff links and the buttons of his jacket looked as though they were probably made of real gold. He had already breakfasted and was drinking his coffee, and I saw that beside the saucer lay a flat brown cardboard box about seven inches wide, ten inches long and an inch thick. My attention was immediately drawn to it, and he caught my glance. The corners of his long lips creased in a faint smile. I guessed that the box concerned me, but I tore my eyes away, unwilling to betray eagerness or anxiety, and examined the third member of our party.

No greater contrast to Captain Gheorgheniu (the captain, precise in all things, had spelled his own name out for me) could have been imagined. My fellow passenger was old, very, very old, with stooped shoulders and a tousled mass of greasy, unkempt grey hair. He wore a white linen suit that was as grubby and crumpled as though he had slept in it, and a droopy, old-fashioned, moth-eaten black bow tie. The shirt was frayed and dirty, though its owner was obviously not poor, merely indifferent and neglectful. The old eyes in the ravaged face were apathetic, only lighting up now and again with a glance of something like cunning or a childish sense of grievance. The old lips pouted beneath the ragged, bushy moustache, sometimes drawing back in a kind of sullen rictus to reveal stained brown teeth. From time to time his long, almost emaciated frame was racked by a really dreadful cough —a smoker's cough to end all smoker's coughs. Yet in spite of the general air of seediness and dilapidation, the hands that lay on the table were strong, square, youthful looking, the skin scarcely puckered or mottled, the fingers short and blunt-ended, but of fine shape. They were splendid, forceful hands.

Their appearance did not surprise me. It was only a few seconds after the captain had said, "May I introduce you to Monsieur Edmond-Amédée Boulanger—B-o-u-l-a-n-g-e-r?" that I realized who their owner was. The pause before recognition was excusable; Edmond-Amédée Boulanger was no longer as famous as he had been forty or fifty years ago, when he was the favourite disciple of Rodin, regarded as the equal of Aristide Maillol. Indeed, he was now practically a forgotten man; time and fashion had passed him by. But in his day his name had been a name to conjure with in the world of European sculpture.

Hastily I tried to call to mind the names of one or other of his more celebrated works. Vast expanses of bronze or marble —I ought to have been able to remember them. But there was no need, for on this occasion I was given no opportunity to do more than wish him good morning. I had scarcely sat down before Gheorgheniu made an almost imperceptible gesture and one of the stewards stepped forward and pulled firmly at the old man's chair. Boulanger frowned at the captain in a bemused way and then began to push himself to his feet. As he did so he dabbed with his napkin at his loose lips, and under cover of dropping it on the table artfully scooped up a handful of sugar lumps out of the bowl in front of him and slipped them in the pocket of his shapeless white suit.

When he passed my chair on the way to the door, I craned around and said to him, feeling a desire to assert myself in front of Gheorgheniu:

"Of course, I know your work very well, monsieur. I admire it tremendously. I look forward to a long talk with you. And may I say that I appreciate your taste in music? Please play your record player as loudly as you like. It won't disturb me in the least."

He stared at me blankly. His old jaundiced eyes wandered in a befuddled way across to the captain. He had not understood me. My nostrils detected a whiff of ingrained grime mingled with a strong odour of freshly ingested whisky. So the old boy had been walloping the bottle before breakfast, had he? I wondered why this poor old wreck was installed aboard Basil Merganser's magnificent ship. It seemed incongruous. Anyway, the smell of whisky explained why the old man had failed to register my remark about his record player. Not that it mattered. Gheorgheniu made no response to Boulanger's look and merely signalled a steward to pour him another cup of coffee. The man who had pulled back Boulanger's chair was helping him to the door, a hand on his arm. Boulanger was gently steered away, and I heard his feet stumble over the threshold. His only contribution to the conversation had been a vague grunt.

I was left alone with Gheorgheniu. He sat watching me as I breakfasted. The sea air had given me an appetite, and I ate my way steadily through the menu to show him how calm I was. We spoke, I recollect, only in a desultory way—about the beauty of Venice; how changeable the weather in the Adriatic could be; how pleasant it was to sail in such a well-found ship. We did not exactly fence with each other: our attitude was neutral. After all, he was not a principal in this affair but only an executive. Possibly he was as much in the dark about the larger aspects of the business as I was. He was just carrying out his orders. But in his own rather remote way he was as smooth and polite as the rest of them; indeed, as an employee of Merganser he seemed a lot more secure and confident than either Bay Russell or Ridgeling. This ship was his kingdom, more tangible and impressive than any of the perquisites which Bay or Ridgeling derived from their employment. And, like me, he had a real profession, a real skill. He was a qualified seaman. He didn't pursue the disposable, exchangeable career of the run-of-the-mill businessman. Indeed, from time to time he was forced to break off our conversation with an apology as one of his crew entered to report to him—a deck officer, a bosun, or a radio officer with a sheaf of messages. He dealt with them briefly, in his clipped, pedantic manner— more, as I have said, in the style of the head of a banking house than the captain of a ship. I learned later that in fact he was the commodore of one of Merganser's three fleets, and had been especially delegated to the *Marmoset* for this particular job. Hence the great air of authority and the almost servile deference shown him by the rest of the crew. In normal circumstances, apparently, the *Marmoset* was commanded by the young lieutenant.

At last I finished my toast and marmalade and pushed my plate aside.

"Now, Captain," I said.

He signalled to the stewards. They filed smartly out of the big cabin. We regarded one another gravely, in silence. The sun, striking off the sea, patterned the walls and ceiling with ripples of quicksilver. We were relaxed yet alert, like two fish basking above the warm, ribbed sand of a shallow pool.

"Could you please tell me," I said, "exactly how long this voyage is likely to take?"

"Seven and a half days." He was lighting a short cigar. The frankness and precision of his answer surprised me.

"And where are we heading for?"

"That, I am afraid, I am not at liberty to disclose."

"A harbour? An anchorage? An island? A canal?"

"I am sorry." His English was flawless but flat, the articulation a little laboured and far back in the throat.

"When my task is completed, will I be returning to Venice aboard this ship? Can you at least tell me that? It will simplify my personal arrangements."

"That, quite honestly, I do not know. I shall receive instructions on that point later."

He picked up the slender cardboard box with a kind of delicacy and rose from his chair. He walked slowly around the table towards me. He was certainly very tall: his sleek head almost touched the ceiling of the cabin. He laid it down with care in front of me. Then he moved back to his chair and regained his seat.

"I was ordered to hand you that package as soon as we were twelve hours out from Venice." He transferred his cigar to his other hand and consulted his watch. "We have been sailing now for eleven and a quarter hours." He smiled. "I think, to use an English expression, that we may 'stretch a point'?"

It was a very small point to stretch. What was the use of three-quarters of an hour when I was a hundred miles out to sea? Yet even this slight bending of the rules, in an organization as rigid as Merganser's, was significant.

Was Captain Gheorgheniu unable fully to control his own curiosity?

He smoked, leaning back with an air of unconcern, watching me. I let the box lie there on the table. I looked at it for a long time. The silver bars of sunlight played across its flat surface.

At last I got to my feet and picked up the box in the same gingerly way as Gheorgheniu. I placed it with great care beneath my arm and moved to the door.

"Thank you," I said.

It gave me a sense of satisfaction to see that the captain seemed disappointed.

XIII

———•◆•———

It was at least another half-hour before I could bring myself
to open the box. I suppose I was indulging in a form of self-
torture. I dreaded opening it, but at the same time there was
a perverse excitement in doing so. For a long time I stood on
the upper deck, holding it in my hands, staring out to sea.
Still no sight of land, on either bow. Gheorgheniu must be
steering a course right down the middle of the Adriatic. Somewhere beyond the sharp sunlit edge of the sea to starboard was
the Abruzzi or Apulia; somewhere off to port was Croatia or
Montenegro. . . . Incredible to think that this time last
week I was seated at a curbside café beneath the acacias, sipping my coffee and working at my notes, after standing in a
tall, cool gallery contemplating my canvas for the day. *La
Vista de Zaragoza*, I believe it was. I remember I spent a long
time trying to puzzle out which parts of the picture, if any,
could reasonably be attributed to Juan Martínez Mazo. Such
were my only troubles, one short week ago. . . .

At last the moment came when I could no longer put off
learning what was in store for me. I walked forward along the
foredeck, intent on finding some hidden corner where I could
open the box undisturbed. After I had taken a couple of dozen
steps I stopped in astonishment. The canvas covers had been

taken off the crates which had caught my attention the previous night. As I had guessed, the larger ones contained animals, the smaller ones birds. There were five of the larger crates, or rather cages, in all, and each of them contained a single beast. I imagine they were being shipped to some zoo: perhaps a personal gift from Mr. Merganser to the private menagerie of some oil-rich ruler in Arabia. As I recall, the beasts were all big cats. There was a leopard, and what looked to me like a jaguar and puma (I am no naturalist), as well as two more splendid creatures whose identities I did not know. One of these was much more active than its companions, which for the most part lay supine, dejectedly sunning themselves, seldom making an effort to shift their limbs and protest at their captivity. But this one animal pounded around and around the narrow orbit of its cage, rearing up on its hind legs to paw at the bars with never-ceasing energy. The same was true of the birds. There must have been a hundred of them, packed fifteen or twenty to a cage—all except one. This one was a particularly beautiful and exotic specimen which, from the fact that it occupied a cage to itself, must have been very rare. It was about eighteen inches long, its plumage of a sumptuous golden yellow, its wings and tail a glossy black, the beak red. It fluttered up and down its cage, restless and with a kind of desperation. Watching it made me forget my own troubles for a moment in the fear that it might dash itself against the bars and the wire mesh of its prison and damage its delicate body.

A steward had seen me stroll forwards onto the deck, and while I stood watching the occupants of the cages he politely set up a canvas chair for me out of the wind. I thanked him and sat down, the box on my knee. The sky was filled with luminous white clouds, set like irregular ovals of enamel in the brilliant blue of the depths beyond. The light was so intense that I screwed up my eyes as I ran my fingernail under the gummed paper with which the edges of the box were fastened. I took off the lid. Inside was a white envelope of the same dimensions as the box. This too was secured with gummed paper. Impatient now, I tore it open. From it I extracted four large black-and-white photographs.

I studied each of the photographs in turn. What I saw utterly bewildered me. The white envelope blew off my lap into the sea; a moment later the cardboard box slipped to the deck. I sat stiffly in my deck chair, trying to take in what my bargain with Bay Russell now seemed to have faced me with. . . .

There were two short, sharp detonations a little farther along the deck. Then two more. Vaguely I turned my head in that direction. From my sheltered place I could see that two men were standing at the rail, holding small-bore rifles. They were dressed in slacks, sandals and gaudy sports shirts. They were shooting at the gulls that slanted around the *Marmoset* as it ploughed its way towards its secret destination. There was no mistaking who the man standing nearest to me was, even though he was not wearing his black uniform: he was the man who had turned on the light in the upper room at the Avenue Fustel-de-Coulanges. His companion was the man who had picked up my suitcase in Venice, and now it seemed to me beyond any doubt that he was actually the same man as Norman Ridgeling's chauffeur. As I watched him he lifted his rifle to his shoulder and let go two shots at the screaming gulls. One of the birds staggered in mid-flight and dropped with the curling motion of an aspen seed into the ocean. The other man turned his head, saw me and gave me a familiar grin.

I saw all this in a daze. My mind was too taken up with the photographs for other events to register clearly.

The four photographs told me that I was not being paid to climb a building. They were photographs of a mountain.

I was being paid to climb into a cave.

XIV

———•••———

A cave.

My God. What had I let myself in for?

From the moment I opened that envelope I really began to sweat the big drop, as *El Albaceteño* would have said. At least with a building you could see where you were going. You could tell what you were up against. You could reconnoiter it in the daytime, walk all around it, work out your tactics with reasonable accuracy.

But a *cave!* . . .

That night I lay on my bed, the curtains drawn back from the portholes to reveal the moon-bathed sea outside. On the counterpane were spread out the four photographs. I had been scrutinizing them in a desultory way for over an hour. Those photographs had made me pass a miserable day. I had eaten no lunch and only a token amount of dinner. My conversation at table had been monosyllabic, to say the least; and as old Boulanger was barely sober, it was left to the captain to fill in the silence. He had treated us to a good-humoured but patronizing discourse that I found intensely irritating.

Two glasses of wine and a small glass of brandy were all the drink I had allowed myself. I was still in training—more strictly than ever, now that I saw what was facing me. I had started to ask myself seriously whether I could go through with it. After Puteaux, my nerves were scraped raw. I know there was a lot of money at stake—an immense amount by my standards. But I was starting to feel more and more like the middle-aged man who had suffered the crushing debacle at Copenhagen. I wondered how I could have been so foolish as to let this eccentric pastime assume such life-and-death importance.

The ship was well supplied with liquor; I envied old Boulanger the treble whiskies he was soaking up. It was his bottomless thirst, as a matter of fact, that revealed to me on my way back from dinner that he was not the person who owned the record player. As I was walking down the corridor towards my cabin I encountered the blond stewardess, or whatever she was, carrying a tray. On the tray was a bottle of Johnny Walker wrapped in its original tissue paper. I saw her take it into one of the cabins on the other side of the corridor, which until then I had thought were unoccupied. I lingered deliberately at my door, waiting to see what happened, and in a few seconds she emerged with an empty tray. Now Boulanger had left—or rather been assisted from—the table before I had, and I had not seen him during my late-night turn around the deck. Therefore I concluded that the bottle was for my elderly companion.

The photographs on the counterpane were arranged in a regular sequence. They were numbered from one to four with neat numerals in India ink. India ink had also been used to make prim little arrows drawing my attention to important points in the pictures.

The first showed a mountain. Some mountain! A monstrous, shale-strewn, boulder-studded disfigurement of the fair earth. The camera angled up from the base towards the distant peak, giving me an ant's-eye view of a colossus. It was the roughest, dirtiest, hairiest mountain I had ever seen. Where it was I hadn't the faintest idea—except that it was set in some exceptionally arid and stony part of the world.

The second photograph was taken high up on the mountain, near the summit. An arrow indicated the entrance to the cave. Black and forbidding, the leaf-shaped aperture was framed by rocks that resembled the cyclopean masonry of Mycenaean tombs, though as far as I could tell the rocks were entirely natural.

The remaining photographs were studies of the interior of the cave. They had been taken by flash, but nevertheless were not revealing. They seemed to portray curving walls of a substance like black glass, splintered or fissured along what looked like faults or lines of stress. The effect was geometrical, like a sculpture by Pevsner or Gabo. The flash had illuminated what looked like a huge cave of black ice. The photographs were magnificent, in an unearthly kind of way, although they told me almost nothing of what I really wanted to know. Probably my employers reckoned that I would see as much as I wanted to when I came face to face with it. . . .

I lay sprawled on my back in my shirt sleeves, gazing up at the ceiling. I debated endlessly whether or not to retire from the entire enterprise. Naturally, it occurred to me that Gheorgheniu, not to mention the two marksmen in the gaudy shirts, might have been given orders to see that I completed the job I had already been partly paid for . . . even if I broke every bone in my body in the process. They weren't playing about, these people. What I had previously taken to be a light-hearted pastime they regarded with deadly seriousness.

I twisted about, tormented. What connection had the copper key with the cave? That, too, I supposed, would become clear to me in Basil Merganser's good time. . . .

At intervals I got up and wandered on stockinged feet into the bathroom to suck water out of the tap. My mouth was permanently dry. I thought of the way *El Albaceteño* must have felt in all those cramped hotel rooms, waiting for a hearselike car like Ridgeling's Cadillac to arrive and carry him off to the plaza. He must have felt, as I did, that time was dislocated; that it could only be put right again at the very moment of supreme terror—when the "Gate of Frights" burst open and the black enemy bounded out to meet him. . . .

It was while I was gulping water from the tap that I suddenly felt an intense curiosity about that music. The beautiful, slightly double-tracked soprano voice had been singing to an orchestral or piano accompaniment ever since I had let myself into my cabin. Who was playing the records if Boulanger wasn't? The stewardess, perhaps? Was an impressionable soul concealed in that muscular body? I wanted to find out. The music was a link with sanity, with a kind of world I understood. I was intimidated by these people around me: the uncommunicative captain, the alcoholic sculptor, the enigmatic men who enjoyed shooting sea gulls. I thought of the strange cargo carried in the cages up there above me on the deck: the big cats and the mass of birds, all with the canvas coverings over them to shield them against the night. I thought of the ship, driving on and on through the darkness, bearing me towards the mountain . . . towards the cave . . . towards a stretcher or a grave. . . .

I felt that I had to do something. Anything. The person playing those records in there might prove to be my only ally aboard the ship. And the tune which was now being played for the third or fourth time tonight, and which had also been played several times the night before, struck me as a good omen. It was a tune with a special significance for me. It brought back the times when . . . But this is not the place to trouble you with all that. Let me just tell you that the tune was the old favourite, *"Plaisir d'Amour"*. . . .

The voice, in spite of its odd, split quality, rendered the fragile melody in a way that touched me deeply. It was not perhaps a great voice, and I would have preferred a piano or a harpsichord to the syrupy orchestral accompaniment; but the singer had succeeded in capturing the elusive essence of the song.

Wagner once said the first eight notes of "Rule, Britannia" summed up the English character. The first four notes of *"Plaisir d'Amour"* seemed to sum up the character of a Europe that was dead and gone. I moved back to the bedroom and sat on the edge of the bed and listened to it. It was painfully evocative . . . reminded me of . . . what? The string trio playing for me and Maggie in the little hotel on the Place Stanislas at Nancy . . . thoughts of a book I once learned almost by heart . . . Manon Lescaut dying on the banks of the Mississippi . . . the Chevalier rooting in the soil with his broken sword . . . digging a grave to protect his loved one from the teeth of the marauding animals. . . .

I sat there musing for what seemed a long time. Then all at once the music stopped.

Nothing strange in that The person playing the gramophone had probably decided to go to bed. But the sudden silence was oppressive, and when it was succeeded by the incessant wallow of the sea it grew more oppressive still. I got up and shut the porthole with a metallic clang that filled the cabin. Uneasy, I went back to the bathroom and listened at the white-painted door. Not a sound. Then, very slowly, I seemed to detect a faint, irregular undertone of something resembling sobbing or whimpering.

I tugged stealthily at the handle. Locked tight. So I started pacing slowly between the bathroom and the bedroom, seven paces one way, seven back, trying to work out how to unlock that smooth, solid, flush-fitting metal door. The snag was that I didn't want to leave any traces. There are always ways of forcing an entrance if you don't care about the mess you make. For example, I could have hit one corner of the door with a heavy object—an iron rail from the side of the bed would do —until it sprung open sufficiently for the rail to be inserted and used as a lever. This is a technique often used in early days for stripping a safe. I won't elaborate on all the possibilities that crossed my mind as I paced up and down. I will only tell you that when I worked in a studio in Battersea I used to have some very funny friends. . . .

In this sphere, as in others, the most effective ideas are often the simplest. It was the holdall containing pins, needles and spools of cotton, thoughtfully provided for me by my hosts, that eventually supplied me with what I hoped would provide the answer. I remembered seeing it in one of the drawers of the dressing table, when I was putting my spare shirts away. I took it out. Inevitably, the initials of Basil Merganser were stamped on the leather cover. I selected the thickest spool of thread and went across to the washbasin. I half filled the basin with hot water, stripped the thread off the spool, and let it soak in the water for a minute or two. Then I wrung it out and dabbed it dry in a towel. I took a pencil and began to pack the thread methodically into the keyhole of the locked door. I packed it in, centimeter by centimeter, as tightly as possible, until finally the inside of the lock was enmeshed by a cocoon of brown thread. The next step was the decisive one. I fetched a wooden coat hanger from the wardrobe and snapped it into three pieces. Two of the pieces I got rid of by throwing them out of the porthole into the sea. After giving the wet thread a minute or two to firm up, I thrust the blunt, splintered end of the coat hanger as far as it would go into the lock. I then turned it gently, as though I was using a key. The splintered end took a purchase in the sodden mass of cotton and I felt the lock click open. Now, when I tried the handle, the door swung free.

Still absolute silence. No sound of weeping now. The door opened into darkness. I switched off the light and wedged the door as firmly as possible with the metal bathroom stool. Then I stepped through the white-painted door. A yard beyond it I bumped into a hard object which shifted and scraped. Exploring it with my hand, I felt the outlines of a steamer trunk, its edges protected by strips of metal. My foot came up against a pile of leather suitcases. I was in a storeroom. Disappointed, I was about to retrace my steps when I saw a line of light on the floor ahead of me. There was another door on the other side of the storeroom.

I felt my way forward, taking care not to knock up against any more obstacles. I groped for a handle of the door. I strained my ears, my heart thumping. Nothing . . . unless it was a little breathy exhalation, like a sigh. Or it could have been the sound of the blood beating in my own temples. Without much expectation of success, I put some weight on the lever of the door and exerted pressure. If I had found it locked, I doubt if I would have had the nerve or patience to go through the damp-cotton routine all over again.

But for once the door was unfastened.

I straightened. I pushed the door open and took a step inside.

The sudden brightness of the light made me blink. The cabin I had entered was of similar size to mine, except that it was decorated in pastel blue instead of a peach colour. It was also very untidy. Clothes were thrown about everywhere: on the floor, on the bed, on the chest of drawers, on the chairs. Everywhere there was a clutter of personal objects.

A woman was seated in front of the dressing table. She wore a plain black slip. Her feet were bare. She had hair of a very intense black that fell on her shoulders and back.

When I entered she didn't turn her head. She was staring into her mirror, lost in the study of her own reflection. She had a very fine profile. I have thought many times that when I first saw her she reminded me of Velázquez's picture of Venus, in the canvas the Spaniards call the "Venus of the Looking-Glass" and the English (who own it) the "Rokeby Venus." Only her features were thinner and paler than those of the woman in the painting. She sat motionless, her hands folded in her lap. The top of the dressing table was littered with scent bottles and other toilet articles, and on the far end of it stood a record player.

The mirror was tilted so that I was unable to see her reflection. At last she turned her head and looked me full in the face. Her eyes were blank. She had the air of a sleep-walker, or of someone under a spell.

The right side of her face was powdered dead-white. The left side of her face, marked off with an accurate line that ran down the forehead and the bridge of the nose, cutting the mouth and chin in half, was carefully painted the colour of midnight black.

She reached out and put the record on over again.

XV

You might have thought I would have had enough sense not to add personal complications to my other difficulties. The voyage was scheduled to last less than another week, and Gheorgheniu was very precise in such matters. I was preoccupied not only by the climb, but by my overmastering desire to earn the rest of my fee, fly back to Madrid and finish my book. My eagerness to get down to the book again was becoming an obsession. During the days that followed I was to remind myself again and again of my original vow to avoid further entanglements. And I would fail.

Mind you, I don't want to give the impression that I actually fell in love with Claudie. The word is inappropriate in a relationship which was always clouded on my side by exasperation: exasperation with her, and exasperation with myself. As for her own side of the relationship—who ever knew what Claudie felt? Quite apart from her special circumstances at the time, I am sure that her emotions were naturally too volatile—I almost said too vacant (exasperation once more!) —to settle at the pitch which one could call love.

It started harmlessly enough. That first time I stayed in her cabin for only a few seconds. I was taken aback, embarrassed—though I remember that even then she betrayed not the faintest hint of surprise. I fancy she had daubed her face with a paste of mascara in that way because she was bored with being locked up in her cabin. She had nothing to amuse her except her gramophone records; she wasn't a great reader, and her faculties were too confused in any event for her to take in a book. Of course, painting her face like that was a symptom of her grave illness, though it was equally an example of the sort of crazy tricks she had played all her life. However, she never did it afterwards; and as I stood there in the doorway, at a loss, she eventually smiled at me in such a way it struck me that she was glad to see another human being.

I retreated hastily, closing the door behind me, and retired to bed. Next morning, however, when I had eaten breakfast and taken a stroll around the deck, I paid her another visit. On going back to my cabin the previous evening, and listening once more to the music, it came to me that she must be confined permanently to her cabin. So when I entered the next morning I leaned against the door and gave her an encouraging little smile. I realized that she was sick and must not be upset. My manner was like that of a man ingratiating himself with a rare and nervous animal. As long as one was circumspect, she would remain calm and trusting.

The black slip had been replaced by a white one. The cabin had been tidied up (by the blond stewardess, I guessed), but by evening it would be untidy again. Once when I was present she went idly through her wardrobe, stroking the clothes or underwear, trying them on, afterwards strewing them about or letting them drop on the floor. I had boarded the *Marmoset* with a single suitcase; but as the trunks in the storeroom revealed, she had come aboard with a large stock of clothes. In fact, I had believed at the beginning that she was Gheorgheniu's wife and that the ship was her home.

For most of the occasions when I visited her she wore a simple slip. Twice she wore a pale-green nightdress; twice a

116

pair of yellow pajamas cut in the Chinese style. Only once did she wear a dress and then, as you will see, she was in such a state that I had to put it on her myself. Why should she need to wear a dress when she could never leave her cabin? One evening when I entered the room she was completely naked. By then I was too familiar with the situation to feel embarrassed; and she herself never showed anything but a kind of sleepy indifference. Much of the time she seemed unaware of my presence, although now and again she would look at me with a shy smile, as if she was grateful for my company. On that particular evening she sat naked in front of her looking glass, dreamily brushing her long hair, an occupation which soothed her and took up a good deal of her time. Neither then nor at any other time did I experience, when I was in her cabin, any stirring of physical desire for her. Not that she was unattractive: far from it. I judged that she was between thirty-eight and forty-two. Her eyes were rather too deep-set and perhaps a little too close together. There were faint creases around her neck and breasts, a slight puckering around the buttocks, and the beginnings of a marbling of the flesh at the back of the thighs. But her body was fine and firm, the skin smooth and a wonderful uniform milk-white in colour. When she had finished brushing her hair she walked around the cabin unself-consciously in front of me. I can only repeat that I was like someone observing a rare animal, taking care to do nothing to disturb it. Her attitude was almost totally withdrawn, a withdrawal caused by her mental illness and the medicines which were being administered to her. Yet you must not think she was mad, or that I had the feeling of being in a hospital ward, or anything like that. There was between us a growing atmosphere of trust and consolation. I was a fellow prisoner, paying a stealthy visit to the neighbouring cell. We had no need of each other as lovers; when that happened, it happened by accident. It was enough for us to spend an hour or two with one another. And as the days went by, and my ordeal kept coming closer, I was not perhaps 100 per cent sane myself. I had taken to drinking, and I used to carry my bottle across the storeroom to her cabin and sit on the floor close to her and listen with her to the music.

On the occasion when she was naked, for example, I merely walked over to the record player and selected a disk or two to put on the automatic changer. Then I settled myself on the carpet beside the dressing table and prepared to enjoy the music. I remember looking at her some time later and noticing that the rounded beauty of her body was marked (I did not say marred) by a very long, jagged scar across her abdomen—a pearly, irregular band with the shine of silk, paler even than her skin. It was like a streak of lightning from which one fork struck up towards the breasts, the other downwards into the triangle of pubic hair.

There were no agonizing choices to be made in choosing a gramophone record. There were only about twenty of them, and with two exceptions they were all recordings made by Claudie herself. The exceptions were two records of violin recitals of the works of eighteenth-century Italian masters, Tartini, Locatelli, Corelli, and so on. There was nothing to explain their presence among the others, but I liked to play them as an alternative to the vocal music, and grew fond of them. They were never played until the time I drew them out from the bottom of the pile, but she did not object when I put them on the turntable. She listened to everything, even her own voice, with the same detached air. She might have been listening to the voice of a stranger.

In one sense that singer *was* a stranger. The recordings dated from several years earlier. One of them was made as many as sixteen years ago, and the latest was already five years old. I learned the dates of the recordings from the backs of the covers, and from the critical notes I gained a good deal of information about her career as a singer. Some of the front covers carried photographs of her at the height of her fame, such as it had been. They showed a sharper, more startling type of beauty, aggressive, flashing. There was no sign of the present melancholy and resignation. I spent a long time, as I sipped my whisky, gazing alternately at the portraits of Claudie on the soiled record sleeves, then looking at her as she was now. In the more obvious sense of the word she was less beautiful; in other ways she was much more so.

On that first morning, when I went in and the music was playing, she was silent, placidly accepting my presence. I seated myself very unobtrusively at the foot of the bed. The record was a selection of Mozart arias, and when it reached "Vedrai carino" she began to join in. The mystery of the superimposed voices was a mystery no longer. Her voice— both voices—was singularly sweet and childlike. She sat at her dressing table and sang without effort, the notes emerging as if from the throat of a bird. She had been endowed by na-ture with a truly excellent if slightly small voice, which had been perfectly trained. It was difficult, as I watched her, to visualize the years of hard work that had gone into the crea-tion of that voice. On the other hand, it was evident, after she had accompanied herself for only a few bars of the aria, that her present voice was only a ghost of her former one. Making allowance for the fact that she was accompanying herself only mezza voce, it was still apparent that the voice had lost much of its resonance and sinew. Whether this was due to her ill-ness or to a natural deterioration I do not know; but the voice that day, without being in any way a complete wreck, was sadly thin in comparison with what it used to be. She would not have been engaged for those same operatic roles again.

At her zenith she had been a star, but not a star of over-whelming magnitude. She had sung with real success in Italy and Germany without conquering New York or London— and it is there, in front of the tone-deaf patrons who pay thirty pounds for a seat, that the international reputations are manufactured. She had sung Tosca, Madame Butterfly,

Mimi and most of the other popular roles in several of the major and most of the minor opera houses of western Europe. In the bigger productions at Milan, Munich and Vienna she was usually engaged to perform secondary roles, for her voice lacked the sheer power needed to make a real impression in the bigger opera houses. In central and eastern Europe, nevertheless, she always enjoyed the reputation of an undisputed prima; and most of her records, I noticed, had been made in Prague and Warsaw. She was more at home there than in, say, Munich or Vienna—for in spite of her name she was neither French nor Spanish. She was christened Claudie, and her surname was the maiden name of her half-Spanish mother, who came from Bayonne. But her father was an engineer from Lienz, and she was born at Szeged.

These facts I gleaned from the covers of the disks. She herself told me practically nothing; in fact, we talked hardly at all. She showed no curiosity whatever about me or what I was doing in the ship; and unlike most artists, she seemed to have little interest in talking about herself. She spoke with the weary fatalism of a prisoner who is condemned and who accepts her fate. She behaved like someone who has run and run, has run into this little cabin, and now can run no farther. When I asked her questions about her present situation she ignored them, withdrawing further into herself. My questions did not alarm her; they did not seem to her to be worth answering. The only times she showed animation or anything approaching gaiety was when we talked about a piece of music. Then her brown eyes would shine and she would demonstrate the shape of a phrase with a gesture of her long fingers. She liked to talk about a technical difficulty—an unexpected modulation or a tricky entry. She would put her head on one side, her hair drifting over her shoulder, and listen with a peculiarly wistful expression on her face to the voice of ten or fifteen years ago solving those difficulties with a youthful ease. Her speaking voice was unexpected, actually quite different in timbre from her singing voice. It was low, throaty and rather weak. She spoke badly, the sentences broken and tripping over each other, hesitant and hurrying. Her speech was a curious contrast with the lucidity of her singing. Part of the trouble may have been that we talked in French or Italian, which she spoke poorly even though she sang in them fluently. She could sing in at least eight or nine languages and talk a little in most of them. Her thoughts flitted impartially from one language to the next, and when she couldn't find a word in one language she supplied it from another. This was very hard on me when she supplied it from what sounded like Czech, or Hungarian, or Rumanian.

Usually, however, we sat silent. She brushed away at her hair with slow, rapt strokes, while I brooded over my bathroom tumbler filled with whisky and water. My thoughts nagged ceaselessly at the problem of the climb; hers were occupied with . . . what? I never found out. In that ship, where secrecy and hostility everywhere surrounded us, we were simply glad of the human warmth of each other's presence.

We had to be careful. At three-hourly intervals the blond stewardess brought Claudie food or medicaments. At the beginning Claudie would warn me of her arrival. With some agitation she would imagine she could hear that almost soundless footfall in the corridor and push me towards the door of the storeroom. I would go back to my cabin and wait till the coast was clear. Soon I could time my exit to within ten minutes of the sound of the stewardess's key in the lock (she never knocked), and I wouldn't bother to go back to my cabin but would sit on a trunk in the storeroom, glass in hand. The blond woman, like all the employees in the Merganser empire, was as punctual as clockwork. Once she came across and tried the handle of the storeroom. Luckily some instinct warned me to put out my hand a second before she did, and when the handle started to move I held it firm. On another of her visits I leaned forward from my perch on the trunk and put my eye to the keyhole. I saw a round white enamel tray on which lay a hypodermic syringe, a bowl of water and a small green bottle. A strong hand with a broad gold watchband on the wrist came into view, picked up the syringe, gave it a practiced shake and disappeared. I felt sick and angry, closer to Claudie.

The stewardess paid her last visit at nine-thirty at night. Then Claudie and I would settle down to a long session with the gramophone records. I would loll on the floor, my back against the bulkhead, savouring the bottle of excellent scotch or bourbon which Gheorgheniu's steward brought me whenever I asked for it. Claudie would toy with her cosmetics or her clothes, or walk up and down on bare feet with a curious light, drifting gait, her look abstracted. We would listen to her operatic records, which were in the majority; but my own favourite was a song recital, recorded by Artemia of Vienna, in which she sang some little-known songs beguilingly, with an unusually sensitive accompaniment. In particular I remember it contained Jensen's enchanting *"Lehn deine Wang',"* and a haunting song of Robert Franz's, to a poem by Lenau, describing a girl walking through the dark woods with her lover.

And then, after some cheerful light-opera nonsense from *Vogelhändler* or *Mädchen aus dem Schwartzenwalde*, we would finish the evening with *"Plaisir d'Amour."* We came to do this by silent agreement. She would smile a little as I filled my glass for the last time, while the orchestra played the opening bars. This was a song we never discussed and about which she never made a technical comment. The voice on the record would make its hushed, thrilling entry, and we would listen, entranced, to the end. Often when I was in that cabin I felt that I, too, was under a kind of spell—and it never lay heavier on me than when her voice, recorded when it was at its richest, sang this song. She never joined in to sing with the record.

I had the impression that she shared my own special affection for this song. When the voice sang the words *plaisir d'amour* we smiled at each other; at the words *chagrin d'amour* we would ruefully turn down the corners of our mouths, as if we both knew what *that* meant too. Well, *plaisir* or *chagrin*, it was probably more than could have been said of Merganser, or Bay Russell, or Norman Ridgeling, or that ice-cold captain and his henchmen. . . .

It was impossible for me to know what was passing through Claudie's mind. But as the song went on I would see her eyes wander towards a photograph that she kept on her dressing table, among the chaos of cosmetics. It was a large photograph in a frame of worn crimson velvet. It showed the head and shoulders of a young man, dark, confident and smiling. He was in a military uniform and wore a cap with a high shiny peak, tilted at a jaunty angle. On his left breast were a pair of silver wings and a row of ribbons. The uniform was not, I was sure, that of Hitler's *Luftwaffe*, or the air forces of Mussolini's Italy or Franco's Spain. I did not recognize the insignia or the medals. It could have been something exotic—Hungary, Rumania, Croatia. I stared at it from a distance for several days before I ventured to pick it up and look at it more closely. When I did so, I was surprised that Claudie gave no hint of disapproval or even interest. I was curious about the long inscription written in a bold, flourishing hand across the bottom corner. It was in German: two lines of poetry that struck a vague chord in my memory. They were melancholy lines, which was strange in view of the youthful optimism in the airman's eyes. *Die Schönen Tage in Aranjuez*, they ran, *Sind nun zu Ende.* . . . The beautiful days in Aranjuez are ended now. . . . And underneath were three words in a language unknown to me, and the Christian name at the end was rendered with such dash and with so many curlicues that I could not decipher it.

I began to be consumed with a ridiculous but definite envy of that young man.

XVI

It would have looked suspicious if I had spent all my time belowdecks with Claudie, so for long periods I would pretend to doze on the foredeck, sprawled in the canvas chair near the cages of birds and animals. I needed the fresh air, and if I stayed below, I found I tended to drink too much.

Old Boulanger would join me there. I would keep my eyes shut as I heard him wheezing his way towards me, holding on to the rail. Then I would catch the odour of stale cigarettes and grubby clothes as he lowered himself into the chair beside me. There would be the smell of the barley sugar he was fond of sucking, or the sound of the wrapper being removed from a piece of the sugar he stole from the dining table. Occasionally he would produce from his rumpled pockets various other fluff-coated eatables which he had filched from somewhere or other, petits fours, dessert peppermints, or cashew nuts. He would blow out his bushy moustache as he popped them between his lips and chewed them noisily. A steward would bring him, unbidden, relays of cognac and Perrier water. In my own periods of dehydration it was irritating to hear him sucking away happily at his glass and crunching up the ice cubes between his stained teeth.

You will not be surprised to learn that in the beginning I

listened to the approach of the unappetizing old personage with some distaste. But I soon grew to like him. He was excellent company and exhibited the ruins of an enormous charm. And he grew to like me, too, although at the outset we were both hostile and wary of each other. I was ignorant of his exact relationship to Merganser and Gheorgheniu; and he for his part was not only an Anglophobe of breathtaking proportions, but I had also been introduced to him as an art critic. As an artist, he could hardly be expected to give a critic the benefit of the doubt, and he only cheered up when I told him that I considered myself not a critic but an art historian, and had once been a practicing artist myself. After several discussions about sculpture, which I took care to limit to the classical masters, he decided that I was not such a bad fellow after all, for an Englishman. By the end of the trip he had so much warmed to me that he kept offering to give me the exclusive opportunity to write the biography of the world's greatest sculptor since Auguste Rodin—Edmond-Amédée Boulanger. There had already been several monographs and critical studies written about him in France, but he did not approve of any of them. None of them, I gathered, was adulatory enough. No artist likes a critical study to be too critical.

In his later years he had become almost as anti-French as he was anti-British. He was a disappointed man: disappointed with life and disappointed with his profession. Like many vital and energetic men, he had been further soured by his inability to come to terms with his aging body. He would talk with baffled regret of the pleasures which he had once enjoyed and which had long ago gone beyond him forever: making love, boxing, riding horses and motorcycles, sitting up all night singing and drinking. Only his ability to sculpt had not yet deserted him . . . and sometimes I would see him furtively stretch out his glass of cognac in the strong, youthful, well-shaped hand and hold it absolutely rock-steady, trying to stop the ice from making the slightest tinkle.

As for his profession, he could not adjust himself to the shift in public taste which had made him a back number. In the most entertaining way—though it was actually rather pathetic—he would denounce France for the ingratitude she had shown towards one of her most gifted sons. In fact he had never lacked recognition at home. He had been granted all the honours, medals, honorary degrees and the rest of it which some artists crave and other artists despise. They had not been enough to feed his vanity or salve his pride. He chose instead to believe that he was shamefully neglected. He was one of those artists who resent the achievements of other artists more keenly than they derive satisfaction from their own. He was a prey to that most sterile of the deadly sins, and the one which is most widespread—envy. Boulanger wanted to sculpt all the statues in the world himself, and sculpt them in his own way. Somewhere during the course of the years he had forgotten that in the realm of art there are many mansions. It has always seemed to me a pity that artists, who have such a craving for the sympathy and generosity of the public, so seldom extend them to one another. They often assail each other in terms more appropriate to describing a mass-murderer than some harmless practitioner of the arts. I was amused, I remember, by a particularly violent diatribe he would launch at intervals at Giacometti—who, surprisingly enough, had been a fellow pupil of Antoine Bourdelle. He talked as though the Swiss sculptor had been a Judas who had betrayed the Master to whom he, Boulanger, had remained faithful. I felt very sorry that the old man was spoiling his last years by so much pointless bitterness.

His denunciations were entertaining, but I soon realized that there was no need to pay close attention to them. When they became wearisome I would cross my legs, gaze out over the water, and do what Dr. Johnson used to do when people started talking about the Punic Wars—"withdraw my attention and think about Tom Thumb." Or else I would turn my head and watch the beasts in their cages. It always astonished me that Boulanger, eaten up by his personal grievances, showed so little interest in them. In particular I would watch the magnificent restless beast that stalked up and down, up and down, up and down its cage. I watched it for hours as it swung its neat, smooth head this way and that, uttering a soft snarl between a cough and a sob. The ground colour of its pelt was not as fine as a tiger's, being a light buff instead of orange-tawny; but the large, irregular, cloudlike patches of black were more exquisite than the parallel bands of the tiger. It had a handsome tail, four-fifths the length of its body and ringed with black, and the pupil of its eye, as I saw when it swung its raking glance in my direction, was not round as in other big cats, but oblong and upright. As for the birds in the neighbouring cages, they were subdued, scarcely uttering a chirp. The food they ate may have been doped or doctored. The only gesture of defiance came from the bird with the yellow body. It flew from bar to bar of its cage, grating at the mesh with its claws, sending at intervals a low, haunting, flutelike note curving out across the water.

It was on the third or fourth morning, when Boulanger was cataloguing the sins of France and I was watching the yellow bird, that he suddenly said:

"Very well, at least I am going to a country where one knows the proper worth of my work! . . ."

At once I gave him my full attention. Today he must have drunk a larger breakfast than usual, because my previous attempts to draw him out on the subject of our destination had all drawn a blank. I eyed him carefully as he sat hunched in his chair, picking some shreds of tobacco off a moth-eaten lump of caramel or fudge. I remember that the two men in bright shirts were at their usual position at the ship's rail, ten yards away from us. Today they were angling, not shooting.

Occasionally one of them gave his line a light tug to feel if a fish was nibbling the hook.

I leaned forward.

"And what country is that?" I asked casually.

"What country? But it is Bulgaria, naturally. As always."

He saw the surprise and dismay on my face, and when the steward had refilled his glass he hastened to reassure me. Nonetheless I felt he took a malicious pleasure in the sight of my frightened expression. I got up and went to the rail.

He clucked his tongue in mocking sympathy when I admitted that I had not had the faintest idea where the *Marmoset* was taking me. He shook his head. Of course, it was very inconsiderate of the captain not to have told me—but altogether typical of such a man. (He had long since made his detestation of Gheorgheniu clear.) But he had heard the captain talking to the first lieutenant, and although they were speaking in Rumanian, he had caught the sound of my name coupled with the name "Kavalla." So there was no need for me to worry that I was being taken behind the Iron Curtain.

I asked him who or what Kavalla was, and he told me that it was a small Greek port not far from the Turkish and Bulgarian borders. The *Marmoset* usually paid it a call on its way to the Bosphorus and its ultimate destination, the big port of Burgas, the third largest city in Bulgaria, on the Black Sea. Kavalla was in Macedonia, three hundred kilometers by sea from Salonika. It was not far from Lemnos and Samothrace, which he spoke of with a sigh as the dream islands of his youth. . . .

He embarked at this point on a flood of reminiscence about the Greek islands which made him forget all about my own little troubles. He was carried back to the years just before World War I, when as a young sculptor he had received an important commission from the Greek government. He had taken advantage of it to make a pilgrimage, wonderful for any young artist, to Athens, Delphi, Mount Olympus, Sparta and the islands of the Archipelago. He was launched on one of his monologues, and I knew it was idle to interrupt him. I stood at the rail, chewing over the meager details he had supplied me with, and finding them as unsubstantial as the details I had been able to glean from my four photographs.

The appreciation of the Greek government in the old days led Boulanger to the appreciation of the Bulgarian government in recent times. France's loss was Bulgaria's gain. Monsieur Merganser had kindly put him in touch with the government of the People's Republic and acted as intermediary for him. Three times now he had made the trip to Sofia aboard the *Marmoset*. He had only had to mention the fact that he disliked flying for Monsieur Merganser to arrange this agreeable (he waved his glass) sea voyage. The only drawback to such a cruise was that he had to endure the tyranny of that odious captain. But thank heaven for the existence of enlightened personages like Monsieur Merganser. They knew what was due a great artist. It had been a privilege to make two separate bronzes of Monsieur Merganser's head: a fine, firm head, full of character, as befitted a true patron of the arts. And when Monsieur Merganser had hinted that the President of the People's Republic would be flattered to have himself immortalized by France's leading artist, he, Edmond-Amédée Boulanger, had been glad to comply. If his journey had helped Monsieur Merganser in his dealings with the President, so much the better. And his initial trip had been so enjoyable that he had returned twice more. His hosts had always been extraordinarily attentive. Nothing was too good for him, nothing too much trouble. He always stayed in one of the largest suites in one of the largest hotels in Sofia. He was given an enormous studio, two assistants—one of them a very agreeable and pretty girl—a valet and a personal interpreter. After his last trip, when he had executed a superb life-size group of Russian soldiers and Bulgarian partisans for the War Memorial in Liberation Square, he had been awarded the Order of the Red Banner, in gold. Now he had accepted an invitation to sculpt a twenty-foot effigy of Vasil Kolarov, to be placed either in his mausoleum or in the Square of the Twenty-first of December.

Vaguely, obsessed as I was by my own difficulties, it passed through my mind that it was all a sad comedown for a man of Boulanger's attainments. It seemed lamentable that the man who had boasted to me of his statues of Clemenceau, Lyautey, Valéry and Claudel should consent to hire out his talents to immortalize a gang of bullies. I had noticed that he never mentioned the great French figures of the last twenty years—Giraudoux, de Lattre, Leclerc, de Gaulle—and I wondered whether during the last war he had been injudicious enough to make statues of Marshal Pétain or other members of the Vichy government. But I may be maligning him. His eclipse was almost certainly due to the radical shift in artistic taste. There is not much demand in the West these days, as he constantly reminded me, for heroic groups of statuary and effigies of soldiers and statesmen. Not even in France.

I stood at the rail, frowning down into the brilliant water as it foamed past the ship's side. Boulanger's voice droned on and on behind me. Through my mind the word *Kavalla, Kavalla, Kavalla* was throbbing in rhythm to the beat of the engines. I only caught the tail end of what he was saying, but now for the second time he suddenly brought me up with a jerk. The peevish old voice came floating towards me:

". . . and you have not seen, I believe, our companion of the trip, the very charming and very pretty Mademoiselle de Carmona? . . ."

He was asking me if I had met Claudie. It was the first time her presence aboard the ship had been mentioned.

". . . Ah, that very unfortunate lady! She knows her own destination, I assure you!"

So he knew all about her. It would have struck me as natural, in this ship of secrets, if he had been entirely ignorant of her existence. After all, I had only stumbled upon her cabin, which resembled some sort of *oubliette*, by chance. But Boulanger knew about her. And he was disposed to talk about her. What Frenchman, particularly an elderly Frenchman, is reluctant to talk about a beautiful woman, especially when he has a glass of a good cognac in his hand?

Claudie's troubles were so harrowing that I had the grace to forget for a moment about my own. Her present predicament was even worse than mine. Boulanger had pieced the story together from various sources, principally a bibulous ship's engineer, an indiscreet steward, and certain items of gossip he had gleaned at cocktail parties during his last visit to Sofia.

I had not been mistaken in suspecting that Claudie was being confined to her cabin. She was being held a prisoner. As soon as Boulanger started to tell me about her, the memory of that random item in the *Corriere della Sera* flashed through my mind. ". . . Singer missing from Private Hospital in Upper Austria . . . Amnesia Suspected . . ." There is no doubt that she was genuinely ill. Even if some of the injections which the stewardess administered were meant to keep her in a trance-like state, some of them probably had a real medical purpose. She needed to be kept going as much as she needed to be kept under. She was suffering from a nervous prostration that had held her in its grip for more than two years. The steward who had helped to bring her aboard at the Punta Sabbioni told Boulanger they had hoisted her over the side strapped on a stretcher, like a dead woman. Of course, she had probably been kept under heavy sedation during the long car ride from Upper Austria, but she had certainly been very seriously ill to begin with. Ironically enough, according to Boulanger the blond stewardess, who had taken part in abducting her from the clinic, was actually a highly qualified and very capable physician. She had looked after her patient well —better, in fact, than she had been looked after at the clinic, which, though expensive, had a poor medical reputation. Merganser, I reflected, never did things by halves. Even his kidnapers had medical degrees. And even his tame acrobats, I thought bitterly, turned out to be art historians. . . .

But why had Claudie been abducted and brought to Venice in the first place? Why had a sick, *passée* opera singer, of no overwhelming repute, been smuggled aboard the *Marmoset* after such elaborate and expensive preparations? Naturally, like Boulanger and me, she must be a card in Merganser's personal pack. But—without flattering myself or Boulanger—what could possibly be her value?

Boulanger, as it happened, was in possession of most of the facts. They meant very little to him. They were a piece of scandal, almost a dirty joke. He rattled away in a happier vein than I had yet heard him, and I was so intent on catching every word, and not interrupting him, that it never occurred to me to be angry with him. Anyway, how could he guess that I had been spending many hours with her and was becoming involved with her at some level which may or may not have stopped short of love? I only wished he would keep his voice down and not wave his arms about so much. The two so-called fishermen were only a few paces away.

He told me that Claudie, with Merganser's cooperation, was being transported to Sofia at the behest of one of the most powerful members of the Bulgarian government. Angel Zidarov was a gifted and determined man. When he was only twenty-two he had gone to Moscow with Georgi Dimitrov, the hero of the Reichstag trial, and had served there during the war years as an officer in the Soviet army. He returned from Russia with Dimitrov in the spring of 1945 and played a substantial part in the overthrow of Stanchev and the executions of Petkov and Kostov. While still in his middle twenties he became assistant to the Chief of Staff, Asen Grekov, when the latter assisted Panchevski, the Defense Minister, to Sovietise the army. He did his job with his usual efficiency; but he was astute enough to see that his superiors were heading for a fall, and by the time Panchevski was disgraced in 1958 he had left the army and become an administrator. However, it was while he was still in the army that he met Claudie. He had travelled to Poland with Panchevski and Grekov in the summer of 1955 to attend the conference that ended with the signing of the Warsaw Pact. Claudie sang at a gala performance at the opera. She became his mistress. She was then at the height of her career; he was a thirty-nine-year-old general. According to the gossip in Sofia, she had borne him a child, after an atrociously difficult delivery. It did not live. He was said to have been hopelessly in love with her and to have put his entire future at risk for her sake. He was married and had three children, and his bosses looked on the liaison with disfavour. He had been heartbroken when, early in 1961, she finally got tired of Sofia and decided to end the affair. He tried to keep her by force, but she pulled strings higher up and slipped away to the West. He made a considerable fool of himself by calling out the country's security forces to try to stop her crossing the border. The whole country sniggered for months.

Now he was one of the most powerful men in the cabinet. Claudie was no longer young or famous, but he wanted her back—and this time it would be on his own terms, and permanently. As a minister he had the influence to arrange it. When he had learned that she was a patient in an out-of-the-way clinic, he knew his chance had come. He therefore dropped a hint to his friend Basil Merganser, who was the head of a consortium of British businessmen for trade with the Balkan countries. A Minister for Metals and Light Industry has many juicy contracts in his gift.

I do not want to do the man an injustice—not even a man who was a protégé of Dimitrov and Chervenkov. It may be that he was genuinely in love with her; it may be that he thought she could be looked after better in Sofia than she could be in the West. Gleeful stories circulated at parties in the capital of the high-handed tricks she had played him when she was his mistress and queened it as prima of the Sofia opera. They had made no difference to his passion for her. Otherwise why would he be bringing about this enforced reunion, seven years later? And what of Claudie? Did she still love Zidarov? Had she actually loved him in the first place? I never asked her—although, as we shall see, it was she herself who poured into my ear details of Zidarov's career which Boulanger could not have known. I can still hear the nightlong whisper flowing on and on . . . "Angel" . . . "Angel" . . . "Angel"—an incongruous name, God knows, for a young Saint-Just who had helped to exterminate ten thousand of his country's leading citizens.

I had the impression that Claudie, in a feminine way, admired his ruthlessness. Her vanity had been flattered by his persistence and possessiveness. I wondered if he was the young man in the photograph on the dressing table? I didn't think so. In the first place, the young man was an airman; his smile was not the tainted smile of the politician; and I could not imagine Zidarov inscribing a sentimental quotation in German. It struck me that that young man possessed Claudie's heart, always; equally, an instinct told me that he was dead. Sometimes I am haunted by the thought that Claudie, like one of the Sabine women, may not have been altogether reluctant to have been snatched up and carried away. She was afraid of Zidarov—of that I have no doubt. But she was also forty, or close to it, and he had gone to extreme lengths to locate her and lay hands on her. Yes, that was flattering. And she was ill, and tired; so who could blame her if she was willing to trade her freedom for some measure of certainty and security? Admittedly, a few hours later I was to hear her pleading with tears in her voice that she only wanted to escape. And I would believe her. Why not? Yet I shall always ask myself if she wanted to escape for a rather different reason. After all, there may have been something that frightened her more than Zidarov. She was seven years older than when he last saw her; her beauty was fading; the defeat and perplexity of her life was showing in her face. She was afraid that when he saw her he would find her unattractive, even disgusting. She dreaded that long first look after a long absence. Returning to Sofia would remind her of what she once was, and of everything she had lost.

Would it seem repulsive to you if I confess that I was drawn to Claudie not because of the marvellous creature she had been, those summers years ago in Warsaw and Sofia, but precisely because she was aging, sick and bewildered? She was more beautiful to me then than she could ever have been when she was the flippant girl who had made Zidarov's life a misery. I cannot explain why this should be so. Perhaps it had something to do with the wreck of my life with Maggie. It was also a matter of circumstance. Why should I become entangled with a woman like Claudie, and at such a ridiculously awkward time? In the final analysis I may have been ensnared, I suppose, by something very obvious and personal: by the look in her eyes of the woman whose heart is vacant, in the Horatian sense; or by the simple curve of her arm as the brush moved down her dark hair.

I can only say that when Boulanger told me about Angel Zidarov I felt jealous of him. I knew that fatuous little stab at the heart for what it was, just as I had recognized it when I had stared for minutes at a time at the photograph in the velvet frame. I thought of Zidarov and suddenly realized the meaning of the sweet, silly words of La Périchole as I had heard them on the far side of the white metal door . . . *Je t'adore, brigand, j'ai honte à l'avouer . . . je t'adore et ne puis vivre sans t'adorer. . . .*

I was no match for Zidarov, any more than I was a match

for Merganser. I sat in my deck chair and brooded about Zidarov and Claudie, and stared up at the sky, and wished I had heard of neither of them. I wished I was a thousand miles away from the hot, bright deck of the *Marmoset*—a thousand miles away—in the galleries of the Prado. . . .

The French chauffeur, in his bilious purple shirt, stiffened and began to reel in his line. Even Boulanger appeared to grow aware at last of the presence of our two guardians. At least, when he spoke again he lowered his voice. He addressed me in an English that was surprisingly fluent for a man so fond of denouncing the Anglo-Saxons.

"I can sense, monsieur, that you are afraid."

"I beg your pardon?"

He moved his shoulders. "It is natural. Everyone who voyages in the *Marmoset* is always afraid."

"Really? In what way?"

"I have seen fear in the faces of the passengers before. On our last trip there was a scientist."

"That's a fairly wide term. What sort of a scientist?"

"He was leaving his own country to make weapons for one of the Arab republics. The admirable Monsieur Merganser had arranged it. I noticed that he possessed the air of a man who never expected to see his native land again. He suffered from many very complicated fears, that man. . . . Like you, monsieur."

"Like all of us, I suppose, Monsieur Boulanger."

The line whined as the reel clicked and the clutch tightened. Our custodians were intent on the fish. Boulanger may have chosen this moment on purpose. He lowered his voice further.

"If you will permit me to say so, monsieur, I like you. On this voyage I have had a great need of someone to talk with. There is only the charming lady whose company we are not permitted to enjoy, and that—that"—an angry shrug of the shoulders—"that miserable . . . *escroc* of a captain." He held up his hand quickly as I opened my mouth to speak. "Our talks have given me great pleasure. I have been most interested in our discussions, especially our discussions of Canova and Thorwaldsen. It is unusual in these sad times to find a younger man who is familiar with such great masters, without whom my own art would not have become what it is."

He levered himself forward in the canvas seat and placed a hand on my knee. He exerted a gentle grip, but nevertheless I could feel how sinewy his hand was. The yellowed surfaces of his eyes were not smooth but divided by reddish veins into a series of convex islands, like the eye of a fly.

"Monsieur, before the *Marmoset* reaches Kavalla it will probably anchor for a day at Salonika. It usually does. If so, I think you would be wise to leave the ship."

"And what would Captain Gheorgheniu say to that?"

"*Ce cochon!* Why should you advise your intentions to him?"

"You think he might try to prevent me?"

"Monsieur, you have that in your face which the German scientist had. I will tell you something. I would like you to finish your fine book on Diego Velázquez."

"Thank you, Monsieur Boulanger. Have you any reason to suppose that I won't?"

He lowered his voice still further. "On my previous voyage the *Marmoset* carried as passengers two young men."

"Yes?"

"Fine, athletic young men. One Swiss, one Danish. Mountaineers. Both of them were younger than you, monsieur. I used to talk with them about the beauty of the mountains."

"Well?"

"In their voices I detected a great fear. And my God, they had reason!"

"In what way?"

"They were both put ashore at Kavalla."

"Well?"

"Four days ago, before we left Venice, I shared a bottle of slivovitz with Svetoslav Gerov."

"And who is he?"

"Our ship's engineer. We are old friends from my earlier voyages, you understand. Only this time *cet amiral suisse* has tried to take it upon himself to forbid me to speak with him. Naturally, I have ignored this piece of insolence. Svetoslav is well informed about what goes on in the capital; this is useful to me. And the other day he told me something interesting about those two young mountaineers."

"What?"

"Neither of them returned from Greece. The engineer of a Greek ship told Svetoslav, at a café in Burgas, that there was a rumour that they had died and been buried near Kavalla."

I stared at him. His hand tightened on my knee.

"So far as I know you are not a skilled mountaineer. I do not know why you are landing at Kavalla. I do not want you to tell me. It is Monsieur Merganser's business, not mine . . . and he does not approve of interference . . . and his reach is long. But Kavalla is dangerous ground . . . and you, like me, are an artist—or were one, once—and if you land there . . . well, it is possible that we will be done for, eh? You will be for sure!"

He settled back in the chair, snapping his fingers with a crack like a pistol shot at the white-jacketed steward who always hovered behind us.

"Do us both a favour, monsieur," said Boulanger. "Say your farewells to Captain Gheorgheniu at Salonika."

All at once the chauffeur in the purple shirt gave a hoarse shout. He was hauling over the ship's rail a magnificent silver fish. Its wet blue eyes were wide and staring, its tail was threshing, the blood was frothing around the hook clamped between its jaws.

XVII

It is very strange. I am seated at a table in a little square, in the shadow of a great church with its soaring spire. The square is filled with the sound of bells. It takes me a long time to realize that I am sitting at high noon in the Grote Markt at Breda. I am seated on the pavement outside the Hotel Het Wapen, drinking a Koninckbier. Opposite me is the town hall with its quaint steps and its odd, asymmetrical façade. As I stare at it I calculate automatically how to climb the outside of the building to the peak of its topmost gable.

Why am I in Breda? Why am I alone in the square at an hour which is normally so busy? Why are the church bells pounding out a stately old chorale of Sweelinck or Pretorius? Why is there a strip of red carpet issuing out of the oaken doors of the town hall and running down the stone steps like a stream of blood? Why does the red carpet reach across the cobbles to the foot of the statue of a woman?

At the sight of that dark metal statue my sense of puzzlement increases. It represents a slender young woman in the bustle and feathered hat of seventy or eighty years ago. Her back is arched and proud; a hand rests firmly on the handle of her parasol. The plinth of the statue casts a rigid geometrical shadow, as motionless and hierarchical as the shadows of the Grote Kerk, the town hall, the hotel. That statue has no right to be there. I recognize it: it does not belong in Breda but in The Hague. It is the statue of Louis Couperus' unfortunate heroine, Eline Vere—beautiful, independent, headstrong, destined for a tragic end. What is the statue doing in Brabant, when it belongs fifty miles away? It should be standing on the banks of a quiet canal a quarter of a mile from the Gemeente Museum. I used to pass it every day when I was working at the museum, gathering material for a section in an art encyclopedia.

What is it doing in Breda? Did Eline Vere walk here in her hobbled skirt—one of those walking statues like the stone image of the Commendatore? The grey metal strikes an incongruous note in the placid square with its old brown buildings. I rise and walk towards it, curious to examine it more closely.

And then my feet are on the red carpet and some dim force propels me past the statue towards the town hall. And suddenly the harsh, bright sunlight, sharp as the daylight in the courtyard of an Egyptian temple, fails and fades. All at once I am groping in a mist. The square has vanished—although I can still hear the clanging of a single deep bass bell in the steeple of the Grote Kerk.

The red carpet is beneath me and I am climbing the façade of the town hall. Or is it the town hall? This is not renaissance stonework: this is smooth modern concrete. There is a light from a window high above me—a pale lemon smear across the fog that gains in intensity every second.

I am labouring. Panting. My fingers are all thumbs. I can't get a grip on the slots or the stringcourse. The surface of the stone is filmed with moisture. My head is level with a big white builder's signboard with the giant black Gothic letters. I try to glue my body against the sticky wall. I press with my hands. But I slide. I slip. My mouth opens to scream. The

Gothic letters of the signboard whirl around me and explode.
M. P. MIDDLE MASS—MIDDLE—MIDDLE—MIDDL—AA——DI—
MI. . . .

Thudding. Shuddering. Shaking. Shouting. My own voice.
Have bitten my tongue. Salt taste of blood in my mouth.
Fighting to sit up. Must wake. Circle of cold white light
burning in the blackness. Hand on my shoulder, pushing me
back. Where am I? Who's there? . . .

It was a minute or more before I was conscious that I was in
my own cabin. The circle of pure white light was the moonlight striking off the sea through the open porthole. I was
having difficulty in struggling upright because I was jammed
hard against one of the mahogany side rails of the bed. The
tangled sheets, soaked with the moisture that was streaming
off me, were lapped around me like a winding sheet. And it
wasn't my imagination that someone was standing close to
me with a hand on my shoulder. I could feel her warmth,
smell the odour of her flesh. Her fingers moved to my forehead; with her other hand she brought the rim of a glass to
my lips. Drinking the water was like drinking the moonlight.

Then the glass was taken away; I heard a silken rustle as
she lay down beside me and put her arms around me.

"You cried out," she whispered. "A bad dream."

She had come through the white door to comfort me. I lay
there, my head cradled in her arms. I was still trembling, the
surface of my skin still crawling, my dazed mind cringing with
the memory of the fall. She held me closer, rocking me
against her breast, her hair falling over my limbs in the dark
like a cool rain. Her lips brushed my temples and uttered
small soothing words.

Little by little the trembling began to die away. For a long
time we lay motionless, clinging to each other like lost children, except that it was our childhood that was lost, and lost
a long while ago. Babes in the wood. *Nel mezzo del cammin.*

The lovers in Robert Franz's song, wandering hand in hand through the dark forest. Who was comforting whom? Did she lie there in drugged wakefulness night after night while I tumbled down again and again into the gulf of my terrible dream?

Was it midnight? Two, three, four o'clock? I had no idea. It was the timeless middle of the night. I often wonder if even plunging into nightmare isn't better than lying awake in the small hours. Though why they are called the small hours, when it's then that one's troubles always loom so large, I never know. At that biting time one's vitality is at the ebb; one's defenses have drifted away. It is the time when one's fears and one's sins come home to roost. Incubi. They sit on one's chest as heavy as lead, their sharp claws twined in one's entrails, their eyes like saucers glaring down at one like the eyes of the hags and monsters and horrible winged things around the base of Goya's statue outside the entrance of the Prado. . . .

I turned and put my arms around her. Her body was firm and smooth. She lay passive and content. It was curious, the tenderness I felt for her. I had not expected this late stirring of my emotions. I accepted easily now that I had a responsibility for her. Because she was a superannuated opera singer, and I was a failed artist, was no reason for us to fall on our knees in front of people like Merganser and Zidarov. Yet how could we possibly escape the vigilant eyes of the two men who stood on the deck, near the cages of birds and animals, and hauled out of the sea the squirming silver fish?

As I put my mouth against Claudie's and felt her move in my arms, I was more than halfway to a decision. Then, lost in her, I felt it was safe at last to let my senses wander. I felt a deeper sleep than I had known for days . . . a deeper sleep . . . and dreamless . . .

When I awoke the cabin was flooded with dawn light as brilliant as a diamond. Over us, as we lay with our limbs entwined, hung the head of the blond stewardess. The sunlight streaming behind it made it look like the mask of the Medusa. We had been incredibly foolish and forgetful. I have never seen such an expression of rage and hatred on a woman's face.

XVIII

I intended to disappear from the ship. And I intended to take Claudie with me.

The question was—how?

It was to Gheorgheniu's credit that after receiving the stewardess's report he kept his mouth firmly closed; but I could see that he would have dearly loved to throw me in the paint locker and keep me there till we reached Kavalla. The general attitude towards me was glacial. No one would talk to me. Without Boulanger's monologues our meals in the captain's dining room would have been sepulchral. Gheorgheniu sat bolt upright in his cane-backed chair, staring at me with the expression of a headmaster unable to punish a delinquent pupil because the boy's guardians are the governors of the school. The first lieutenant never lifted his head from the tablecloth; and the stewards were too frightened to murmur a single word as they slipped my plate in front of me.

Fear. Boulanger was right. Everyone in the *Marmoset* was afraid. They had been afraid from the beginning, but this little crisis had brought their fear bobbing to the surface, naked and undisguised. It was not moral disapproval that made them shun me: they were frightened. Even Gheorgheniu was afraid. He was nervous that the story would reach Sofia—and from the venomous way he now looked at Boulanger he showed that he knew who would probably carry it there. As a friend of the President, and the sculptor of the projected monument to Kolarov, Boulanger could make sure that the story reached the ears of Angel Zidarov himself. The old man was revelling in the situation. He was paying Gheorgheniu back for what he regarded as his lack of respect. He would grin at the captain—then wink at me. The exaggerated wink of an old lecher. It made me uneasy. I considered that I would be wise to be back in Madrid by the time Boulanger's tale of Claudie de Carmona and the Englishman began to circulate in Sofia, the Bulgarian capital. . . .

Gheorgheniu was uncertain what course to adopt; but I was sure that he would not remain uncertain for very long. As a first step he had removed Claudie from the cabin next to mine. This was predictable, though it angered me. And it angered me even more when I realized that they had taken her record player away from her. I suppose they did it so that the sound of the music would not enable me to identify the cabin they had put her in. But it seemed petty, vindictive. I thought of the poor woman locked in her cabin without even her records to solace her—and I started to dislike that cold sea captain in the same way that Boulanger did. Their determination to keep her away from me for the rest of the voyage made me equally determined to regain contact with her, although I realized that this would not be easy. They meant to give nothing away. For example, I no longer encountered the stewardess, who was obviously under orders to keep away from the corridor whenever I was belowdecks, with a view to making quite certain I could not discover where Claudie's new cabin was. In order to enable her to pay her medical visits to Claudie, the crew must have been keeping a careful watch on my movements.

Of course, if it had not been for Claudie I could easily have avoided Gheorgheniu's watchdogs and escaped from the ship without delay. True, there were snags. To begin with, when we finally reached Salonika I found to my dismay that we had dropped anchor half a mile offshore instead of entering the harbour. I had not counted on this. During the afternoon I leaned for an hour on the rail, impotently watching the distant bustle across the water. If there had only been myself to consider, I could have waited till nightfall, slipped into the sea and swam ashore. I am a good swimmer, and even if they had searched for me with a launch I could have escaped in the darkness. As it was, knowing that their suspicions were already inflamed, I made no attempt to go ashore. I guessed that my request would be refused in any case, on one excuse or another. But Boulanger insisted on visiting Salonika; and as the dinghy puttered away from the ship's side the old man glanced up and gave me a sly smile. He patted his pocket. In that pocket was a letter I had prepared for the British Consul. He had promised to post it for me. I had written to tell the consul that I would be landing at Kavalla within the next day or two and might find it necessary to consult his colleague there in a hurry. I could not be explicit, but I made it sound mysterious and important. I asked the consulate to phone through to Kavalla and ask them to stand by. If I didn't disembark from the *Marmoset*, they were to send out a boat for me and fetch me off.

Why, I wonder, was old Boulanger so anxious to help me? No doubt he was keen to spite the captain. And as I have said, I think that at heart he resented being kept on a string by Merganser and his Balkan friends, much as he needed the opportunity to work and feel he was still needed. Watching him settle back in the bows, under the eyes of the first lieutenant, I thought that he also possessed an innate propensity to stir things up, to make mischief. The old boxer, bicycle-racer and general hell-raiser of the long past days at the Dôme were by no means dead in him.

· · ·

When he returned, at dusk, I happened to be standing once again at the rail. The first lieutenant, spick-and-span as ever, helped him up the companion ladder. It was a tricky business. There was a heavy swell on the water, and evidently the old man had been making the rounds of the waterfront bars. My heart leaped as I noticed that the crew of the dinghy secured it to a ringbolt beside the companionway by means of a single painter, with the lanyard of the outboard motor dangling invitingly over a thwart.

Here, if I could only get as far as the companionway, was the opportunity for me and Claudie.

But I had no intention of rushing things. After all, I had first to locate her. I turned away from the rail as though I had noticed nothing. The rays of the sun were spreading like stripes of rough red silk on the surface of the sea as I strolled below. I was sure someone would be watching me leave the upper deck, but I saw no sign of anyone following me below. They were not crude enough for that. I had the twin corridors of the passenger's quarters to myself. I walked down the brightly lit, soft-carpeted passageways, listening to the subdued whirring of the air conditioning. Which of the dozen cabins contained Claudie?

I tapped with a knuckle at each door in turn. Nothing. I half expected the angry stewardess to pop out at me, boiling with fury. But if she was there, she stood silent behind the door, lying low. On an impulse I suddenly started to whistle the first tune that came into my head. I stopped and listened. Nothing. I whistled another few bars, a little louder. Again nothing. Then, as I was about to give it up as a bad job, the answer came. My heart gave a sudden leap as I heard Claudie's voice sing the following line of the song. I was very moved to hear the flawed but still beautiful voice shaping the words into an exquisite, flowing phrase—"*Chagrin d'amour dure toute la vie . . .*" Then all at once, in mid-note, for no reason that I could guess, the voice was cut clean off. But my little ruse had been successful. I took note of the position of her new cabin. They had transferred her from the port to the starboard side of the ship. I knew now where she was.

I walked away, towards my own cabin, whistling gently again. I felt rather like Philipp Koenigsmarck, the night he whistled the venerable old tune *"Les Folies d'Espagne"* beneath the windows of Herrenhausen, as a signal to the Princess Sophia Dorothea. Then I remembered what had happened to Koenigsmarck, and the comparison suddenly seemed a lot less glamorous. . . .

I felt uneasy all through dinner. I forced myself to eat and drink and behave normally. Nevertheless I found the silence of the ship's engines rather unnerving; I kept on wondering how soon they would start up again and rob me and Claudie of our chance to run for shelter in Salonika. As I went through the motions of eating I thought of the photographs of the mountain. I kept telling myself I was doing the right thing. By backing away from the climb I was guilty of physical cowardice: I admitted that. But hadn't I been guilty of an equally serious form of cowardice—moral cowardice—in letting Bay Russell talk me into it in the first place? It was not even as if Bay had played fair with me; so what was the point in killing myself, simply in order to spit in Bay's eye and to satisfy my own stupid vanity? Yet . . . I don't know . . . running for cover would still rankle a little, in some obscure way. . . .

When dinner was over, Boulanger snatched an opportunity to give me a message before the stewards came to help him out of his seat. Gheorgheniu happened to be standing with his back to us, conferring with the first lieutenant. Boulanger leaned sideways and dabbed at his stained moustache with his table napkin.

"My friend Svetoslav . . . he tells me the ship sails at ten o'clock. It is necessary for you to hurry, monsieur!"

That was all he had time to say. He shuffled quickly away.

But his words threw me into a positive fever. I had less than an hour to act—and only the sketchiest notion of a plan.

It was not easy to rise slowly from my chair and saunter from the dining room. I reached the upper deck and began pacing slowly along it as if I were taking my after-dinner stroll.

This was the moment I had been waiting for. My two chauffeur-fishermen always ate elsewhere, and it usually took a few minutes for them to receive the information that I had left the dining room. It would be three or four minutes before they fell into position astern of me, so to speak.

In a deliberately casual way I made tracks for the starboard side and paused opposite the flag locker. I pretended to examine the birds and animals, now settling down for the night. Soon the crew would come with lamps to fasten the tarpaulins. The darkness was thickening fast, and the birds, more haunted than ever at this hour by the wastes of the sea, huddled together with a dry rustle of wings. As I stood there, an innocent look on my face, I felt for the two picklocks in my trouser pocket. One of them was a makeshift affair, made of bent wire from the hook of a coat hanger; the other, more elaborate, I had fashioned from the spoon which came with the Tom Collins I had made a point of ordering that morning. The steward had not noticed it was missing when he fetched the empty glass.

I had no need to use them, for when I reached behind me and tested the lid of the flag locker I found it was unfastened. Even Merganser's men could be too trusting at times.

I took out a string of signal flags, lowered the lid of the locker safely, and stepped over to the rail. I went to a spot about twelve feet from the locker and dropped the long line of bunting overboard. Pressing against the rail, using my body as a shield, I lashed the free end of the cord to one of the uprights. My fingers refused to hurry, and instead of the neat fisherman's bend I had intended, I had to be content with a rough-and-ready overhand knot. I finished it off with a half hitch, praying it would hold.

I moved away from the rail and had walked less than a dozen paces before I bumped into my pair of "keepers." To my relief their faces were blank. I didn't think they had seen anything. It was too dark now. Nor did I think anyone would spot the cord or the flags, hanging as they were on the windward side of the ship.

My step as I went towards the companionway was the leisurely step of a man who has taken his fill of the evening air. This attitude changed as soon as I reached my cabin. I turned the key in the lock and thrust securely under the door a pair of wedges I had previously cut from the cork bathmat. Then I stripped off my coat and trousers and threw on my black sweater and my grey slacks. The Arco boots were already tied together by their laces; I slung them around my neck. I opened the porthole, climbed on the dressing table, wriggled my legs through and dropped.

I thought I had made sure that the side of the ship beneath the porthole fell straight to the sea without any obstruction. But as I hit the water my knees cracked against some kind of ridge or ledge. I don't know what it was—some sort of projection on the hull. I only know that the upper part of my shins felt as if they had been splintered to bits. I have never felt such pain in my life—not even at Copenhagen. I hit the water like a stone, and I may have fainted, because I have a confused memory of salt water choking me and being unable to strike out with my arms and legs. I probably plunged a long way under before I started to come up. It was a miracle I escaped drowning. Another miracle I didn't cry out and give myself away. I must have made much more than the gentle splash I meant to. Anyhow, somehow I rallied and began swimming slowly around the *Marmoset*'s white-painted hull, half-dead with the pain in my legs. They soon began to feel as numb as if they had been snapped off sharply just below the kneecap.

When I reached the line of flags where it trailed in the sea I had to hang on and tread water for a while. The huge black iron bulk of the ship loomed above me. My lungs were full of water; water dribbled from my nose; there was a tremendous roaring in my ears. I had pictured myself seizing the rope and "walking" straight up the side of the vessel to the point where the light from Claudie's porthole shone out like a beacon fifteen feet above my head. But even with the help of the rope the short climb was one of the most laborious I have ever made. I seemed to have no sensation in my legs at all. I clung on tight and inched myself upwards like the fat boy of the form on the rope in the school gymnasium.

Fortunately I had measured off the distance correctly from the flag locker. The rope exactly bisected the shining circle of the porthole. I managed to twine the rope around my foot and hung there, peering through the thick glass.

Claudie was sitting at the dressing table. This was predictable—although for an instant I was disconcerted by the fact that in her new cabin all the furniture was facing the other way around. Much more disconcerting was the sight of Claudie with her cheek flat on the top of the dressing table, her head turned away from me, naked arms sprawled out among the jars and bottles. She wore a pale-blue nightgown and her feet were bare. It came to me with terrible alarm that the stewardess might be keeping her under heavier sedation. She might have been slumped there unconscious—in which case we were sunk. There was something unnatural about the appearance of the cabin. It was so tidy. It almost looked as if Claudie had given up all hope, as if she hadn't even got the heart to scatter her clothes around any more.

I tapped on the glass. I didn't like making a sound, but I had to—and unless I tapped loudly I knew she wouldn't hear me. At any moment I expected a head to lean over the rail and a mouth to open in a shout. I slapped on the glass with my wet palm. Hard. Harder. And at last, with a relief you can imagine, I saw her stir and her head began to come around. Her arms moved and two bottles were swept soundlessly to the floor. I felt as if I were staring into the lighted interior of a fish tank. Her gaze roved in a vague way towards the window. Her eyes regarded me emptily and without focus through a black thicket of unruly hair. I had to keep slapping at the glass before she registered that someone was trying to attract her attention. More bottles tumbled to the carpet, inaudible to me, as she struggled to get to her feet. Her legs seemed almost as unruly as mine were. My arms were aching and I wished she would hurry.

She had to drag herself across the cabin, clinging on to one piece of furniture after another. Her mouth was open and her eyes held no comprehension at all. My next worry was whether she would be able to unfasten the metal catch of the window. She fumbled with it ineffectually, while I made encouraging faces at her. At last, just as I thought my strength would give out and I would receive another ducking—and another bang on the legs—she managed to slide back the stainless-steel catch. Fortunately, like everything else on the *Marmoset*, it was kept well-oiled and in perfect condition. I heaved the upper part of my torso through the porthole and toppled, dripping and exhausted, onto the carpet at her feet. She stared down at me with her hands hanging straight at her sides.

There was no time to lose. I didn't—I dared not—even pause to roll up my trousers and investigate the damage to my legs. I steered her to the dressing table, sat her on the chair and pulled off her nightgown over her head. Opening the window seemed to have used up all her strength. She waited, placid and motionless, while I tore out of the wardrobe the first summer dress I could lay my hands on. We must have looked rather comic as I crammed the dress over her head and wrestled her arms into the armholes. I hauled her to her feet and smoothed the material down over her hips. I couldn't be bothered with underclothes. At first she leaned against me, dead weight; she had certainly been injected with a massive dose of some drug or other. But gradually she roused herself and became more animated. At least she managed to put on the sandals I found for her, although I had to help her with the buckles. The zipper at the back of the dress stuck halfway up. I left it.

Now I had to face a particularly difficult moment. I had managed to get into Claudie's cabin. Next I had to get us both out of it and into the dinghy. Going back the way I came and trying to reach it by swimming was out of the question. I didn't even know if Claudie could swim. We had to run the gauntlet of the corridor and reach the companion ladder. The latter route was hazardous and exposed, but it had the advantage of being short. It was certainly easier than splashing my way around the bows of the ship with a comatose woman. With any luck we could gain the dinghy in less than two minutes.

But first we had to leave the cabin; and of course the stewardess had locked the door. I took my picklocks out of my pocket and got to work on the lock. My heart was beating a lot faster than the regulation eighty times a minute. Everything depended on my ability to open the door. If I failed, there would be nothing for it but to admit defeat. Claudie would sail on to Burgas; I would have to climb that damned mountain. I had been riding my luck hard. If only it would hold up for five minutes longer! . . .

I scraped around with both my picklocks in turn, trying desperately to get a purchase on the tumblers. Once I thought I had them—but the bent wire slipped. Sweat ran down my wrists to mix with the salty dampness still on my hands. It was no use. I buckled one picklock after another and threw them on the floor in disgust.

Claudie and I stared at each other. She clasped her hands

together as if in prayer, as if she was pleading with me not to abandon her. I wondered if she was afraid I would treat the crisis as a *sauve qui peut*, dive into the sea and swim off to Salonika on my own.

What could I do? I could hide behind the door, wait for the stewardess and take her keys. But I reckoned it must have been at least a quarter to ten by now. The stewardess might not come in until the ship was under way and we were miles out to sea.

I gazed around wildly. It was a poor moment to start improvising.

High up on the wall to the right of the door was a fire hose. It was enclosed in a glass-fronted box let into the wall. The glass was on two sides, giving access to the box from both sides, cabin or corridor. I dragged a chair across and stood on it. My one frantic hope was that the hose was accompanied by an axe.

It wasn't. No axe. I realized the extent to which I was losing my head by asking myself what I thought I could have done with an axe, anyway? Against a steel door? For one mad second I even considered smashing the glass and grabbing the copper nozzle attached to the hose and battering at the lock with it.

That bloody lock! I was angry enough to jump off the chair and kick it. Claudie ran forwards and twisted and twisted at the door handle. Tears ran down her face. Wearily I took a heavy step off the chair, forgetting my sore legs and jarring them in the process.

As my foot touched the ground the idea came to me. It was a ghost of a chance—but the only chance we had. At a bound I crossed to the bed and snatched up one of the pillows. I clambered back on the chair. I put the pillow against the glass and hit the middle of it a good hard smack. Even with the pillow, the crack of the glass sounded like the breaking of a jeweller's shopwindow. I suppose the sheet of glass on the opposite side must have muffled the noise from the corridor.

Claudie stared in a bemused way as I lifted out the nozzle and got down from the chair. I stuck the tip of the nozzle in the lock and reached up and twisted the knob that controlled the water. I turned it full on.

Everything depended on the force of the jet.

The canvas pipe swelled like an engorging snake and the jet shot out and ripped the nozzle out of the lock. Water gushed all over the cabin. If the jet had struck Claudie it would have knocked her legs from under her. She gave a little cry and skipped backwards.

I pounced on the nozzle where it was threshing about on the floor and turned it on the door. The jet drummed like thunder on the metal. The water was gouting out with tremendous force. Ship's hoses are always extra powerful. I placed the nozzle at an angle in the keyhole and aimed the jet at the back of the lock. The water pressure was a thousand times greater than any pressure I could have brought to bear with my wretched bits of wire. The tumblers were pushed back. When I turned the handle—it gave.

I hurled the nozzle through the bathroom door behind me. It clattered on the floor, scything out water. I seized Claudie by the hand and pulled her out into the corridor. I was reckless now. Trusting to luck. No time to hang about. Turning on the fire hose must have alerted the engine room. They would raise the alarm. And any second I expected the deck beneath our feet to tremble with the beat of the engines.

We ran down the corridor and into the other corridor on the port side, where my own cabin was situated. I now saw that Claudie was carrying a pile of her precious gramophone records and the photograph in the velvet frame. She must have snatched them up as we were leaving the cabin. She held them clutched tightly against her chest. It was too late to take them back now. A few steps in front of us we could see the stairs that led to the upper deck and the gangway with the dinghy

Claudie ran like an automaton. I was afraid her legs would buckle under her; my own were hurting like hell. She was making a heroic effort. Her nails dug into my hand as if she was willing me to give her courage and strength.

Wet and bedraggled, we made a strange pair. But I was filled with a sense of elation. I was Perseus rescuing Andromeda. What did it matter if the hero was grey at the temples and weak in the legs; or if the maiden, like the lady in Rembrandt's little picture in the Mauritshuis, was beyond hailing distance of her first youth?

We were actually climbing the stairs when I heard the voices coming down from above.

We were right out in the open. No chance of retreat. No time to run back down the corridor to Claudie's cabin. Too far. And no chance of seeking shelter in mine. I had wedged the door too firmly with my bits of cork.

My sense of exhilaration evaporated. Now I was paralyzed, played out. I swung around and went back down the stairs. I stood uncertainly in the corridor, holding Claudie's hand. The voices grew louder.

Suddenly the door of the cabin which was nearest to us opened with a loud click. I spun around. It was Boulanger. He was about to leave his cabin and was unsteady on his feet. But his reactions were extraordinarily alert. He stared at me, then stared at Claudie. He had never seen her, and she must have looked startling, standing there barelegged, with her dress half fastened; but I could see from the light that came into his dulled eyes that he guessed who she was. And he took in at first glance that I was trying to get us both off the ship.

His head turned to the stairs as he heard the approaching voices. He understood. He opened the door wider and crooked a finger at me. I leaped forwards and dragged Claudie in after me. Old Boulanger moved into the corridor and closed the door behind him.

We stood in the cabin, holding our breath, as the voices came close. Boulanger was racked with a fit of awful coughing as he waited outside the cabin door, and then we heard him exchange a few remarks with the newcomers.

I looked around the cabin. My main impression was of empty brandy bottles, the smell of grubby clothes, ashtrays over-flowing with cigarette ends. What a cancer of despair gnawed at that old man. There were also at least a score of charcoal drawings fixed to the bulkhead with Scotch tape. They were all studies of the nude, evidently all studies of the same strong, fleshy, statuesque woman. A second glance told me who the woman was. She was the stewardess. Extraordinary to think of the old man inveigling that woman to enter his cabin and take her clothes off and pose for him. I am sure the captain knew nothing about it. What persuasive powers the old man must have had; and what pride the woman must have had in her body for all the barriers of her training and her position on the *Marmoset* to be borne down. Probably Boulanger had bribed her with a gift of some of the drawings. Perhaps she would save them to give to a boyfriend— some gigantic captain in the security police, or the commandant of a correction camp. It made me realize that Merganser couldn't buy up the total personality of even his closest employees: there must always be a tiny part that remained inviolable. I suppose I waited there holding Claudie's left hand for only a few seconds (with her right she clung even tighter to her personal belongings), but even then my critical instinct was alive. I remember I thought how masterful the drawings were, although somewhat hard and insensitive. They had enormous bravura. The fire of still life still burned high in that old man of seventy or more. I was moved by the intensity and sensual longing of those black lines.

This was no time for a private view. When the voices had

ceased I jerked open the door. As if the door had been connected to the engine-room telegraph, the ship began to vibrate before my hand left the door handle. Boulanger was standing there. I gave a brief nod of gratitude and pulled Claudie towards the stairs.

It was now a question of a dash for the gangway. We scrambled up the stairs and along the short darkened passageway leading towards the square black hole in the side of the ship. Through it I could see the starlit sky and the distant line of lights along the Salonika waterfront. The beat of the engines was loud in my ears. The ship was shaking herself like an animal aroused from sleep.

My main fear was that the dinghy might have already been brought inboard. We covered the distance without interference. All at once we found ourselves standing on the threshold of the gangway. Below us on the swell bobbed the dinghy: I could see the faint bars of its cream-painted thwarts. It was no more than ten feet away. I squeezed Claudie's shoulder, turned and started to scramble down the rope ladder. My aim was to haul the dinghy, floating on its painter, directly under the gangway. Claudie would then have to do nothing except drop into the boat and I would stand there ready to break her fall. It was all makeshift, and faintly comic, but what else could I do?

I twisted on the ladder, steadied myself and leaped into the boat. I sprawled across the thwarts, doing my damaged legs no good at all. I bit back the stab of pain, stood up and craned my head back towards Claudie. Lights were going on all over the ship. There were sounds of activity. Waves slapped the steep side of the *Marmoset*. The dinghy pitched steeply under my feet. I pulled her in close to the ship's plates. The vibration of the engines was more marked close to the water line. When the dinghy's gunwale scraped against the ship it was as if it touched an electric fence.

I called up:

"Jump, Claudie. Jump!"

No response. She had frozen in fright.

"It's easy. Jump!"

Still she hesitated.

"Claudie—be quick!"

The events of the next minute are impacted on my brain. They are like the impressions one receives as one twists the wheel before a crash. The collision drives them into the mind like a nail hit by a hammer.

Powerful lights were switched on in the passage where Claudie was standing. The light streamed out behind her, outlining her figure, stiff and indecisive, turning the tips of the waves around the dinghy into the edges of knife blades.

Two members of the crew, ropes in their hands, stared down in surprise at the pale oval of my upturned face. At once they shouted and hurled themselves into the dinghy. They landed on top of me, and the three of us started to lunge and grapple in the wildly rocking boat.

I looked through a mass of whirling arms and saw two other members of the crew, their white uniforms glaring in the light like those of male nurses, appear and seize Claudie. She struggled. I tried to shout out her name.

One of the men was holding me as the other pounded me. I managed to get to my feet and hurl them away from me.

"*Claudie!*"

Something struck me a gigantic blow on the back of the ear. I heard Claudie cry my name in a shrill, dying voice like the voice on a record suddenly switched off in the middle. There was an odd swishing sound and my fading sight saw several square objects hit the gunwale and bounce into the sea. Claudie had dropped her collection of records.

I lay with my head on the gunwale. My senses were clouding. I don't know whether it was just the roaring in my ears as consciousness was swamped by a wider darkness, but

I seem to remember the ship's siren suddenly blaring out a tremendous blast.

The last thing I remember was the photograph of the young airman in the velvet frame splashing into the water a foot from my glazed eyes. The light from the gangway glittered on the glass. I fell into bruising blackness at the moment when it started to spiral downwards, carrying the young airman to a second death in the depths of the sea.

XIX

—•—•—

The steward who brought me the message that the captain would like to see me in his quarters stuck close behind me every step of the way. He was like an escort at a court-martial. He did not turn aside until he had delivered me, so to speak, into the very custody of the captain. Even then I had the feeling that he would remain on sentry duty outside the door.

We had to wait a few seconds before I was marched in. Voices were raised inside the cabin . . . or, to be exact, one voice was raised. I was exhausted. I had been unable to eat any breakfast, and I still had a cracking headache from the clout the seaman gave me in the dinghy the previous night. I had had to ask a steward to bring me a roll of adhesive tape with which to bind up my shin, which was gashed in three places. So it took a little time for my muzzy intellect to register the fact that the voice was Boulanger's.

I was leaning against the bulkhead with my eyes closed and my forehead resting against the cool metal when Boulanger came out. He emerged, followed by yet another of the army of white-coated stewards, and stopped when he saw me. What had happened in the cabin had made him furiously angry. There was a red glow in his faded eyeballs and the purple veins in his cheek and nose were splendidly suffused with blood.

He did an unexpected thing. He took a shaky step towards me and gripped my arm . . . a grip that could still bite to the bone. I smelled the brandy on his breath as he gave me an oddly wild look. It wasn't much; but it was enough to confirm my earlier guess that he, like me, hated and feared being carried in this ship, for all his whistling in the dark.

Then he was shuffling off down the corridor, the steward's hand firm beneath his arm; and the cabin door was still open, and Gheorgheniu was ready to attend to me.

As I stepped inside I saw that the well-appointed cabin was dominated by the coloured photograph of a portrait in oils. The portrait was fully four feet square and mounted in a sumptuous gilt frame. It occupied most of the wall behind the captain's neatly barbered head.

It was easy to guess whose portrait it must be. The sitter had grey hair, a long, rather underslung jaw and a sallow complexion almost the same colour as the gilt frame. The eyes were pouchy, watchful, with a wary humour in them; the mouth narrow, and curved in an oddly paternalistic smile. I recognized the style of the portrait as that of a painter of a previous generation who sometimes, for a fee nicely calculated on both sides, would turn aside to oblige an exceptionally wealthy client. Sometimes his clients were people of such forceful character that their features could survive the cynical assault the artist launched on them in order to assert his own independence. The present client was one of them. In spite of the crooked mouth, crafty eyes and jaundiced complexion, Basil Merganser stared across at me with an expression of irreducible authority.

Gheorgheniu sat behind his broad table with a magisterial air that irritated me. In front of him were ranged a series of gold coins, large and small, new and old, together with a sumptuous album of crimson morocco whose pages consisted of sheets of transparent plastic. The sheets had pockets into which the coins could be inserted for purposes of display. The album already seemed to be filled with gold coins, fifteen or twenty to a page.

Without being asked, I dropped my aching limbs into a chair in front of the table. The light hurt my eyes and I had to put up a hand to shield them. As usual we talked in French.

"I deeply regret the events of last night," he began. "I asked you to be kind enough to step along to my cabin so that I could apologize. Of course, when they attacked you my men made a mistake. They thought a thief had swum out from Salonika to try and steal the dinghy. They sometimes do that sort of thing in these Greek ports, you know."

His manner was bland. If anyone had raised his voice during the previous interview with Boulanger, it had not been the captain. I sat up straight and grasped the arms of my chair. He had given me an opening for the question I wanted to raise with him.

"And what about Mademoiselle de Carmona?" I demanded. "I suppose your men mistook her for a thief, as well?"

He picked up a coin and delicately buffed it on the sleeve of his uniform, above the gold rings of his rank.

"Mademoiselle who, monsieur?"

"Mademoiselle de Carmona."

Slowly he shook his head. "We have no one of that name aboard this ship."

I was slightly shaken by such a blank denial, but I laughed. "Oh, come now, Captain!"

He slid the coin into one of the transparent pockets in the album. Then he touched his temple and said courteously:

"Perhaps the regrettable blow you received from one of my men? . . ."

I said, "The game seems rather pointless, doesn't it? Why bother to make such a mystery out of it?"

"You may ask the purser to show you his lists of the crew

and passengers, if you like. You will see that the only woman whom we carry in this ship is our stewardess, Mademoiselle Franciska Brody." He spelled it out: "B-r-o-d-y."

"Then I suppose you will reprimand Mademoiselle B-r-o-d-y for putting me in a cabin next to Mademoiselle de C-a-r-m-o-n-a? Without even checking that the doors were properly locked?"

He gave me a searching look. I smiled briefly and went on:

"You have absolutely no right to keep Mademoiselle de Carmona locked up aboard this ship against her will. As soon as we reach Kavalla I intend to see that she is released and taken back to Austria."

He stopped toying with the coins and stared at me, his hands in the silk cuffs with the gold links inert on the table.

"You seem to be very well informed, monsieur."

"Perhaps." It was my turn to be unforthcoming.

"I think you ought to see the purser's list." He paused. "You will also notice that it contains the name of only a single passenger. Monsieur Boulanger."

This was rather jarring news, even though all along I had half expected it. Why else had I been brought aboard at night and not encouraged to go ashore? Gheorgheniu was threatening me; but after the precautions I had taken I did not feel in the least uncomfortable.

"I am going to take Mademoiselle de Carmona off this ship," I repeated. I was astonished at my own assurance. "It is stupid to think you can conceal her presence aboard this vessel. For example, Monsieur Boulanger knows as much about her as I do."

I could have bitten off my tongue as soon as I had spoken. It came of being too confident, desiring to score off someone I disliked. The eyes in Gheorgheniu's narrow, handsome head seemed to darken. They hooked themselves into my face like the eyes of a shark. I don't believe he would have uttered his own next words if I hadn't provoked him; but mutual dislike had made him, too, imprudent.

"It will not be difficult to track down Monsieur Boulanger's source of information," he said, speaking slowly. "In fact, I believe I have already done so."

Something in his voice struck a chill into me, in spite of my resolution not to let him intimidate me. There was a certain ship's engineer who would probably not be available for the next voyage. . . .

"As for Monsieur Boulanger," the captain went on, "he is a very old man. Who knows whether the climate of Sofia will continue to agree with him?"

Again his tone chilled me. He was a very dangerous man, and I had caused him a great deal of trouble. He was staring at me with a kind of suave savagery. I had to nerve myself not to flinch.

My careless words may have put Boulanger in peril. It would be quite simple for Angel Zidarov to arrange for him to succumb to pneumonia or some other convenient illness. I had come to like the old boy and felt somehow responsible for him—just as I felt somehow responsible for Claudie. We were all on the same side.

Gheorgheniu's remark nearly provoked me into a biting reply. I could have told him something that would flatten him. This time I had the sense to keep my mouth shut.

He read my mind. He lifted the cover of the crimson album and picked up something that had been concealed there. He flicked it towards me with two fingers, as if it had been a playing card. It slid across the polished table and came to rest in front of me.

It was an envelope. The address was written in my own handwriting. There was a stamp in the corner, but it had not been cancelled. The envelope had gotten no farther than the sorting office.

Well, the stamp showed that old Boulanger had tried. . . .

It was the captain's turn to smile.

"You are a very enterprising and resourceful man. I have no doubt that you will do a great deal better than the others, when you enter the Cave of the Cyclops—C-y-c-l-o-p-s."

He had done more than trump my ace. He had pulled it out of the pack.

There would be no launch to sail out to the *Marmoset* if I failed to disembark.

Boulanger and Claudie and I were in deadly danger. I suddenly saw that there was no intention of letting Boulanger or me carry the news of Claudie's whereabouts back home. Nor had the other two climbers, the Dane or the Swiss, returned home after their trip to the mountain. Successful or unsuccessful, I realized that they were never meant to leave Greece.

Cave of the Cyclops . . . So he had known about that, too, all the time?

I looked at him, toying with his bits of gold, like a tame pirate. I feared and hated him. The cabin seemed to grow smaller, more constricted. The light seemed stronger, pricking my eyes. My legs were stiff and painful from their battering the previous night. I had been drinking too much these past few days . . . not sleeping well. . . .

How could I climb the mountain—enter the cave—make the leap? I was sick. It would be worse than Copenhagen. . . .

But one thing I knew for certain. My only chance of getting off the *Marmoset* and helping Claudie and Boulanger was to go through the motions of preparing for the climb. Locking myself in my cabin or refusing to leave the ship would be the quickest way to destruction. Probably the captain had instructions to eliminate me without any further argument if I proved uncooperative. So I must at least pretend to collaborate. Not that I actually had to make that final leap, of course. . . .

Gheorgheniu bared his fine teeth.

"You have been given a very important task, monsieur. Monsieur Merganser is counting on you."

The smile in the life-size photograph above his head was as mirthless and uncompromising as his own.

XX

———•━••━•———

The ship reached Kavalla late the next night.

I was lying awake with the light on, counting the rivets on the bulkhead above my bed, when the ship's engines suddenly slowed. They beat with a menacing deliberation for some minutes, then stopped. The vessel glided on in silence through the darkness. Another shuddering burst from the engines—shouts on deck—boots ringing on metal—scrape of hawsers—rattle of anchor chains. After that—for the remainder of the night—silence. Profound silence.

The unnatural quiet robbed me of what little calmness of mind I could still muster. My voyage was over. I had reached my destination. Is it any wonder that I grew increasingly restless and wakeful as the hours dragged by, and that it was only when the first gritty light of dawn was beginning to filter through the porthole that I managed to drop into a doze—my usual dream-ridden, unrefreshing doze?

All the time I lay there I was conscious of the empty cabin next to mine, on the other side of the locked white door. Oddly enough, they had made no effort to lock that door and prevent me from gaining access to the cabin that had once been Claudie's. It may have been a touch of malice on their part. Several times since they had moved her away I had wandered through the white door into the cabin beyond. The storeroom between had been cleared of her boxes and suitcases. There was no trace of her presence in the cabin she had occupied. The porthole stood open as though to let the sea air scour any remaining scent of her clothes, body, or cosmetics from the atmosphere. The floor had been swept, the furniture dusted and rearranged with mathematical severity. I could almost smell disinfectant. There were crisp new sheets on the bed. I laid my hand on the freshly laundered pillowcase where her head had once lain. Nothing. Not a vestige of her. She was gone. I would not see her again. I looked aimlessly around the place which had become familiar to me, where I had felt at home. Nothing. No fugitive snatch of "Plaisir d'Amour" could possibly linger in those sterilized crevices and corners. . . .

My breakfast was brought to me in my cabin at eight o'clock. Again the steward set it down hastily, avoiding my eye, making his exit quickly. There was the same attitude towards me when I went up on deck. Members of the crew who had not previously shown much interest in me now seemed almost visibly to shrink away from me. I was rather flattered —in the bitter sort of way a man who is the carrier of a rare bacillus might be flattered by the respectful gaze of the nurses, or a man on his way to the gallows by the bashful glances of the spectators.

It was a day of dazzling sunshine. The sun hung in the sky like one of Gheorgheniu's gold coins. I stood by the rail, drinking in the scene of activity on the deck and the quay, feeling vaguely depressed by it. I was in a state of suspended animation. I had been given no intimation of the moment when I would be called to go on shore. I had dressed myself with care in the same clothes I had worn for my climb in Paris: the black wool jersey, the dark wool slacks, the soft suede boots. I had put them on with the same sense of comfort a bullfighter feels when he dons a uniform in which he has scored a previous success. They had helped me to overcome the hazards of the Avenue Fustel-de-Coulanges; they might possibly help me to overcome the Cave of the Cyclops. I carried the same small flashlight and pigskin gloves. The only addition to my outfit was a table knife which I had sneaked from the serving table in the dining room the previous evening. Its edge was not particularly sharp to the touch, but it was all I could obtain in the way of a weapon. I wrapped the blade in a strip torn from a towel and thrust it down the side of my right sock.

I noticed that Merganser's house flag had been removed from the jack staff. In its place was a flag consisting of equal horizontal bands of white, green and scarlet, with a small device surmounted by a red star in the top left corner. Why there was any necessity for this elaborate by-play with the flags I am unable to say. The new flag hung straight down from the slanting staff in the windless air, like a square sheet of metal enamelled in brilliant colours.

I tried to compel myself to remain calm, and on the whole I succeeded. Every now and again, however, I took a slow stroll around the deck, hoping to catch some glimpse of Claudie, or at least to gain some clue as to her whereabouts. It was mortifying to realize that she was hidden away in this great steel ship, perhaps no more than a few feet from where I was pacing up and down.

Then I would return to my former position at the rail, near the gangway. I knew very well that if I attempted to walk off the ship my path would be politely blocked by the young first lieutenant and the two seamen who stood at ease at the head of the gangway, studiously refraining from looking at me; but it soothed me to watch the bustle of the loading and unloading. Much of the deck cargo, including the cages containing the birds and animals, was being secured with ropes and chains and swung onto the quay by means of a mobile crane. The crew of the *Marmoset* worked in disciplined silence, but the Greek stevedores bellowed and ran about, frightening the creatures in the cages. The birds flapped and shrieked, the big cats lurched around on the tilting platforms and howled. I saw with a kind of pride that my yellow bird fluttered more fiercely than the rest, while my tawny leopard flung his muscular body against the bars and lashed out with his claws. I was amused to see that the men who handled the cages did so with a gingerliness that was almost comic. The beast's hoarse roars of rage must have been audible all through the town. The stevedores clapped the sides of the crates into place as soon as each cage was landed on the quay. At last there was nothing to see but a long row of tall wooden boxes from which came suffocated roars and muffled squeaks. It was with a real sense of loss that I watched the shutters being put up for the last time over the leopard and the yellow bird. Then they were just invisible prisoners with the rest. A very short lame man in blue denims, almost a dwarf, was scuttling from one crate to the next with a stencil and a rag soaked in black paint. On every crate he daubed a symbol, which I took for the forwarding address of the consignment. As far as I could see, it read "Medus"—something like that. At the time I did not pay it much attention.

Kavalla struck me as a port of moderate size. It was interesting to note the modern appearance of the harbour and its equipment. The installations were efficient and up-to-date, and from the prevalence of the M monogram on the sides of warehouses and dockside buildings I guessed that the money for them had been provided by Merganser. The place had the air of one of the staging posts of his private empire. There were no other ships in the harbour at the present moment, and the whole labour force was busy with Mr. Merganser's business. When the cages had been off-loaded, it was time to hoist inboard a number of slim wooden cases, five feet long and securely fastened with wire and lead seals. There must have been several gross of them. Beyond the harbour the house flag of Basil Merganser, resembling a tasteful brand symbol, flew everywhere like a discreet endorsement beside the blue-and-white stripes of Greece. For the most part the buildings on which they flew were flat-roofed and whitewashed, in the traditional style; but they also flew on two or three buildings that towered above the rest, aggressive structures of glass and steel, more appropriate to Manhattan or the south bank of the Thames than an out-of-the-way town in the eastern Mediterranean. One of them, with sloping sides and blunt top, was taller than its neighbours and dominated the center of the town. And taller again than the tops of the tall buildings rose up the distant mountains, range upon range of them. Those that were farthest away were hazy, their summits laced with a pinkish-gold snow; while the lower hills in the foreground were clear and sharp, like a palisade or a row of jagged brown fangs. And waiting for me somewhere among those mountains was the Cave of the Cyclops.

From the Calle Doctor Pedrell to the Rhodope Mountains. Twenty-five hundred miles in the space of a few days. It was a long way for chance, vanity and necessity to have brought me. Not, I insist, that my motives were entirely haphazard or unworthy: I had my sufficient reasons. But I had to face the fact that my plans now lay in ruins. Whatever it was that I had been hired to do, younger and fitter men than I had been killed attempting to do it. And even if I succeeded where they had failed, and came alive out of the cave—well, I had already made a dangerous enemy of Gheorgheniu. Worse, I had discovered the ship's woman passenger and knew her identity.

How could I have expected to find myself surrounded by so much violence and deceit? I should have left the heroics to *El Albaceteño*. Velázquez had only painted the capture of Breda; he had not volunteered to take part in the assault.

I tell you, I felt very small and lonely, standing there at the rail. What sustained me, I suppose, was my determination to liberate Claudie. I clung to that. It gave me strength; it took my mind off my own troubles; it gave me a larger goal to aim at. Somehow—I didn't yet know how—I had to get through the business in the cave and return to the harbour before the *Marmoset* sailed. I prayed that I would stay alive long enough to get back to Kavalla before Claudie was carried on to Burgas. I was counting on the fact that Gheorgheniu would not leave Kavalla before whoever escorted me to the cave had returned to report to him that my task was concluded—one way or the other. I clung to the hope that the *Marmoset* would remain at anchor for at least another twelve or fifteen hours.

I remember that I was calculating how long the mound of cargo on the quay might take to stow in the holds when my eye was caught by a car edging its way along the crowded waterfront. It was a black Mercedes saloon, coated with red dust. It stopped at the foot of the gangway, and my so-called French chauffeur, in his familiar check shirt, got out from the seat beside the driver. I could not see, from my bird's-eye angle, who was behind the wheel; I guessed it would be his Spanish counterpart. He opened the rear door and old Boulanger emerged, clad in an ill-fitting suit of dirty white duck, his limbs very shaky. Holding on to his fellow countryman—if a Frenchman was what the chauffeur was—he stumbled on his sticklike legs up the gangway. He ignored a polite salute from the first lieutenant. He ignored my smile of greeting. He was in the grip of some terrible, consuming anger. He was angrier, far angrier, than when I had seen him come storming out of Gheorgheniu's cabin the previous morning. His lips were bluish, necrotic, like those of a man who has suffered a stroke; his cheeks were ashen. His eyes seemed to have sunk into their sockets, and when I looked more closely at them I saw that tears were trickling out of them. He made no effort to conceal the tears or staunch them. As the chauffeur led him past the gangway, I saw the latter exchange a smile of secret amusement with the first lieutenant behind the old man's bent back.

I started to move forwards to help him, but he hobbled away from me towards the companion ladder.

He must have gone ashore at first light, or at the latest when I was eating my breakfast at eight o'clock. Why had the old gentleman wished to visit a place like Kavalla in the first place? What had so upset him when he got there?

The answer was given me a half-hour later. He suddenly reappeared on deck and walked straight up to me. He held his hand out and took mine in his and crushed it with a power that made me wince. He had a grip like a bear. His yellowed eyeballs were still swollen and watery, his features twisted and stiff.

"They laughed, monsieur! They all laughed. That captain —he laughed at me. . . !"

He had suffered some profound setback, some piercing humiliation. I didn't know what to say. I led him gently to a stack of the narrow wooden boxes that had been shipped inboard and made him sit down on them. His doddery legs folded under him and I had to catch hold of him to stop him falling back against the rail. In spite of the power in his hands his body was as light as paper. As I settled him on the boxes it was like handling a bundle of dried reeds.

". . . *That man LAUGHED, monsieur. . . !*"

Knowing Gheorgheniu as I did, I realized that his laugh would have been neither vulgar nor loud; it would have been as thin and cold as a knife blade sliding between the ribs. It would have been intended to demolish the old man. The bearing of the story on everything that happened to me later was so startling that I would like to relate it in the way he poured it out to me against the background of the clatter of the cranes and the squeal of the winches.

"You will perhaps remember, monsieur, that I told you how fifty years ago I was asked by the enlightened government of a country—alas, not my own—to make a statue to commemorate the death of your Lord Byron?" He had not, in fact, mentioned that the statue concerned Lord Byron, but I did not interrupt him. *"Eh bien,* I carved my statue in Athens and delivered it to the Ministry of Home Affairs there; but afterwards it was taken north and erected at a small bay called Kelos, where Lord Byron accepted the command of a body of volunteers who came to fight under him in the struggle against the Turks. A noble man, monsieur, and magnificent with women. I honour him, I salute him!" He paused. "Well, monsieur, it so happens that this place Kelos is situated sixty-two kilometers west of Kavalla. I verified this from the Greek Legation in Marseilles before setting out on my present journey. I was informed that it could only be reached by means of a hard drive along a rocky road, but that such a drive was not at all impossible to an experienced driver and a strong car.

"Although I had been aware for many years where my statue was situated, there seemed little likelihood that I would be able to visit this remote spot. Thus I had resigned myself to memories of my statue—in some ways the work that first revealed my genius to the world. I would look with nostalgia at the photographs of it on the walls of my studio, or in the many books devoted to the progress of my art. Who could have foretold that in my extreme old age a ship would bring me, not once but three times, within a measurable distance of it?

"On my first voyage I was totally ignorant of the route the ship would take to Bulgaria. I had no idea that the vessel would actually touch at Kavalla. But that first trip the ship only docked briefly at nightfall and was off again before dawn (that was the voyage when your two unfortunate predecessors were landed), and it was not until the following afternoon that I learned, in answer to a casual question, that Kavalla had indeed been our port of call. So on the next voyage I went prepared. I told the captain as soon as we left Marseilles that when the *Marmoset* reached Kavalla I wished to be put ashore. I asked him to arrange for a motorcar to be waiting to take me to the Bay of Kelos. He promised to do so; but since we do not like each other, and being the man he is, he broke his promise. He had no intention whatever of gratifying my wishes. He pretended that there was no motorcar available. No motorcar—when the streets of Kavalla are filled with Monsieur Merganser's motorcars and camions! He compelled me to wait in my cabin for the arrival of a nonexistent motorcar, a motorcar that he had never ordered. He had realized how passionately I desired to see my statue once again, no doubt for the last time. It gave him a cruel, cold pleasure to play on my impatience and my longing.

"But this time, on the voyage on which we are now engaged, I was prepared for him. Before I sailed I procured a letter from Monsieur Merganser's principal officer in Paris, a Monsieur Russell, a most sympathetic man, giving Captain Gheorgheniu categorical instructions to provide transport for me to the Bay of Kelos. I withheld the letter until yesterday morning, the eve of our arrival, because I wished to produce it at the moment when it would make its greatest impact." There was a flash in the sunken eyes, a twitch of the feeble limbs. "Even then the man tried to defy me! He made excuses, raised objections. He declared that the routine of a busy vessel could not be interrupted to satisfy what he was pleased to call a whim. We exchanged bitter words. In the end he was compelled to bow to Monsieur Russell's orders.

"This morning, monsieur, I bade the steward rouse me at dawn. I confess that I was too excited to do more than swallow a single cup of coffee. Can you understand that excitement, monsieur? I think you can. A sculptor or a painter is not so fortunate as a writer or a composer. If a writer wants to renew acquaintance with one of his previous books, he lifts it down from his bookshelf; if a composer wants to listen to one of his previous works, he puts a disk on the turntable or a tape on the recorder. Though I think it would be an inferior sort of writer or composer"—he smiled—"who troubled himself too frequently about his earlier endeavours! But with the sculptor or the painter, it is far different. His works are uniquely themselves, and they are like children who have married—too often, alas, beneath them—and gone to live abroad. Their creator is fortunate if he ever sets eyes on any of them again. My own family, monsieur, is scattered all over the globe, in museums or private collections, in Montreal and Los Angeles, Montevideo and São Paulo, Sydney and Tokyo, Leningrad and Tehran. Some of these are among my favourite children, my most successful ones. I am unlikely to set eyes again on most of them in the few years remaining to me. They are even farther away that Kavalla once seemed. And since my own particular children, monsieur, are a veritable race of giants, in stone and bronze and iron, it is not likely that they will ever be sent on expositions to Paris. No, we sculptors, like elderly parents, must resign ourselves to living on our memories of the days when our children were not yet grown up and had not been torn away from us by the greedy world.

"We do in fact spend much time in the company of our individual works, moulding them as a man moulds an infant. That is why I hate a heedless critic: because he is too insensitive to see that a work of art is not merely marble or ink or paper; that it represents an actual, literal portion of an artist's life, part of his nerve and tissue, part of his time on earth. And the statue at the Bay of Kelos was peculiarly precious to me. The captain, of course, sensed this. It was my first important commission. I lavished all my love on it, at a time when youth, hope and energy were in their prime." He paused and tilted his silvery head to look at me where I stood propped against the white rail, listening with half an ear to his story as I continued to scan the dock. "But there was another reason why I loved that statue," he went on. "Not just because it brought back my youth—but because I was in love with the woman who posed for it."

For a moment he was silent, taken up with his thoughts. Then he said:

"The Byron Memorial is a statue of a young woman. It is twelve and a half feet high and carved from a very fine block of Pentelic marble, specially quarried for me by the Greek government. The young woman stands in a simple posture, her head thrown back, her hands hanging by her sides and slightly open, one leg advanced a few inches in front of the other. It is a pose that one sees in early Attic sculpture and in the sculpture of Egypt. The thick tresses are caught up and pinned to the crown of the head with a single comb. Except for the comb the young woman is naked.

"It takes a remarkable artist to invest such an unadorned figure with vitality. I need not tell you that my figure was vibrant: a young woman of two-and-twenty, bursting with juice and sap. The strong thighs—the deep belly—the generous breasts—the small shapely head on the strong neck . . . that is how my statue looked—and that is how Jeannine Ducaux looked fifty years ago, when I made my marvellous image of her. That is how she looked whenever she stood with her unbuttoned skirt and fallen petticoat around her bare feet, ready to step out of her clothes and take one light stride onto the studio sofa where I was waiting for her.

"Jeannine was not a professional model; she was a girl of good family. Many years before my mother had been a maid in the house of her parents. We were very much in love. I do not know if I have ever been seriously in love with anybody since. I was twenty-four. It was impossible for us to marry or for her to live with me. She was engaged to a young man, the son of close friends of the family; it had always been arranged. She married him when she was twenty-three, on his return from a long business visit to the colonies. Two months later she went with him to Constantine in Algeria. With the exception of brief visits to Paris, she lived there without interruption for forty-four years, until she died. I know from the letters

178

which we exchanged each month for forty-four years—she was the only person with whom I ever maintained a continuous correspondence—that she was rich, comfortable and tolerably happy. Her husband was a very nice man. She had four daughters. Nonetheless I did not envy him, for I think he never knew the best of her. In many ways it is a pity that people should fall in love; it is an exhaustive emotion that drains other and often significant emotions of much of their force. One of the few things we know for certain about it is that it usually produces disruption and confusion. For example, I can never decide the simple question as to whether my passion for Jeannine helped to make me a more or a less significant artist than I might otherwise have been. It may have compelled me to use up certain of my emotional resources too early. But perhaps it was enough that such a passion enabled me to create that single wonderful image." He coughed a little and gave a wan-sounding chuckle. "It is not for nothing that it is we artists who suffer love and celebrate it. The effective men, the men of action, they do not feel it, they are never saddened or paralyzed by it. Love does not mix with money or politics. Thus the politicians and the businessmen are able to preserve their uncomplicated greed and optimism to the end. One can scarcely imagine Monsieur Merganser falling in love. As for Monsieur Zidarov"—another cough, another chuckle—"falling in love is a disaster for a man in his position. It would have been well for him if he had spared a moment to read the piece about Britannicus by our Jean Racine, or the piece by that strange, wild poet of yours about Marc Antony. Do you know what love will do for Angel Zidarov? It will put him on his knees in a cellar, with the muzzle of a pistol on the nape of his neck.

"I saw her again. Once. At least, I *think* it was her. It was on a sunny Sunday morning in June, nineteen thirty-nine. At that time I had an apartment in the Boulevard Suchet, and at lunchtime on Sundays I would stroll beneath the chestnut trees, past the boule players and the racecourse, to eat at the Roi d'Yvetot at the Porte d'Auteuil. On that particular Sunday I was accompanied by the painters Albert Tronçon and Philippe Thionville. Their work will be familiar to you. We spent most of our time at the lunch table discussing, like everyone else in Paris that summer, not art but the international situation. As I was taking my coffee I happened to glance around and saw a woman seated at a table in the corner. I felt as I once felt when my chisel slipped and almost severed my left thumb at the base." He held up his hand so that I could see the thickened scar. "She was looking at me. She continued to look at me for a full ten seconds before she dropped her eyes. Her eyes were the same colour of very dark *terre d'ombre* as Jeannine's. I watched her carefully, my heart pounding. She was with a stout, bald, good-natured man who dabbed contentedly at his lips between mouthfuls of food. She remained staring at her plate, her hands folded in her lap.

"I have never been able to account for the fact that I failed to go over and speak to her. There was no question of ordinary social embarrassment, the fear of making a fool of myself if I was mistaken. Surely after a separation of nearly thirty years I was entitled to a smile and a handshake. In any case, such considerations would never have weighed with me. No, it was some stricter inhibition. I had a feeling that she would not encourage such an intrusion. She must have been fifty. She was plump, double-chinned, her hair cut short, marcelled and tinted. The once magnificent complexion had been roughened by the rasping winds of the Maghreb—if, that is, she *was* Jeannine . . . if those really *were* the cheeks and forehead I had kissed and fondled and cast in marble. . . .

"I recall that I wondered why she had passed so close to the place where I lived, and whose address she knew, without coming to see me. She could even have brought her husband, if necessary; as I have said, our relationship was ancient history. But I realized that she did not want to see me—not as we both were now. And instinctively I understood her reasons and respected them. She lowered her head and stared thereafter at her plate with a fixed expression. I was very moved. With my head I wanted to believe that she was not Jeannine, but with my heart I have always believed that she was. Neither of us referred to the casual meeting in our next monthly letter.

"My friend, can you therefore put yourself in my place as I took my seat in that motorcar five hours ago? Can you understand how I felt when I heard my oafish companion tell the driver to make for the Bay of Kelos? I was once more the young sculptor of twenty-four, rushing back to his studio where he knew that the woman—he had given her her own key—would be awaiting him, her shoes kicked off, her bodice unbuttoned. I was as excited as a boy. I was bound for a rendezvous with a marble statue—how ridiculous love is!—but that statue represented Jeannine. It *was* Jeannine—exactly as I had wheedled her into posing for me so that I could make some sketches of her. They are much sought after nowadays, those sketches. Those were her limbs, that was her small shapely head. Do not think me foolish, or a little insane, if I assure you that, to me, my statue was—literally—the woman it portrayed. When I carved it I intended it to be her twin self, her simulacrum. That was a trick that fashioning the Byron Memorial taught me, a trick which has since helped to make me celebrated. To me the creation of a statue always afterwards possessed something of the meaning it had for the sculptors of ancient Egypt. To the Egyptians a statue enshrined the soul of its subject. It was meant to stand in the sunlight of a temple courtyard or the darkness of a tomb and figure forth its subject for all eternity. It was meant to be magical. And no statue of mine, I thought as the machine whirled me across the dusty brown plain, had ever embodied so much of that quality as my statue of Jeannine Ducaux."

He broke off and leaned back, slumped against the rails, his brittle body twisted sideways on the wooden box. His voice was growing gradually fainter; I felt concerned for him. It was becoming more and more difficult to catch what he was saying above the rattle of the crane; and I must admit that my preoccupation with my own troubles made me a poor listener. I was continually glancing down at the dock or scanning the bridge of the ship—watching for Claudie, waiting for my summons to action to arrive. I would have given him a tactful hint that he was tiring himself and ought to withdraw to his cabin, but before I could say anything he sat up straight and squared his angular shoulders.

"From time to time as we drove along I had a glimpse of the sea. It was the colour of the beautiful clear cobalt employed by Thionville in his Orphic period. Its burnished surface was speckled by fishing boats. Then we left the plain and began the steady climb into the hills. The sea was lost to view. The road was as primitive and boulder-strewn as the Greek Legation in Marseilles had promised me it would be. We passed through great cold pools of shadow cast by the high peaks. Then, as though the motorcar were a toy tipped backwards and forwards on a plate, we embarked upon a series of violent climbs and drops. The machine seemed to lurch from one declivity to the next. Yet I was not frightened: I was too wrought up by the prospect before me. And then at last we emerged from the mountains and drove along the curving sweep of the Bay of Kelos. I sat forwards like an excited child on the edge of my seat. As for my escort, he leaned back in his corner, bored by the quest, indifferent to the shining classic landscape unrolling itself before him.

"The road was rutted and full of potholes. *N'importe!* We bumped through a poverty-stricken village. Barefoot children chasing the machine—old women in black—nets hanging on wooden racks to dry—more fishing boats tied up in the harbour. Soon we were driving again up a gentle incline towards the distant curve of the bay. The great arc of sand, sky and water was magnificent. I rejoiced when I reflected that my statue had been placed in such an incomparable setting.

"And there at last I could see it! I could make out a white spot on the tall promontory that sealed in the far end of the bay. My heart beat faster. I was going to see my Jeannine again! I recognized in myself one of those moments when the division between heart and head, man and artist, is obliterated, and all the elements of personality are fused together. Rare moment! Holy moment!

"It was necessary to leave the motorcar at the base of the promontory and make our way up to the memorial on foot. We ascended by means of a goat track. It was a hard climb for an old man like me, and although it was repugnant to me I was compelled to hold on to the arms of my two companions. But I was comforted by the smell of the thyme and the springy turf, the salt tang of the ocean, the singing of a cloud of larks that shot up all around us—and above all by the knowledge that at any moment I would come face to face with my statue." He lifted his hands in a peculiarly graceful gesture. "Monsieur, I was happy!"

He said it as if it was the last time in his life that he expected to feel that emotion. He went on:

"After what seemed like an hour, but was no more than twenty minutes, we reached the summit of the promontory. There was a wind at this altitude, blowing off the creamy waves far below, and it played with my hair as I shook off the arms of my helpers and advanced alone across the goat-cropped triangle of grass towards my memorial."

A loud crash from the quay below made me jump and turn around. One of the wooden boxes had fallen from a sling as the crane jerked a load of them skywards. A foreman hurried forwards and bent over it to make sure that it had not broken open, waving back the rest of his gang. Boulanger did not hear the noise. He continued with his story, as if he was now talking to himself as much as to me.

"The first glimpse told me that something was wrong. The joy and excitement died from my heart. Shall I tell you what I saw? Shall I?"

His arms were propped on his bony knees. I could see that the wrists protruding from the grimy cuffs of the white duck suit were trembling.

"She was mutilated. She was spoiled past mending. The unblemished eyes were fixed upon the sapphire sky—but the lower half of an ear was cracked away, the nose snapped off; a cleft like an open wound ran from the smooth temple down the cheekbone. One arm was broken off below the elbow. There was no trace of it on the ground around the plinth; probably it had been thrown over the cliff onto the rocks. Two fingers and the thumb of the remaining hand were missing. The left leg was split across at the kneecap so that the ridges of the marble overlapped one another like comminuted bones. The lower half of the body was blackened and blistered, as though fires had been lit between the legs. The insides of the thighs were seamed with malicious, obscene scratches. And the entire surface of the statue on the left-hand side was pocked and chipped with pits and runnels."

He clasped his hands together and stared at the scrubbed deck beneath his feet.

"Ah, my poor Jeannine! What have they done to you?"

I stared at him, my personal difficulties forgotten for the moment in the anguish that had gripped him. He said at last:

"I do not recall the return to the motorcar. I seem to remember someone prizing my arms loose from the shattered stone. I have a dim memory of the machine stopping in the fishing village and one of my companions forcing a vile local brandy between my lips. He must have questioned the villagers about the statue, for I have some memory of him saying something to me on our homeward journey . . ."

"'. . . Local vandals . . . Turkish soldiers in the war of nineteen twenty-two . . . damage by the Greek communists in the struggles of nineteen forty-eight . . . used to throw their prisoners off the headland . . . target practice from the beach below by volunteers organized by a Cypriot fanatic in nineteen fifty-nine . . .'"

I stood quite still, searching for words. What could I say? He shivered like a weary old dog.

"Monsieur, I swear to you. Seated in the Mercedes-Benz as it wound its way back through the mountains . . . I realized for the first time in my life that Edmond-Amédée Boulanger was no more immortal than the rest of mankind. You may think me naïve, but until today I sincerely imagined that my statues would make me live forever. When the names of Jeannine Ducaux and Edmond-Amédée Boulanger and Lord Byron were forgotten, and when no one could decipher their names chiselled on the base of the memorial, the image, the essence, the very soul of that beautiful woman would nonetheless survive. . . ." He coughed and choked. "But when I saw her there—insulted—it came upon me for the first time that everything perishes . . . love . . . the perfect images that artists have created . . . I saw that men will destroy them as easily as they must eventually destroy themselves. . . ." He rose. His tall thin figure was like a prophet's. "I saw then that what I had always privately believed to be inconceivable must come to pass. I realized in a moment of terrible clarity that my own works were not exempt, that they must suffer the same fate as the statues of antiquity. Jeannine would stand up there on the hill and be battered to pieces. Oh, my friend, what hope is there for humanity if men will even murder marble, dumb, blind stone, the very matrix of their planet? I saw that it would have made no difference if they had put my Jeannine on a pedestal in one of their well-appointed museums. She would only be awaiting the ultimate grinding of the bomb." He raised his arms. "Dead men and bits of marble . . . Flames and falling stone. . . !"

I thought he was about to fall forwards. When I tried to catch him he brushed me away. He sank back on his wooden box.

"When I had returned the captain knocked on the door of the cabin. He came in. I could tell he had been told what had happened by the men who accompanied me. He was smiling. He saw my tears. He asked me how I had enjoyed my little trip. He reveled in my distress. He crowed over me in triumph. He wanted to know if I was pleased with the arrangements he had made for me. *He laughed at me! That man laughed at me! . . .*"

I put my hand on his arm. He let it stay there.

Again I searched for something to say; but as I was opening my mouth to speak I felt a sharp tap on my shoulder.

I spun around. Standing close to me were the French chauffeur and the man whom Ridgeling had called José-Luis. The Frenchman's face bore the same insolent half-smile I had always seen on it. It was the same half-smile that must have appeared on it when the panting, tottering old artist advanced towards the statue of Jeannine Ducaux. The Spaniard's expression was as solemn as usual.

They no longer wore their garish sport shirts. Holidays were over. Like me, they wore close-fitting wool shirts and slacks. They carried coils of rope.

They were ready to conduct me to the Cave of the Cyclops.

Something in their manner made me feel certain they had been there before.

XXI

———•◆•———

I sat in the front of the jeep, beside the Spaniard. The Frenchman sat in the rear. On the floor at his feet, its breech protected by a canvas sheath, lay the rifle with which he had been shooting at the gulls.

The Spaniard drove quickly and surely, as if he knew the way, and as if he wanted to get me out of Kavalla as rapidly as possible. My two companions may also have had an idea in the back of their minds that I might try to jump out. There was very little motorized traffic in proportion to the numerous carts drawn by horses, donkeys, even oxen, and the Spaniard had to thread his way through them. He leaned mercilessly on the horn, and we were thrown about continually from side to side. He was only able to keep up his speed because we were driving down a wide new highway, built mainly, I imagine, for prestige purposes, leading from the dockyard gates to the far side of the town. It ran through the main square, beside the tall building with the blunt top and sloping sides that I had noticed from the ship. Fountains splashed in concrete basins, and men were busy hosing down newly planted trees and plots of fresh emerald turf. Above the glittering doorway, guarded by two commissionaires in wine-coloured uniforms, was Merganser's cipher in its circlet of gold. Kavalla was evidently being developed as a company town, strategically placed as it was between East and West.

Let me say at once that I was certainly tempted to jump out of the jeep, even though it was driving along at forty miles an hour. I thought my chance had come when we approached a thronged crossroads with a white-coated policeman in the center. For a moment I thought he was going to put up a cotton-gloved hand to stop us; but three crisp bleats of the horn made him look more closely at the jeep and he hastily waved us through. There were cobbled streets and unpaved alleyways to be seen on each side of the central highway. If I could have tumbled out of the jeep and gained the shelter of one of those alleyways, I might have been able to twist and dodge and lose myself in the poor quarter of the town. But ten to one the Frenchman and the Spaniard knew their way around Kavalla pretty well—and probably most of the local population were in Merganser's pay into the bargain. My chances of getting away were practically nil.

The concrete highway ended abruptly before we were clear of the suburbs. Its engineers evidently considered that there was no point in wasting good materials on the inhabitants of the shacks and wooden huts on the outer fringes of the town. From that point onwards we travelled on a very problematical kind of dirt road. As far as I could judge we were going northeast, in the direction of the Turkish or Bulgarian border, and as we approached the mountains I expected even the track to peter out; but before we reached the end of it the Spaniard swung the wheel and we bumped on to a meager side road.

The gradient grew steeper. The Spaniard pushed in the red-topped gear and engaged his four-wheel drive. We lost the track and ground our way over bushes and patches of scrub. The sun was high in the sky and the canvas roof was hot to the touch. My mouth was dry. From time to time the Frenchman leaned forwards to speak to the Spaniard about the direction, and the latter nodded and drove on without slackening speed.

Neither of them spoke to me. They seemed indifferent about whether the trip would be a success or a failure. It struck me that they had made up their minds already that it was bound to turn out badly. Presumably they had witnessed similar failures in the past. I remembered the Dane and the Swiss. The two men were behaving as if they were simply doing a routine job. Something to humour the boss. Something for which, win or lose, they didn't expect to receive either any blame or any bonus.

Then we rounded a grey-coloured bluff crowned with a few discouraged-looking olive trees: and at last I saw it ahead of me. The mountain. I recognized it from the photographs.

The jeep clawed its way over the scree, and when we reached its lower slopes we stopped and got out.

I was stiff from the ride. My legs were still sore from the knock I gave them against the ship's side. I stamped my feet in a tentative way to get rid of the pins and needles and stared glumly at the summit of the mountain above me. Its squat bulk, outlined against the more majestic peaks beyond, gave it a touch of additional menace.

My companions produced food and drink from a well-stocked wicker hamper. There was rye bread, hard-boiled eggs, pâté, various kinds of preserves and sweet rolls. We ate standing up beside the jeep, the food laid on the hood and mudguards. To my surprise, I found myself eating heartily, scanning the mountain as I tore at the rolls with my teeth. I noticed that the Frenchman buttered the bread and handed it to me, without letting me get my hands on the knives or forks. From an aluminum cup I drank three lots of scalding black coffee. There was no wine or alcohol. The other two ate in a leisurely way, as if they had the whole afternoon in front of them. They were not worried by the excessive warmth of the sun, hanging motionless at the zenith above the top of the mountain.

Methodically they packed the hamper away in the back of the jeep, carefully wrapping up any food that was uneaten. They took out and laid on the ground the equipment which we would carry up to the cave. It was light and compact, but as though solicitous for my strength, they carried the bulk of it themselves. My share consisted only of one of the three sections of a light-alloy ladder, one of three large electric lamps and two coils of nylon rope. The others thoughtfully carried all the material which was sharp and might be used as a weapon: a set of spikes, pitons, crampons and axes. I noticed that the Frenchman secured the rifle across his back with the webbing sling. He slapped the pockets of the canvas jacket where he had put the spare clips of ammunition.

We then had a long, bitter argument.

They told me to rope up. They started to get the rope ready and ordered me to take my place in the middle.

I had always felt that we would have to use a rope to reach the cave. The photographs confirmed that there was a tricky overhang and other moderately difficult features. But it was no part of my pathetic little scheme, such as it was, that I should be number two on the rope.

I refused. I said I would go up as number one or not at all.

The Frenchman told me to hook on and be quick about it.

I got back into the jeep, slammed the door, folded my arms and sat looking out at the bank of grey shale rising in front of the windshield.

They stood at the rear of the jeep and conferred in low tones. Their words were inaudible. They could dispose of me on the spot and report to Gheorgheniu that I had been "lost" in the cave like my predecessors. It would save them a lot of exertion. As I listened to their voices behind me there was a pricking sensation at the base of my skull. I almost expected to feel there the cold pressing circle of the hunting rifle.

The Frenchman came around the side of the jeep and asked me to get out.

I got down and stood facing him. If he had wanted to shoot me, I could have made no resistance. I was too scared even to move my weight off my heels or close my hands into fists. I simply stood on the parched hillside blinking at him.

He gave a shrug and said I could go up first on the rope, if it meant so much to me.

He and the Spaniard were studying me with a kind of grudging curiosity. I had a feeling that they were interested in seeing how I meant to tackle a job that they were not qualified to tackle themselves.

They smoked a cigarette as I adjusted the rope around me. It took a little time. My fingers were shaking.

I made a sign to show I was ready.

We moved off.

It was the climb that restored me. The rhythm of striding uphill settled my breathing into a slow, regular pattern that made thinking easier and gave me a measure of confidence. After all, I was an excellent climber. I had done a fair amount of good-class climbing in my younger days.

For a man walking to his own funeral I set a vigorous pace. I did so deliberately. Soon I heard my companions swearing and stumbling behind me. I was surer footed than they were on the broken rocks underfoot and less encumbered with equipment. I gave them no respite. Every time I heard one of them slither back or trip over and scrabble at the shale with his hands I felt a little better.

They must have thought I was mad to go bounding over the lower slopes like a mountain goat. If they had known I was going to act like that, they would have postponed the roping up until we reached the foot of the overhang. And then they would have made quite sure that I went second on the rope. As it was they must have reckoned that I was eccentric, or demoralized. All the same, tethered to them as I was by the nylon rope, there was no danger of my slipping away from them and vanishing into the beckoning mountains. And if they had seen me trying to untie the rope, the rifle would have been unslung and that would have been the end of it.

It took us twenty to twenty-five minutes to reach the overhang below the entrance to the cave. I was blowing a good deal myself by that time. I halted and looked up. The mouth of the cave was invisible, but a hawk was soaring and stooping in the sky above the summit. The bird's movements were so bold and free that I took it for some reason as a good omen. I breathed in a few deep lungfuls of mountain air, already colder and more invigorating than the tepid air of the plain. Then I started to negotiate the overhang.

There were shouts from below. I took no notice. I paid out more rope and went up hand over hand, my Arco boots kicking for any nick or crevice in the cliff wall to sustain me. My leg, bound with the adhesive tape, was stiff, but not stiff enough to slow me up.

More cries from down below. I imagine that when they had escorted the previous party, everyone came on slowly and rested for a while at the foot of the cliff. Everything would have been taken very methodically. Only after a suitable breather would they start to cope with the overhang, using their axes and pitons. I am sure the Swiss and the Dane were more trusting than I was. This time my companions must have been amazed as they struggled over the last few yards of scree to see me flitting up the surface of the cliff like a bluebottle on a windowpane. But such unorthodox, extempore climbing was, after all, my specialty.

Do not mistake me. I am not an outstanding mountaineer and never will be. I bear the same relationship to a mountaineer that a stunt man does to an athlete. But after all, it was as a stunt man that Bay Russell had hired me. And it was important that my stunt should begin then and there, at the foot of the overhang, and not in the mouth of the cave.

It was a tall overhang, at least fifty feet. I was taking a most appalling risk, freewheeling in that crazy way. It was actually the only part of the business in which the set of photographs were of the slightest use to me. I was glad now that I had studied them so carefully during my sleepless nights aboard the *Marmoset* and had worked out what appeared to be the most feasible route.

The Frenchman and the Spaniard cursed and yelled at me. If they had wanted to, they could have pulled at the rope and plucked me clean off the cliff face. They must have simply concluded that I was off my head; and they stood there together for a minute or more, taking a breather before committing themselves to the overhang.

That was when they made their mistake.

I needed a breather myself, by the time I threw myself onto the ledge at the top of the overhang. It is remarkable how nimble you become if you find yourself clinging practically upside down with a gun, for all you know, trained on your back. It was hardly surprising that I wasted a few valuable seconds slumped on the rock with the knees torn out of my slacks and a good deal of skin rubbed off my fingers. I was too done in to get up.

The Frenchman had lost his opportunity to shoot me. He and the Spaniard were now out of sight below the overhang. No doubt they were wondering what the English lunatic was up to. The rope between us was slack. But what advantage could I gain by untying it and making a dash down the other side of the mountain? They had obviously chosen this route because it was the easiest. They could scramble down to the jeep ahead of me and drive to any point at the base of the mountain to cut me off.

I acted in a way that was intended to put their doubts at

rest. I coiled in the rope and drew it tight—but gently. I wanted to give them the impression that I was being cooperative. I wanted them to think that my sudden jump ahead had been caused by nothing more than an exuberant impulse.

I crawled up the ledge to the cave, carefully keeping that same inviting tightness on the rope, as if I wanted them to ascend. There was a boulder in the heap of stones outside the mouth of the cave, a big black irregular hexagon. Still on my knees, I belayed the rope around the boulder and secured it strongly. When it was fastened I gave it an inviting tug or two, to signify to the two men down below that it was fixed ready for them to climb. Then I stood upright against one of the megalithic uprights that formed the entrance to the cave, watching the slender thread of green nylon as fixedly as a man watching a snake. Only this time I was the snake.

Almost at once it grew taut and started to make small twitching movements from side to side. I passed my tongue over my dry lips. The twitching meant that my companions had finished their deliberations and were climbing the rope. The point was, were they both climbing at the same time? Everything depended on that. If the overhang had been twice as high and awkward to negotiate, and if they had had any great cause to mistrust me, they would have climbed the rope separately. One of them would have stayed at the bottom, covering the other.

I dropped on my knees and cautiously put my head over the edge. The Frenchman was about thirty yards below me. He sensed that I was looking at him and glanced up. His face was a white blur in the harsh sunlight. A few yards below him the Spaniard was moving purposefully up the cliff face. The Frenchman put his head down and kept on climbing, his boots scraping against the granite.

They were tough, fit men, competent mountaineers. They could expect to reach me in two to three minutes.

I took out the table knife from my sock and unwound the

scrap of towelling from the blade. Kneeling there, I tried to take the rope in my left hand in order to lift it an inch or two from the rock so that I could sever it more easily. There was so much weight on it from below that I was unable to get my fingers under it. It was jerking backwards and forwards in a purposeful way that was very frightening. If the Frenchman and the Spaniard arrived on the ledge and caught me trying to cut the rope, my end would be short and brutal.

The seconds were passing. I was making no progress. The blade of the knife was of a fine-quality silver, and silver is soft. It seemed to make no impression at all on the smooth surface of the rope. It was like trying to cut a thick piece of gristle. I could hear the Frenchman panting, groping for holds, his boots smacking the stone.

Frantic, I chopped and sawed at the rope, wedging it flat on the ledge now, striving to hold it still. At last I thought I was making a slit in the outer skin. . . .

In retrospect the scene is an evil dream . . . crouched on the ledge, the sweet-tasting sweat running into the corners of my mouth . . . everything is slow slow slow slow slow slow slow slow-motion . . . hacking at the rope with movements that I know are frenzied but which look as slow as the movements of a fish swimming in some viscous liquid, in some kind of jelly or glycerine . . . slow slow slow slow slow . . . no means of escape . . . slow slow . . . limbs shaking and sheathed in lead . . . slow . . . the sun in the empty sky beyond the ledge made a million times brighter by a black corona of faintness and terror . . . slow . . . and the murderer climbing closer closer closer closer closer closer . . . until at any moment his fingers are about to wriggle over the rim of the ledge a yard from my eyes . . . slow slow closer slow closer closer slow . . .

How am I expected to describe what happened in the next half-minute? What language am I to use? It was beyond language. Did I feel relief or horror? Was I pleased or sorry? What do such words mean? Violent action has a language of its own.

I will be honest and admit that I felt a barbarous exhilaration. At the moment when I sundered the rope I experienced a dreadful feeling of joy. I heard my voice issuing from my dried-up throat in what sounded like a yelp of laughter.

Screams and sounds of falling . . . splatter on rocks . . . bumping of flesh and banging of metal . . . a distant liquid groan . . .

I was kneeling with my chin dug into my chest, eyes screwed shut, muscles locked, fingers clenched. Only when it was silent again and my ears could hear nothing but a soft wind did I open my eyes. Like a small frightened animal I lifted my head and squinted about me. The hawk was hovering level with the ledge, inquisitive. It folded its wings and dropped out of sight, attracted by the bright debris on the rocks below.

I was staring at the silver knife in my hand. Its blade was dented and blunted. On its handle was a delicate monogram: a Gothic letter M in a laurel wreath.

XXII

———•◦•———

I entered the Cave of the Cyclops and went into the cold, dark interior.

I switched on the big flashlight as I walked across the twilit antechamber beyond the massive blocks of the entrance. The antechamber was like a huge natural atrium, leading into the depths of the vast subterranean cathedral in front of me. The beam of the flashlight strayed across the vaulted recesses of the roof. It played on the jumbled blocks that formed the walls. I was surprised to see that at the foot of the walls was piled the flotsam left by previous visitors to the cave. There had evidently been a good many of them. The light revealed mounds of what looked like decayed canvas, heaps of mouldy webbing and leather interspersed with rusty bits of metal of all shapes and sizes, and discarded water bottles and enamelled mugs and plates. I investigated some of the rubbish with the toe of my suede boot. Some of it was expensive. There was the remains of a camera with an elaborate lens, and fragments of a surveyor's theodolite, the tripod entangled with the rust-red measuring chains. As I approached the rear of the cavern I found myself wading shin-deep through stacks of what looked in the beam of the flashlight like discarded military uniforms. The tattered shreds gave off a musty smell and the dust curled around my ankles as I trod over them.

The cavern narrowed down into a rock funnel. I made my way along it with a great deal of hesitation. The rough rock beneath my feet sloped gently downwards. I had a fear of getting jammed in or cut off. The feeling was irrational but strong, more the product of the darkness and constriction of the tunnel than anything else. I was still shocked by the savage events of a few minutes before. I trembled as I reminded myself that if I was trapped I would die here, inside the mountain. Or if a party from the *Marmoset* came out to investigate—and stumbled on what lay below—then I would die anyway. . . .

I lost all sense of time as I was moving down the funnel. It could not have been more than three hundred yards long, but it felt like three hundred miles. The freezing cold was making me sweat. Fortunately I was travelling slowly, braking my body against the slope—because all at once some instinct told me to halt. Half the circle of yellow light at my feet had been swallowed up by an opposing circle of darkness, black as tar. I stopped dead, staring at it as if it were a Yin-Yang sign spread in front of me. The torch wavered. I realized that it was no simple pool of darkness: it was a void, a gulf. I probed with the light ahead of me. Blackness. Infinite blackness. Then the beam picked up a gleam of rock on the far side of the abyss.

The flashlight established that I was standing on a very shallow, irregular ledge. It curved away to left and right and ended against impassable rock buttresses. It was little more than three feet wide at the center, where I was standing. The rock down here was of a curious dark glistening substance, like jet or black glass. The edges of the rocks were geometrical and razor-sharp, snapped into clean straight planes. The rocks looked smooth and slippery.

Further examination told me that the chasm was about

twelve feet wide. The wall on the far side was not the featureless blank I had first imagined. It was pierced by what, after reflection, I took for the continuation of the passage from which I had just emerged. My light would not penetrate the far passage. The beam was absorbed in the dark irregular oval.

At some stage the two passages had been continuous. Then some cataclysmic movement of the earth had sundered them. They were split apart by the twelve-foot gap.

The entrance to the opposite passage was slightly above and to the right of me. At its lower left-hand corner jutted a splinter of rock. Caught around the rock was a twist of white, like a coiled spring. One end of it extended as a thin white line straight down the face of the rock below. It hung as precise as a plummet, heightening the effect of infernal geometry which characterized the whole of the bizarre locality. After a moment I saw that the white line must be a climber's rope, sheathed in some kind of white plastic. The bottom end of it was invisible. What the weight was that held it so rigid I was unable to see. I was grateful for that.

A rusty spike had been driven into the rock eighteen inches above the projection. From the spike a short metal ladder hung askew. The last rung had broken loose and drooped forlornly. The rock beside the ladder was scored with several shallow, parallel, grey-coloured scratches.

Basil Merganser wanted someone—someone like me—to leap the gap between the end of one passage and the opening of the next. It was obvious why an ordinary climber would have been of no use to him. There was simply no way in which he, however skilled, could have got an initial purchase on those hard, glossy rocks. There was no tackle known to me which could have secured a grip on them. The Dane or the Swiss, or both, had done well to have driven in that spike and fixed that ladder before making those scratches on the rock and going spinning down into nothingness. I saluted them.

The only way of reaching the opposite passage was to leap

the crevasse. Around me on the ledge was the evidence that the previous climbers (there seemed to have been many more than two) had tried all manner of hooks and grapnels. The ledge was littered with various bits of discarded ironmongery. The flashlight shone on the dulled tips of their still wicked-looking barbs.

I stood for a long while looking down into the void.

Twelve feet. A standing jump. No opportunity of drawing back and taking a run at it.

A standing jump. High and to one side.

Bay Russell hadn't offered me enough. He hadn't come within a million pounds of it.

It gave me a strange feeling, gazing into the blackness below. I suppose I was no more than halfway down the mountain, hundreds of feet above the level of the plain. But I felt as if I were buried deep under the earth.

I stooped and picked up a stone whose sides were planed into diamond-shaped facets. Extending my arm over the void, shrinking back a little, I let the stone drop. I listened. Time passed. There was no sound of the end of the stone's journey.

No echoing rattle of rock.

No faint plop of water.

No signal from the heart of the mountain.

Nothing.

Carefully I transferred the flashlight from one hand to the other. I felt in my trouser pocket and took out the key, holding it in the light. It was a beautiful thing. The beam shone warmly on the delicate ivory head and copper body. It lay soft in my palm.

What lock did it belong to, over there on the other side? What treasure was it meant to yield? The prize must be very considerable. Merganser had thrown the resources of his whole organization, the abilities of his leading cadre into the search. He had persisted in the enterprise for several years. He was the master of Geddingley Park, a mansion stuffed with the artistic wealth of Europe and the Orient. He owned Rembrandts and Turners, Manets and Monets, rare china and porcelain, tapestries, precious books and bindings. What could be hidden in this remote place that he coveted so highly? And who had brought it here in the first place? Was it booty from some past war—Graeco-Persian, Turko-Venetian, Russo-Bulgarian, Turko-Greek, World War I, World War II? . . .

Scarcely aware of what I was doing, I put the key in my pocket, stepped away from the ledge and carefully laid the flashlight at my feet. Slung across my shoulder was the coil of nylon rope. Clipped to my back by means of a snap link and a short length of cord was the section of the light-alloy extension ladder. During the excitement of the climb I had forgotten that I was still carrying my own minor share of the equipment.

I must have been in an extraordinary mood of exhilaration. Exaltation is the better word. My fingers shook and fumbled as I groped in the splash of light for one end of the nylon rope and knotted it around my waist. I bent down again and picked up the light and loosened the separate strands of the rope to make sure that it would run smoothly and that there were no tangles in it. I passed one end of the length of cord that had been used for the ladder through the metal tag at the base of the flashlight. The other end I tied to my wrist so tightly the flesh hurt. I was glad the lens and bulb were protected by a thick flange of rubber and glad, too, that the beam was a powerful one. I wished the lights carried by the other two had been available.

Everything I did I did quickly, to stop myself from thinking too much. Before I knew it I was stumbling back along the rock tunnel towards the entrance. I was shivering now and banged and blundered into the rock walls. It seemed to take an age to reach the antechamber, though I must have covered the distance in half the time it took me when I was walking down it the other way. It is a curious thing about human beings that they only have to visit a strange place a couple of times to feel thoroughly at home in it. As I went I pulled lightly at the nylon rope, paying it out behind me and giving it a slight twitch now and then to free it from any snags.

My resolution almost failed when I reached the antechamber and saw the daylight seeping into the chamber past the tumbled blocks around the entrance. That weak daylight was very inviting. When I speak of my resolution, I must emphasize once more that I was acting instinctively, feverishly. I suppose I was driven by that old mysterious compulsion to prove something to myself. I deliberately turned my back on that glimmer of light—so sane, so matter-of-fact—and went on with my hurried preparations.

I tugged at the nylon rope until the loose end came into my hand. Then I picked up the metal tripod of the discarded theodolite, carried it awkwardly across to two of the biggest of the fallen boulders and wedged it horizontally behind them. I tied the end of the rope around the middle of the tripod and gave it a quick, nervous pull with all my strength to test that the knot would hold. Nylon or Perlon, or whatever the outer sheathing of the rope was made of, is a slippery material and it is easy to have accidents with it.

Paying out the cord behind me, I went back down the passage towards the ledge. Why I hadn't simply carried the coil of cord with me in the first place and tied it around my waist when I got to the antechamber instead of when I was on the ledge is a mystery. I suppose I was too excited and confused to think matters out in a sensible sequence. It just didn't occur to me.

Somehow I got back to the ledge without making a bird's nest of the rope. Worked up as I was, I am pleased to say I still had enough sense left not to plunge straight ahead with the most obvious and perilous expedient without trying other methods first. Slightly encumbered by the flashlight tied to my wrist, I picked up the ladder section. In spite of the cold down here inside the mountain, I was sweating even more than I had in the Avenue Fustel-de-Coulanges.

As soon as I maneuvered the ladder out over the chasm, juggling it so that the other end dropped on the far ledge, I saw why it was that even the most up-to-date climbing equipment was of little use. True, the geological fault that had split the tunnel had made the far ledge higher than the one I was on, so that the ladder tilted up at an angle. But this would not have been so bad if the ladder had not been canted sideways thirty degrees because the jagged edge of the shelf on the far side failed to provide it with a flat surface to rest on. Even then I might have tried to crawl along the ladder, risking being tipped off into the chasm beneath—for it was, after all, only a relatively short distance to travel. But even as the other end of the ladder had fallen with a metallic ring on the opposite ledge there came an ominous little rattle of stones falling into the abyss. And when I extended a foot and cautiously leaned my weight on the first rung there was a dreadful creak and grinding and an even louder rattle of rock from the other side. I felt the ladder give a good four inches under the thin sole of my suede boot. I drew my foot back in a stomach-squeezing reflex of alarm.

Whatever kind of stone it was, it was horribly fissile and friable. It was soft as cheese. I couldn't trust my full weight to that ladder in case it collapsed and went crashing down. Heaven knows how my predecessors had managed to drive a peg into the far side of the cliff. They must have been pretty good mountaineers. They really had deserved a better fate than the one meted out to them.

I withdrew the ladder—trying not to dislodge any more of that weak and treacherous lip—and steered it straight back into the tunnel behind me. I hauled in the slack of the nylon rope, arranging it in a loose coil on one side of the ledge, and gave a last tug to satisfy myself it was firm.

The moment I had feared for many days—for years, perhaps, ever since I fell out of the fir tree as a boy—ever since I used to jump across Fox Lane—ever since the night at Copenhagen—had arrived. But why, why did I do it—I mean, when there was absolutely *no need?*

I backed away diagonally to get the best run at the thing that I could. It would have helped if the ledges had been parallel with the entrance to the tunnel behind me—though in any case the angle of the tunnel itself cut back at a tangent to the ledge. But in that case there would have been no need for my special talents. Four meager paces back and my spine was jammed hard against the black edges of the wall.

This was it, then. No more excuses. No more hesitation. No holding back. No more reservations.

I heaved my shoulders away from the wall—then let myself relax and sink back against it once more. My legs were firm enough, but my breath came jerkily and I knew I needed to gain more control over my lungs. My bowels felt as though they were full of lead shot.

I told myself that even if I dropped into the chasm the rope would support me. Yes, said a small voice—and a fat lot of use that would be if the rope snapped or tore loose from its metal moorings in the antechamber. Or if I busted a leg or an arm as I fell. I could dangle down there until I rotted. Dangle down there forever.

Then—as I did on the roof of the stables in Paris—I pushed myself forwards and made my leap. I was taking the third of the four short paces before I really realized I was committed. The flashlight was thrust out straight ahead of me. On the final step I stooped as if warding off a blow. Again as in Paris I felt the lip of the ledge crumble under me as I took off and hurled myself into emptiness.

The arc of the light veered crazily out of sight. Through

my mind stabbed the irrational image of making a lunatic reverse jump from the roof above Ridgeling's room upwards onto the roof of Bollow the baker's—an insane, impossible, unthinkable leap. . . .

I hit the opposite ledge with my sore shin and the inside of my skull went white with pain. Somehow I was ploughing along on the backs of my hands, taking all the skin off my knuckles.

The pain in my leg ebbed as I struggled to my feet. My chest was bursting with the effort to suck in air and with the sensation of surging triumph. I had made my jump. I had reached back over the past, across the gulf of the years, and joined hands with that young man at Cambridge. This was more important to me than any transaction with Merganser. I was in the grip of that long-forgotten, drunken, barbaric, all-or-nothing emotion Bay Russell and I used to feel and which comes less and less often as you grow older. . . .

Anxiously I groped for the flashlight on its cord—grasped it—switched it on. It worked.

The light scampered around the gleaming, glassy walls. The nylon rope had got itself twisted around my ankle. As I staggered on down the passage ahead of me I bent down and flung it off.

I lurched along, scuffing my Arco boots against piles of rubble and loose stones. There was no glimpse of light here. I was moving deeper into the heart of the mountain. Gradually my heart stopped thumping, and I began to calm down and examine the track and the walls more systematically.

The tunnel was much narrower than on the opposite side and the roof was lower—though it was not so much a roof as the pointed apex of a gigantic geological landslide. It was curious that the rock should look like black polished steel and yet shear off and cleave so easily. The tunnel began to shrink rapidly, and after twenty yards my shoulders were beginning to brush against the walls on either side. Another ten yards and I fetched up suddenly against a solid face of rock: large fallen blocks that barred any further progress. My light played over their facetted surfaces. They were packed tight and there were obviously more of them beyond.

End of the road.

I was conscious of mingled relief and disgust. I made a feeble attempt to drag one of the blocks away, but gave up when I realized it was hopeless.

It was only when I turned around to go back, my heart heavy with disappointment, that I saw it. It was hard to understand how I missed it the first time—I suppose because of the fitful light and because its surface was almost as smooth as the surrounding rocks.

As doors go, it was smaller than normal. It was about five foot six inches high and consisted of a slab of solid metal. At first glance it reminded me of the front door of Number Twelve, Avenue Fustel-de-Coulanges. But whereas the latter had been painted battleship grey, this door was innocent of paint. The metal was as naked as the rind of a tree when the outer bark has been stripped away—except that in this case the underlying material was dark in colour and grainy or mineralized in texture. The surface was oddly warm to the touch—or at least noticeably less cold than the chilly rocks in which it was set—and when I put my hand on it I had the impression of laying my hand on an area not of metal but of human skin. The pitting was curiously uniform in character, extending over the entire surface of the door, and had a satisfying sort of aesthetic quality, as if it were not so much natural as artificially applied. On the left side of the door was a small triangular aperture which I took for a keyhole. Otherwise there was no sign of a lock or handle. The basis of the triangle was uppermost; and coupled with the fact that the keyhole was on the left instead of the right, where it is usually situated, it struck me that for some reason the lock had been put in on the wrong side and upside down. You see locks inserted in that eccentric way in two- or three-hundred-year-old houses in England, France, Italy and elsewhere.

Now I studied it, the door could easily be several centuries old. Even older. Somehow it had a very old-fashioned, antique look about it. It intrigued me.

I fished in my pocket for the key. I focussed the beam of the flashlight close to the triangle of the keyhole as I took out the key and inserted it into the lock. The bright copper shank made a glittering contrast with the dulled metal of the door.

I wiped my fingers on my wool shirt and grasped the key gently. Slowly, oh so delicately, I turned it in the lock. I thought I felt something yield a little . . . Then it stuck. I applied a little more pressure. The interior mechanism of the lock seemed to budge another quarter of a turn. Then—immovable resistance. I wiped my hand once more on my shirt and gripped the key more firmly.

I turned. Harder. No use. Turned again. Nothing.

I was afraid of damaging the carved ivory head of the key. It was obviously not designed for brutal treatment. And indeed, when I made another attempt to turn it I felt the fluted neck between head and shank buckle slightly. Instantly I relaxed the pressure. Forcing it would snap off the head and leave nothing but a useless copper spike jammed in the lock.

I gave a final soft tentative twist—then gave up. Whatever was in the room or cavern beyond would have to remain hidden. I stared thoughtfully at the key as it lay in my palm, and a thought occurred to me. I could have the key copied in a stronger, unbreakable metal. I could have several keys made, variations on this one. One of them would be bound to fit. Or I could work out some method of bridging the chasm in such a way that I could bring an expert back to the cave with me—a professional safe-cracker, perhaps? . . .

I was turning these ideas over in my mind as I walked back through the tunnel towards the ledge. But everything else fled swiftly from my brain as I found myself standing once again on that ledge. This was immediate. This was real.

And at this extremely critical moment a terrible mishap occurred. I dropped the flashlight and it went out. I had forgotten that I had untied the knot of the cord around my wrist with my teeth to give me more freedom when I was manipulating the key. It sounds stupid: but I simply opened my fingers and let it drop—and remembered about the cord only as it went smack on the ground. I snatched it up in terror and clicked and clicked at the button. Useless. The bulb had broken. I shook the light frantically, slapped it, went through a whole series of silly, futile actions. The tiny filament inside the little globe had disintegrated. A fragment of wire, a blob of glass—and that was that. I was pretty well done for.

I was alone. In pitchy blackness. On the wrong side of the chasm. In the middle of the mountain.

For what seemed an hour but was probably ten minutes I did nothing. I squatted on my heels, holding the defunct light. I could hear my breath rasping horribly through my lungs. Then it dimly occurred to me that squatting would give me cramps, so I rolled sideways and lay sprawled on my belly—taking care to cringe away from the edge of that appalling gulf. The coldness of the rock platform struck up through my damp shirt and slacks.

What I actually thought about in those minutes is beyond recall—if I thought of anything at all. Finally I raised my knees under me and started to crawl forward an inch at a time towards the rim of the ledge. I explored it with my fingers like a blind man. I could feel the curiously regular indentations of the little cracks that had been caused by the ladder or by the boots of previous climbers. Parts of that fragile edge were almost as sharp as the blade of a knife. And all the time I was striving to visualize where precisely the other ledge ran in relation to my own. I knew it was roughly parallel, though at an appreciably lower level. That should make it easier: I would be jumping downwards this time, not upwards. A flying leap in a downwards direction ought not to be utterly beyond me.

Yes—but in the dark! . . .

For a while I pondered the possibility of lowering myself on the nylon rope into the crevasse and letting my own weight carry me across to the far side. But I couldn't think clearly enough: it was all too confused. I was long past clear and vigorous reasoning. There were too many contingent factors, too many imponderables. What if the rope slipped, or I did, or if it broke or frayed on that sharp edge? It was all too much of a gamble and I was too weary to think it through to a conclusion.

Slowly I stood upright. I was mortally afraid of losing my balance and swaying outwards and dropping head first into the chasm. In my state of fever and terrible fatigue I fancied that the chasm was filled with all sorts of demoniac horrors of the kind you shudder at in Bosch and Grünewald. As I inched up to my full height and struggled to keep perfectly motionless and upright I felt as I must have felt when I stood on the roof of Bollow's, knowing that I had drunk too much and it was four o'clock in the morning and if I failed to clear the darkened gap above Fox Lane I would hurtle down on those rusty rows of spikes on top of the college wall and my flesh would be sliced to shreds. . . .

I started to panic. My mind went numb and I suddenly lost the capacity to visualize the opposite ledge. It seemed to be alternately rushing towards me, then rushing back again in a kind of malicious rhythm or spasm. It seemed to perform this teasing trick in time to the swelling and emptying of my lungs and the thunderous pumping of my heart that caused a tremendous roaring in my ears. The inside of my chest was sore with fear.

There was no question here of taking a run. Not even two steps. Not unless I wanted to miss my footing.

I stood in the dark, struggling to fight down the little spring of hysteria that was flooding up from somewhere inside the core of my being. I remember I had to clamp my teeth together as if to stop myself from being physically sick.

I sort of shrank back a little—not so much recoiling as coiling myself like a spring or a snake about to strike. I waited until the moment when the inner vision of the opposite ledge was as clear as it was ever going to be—then I gave a mighty thrust with my legs and drove my body forward into the black nothingness.

I jumped straight and level, legs flailing, arms swinging, brain bursting with the effort of summoning up every last scruple of energy. The veins in my neck and temples felt as if they were going to burst. A terrific cry forced itself out from between my jaws.

Then I dropped, legs still threshing—and the instant I felt a part of my body touch rock I hurled my whole weight forward with a final mighty kick.

I caromed into a barricade of rock with a thump that jarred all the remaining breath from my body. My head snapped forward and I would certainly have cracked my skull like an egg if the impact had not been cushioned by a luckily interposed forearm. I collapsed and lay quivering. I had lost my bearings utterly and had no sense of where I was for many seconds. My first thought was that I had missed my objective and fallen into the chasm. My faculties were so scrambled that I was unable to judge whether I was lying on my side, my back, or my stomach. It was like being bundled into a tomb—buried alive. The darkness pressed down on my eyes like a velvet pad. I felt as if I was going out of my mind.

What saved my sanity and brought me back to normality was a tingling sensation against my cheek. After a moment

I realized what it was: it was a current of air. I moved my bruised limbs to test them—nothing broken—and dragged myself—painfully, wearily—towards the source of that faint current. Sweeping about with my hands, my heart gave a great bound as I recognized what it was. The air was coming from the tunnel that led to the antechamber.

I had made my greatest leap perfectly. I had landed on the ledge on the exact spot, a foot or two to the left of the tunnel, from which I had made my original jump.

I levered my body upright. I tottered, dizzy in the darkness, and clung to the rock wall like a scared child pressing itself against its mother. Two or three minutes more and I would be free.

Then I was struck by a thought. I hesitated, turned back and took a single pace in the direction of the unseen chasm. One pace—no more. The nylon rope was tangled around my leg again. I shook it off. Once again I took the key from my pocket. In the dark I could feel the intricate carved shape of the head.

I knew in that moment—knew for certain—that I would not be returning to the Cave of the Cyclops. It suddenly came to me that, more than anything else in the world, I wanted to keep whatever treasure lay hidden in the mountain safe from prying eyes, safe from the snuffling, acquisitive muzzle of Merganser.

Let it remain where it was, wrapped in its secrecy and potency. Merganser would have to rest content with the spoils he already possessed. Let something still belong to time, to the recesses of the spirit, to God. I would not have touched that locked door if behind it lay the hundred lost tragedies of Aeschylus and Euripides, or one of the lost pictures of Diego Velázquez, or even the Holy Grail. Let what was lost remain lost. Let the mystery abide.

I reached forward and pitched the key into the void.

It was easier to throw away one key than to lay hands on another.

I now had to go down the mountain and rummage in a red mess for the small, cheap, mass-produced, bloodstained key that would enable me to start the jeep.

XXIII

When I emerged from the cave, before I could even begin the descent to the jeep, I blacked out.

My impression is that I actually lost consciousness for a time, but for how long I cannot say. But when I came around I remember the rough grain of the granite under my cheek and the orange blur of the late-afternoon sun. My limbs seemed paralyzed, shot through with a profound pain. I had no desire to get up. Once I did so I would have to abandon this warm nook and embark on the final stage of my odyssey; and I was exhausted, and afraid. I suppose there was a natural mechanism inside me which urged me to put a period of sleep, or unconsciousness—any kind of mental blank or full stop—between me and the terrible events of the past hour.

I was shaken and knocked sideways by what I had done. I was no ruthless man of action; I should have stuck to my art-history. It was no good telling myself that I had only obeyed the sensible injunction: "Do unto others as they would do unto you—only do it first." I suppose some men are born to be heroes, other men to watch them or paint them. I was no iron-willed Spinola—just one of the throng who stood around respectfully as his beaten enemy handed him the key of the stricken city.

Eventually I managed to rouse myself and climb into the jeep and begin the long drive back to Kavalla. The return journey to the city took twice as long as the journey to the mountain. Partly this was deliberate, because I dared not arrive back in daylight. Partly it was incidental, because the events of the day had weakened me. Nor had I enjoyed the final horror of having to root around in the moist mess at the foot of the overhang. After it was over it was necessary to wipe my hand on a tussock of coarse grass. I drove at a grim forty, eyes fastened on the dusty road. On my right the sun showered down arrows of fire across the empty plain as it sank in a barbarous blaze.

I wondered dully whether the *Marmoset* had already weighed anchor and sailed. Perhaps by this time it had already set course for Burgas. Claudie would be sitting there, in her tidy new cabin, without her phonograph or her records, sick, guarded incessantly by the creature with the syringe.

I had the jeep: I could have made a run for it. There were half a dozen spare cans of fuel in the back, and I knew they were full. I had four-wheel drive. I could have left the road and driven baldheaded across country for Thessalonika, skirting Lake Arethusa. The distance was only about a hundred and fifty kilometers. At Thessalonika I would find sanctuary. The influence of the British Consulate at Kavalla was problematical; at Thessalonika the consulate would be large and important enough to resist the pressure of the Merganser organization. Yet here I was, with an excellent chance of saving myself, consumed with the suicidal desire to drive back to Kavalla.

Why? Thus far I had managed to emerge on the credit side of the ledger. I had prudently banked at the Rue des Capucines, on my way to Orly Airport, the two checks which Bay Russell had handed me on the night before my departure for

Venice. Therefore I had already achieved my main aim: to make enough money for me to complete my book. Yet here I was, getting closer minute by minute to Kavalla, obsessed with the idea of liberating someone I had not even met a week before. Apparently I had stumbled on something of more consequence to me than finishing my book. But had she really succeeded in touching some inner spring in me, or was it more a question of my desire to defy Merganser, Gheorgheniu, Bay Russell, Norman Ridgeling, and the rest of them? These were questions I had asked myself repeatedly during the last few days of the voyage. They were questions I was asking myself now, as I drove.

I reach Kavalla at the time that I had planned. It was just after dusk when I entered the outer suburbs and felt my wheels leave the dirt road and run onto the smooth surface of the asphalt highway.

I drove only on my sidelights, and I drove as fast as I dared without attracting attention, heading for the alleyways of the old town where I hoped to lose myself as quickly as possible. Now that it was dark I felt I had a better chance of escaping a general pursuit.

I managed to avoid the main boulevard and the central square, and I was relieved when the darkness grew more intense as I began to drive down the ever-narrowing streets of the poorer section, the car whining in second gear. The houses closed in on either side of me, and I quickly lost my sense of direction and felt like a rat in a maze. I had to drive more and more slowly, for the pedestrians were wandering down the middle of the high-ridged cobble streets, ignoring the cars. Once several people ran alongside and yelled at me, and my heart sank; but I think they were only shouting at me because I was going down a street the wrong way. I nodded energetically as though I understood and pressed on. But in the very next street I became boxed in behind an old lady in a long black dress, trudging behind a handcart laden with vegetables. No amount of discreet tooting would make her either go faster or give way. She was deaf and blind.

I realized that I was not going to get very far like that. Driving the jeep made me conspicuous, particularly driving it so slowly, and I could travel faster on foot. Looking to my left, I saw an archway with the paint and plaster peeling off it, with an empty, neglected-looking courtyard beyond. On an impulse I swung the wheel and bumped my way across the uneven pavement into the unlit courtyard.

I was right: the buildings looked like a tumble-down, deserted barracks. It must have been official property, whatever it was, otherwise it would have been packed with squatters and down-and-outs. The façade of the main building had once been handsome; over its doorway a dilapidated flagpole was fastened to the crumbling stonework with rusty clamps.

I ran the jeep hard up against a wall in the farthest corner, where it would be invisible from the street. With its lights off, at a dozen feet it would be nothing more than a dark, undistinguishable mass. I locked it, slipped the key into my pocket and walked back through the archway.

I was thankful for the darkness now. The streets were not illuminated, and the paraffin lamps that lighted the stalls, shops and houses were dim. I was able to sidle along, side-stepping the passers-by, pressing myself against the wall at the approach of anyone whom I thought looked dubious. My dark shirt and slacks were useful here, but I had to remember that in that population of white-shirted males I was the odd man out. The clothes that gave me protective colouring could also give me away.

Some instinct like that of a small burrowing animal drew me towards my goal. I had nothing else to guide me. It was fortunate that Kavalla was not the size of Le Havre or Genoa. It seemed to take me hours to reach the waterfront, though I probably reached it in less than thirty minutes. I walked as fast as I dared through a network of alleyways whose high walls had retained the sweltering heat of the day. There was a fruity reek of garbage, hot olive oil and horse manure. I was glad when I suddenly stepped out onto a wide new concrete road and smelled the sea. I recognized the road from my noonday ride. It was the road that led to the dock gates. In another five minutes I was a hundred yards from the gates themselves.

I had enough sense left to realize that from this point on I would have to move with greater care than ever. I kept to the side of the road nearest the old town, out of range of the violet glare of the string of sodium lights inside the high protective wire of the dock fence. The brightness of the lights intensified the shadows in which I stole along like a spy, ready to duck back into the streets of the town at the first hint of danger. My rubber-soled boots were soundless.

As soon as I saw the dock gates I knew there was no chance of sneaking through them unobserved, or even walking through them boldly and openly. A knot of men were loitering close to the massive double gates, one side of which was shut. As I walked safely by, I felt a little ball of fear bunching in my stomach. However, I took the presence of the watching men as a promising sign. It suggested that the *Marmoset* was still in dock, after all. Gheorgheniu was still waiting for my two companions . . . or waiting for me. . . .

How was I to reach the ship? I suppose I could have scaled the fence: it would have taken me about two minutes, in spite of the triple strand of barbed wire at the top. But the possibility of my being spotted in the glare of those harsh sodium lights was almost a certainty. I reminded myself of the old cat burglar's adage: "It's always a lot easier to get in than it is to get out." If I were caught on the wrong side of the fence, the two minutes it would take me to climb back out again would last as long as eternity. I would be shot on that exposed wire like a prisoner trying to escape from a Communist detention camp.

I walked on and on for over another mile. This took time, but there was no alternative. For the last half mile there were no sodium lamps, only the blank stretch of the fencing. Nevertheless I made myself walk, not run. I guessed—correctly—that I was going to need all my remaining stamina when I reached the *Marmoset*.

The fence ran past the warehouses and quays and came to an end on the curving shelf of the pebbled shore. The fence continued straight into the sea. It was built right out over the sea bed until the waves closed over it. I could just about make out the acute angle where it met the water by the light of the rising moon.

I sat on the pebbles and took off my socks and my suede boots. I regretted those Arco boots. They had cost me a hundred and fifty new francs, and they were the last pair in the shop. Then I waded into the sea and struck out towards the end of the fence.

The waters of the Aegean were cool on my limbs. I swam slowly, almost luxuriously. Soon I felt sleepy. It was hard to remind myself that this was not a leisurely holiday swim in an enchanted, moonlit sea, but the culminating act of a murderous drama. The thought made me swim more purposefully.

I suppose the local fishermen knew better than to try to enter the inner harbour in this particular way. It was certainly a very long swim. I imagine in view of what happened when I landed that the water around the fence must have contained buoys fitted with radar, or some sonic apparatus of that kind. The thought crossed my mind before I entered the sea. I accepted the risk. I reckoned that it would be more difficult to hunt me down in the ocean, in the dark, than to hunt me down on land, inside the wire.

The *Marmoset* was there all right. She was tied up in the

same berth as before, next to a big tanker that had not been there that morning and which must have come in on the afternoon tide. The *Marmoset's* white outline was superimposed on the tanker's black bulk. Her decks twinkled with light, her sides stuck with the tight rows of bright yellow drawing pins of the portholes. Which one of those portholes was Claudie's? . . .

I swam on with a steady stroke. No one could have approached that ship more silently. I floated like a mine beneath her ghostly hull. I paddled around her, the sound of my movements disguised by the suck and slap of the wavelets. I was looking for a rope, a ladder, a hawser. I cruised about, sticking close to the waterline, quivering at the thought that at any moment the ship's screws might start up a few yards from where I was swimming.

My search was in vain. There was nothing for it: I would have to leave the water and see how matters looked from the quay. There was a flight of stone steps dripping down into the water near the bow, between the *Marmoset* and the tanker. As I headed towards it with a quiet sidestroke I could hear men moving about, talking and laughing on the deck of the tanker. Aboard the *Marmoset* the usual decorous silence seemed to reign. I had the feeling that I used to have in my cabin, staring at the white-painted door: that I was very close to Claudie now.

I swam slowly through a broad cone of red light shed by the lantern at the end of the tanker's bridge. Another minute and I felt the first slimy stone step under my naked foot. I was curiously reluctant to leave the water, which wrapped me around with a protective warmth. I lingered in it for a moment, lazily moving my arms and legs. I took no pleasure in the drying land breeze that already blew on my neck and shoulders. Then I made out, near at hand, a glimmering mass wallowing towards me. From its fetid smell I recognized it as one of the rafts of rubbish with which maritime nations like to festoon their harbours. I clambered up the steps just as it threatened to fold itself around me.

At the top of the steps I bent double and raced blindly for the dim shape of a pile of crates assembled on the dock, twenty yards from the edge of the quay. I ran for cover, spraying water as I went. Then all at once the muffled noises of the harbour seemed to explode like artillery. They blew up into a great balloon of shouting.

So Gheorgheniu's men had been waiting for me. Or so I thought. I expected a hundred hands to grab for me, a hundred legs to be thrust out to trip me up.

I went flailing towards the shelter of the crates. The sound of shouting seemed to swell to a monstrous intensity. I dived behind the mountain of cargo and lay face down, weak and panting. I went limp and waited to be found and finished off. With my cheek raking the stones, I thought:

Good-bye, Claudie . . . thank you for nothing, Bay Russell . . . won't finish the book now . . . angels singing "Plaisir *bloody* d'amour" . . .

There was a roaring in my ears and I seemed to be falling into a vast black pit . . . *Cyclops . . . Copenhagen . . . Mr. Bollow the baker . . .*

Then I realized that nothing was happening. The night still rocked with the noise and shouting. But as the seconds passed it became more and more obvious that the yelling was directed not at me but at something else.

I lifted my head from the stones. I became aware that a wavering light was playing on my eyelids. I opened my eyes, squirmed forwards on my forearms and peered around the stack of crates.

I was staring at a fire. Flames were shooting up from the foredeck of the *Marmoset*.

She was burning.

Keeping my head down, I climbed the tarpaulin-covered boxes and lay prone on the top. Was it my imagination, or could I feel some kind of fluttering from inside one of the boxes, as though it contained a bird—a gold bird? . . .

I peered across at the *Marmoset*. Its white flank lay diagonally towards my vantage point, not more than sixty yards away from me. I was admirably placed to see what was happening. Flames the height of a three-story house were crackling out of her midships, between the main hatch and the bridge. Someone must have set fire to an oil tank or something equally combustible. The fire was eating up the ship at a fantastic rate. Waves of heat fanned my face. There was no need for me to cower down; nobody was going to bother about me in the crisis that had now engulfed Kavalla.

The raving of the flames grew into a noise like a forest fire. The tanker's siren began to bray with a high demented note as her engines came alive and the crew struggled to cast off the cables. She was already beginning to shudder backwards away from her burning companion. Men were streaming like ants across her decks and across the decks of the *Marmoset*. The men on the white ship ran about like drops of fat in a frying pan. Even at this disastrous moment they seemed to retain some semblance of discipline. They scurried to and fro in a noticeably more purposive way than the crew of the tanker that towered over them. I spared Captain Gheorgheniu a half second of admiration.

The tanker's officers appeared to have lost their heads. I could scarcely blame them. At any moment the heat or the sparks could ignite the oil in their holds and send the whole vessel sky-high in one incandescent explosion. The *Marmoset* would blow up with her. So would Claudie. So would I.

I watched with frozen fascination as voices bellowed, sirens shrieked, whistles shrilled and the bells of the port's fire engines clanged somewhere behind me. On board the *Marmoset* thick white strands of foam were already being directed towards the seat of the fire. Brave but hopeless: secondary fires were already pulsing like the rays of a starfish from the main blaze. In the stern a gang of men were labouring heroically to save a portion of the cargo. They were heaving onto the quay the long oblong boxes which I had noticed earlier. They must have been precious—for those men down there, tottering to the rail, three to a box, were risking everything for them. Strange how a man like Merganser can always persuade people to risk their lives for his property . . . hadn't I risked mine? . . . One by one the heavy boxes burst open on impact with the quay and I saw the shapes of guns come rattling out of them like black metal match sticks, and shiny black pellets like caviar that must have been hand grenades or mortar shells.

And all this time, on the open end of the bridge beyond the enclosed box of the wheelhouse, Gheorgheniu stood calling orders through a megaphone. And his crew listened to him and obeyed him. There was something undeniably impressive about that immaculate figure, framed against the glowing square of the wheelhouse. The conflagration shed a light of an almost atomic intensity that enabled me to make out his form and features with perfect clarity. His gold-braided cap was set as squarely on his head as if he was making his morning inspection. I could see the glitter of the gold buttons on his white tunic, the gleam of the gold band of his watch as he held the megaphone to his lips.

As I watched him, perched there on my tarpaulin, I saw a figure taller even than his, though stooped, come into view inside the wheelhouse. Then the door of the wheelhouse was flung open and the figure advanced with an oddly deliberate gait along the open portion of the bridge. The figure wore a rumpled white suit—and as it closed on the captain, who stood oblivious with his back turned towards it, I thought—I don't know why—of the figures of Don Giovanni and the Commandatore in one of those productions in which Claudie must have taken part.

It was a prophetic thought. In the very second that I realized that the bowed and crumpled figure was Boulanger, the latter shot out his long spidery arms and gripped Gheorgheniu by the throat. The megaphone spun out of his hands over the bridge. His knees buckled. I swear I could hear him gag as he twisted around beneath the pressure of those fingers. I knew those hands. Smooth, youthful-looking, lending the impression of a colossal strength. They were the hands that had hewn out the woman of the Byron Memorial; and the throat they squeezed was that of the man who that morning had laughed at what had happened to it.

Gheorgheniu swayed and writhed, clawing at the old man's wrists. Then the flames below belched up and a curtain of smoke veiled them. When it cleared Boulanger stood alone on the bridge, his back hunched above something inanimate at his feet.

His attitude reminded me of the hawk staring down at the dead men lying at the bottom of the mountain.

I am confused about what happened next. The ship appeared to shake itself like a creature in pain. There was a tremendous twanging sound which mystified me until I saw that the tanker, churning madly astern, had snapped two of her anchor cables and torn a big steel bollard clean out of the stone quay. The bollard clanged against her plates like a cannonball. When my eyes went back to the bridge Boulanger was no longer there. Nor was the bridge. There was a gap: a glare like the mouth of a furnace; an aureole of spark and flame. The whole middle section of the *Marmoset* was a molten mass.

I shrank back. I could feel the tentacles of heat whipping across the dock. I couldn't bear to watch the death of the *Marmoset* and its crew, which also meant the death of Claudie. I pressed my face down on my bare forearm, blood on my tongue again.

But I had to look. And when I narrowed my eyes to peer into the heart of the fire I saw a little group of people jostling down the gangplank towards the quay.

One of them tripped and was jerked up again like a doll by the man in the lead.

He was the fair-haired lieutenant. The doll he pulled upright and dragged after him was Claudie.

I slipped down from my stack of boxes. I crushed myself back in the lee of my hiding place to watch them go by. They passed within six feet of me.

Claudie's face, caressed by the flames, had the same resigned look that it had worn so often during the voyage. She walked like a mechanical toy, wide-eyed, staring straight ahead. She wore a white overall with the top button undone which I guessed must have belonged to Franciska Brody. The left sleeve bore a big dark smear which was hard to identify in the wavering red light. Was it dirt, where she had fallen over? Was it a burn? Was it blood? The lieutenant pinioned her by the right arm, while on the other side of her marched the vigorous figure of Franciska Brody herself, fingers fixed like pincers around Claudie's upper arm, blond hair like burnished bronze in the glow of the fire. Two sailors, laden with baggage, brought up the rear.

Captain Gheorgheniu, faithful to his employer to the end, had succeeded in discharging the most valuable item of his cargo.

I padded in the wake of the little party, moving from one piece of cover to the next. I kept Claudie's white-clad figure, an unnatural dot of repose in the chaos around us, always in view.

There was such a horde of men running about all over the dock that there was really no point in all the precautions I took to stay out of sight. In any case, who would have recognized my dripping, bruised, blackened, Caliban-like figure as the English passenger who had stepped off the *Marmoset* a few hours ago? Anyone who bothered to notice me would take me for a sailor escaping from the hell of the *Marmoset* or the tanker alongside her.

Nor was there any point in my fear that I would be unable to bluff my way out through the dock gates. The lane to the gates was choked with townsfolk pouring onto the dock to see the fun. The lieutenant and Franciska Brody, tightening their hold on Claudie, had to fight their way through. Soon I had moved so close to them, fearful of losing contact in the crush, that I was practically treading on their heels.

There was nobody on guard at the gates. They hung wide open and people streamed in and out at will. All trace of discipline had collapsed. The guards were probably helping the firemen, or trying to throw a cordon around the doomed ships. Or else they had fled.

I was level with the gates when the event occurred which earned Kavalla its fleeting place on Europe's front pages. The ground suddenly heaved up beneath my feet like the skin of boiling milk. There was an immense grating, crunching sort of sound. Everyone in the crowd packed around me shouted or screamed. We were all thrown on top of each other and rolled around like beans in a coffee grinder. Night turned to day. The sky was a sheet of blue and white flame. My mind formed the word—*earthquake*. An instant later the explosion that followed the ghastly glare that was splitting open the sky showed me that I was mistaken: the tanker had blown up. In that moment eighty-four seamen, thirteen fire-fighters and twenty-seven other people died.

The lieutenant and Franciska Brody had strong nerves. They were the first persons on their feet, hauling Claudie up with them. A black rain was weeping from the sky, from which the lightning flash was ebbing. Dark splashes pattered on my chest and shoulders, on the white overalls of Claudie and the stewardess, on the white cap and tunic of the lieutenant. It was raining oil. The lieutenant pushed Claudie through the gates, over the prostrate, stupefied townsfolk on the roadway, and got her across to one of a line of cars. The driver was lying on his back, stunned. The lieutenant kicked him in the ribs. The roof of the car was sticky with the spots of oil that sifted onto it. I pressed myself against the wall behind the gatehouse. I saw the lieutenant open the door and deposit Claudie on the back seat. He spoke one word to the driver.

"*Meidias*," he said—or what sounded very like it.

The car drove off, wipers clicking to clear the drops of oil that clung to the windshield.

XXIV

It seemed to take me hours to find my way back to the barracks or whatever it was where I had parked the jeep. Just when I thought I was lost and would have to abandon the search I suddenly caught sight of the battered archway with the darkened courtyard beyond. I almost wept with joy.

Fortunately the jeep had not been touched. In spite of my recent exertions the personal belongings in my trouser pockets were still intact. I had the key.

My destination was obvious. The lieutenant and Franciska Brody could only be heading for one place: the tall building in the main square that I had seen from the rail of the ship and which I had passed on my way out of Kavalla a few hours ago. It was the tallest building in Kavalla: where else could the Merganser organization have its headquarters?

No one paid me the least attention as I drove in what I thought was the direction of the square. At first I was caught up in a terrible confusion. The town was half destroyed, a blanket of gritty smoke was drifting landwards, and people were reeling along the streets as if they were drunk. Then came a section which had not felt the impact of the explosion quite so severely and where the poorer citizens were flocking almost happily towards the docks to see what for them was a tremendous free show. And the farther from the docks I went the atmosphere became increasingly normal and the passers-by appeared less dazed. Here the street lamps had not been blown out by the explosion like the lamps at the docks, and the bright lights lessened the menace of the red glow in the sky. The cars were heading towards the scene of the disaster at a more leisurely pace.

Then, turning into a long, wide street, I saw ahead of me the square and the great building. The building dominated the whole of one side of the square, its upper floors mushrooming above the pool of light that spread over the asphalt apron at its base.

I had been driving like a somnambulist, my eyelids raw with the smoke from the blaze, the windshield filmed with oil. Now I made a special effort to concentrate.

What I was after was an unobtrusive place to park. I cruised around the streets in the vicinity of the square, without actually entering the square itself. After ten minutes I finally came across a deserted shopping street only a few yards away from the main square and the rear of the building. I drew up in a patch of shadow opposite a construction site hidden behind primitive wooden scaffolding. I got out and placed the key with elaborate care deep in my right-hand pocket.

Cautiously I entered the square and mingled with the pedestrians. I kept to the extreme inner edge of the pavement, where there was plenty of shade and where I could dodge into shop entrances if I needed to. I wanted to work around slowly to a spot where I could get a good view of the building.

It seemed to grow taller and more monstrous with every step. It was basically a modern office building of a familiar type; but there was something about its sloping sides and truncated top that reminded me of a Babylonian ziggurat, or a flat-topped Aztec pyramid where the priests danced laced in the flayed skins of their victims. My feet carried me forward as if I myself were an involuntary sacrifice at some deadly rite. I craned my head back to look at the bulk of the tower as it wheeled overhead. The rooms were dark, but the lights from the square struck upwards against the steel rims of the windows and made the building look as if its framework consisted of huge steel razor blades. The ruby light of the distant conflagration beat against the windowpanes.

I stopped when I saw the two white-coated policemen with their backs towards me. They were standing near an oil-spattered car that was parked in the forecourt. The forecourt was provided with an ornamental chain which could not have prevented a child or an old lady from entering if either had wanted to; but I am sure that no one in Kavalla ever trespassed on that forecourt. The crowds on this side of the square were noticeably thinner, as if they wanted to keep away from the building, and the people who passed it hastened by with quickened steps.

I had no intention of setting foot on that forecourt or entering the building by the tall glass doors, on which I could now make out an inscription consisting of seven large gold letters. My Greek was just about good enough to enable me to transliterate the letters as the name *Meidias*. In the darkened hallway beyond I could see a man in maroon uniform seated behind a desk on which stood an gooseneck lamp. It seemed to me that there were other men in the shadows behind him.

Nonetheless I knew that I must enter that building, because it was there that the American car had brought Claudie. I melted back into the crowd again and made a complete circuit of the square, trying to force my fagged brain into giving me an idea of what I should do.

I rounded three sides of the square, gulped down two mugfuls of water from a drinking fountain, splashed more of it plentifully over my face and neck, then plunged down a street that ran along the right-hand side of the Meidias Building.

The street itself was dark, and when I looked up and saw the lights in one of the upper stories of the building they seemed to shine out with an exaggerated brightness.

I think that the fact that the spring night was so warm helped me to climb the wall into the compound at the back of the building. The soft warmth seemed to coax some of the stiffness out of my weary limbs. The blocks of the wall were set flush, but somehow my bare feet managed to get a purchase. However, it was only when I reached the top of the wall, which was about ten feet high, that I realized why it was so deceptively easy to climb. Underneath me a uniformed guard with a dog as tall as his thigh was just strolling away from me. I could hear the animal's deep-chested breathing. It looked like one of the breed from Geddingley Park that dealt so efficiently with anybody who tried to take an uninvited peek at Mr. Merganser's pictures or silver. If I had arrived at the top of the wall three seconds sooner, the brute would have spotted me, dragged me into the compound and ripped me limb from limb.

I lay prone on the wall and gave the guard a full minute to get clear. He disappeared behind a stack of boxes, and I made sure that everything was absolutely silent before dropping into the compound, landing as softly as possible in order to spare my damaged shin.

I had to explore the rear of the building as best I could by the glimmer of light that filtered into the side street from the distant square. Fortunately I soon came on what I was looking for. The big frosted windows leading to what I imagined were kitchens were all barred from the inside; I could see the black shadows of the bars through the frosted glass, reinforced with wire. But behind a row of aluminum ash cans, emptied and turned upside down in neat ranks, were two smaller, lancet-like windows. They consisted of the same reinforced glass, but as they were so narrow the architect doubtless reckoned they did not need bars. At least, I could see no sign of any in the dull glimmer that shone from inside. The breadth of the windows was no more than six to seven inches, but that was enough. If there is room for a man's head and a single upstretched arm to pass, then a man's whole body will go through. I hauled up my tattered trouser leg and picked at the end of the adhesive bandage on my right leg. It was soaked with water and difficult to unwrap, but I managed to peel it off without getting it into a tangle. I hoped that the adhesive on its underside had not been affected too badly by its wetting, and stuck it on the pane of one of the little windows, covering as much of the glass as possible. I smoothed it down flat with my palm, holding one of the ends in my right hand. Then I pressed my left shoulder against the pane and pushed hard until I felt the whole thing give beneath my weight.

The window crumpled inwards, held by the adhesive. Except for the tinkle of a single sliver of glass, there was no sound. I lifted out the string of broken glass sticking to the bandage and laid it on the ground behind one of the ash cans. Now I had to pick out the remaining bits of glass. By a stroke of luck the putty was not too old and too bone-hard, and I worked most of the longer bits out in their entirety. One or two of the shorter ones snapped off more or less flush with the frame, and this I could do nothing about. I had to work quickly. I was very afraid of that dog scenting me and coming back.

I dropped the fragments of glass out of sight behind the ash cans, then put my head and my right arm through the window. It was a terrible squeeze. I grunted and wriggled. Had I misjudged the width of the opening? What an undignified end to the affair—wedged in a window with a dog snapping at my calves! . . .

It seemed to take an hour to worry my body through the gap—and the stubs of glass scratched furrows in my wretched carcass, already scarred enough since that distant, peaceful afternoon in the Prado. Then, thank God, I was through and dropping forward on my elbows on to a cold cement floor.

I was in a cellar or a storeroom. A subdued light came from a low-powered red control light set high up in the wall at the far end. I crept forward. As I passed the boxes piled in the center of the enormous room, I caught the faint sound of rustling and chirping close to my ear. These were the crates that had been unloaded from the *Marmoset* while I was listening to Boulanger's recollections of Jeannine Ducaux. My fellow prisoners were in there, my companions of the voyage, under their tarpaulins, stirring as I went by.

I knew then beyond any doubt that I had hit on the right place to find Claudie.

I could hear voices. They were little more than a murmur, as though their owners were keeping watch. They came from the vestibule, which was evidently reached by a half-staircase from the rear of the building. I put my head around a door from the basement, but all I could see was the uniformed figure at the desk and the tall glass door beyond. Through the doors I caught a glimpse of the square in reverse: fountains playing, cars and taxis driving by, people hurrying with averted faces past the façade of the Meidias Building. There was a great spread of plush carpet, probably crimson in the daytime, but a dark purple like the colour of an old bloodstain in the half-light. The furnishings were very luxurious, more suitable to a capital than to a small city which was almost off the map.

Problem: how to reach that brightly lit suite of rooms which I had noticed from the side street?

It would be asking for trouble to try to sneak up the half-staircase and around the back of the vestibule, to the point where I supposed the main staircase and the lifts were situated. I closed the door very quietly and went back into the basement.

I spent the next ten minutes looking around. My bare feet made no sound as I examined the basement, the kitchens, the laundry, which were all connected with one another. They were well laid out and furnished with the most modern equipment. The same dim red guard light played everywhere. I roamed about in a mood of distraction. What if Claudie were being kept in the building for only a short time? What if Zidarov had been told what had happened and had already sent his men to collect her? It was unlikely that anyone from Bulgaria would reach Kavalla before tomorrow morning; but a man who had been so eager to bring Claudie back to his side was unlikely to waste any time.

I wanted to hurry, but I also wanted to keep my head out of a noose. What was I to do? I picked up a shining steel screwdriver which had been left on top of a deepfreeze and tapped it idly on my palm, struggling to get my thoughts in order. My actions thus far could hardly be described as brilliantly constructive. I pushed the screwdriver into the pocket of my tattered slacks.

I started to open cupboard doors. It seemed to me that there must be some sort of air duct or service duct in a building like this. I was no architect; at least, I was interested only in the aesthetic, not the practical side of architecture. But I knew there was a service duct running from the top to the bottom of most apartment and office buildings. There was one in my apartment building in Madrid; I opened a door on the landing one day and walked into it by mistake. So for several minutes I walked around opening broom cupboards, jam cupboards, every other sort of cupboard. And then, suddenly, I found it.

The duct, covered by a heavy fireproof door, was alarmingly small in size. It was about six feet deep and only four feet wide. Bolted to the wall was a cat ladder, its upper rungs disappearing into the gloom above the first little crimson guard light. On either side of the ladder were big fat pipes and cables, through which ran the building's drainage and electricity supply. And hot! . . . The May night outside had been hot enough—but this! . . .

Well, there was nothing else for it. At least the duct would carry me a few floors above the vestibule, where I could creep out unobserved and continue up the main stairs. I wedged the thick door with a cardboard carton containing cans of food which I dragged from under one of the white-topped tables in the kitchen. It would keep me from locking myself in the duct and might even create a bit of a draft.

I went up to the cat ladder, gasping for air as I climbed. The sweat poured down my ribs; a salty stream trickled into my eyes and made them smart. One of the sets of pipes that ran beside the ladder was lagged with some sort of fiberglass material. The pipes scalded my body when I came into contact with them, and the fiberglass gave off an abrasive white dust that got into my throat and under my eyelids. After about two dozen rungs my right shoulder came into contact with a protruding valve, sending a wave of pain through my body and making me feel sick. I slotted my left arm through the ladder and hung there for a moment, waiting for the first shock of pain to subside, wondering if the heat would eventually defeat me and force me back.

I hauled myself upwards rung after rung. The heat began to affect me. The Meidias Building and the cave in the mountains were becoming fused together in my smouldering mind. I was only brought back to reality by hitting my head sharply against a metal trap door. For a moment my heart sank. My ascent seemed blocked. Then to my delight I found that the trap door could be pushed upwards away from the cat ladder. The door was a firetrap, hinged so that it could be quickly lifted up or down. On the other side of it was a door in the side of the duct similar to the door in the kitchen. I turned the handle and found it was locked; but on a nail beside the door I saw hanging one of those square-ended keys like the keys railwaymen use to lock carriage doors. I used it on the lock and stepped out with inexpressible relief into the corridor.

It was warm in the corridor, but after the stifling atmosphere inside the shaft I felt like an Arab leaving the desert and entering an oasis. I judged that I had emerged on about the third or fourth floor of the building. The corridor glowed with a shaded yellow light, several degrees brighter than the guard light in the shaft. At first I found it almost blinding. The stairs were to the left of me, beside a triple bank of elevators. I started to mount the stairs three at a time, revived by the comparative coolness of the air. My bare toes sank into the pile of the carpet. I mounted so rapidly that I rounded the corner of the next floor and nearly ran into the arms of two sentries.

Luckily they were standing with their backs to me, staring out of the landing window. In that first half second their image was imprinted on my mind. They wore the now familiar black uniform, like the French and Spanish chauffeurs, and on their shoulders were draped short-barrelled carbines. They stood stock-still, silent, the flames from the conflagration in the distant docks casting a flickering orange shadow across their faces.

I shrank back. For a second I stood motionless, certain that they must at least have heard the thumping of my heart. Then I stole downstairs again, one delicate step at a time, very much more slowly than I had come up.

I looked at the door to the service shaft with loathing. By a sheer fluke I had left the key in the lock in my haste to get out, or else the door would have clicked shut. Going back into the shaft was like re-entering the mouth of a furnace. The rungs of the cat ladder seemed to sear my bare feet. I slipped the key in my pocket and embarked once more on my purgatorial ascent.

It is a mystery to me why the heat failed to knock me out.

If I had fallen off the ladder I would have dropped at least twenty-five feet onto the iron trap door on the next floor below. I thought of this every time I struggled with one of these heavy trap doors on my slow progress upwards. I could lie with all my bones broken on that sizzling sheet of metal until I suffocated or died of internal injuries. Even if I still had enough strength left to cry out, no one would hear me. The fireproof cladding on the doors and traps would make sure of that. Every time I lowered one of those traps I felt that I was sealing myself more permanently into my tomb.

Mercifully, the next trap door I pushed up proved to be the last. I could not have pulled my protesting limbs up many more rungs of that ladder. I crawled through the trap and found myself in a huge room with metal walls. It was cluttered with machinery. The ceiling was at least forty feet high. All around me were parts of a refrigeration plant, electric motors. I was in the top floor service area.

I lay prostrate for a moment to get my breath back and allow my head to clear. There was a door. I rose to my feet and used my square-ended key to open it. Because of my experience a few minutes earlier I was careful—and was glad I was. Three men with carbines were talking in low tones outside a massive, elaborately carved and gilded doorway, designed in a kind of Hollywood-Assyrian style. On each side of the doorway were gold stands with sheaves of tall spiky flowers of a deep copper colour. I could smell their musky scent. The head of one of the guards started to swing in my direction. Quickly I closed the door, relocked it and stepped away from it.

I waited. Trembling. Hoping no one had seen the door move or heard it click. After half a minute I put the key in my pocket and let my body slide to the floor. For what seemed an age I simply sat with my bare back against the lukewarm plates of the wall, staring stupidly at a long row of enormous dials, marked with red numbers, six inches away from me. They stared back at me, like the baleful, bloodshot eyes of the Cyclops in their cave. . . .

How could I gain access to the suite of rooms behind their gilt-encrusted doorway?

There was another cat ladder running up the wall to a trap in the ceiling. My calf and thigh muscles were shrilling with tiredness as I clambered up it and thrust my body through this ultimate trap door.

A great chill suddenly caught hold of me. Above me the stars shone down with an icy vindictive glitter. I lurched out onto the roof.

Behind me were the black shapes of the mountains, with the moon rising behind them. In front of me the whole water-front of Kavalla appeared to be ablaze. Seen from up here it was a spectacular sight. Obviously it would be many hours before the conflagration was brought under control. Kavalla was paying very dearly for Basil Merganser. Somewhere in those sulphurous flames lay the wreck of the *Marmoset*, with the bodies of Boulanger and Gheorgheniu. I had no doubt that the old man, in a fit of hate or self-disgust, had set the ship alight. Or else he had done it, apparently by accident but actually with unconscious purpose, by means of one of his interminable cigarettes, setting his bed or his cabin curtains on fire.

Then, as I let my gaze wander across the roof, I saw that I was not going to be allowed to conclude the affair, after all, without having to undergo one final test of my powers as a nightclimber. . . .

The difficulty was not reaching the other side of the roof. That was easy. There was a raised catwalk all the way around, skirting the thicket of television and radio aerials. I made my way to what I judged to be the point above the top-floor suite without any mishap. True, I found that I had to cling tight to the rail of the catwalk, and I dared not look down.

There are few people with a better head for heights than I have—but by that stage I seemed to have lost my zest for peering down into several hundred feet of empty space. Such pleasures are wasted on a man with an exhausted mind, an empty stomach, sore hands and feet, an aching right shoulder, and a body excoriated by jagged glass and punished by the landward breeze.

I searched methodically all around me. There was not, as I had confidently expected, a trap door corresponding to the one from the service area that would give me access to the set of rooms below.

I crawled on my hands and knees to the parapet and stuck my head between the bars of the catwalk. When I looked down my stomach somersaulted. It was a horrible sight. This was not Fox Lane as seen from the roof of Bollow the baker's. This was a quarter-mile drop into the square below. It looked the size of a pocket handkerchief. The fountains were little twisting rods of glittering glass.

I was compelled to shut my eyes for a moment. Then I forced myself to open them in order to perform my famous *coup d'oeil*, the expert glance that would show me the exact lie of the land. When the dizziness had cleared, I noticed the balcony. The apartment below me was unique in the entire building in that it possessed a diminutive balcony. I hardly supposed that the occupants of the executive suite would be rash enough to use it, but no doubt it enabled them to open the wide windows and let in some fresh air. It was only a token balcony. Its metal struts had been made deliberately slender and frail, in order not to spoil the symmetry of the front face of the building—and I must say that it looked the very opposite of robust. At least, to a man who would have to drop onto it from a distance of twenty feet. Which is what I had to do now.

This would be no grand flying leap. This was something much more cold-blooded.

My nerves were screaming a protest as I climbed over the catwalk, hanging on grimly to the rail. The muscles in my arms were fluttering. I felt as weak as water.

Slowly I turned inwards, lowering my body over the edge of the building. The smooth stone was still hot from the sun, and I had the hallucinative feeling that the red light from the dock fire which played on it was somehow helping to keep it warm. It felt as warm as human flesh.

I hung full length from my arms. I could not look down. I strained my neck back and stared up at the chalky stars in the jet-black sky. My mouth was open and my throat was emitting a strange dry roaring sound like a wounded horse.

I wish I could claim that I willed myself to drop onto that balcony. I don't believe it was a purposive act. I think I dropped because my wrists and forearms hurt so much, and because my right shoulder felt as if it had been torn out of its socket.

I just loosened my fingers and fell down the face of the building.

XXV

If I hit the rim of the balcony I would either be tipped backwards into space or hurled forwards to smash against the wall or the windows.

I managed—for once—to do something right.

The soles of my feet smacked on the terrazzo with a noise that must have been audible inside the apartment. I stayed squatting, in the position in which I had broken my fall, waiting.

Nothing happened. I suppose the closed windows and drawn curtains must have muffled the sound. Or else they thought it was a minor reverberation from the docks, a side effect of the destruction of the tanker, not violent enough to merit attention.

As I straightened up I gave an involuntary glance over the parapet. A mistake. The sight of the town stretched out below, half obscured by angry, cindery smoke, made my mind reel. I had to put my hand against the wall to steady myself. I felt so light-headed, the whole of my tired body felt so paper-thin, that I had the illusion that the mild breeze would whirl me away from the balcony into the void. . . .

It was at least a minute before I recovered enough to examine the windows. They were french windows. The catch had been slid across on the other side. I took the square-ended key from my pocket and carefully jabbed at the glass around the lock. I was poking out a half-circle of glass, intended to be large enough to put my hand through, when the cracking of the pane finally aroused the people in the room and the curtains were suddenly whipped back.

I was confronted through the window by the face of the young lieutenant. With a wild satisfaction I saw that he was more startled to see me than I was to see him. For once the meaningless polite smile was absent from his face.

Then he snicked back the catch and took a pace backwards. The windows flew open. I stepped into the room. It was cool, cooler than it was on the roof. Behind his head, high on the wall, an electric fan was whirring. The light from a tall floor lamp beside the desk in the corner struck the metal fins, and some of the wavering light of the dockside fire now entered the room and provided a strange, alternating kind of illumination.

The lieutenant was about to throw himself on me and overpower me. I suppose it was because I looked so feeble that he didn't bother to call for help. I was aware that a second man was sitting in the shadow behind the desk.

Before he attacked me the lieutenant stared at me for a second. There was a baffled expression on his face that added to the elation I felt. I could see that he was asking himself how this half-naked, scarecrow figure could have caused so much havoc: killed Gheorgheniu; sunk the *Marmoset*; destroyed her cargo; upset all the intricate arrangements concerning Claudie de Carmona. How could one man—a mere painter, an art critic, or whatever he was said to be—defy Basil Merganser and Angel Zidarov, set half a town on fire and appear without warning on the top floor of the Meidias Building? His pale-blue eyes showed his bewilderment and incredulity. How was it possible for a single weak individual to disrupt the workings of the Merganser organization? His face was pale with hatred for the inconvenience and indignity I had inflicted on him and his masters.

Then he came at me, aiming a savage blow with an object he held in his hand, his head lowered to butt me in the face. As his arm swung I swayed away and he lurched past me. He should not have given me that short second of respite. I had gotten the kitchen screwdriver out of my pocket, and as he stumbled against the still undulating curtains I brought it down hard between his shoulder blades. It sank in. As I let go of the shaft, he slipped to his knees and pitched forward on his face. Blood began to widen around the shaft, soiling still further the once-perfect white uniform already disfigured with oil stains.

I stooped and picked up the object which had fallen from his hand. A ray from the lamp shone on it and showed me that it was a big block of colourless plastic, its edges sharp and square. In the middle of it was embedded a large, glittering, newly minted gold piece. He must have picked it up off the desk when he heard the glass breaking in the window.

I was still staring at the gold coin when there was a sharp snapping sound behind me, and I felt a burning sensation in the side of my neck, under the jaw. I put my hand there and it came away a sticky red. There were three more sharp reports and three thumps on the curtains not far from my head, as if someone was slapping the velvet drapes with a carpet beater.

From that point on my recollection of the rest of what happened is very hazy. I have a definite impression that I thought I was bleeding dangerously and that the loss of blood was making me feel faint. The level of my consciousness now began to oscillate violently between extreme poles. It was as though my heart had started to pump with a frenzied action, now strong and now sluggish. At one minute my sight would register the objects around me with a fantastic clarity—and the next minute everything would be fading and I would be groping about half-blind. From then onwards I felt increasingly that I was fighting to hold off a tide of darkness that was beginning to pour over me. I felt that the black smoke from the burning docks was drifting through the open windows and trying to engulf me. I was willing to fight on to the end—but what reserves could I expect to summon to keep me on my feet much longer?

I whirled around. In a mist I saw that Franciska Brody was standing beside an inner doorway from which the light flared out and was firing at me with an automatic. Her first shot had hit me, but it was a small gun without much stopping power, and she was evidently inexpert in its use. Like the lieutenant, she was no longer the cool and decisive figure she was in her own setting, aboard the *Marmoset*. That big icy woman was panic-stricken. Her hand shook. I hefted the solid block of plastic and threw it at her with all my remaining strength. The corner of it hit her square on the temple, and as she fell back she hit the side of her head a horrible blow on the doorpost.

In the little room behind her I could see Claudie. I cried out and started towards her. She was standing still and upright in the little gleaming white-tiled room, dressed in her white coat. The buttons down the front were unfastened, and I could see that beneath the coat her body was naked.

The light was waxing and waning, now brilliant, now cloudy, and there was a ringing noise in my head.

Then I remembered the second man, the figure behind the desk, and something made me turn to look at him.

My eyes could scarcely penetrate the shadows. The ringing noise was like the droning of a huge cracked bell. My legs felt as if they had diving boots fastened on them.

The first thing I noticed about the man was that his hands lay on the desk. But the light in the room was so vague and I was so faint that I could not see properly. My brain felt as if it had turned to pulp or floss. The face was a blur: smooth, featureless, the skin stretched tight across it. I had a fantastic sensation as I waded towards Claudie, craning my head backwards towards the desk, that the hands weren't hands at all, but talons . . . and the skin of the face wasn't skin—it was horn or cartilage . . . And a great beak was growing out of the center of it and beginning to grind and chew like the beak of a parrot . . . And the ridge on top of the skull was sprouting a floppy, leathery crest, and its scaly old eyes were shedding thick skins of mucus like tears of liquid gum . . .

Then the figure rose slowly to its feet, and the awful mist of fatigue and unreality shredded away for a moment, and as the face was thrust forward into the light of the floor lamp, I saw who it was.

Basil Merganser.

XXVI

It must have been thirty years or more since Augustus John or Wilson Steer or whoever it was had painted the portrait I had seen in Gheorgheniu's cabin. Merganser was then in the prime of life. Now he was old. Very old. His face was seamed and twisted like an old turtle's or a gargoyle's. He looked incredibly ancient as he stood there, stooped behind the desk, the metal fan whirring behind his head; yet his shoulders still retained a hint of their strength and authority.

I had little time to waste on asking myself why he was here. I was putting up a more-than-human struggle to remain conscious and get to Claudie. I was ploughing across the room to her, and the floor was rocking like the sea, and the ringing noise was shattering my eardrums. Someone must have set off the alarm bells and the shrill peals were reverberating through the shell of the huge building. My head felt as if it was swelling and splitting along the sutures. The blood seemed to be streaming in a continuous gout from my wounded neck.

It dimly occurred to me that Merganser must have come to Kavalla in my honour. Partly he must have come to meet the *Marmoset*—to supervise the landing and transshipment of her lethal and profitable cargo. Also to see to the disposal of

Claudie. But mainly he must have come to the Meidias Building to be on hand when I did my stuff in the Cave of the Cyclops. He had come to lay claim—personally—to his booty. Whatever was in the cave must have been something altogether exceptional to bring the great man from Manhattan or Geddingley Park to this remote corner of Europe . . . And I had disappointed him . . . and was unrepentant . . .

Somehow I had reached Claudie now and pulled her roughly out of the doorway in which she was standing. At any moment the guards outside would burst in and the whole room would explode around us. I knew what to do if only I could stave off this terrible creeping numbness.

I had seen the door of the private executive elevator a few feet to the left of the door of the bathroom. I banged the red button on the wall with my palm and at the same time reached down with my other hand for Claudie's wrist.

Then behind me I heard a scuffling, shuffling sound. To my flagging senses it sounded like the muffled clicking of the claws of a lobster. Again my mind and vision were furred over; again it seemed that it was not Merganser but some sort of monster which was coming around the desk and making for me. In spite of its age I knew it was enormously powerful. Its iron claws would sink deep into my bruised flesh and rip and tear me . . .

My sight seemed to be going; the clangour in my skull was threatening to burst it; the hands with which I pushed Claudie towards the door of the elevator seemed to have no vitality left in them . . . So this was how *El Albaceteño* must have felt . . . the last fight . . . one toss too many . . . worn out . . . sold out . . . clapped out. . . .

Something that felt to my overwrought imagination as cold and heavy as a metal gauntlet fell on my shoulder. I felt the long nails crisping and hooking themselves into the muscle. I no longer knew what I was doing. I more or less fell away from it . . . covered Claudie with my body . . .

It is obvious that Merganser yanked at my shoulder and that at this point I was so defenseless that although he was an old man he managed to pull me away from the elevator. Either he tripped me or I stumbled. I staggered a few steps and went sprawling. My feet hit something and I went full length and lay there dazed, stretched out on my back with the winking, flickering light in my eyes. Beneath me I caught a glimpse of an oil-smudged white overall and realized I was lying across the great soft, inert body of Franciska Brody. I twisted and tried to get up and then my head sagged back.

I saw a misty form looming above me, blocking out the wavering light. Merganser . . . but my crazed and exhausted brain saw only a burning yellow eye, a flopping crest, a talon reaching out with a reptilian ruff . . . The nightmarish images coined by my racing mind—imagination plunging out of control—drained the will out of me. I pawed ineffectually at the deep, soft carpet.

Merganser sank to his knees beside me where I lay across Franciska Brody. I felt her big limbs stir slightly. Then my brain clicked as I realized what he was groping for—the gun the woman dropped when the plastic block knocked her out. I could see Merganser's burning yellow eye in its creased and puffy socket. It was fixed on me with an intense and insane hatred, unwinking and venomous as a reptile's. Think of what I had done to him, what I had robbed him of. The *Marmoset* —its cargo—Gheorgheniu—above all my refusal to procure for him the wealth in the cave. He glared at me with an atrocious, baffled greed. What was I compared with him? A nothing. And I had dared to challenge and defy his whole organization.

The old man meant to kill me. But for once he was going to have to do his own dirty work. Who else was left up here now to do it? I slid my hand sideways across the carpet with a sudden spurt of decision and my fingers knocked against the cold butt of the gun. He reached for it just as I made a second

247

snatch and got hold of it. His nails scraped across my wrist, dug in. He tried to shake and wrestle the gun out of my grasp. I dropped it; his hand fastened on it—lifted it. The barrel came around. I grabbed at it. He was making a groaning, creaking, wheezing sound. I smelled lavender or attar of roses —the pomade on his hair. Now he was going to shoot me. His eye was enormous. Close to mine. Then I ripped the gun out of his hand. His jaw was working and grinding with an insensate, lunatic motion. I strained back and thrust the gun in his face and jerked at the trigger three times.

I didn't hear the noise. At least I don't remember hearing it. That gun may have been small, but at that range its effect was horrifying. It blew three holes in his face. There was a spray of shreds and ribbons. The red ruined head shook out blood over me; and though I can't remember the three explosions I can remember distinctly how surprised I was that his blood wasn't cold. A kind of thin leathery cry rattled out of his chest. I was appalled at the thought that he might topple across me and reached up a hand and jammed it defensively against him. Then suddenly and swiftly he arched upwards and away from me, and there was a thump as his shoulder hit the carpet, and the light was shining full in my eyes again.

All this seemed to take an infinity. In actual fact it must have occupied less than half a minute.

Franciska Brody was regaining consciousness. After a second I managed to sit upright. I felt someone pulling me to my feet. Claudie. From this point on she seemed possessed by one of those mysterious accesses of energy and decision which had visited me, too, several times in the past few days. There is certainly some kind of enhanced physical strength and mental quickness that comes to you in dangerous situations.

It was Claudie who dragged me across that soiled and haunted room towards the elevator. Its door stood open. It was Claudie who maneuvered me into the glaringly illuminated box, padded with emerald-coloured satin, pressed the button to close the door, started the elevator moving downwards.

As the door was hissing across I caught sight of the door of the apartment bursting open and seemed to hear the mingled sounds of shouting and firing. Wood splintered near the roof of the lift . . .

By good luck she had pressed the override switch that would send us straight down without anyone on the other floors being able to intercept us.

It was a high-speed lift. It started dropping like an express from top to bottom of the building. It seemed to go on and on and on.

Claudie was close to me. She held me upright. Weakly I put my arms around her. (If only someone would shut off those alarm bells!) She looked up at me. I held her against me. I smelled the familiar faint milky scent of her body. I cupped my hands around her cheekbones and moved my thumbs with vague tenderness across the pale forehead with its faint lines.

But the cindery fog was settling around me. I struggled against it. The elevator hummed downwards . . . faster. I must make a supreme effort. Soon we would reach the basement, a few steps ahead of the guards in the vestibule . . . we must cross the kitchens and the storeroom and find a way out to the compound at the rear . . . dodge the dog handler and his murderous companion . . . get over the wall . . . find the jeep . . . way to the British Consulate . . . speak no Greek . . . leave Kavalla . . . Thessalonika . . .

Claudie murmured my name and stretched upwards in my arms and put her cool lips against my fevered mouth.

Why were we falling so fast? Why were her face and body melting away? Lights dissolving? . . .

The elevator cable seemed to have snapped. We were plummeting downwards . . . hurtling towards the bottom of the shaft . . .

Something had turned over in my brain, and there, enclosed in Merganser's luxurious satin-upholstered elevator, I was experiencing a moment of hallucination. Illusion and reality fused and ran together. Mind had slithered over the frontier of actuality into the realm of the dream . . .

. . . The bells were ringing not here in the Meidias Building but in the Prado . . . Closing time in the great gallery . . . Bells ringing in the cool high corridors to warn the visitors it was time to leave . . . A black-coated attendant with a peaked cap and the face of José-Luis was smiling down at me with a Spaniard's good-humoured courtesy and shaking me by the shoulder to wake me up . . . I had been sitting there dozing on the bench in front of Velázquez's picture . . .

. . . So the burning city of Kavalla was the burning city of Breda . . . A bank of smoke and flame . . . plumes . . . lances . . . a blood-stained jacket . . . And a key on a long silken ribbon with a woven tassel handed ceremoniously from one man to another . . . A fine old key of elaborate workmanship . . . A key of special design . . .

A nightmare . . . A recurring nightmare . . . In a minute I would rouse myself and rise and the bells would stop and I would walk out of the side entrance of the Prado . . . pay my respects to the statue of Goya . . . stroll beneath the acacias to the Plaza de Cibeles . . . order a cold drink . . . a horchata *. . . a* Cruz Blanca *. . . a* zumo de limón *. . .*

. . . Not dining with Professor Obregón till nine-thirty . . . Plenty of time to saunter home along the Calle de Serrano . . . When I reach my apartment building, must try to be sensible . . . Respectable art historian . . . Barracks of the Guardia Civil on the corner . . .

. . . And Ridgeling will be there . . . talking about Conderton Building . . . bribing me to go to Puteaux . . . Ven-

ice . . . Marmoset *. . . the cave . . .* Meidias Building
*. . . the room above us at the top of the tower . . . this de-
scending elevator I was now in . . .*
   *. . . On and on and on . . . forever . . . Locked in a
dream . . . Living it over and over again . . . Moving perhaps a stage or two further each time I relive it . . .*

There was a whir as the door of the elevator opened and
Claudie ran out holding my hand.

A current of cold air hit me in the face. Not really cold air
—but colder than the air in the penthouse, colder than the
air in the elevator. Enough to revive me.

I shook myself awake, fighting to dispel the fume of dream
and fantasy. Muzzy, I forced myself to stand still for a moment and take stock.

The elevator had come to rest at the vestibule or half-
staircase where the tall glass entrance doors of the principal
entrance were situated. I recognized it. It seemed a thousand
years instead of twenty minutes, but I recognized it.

Rapidly I steered Claudie down the stairs towards where I
knew the door of the basement was. She moved confidently.
Probably Merganser had told Franciska Brody to stop ad-
ministering drugs to her during the immediate period before
she was reintroduced to Zidarov. Merganser would want the
consignment to arrive in prime condition. I noticed that when
she ran down the stairs at my side her movements were fluent,
graceful. She had buttoned the front of the white coat on our
journey down in the elevator—and this time the buttons were
properly fastened.

I could hear the sounds of commotion filtering down from
the upper floors. I opened the door of the basement. There
was very little time. Another minute or two and the guards
would come riding down in the main elevator, hunting for
us. I prayed they would jump to the conclusion we had bolted
out through the open glass doors across the square.

I had the presence of mind not to slam the metal door of the basement behind us. I shut it gently. Claudie went on ahead of me down the steps. The same dim red control light threw a hollow glow over the storerooms and the kitchens beyond.

It took me less than five seconds to discover that there was no lock or bar on the inside of the door. Bad. I descended the steps two at a time and took Claudie by the wrist and led her through the kitchens in the direction of the window that gave onto the compound at the rear. She looked wonderingly at the ranks of electric cookers, the rows of stainless-steel sinks and white-topped tables all gleaming pinkly in the roseate light.

We stopped at the window. Quickly I indicated how she was to wriggle her body through the gap where the pane had been. She smiled briefly and gave me a nod to show she understood.

I murmured, "Wait for me outside. Keep in the shadows. Close to the wall."

Another nod. Immediately she put her shoulder into the frame in the way I had demonstrated to her and started to ease her body through. There was a slight tearing sound as one of the slivers of glass that had excoriated my own body ripped the stiff linen of the white coat. She was unpracticed, and went at the thing awkwardly but with plenty of determination. I had to risk the dog handler coming back through the compound and finding her. That slavering beast. I put the thought out of my mind. . . .

My main concern was with the guards inside the building. I ran back through the kitchens into the storeroom and looked around for something—anything—that would block the unlocked door for a few precious moments. A wild idea came to me to try and manhandle a deepfreeze or refrigerator up the stairs. Stupid. Then I went over to a pile of crates made of glistening new wood and heaved at one of them. Equally stupid. It refused to budge.

Then I remembered the sounds of rustling and chirping I heard when I crossed the storeroom on my way in. The birds. Their boxes were stacked up in the center of the room. There were twelve or fourteen of them in all, and they were cumbersome to shift. But at least they were half the size and a quarter the weight of the crates.

Rapidly I started to drag them one at a time over to the steps. In this way I managed to pile five of them one on top of the other against the inner side of the door. A flimsy enough barrier—but the guards would get a shock when they wrenched open the door and dashed in. With any luck there would be confusion and a few broken legs as they tripped over each other down the stairs in the semi-darkness. I strewed more boxes on the steps and at the foot of the staircase.

A shrill twittering rose from the boxes as I moved them. The sides were covered with coarse sacking or canvas, and I could hear feeble frenzied bumps as the small feathered bodies hurled themselves against the inside of their prison.

As I was dumping one last box at the bottom of the stairs the sacking tore partly away. It showed me that the inside of the box was made of wire mesh. The mesh didn't seem unduly strong. It didn't need to be.

I had an idea. Lying on one of the crates of new wood I had noticed a long, smooth bar of metal. One end of it was split or forked. It was a tool for prizing open the nailed-down lids of crates and boxes.

I snatched it up and went back to the bird boxes and started to slash the sacking off one side of each of them and rip away the top fastenings of the mesh. I worked hurriedly—but my efforts, if sketchy, were effective. Immediately swarms of small birds began coiling out of the punctured mesh like streams of smoke. In the enclosed space of the basement their thin shrieking and cachinnation seemed deafening. Several of them struck me in the face with a surprising force. It was uncanny, that flock of frightened, liberated little creatures dipping and swooping around me in the darkness.

I had the metal bar in my hand as I returned to the window. Claudie had gone. As I put my right arm through the frame a skein of birds was already pouring out into the compound. They collided with my face and neck as I heaved and squirmed, buffetting my bare skin.

I climbed out more easily than I had climbed in. My limbs went through the sequence of movements without hesitation. Every second I expected to hear the guards come crashing through the door and into the storeroom behind me. As I dropped headfirst out of the window frame, threshing to free my legs, my hands on the ground, I saw Claudie's white-clad body crouched down against the wall beside the row of up-ended ash cans.

I had to spend a few valuable seconds getting my breath back. Then I scrambled up, caught hold of Claudie and propelled her ahead of me across the compound. The sky above the city still oscillated with the angry blaze from the docks. The underside of the low-lying pall of smoke was lit by a sullen glow.

I pointed at the wall. Claudie nodded. I put down the steel crowbar, gripped her tightly around the waist and hoisted her up. She pushed hard, scrabbling with her foot for my shoulder, then reached the top of the wall and abruptly disappeared. And at that moment the long-expected pandemonium broke out inside the basement. I picked up the metal bar, felt for a foothold on one of the rough blocks of the wall, found it, hauled myself up after Claudie.

The crowbar was an encumbrance; but just as I was scrambling to gain a purchase on the top of the wall the guard dog suddenly came bounding around the corner of the compound and headed straight for me. There was no sign of its handler. Silently, with no more than an enraged rasp in its throat, it leaped up against the wall over and over again, snapping like a wolf at my heels. Its teeth brushed my ankle.

Leaning down, I waited for the next leap. Then I hit that damned brute a terrific crack with the steel bar at the top of the snout, just below the eyes. It slumped in a heap into the shadow at the base of the wall.

Claudie was below me, once more hugging the stones. I was just about to jump down when some instinct made me glance back across the compound at the window. I heard a soft dry flutter. On the sill I could just make out a shimmering oval shape the colour of pale sulphur.

It was my big golden bird from the *Marmoset*. It perched there on the sill, motionless, not uttering a sound, while the myriad smaller birds fluttered out on either side of it. Unhurriedly it looked around. Then a light clicked on in the basement behind it, making its plumage glitter with a marvellous brilliance. Still unhurried, it pecked at its breast, then gathered itself together and with one straight slow beat of its strong wings launched itself into the troubled sky and flew away into the darkness.

Claudie's white face was staring up anxiously at me. I rolled off the wall and landed beside her.

Together we ran across the street at the rear of the Meidias Building and made our way by a circumspect route to the place where I had parked the jeep.

We were not pursued or molested as we drove out of Kavalla. Merganser's men must finally have lost heart and given up, now that their leader was dead, the city razed, their organization destroyed.

When dawn came two hours later we were well on our way towards the mountains. In the heat of the day we stopped and slept for several hours in the shade of the jeep; then we filled the tank with the spare cans of fuel and turned west for

Lake Arethusa and Thessalonika. We reached Thessalonika after dark and drove straight to the Consulate.

Three weeks later I was back in the Calle Doctor Pedrell. The check had arrived from my publishers; the concierge told me it was delivered twenty minutes after I left in Ridgeling's Cadillac for Paris.

Claudie likes the apartment. She also accompanies me on the three or four afternoons a week when I work in the Prado, though at the moment she is mostly taken up with long, leisurely (and costly) shopping expeditions in the Calle de Serrano and the Gran Via.

I am engaged on the last few pages of *Diego Velázquez and His Circle*. When it is finished we may decide to take a trip to England.

the game of troy

To

JOHN O. WEST

I

YOU know, I thought we'd covered our tracks pretty well, Astrid and me. I thought we'd avoided careless mistakes.

It sounds sordid when I talk about it in this way. It sounds like any other furtive little adultery. It wasn't like that at all. If we were secretive about it, it was because she was determined to spare Gabriel pain. It's true she was scared of him. He was unpredictable. They still have a code about that kind of thing down here in Texas. But there was more to their relationship than that. It wasn't an ordinary relationship, because Gabriel wasn't an ordinary man. But if she didn't love him, she had a very real affection for him. They'd been married nearly ten years and he'd never treated her in any way that could be described as mean or unpleasant. The legend said he was a great kidder, a great practical joker—which was why it was surprising to find him married to a woman like that.

Until I came along she'd been completely faithful to him. This was certainly the first love affair she'd ever had. Her gentleness and shyness—not feminine qualities usually encountered in the high-spirited state of Texas—were what attracted me to her in the first place. She was standing on the fringe of a noisy party. I remember the nervous little gesture with which the tall, fair girl tossed the strand of white-blond hair out of her eyes as I went across to speak to her. I remember her soft breathless laugh when I told her I was a stranger to Texas, too. I said we looked like Babes in the Wood. She laughed because, as she told me with a little stammer, she *was* a Texan—though not, I could see, the usual type of female Texan—strong, confident, extrovert. I was being a bit patronizing, taking pity on her like that. I wondered why her husband wasn't at the party. I didn't know then that he never attended parties, but spent all his free time puttering about his huge place at El Pardo. In any case he was thirteen or fourteen years older than she was, and didn't have much time or energy left over from his responsibilities as head of Sarrazin Resources. I didn't invite her out to dinner after the party. I was sure she'd refuse, and as I was eager to see her again, I wanted to avoid a false step.

I ought to say right away that I'm not any kind of Don Juan or professional seducer. In fact, I'm a little like Gabriel, in that the assurance of my conversation and bearing lead people to assume that I'm equally assured underneath. That's not so. But at least my air of assurance, like his, is based on the fact that in my own particular field I do happen to know exactly what I'm talking about. If that sounds bumptious, I assure you it's true. Not many modern architects have mastered their craft as thoroughly as I have. In New York, Pittsburgh, Chicago, St. Louis, New Orleans, Toronto, Anchorage, San Francisco, Houston, Dallas, San Antonio, El Paso—even Rio, Buenos Aires, Hobart, Wellington—you can see the buildings that I've designed which prove it.

On the other hand, most of my energies up to that first evening had been devoted to my profession. There hadn't

2

been much time to spare for anything else. My personal life had been pretty spartan. I'd built myself two fine houses. I liked to buy fast and expensive European cars and drive them in the way they were meant to be driven. But aside from a few college friends, I hadn't developed any profound relationships. My relationships with women were superficial. I kept them that way. I was always up to my ears in commissions, conferences, schedules, always working early and late. I fought shy of entanglements that might encroach on my professional activities. I was very jealous of my time. I doled it out grudgingly. As an Easterner, largely employed during the past three years in Houston, Dallas, and San Antonio, I'd recently become even more of a slave to my office and drawing board. Socially, I'd always been rather a fish out of water. So I turned the situation to my advantage and retreated further into my shell.

This explained why, when I finally encountered Astrid at Patti Danziger's party, I went so wild. Wild, that is, for a normally highly controlled man. Actually, I'd almost given up going to parties. Of course, they're a good way of making contact with would-be clients. But I had too many clients already. In actual fact I was reluctant to take on any new assignments. This was an enviable position for a thirty-three-year-old architect—but thanks largely to Texas, I *was* a very enviable young architect. Naturally, there was a price to pay. I worked sixteen hours a day and wound up by presenting myself with a small but definite drinking problem. As a matter of fact, I felt as guilty about not working this evening as I felt about the number of martinis I was drinking. I'd only come along to Mrs. Danziger's party because I'd just completed for her the house we were standing in—though "oriental palace" might be a better description. And after all, she *was* Mrs. Ralph Dan-

3

ziger. I wasn't so busy I was keen to indulge in the social and professional suicide that turning down her invitation would entail.

I won't say it was a case of love at first sight. Let's just say that there was an overwhelming immediate attraction. I'm not an authority on these things, but some people seem to know right away that someone they're introduced to is destined to have a special meaning for them. That's what Astrid and I felt, there in that sumptuous Arabian Nights drawing-room that I'd designed. Anyone looking at us would have thought he was looking at two tongue-tied people without much to say to one another. We stood there shuffling our feet and twirling our martini glasses. In reality we'd exchanged what a French writer called *le regard rouge*, the secret glance of a man and a woman who know they desire each other.

Three days later she came along with Donna Vorbeck to my office in the Fargeau Building in downtown Houston. Donna wanted to consult me about some additional landscaping she wanted at the house I'd built for her and her husband (the subject of a special number of the *Architectural Journal* last Easter). Astrid, it turned out, was Donna's cousin. As a rule I'd have thrown the job to Ed Edmondson, the expert in Westport who usually does my landscaping for me. Besides, Donna was tiresome—silly and talkative. She ran an art gallery in Dallas specializing in far-out sculpture. She only ran it as a sideline, as her husband was a vice president of Sarrazin Resources. She scarcely needed the income. Still, though I didn't like her, this time I took the job myself. I intended to see as much as I could of her beautiful and timid cousin.

From there on, it was easy. We met three or four times when I went to Donna's to make notes and measurements.

4

Soon I knew her well enough to inquire casually whether she'd be going to the first night of a play at the Alley Theatre, a concert by the Houston Symphony, or the opening of an art exhibit. Five times out of six, she'd find a way of turning up, and we'd be able to have a drink and exchange a few words. Gabriel never went to these cultural affairs.

For two people as predisposed toward each other as we were it wasn't absolutely necessary for us to have a great deal in common. But we did. She'd majored in art and history at Austin, then spent a year in Paris and eighteen months in Switzerland. It was obvious that Gabriel, considerate though he was in other respects, had starved her mentally by denying her any participation in his own work and interests. Perhaps it didn't occur to him that she might get bored, or might find the operations of his engineering and aircraft industries interesting. Certainly she was quickly absorbed by the theory and practice of architecture. I gave her architectural books and magazines to take home to El Pardo. There was also something else. We laughed a lot. Her sense of humor took some time to emerge. It didn't surface all at once. But when I finally reached it, I found it abundant and delightful.

If he neglected her to some extent, Gabriel wasn't stuffy or Victorian. He didn't act as if he believed that a woman's place was in the home. She came and went as she liked, without giving more than the token explanations customary in apparently happy marriages. Altogether, from the little she told me, I was quite unable to credit the stories I'd heard about his being devious and vindictive. I put them down to gossip. I didn't even take it seriously when Axel Johnson, an architect whom I respect, happened to mention that Gabriel had effectively driven him clean out of

5

Texas when Axel had sent in a bill for some work on a Sarrazin Resources plant with what Gabriel thought was impertinent haste. He said Gabriel pursued him with extraordinary violence. I attributed all this to Axel's well-known excitability and tendency to exaggerate.

If we'd been reasonably discreet, we could have had the run of the fabled kingdom of East Texas for as long as we wished. If, that is, we'd wanted to remain just good friends. But we didn't. It rapidly became clear that we wanted to progress far beyond that tepid condition. Her elder sister, Beatrice, was married to a California real-estate man and had a home on the Pacific coast a few miles beyond Oxnard, north of Ventura. One of the two houses to which I liked to return between bouts of activity was in Beverly Hills. I'd torn down a mock-Mexican horror on Whittier Drive to create room for it. It was private and secluded. The journey from Oxnard through Malibu and along Sunset Boulevard to Whittier Drive takes a woman driver forty-one minutes. We first fell into bed together on September 13th. We had met at the redoubtable Mrs. D's party on June 28th.

The appetite grows by what it feeds on. These *cinq-à-sept* meetings were insufficient. Twice, therefore, she went on "skiing vacations" to Oregon—only the closest she came to Oregon was Whittier Drive. Her sister had a Texan sense of morality, so we thought it kinder not to tell her what was going on. Astrid used to run her red Porsche (like me, she had a taste for European cars) into the garage. Her skis were never unstrapped from the roof-rack. Once we spent a whole week together and never left the house. It was an obsession, a *folie à deux*. Parting from her was a small death. When you remember that she was a Texan, and had been brought up as strictly as her sister, you'll understand that to behave in the way she did she must have been swept right away from her emotional moorings. So was I.

As I said, I was sure we'd covered our tracks. Los Angeles is an enormous and anonymous city. Dallas was fourteen hundred miles away. She was in California on a routine family visit. Every other night she called Gabriel as if she was calling from Oxnard. There was absolutely no reason for him to suspect that she was having an affair with another man. True, a curious thing happened during her second stay with me. I came downstairs late one afternoon to put through a call to my New York office and found that a window was unlatched and a thief had sneaked in. A wooden kachina doll had been knocked to the carpet and trodden on. A portable television set on a side table was missing. Nothing else. I suspected the Spanish-American gardener. He had previously stolen a couple of power tools from the outside workshop. I decided to say nothing about it because it was all so trivial, and forgot about it.

Astrid was always a different woman once I got her away from Texas. She didn't lose that delightful shyness that first attracted me, and which struck some deep chord in my own nature, but she was altogether more relaxed and alive. She reveled in the intimacy and domesticity of our long days alone together and enjoyed escaping from the role of wife and hostess to a millionaire and businesss tycoon. She even involved me, the least domestic of men, in her homemaking games. I remember I spent almost the whole of one afternoon, after we had eventually managed to get out of bed, obediently rearranging furniture as she stood in the middle of the floor with her blond head cocked

7

on one side and issued gentle but decisive commands. I actually thought this coolie labor was great fun. She also turned out to be a splendid cook: her eighteen months in Switzerland had been put to good use. Obviously, in spite of recurrent feelings of guilt and apprehension (sometimes she woke trembling with fear in the middle of the night), she was happier than she had been for a long time, years perhaps. During the day her terrors left her. Eventually she was even willing to risk leaving the house and taking a drive. At first we stayed in the car and would park on a cliff or headland, sitting hand in hand and watching the sun go down into the Pacific. Occasionally we would stop long enough to order a cup of coffee and a sandwich at a drive-in. At last we grew more adventurous and twice had dinner at a fish restaurant on the beach at Malibu. And finally we took to walking for hours after dark along the shore at Ventura, where two or three times, when the warm night and the waves and the damp sand under our feet had fanned our feelings for each other, we found a place among the rocks and lay down to make love. Which didn't prevent us from going back and making love all over again an hour later. She gave herself up to the business of lovemaking without reserve, with an overwhelming sense of hunger and abandon. It was as if she was discovering an immense and unexploited capacity for pleasure in her slender soft pale body and could arouse a similarly unexploited capacity in mine.

My house in New York was in the upper seventies, near the Park. From the outside it was a dignified old brownstone, but I'd gutted and remodeled the entire interior on unorthodox lines. Astrid was in the habit of flying to New York every October or November to visit the

8

stores. Although Nieman-Marcus has everything, even Big D isn't New York, and when we were still in Los Angeles we'd made detailed plans to meet back East two months later. She wasn't happy about it, but she was in love with me. Again and again I'd urged her to marry me. In the space of a few weeks she had soothed and satisfied me in a way I never suspected or believed was possible. She had even managed to make some headway with the drinking problem I mentioned. I was growing dependent on her, on being with her. But she couldn't make up her mind to leave Gabriel. She shrank from hurting him. She also seemed to have some kind of a frightening picture in her mind of the moment when she'd have to explain things to him.

We saw each other five or six times in the interval, always in the company of other people. We exchanged the purest banalities and didn't betray our feelings by as much as a glance across a dinner-table. She hated all this deception, and I'd see her mouth quiver as she raised her glass, carefully avoiding my eyes. I'd see her fingers tap the cloth, frail and pale beneath the Colombian emeralds or South-West African diamonds Gabriel constantly gave her. Not to be outdone, I'd gone to Van Cleef and Arpels and bought her a magnificent sapphire, the color of the first dress I'd seen her in. I gave it to her at La Guardia just before she boarded her plane. She could always explain it away—if Gabriel even noticed it—by saying she'd happened to see it and couldn't resist it.

We were scrupulously careful during that extraordinary week, when the trees in the park were turning a tender gold. We tried to be more discreet than we had been in California. We kept the drapes across the windows and came and left by the rear entrance. We stayed in as much as possible during the daytime. When we went out at night we frequented out-of-the-way bars and restaurants. At first, as in Los Angeles, she was restrained and on edge, as if she couldn't shake off the effects of whatever it was that worried her at home. But after a few hours she relaxed. As in California, she made love with a marvelous frenzy that at first disconcerted me in such a quiet woman. I knew there must be a reason for it, but at the time I simply accepted it with pleasure.

I suppose we did behave now and again like the pair of happy children we were. Some of the expeditions we finally couldn't resist making were probably injudicious, at that. The one to the Met, to hear *Tosca,* or the one to the Museum of Modern Art. My mood was so exalted I was taken completely by surprise when she told me she had a feeling we were being followed. She first said it at the Frick Collection, only a ten-minute walk from my house and where we went one morning. She said it again at Marta's, down in the Village, where I'd reserved a table that same evening under another name. Each time I only laughed and put an arm around her. But she couldn't get rid of the impulse to look over her shoulder, so afterwards we stayed indoors and rustled up our meals ourselves.

2

IT was during the long wet spell in March that I got the call from Gabriel Sarrazin. It came through about three-thirty in the afternoon. The rain was pelting down. It was so dark the lights in the office were on. I was standing at the window watching the cars plowing through the deluge created by the clogged gutters in South Main Street. There was no point in returning to my rented house in River Oaks while the downpour kept up. I'd work late. I'd send down to the coffeeshop for coffee and sandwiches. I'd sleep on the couch in the inner office.

Then my secretary came on the line.

"A call for you, sir. From Dallas."

She was flustered. She wouldn't have put it through unless it was important. I'd told her not to disturb me.

The name of Dallas had an emotive effect on me because of Astrid. But she'd never called me at the office. I expected Evie to say that the call was from one of the hundred people I worked with there—contractors, surveyors, suppliers, and so on. Her next words shook me.

"Mr. Gabriel Sarrazin, sir."

For a second I thought she said *"Mrs.* Gabriel Sarrazin."

I'd never even met Sarrazin, let alone talk to him. As I picked up the phone, it crossed my mind that Evie might be flustered because she knew (did the whole office know?) about Astrid and me. Then I realized she was excited because the great and legendary Gabriel Sarrazin was on the line in person.

I held the phone a little more tightly.

"Mr. Sarrazin? What can I do for you?"

I heard him say something about just getting back from a meeting in Amarillo. Then he added:

"I think it's about time we had a talk."

"Oh? What about?"

I'm not sure there wasn't a trace of uncertainty in my tone. This was the voice of the man whose wife I'd been sleeping with. It sounded vaguely familiar. After a moment, with a shock, I realized that it reminded me of Astrid's—light, charming, polite. The Texas accent was slightly more marked, and there was a definite hint of a drawl. Of course, he didn't indulge in *Howdys* and *You-alls* and that sort of thing. Nevertheless, the basic trait of the Texan was still there, and I'd have been wiser to have taken more heed of it.

He greeted me by name and said that I'd been recommended to him by mutual friends. He complimented me on my work. Evidently he'd been checking up on my performance as an architect, for he went on to say how impressed he'd been by five or six projects of mine in and around Dallas, Houston, and San Antonio. It was obvious that he'd actually taken the trouble to go and view them.

I quickly realized I wasn't going to be required to discuss Astrid. The agreeable flow of his words was a clear indication that the poor chap hadn't even remotely suspected what was happening. He was asking:

"How'd you like to take on a job for me?"

"A job?"

A job for Sarrazin could signify a factory, a major installation, a big block of offices. Could I help it if my mouth started to water?

"Here at El Pardo?" he said.

There was no point in pretending I hadn't heard about the wonders of El Pardo. The house and the surrounding ranch occupied about a third of Otero County. I tried to sound like an informed and intelligent stranger.

"Oh yes? At El Pardo?"

"A very big job. Very. In fact, unique. It'll appeal to you enormously. It's a very great challenge and a very great opportunity."

"Oh? Exactly what sort of job is it?"

"Why not come down to El Pardo so we can talk about it?"

"To El Pardo?"

"Why not stay a few days? You'd like it. It's a showpiece. A fun place. I love getting people down here and showing them the sights. Especially someone like you, who'll appreciate it. Mrs. Sarrazin and I would be delighted to entertain such a distinguished guest."

I'd been thinking.

"Mr. Sarrazin, I appreciate your calling me this way. But I'm afraid at the moment I'm pretty overloaded. I hate to turn down what sounds like a very fascinating job, but at present I'm absolutely swamped."

"Believe me, I'm not in the least surprised. A man of your ability and reputation is bound to be in terrific demand. I ought to have got in touch with you sooner. A lot sooner. But won't you at least think it over for a while?"

"Think it over?"

13

"Please?"

"Well—"

"People say a lot of hard things about me, but I've never heard them say I'm not a generous employer. I assure you you'll find the job rewarding financially as well as professionally."

I hesitated.

"What—what did you say about it being—unique?"

He laughed. "Never mind! Just you come on down here and see! What about it? Could you come tomorrow?"

"Tomorrow?"

"Yes."

"I'm afraid—"

"Then what about next weekend?"

"I can't possibly get away from Houston before—"

"I can make it very simple. I'll send a plane."

"Mr. Sarrazin—"

I'd made up my mind to turn him down as soon as the job was mentioned. But he sounded so eager and friendly I was finding it hard to refuse him. I was still under the illusion that Astrid and I had handled everything prudently.

His light, pleasant voice came pouring on through the phone.

"Now, don't you go turning me down. Give me a chance to explain this thing. After all, it could put a hundred or a hundred and twenty thousand dollars in your pocket."

He heard me catch my breath.

"Yes," he said, "it's that big. Or should I say—that *wild?*"

"Wild?"

He'd certainly gripped my imagination.

14

"Look," he urged. "Why not let the idea simmer for a while? I'm sure if you brood about it you'll find a way of rearranging your plans." Again I heard the ingratiating little laugh. "If not, damn it, throw something out! Why don't I give you a call in the morning? At ten-thirty, say?"

It was my turn to laugh. His charm was getting through to me. I'd already half-forgotten he was Astrid's husband.

"That's just about eighteen hours," I protested. "You obviously like people to make up their minds in a hurry?"

"Certainly!"

"Still, whether you call me tomorrow or a week from tomorrow, the answer's bound to be the same. For one thing, I'm due to start work on a big new house that some people called Cunningham—"

"Cunningham? Jack and Margie Cunningham?"

"That's right."

"Well, I don't see Jack and Margie too often, but they happen to be very old friends of mine. Jack's closely tied up with one of my companies, as a matter of fact. I think I can manage to persuade him to stay in his old home for a while, while you're engaged on this little enterprise for me."

"Mr. Sarrazin, perhaps I didn't make it quite clear—"

"Why don't you call me Gabriel? Now, you go and sleep on it, there's a good chap. Don't rush into a refusal. That's always a mistake. I'll call you at ten-thirty tomorrow. All right?"

He hung up. I could see where he got his reputation as a brisk negotiator.

I was standing with the phone in my hand when Evie burst into the room without knocking. She was well over forty, but she was practically running. Her big bosom was heaving with excitement. Her heavily made-up eyes were brimming with reproach.

"Oh, sir! Mr. Gabriel Sarrazin! You can't turn him down! You simply can't!"

We had some wealthy and prestigious clients here in Texas, but none, it seemed, with the money and glamor of Gabriel Sarrazin.

I smiled into the gummy depths of Evie's mascara.

"I'm flattered, Evie. But I don't think we'll be taking up Mr. Sarrazin's kind offer."

The big blue eyelids fluttered with dismay. Evie, a native-born Bostonian whom I'd brought with me to Texas, was a tremendous snob. Perhaps she'd already been cherishing visions of weekends at El Pardo?

"Oh, sir!"

"If you'll fetch your notebook," I said firmly, "there are several letters I'd like to dictate . . ."

3

THREE days later I was on the road to Dallas.

It was still raining hard. I'd declined Gabriel's repeated offers to ferry me down there in one of his planes
and was driving the Maserati I'd imported from Modena
six weeks before. This was partly because I didn't want to
be endebted to him and partly because I always found it
soothing to get off by myself in a fast car and drive along
those magnificent Texas highways through that marvelous
Texas landscape. I did a lot of my thinking and planning
on those trips.

So there I was between Houston and Dallas with the
spray pluming up beneath my tires. The broad green expanse of the Texas ranches went rolling by. I was warm,
I was relaxed—and I was exasperated. Why had I given
in? Why was I on my way to El Pardo? If it was embarrassing to talk to Gabriel on the phone, wouldn't it be a
hundred times more embarrassing to talk to him face to
face?

The reasons for my decision were complicated. There
was no doubt that Gabriel had succeeded in generating an
interest in his mysterious proposal. On the other hand,
there was my instinct to stay clear of him and his ranch.

By going there I might accidentally stir up trouble for Astrid. I kept remembering that warm soft body at Whittier Drive and in Seventy-Eighth Street, pressed against mine, suddenly coming alive with a small jar of terror in the early hours of the morning. I remembered the sleepy hiss of fear, the film of moisture breaking out on the satin skin. I remembered the soft jerk and little moan. I didn't know then why she felt fear, or what she needed to be afraid of. I thought she was just a naturally shy and nervous woman. But her reaction, justified or not, was bound to rouse strongly protective feelings in me, deeply in love with her as I was. There had been nothing in my phone conversation with Gabriel to suggest he was some sort of ogre or to make me anxious on her behalf. Quite the contrary: he sounded eminently sane and civilized. All the same, something prompted me to get down to El Pardo to reassure her, to satisfy myself that she was safe and well. I couldn't have told you what it was. On the other hand, I was a little troubled about calling on Gabriel for business reasons because I didn't want her to think that I'd been cultivating her for an ulterior motive—because I wanted a commission from Sarrazin Resources and could use her to get an introduction to Gabriel. However, since the initiative had actually come from Gabriel, I didn't feel too badly about it. In any case, she knew me too well by now to think I'd stoop to anything like that.

It wasn't the immediate prospect of a succulent commission that had snared me and put me on the road to Dallas, although admittedly an operation like mine requires constant injections of cash. It wasn't greed for money: it was greed for reputation, greed to excel. Texas had been good to me in this respect. When I first flew down there four years ago to carry out what looked like a quick but lucrative little job, I had the lofty attitude to Texas of the typical New Yorker. My friends made the usual snooty remarks when I told them I'd accepted a small official undertaking in the state capital. I'd never been to Texas in my life. At first I couldn't adjust to those exuberant and outward-going people. Moreover, in spite of the large-scale constructions to my credit, I was disturbed by the swaggering and outrageous demands that Texans made on their architects. I began by being very condescending about them. I sent witty and superior messages back home to the suave citizens of Manhattan.

The truth is, I was too Eastern, too buttoned up. Texas shook me to the depths of my competent and complacent soul. The first big assignment I accepted there was to build a house for Felix Stump near Corsicana. Like most Texas oilmen, he had a mania for big-game hunting. On one of his trips he'd visited Nepal and Bhutan and been struck by the rulers' palaces. So he instructed me to build his house (it cost nearly a quarter of a million dollars) in Nepalese style. To begin with, I treated the whole thing as a joke. Then I became engrossed. Finally I had to admit that I'd never had so much sheer fun with anything I'd built in my whole life.

My second job was similar. Pete Uys had also hunted in India. He'd been impressed by the imperial splendors of Sir Edwin Lutyens' New Delhi. At enormous expense I erected at Ozona a florid purple pile that would have looked more in place on the burned plains of Bengal than in the soft pastures of Texas. It was a feat of pure bravura, a crazy gloss on the work of the great Englishman. But I had to admit I'd enjoyed it enormously.

By the time Richeson Smith and Mrs. Bonnie Huddleston came along, I was more or less broken in. For the former, who'd recently married a girl thirty years younger than he was from one of the old Mexican dynasties of Laredo, I built a miniature version of the Alhambra. For Bonnie, who was mad about mirrors, I built a mansion that was partly a Persian seraglio and partly the palace of Versailles. As for Patti Danziger, I had no difficulty in meeting her request for a home that would embody water, water, and more water. Havelock Ellis, Simone de Beauvoir, Pierre de Mandiargues, and other students of Undinism could have devoted an entire chapter to Patti Danziger's fountains and waterfalls, some of them soaring forty feet high and lit by sealed-in spotlights that changed color. The principal feature was an indoor pool in the main bedroom, large enough for the Ladies of the Lake to have ferried King Arthur away to Avalon.

Texas liberated me. It freed in me some buried spring of extravagance. In turn, it reacted on my buildings elsewhere and made them more striking and intriguing than they would have been otherwise. After four years in that enchanted land, crackling with energy, where there is a grand sparkle in the air, I was ready for anything. No architectural extravagance of any kind was too fantastic to envisage—not to someone who'd reproduced New Delhi, Versailles, Granada, Katmandu, and Shangri-la. So when the summons came from Sarrazin, the king of them all, I was already prepared for it, unconsciously lusting for it. What monstrosity or fantastic novelty might he ask me to dream up for him?

Needless to say, there was more to my change of intention than just the spur to my professional curiosity. There was a complex of personal reasons. I tried to isolate and examine them as the well-bred growl of the engine carried me through the deluge at what my Italian odometer told me was between a hundred and seventy and a hundred and eighty kilometers a minute. For one thing, Astrid and I hadn't been alone together since I'd put her on the plane at La Guardia in late October. Three months and nine days ago. We'd met twice, in company, on neutral ground, and exchanged nothing more than a few polite inanities. I was starving for her. It hadn't been so bad up to the New Year, when I was still basking in the memories of Los Angeles and New York. There had to be a period of separation and recuperation. Like her, I was drained, exhausted, and bruised. But then, in January, my mood began to change and sharpen. My body started to shiver with hunger. I thought of her so incessantly, wanted her so badly, and was working so hard that I began to sleep badly. That's when I started taking those phenobarbitone pills. I couldn't resist this chance Gabriel had suddenly given me of being close to her.

The irony of poor Gabriel's situation wasn't lost on me. Inviting me right into his house! A man who wasn't just engaged in making love to his wife, but was intent on taking her away and marrying her. Actually, I was troubled about her. When I saw her at Harry MacMaster's place just before Christmas and at Wayne Lewkowski's just after it, I though she seemed listless and unresponsive. I tried to seize a moment when we were alone to take hold of her hand. I tried to create opportunities to get her on her own for a few minutes so that I could talk to her. I wanted to find out what was wrong and how I could help. It was idiotic to behave as rashly as that and risk embarrassing her, and I can't blame her for avoiding me. Nevertheless, I was disturbed by her behavior, and all my protective instincts were well and truly roused. Also her evasiveness only made me desire her more. As I drove I kept seeing her strained, pale face in front of me and remembered that fair hair and slender body fleeing away from me into the darkness of a terrace or the shadows at the end of a corridor. It wasn't that she'd fallen out of love with me—I was sure of that. But why, oh why, wouldn't she marry me, when she knew by now that we so rightly and inevitably belonged together?

Did I nurse some idea that by going to El Pardo I might persuade her to run away with me then and there? Was I heading, perhaps unconsciously, for some Texas-type showdown with Sarrazin? Maybe my cool Eastern temperament had been more infected by Southern romanticism than I realized. And if a showdown was in the cards, wouldn't I have been wise to bring someone along to back me up? For a moment I wished the rugged frame of Wendell Barratt, my technical assistant, who'd been nominated for the Heisman Trophy as a tight end, was wedged in the passenger seat beside me. And for a fleeting second it even crossed my mind that perhaps I ought to have brought something to protect myself with—a thought that had never previously occurred to me in the whole of my adult life. I pushed it aside as melodramatic and puerile.

What was Gabriel like? The closer the wet wheels took me to El Pardo, the more curious I became. He didn't like being photographed for the newspapers, that much everyone knew. Not that you can tell much about a man from a photograph, anyway. Was he five feet tall, or seven feet tall? Was his hair black or blond or brown? Was his handshake limp, or was it the bone-fracturing clasp of the native-born Texan?

All I had to go on was his voice. It sounded good-natured and engaging. So why had I been blowing up his image into the likeness of a fire-breathing monster? Oddly enough (again I felt a pang of shame) we'd probably get on very well together . . . poor devil.

Yet I didn't deceive myself. I was prepared for something unpleasant. Sarrazin carried plenty of muscle. He could run me clear out of Texas, as he was supposed to have done with Axel Johnson. Tales of Texan revengefulness aren't fairy stories. Texas is the last stronghold of the vendetta. I seemed to remember hearing at some dinnertable or other that Sarrazin's grandfather—or could it have been his actual father?—had been mixed up in one of the most notorious of the Texas feuds, a private war that went on for nearly ten years and reduced a sizable chunk of the great raw state to a shambles.

The long hood of the Maserati split the oncoming torrent like the bows of a yacht. It was teeming so hard I sensed it must soon lift. There was a silver radiance on the rim of the horizon. I kept my foot down.

Another thirty-five or forty minutes, and I'd be seeing Astrid. This time she wouldn't be able to evade me—not at El Pardo, in her own house. This time I'd find out what was frightening her, what was wrong. I glowed with the fire of knight-errantry. I was El Cid, and the Maserati was the steed Babieca. I was riding to Astrid's rescue whether she liked it or whether she didn't.

Extraordinary as it sounds, I was really and truly looking forward to my visit to El Pardo. Yes—actually *looking forward* to it!

4

GABRIEL'S estate began eighty miles south of
Dallas. I knew I'd reached it when I began to encounter on each side of the road a tall and shining chain-link
fence, made of more solid and expensive materials than the
usual run of rusty barbed wire. The Maserati ran on beside
the shimmering silvery barrier for over thirty miles.

The entrance was a turning off the highway on to a wide
dirt track. A triple cattle-grid covered the opening, and the
entrance was spanned by a gleaming steel archway surmounted by the ranch brand and the words *El Pardo* in
modern lettering.

I swung the car off the highway and across the cattle-
grid. Obviously it would take an age to cross Gabriel's
land and reach his house. The land was flat, but the grass
was thick and green. Neither pains nor money had been
spared to irrigate it. The whole huge plain was seamed with
a concourse of nearly engineered canals. There were pumps
and water tanks around which the cattle were clustered
thickly. The entire landscape was dotted with them. I saw
Herefords, Guernseys, Friesians, Jerseys, and a bulky
breed of flawless cream-white color that I couldn't iden-

tify. Screened by trees, the houses of the ranch hands stood on either side of the dirt road.

The rain had stopped. There was a brilliant rift of lemon yellow in the gunmetal sky ahead. The weather was clearing. There would be one of those spectacular sunsets I enjoyed so much—a Texas fruit salad of pinks and purples, mauves and lavenders, scarlets and saffrons. I drove faster, feeling the broad bite of the tires in the damp dirt of the road.

Ahead of me, through the crescent on the spattered windshield, I could make out a dark line. It was a wide arc of trees. They marched toward me down a rise like an old-style army advancing *en masse*. The flanks came crowding in like encircling cavalry. In the center I glimpsed a white rectangle. Then I was among the woods, the pines pressing all around the car like giant grenadiers.

They were pines of the type which smother the whole of northeast Texas from Texarkana to Greenville with a sumptuous pelt. I guessed that the white square in the middle was the roof of the upper portion of El Pardo itself, lurking behind its lance-like rampart of trees. And there, only a few short miles away, Astrid was waiting to meet me.

She was closer than I thought.

Where the shoulders of the dirt road converged to a dark brown point I made out a bright crimson dot.

I slowed. It was Astrid's Porsche, parked diagonally across the road, door wide open.

I drove past it and pulled to the side and stopped. I switched off the engine. Astrid was already running out from behind the trees on the other side of the road. The toes of her high black boots kicked up small scads of sodden dead leaves and pine needles. She was dressed in creased white linen trousers and a short black reefer jacket with brass buttons. Her fair hair was caught back by a cream silk scarf.

My smile of greeting disappeared as soon as I saw her expression. She hurried to the window that I'd started to lower as soon as I'd spotted the Porsche. She was fighting for breath, like a deer with the pack after it in full cry. She shot a glance over her shoulder as if at any second she expected to hear the hounds baying and see them come bounding out of the wood.

"Quick!" She had the key of the car in her hand. "*Quick. Please!*"

"Darling, what the—?"

"Follow the Porsche. I've got to talk to you."

She darted away from the window toward her own car. She slipped behind the wheel, slammed the door, started up, and came lunging by me in one continuous movement. Mystified, I pressed the starter and took off in pursuit. A hundred yards down the road, without any warning, she veered to the left and shot down an inconspicuous side turning. I was caught napping, overshot, and had to reverse. She went on ahead without slowing down.

After about a minute of furious driving I found myself spinning along the raised levee of an enormous lake. We came on it abruptly. It reminded me of a wooded lake in a corner of Europe, in the Black Forest, or in the wilds of Scotland. It was extraordinary to stumble on that dark and romantic stretch of water in the middle of a Texas plain. That evening it looked somber and reedy and forlorn. A band of lemon-colored sunlight irradiated the distant shore.

The Porsche gave me no time to savor my surroundings. I had to push hard to keep up with it. Leaves and pine needles lay thick on the track, and we ran on between the mournful glades and the curving shore with a muffled softness. Then the Porsche's brake lights winked briefly as it swung left over a small stone bridge.

The bridge connected the shore with a little island about an acre in extent. In the middle of the island stood a white belvedere or gazebo. It was constructed to command a wide view of the lake. Astrid drove in behind it where her car would be concealed in the stretch of shadow between the belvedere and the trees. I followed suit.

The belvedere was a replica of an eighteenth-century original. It had bulging bow windows and a pair of glass doors flanked by stucco columns. It resembled a rustic folly at Versailles or Schönbrunn. The white wooden exterior, with its Greek-key patterns around doors and windows, had been allowed to weather to a natural patina. It had an air of disuse. Astrid left her car and jerked open the glass doors and vanished inside. In a moment I saw her motioning through the panes as if beseeching me to hurry.

As soon as I entered, she shut the doors and leaned with her back against them. The belvedere was unheated. I regretted the warmth of the car. Then she rushed toward me and we embraced and I forgot all about the chill and the smell of damp and the long drive and the three-month separation.

We sat side by side on a black leather sofa in front of a marble fireplace with an iron bucket piled with logs. The leather was cold and musty. There was a film of dust on the dry surface of the logs.

She was staring at me with big nervous eyes. Her voice shook.

"I'd been waiting for you . . . hours . . ."

I wrapped my arms around her more tightly. Above the fireplace and nailed on the walls were trophies of skulls crowned by spreading horns with tiny delicate twisted spikes. The skulls were arranged in fancy designs. They looked like a sort of florid celebration of death.

"Why did you come? I couldn't believe it when Gabriel happened to mention it last night."

"Why? Because he phoned me—"

"Phoned you? Gabriel did?"

"Yes."

"He called you? But what about?"

"He wants to consult me."

"Oh?"

"Professionally."

"Oh!"

"And it was a great chance to see you."

"What's he up to?"

"How do you mean?"

"I know Gabriel."

"What would he be up to?" A sudden thought struck me. "Or did you talk to him?"

"Why should I do that?"

"Because you wanted to see me as badly as I wanted to see you. Did you suggest I might do some sort of a job down here?"

"Darling, do you imagine I'd have talked about you to Gabriel? Ever?"

"It might have come up quite innocently. Anyway, there's nothing very odd about him getting in touch with me, is there?"

"No?"

"He said he'd heard of me. He'd have been bound to, wouldn't he, sooner or later? He's always needing architects. His companies are putting up plants and factories all the time."

She was unconvinced. She kept saying she couldn't believe the whole thing had happened in a perfectly ordinary way. She thought there must be some deep dark plot.

I cupped my hands around her face. She didn't want to look at me. She sat with her hands thrust in the pockets of her jacket. Her cheeks were very cold. There was a line between her gray eyes as if, like me, she'd been sleeping badly.

I said softly, "Astrid, listen. I know you've been troubled. I know you've been unhappy. That's exactly why I came."

But all at once she broke out of my arms and stood up. Clumsily she leaned down and clasped her hands around my face. I was astonished to see that tears were spilling out of her eyes. She bent and pushed her mouth with greedy tenderness against mine.

"Astrid!"

She took my hand and pulled me to my feet. Her fingers were shaking.

"We can't stay here. He'll miss us. He'll get suspicious."

"So what?"

She fumbled a small scrap of a handkerchief out of the pocket of her slacks and scrubbed at her cheeks and eyes.

"He'll see I've been crying."

"What if he does? What *is* this?"

She balled the damp handkerchief in her palm.

"If only I knew what we could *do*—"

"Do? How do you mean, darling? There's plenty we can do."

"You don't know him . . ."

"Darling, we can do whatever we want. You've only got to make up your mind about marrying me. I'll speak to him at the first possible moment."

"No!"

"But why not?"

"As I said—you don't know him—"

"But I'll have to, sooner or later."

"Promise me you won't say anything till I say so."

"Darling—"

"Promise!"

"I don't—"

"And you've got to promise something else, too—"

"What?"

She stepped closer to me. "That you'll go away tomorrow."

"Go away?"

"Leave El Pardo. Tomorrow morning. And whatever it is he says he wants you to do for him, you won't do it."

"Astrid—!"

"Promise!"

"But what's the harm in at least hearing what he—"

"No! You must get away as quickly as possible. Make some excuse. And you must stay away."

"Why are you making such a big thing out of all this? I don't under—"

"Stay away! This isn't just the sort of routine affair you could have with another woman. Don't you understand

30

that? I wish I'd never got you into this. Darling, go away and stay away!"

"But, darling, be reasonable. What could he possibly be—"

"I don't know. But there's bound to be *something!*"

She had already turned away from me and was walking quickly toward the door. I shook my head as I followed her. At the door she swung round and thrust her arms round my neck. I held her, embracing her hungrily. Her unhappiness and uncertainty tore my heart. Then she pulled away and opened the glass door. A cold gush of air nipped into the belvedere.

Just behind the door as she tugged it open I saw a squat metal contraption like a miniature computer. It had a kind of console studded with thirty or forty black buttons and a line of red ones. Without thinking, and out of pure curiosity, I put my hand out toward it. I thought it was some kind of giant hi-fi. My fingers strayed over the red buttons.

"*Don't touch it!*"

I jerked my hand back as if I'd been stung.

She said, "You'll set off the nightingales or something . . ."

"Set off the *what?*—"

She lifted a hand through the open doorway in the direction of the lake.

"It's all connected with that."

"Ah!" I nodded appreciatively at the darkening expanse of water. "He was lucky to find a stretch of water like that when he came here."

"Find it? He made it."

"*Made* it?"

"Yes."

"But it's vast! Like a small sea!"

"That wouldn't worry him. He never does anything by halves."

"Obviously." I could just make out what looked like a long line of slipways about a mile away. They were almost invisible against the evening-shadowed woods. "I suppose it's quite shallow, then?"

"Shallow?" She was impatient to be off. The chill breeze ruffled her hair, and she put up a hand to smooth it down. Her voice was rapid and indifferent. "I wouldn't call it shallow. It's forty feet deep."

"Forty *feet!*"

"Yes." She was hurrying toward the Porsche and spoke without bothering to turn her head.

I started after her, giving a low whistle.

"Forty feet! . . . You're right . . . He doesn't do things by halves!"

I could see Wendell Barratt's big body huddled over the drawing-board as he puzzled out the calculations for a big job like that. I could picture the bulldozers and earth-moving equipment.

She had reached the car and was looking back at me as I came up.

"Let's hurry. He's got some kind of a gadget on the front gate of the ranch. A camera, and some sort of timing device."

"If it's worrying you that much, I can always say I stopped to admire the view, can't I? But why don't we simply tell the truth? Why not tell him you came to meet me? You're going to be my hostess, aren't you?"

She nodded, managing to smile.

"And he told you I was coming, didn't he?"

Another nod.

I squeezed her hand. "Well, then!"

She shook her head. "You don't understand." She stood there in the dusk and gave me a curiously intent look. "Darling, I'm not behaving this way because I don't— If I could—"

She gripped my arm and stood on tiptoe to give me a swift darting kiss. Before doing so, she glanced round quickly as if the nearby pine trees might be full of eyes. Her lips were dry and hot.

Then, with the same furtive grace of the hunted animal she'd shown when we met, she slid behind the wheel of the Porsche. She looked up out of the window and spoke in a rapid voice.

"You drive on ahead, darling. Just go back around the lake to the main drive again and turn left."

"What about you?"

"I'll go the other way and come in by a different road. I told them at the house I'd be visiting the wife of one of the foremen. I'll drive down there now. She came back from the hospital yesterday."

I shrugged and nodded. It all seemed rather melodramatic.

She went on, "I won't reach the house until at least half an hour after you do."

She drove off rapidly without switching on her lights. The car was swallowed up by the gathering darkness as soon as it crossed the small stone bridge.

I got into the Maserati and drove in a leisurely way in the direction she told me. No need to hurry now. I put the window down and enjoyed the fresh damp air. The whole unexpected scene had surprised and slightly unnerved me. I put on my headlights, thinking about the summerhouse as I drove. Across the lake, above the shrouded purple of the pines, a last thin band of light shone a clear topaz yellow as the night dropped down.

I glanced at the inky water. I didn't know it, but tomorrow morning I was due to return there. I'd be given a special tour of the ranch, the lake, the summerhouse, and a score of other features of the estate. My guide would be none other than their owner and my prospective employer himself. The summerhouse, like everything else, would turn out to be highly original and ingenious. The console I'd almost touched would prove to be fitted with a battery of special devices, all of them connected with the lake. As I'd been warned, one button set off recordings of artificial nightingales, transmitted by amplified microphones situated at strategic points. There were buttons that set off owls, nightjars, warblers, and various other kinds of bird noises. Other buttons released swans, mallards, pintails, teals, and Muscovy ducks from a collection of individual breeding pens. Still other buttons controlled invisible dams and sluices that raised or lowered the level of the water. There were buttons that sent music floating dreamily across the lake, while a whole array of rheostats made possible a fantastic combination of lighting effects. Spotlights were positioned among the trees, along the shore line, and right under the surface of the water. There were lights of every size and color. On summer nights it must have looked like fairyland. There was also a special row of buttons that served a very different purpose. These were the red ones. A touch of one of the red buttons and the mild summer night would be filled not with the warble of nightingales but with the howling of coyotes and jackals. And to make the flesh creep further, another button could send a shoal of horribly realistic plastic crocodiles slithering into the water. These could be steered electronically in any direction and made to creep up on any unsuspecting swimmer or fisherman. Finally, as the *pièce de résistance*, another button unleashed the plastic black fins of a school of sharks. These too were controlled from the panel in the summerhouse. They could be maneuvered right up to the rim of the shore and made to dance a sinister ballet. Gabriel demonstrated for me. He had a very light and delicate touch on the console.

Even though I still thought Astrid's fears were groundless, I couldn't help feeling a slight flutter in the pit of my stomach as I stood at the foot of the portico with its soaring pillars and spreading pediment and watched my car being driven into the falling darkness. A burst from the exhaust, a spurt of gravel, and the Maserati rounded the far end of the long white building and disappeared from sight. I felt oddly alone and naked, like someone caught in the middle of a wood with the darkness crashing down.

I turned and walked toward the front door, flanked by two of the servants who had been waiting for me at the foot of the portico. They seemed to materialize out of the air. They wore slacks and red turtleneck sweaters. The leader, who also wore a black blazer with silver buttons, smiled briefly and murmured a polite "Good evening, sir." He wore spectacles with smart square black frames. The impression he gave was intelligent and studious. They were young men, all three of them: serious, concentrated, well-barbered, athletic, more like junior executives than servants.

My bags were out of the trunk before I climbed from behind the wheel. I ascended the front steps with my two-man escort. This was an efficient and purposeful household.

The front door swung open at our approach like the gate of an enchanted castle. My glimpse of the belvedere had already prepared me for Gabriel's mania for gadgeteering. Nothing would be done by hand if it could be done by means of a photoelectric cell.

I gave the building a brief professional glance before I went inside. There was hardly any light left in the sky, but it confirmed the glimpse I'd caught as I came up the drive. The house was grand but not very distinguished, a copy or a heavily restored version of one of the antebellum mansions of the Old South. I was disappointed. I'd imagined the house would correspond to the reputation of its owner. I'd expected it to be one of those weird Texas follies I'd come to like. El Pardo only succeeded in giving me a feeling of elephantiasis. It didn't strike me at all as being the "fun place" Gabriel had described. But I'd already been wrong about the belvedere, which also looked perfectly ordinary on the outside and obviously contained plenty of surprises once you entered it. Maybe the house was the same. Was Gabriel secretive?

We passed through a huge hallway and up a broad stairway. Like the summerhouse, the hallway was festooned with the skulls of dead game. I found that the suite of rooms I was to occupy were also laid out on what might be called an electronic basis. At strategic points—beside the bed, on consoles and coffee tables—were miniature remote-control panels with neatly labeled buttons. Without leaving my bed I could open and draw the curtains, raise and lower the blinds, operate the radio and television, slide back the doors of the closets, switch the lamps on and off and make them dimmer and brighter. The master of El Pardo seemed to have an inclination to play the magician.

The bathroom was laid out as lavishly as the bedroom. There were electric razors and safety razors and a choice of hot lather from dispensers or cold lathers in ordinary cans. A regiment of lotions stood on the marble basin beside the gold taps. The bath and the shower were sunken affairs that would have pleased the Emperor Tiberius, their enormous gold fittings massive enough to gladden the heart of Patti Danziger, my Houston client who spent half her life immersed in scented water.

Although I fought against it, I still couldn't prevent myself from feeling tense and uneasy as I put on a fresh shirt and a dark suit and made myself ready to meet my host.

5

AT first sight my fears seemed groundless. It would have been hard to imagine a friendlier reception than the one Gabriel gave me. It didn't seem possible that he could ask me to build anything sinister or monstrous.

He was talking on the phone. As soon as I entered the drawing-room he put down the receiver, picked up a glass, and walked across the room with it.

"I expect you can do with this." He smiled. "Welcome to El Pardo. I'm afraid you aren't seeing it under very agreeable circumstances."

I was putting out my hand to take the glass.

"I beg your pardon?"

"The weather. Perfectly foul. You like martinis, I suppose?"

He put the glass in my hand.

"Oh, yes," I said. "The weather. Horrible!"

"You *do* like martinis?"

"Oh, yes! I like martinis!"

"Good. My wife will be down in a minute. She went out after lunch and came back only a few minutes ago. I know how much she's looking forward to meeting you."

I sipped my drink and said carefully, "Your wife and I have met before, actually."

He took my arm and steered me over to a sofa.

"So I gathered, but that was only casually, wasn't it? At the house of some friends?"

He was standing over me, smiling down at me. He'd picked up a half-full glass of what looked like milk from the top of the bar as we walked past it.

"How's the martini?"

"Fine!" I indicated the glass in his hand. "But aren't you having a drink yourself? Or is that a brandy Alexander?"

"This? Oh, I don't drink! Never have. I don't smoke, either. But don't you get the idea I'm some sort of a puritan. I like to see other people enjoying themselves. Actually, I think I mix martinis rather well, don't you?"

"You mixed this?"

"El Pardo's famous for its man-size martinis . . . You're sure you like them?"

"How do you know how to mix them, if you don't drink them?"

"Ah! I have a great gift for pleasure at second-hand. Does that sound strange?"

"Well, a little unusual, perhaps."

He laughed. His laugh, like his smile, was attractive. He had charm. His warm brown eyes twinkled continuously. His rather fleshy lips were constantly drawn back from the fine square white teeth. He was rather smaller than I'd imagined, not big for such an important man but broad-shouldered and strong-looking. His complexion was very brown—though whether this was due to what I'd heard about a touch of Mexican ancestry or the effects of outdoor life I didn't know. The main impression he gave was of abundant energy. He liked to stand with his legs apart, thrusting his body squarely toward the person he was talking to. He tended to step close to you, invading your private space, pressuring you. If you were taller than he was, he liked to make you sit down so he could remain standing, making it easier to dominate you. His manner was friendly but relentless. His restless vitality was visible in the way he had of twitching his shoulders, the constant movements of his head and hands, even in the waves of his thick auburn hair that seemed to crackle with electricity. One thing in particular that immediately struck me about him was the unlined appearance of his face. He was ten years older than I was, but we looked the same age. He was dressed informally, in the same red turtleneck sweater and dark blazer as the young man in the driveway. He was putting himself out so strenuously to be agreeable that I don't know where I got the impression that he might be sly and dangerous.

We were talking in the same desultory way when Astrid came in. She entered the enormous room quickly, still as rushed and flustered as she'd been an hour before. She'd put on a green silk dress, and her hair looked freshly combed and slightly damp, as if she'd just hurried out from under the shower. Gabriel went up to her and wrapped an arm around her. He drew her toward me, the picture of fond possessiveness.

I rose politely and shook the hand she held out to me. I gave it a little squeeze but felt no response. Beaming, Gabriel effected the introductions, telling me that now Astrid and I had met properly he was sure we'd get along splendidly. He made her sit down beside me on the sofa. His brown eyes shone happily down at us, as if he was delighted at the cosy spectacle of his wife and his new friend seated so close together. His lips were drawn back in the familiar grin, and his slightly snub nose was wrinkled with pleasure.

He gave a start and touched Astrid on the shoulder.

"Forgive me, darling! I was forgetting. You'll have one of my specials, of course? We've plenty of time before dinner."

He moved smartly to the well-stocked bar on the far side of the room and picked up a silver pitcher. Astrid and I exchanged a quick glance. She looked pale. Her eyes seemed to be begging me to keep quiet and not stir things up. When she was in her husband's presence, she was a totally different person from the lively and amusing woman I was in love with.

When Gabriel handed her her drink, I smiled at her and said, "Well, I'm glad to see *you* drink, Mrs. Sarrazin. It's nice to have company."

She looked up nervously at Gabriel, looming above us, legs straddled, a newly replenished glass of white liquid grasped firmly in his hand. He smiled down at her fondly.

"Oh, well, I've done my best to break her of these nasty habits—though I haven't had much luck, as you can see!"

"Why don't you drink, yourself? Did you have parents who were good Texas Baptists?"

"Oh, no, nothing like that! No, I tried drinking once, but it just didn't suit me."

Astrid had tilted her chin up at Gabriel's reference to her. She took a mouthful of her drink in a way that struck me as quietly defiant. I was rather annoyed to notice that she wasn't wearing the sapphire I'd bought her, only one of Gabriel's gross-looking diamonds. Then the flash of defiance vanished almost as soon as it appeared. She stared down into her lap.

As I made efforts to make conversation I studied the drawing room. It was ornate and conventional, like the house itself. There was no indication that Astrid had had any hand in designing or decorating it. It was impersonal. The only individual touch was a large picture over a buffet near the door at the far end. It was too far away for me to make it out. It looked interesting, and I decided to take a look at it when I had a chance. Otherwise, the place was bland and almost barren, though I had no doubt that it was strung with the same invisible spiderwebs of electric wiring as all the other rooms in the house. One of the control devices lay on the coffee table in front of me, beside a chessboard with a set of streamlined chessmen cut out of polished steel. The chessboard wasn't just an ornament. A game was in progress. I hadn't played chess since I left college, but it looked to me as if the opposing sides were locked in a particularly intricate and bitter end-game. Was he playing against himself? Or with one of the young men who waited on him?

I complimented him on what I'd managed to see of his house and ranch. I told him how impressed I'd been by the sight of his rolling acres. I mentioned the fine herds, particularly the white cattle that had been unfamiliar to me.

His eyes lit up. He swayed back from the hips.

"Ah! You noticed my Charollais! It's not exactly surprising you didn't know what they were—very few of my guests do. Still, I doubt very much if there's really much you don't know, is there? Everyone tells me you're a very clever chap and that I'll be very lucky if I can get hold of you!"

He said it without any apparent tinge of irony.

I explained that my grandparents had come from the pastures of Leicestershire to be dairy farmers in Vermont. When I was a boy, my father took me to livestock shows all over New England. This interested Gabriel. Waving his glass of milk (I was pretty certain it was milk now) he launched into an eloquent account of the care and rearing of Charollais. He went into details of their behavior in their native France and in different parts of America. He talked about lactation and milk yields. He was a fanatic about cattle, as I suppose his Texan ancestors were before him. From childhood I was used to men who were crazy about farming, and at first I listened tolerantly, even with pleasure. Astrid sat with a glazed expression, as though she'd heard this same dialogue a hundred times before. But she began to grow restive and embarrassed when her husband insisted on going into the finer points of breeding. There was one outstanding bull he owned called Leonidas. Its sexual prowess seemed to satisfy him and cause him tremendous satisfaction. It must have been one of the most potent animals in Texas—in America—to judge from the figures Gabriel reeled off concerning the number of cows it could cover and the number of offspring it produced. It was currently the most expensive stud bull in East Texas, pumping out seed in a seething flood. I gathered that Gabriel was fond of riding down to the corrals to watch Leonidas do his stuff, and liked to take parties of visitors down there for the same purpose. I could feel Astrid growing tense on the sofa beside me as the description went on and on and became more and more anatomical. It was certainly rather a strange monologue. I looked up into Gabriel's face as he bent over us, sawing away with his glass. I'm moderately fond of milk, but I eyed that glass with distaste. His eyes were bright, his rather prominent lips wet. There was a filament of spittle at the left-hand side of his mouth as it opened and shut.

I think I was growing a little crimson myself, when we were saved by an interruption. The bespectacled young man who had supervised my arrival was standing in the distant doorway. He waited until there was a fractional lull in Gabriel's discourse. Then he raised his voice, to make sure it reached us, and announced that dinner was ready. He was still wearing his previous outfit of slacks, sweater, and blazer. It must have been the El Pardo uniform.

Gabriel looked cross at being forced to terminate his recital of Leonidas' amorous achievements. If I hadn't happened to be actually watching him, I wouldn't have witnessed it, but for a second his smooth face was transfigured by an oddly devilish look. It was like the stroke of lightning that fissures a summer landscape and reveals it in a completely new light. He paused a moment, looking down at the chessboard. All at once he moved a queen and removed an opposing knight from the board. Then he stood back and suddenly smiled, motioning us to leave the sofa and walk ahead of him, side by side, toward the door. The young man stood aside for us in the easy but respectful attitude with which he had previously seen to the disposal of my car and luggage. If he knew that he had momentarily annoyed his employer, he didn't show it. Perhaps Gabriel's forked-lightning reaction was too frequent to be significant?

Before leaving the room, I paused briefly to examine the picture over the buffet. It disconcerted me. Nothing I'd

44

seen so far in Gabriel's surroundings led me to suppose he was particularly concerned about the arts. And now I found myself admiring a modern painting of exceptional quality. It was unsigned, though I rather thought it must be by Masson. It was painted very freely, in acid greens and scarlets with a few small areas of violet and amethyst. It showed a man and a woman, their bodies bent and gashed, running with hair streaming and heads strained back in terror. They wore classical robes, stained and rent, ripped away to show their sexual organs. They were posed together on a kind of plinth, as if they were statues, and enclosed in a room or shrine. They were pursued by a swarm of winged insects, ants or hornets, that had either flown into the room from outside or which emanated from their own suppurating wounds. In a square window or doorway behind them a volcano was erupting, spitting out great blocks of glowing granite into the somber sky. On its slopes a building with columns and a pediment was being blanketed by molten lava. Long grass and poppies grew around the foot of the plinth. What was particularly striking was the way in which the man and woman were fused together. They were literally one flesh, joined or hinged into a single scampering figure. The sexual organs were exaggerated, the man's clutching hands fastened on a jutting breast and on a swollen vulva whose gaping interior was furnished with interlocking tines like the inside of a gigantic conch shell.

I heard Gabriel's voice behind me. He laughed.

"Quaint, isn't it?"

"A very fine painting."

"Like to know how I got it?"

"How?" I turned round and moved closer to it.

"I was at Ranald McFee's place, up in the Panhandle. He buys a lot of that kind of stuff. It's for investment, though I suppose he's got to have some sort of hobby since his umpteenth wife left him and he got busted up playing polo at Midland. Anyway, it was on his wall, and as we were eating he saw it'd caught my fancy. I couldn't tell you why, but it had. It wasn't like any of his other pictures, which were mainly hunting and racehorses. He said it'd got sent down from Washington or somewhere by mistake with a regular shipment and he hadn't bothered to send it back. He's got paintings all over his walls, even the lavatories. When he saw the way I kept looking at it he called in a gardener and told him to take it down and fetch it along to the airstrip. He gave it to me as a little sweetener to help along the deal we'd been roughing out. I brought it home in the jet and had Larry here—" He put his arm around the shoulders of the young man with the spectacles. "He tried it out in various places until it wound up in here. Larry's awfully fussy about little things like that, aren't you, Larry? Queer picture, isn't it? One of these days I'm going to get Ranald's art dealer down here to explain it to me and tell me if it's worth anything."

I turned back to face him. He took his arm from Larry's shoulders and put it round Astrid's. He pulled her close to him. Once more he was beaming and boyish.

This seemed a good moment to ask him something that had been on my mind ever since he called me in Houston.

"Mr. Sarrazin," I said, "I'm naturally eager to learn why you've asked me to come here. Tell me, exactly what kind of a building is it you want me to design for you?"

"Building?" He grinned. "What sort of building?" He and Larry looked at each other, as if what I'd said had

46

amused them. "Oh, I don't want you to design me a building!"

"No?"

"No!"

I frowned. "Well, what *do* you want me to design, then?"

The brown eyes became slightly opaque without losing anything of their charm or good nature.

"If I asked you to guess, do you think you'd be able to?"

"Guess?"

"If you tried from here to next week?"

"Mr. Sarrazin—"

"Oh, please, won't you call me Gabriel?"

I was impatient and couldn't conceal it. He laughed again. He was enjoying himself. I saw that the depths of his eyes were growing quite thick and muddy.

"It's something that'll intrigue you," he declared. "I can promise you that!"

"Well?"

"As I said when I called you, you'll find it a challenge . . ."

"What sort of challenge?"

"Why don't you wait and see? We've got the whole of the weekend ahead of us to talk about it."

I made a sound of such unmistakable irritation that he decided to put me out of my misery, at least partially. He was walking past me, taking Astrid with him. He spoke as they went through the door with a note of amusement and something like triumph in his voice. The Texas accent was slightly more noticeable.

He said, "It's a maze."

I stared. "A—a—?"

"That's right." Another laugh. "Didn't I say you'd

47

never guess, not if you took all week?"

I thought in my ignorance that he was just playing one of his jokes on me.

He gave a final little bubble of laughter at the look on my face. Then he gave Astrid a peck on the cheek and a proprietary pat on the bottom and steered her through the door before I could think of anything else.

The bespectacled young man stood back, waiting for me to pass. His eyes behind their black frames were now expressionless.

6

IT seemed a wild and even crazy idea until you became more familiar with El Pardo.

The house wasn't at all what it seemed at first sight. It really did conform to Gabriel's conception of a "fun place." I should have remembered the belvedere and the plastic sharks. A maze was exactly what El Pardo needed to round it off. Let me explain.

The drawing room and the dining room were neutral and conventional. They were meant to be for orthodox occasions and for orthodox people. For people he thought had stronger stomachs Gabriel unveiled the extravagant side of his nature. He took me on a conducted tour that same evening, and we continued it the next day and the day after that.

Build a maze! The suggestion first began to make sense when I set eyes on the penny arcade. It was a barnlike room built on behind the house and crammed with extraordinary machines. Some were modern; others were fifty or sixty years old. Gabriel, I discovered, spent hours in this room. He'd start up one or other of the player pianos, mechanical organs, or jukeboxes that lined the walls. Sometimes he'd start them all up at the same time. Then he'd plunge his hand into one of the sacks of pennies that were propped against the walls of the arcade and rush about popping them into one slot after another.

The arcade had a glass dome that splashed the whole painted glittering metallic scene with brilliant splotches of crimson, mauve, emerald, and orange. Gabriel reveled in it. To the wheezing and puffing of "On the Banks of the Wabash," "Paper Doll," or "Meet Me in St. Louis" he'd scamper up and down pulling levers and pumping handles. There must have been a couple of dozen fortune-telling machines and tell-your-weight machines. Then there was a series of machines that played out little dramas as soon as you dropped your coin in. One of them was an antique English contraption in which a pair of black gates creaked open to reveal a prison yard with a scaffold in the middle. Little figures representing the prison governor and chaplain jerked their arms and gesticulated, a top-hatted executioner threw a shining silver lever, and the condemned man shot down through the trap and the rope twitched backwards and forwards above the dark aperture. Another English machine of Victorian vintage showed the execution of Mary Queen of Scots. A black velvet curtain parted, the headsman slowly hefted his axe, the blade fell, the royal head plopped into the basket. The wire in the neck by which the head was fastened had been painted bright red to suggest when it dropped that an arc of blood gouted out. Gabriel seemed to be fond of such scenes. Another glass case depicted the beheading of Charles the First outside the Banqueting Hall in Whitehall, a building I'd always admired. Another showed the execution of Louis XVI outside the Louvre. There were deaths in the electric chair and the gas chamber. The last pair struck me as distinctly creepy, as I got the definite impression they weren't penny-arcade machines at all, but were specially manufactured. They were smooth and well-oiled in their movements, and when the current went through the victim, or he sniffed the cyanide, the shudders that went through his body were horribly lifelike. Gabriel enjoyed pressing the buttons and watching the miniature tragedies taking place to the accompaniment of "Sweet Adeline" or "Casey Would Dance with the Strawberry Blonde."

He also made me play for a whole afternoon on the group of machines that featured games played by opposing sides. Little figures clicked ice-hockey sticks backwards and forwards or lashed up and down with stiff right legs in English-style soccer. The object was to propel a ball-bearing into the goal. There was also a baseball game where the batter got three strikes and out. We thumped at the brass handles, and Gabriel was elated when he won and childishly upset when he lost. Or we cranked madly at little wheels that sent racehorses and racing cars circling a track, urging on our mounts and machines with cries and curses. At first I thought the entire business was pretty silly and only joined in to indulge Gabriel. Then somehow I got fired up and entered into the fun of the thing. Gabriel had that effect on you. It didn't take him long to get other people going his way. He acted like a small boy who'd found somebody new to play with, and I honestly thought he liked me.

We seemed to spend a great deal of our time on the shooting machines. They had the butts of pistols or the stocks of rifles sticking out of them and you swiveled them to shoot rows of ducks or cats sitting on rooftops. We spent hours popping away. He also had a full-size real-life

51

shooting gallery in the basement, where I watched him shoot both hand guns and rifles. He had rows of shotguns and hunting rifles in glass cases in his gunroom. He loved to display them, handle them, fondle them, lubricate them, work the actions. I didn't take much notice of it at the time. It struck me as just another example of a well-known Texan hang-up.

Apart from these pastimes he had another gallery, upstairs, where the entertainment was more sophisticated. This gallery was kept in total darkness. He loved to take you right over the threshold before he snapped the lights on. What burst on you then was a kind of Aladdin's Cave. The place did in fact resemble a cave because it was provided with walls and dummy buttresses leaning at all angles and painted in different primary colors. It was like walking into the set of a German Expressionist movie—*Caligari, Homunculus,* or *The House Without Doors or Windows.* The ceiling had been lowered to a height of less than eight feet. As in all pastimes associated with Gabriel, there was plenty of noise. He told me later that as a professional plane and instrument maker he was particularly interested in noise. He'd written a thesis at Rice (he was a Ph.D.) on the effect of noise on human physiology. The noise in the gallery was an eerie and resonant blend of electronic computer music.

In niches against the left-hand wall were ranged a score of perpetual-motion machines. It was a collection that any scientific museum would have given its eyeteeth for, since it contained what looked like some very early and valuable specimens. Two that I especially remember were one that had a little fluted glass rod that kept twirling around and around in imitation of a jet of water, and another in which a steel ball ran endlessly up and down a series of brass plates tilting delicately backwards and forwards in response to its weight.

Against the right-hand wall was a row of kinetic sculptures. Like the machines, each had an individual light focused on it, operated by means of an invisible rheostat. The sculpture you were looking at brightened while the ones on each side of it dimmed. Gabriel explained that Donna Vorbeck had a standing order to provide him with unusual examples. He wasn't interested in them as works of art. What interested him was the fact that they resembled complicated and ingenious toys. They were constructed of steel, plastic, or Plexiglas and presented images that constantly shifted. Some were arrangements of light; others presented varied effects of refraction or altering perspectives. One of them had geometrical shapes that dropped into different positions as the whole thing revolved on the wall behind it. They were beautiful and precise. It was easy to understand why a man with a technical background would be fascinated by them.

At the far end of the gallery was a row of large black boxes that turned out to be peep-shows. You looked through a pinhole and saw a whole room magically displayed before you. The oldest of them looked like a Dutch interior, another like the parlor of an old-fashioned doll's house, and a third resembled a modishly furnished drawing room. I stared at this last one a long time while the weird music plunked and mooed away. I stared at it because—inadvertently, of course—the maker had given the room an extraordinary resemblance to the drawing room of my house in New York. Two tiny puppets representing a man and a woman had been inserted into the room, but for some reason they had fallen over and were lying face down on the rug. The rug was a burgundy color, oddly like the color of the rug in my house on Whittier Drive.

Gabriel didn't give me much time to study the peep-shows. He was eager to hustle me out of the gallery and up to the third floor. The third floor was his own personal hide-away. He had a room there that housed his own computer, a product of one of his companies, and when he demonstrated it he proved to me that he had an impressive grasp of mathematics and what looked like a highly individual approach to the possibilities of programming. Most of the top floor, however, was devoted to the layout of a model railway. It was the model railway to end all model railways. It ran down corridors and in and out of rooms and contained every item known to the model railway maniac. A few of the locomotives and freight cars were old and battered, as if they were survivors from Gabriel's childhood. But the model railway was only part of it. In one room was a banked track, a replica of Monza or Indianapolis, around which racing cars and sports cars whirled in an amazingly lifelike way. And there were colossal armies of model soldiers of every period and nationality. The floor of one room was entirely given over to a tableau depicting the jungles of Southeast Asia. American troops were attacking guerrillas. Planes dropped down from the height of the ceiling to deliver imitation napalm, and Gabriel activated a platoon of flame-throwers for my benefit, literally burning up a native village. The battle was enhanced with sound effects played at a deafening pitch over a battery of speakers. And while the village was blazing, he photographed it with a Polaroid camera, showing me the results with great satisfaction. It all looked real—columns of flame and smoke and burning thatch. There were heaps of photographic equipment lying around. He used it to take photographs of care-fully staged racing-car and railroad crashes. Blown-up versions of the more striking photographs were thumb-tacked to the surrounding walls. One showed a train with a long string of boxcars leaving a viaduct and dropping into a ravine. It looked frighteningly like an actual disaster.

7

GABRIEL'S pleasure in his possessions was so child-like and whole-hearted it was easy to overlook its destructive side. That first evening—before he'd shown me his treasures—he made such an effort to charm me that I'd have felt a swine not to try to respond to it.

He didn't drink at dinner, but he'd made a study of wine and vintages and pressed on me a really superb hock followed by a splendid Burgundy. He produced a little printed card from his billfold and studied it attentively before making his selections. Later there was a thirty-year-old Calvados and a Cuban cigar—an Upmann, no less—to round off an excellent meal. I felt very relaxed.

We were waited on by the three young men in blazers. They moved around the dining room, their hands and faces appearing for a moment in the warm pool of light from the candelabras before melting back into the obscurity beyond. Larry, the senior of the trio, served Gabriel himself, putting down the plates in front of him in a deferential but faintly possessive way. All the time, taped music played softly—Boccherini, Telemann, Vivaldi. I don't think Gabriel was any more fond of music than he was of art (though I may—again—have been underrating him), but he had a great sense of how he ought to behave and what was expected of a gentleman and a millionaire.

Naturally, I was aching to ask questions about the project he'd mentioned. But in a playful way he kept heading me off, so I decided not to press him. In his capricious way he ignored my hints and overtures and steered the conversation in other directions. Astrid sat motionless while he talked and stared down at her plate. She ate almost nothing.

Chiefly he talked about his parents. He was in a reminiscent mood. Their life-sized portraits hung on either side of the fireplace, separated by the artificial flames that leaped up from a pile of synthetic logs. The portraits were kept apart by the blackened muzzles of a crossed pair of old-fashioned muskets. Their subjects were dressed in the evening clothes of the 1920s, though Gabriel's father, obviously ill at ease in his boiled shirtfront and wing collar, managed to suggest the stance and attitude of an earlier age. There was something of the frontiersman about him. He didn't look the sort of man you'd want to pick a quarrel with. His wife was different. She looked almost thirty years younger than he was, and a million light-years more agreeable and sophisticated. I felt I could have talked to her, but not to him. She wore a simple and elegant gown of black velvet with a long train. It was cut low to reveal a generous white-powdered bosom. Her arms were firm and fine. Except for a pair of heavy jet bracelets, she wore no jewelry. The painter was no John Singer Sargent, but he managed to convey an air of poise and assurance. Her hair, drawn back tightly from her forehead and held by silver combs in a great knot on her creamy shoulders, was so black and glossy and her face so distinctively oval that it struck me she almost certainly had ancestors who came from south of the Pedernales and the Nueces. Texas, after all, has only been independent for not much more than a century. Her ample body was redolent of pride and sensuality.

A feature of her portrait was that she had insisted on having her only child painted with her. Little Gabriel, in a sailor suit, with short white socks and black leather pumps, stood beside his mother and stared down at us as we sat around the dining table with big solemn eyes. He leaned against his mother's velvet dress, locked close against the full curve of her hip. The little fellow was literally crushed against her, though he didn't seem to find the awkward stance unpleasant. He looked pleased to be huddled close to her. Her chin was lifted in an attitude of hauteur, almost of maternal defiance, in the direction of her husband's portrait, as if she wished to shield the boy from his father.

I doubt if Joel Sarrazin had ever been cruel to his son. There was humor and a kind of rough tenderness in the mouth beneath the heavy black mustache. Still, from what Gabriel was saying, it might have been a good thing to have been shielded from him in certain of his moods. Gabriel related how his father had killed at least four men in his time. He was extremely entertaining on the subject of the celebrated Kohls County feud of 1898, in which his father took part as a principal while still a very young man. It was then that he had disposed of three of his four victims. The affair masqueraded as the usual quarrel over grazing rights, but it was easy to read between the lines of Gabriel's narrative and divine that it was really a case of *pundonor*, even of simple revenge. I thoroughly enjoyed Gabriel's account of it, which had obviously been polished to a fine point by repeated re-telling. I leaned back in my chair and savored my Calvados. I was amused by this picturesque tale of bloodshed and violence, characteristic of an age that was long dead and buried. He told how his father had shot down the two Levitt brothers by hiding in the bushes outside their house and bushwhacking them, and how he rode down their cousin Bob Everest on the open range. It was stirring stuff. As he spoke, he kept his eyes fastened for long periods on the pictures beside the fireplace. I noticed that although he was talking about his father, it was his mother's picture he mostly dwelt on. There was a soft smile on his face, and I supposed that he was amused by the spectacle of himself in his sailor's get-up.

As the story continued, I let my glance stray between the portrait of Isabel Sarrazin and the daughter-in-law whom she had never known. I wondered how Isabel would have got on with Astrid. Gabriel told me with engaging directness, during the course of his family reminiscences, that she died in giving birth to a daughter when she was only twenty-nine. The girl was stillborn. He was as frank in mentioning these obstetrical matters as he was in talking about the sex life of the bull Leonidas. He even told me—with what seemed the same apparent cheerfulness—that his father had been twice married before he'd married his mother and married twice more after her death. He'd loathed both his stepmothers. He seemed more amused than bitter and embroidered his account with tales of the tricks he'd played on them to make their lives miserable. He was such a bad boy his father had sent him away to military school in Louisiana. He'd hated that, too, ran away three times, and finally forced them to expel him by setting fire to the dormitories.

After dinner, when we were drinking coffee in the drawing room and it was already past eleven o'clock, he finally came to the point.

"Well?" he inquired. "I expect you're about ready by now to talk about this business of the maze?"

I remarked a little testily that I'd been ready to talk about it for the past four hours.

He motioned to Black Spectacles to bring me another Upmann and waited while I lit it. He rose and turned to Astrid.

"Would you like to accompany us, dear?"

"Accompany you?"

"Downstairs."

She stared at him for a moment, then lifted her hand vaguely toward her forehead.

"Do you mind if I don't? I've got rather a headache. I think I'll go to bed . . ."

He was solicitous. He suggested hot milk and aspirins. He said that he had thought she looked a bit washed out when she came in from seeing the foreman's wife that afternoon.

She was faintly impatient.

"I'll be all right." She rose, hesitated, then added, "I expect I'll be asleep by the time you're ready to come to bed . . ."

He nodded. "I expect so, but I'll just put my head around the door. Just to satisfy myself you're tucked up and asleep . . ."

She came across to give my hand a brief formal squeeze. Her hand in mine, I commiserated politely about the headache. I mentioned I'd been rather out of sorts and sleepless myself lately, and offered her one of my sleeping pills. I told her they were a special prescription. She declined.

"No, thanks. It's nothing serious." She withdrew her hand. "I hope your room is quite comfortable? Are you sure you have everything you want?"

"Yes, thank you, Mrs. Sarrazin. I hope you'll feel better in the morning . . ."

She went out quickly, without looking around.

Gabriel turned to me and sighed. "I knew she wasn't well. She's been rather overdoing things lately. Did you notice how silent she was at dinner?"

He indicated the other door.

"Shall we be on our way?"

I felt a faint pricking on the back of my neck as I walked down the long drawing room. Gabriel was ahead of me and Black Spectacles behind me. I dismissed the feeling as childish. There'd been absolutely nothing in Gabriel's behavior to indicate that he had any idea at all of my relationship with Astrid.

We marched in line astern down a dozen well-lighted corridors. I lost my sense of direction. Then we stopped in front of an elevator. Gabriel pressed the button. The door slid open, and we entered.

The elevator started to move downward. The journey only lasted a few seconds. The door slid back, and we emerged directly into an underground room about twenty feet square. It was warm, well-carpeted, and softly lit.

It was a vault. A bank vault—not the kind you keep coffins in. There were a couple of antique chairs and a rosewood table, and the atmosphere was cosy. There was piped music down here, too, no doubt in accordance with Gabriel's acoustical theories. Or perhaps he simply had an aversion to silence? There were no iron bars or grills. The place didn't need them. In the wall in front of us was a massive steel door with the glass-covered mechanism of an elaborate time lock bolted in the center like a robot with its intestines protruding. It looked solid and impenetrable.

Gabriel took up a position on one side of the steel door. His smile was genial and eager.

"I won't go into the whole thing deeply until tomorrow," he said, "when you're rested and refreshed. Tonight you're tired after your drive. But I thought I'd just give you something to sleep on. Actually, I'm terribly interested in the way the human brain works. Computers, and all that. It's a professional interest as well as a personal one. I'm fascinated by the way the brain functions when it's asleep, the way it can feed problems down into the unconscious and come up next morning with the most extraordinary ideas and solutions. So I thought we might at least get you started on the project on your first night here." He smiled. "Who knows what brilliant notions you'll throw off tomorrow morning, at the breakfast table?"

He tapped at the steel door with his knuckles. It was so thick it gave off practically no sound.

"Not that there's much to show you inside this thing. I don't use it. It came with the house. Our original family place is eighty miles away, at Corinth. El Pardo was always a thorn in our side. It wasn't a big estate in itself, but it cut our land practically in half. It was just big enough to bite into Sarrazin land and stop us becoming a consolidated block. See what I mean?"

I nodded. He leaned back against the rosewood table. He was taking it very much for granted that I'd already begun to go along with his plans.

"The family who owned El Pardo wouldn't sell. They were distant relatives of ours, actually. Second cousins or something. They'd come here from South Carolina and persisted in holding on. They weren't poor—not to start with—and wouldn't be pushed out." Another smile. "Used to make my old dad hopping mad. Of course, he never showed it. He could be patient. Very, very patient." The smile widened. "He got them in the end. In the end he always got everybody. It took him years to do it, but bit by bit he wore them down. He'd got into oil, and they'd stayed in cattle. Foolish of them. So they handed him the advantage. The way he went about it was very ingenious. Finally they had to knuckle under and sell. Dad got the house and land for a song." He paused, then added, "of course, the joke was—! Know who the original owners were?"

"Who?"

He laughed. "Why, Astrid's people!"

I stared at him and he laughed again, more loudly.

"Mean to say she never told you?"

"Tell me? Why should she tell me?"

"Oh, yes. Sorry! I was forgetting. You've hardly met, have you?"

He pushed himself away from the table.

"This is what I've got in mind. This vault's been empty ever since the Hamiltons left El Pardo. It was empty before they left, as far as that goes—no money to put in it. I own a bank in Houston, so what do I want with a private vault? For years I've been racking my brain for some way to use the thing—it seemed a pity to rip it out. And finally it came to me. I'd been wondering how to round off the entertainments El Pardo's got to offer—the slot machines, the sculptures, the time machines, and all the rest of it. And somehow the subject of a maze cropped up—"

Here I cut in. I said I didn't see how an out-of-the-way subject like a maze could just "crop up."

He smiled. "I was showing a party around my new computer research plant at Corpus Christi. One of them was a biologist, a very sharp fellow. Over lunch he started comparing a computer with the human brain. That got me interested. He began to describe a series of experiments he was doing at the University of New Mexico. Experiments with rats. In mazes. He'd been struck by the resemblance between the pattern of his mazes and the pattern of the human cortex, with its tangled masses of axons and dendrons, its nerve pathways, its millions of synapses. Rather like a computer, when you come to think of it. Rats in mazes. Fascinating, eh?"

He was talking with the same enthusiasm with which he'd talked earlier about his Charollais, or the Kohls County feud. He'd started pacing around the underground room, warming to his subject. I remember the soft lights, the deep beige carpet, the music playing "Someone to Watch over Me," the crystalline reflection from the square glass cover of the time lock, the glint from Larry's spectacles as he waited patiently beside the door of the elevator.

I was only half listening to his voice. I was chewing over the curious fact that Astrid and Gabriel were cousins . . .

". . . Lots of fun for guests . . ." I heard him saying ". . . Something really unusual . . . Kind of a grand finale . . . It'd be absolutely original—unique! El Pardo'd be celebrated. A great American showplace. Imagine it! A genuine, all-out, slap-up, full-blown, full-fledged, whole-hog modern maze! The Eighth Wonder of the

Modern World! And who'd have designed it? You would! You'd be the only living architect ever to design and build a structure like that. Doesn't that appeal to you? Isn't that tempting? Isn't that the challenge I promised you?"

He slapped his hand on the glittering steel door of the vault.

"Ideal site . . . Guests have dined . . . Shoo 'em into the elevator . . . Bring 'em down . . . Open the door . . . And right there facing them . . . That's when the fun really begins!"

8

I must admit I was genuinely excited about the prospect of constructing anything so original as a maze. Yet at the same time some profound instinct was warning me against it. Gabriel gave me ten days to make up my mind, and a dozen times I was on the point of calling Dallas and saying no. Then I thought of all my friends and rivals in the profession who would be only too eager to grab such a ripe job if I let it go, and I couldn't bring myself to pick up the phone. It was almost as if I finally agreed to take it on against my will, and it was against Astrid's will, too. She actually called me in my office on South Main Street, breaking our agreed pact not to call one another, to beg me to drop the idea. If only she had been more specific about her objections, and had told me exactly why I shouldn't take it, I believe I'd have dropped it there and then. Even so, the terms I presented to Gabriel were stiff, as if I unconsciously wanted him to turn me down. To my surprise, he accepted them with only a few minor modifications.

All the same, I began work at El Pardo in a defensive frame of mind. I was always looking forward to the moment when the job would be over and I could get away. That was what I was longing for: the time when Astrid and I would break free and begin our own life together. I wanted that desperately. In the weeks ahead I snatched at every opportunity to ask her to marry me; I asked her and kept asking her. And she always hesitated, always refused.

In the end I probably accepted the commission because of the chance it gave me to be at El Pardo and stay close to her. I could keep up the pressure on her with regard to marrying me—and also be on the spot to shield her, if any of her obscure fears turned out to be real—which, however, I secretly doubted. Nevertheless, the agitation she always showed at the prospect of my being at El Pardo infected me, too, with a nagging uneasiness. During the coming weeks I was constantly in the grip of a troubled mood.

Still, I've got to confess that I got down to the job with a genuine relish. Not only was Gabriel a persuasive advocate, but I discovered he was right. No architect had been called on to provide this particular commodity for almost two centuries. I took a bright girl called Jenny Anderton out of my office in New York and made her a full-time researcher. I got her to turn up all the material she could on the subject of mazes and labyrinths.

There wasn't much. But what there was was fascinating. The whole history of the maze is extremely ancient. It seems to have derived from the dark and frightening depths of the caves in which our ancestors lived in the old Stone Age. The interior of these caves could only be reached by narrow winding paths, and it was in these deep and inaccessible places that primitive hunters painted the images of the wild beasts and weird deities they worshipped. The maze might also be a symbol of the great primeval forests in which early man was terrified of losing himself. The old sign of the swastika is a maze pattern. On the wall of the Casa Grande in Arizona is a maze whose center represents the spiral hole through which the Pima Indians believed they had emerged from the Underworld.

It was in Ancient Egypt that the maze really came into its own. According to Herodotus, the Great Labyrinth at Crocodilopolis was a larger and more impressive structure than the Great Pyramid at Gizeh. He wrote that it had twelve huge covered courts and thirty thousand rooms. Jenny Anderton dug out for me all the references to the Great Labyrinth in classical literature. Strabo, Diodorus Siculus, Pomponius Mela, Pliny, Plutarch—she prepared dope sheets with extracts from all of them. I remember a striking quotation from Pliny's *Natural History* to the effect that "some of the passages and rooms are made so that the opening or shutting of a door makes a terrifying sound like thunder, and most of the Great Labyrinth is plunged in perpetual darkness . . ."

The Greeks and Romans took over where the Egyptians left off. Virgil mentions in the *Aeneid* something that he calls "The Game of Troy," in which horsemen perform intricate operations resembling the windings of a labyrinth. The ceremony spread all over the Mediterranean. It survives in modern dances in Spain and Sardinia and reached even farther afield to Scotland and Wales. The Romans were also very fond of incorporating mazes into the designs of their mosaic pavements. A famous example is in the Casa di Labarinto at Pompeii, and others are recorded from remains of villas in such places as Tunis, Marseille, Salzburg, Paris, and Caerleon in Wales, the latter associated so closely with the legend of King Arthur. The maze design and the maze dance survived into the Middle Ages in Christian churches. On the floors of more than thirty churches and cathedrals existed pavements laid out in the form of elaborate mazes. These holy mazes could be found at Rome, Ravenna, Cremona, Pavia, Piacenza, Chartres, Reims, Amiens, Sens, Bayeux, Poitiers. Sir Giles Gilbert Scott restored a maze on the floor of Ely Cathedral in Cambridgeshire as recently as 1870. What purpose did they serve? No one knows. Perhaps they were *Chemins de Jerusalem;* that is, instead of taking the actual road to Jerusalem as a pilgrim or Crusader, it was possible for a devout worshipper to make the journey in his imagination within the precincts of his own church. Perhaps the church mazes were also associated with the idea of penance. If you were a sinner, you would be instructed to go to the *Chemin de Jerusalem* and follow its winding course on your knees. I suppose there was also the idea of following the tricky and tortuous path through the snares of the world until one found oneself finally arriving at the Gates of Paradise.

During the Renaissance and the *ancien régime,* mazes maintained their popularity. Entire gardens were laid out in the form of labyrinths. In 1560 Lord Burghley built a maze at his estate at Theobalds, and there was another at Hatfield House. Cardinal Wolsey ordered one to be built at his seat at Hampton Court. The present Hampton Court maze dates from 1690 and was described by Daniel Defoe.

Hampton Court maze was tiny in comparison with the French "Labyrinthe de Versailles," designed by the great architect Hardouin-Mansart for Louis XIV. This vast maze was furnished with thirty-nine groups of statuary representing incidents in Aesop's Fables. The statues were worked by hydraulic machinery activated by fourteen water-wheels driving two hundred and fifty pumps. Sarrazin would have loved the Labyrinthe de Versailles. It set the Sun King back half a million dollars in modern money. Unfortunately, it was completely dismantled in

1775—but Jenny Anderton found illustrations of it in a book published in Paris in 1677 and written (appropriately) by Charles Perrault, creator of such fairy tales as that of Cinderella.

I thought the Versailles labyrinth was the model Gabriel would go for. It was ingenious like his time-machines and kinetic sculptures. It was also expensive, and he wanted the El Pardo labyrinth to be expensive, too. It was to be an example of conspicuous consumption. He was prepared to spend three-quarters of a million dollars on his Texas whimsy. But to my surprise, the labyrinth he kept referring to again and again was the most renowned one of all. This was the legendary labyrinth of King Minos at Knossos in Crete. Gabriel had evidently been doing some research on his own account. He was well primed about all aspects of the Cretan legend. It occurred to me that it must have been Crete that had set him off on the subject in the first place. He'd probably heard about it from a friend who'd been cruising around the Mediterranean with a Greek millionaire, or from a magazine article.

He'd accumulated a mine of information about it. He'd even gone to the length of collecting specimens of the twelve or thirteen Cretan coins that feature the labyrinth on their reverse side. Some of them were extremely rare and must have cost him a fortune. He carried them around in his hip pocket. As he talked, he'd produce one and fondle it, smoothing its silver surface with his thumb. He talked constantly of the labyrinth, dwelling on different details of the story. He brought me references about it from Claudian and Catullus. He produced a passage from Apollodorus that stated that it was modeled on the Great Labyrinth of Egypt.

70

Its history was certainly colorful. King Minos' wife was called Pasiphaë, and she conceived a monstrous passion for a beautiful white bull. She got the great artist and artificer Daedalus to fashion a simulacrum of a cow into which she could creep in order to position herself to have intercourse with the bull. She became pregnant and in course of time bore a gigantic creature which was half-man and half-bull. Minos then called upon Daedalus to fashion a place where the creature, called the Minotaur, could be imprisoned, and Daedalus conceived and executed the idea of the labyrinth. Later, a son of Minos called Androgeos was killed by a gang of brigands when he was traveling through Attica on a visit to the mainland. His father thereupon laid upon Aegeus, the King of Athens, a tribute to be paid every nine years. It consisted of seven youths and seven maidens, who were sent to Crete to be shut up in the labyrinth and sacrificed to the Minotaur. On one voyage the freight of doomed youths and maidens included Ariadne, with whom Theseus, a son of King Aegeus, was in love. He sailed to Knossos, entered the labyrinth, and rescued Ariadne by using the famous device of the thread of wool. When he returned to Athens, he forgot to hoist the white sail his father had asked him to raise if his expedition had gone well. When the poor old king saw the black sail, he rushed down the cliffs and threw himself into the sea. The sea has been called the Aegean ever since.

A very dramatic and tragic series of events.

9

IT took a much shorter time to build the thing than you might have thought. It was a job that under other circumstances I'd have liked to dawdle over. It would have been fun to fool around with it. But Texans aren't that sort of clients. They're people in a hurry. And Gabriel for some reason had suddenly become in a greater hurry than most. It seemed he couldn't wait for his new toy to be finished and ready.

We were on very good terms during the nineteen weeks it took me to finish the Great Maze of Texas. We got along very smoothly. He was considerate and courteous and gave me a completely free hand. But for me, at least, it was bound to be an uneasy association. I was glad that for at least twelve of those nineteen weeks he was dodging around the country in his jet, busy with business affairs— principally a merger between Sarrazin Resources and some mammoth printing company in Indiana. I had expected that during his absences Astrid would be more at ease. I hoped that at least we could spend more stolen time together. On the contrary, she was almost as defensive as if he was still in the house, and continued to be petrified that our meetings might be detected by Larry or the other servants. I managed to persuade her to see me a little more frequently—but if I imagined her confidence would increase in proportion to the distance between Gabriel and El Pardo I was disappointed. However, as far as I was concerned, the furtive and frenzied nature of our hours or half-hours together only inflamed my feelings for her and strengthened my determination to carry her off once the maze was finished.

My first step was to decide what type of structure I wanted to design. I had to choose between a maze that was unicursal (that is, with a single twisting path leading to the center) or one that was multicursal (offering a number of different paths dividing up at intervals into two or more branches, most of them going in wrong directions and finishing up in dead ends). Most of the early mazes were unicursal—simple affairs intended for childish amusement and not for taxing the brain. This would not have suited Gabriel at all. This type of maze would have provided his guests with a pleasant little saunter to round off their tour of the penny arcade and the rest of the house. It would have been little more than a stroll along an underground gallery with a number of innocuous features to negotiate on the way.

Gabriel's instructions were quite specific. He pointed out that most of his guests were very shrewd operators who wouldn't mind having their intelligences tickled. It wouldn't even hurt if one or two of them got bogged down or even well and truly lost for a while. Think of important men like Phil Braxton or Bo Lattimer stuck in a maze, roaring and cussing and fit to be tied! Wouldn't that be rich? Of course, not that they'd have anything to worry about. The place would be provided with a whole regiment of devices to reassure people and keep prodding them forward along the right lines.

So I got out a ground plan and went over it with Gabriel in order to get it formally approved. It was a large multicursal labyrinth of complex and symmetrical design, rather like a gigantic subterranean three-dimensional chessboard. In fact it was a highly elaborated version of one of the Cretan labyrinths depicted on Gabriel's coins. It featured steps or ramps leading up and down from one level to the next, some of them shallow and some of them sudden and steep.

I put Wendell Barratt in personal charge of construction. He wasn't particularly happy about it. Not because of the job itself—that was easy. As a serious-minded and somewhat humorless young man he simply couldn't understand why I was postponing work on several important projects to devote my energies to something he considered frivolous and downright crazy. He came from Minnesota and had been brought up to disapprove of Texans. But he never questioned my decisions and contented himself with making a private vow to clear the thing out of the way as speedily as possible.

There weren't many logistical headaches for him to cope with. Gabriel already owned most of the equipment we needed. We only had to employ outside contractors for some of the relatively minor aspects of the job. For example, Gabriel had a fleet of excavators and earth-moving machines at one of his Texas plants. We took down the gates at the entrance to the ranch and widened part of the dirt road through the wood, and the machines duly arrived on their flatbeds from Galveston a day before they were scheduled to go into action. Everything else we asked for reached us with similar promptitude. Wendell was like a dog with two tails. For once, a job went off without a single one of the customary foul-ups. I think it shook even his solid nerves a bit.

The maze was to be situated so deeply under the ground that the platoon of excavators went on gouging away day after day, filling the air with their unholy racket. During the first three weeks, the heavy summer rains I'd encountered on my first visit to El Pardo continued. But this was the time when I was largely occupied with finalizing the design, so it didn't greatly inconvenience us. It didn't seem to worry the machines or their operators. The Euclids and Lubeckers and other metal giants went on tearing great gobbets of soil out of the landscape and spewing them onto the dumpers. The whole area to the west side of the house, acres and acres of it, extending from the west wing right to the far-distant fringe of the pine woods, took on the appearance of a titanic battlefield. Mountains of soil were thrown up over the entire area, as if any army was digging itself in. The dark brown ranges stretched away almost as far as the eye could see. The din was really beyond belief. A huge expanse of lawn, three fruit orchards, and the whole of El Pardo's celebrated rose gardens—a legacy from Gabriel's mother's time—were eliminated, though we intended to replant them when the topsoil was replaced. We meant to bury the maze so far under the earth that no vestige of it would be detectable. There'd be no hint of its existence. Even the vents of the air conditioning and other apparatus would be hidden by groves and bushes. The whereabouts of the great structure would be secret and enigmatic.

I used many of the techniques employed by the special-

ists who build underground garages. The business of preparing the enormous basement-like construction and
pouring the concrete proved to be a colossal undertaking.
The scene at El Pardo must have resembled the scene at
Hawara when the Egyptian masons were building the
Great Labyrinth for the Pharaoh Amenemhat. We also
hit a snag that caused us a good deal of amusement. Some
of our workmen were always getting lost. Before we
capped the maze with its concrete roof, it was easy for
someone to stand on one or other of the fifty-foot-high
towers we erected at intervals around the rim and give
directions to anyone who'd gone astray. If they were very
close to the center, it was a bit more difficult; they were
lost to the view of the men on the towers. Once or twice,
workmen got lost for upwards of an hour, and all we
could hear were their faint yelps as they blundered invisibly
round and round. It was like hearing men drowning far out
at sea. As a rule they were good-humored about it and put
up with the ribbing they got when they emerged. But now
and again an elderly workman or an adolescent one would
lose his head and panic and be finally brought out in a
state of near-collapse. To counter this we rigged up a
thick red cord as a guideline down the central corridors
leading to the exit. A series of blue cords designated the
corridors that fed into the central corridors, and a series of
black cords designated dead ends. All a man had to do was
follow a blue cord until he came to a red one, then follow
that. The system worked very well, and from then on,
only the stupidest workman got lost.

Gabriel's crews were exceptionally well-trained and
well-disciplined, as was to be expected of employees of
Sarrazin Resources. Wendell was a capable organizer, and

as for me—well—I can flatter myself that I'm pretty calm and clear-headed. I devoted a great deal of thought to the material I was going to use to face the raw concrete walls of the network of passageways. Everything was suggested: wood panels, specially treated to withstand the underground damp or warping from the air conditioning; marble, to be imported from quarries outside Tucson; a newly developed light porous brick; and sheets of steel. After carrying out a series of tests, I chose the latter. I'd reckoned that Gabriel might insist on marble, in view of the close associations of the El Pardo labyrinth with Knossos. But he said he welcomed the modern character steel would give it. Moreover, there was a steel company in Trenton that supplied high-grade products to Sarrazin Resources. Mohner and Lewis would give him a good price on the sheets we required—we'd need several miles of it—and turn it out to the specifications we wanted. So Mohner and Lewis received the contract, and six weeks later the first consignments began to trundle down the dirt road across the ranch.

The sheets were beautifully cut and even more beautifully finished. They'd been buffed and re-buffed until their surfaces were as shiny as a mirror. I remember the astonishment and admiration of the crews when they lifted them off the trucks and uncrated them in the sharp summer sunlight, laying them on the raw and roughened ground to one side of the mammoth opening in the earth. They whistled as the glittering squares were removed from their individual wrappings, each team handling them as if they were glass, reverently placing them in ten-foot-high stacks with layers of sacking spread carefully between sheets.

I stayed on the site with Wendell almost continuously,

though once or twice, like Gabriel, I had to go away on business trips. One of our biggest headaches, and one for which we ought to have made more adequate preparation, was the national press and television. When they got wind of it, they came swarming around like bees. This was a project as ambitious and as remarkable in its own way as Buckminster Fuller's astrodome over at Houston. There was bound to be keen public excitement about it. One or two reporters got past the vigilance patrols Gabriel recruited from his factory police, but in the main, security was tight and effective. On the other hand, you can't keep out helicopters, and to Gabriel's intense fury some excellent aerial shots of the maze in its unroofed stage appeared in the papers and magazines. The pressmen called it one of the marvels of the twentieth century, though they couldn't resist some lofty remarks about Texan extravagance and megalomania. One Sunday one of the television networks even carried a thirty-minute special feature gleaned from various snippets. I tried to explain to Gabriel that you can't expect to build an underground structure the size of several football fields without attracting maximum attention. As he became increasingly enraged, his orders to his private police force became harsher. Several too inquisitive reporters got bloody noses and broken cameras. One was severely beaten up.

IO

IT was on one of these final hectic days as the job
was nearing completion that Astrid and I had the
last and most frantic of our meetings. Putting up a building
is always a struggle. This one was no exception. Her presence at El Pardo became a terrible added strain. She was so
close—yet most of the time a million miles away.

We managed to meet in the house or on the estate two or
three times a week. It was easy to exchange whispered
messages when we saw each other every day. We'd snatch
a few minutes together in an out-of-the-way room or in the
sculpture gallery or the summerhouse. There was a secluded spot in the pine woods near the lake that became a
favorite rendezvous. Whenever it was safe to go to the
summerhouse, we went there because it was there we could
make love. It wasn't comfortable or romantic, and all the
time we were aware of the distant noise of the work going
on on the maze, but being under the same roof had given us
a sharp and gnawing sense of physical need.

It was one of these last trips to the summerhouse that
produced the urgency of our final meeting. I'd gone up to
my room hot and sweaty at the end of a working day and
was looking forward to soaking myself in the gold-and-

marble tub. I'd got my jacket and shirt off when the door opened softly and Astrid slipped into the room. She closed the door quietly and ran across the carpet to where I was standing between the bed and the window. She wasn't wearing shoes. She saw my look of surprise. Up to then, we'd always been careful. Coming to my room like this was taking a fearful risk. It was true Gabriel was in Missouri on business, but his three young men would be lurking somewhere in the background. I moved to the window, grasped the cord that closed the curtains, and quickly drew them shut.

Even while I was standing with the cool body in the yellow linen frock in my arms, she was murmuring that she could only stay a minute and would have to leave almost at once.

"Don't worry." I pressed my face into her sweet-smelling hair. "It'll be easy to invent an excuse. What's so unusual about you're coming into my room for a second to ask me something? I'm practically a member of the family by now, aren't I?"

"Darling, I had to see you. I've been looking for a chance to talk to you since Gabriel left. I couldn't seem to escape from Larry."

"Where is he now?"

"Out in the drive. He and the others are helping to unload the furniture Gabriel ordered for the party next week."

"Good. We've got a few minutes."

We exchanged a long, hard kiss. I drew her over to the bed, gently pushed her down, and knelt beside her. She relaxed on the coverlet. It was nearly a week since I'd been able to snatch a few moments with her.

"God . . . I've missed you . . ."

She gave herself up eagerly to an embrace, then stirred and struggled upright.

"No . . . no . . . We must talk . . ."

I let her sit up. Much as I hated it, I had to admit this wasn't the time or place for lovemaking. She looked up at me, eyes troubled. Something was the matter.

"What is it?"

It wouldn't come at once. She laced her hands in her lap and bowed her head. The room was shadowed, now the curtains were drawn. The noise of pile-drivers and jack-hammers filtered in from outside.

Finally she said, "Darling—"

She couldn't go on. I cradled her head against my stomach and stroked her face as you'd stroke a troubled child.

"Please, darling—what is it?"

At last she said, "Darling—"

Another pause.

"Well?"

"I—I think I'm pregnant . . ."

My fingers tightened on her face. Then they relaxed.

Neither of us moved. Finally I got off the bed and knelt in front of her and forced her to unlock her hands. I took them in mine.

"Does Gabriel know?"

She didn't look up. She gave a little doll-like shake of the head.

I picked my words carefully.

"He doesn't?"

Now she looked up at me.

"It isn't his."

I said nothing. She frowned, her eyes searching. Her tongue moistened her dry lips.

"I haven't been—*with* him . . . Anyway, it isn't his, because . . . well . . . it *couldn't* be . . ."

"*Couldn't* be?"

"No."

"How do you mean?"

"I mean he couldn't . . . *can't* . . ."

"*Can't?*"

"No."

It began to sink in.

She said, "Never . . . Not before . . . Or ever . . ."

That was it. The meaning of the years of childlessness. Her sexual exigency. The frenzy and abandonment.

Leonidas . . . glasses of milk . . . little boy in a sailor suit squeezing against an ample female thigh . . .

At that moment I regretted the delicacy that made us avoid talking about Gabriel during our days in Los Angeles and New York. It was something I ought to have known. I should have guessed. I'd done him a worse injury than I'd dreamed of. To deceive a man was one thing . . . To deceive a man who was . . . *well!* At that moment, spraddled there above the bed with my arms around her, I didn't like myself much.

"How long have you known?"

"I'm not sure, even now. I suspected about three weeks ago . . . the end of the month."

"Have you seen anyone?"

"A doctor?"

"Have you?"

She nodded.

"Oh? You have? And?"

"It's too early to be certain." She paused and said in a voice so low I could hardly catch it, "If it's true, you—wouldn't be angry with me?"

"Angry? . . . Delighted!"

"Delighted?"

"Of course! Now you'll have to do what I've been asking you since the spring. You'll have to tell him you're leaving him."

I felt a shudder go through her. She pressed closer against me. I knew that didn't mean she was reluctant to leave him and come to me. But I also knew how unwilling she was to hurt him. So why had she let herself have a child? And at this time? It hadn't occurred to me to ask if she was being careful. I thought being pregnant was the one thing she'd be anxious to avoid. Probably she felt that refusing to go the limit made our relationship small and squalid. All the same, I couldn't help asking myself what sort of a situation I'd unknowingly walked into.

Her lips tightened and trembled.

I went on, "I know you're unhappy about telling Gabriel. I can handle Gabriel."

To my dismay, she started to cry.

"Hey!"

"*Handle Gabriel!*"

Her voice held a note of scorn and fear. My voice hardened.

"Listen, darling—"

"Have you any idea how many men have thought they could 'handle Gabriel'?"

"Look, I'm not an idiot. I've been thinking about things —making plans."

As had happened during almost all our meetings during

the past four months, reproaches began pouring out of her about my taking the job at El Pardo in the first place.

I said, "Darling, what's the use of arguing about all that now?"

She rose and faced me.

"We've got to go away. Tonight."

"Tonight?"

"That's what I came in to tell you."

"Darling, you know there's nothing in the world I'd like to do better. But I'm right in the middle of finishing the—"

"Tonight! Before he gets back."

"Darling, listen to me. There's only another week or so to go. You said yourself the doctor wasn't sure. Why don't we wait at least until after we've had the party?"

"This is the best chance we'll have."

"Look, we can't hide from him, wherever we go. And what difference do another few days make?"

"You sound as if you want to stay? As if you want to attend that silly party?"

"Well, it's to celebrate the end of the job. And it's not just me—it's for my own men and for Gabriel's men. Everyone who's slogged his guts out on it."

She was growing increasingly angry and impatient. I tried to calm her down. We stood there arguing, though instinctively keeping our voices down.

"Listen, darling. The day the party's over—the day after!—we'll tell him together and go away. I promise!"

She accused me of vanity. Perhaps it was. I only knew in a dim sort of way that I was genuinely looking forward to the party. It would round off the whole business. There'd be all my own people and seventy or eighty important guests. I'd already seen a list of the invitations. There'd be representatives from television and the other media. It would be a pretty big occasion. It all goes to show how deeply Gabriel had succeeded in hooking me on the idea of the El Pardo Maze.

Oh, yes, I was looking forward to that party. Really looking forward to it.

II

THE night before the party, just before dinner, I got a call from Evie in Houston. She said she'd been trying to reach me all day. I'd been dodging about all over the enormous site, and she hadn't been able to contact me. Apparently she's left various messages for me at the site office and elsewhere, but I certainly hadn't been handed any of them as I'd dashed in and out, up to my neck in the business of putting the finishing touches to my bizarre masterpiece. The final stages of any large-scale piece of construction are bound to be a hectic rush. Evie said a firm called Ling-Meyers Electronics at San Antonio was anxious to set up an early meeting with me to discuss building a new plant down south on the Texas coast between Harlingen and Brownsville. In the past month I'd talked about it a couple of times on the phone with the Ling-Meyers operations manager, but the whole thing had been desultory and speculative, because nothing could be done until the managing director returned to the United States from Brussels, where he had been setting up a European subsidiary. It seemed that he had now gotten back to Texas and within twenty-four hours of his arrival was fuming and fussing about his new plant. He wanted to see

86

me urgently—next day, in fact. By this time I'd gotten used to this Texas precipitancy, and the chance to work for a growing concern like Ling-Meyers, whose shares had recently been quoted on the New York Stock Exchange, was not one I wanted to pass up.

It so happened that I had tidied up most of the odds and ends at El Pardo that day, so as we were going into dinner, I asked Gabriel if he would mind my slipping down to San Antonio the next morning. I assured him that Wendell Barratt was well equipped to look after everything and that I'd take care to be back in good time for the party. He was very understanding about it—positively gracious—and said that of course I must go. He was very interested in the project, as Sarrazin Enterprises had an interest in Ling-Meyers. He made a lot of shrewd suggestions and asked a lot of questions, though at this early stage there wasn't much that I could tell him. As soon as dinner was over, I got back to Evie and told her to call the managing director and the plant manager at the numbers they'd given her and let them know I'd meet them at their head office in San Antonio sometime in mid-morning.

The distance between Gabriel's ranch, south of Dallas, and San Antonio was less than two hundred and fifty miles on Interstate 35. In the Maserati I could eat it up—and in fact recently I'd been driving, when I was between towns and out of range of the local sheriffs, with unusual recklessness. What is the use of having a car that will touch 180 if you plug along at 70 the whole time? I daresay I was using the Maserati to drain off some of the frustration I was undergoing with Astrid at El Pardo. Anyway, I was in conference with the Ling-Meyer people on New Braunfels Street just before eleven, and remained shut up with them there till well after four. It was an intensive session, with no incoming calls and only coffee and sandwiches for lunch. I felt fairly done in at the end of it and was glad to tear myself away and scoot back to El Pardo. Macdonald Fraser, the managing director, was a nice enough man, but a bit of an old woman. He seemed determined to keep me there as long as possible, even though I kept looking pointedly at my watch and hinting that it was time for me to leave.

The weather was thundery and overcast as I drove up the long approach to the house, as it had been when I first came to El Pardo, though it wasn't actually raining. The dirt driveway, inside the point where the steel posts of the ornamental gateway lay dismantled by the side of the path, was still cut up and rutted by the giant wheels of the trucks and flatbeds that had hauled the materials and machinery to the site. The night had set in black and close by the time I swung to a stop in front of the portico. It was six o'clock, and the party wasn't to begin till nine. All the same, I was surprised to find the wide area around the entrance was devoid of cars and people. After all, even if Gabriel and Astrid had restricted the number of guests to between eighty and a hundred, many of them were celebrities. They were to include two ex-Governors of Texas, a Hungarian opera singer who had just married the richest oilman in Wichita Falls, the owner of the Dallas Cowboys, the owner of the two largest hotels in Houston, two members of the King family, and the president of Baylor. I would have expected a throng of cameramen and reporters, and a horde of technicians setting up loads of equipment. This was the night that Gabriel had promised the media that he would come through with the information and the big story for

88

which they had been needling him. I'd have thought they would have been getting ready since mid-afternoon. However it was still early, and no doubt Gabriel had made his arrangements with the people involved. They'd be along soon.

Gabriel's young men appeared with their usual creepy promptitude to park the Maserati for me. Somehow I imagined that they'd have more important things to attend to on this particular night. As usual, one of them carried my briefcase up to my room and made sure I had everything I needed. In the last five months it had all become such routine procedure that I'd been lulled into a state of mind where I thought nothing dramatic was ever likely to happen. I was guilty of letting down my guard because I thought it was the last round and foolishly fancied I was well ahead on points.

I took my time about showering and shaving and putting on my evening clothes. Oddly enough, I had an unexpected feeling of melancholy now that the end of the job was in sight. There is always a sense of loss and let-down at the completion of a big project. Even so, I was dressed and ready by seven and wasn't sure whether I ought to skulk in my room for a while or go downstairs and hang around. I had half been expecting Wendell Barratt to call me, but he hadn't. What finally decided me was my need for a drink. As a rule, either Larry or one of the others would have brought in a martini, a silver tray with a frosted glass on it, and a small pitcher of the famous El Pardo brew. Tonight, after a five-hundred-mile drive and a day-long session with the finicky Fraser, I found myself compelled to wait in vain. I was growing thirsty. I went over to the window and pulled back the drapes and stared out at the dark trees and somber sky for a while. It was beginning to rain. I could hear the first heavy drops. At last I decided that the chances of getting a drink, or pouring myself one, were a lot brighter downstairs. I also thought I might as well cast a discreet eye over the preparations that had been made. When all was said and done, to some extent I was the evening's main attraction. Gabriel had conceived and financed the El Pardo Maze, but I had designed and executed it. I stood in front of the mirror and fiddled with my evening tie and felt proud and increasingly excited.

Walking slowly down the broad sweep of the main staircase, I was astonished to see how empty the house was. Quarter after seven. Less than two hours to go. Wasn't Gabriel leaving it a little late? If I hadn't known how efficient he was, how he would have everything under control down to the tiniest detail, I would have been faintly worried. But trust Gabriel—he wouldn't leave anything to chance. Still, I would have thought there'd be hired waiters and maids and bartenders scurrying about. Larry and his friends were extremely capable, and it was remarkable that they ran the whole house by themselves except for the sizable but always invisible kitchen staff. I had often seen the three of them cope easily with a dozen dinner guests—but tonight was different, a large and important occasion, and I had imagined that Gabriel would have drafted in a whole battalion of supernumeraries to lend them a hand.

I wandered into the drawing room. All the lights were on, and it shone with a hard, shadowless brightness. It was totally empty. A fire—a real fire of big blazing logs—was burning in the fireplace, a large recess in the wall normally covered by a panel that slid up and down at the touch of a button. A fire was completely unnecessary in a house that was more than adequately furnished with every kind of heating and cooling: but the night outside showed signs of being raw and damp, and I sauntered down the enormous room to warm myself beside the comforting flames. There is something primitive about a fire that is reassuring.

I stood there for two or three minutes; then, undecided and growing restless, I thought I would take a look at the dining room. There an elaborate buffet would have been laid out. I started to make my way toward the door at the far end that led to the corridor that would take me to the dining room. Beside the door was the weird painting of the man and woman in classical costumes running for their lives beneath the menace of the volcano. I had nearly reached the door when I heard an echoing footstep at the other end of the room. I turned around. Astrid had just descended the stairs and was crossing the polished parquet of the hallway toward the high double doors of the drawing room.

She was dressed in a simple white gown with a wide gold belt and golden trimming. Her pale yellow hair was upswept and fastened with gold combs. She wore no jewelry. She looked pale but composed, and I thought I had never seen her look so beautiful. I was reminded of the first time I saw her, at Patti Danziger's party ten months before, and my heart turned over in exactly the same way that it had then. I watched her walk toward me and wanted to run to her and take her in my arms. That would have been imprudent—but if someone had been in the room, he must have seen my naked feelings showing in my face. I went as far as to take hold of her hand and draw her over to the fire. There I could look at her without anyone noticing.

Speaking quietly, I told her how lovely she was. She

dropped my hand and stared quickly around as if the whole huge room was filled with eyes and ears. I saw she wanted me to change the subject.

I asked, "Where is everybody? I thought they'd be rolling up in droves by now. Has Gabriel decided to postpone things for an hour or two?"

She frowned. "Postpone things? No, I don't think so."

"You don't know?"

"Gabriel hasn't told me much about it."

"You helped arrange it all, didn't you?"

"Only part of it. He asked me to order the food and wine, and go over the guest list with him."

"But you've been busy with it all today, haven't you?"

"I would have been, but there wasn't any need."

"No need?"

"Gabriel said that Larry and the others would look after it."

"I suppose you attended to setting the tables, and the glass and silver and flowers, and the rest of it?"

"I didn't, actually."

"No?"

"Larry told me it was all being taken care of."

I examined her carefully as she stood looking down into the fire, with the flames throwing crimson splotches on her white face and whiter dress. Her manner was offhand and listless. I realized that once again she had fallen victim to that awful mood of fatality that took hold of her whenever she was at El Pardo. It was as if she was afflicted by some sort of sleeping sickness. It always angered me and made me feel helpless, particularly since I could never see the justification for it. As a man of business, Gabriel was a powerful and formidable figure; everyone acknowledged that. But in a private and personal capacity, apart from his obvious eccentricities, he had done practically nothing to alarm or offend me. Given the situation Astrid and I were in, it was sensible to treat him with caution. Other than that, I rather liked him. What particularly infuriated me was to compare Astrid in this zombie frame of mind with the vital and passionate woman I had known in New York and Los Angeles. However, there was no use saying anything about it. She wouldn't come alive again till I took her away from El Pardo. So I held my tongue.

"Let's go into the dining-room," I suggested. "I'd like to see how Larry and his friends have coped. And I might be able to steal a sandwich. I'm starving."

She looked up, the firelight tangling like a red snake in the piled-up masses of her blonde hair. Then all at once she smiled—a warm, animated, brilliant smile that made my blood leap. She leaned forward and laid her hand on my cheek and kissed me on the lips. We stood there motionless, lapped in the glow of the flames. At last she broke away. I was conscious of an immense relief and happiness.

Again I took her hand and led her away from the fireplace in the direction of the drawing room. Then my eye fell on the tray of drinks standing on a long table under a curtained window on the other side of the room.

"First things first," I said. "What I can really do with is a drink." I started to walk across the room toward the table. "I expect you can, too."

I had almost reached the table when Larry suddenly walked through one of the other doors, carrying a silver salver with the long-awaited pitcher filled with straw-colored liquid. It was almost as if he had been watching me from the doorway and waiting for the moment when I stretched out my hand toward one of the decanters before making his entrance. When I saw the pitcher, I stopped and smiled. I was very partial to martinis mixed according to Gabriel's patent formula. I had drunk enough of them in the last five months to appreciate them.

Surprisingly, Larry still wore the black blazer and red sweater that were his everyday garb. I had expected that by this time he would have changed into something more formal. However, he was exceedingly agreeable in the way he ushered us to the sofa and installed us there, one at each end. He served us our drinks with a little flourish. I looked at Astrid and raised my glass in a covert toast.

I asked Larry, "You're cutting things pretty close, aren't you? When are the guests arriving?"

He stood with the pitcher at his side, his body inclined slightly forward.

He said politely, "Oh, I think you'll find we've made all our preparations, sir."

He was watching us intently. I thought it was strange that he was lingering in the drawing room instead of simply serving the martinis and leaving. He must have had a great deal to do. And it was probably at that moment, when I was already half-way through that welcome first drink, that it broke in on me that something was wrong. It was all too pat.

Why were we dressed up in our evening clothes, and no sign of any other guests?

I reached out to put my glass on the small table at the head of the sofa. My movement was so strangely stiff and clumsy I hit the bottom of the slender-stemmed glass on the edge of the table and snapped it off. Both halves of the glass dropped on the carpet, spraying out the last remaining drops. I stared at them numbly. On the table was the chessboard with the glittering steel chessmen. It occurred to me in a bemused way that a regular game was in progress, just as one had been on the first night that I ever set foot in this drawing room. My brain seemed fuddled— but it was still clear enough to register that the king on the row of squares nearest me was pinned in what looked like an unbreakable check by a ring of opposing pieces. The queen, too, was about to be removed from the board.

There was a roaring in my ears. I turned toward Astrid. All I could see was a gold-and-white blur. I looked up at Larry. His features were hazy, but I realized that he was standing in the same attentive, predatory pose. I tried to rise. My legs wouldn't obey me. I struggled harder. Nothing. It was as if I was paralyzed. My tongue felt swollen and tender and fiery.

Checkmate . . .

The effort to get up unbalanced me. I have a dim memory of toppling forward, flinging out a hand as I did so, catching the leg of the table, and bringing it crashing down beside me. The steel chessmen fell all around me with a curious effect of slow motion, describing elegant lazy arcs in the air and scattering on each side of me like a shower of meteorites.

As I lay on the carpet, it seems to me that my vision cleared for a second or two. There was an instant of pristine clarity. The drawing room appeared vast and cavernous, and the ceiling was receding, and everywhere there was a high continuous ringing noise like a million martini glasses breaking. Gabriel's face—grinning—hung in the air above me. Far away, behind his pendulous head, I could see two white-clad forms, bodies fused together and hair streaming, fleeing through a landscape like a dream. I thought it was very curious that Gabriel, like Larry, wasn't dressed for the party, but was still wearing workaday clothes. I wanted to get up and urge him to go and get ready—but the lights were fading. I tried to shout. Blackness was washing over me like a great pitchy wave. As I went under and drowned, I thought I felt a terrific blow in the side . . . then another . . . and another . . . another . . . anoth . . . ano . . . an . . . a . . .

12

. . . Sensation of choking and burning . . . dream
. . . nightmare . . .

Black. Black. Black.

. . . What's that music all the time? Some sort of crazy
waltz?

Why am I lying in my shirt and trousers? And my
mouth—sore, as if it's been punched? And my ribs—as if
someone's been kicking me?

Up. Get up. Slowly.

Weak. Very weak. Legs like water. Take it easy. Try
and crawl a couple of feet.

Head's full of smoke . . .

Here. Yes. That's it. That's the wall.

Grope my way along. Gently. Surface is freezing. Use
fingertips. Keep body away.

Ah, that choking sensation . . . burning . . . smothering . . . smothering and burning . . .

That damned music! If you can call it music. Lot of
noise and distortion. *One-two-three. One-two-three.
One-two-three.*

Legs like rubber. Certainly could do with a nice cool—
Blast!

Slipped. Lost balance. Bumped wall.

Cold. Hard. Fingers sliding.

Hand's coated with sweat. Feel it dribbling down my wrist.

Bloody dream! Bloody nightmare!

Won't panic. Won't panic. Won't panic.

Head's still woozy. Blackness keeps churning in front of me. Tar bubbling in a cauldron. Something horrible about dragging yourself along like an animal. God almighty, this thirst. And still the soreness round my mouth and ribs.

Stupid waltz. Hammering. Hammering. Hammering. Hammering.

. . . Could I be dead? Is that it?

. . . Limbo? . . . Hell? . . . Or some sort of tunnel? . . . Something we've all got to crawl through after we die?

Die? . . . So confused . . . sleepy . . . How could I have died? . . . All the rain and slush? . . . Don't remember anything like that . . . Surely something of that kind—Maserati skidding—other car or tree or side of bridge or white face sliding toward you at a hundred and thirty . . . Bloody smash . . . Agony . . . Surely I'd have remembered that?

. . . Can't pretend any more I don't feel panic . . . Sour taste . . . Sweat on my body smells acid . . .

I've got a sense I'm not alone in this tunnel, or whatever it is.

I've got a definite feeling there's someone else. Someone crawling behind me.

God almighty, it's growing lighter! Only a softening of the darkness. But it's lighter. Black ice beginning to snap and melt. Darkness dissolving like chocolate in a pan.

Relax. Slacken your limbs and empty your mind and

hoard your strength and wait for the moment when the light is—

My God—there *is* someone else! I can *see* him! Over there! Another man! *The* other man! The one who's been following me—crawling after me!

Shout!

HEY! You there—!

He's moving. Crawling toward me. On all fours. Like a dog. Big dazed draggled dog. Is he vicious? Coming close—!

HEY! . . . !

Good God—*laughing* now. Hear him laughing. *Myself* laughing.

Me!

Just light enough to see that he's *ME!*

Reflection. Sheets of polished steel. Mohner and Lewis. Buffed like a mirror.

Hair over sweaty forehead. Eyes burning fever. Shirt. Trousers. No socks. No shoes.

Can make out the whole corridor now. Very long and very wide. Very high. Beige carpeting. Lights in slits high up in the wall. Convex lenses of the all-seeing eyes. Square glass indicators of the emergency guiding system.

Which way am I going? Toward the entrance? Toward the center?

Corner. Corner. Don't know what good I'm doing just aimlessly walk——

Astrid!

13

ASTRID!

When I saw her sitting on the floor, her back propped against the steel wall, I knew I wasn't going to wake up. I wasn't going to wake up because I hadn't been asleep. Everything clicked into focus. There hadn't been any nightmare. It wasn't any bad dream I'd been having. The dream wasn't a dream at all. The dream was real.

WE WERE—IN THE MAZE!

Astrid was slumped down in an attitude of despair. She looked sick and defeated. She didn't hear me approach because of the thickness of the carpet (oh, no, her husband hadn't spared any expense!). She didn't see me because her head was turned away, lolling on her shoulder as if her neck had snapped. Her fair hair, which had been elaborately arranged, broke and fell in an untidy wave across her face. She wore only a silver-colored negligee, and her legs and feet were bare. On her finger was the sapphire ring from Van Cleef and Arpels.

I knelt down in front of her. Her eyes were closed. I could smell a sharp perfume on her skin. Her lipstick and mascara had been carefully applied, but the sweat on her face had smudged them. I was afraid of frightening her. When I put out a hand and touched her naked shoulder, I did so as lightly as I could. No response. My own heart was beating fast, and I was in a state of semi-shock. I still hadn't recovered from the terror of waking to a state of things more fantastic than any I could have experienced in a dream. I cupped my hands beneath her chin and pulled her head sharply toward me.

Her eyelids fluttered and opened. She gave a little weak gasp.

I leaned forward. She shrank away, as if the rapidly brightening light was hurting her eyes.

My voice was like a stranger's. It was harsh and remote, and I could hardly believe that it was mine.

"It was you? In the darkness? It was you I could hear?"

I had to wait for what seemed hours before she answered.

"I guessed it was you . . ." Her voice was as different-sounding as mine. "I tried to keep up . . . You were going so fast . . ."

My head was throbbing. I squeezed my eyes shut and kneaded the nape of my neck. I had to throw off this dizziness. I had to start thinking clearly.

She sat upright. Suddenly there was a harder, if still trembling, note in her voice.

"I told you! Didn't I tell you? Would you listen to me? Didn't I beg you to be careful?"

I lowered myself to the carpet, watching her. She was still drowsy, but a little more awake now. Like me, she was starting to snap out of what she must have taken for her own bad dream. I tried to sound reasonable, but my voice was still shaking.

"Darling, I *was* careful. I never said a word or gave a hint—"

"I tried to warn you! I did! Didn't you realize the risks we were running?"

I reached forward and caught her arms. They were sweaty and clammy. I gripped them fiercely.

"We'll get out of this—"

"How? You imagine he hasn't thought of everything? Every twist and turn? You don't know him!"

"We'll get *OUT* of this!"

"Remember what you said?—about 'handling Gabriel'? Well—Gabriel's handling *YOU!*"

"Good God, does the man really think he can ever get away with anything as mad as—"

"He *is* mad! Don't you see? He *is* mad! Do you think I've lived with him all this time and I don't know? Do you think I didn't know it when I was a girl and his vicious old father swindled us and drove us out of El Pardo? Didn't you see I was doing everything I could to—"

I shook her.

"Listen! If he thinks he's going to scare us—"

"You think he only means to *scare* us?"

"*Listen*, will you? This is just another of his silly stunts, that's all. Another of his silly tricks."

"If you think it's just a—"

"Do you honestly think he'd risk everything? Sarrazin Resources? Throw everything away?"

"He'll have *considered* all that!"

Her words brought back to me the memory of the computer on the top floor. I remembered the bright metal chessmen in the drawing room.

When she started to talk hysterically, I shook her again to silence her.

"All right! Perhaps he *is* mad. But I promise when we get out of here—"

"Get out of here? We aren't going to get out of here!"

"I wish you'd *listen* to me—!"

"You know what he's done? He's made you build a trap for yourself! Build a tomb for yourself! For both of us!"

She started to laugh. I felt my face go cold.

Rats . . . in mazes . . .

I scrambled to my feet and looked down at her. I was frightened, but angry, too.

"We're wasting time and energy. The sooner we give this thing some thought, the sooner we'll be out of here. The sooner I can tell that maniac—"

She heaved her body upright against the wall and shouted, "There's nothing you'll tell him! Nothing! Ever!"

"Oh, come on, darling—this is simply one of his sick jokes!"

I tried to smile. But I knew she was right. Automatically I lifted my eyes and looked at the ceiling. In contrast to the brilliant metal walls the rough-cast concrete of the ceiling had been painted a jet black. Set into the center was the round eye of one of the scanners. The ceiling was five feet thick. It was reinforced, stressed with steel mesh, crisscrossed by internal ducts that carried wires for the heating and lighting and dozens of other things. And on top of the five feet of concrete was eight feet of red Texas earth. I'd had the mountains of soil from the excavations shoveled back into place by the squadron of bulldozers. I'd had them flattened and rolled and tamped down ready to be sown with grass seed and planted with shrubs.

She was following my glance. She'd often visited the site and seen what was going on. The same thoughts were going through her mind, too. I cursed myself for accidentally underscoring the full misery of the jam we were in. From now on, I'd have to try to stop reminding her of the basic horror of the situation.

A muscle in her neck was quivering like a tiny animal. I reached down and took hold of her hands. Like her arms, they were clammy, in spite of the fact that the temperature down here was warm. She got up and followed me down the corridor. She walked almost meekly and dragged one bare foot after the other. All at once she stopped.

"What time is it?"

I didn't answer. I kept urging her along.

"What *time* is it?!"

It was a pointless question. What difference did it make what time it was? Anyway, I didn't know. It could be morning, afternoon, or midnight. There *was* no time down here. The only time that existed was the time it would take us to die.

I'll confess that at that moment I was tempted to give up the idea of struggling and fighting back. I was still weak. Why inflict on ourselves all that pointless torture? Wouldn't it be less painful to lie down in the corridor and wait for the end? Gabriel held every one of the cards. He'd thought it all through. He'd had the nineteen weeks it took us to build the maze to make his plans foolproof. Probably he'd been working on the idea for months before that. Somehow he must have found out about Astrid and me.

I was bruised in body and mind. I knew now the pain in

my mouth and chest were the result of a desultory beating-up I must have received when I was lying unconscious, either down here or upstairs in the drawing room. A few casual contemptuous kicks in the face and ribs. Touching these painful spots, I was suddenly aware of the first stirrings of the desire to hit back. I wouldn't let him get away with it. He'd better make sure I never got out of here, because if I did, I was going to make him sorry he'd ever picked up that phone and called me at South Main Street.

Astrid was asking what time it was because she was trying to orientate herself. She was groping toward reality. A healthy sign. The first step was to start thinking rationally. We'd go back to the beginning and try to unravel what had happened. It would make us feel we'd got back on a logical track.

I was guiding her down the corridor. I wanted to reach a point where we'd be out of range of the scanners in the ceiling. Also out of range of the sensitive microphones associated with them. The scanners were placed at strategic intervals. Usually there was one to a corridor, but in some of the longer corridors there were two, one at each end. There was usually a slight gap in the middle where the scanners failed to overlap. I was pretty certain someone—Gabriel or Larry—was watching us. If I couldn't stop them watching us, at least I could get us more or less out of earshot.

I whispered to her to keep her voice down. The inane music was still blaring out. Now it was a bright Strauss-type polka. Probably Gabriel had made his selections precisely because of their incongruity and irony. Well, it would serve to drown what we were saying to each other. I squatted down and motioned to her to do the same.

I said quietly, "He knocked us out with those martinis." Again I caught the mingled smell of sweat and perfume. I smoothed the fair hair from her cheeks and forehead.

She raised her head. She saw the bruising around my swollen mouth and put out a hand to touch it.

"It's all right," I said. "They didn't hit me too hard. They wanted to save me for . . . well!" I stroked her hand.

She spoke in a thick whisper. "The party . . ."

I gave a grim nod. "The party. He had it all worked out, didn't he?"

It was easy to see how he'd outmaneuvered us. It had been childishly simple. Now I understood only too well why there hadn't been any cars and reporters in the drive, and why there hadn't been any signs of preparation, and why there hadn't been any guests, and why Larry and Gabriel hadn't bothered to change. I saw why Larry had appeared so opportunely with his silver tray.

Probably there had never really been any party in the first place. The party had never existed. It was a fiction, a make-believe. Yes—but those invitations? Astrid and I had handled the actual invitations ourselves. They had been specially printed over a month in advance. They were large, handsome, deckle-edged, engraved in golden script on a thick creamy card. The invitations had definitely existed. Yes—and they were fakes. I remembered the big printing corporation up in Indiana where Gabriel had recently been spending so much of his time discussing a merger. He'd probably had the invitations run off privately, on the side. Most likely, they'd never actually been mailed; but if they had—just to make the hoax look entirely authentic—he had only to call up the people involved at the last minute and say the opening was canceled or postponed because of ill-

ness or a last-minute hitch. I'd left the whole thing to him—
it was his affair—and simply jotted down the date in my
diary. Then, as a last consummate touch, he'd arranged to
have me called away from El Pardo on the very day of the
supposed party. That way he could get rid of Wendell Barratt and anybody else who'd worked with me on the project, so that they wouldn't be able to tip me off or see what
was happening when I got back from San Antonio. I remembered that Sarrazin Resources had an interest in Ling-
Meyers. Probably he'd been instrumental in encouraging
Macdonald Fraser to inveigle me down to San Antonio.
No doubt he'd also found a good excuse to send off the
kitchen staff, leaving just him, Larry, and the two others
to handle the business alone. For the first time, I began to
see just how crafty and thorough he was, and what crazy
lengths he was willing to go to. Astrid had been right about
him all along, and I'd been a blind idiot.

Huddled there on the carpet, I sorted out the probable
course of events. There were a few unavoidable gaps, but
I felt that, evil as the picture was, I was giving myself a
solid foundation to build on. I forced myself to think the
thing through. At least it would stop me feeling that my
troubles, bad though they were, hadn't been inflicted on
me by a supernatural agency, but by a human being like
myself. It reminded me that Astrid and I weren't the victims of divine retribution, but the victims of Gabriel Sarrazin. Trying to reconstruct what had happened re-estab-
lished the sense of continuity and got me going again. I had
to get my mind in motion if I was to work out a plan of
action.

Astrid watched me without saying a word.

"All the same," I said to her at last, "I can see why he'd

want to do this to *me*. But you? What pleasure can he get out of dragging you down here with me, kicking and screaming?"

She pulled herself up, looking rather shocked by the idea I had presented to her.

"I don't know." She shook her head. "I don't understand. It's hard to explain—but he's always been—well—." She hesitated.

"Been what?" I said.

"So—gentle—," she said. "So—tender. Even during these last few weeks."

"Gentle?" I asked.

"Yes."

"Tender?"

She was roused by the irony. She said, "Yes! Even though he . . . well! . . . even though he . . . couldn't . . ."

I said abruptly, "What about tonight, then? Why did he put a little pill in your drink, as he did in mine?"

Again she shook her head, frowning, confused, trying to work it out.

I quickly saw that there was no point in disturbing her by going on with this negative line of talk. What did it matter why she was down here? She was. That was the reality of the matter.

I said: "Darling, listen. I want you to sit here while I go and check on something."

"Check?"

"I've got to walk a slight distance . . . only thirty or forty yards . . . but I'll have to leave this corridor and go into the next one."

"You mean—leave me here?"

"Don't worry, we won't get separated."

"Please, darling—don't go . . . "

"Honestly, it won't be for more than a minute—"

She was agitated and tried to get up. I had to force her to stay where she was. I told her to keep her voice down and repeated that I wouldn't be long. I didn't blame her for feeling terrified. The previous week, Gabriel had brought her down here to show it to her. He'd told her funny stories about the workmen who'd gotten lost. At one point he'd pretended he'd lost his own bearings and couldn't find the way. Considering what he already had in store for her, he must have spent a very amusing afternoon.

I could have taken her with me easily enough. But I wanted to try out the emergency devices. If they weren't functioning, I wanted to spare her the added sense of hopelessness that would result. I hurried down the corridor and turned the corner. I was confronted with a fan-like junction of three corridors, all of them stretching wide, bright, empty, inviting—and treacherous. I stopped and considered. Easy enough to promise Astrid I wouldn't get lost. I resolved that I wouldn't go too far. I'd give up as soon as there looked like complications. I took the left-hand corridor.

To my relief, a few yards down on the right-hand side I found what I was looking for. On a small red-painted panel on the wall was a shiny black button. Eighteen inches above it were two small glass squares. When you pressed the button, a light came on behind one of the squares, either a green light or a red light. On each light was an arrow, one pointing one way, one the other. Anyone who was lost or felt anxious could press the button. The green light showed him he was on the right path, and the green arrow showed him which way to go. If the red light came on, the red arrow sent him back the way he'd come, in the direction of the previous button. He kept on pressing buttons until he found the right one.

I pressed the black button.

Nothing.

I had expected that.

If anyone became completely muddled and started to lose his nerve, he could press one of the alarm buttons. These were red buttons that set off a buzzer in the anteroom upstairs. Someone was always supposed to be on duty up there at the control panel when the maze was occupied. The controller then acted to guide the person concerned out of the maze as quickly as possible, switching on the microphone system to do so. Naturally, it was considered a confession of failure to push the alarm. It was regarded as chickening out. Gabriel would treat anyone who begged to be led out of the maze with merciless jocularity. The person concerned would never be allowed to live it down.

I pressed the red button.

Nothing.

Dead.

Press.

Nothing.

Dead.

Obviously Gabriel had been making meticulous preparations. He hadn't overlooked any of the minor details.

14

I was standing there, dejected, staring at the useless red button, when I heard Astrid's voice. She was calling my name in a frantic way that told me she must be running. I swung around in the direction her voice was coming from. I was afraid she might run down the wrong path at the junction and we'd get separated. That was the principal fear that was bound to haunt us.

I barely reached the corner of the corridor when she ran into my arms. I caught her and held her fast. She dug her face into my shoulder, and I put my face against her hair, hard and springy with lacquer, trying to calm her down.

"Darling . . . it's all right . . . I was coming back . . . another minute and I'd—"

I broke off as I felt her suddenly go rigid in my arms. There was a violent ear-splitting electronic wail from the loudspeakers: a high-pitched, nerve-scraping squeal. It was so fiendish-sounding it made us catch our breath.

It lasted ten long seconds, then stopped. Dead silence. For the first time, there was no music. Complete absence of sound. The silence was so dense and palpable I'd almost have welcomed the return of the brittle music of the waltz.

We waited.

A voice came over the speaker. At first it was distorted;

then the level was adjusted until it came through crystalline and sibilant.

Gabriel spoke slowly.

"Well . . . well . . . well! . . ."

He was making what immediately struck me as a highly unnatural attempt at self-control.

"As you both know, I'm not fond of parties. Still, I'm not a spoilsport, either. I like to see people enjoying themselves. So why should I rob you of the pleasure of your little party? We'll have a little private celebration party of our own, shall we?"

Astrid was beginning to tremble. I folded my arms around her more tightly.

"I don't intend to bore you with any long speeches . . ."

Suddenly he spoke her name. The syllables came out like two cracks of a pistol. She jumped.

"What attracted you to your friend there? His good looks? His cleverness? If he's so clever, let's see how he's going to help you now, shall we?"

The metal walls made his voice whine eerily.

"*You* weren't very clever, were you, my dear?"

She was about to cry out. I pressed my hand over her mouth. I knew this was going to be a war of attrition. We'd last only as long as we could stop him breaking our nerve.

"Shall I tell you how you slipped up? Shall I tell you how many mistakes you made? That little business in Los Angeles—when someone got into your friend's house and stole a television set? Did you really think that was due to a thief or a casual prowler? And those meals in the restaurant at Malibu, or the walks on the beach at Ventura? Did you imagine you wouldn't be followed?"

She moved in my arms. I kept my hand in place and

gripped her more firmly. I wasn't going to let her plead or argue with him. I knew in my bones there wasn't much point. It had all gone much too far for him to turn us loose.

"And what about your visit to New York? You think it wasn't easy to find out where you were? To hire someone to check on your trips to museums, concerts, restaurants? And how about that sapphire ring you've got on your finger? How did I find out about that? No, I didn't look in your jewel case. You didn't quite reduce me to that. Your cousin Donna told me. Not intentionally. Blurted it out, in her usual chatty way. Told me how generous I was to be always buying you jewels like that. So I checked up on that, too. How many stores do you think there are that sell sapphires of that size?"

Astrid had relaxed as the monologue went on. Cautiously I removed my hand. I then did something that surprised her. I kissed her. I pulled her hard against me, crushed my mouth on hers, and held it there while Gabriel went on talking. He spoke more quickly now. The self-control was wearing thin. I'd never heard him like that. I could have sworn that for once he'd spiked his glass of milk with gin or vodka. Strangely enough, his speech didn't fill me with increased fear, but with a sense of elation. He was making his first tactical error.

"Of course, once I'd encouraged Donna to gossip—it doesn't take much doing—other things came out, too. Who made that stupid remark about the husband being the last to know? You imagine I didn't discover why you sneaked off three days ago to Dallas to see that Doctor Richtersveld?"

He was beginning to sound overwrought and confused, unable to control the intensity of his emotion. He was directing his monologue only to Astrid. He couldn't bring himself to acknowledge my existence. He was going to wipe me out like one of his tin soldiers.

Then he did an extraordinary thing. He stopped talking and started to play back the tape of a series of conversations. At first, I didn't recognize the voices. A man and a woman were exchanging disjointed remarks with long gaps in between. " . . . *Don't touch it! . . . Set off the WHAT? . . . Find it? He MADE it! . . . Isn't his because it—well—COULDN'T be . . . I mean he COULDN'T—CAN'T . . .*" Then I knew what it was. It was a composite tape of the conversations I'd had with Astrid in the previous weeks. Conversations in the summerhouse, the sculpture gallery, the drawing room, my bedroom. He'd had the whole damned place wired. He'd known what was going on right from that first afternoon.

I could imagine him seated up there in the control room. I'd had the steel bars in the vault removed, and it was now a pleasant room, most of it taken up by the giant control panel. I'd kept the massive steel door and the time lock. They looked mysterious and intriguing. The panel contained the warning lights and alarm buzzer, the speaker system and television screen. It also incorporated a special system in which beads of light moved around a plan of the maze, showing the operator how any or all of the people inside were making progress.

Gabriel would be sitting there, glowering at the screen, preparing to go on mouthing his diatribe into the microphone. On the wall behind, I could visualize the mounted heads of a row of stags he'd stalked and shot surrounded by the antlers of a host of smaller horned animals. Beneath was a pedestal with a bronze statue of a Texas longhorn steer.

He'd had it brought down from his study to ornament the control room.

He allowed the tape to run through to the end, even though it must have caused him bitter torment. For some reason, he hadn't even cut out passages recording our love-making in the belvedere. But hardly was it finished when his voice came pouring back through the microphone, thick and agitated. Trying to cling to a last pathetic shred of control, he abused and threatened us. There followed a turbid passage about how the Sarrazins clung to their own, how nobody had ever taken away from them anything that was theirs. Then came a garbled rigmarole about divorce. There'd be no divorce. He went on and on about divorce. I realized he was terrified at the prospect of the legal proceedings and the personal revelations that might get dragged out in public. That was why he was now making quite certain that the only two people in the world who knew those intimate private details would never be able to open their mouths. It was curious to hear a definite note of appeal and suffering in the way he talked to Astrid. He was a little boy in a tantrum stamping and dancing on his favorite toy.

Then he started to weep. His voice was shaken by sobs. The microphone enlarged it to a primitive screech. At any other time it would have been embarrassing; now it was frightening. Astrid and I stared at each other at a loss. I put my finger to my lips and motioned her to keep quiet. I reached down for her hand, grasped it, and drew her away in the direction of the corridor we'd been standing in originally. While he'd been talking I'd been trying to use my brains, striving to think of something constructive. And I'd noticed something encouraging. Gabriel was shouting about a red thread—about us not having a red thread to help us now. He sounded on the verge of going out of his mind. He seemed on the point of exhaustion, and it was at this stage his voice began to die away, as if he couldn't go on any longer. And as his voice tailed off, so the lights began to dim. It was almost imperceptible, but both of us noticed it.

I hurried her along more rapidly.

She said breathlessly, "Where are we going?"

I'd happened to notice that the chrome ring around one of the tell-tale eyes in the ceiling above us had been cheap and rough in texture. That told me one thing: that we couldn't be far from the entrance. The light was growing dimmer as I hustled Astrid along and kept my eyes fixed on the ceiling.

Yes! The chrome around the ring on the next light was also rough-textured. I knew there were only five or six rings of that type. All the other thousand-odd in the maze were smooth and shiny. The small number with the rough finish had been included by mistake in one particular batch. We'd put them on the lights nearest the entrance so as to make it easier to replace them when the proper rings arrived. So it stood to reason that we weren't far from the vault door. What's more, they'd hardly have bothered to drag two drugged people too far into the maze. They'd simply haul us a little way in, then drop us. There was no need to do more.

I also realized why we were only partially clothed. They'd stripped us of anything that might have been of conceivable use to us. My pockets had been emptied. I had no keys, no coins, no penknife. No wristwatch or comb. We had been deprived of anything that with a little ingenuity might remotely have served as a tool or a weapon. I was rather surprised they hadn't pitched us in there stark naked while they were at it—except that I suppose Gabriel wouldn't have been able to bear the sight of it.

But, of course, he also had a practical consideration. It's not easy to put clothes on a corpse—especially a corpse whose limbs might already be growing rigid. What he intended to do, I guessed, was to let us die. Then he'd enter the maze, find our bodies, and chuck down the rest of our clothing in a heap beside us. Then he'd leave. Next week, next month, even next year, our putrescent bodies would be discovered—by someone else . . . not by *him*. Perhaps by the first group of innocent visitors to the maze. The police, the public, and Gabriel's friends would suppose that, unable to slake our appetites anywhere else in the house, we'd crept down into the maze. After all, it was warm and well carpeted. And the iron door of the vault had somehow slammed shut on us . . . As for Gabriel, he wouldn't know a thing about it. He'd thought Astrid was visiting her sister in California, and that I was away on business. Or if pressed harder, he could say he knew we'd fallen in love and assumed we'd run away together. Sympathy all around. Better to be taken for a husband who's been deceived by a worthless wife and a treacherous Yankee than a husband who's been deceived because he's impotent. There wouldn't even be any marks on our bodies, except for some superficial bruising around my mouth and ribs, which could be easily explained and might in any case disappear during the first stages of decomposition. I saw now why I hadn't been kicked and beaten more thoroughly . . .

We'd reached the entrance of the maze. It had only taken us a couple of minutes, perhaps less, after I'd spotted those chrome rings.

The door of the vault was shut fast. I went up the five

steps and gave it a half-hearted push with my shoulder. It didn't budge a millimeter. It was thirty inches thick and made of armored steel. The slab of smooth, cold metal, glistening in the slowly fading light, was like the marble door of a mausoleum.

I placed my hands wide apart on the door, gave it another shove, then let my head drop forward with an air of defeat. It was a convincing performance. I wanted Gabriel to see me on the monitor screen and think I was in the process of giving up. It would make him happy. It would also give him a false sense of security. True, it wasn't a difficult part to act; I wasn't exactly brimming over with good cheer. But beneath my drooping exterior I was tingling with suppressed excitement. In another minute or two, I'd know whether we'd received a brief reprieve or whether our one and only chance was gone . . .

I bumped my way heavily down the five steps and dropped down on the bottom one, propping my head in my hands. When Astrid sat down beside me and laid a shaking hand on my forearm, I whispered, "*Ssssh!* . . . *Keep still!*" I was waiting for the lights to fade away completely. I couldn't move till then. It seemed to take an age for them to dwindle and die out. I fastened my eyes on my bare left foot and kept as still as I could. I was reminded how thirsty I was. Hungry, too. God knows how long it had been since either of us had had anything to eat or drink.

15

WHEN the last glimmer of light had gone, I forced myself to sit still a minute or two longer. Then I slid off the bottom step and lay full length on the ground. I could hear Astrid's light and shallow breath above me in the darkness and smell the warm spice of flesh and perfume. What I was searching for was one of the steel screws that held the polished metal plate onto the concrete riser. Everywhere in the maze the drab surface of the basic concrete was disguised by steel, carpet, or paint. I fumbled frantically for the screw and found its domed outline. It felt enormous in the darkness. What I was looking for was behind that metal plate. And here was the snag. I'd taken care to tighten up the screw only very lightly—but without a screwdriver I was helpless. I groped for the second screw, at the other end. Same thing. Impossible to turn it with a thumb and forefinger.

Now I was really beginning to sweat. Could an over-conscientious workman have been doing a last-minute check, found those two slack screws, and tightened them? Our lives depended on my ability to get into the space behind that panel. I could feel my heart pumping crazily in my chest. My tongue felt several sizes too large for my mouth.

I scrabbled at both screws in turn with my nails. Useless. I was glad Astrid couldn't see the look on my face.

She whispered, "What are you doing?"

I hunched myself on to my knees.

"Astrid—"

"Yes?"

"Your bra—"

"What?"

"Take it off."

"My—?!"

"Take it off and give it to me."

She didn't argue. A bare thigh or forearm—something too firm to be a breast—brushed across my shoulder as she twisted and reached behind her to unfasten the bra. Her hand struck my neck as she handed it to me. It was lacy and warm. We bumped into each other in a soft tangle, and it took a second to straighten ourselves out. In the confusion I dropped the bra, feeling a little flare of panic as I brushed my hands over the carpeted floor. A crazy spurt of release flowed through me as my fingers closed over it. On that ridiculous scrap of fabric hung whatever future we had.

My fingertips explored the straps and found what they were looking for. The bra was fastened by means of a small flat metal tag. I let out my breath in a sigh. If it had been fastened by hook-and-eye, we would have been done for.

Grasping the tag, I put out my other hand. I knocked against the metal plate as I searched for the first screw. I guided the corner of the tag into the slot of the screw and gave it a gentle twist. It wasn't easy to manipulate, since it was a Phillips screw, and the blackness didn't make the operation easier. If the screw had really been tightened by a workman, that would have been the end of it. The little tag would have buckled and snapped.

The screw yielded. My spirits gave a jump. No one had tampered with the plate. No one had detected my hiding place. And it had been right under their noses. They'd made a clean sweep of the other safety devices. This one they'd missed. I'd noticed there were hollows under each of the five steps. I did nothing at that time. I'd waited. Only when I had a chance to slip into the maze on my own, late one night, had I unfastened one of the metal plates fixed over the hollow batten behind. I wanted to use it for some make-shift and hurriedly assembled safety devices of my own.

Why had I done that? What feeling came over me? What second sight warned me? It isn't at all easy to explain. Briefly, I hadn't been so blind to Gabriel's tendencies that I didn't realize that he was an incorrigible practical joker. Half an hour alone with him or a superficial glimpse of his weird house would be enough to put any intelligent person mildly on their guard with him. Astrid hadn't managed to persuade me, worse luck, that he was actually dangerous— but I'd seen over and over again with my own eyes that he had a natural propensity for all kinds of joshing and haz-ing and schoolboy tricks. I'd heard him describe with gen-uine glee how we were to build a maze that would be diffi-cult enough to reduce his closest friends to the condition of blubbering jellies. I'd seen how he'd always shouted with laughter when one of the workmen managed to get himself lost; you'd have thought it was the funniest joke in the world. And Astrid had told me all about the little epi-sode of how he'd taken her into the maze and pretended that they'd gone astray and couldn't get out. I wish I'd taken her account of the incident more seriously. All the same, I never in my wildest dreams imagined he'd go as far as he'd done now—let alone contemplate homicide. Nevertheless, I did recognize that he was quite capable of playing a malicious prank on me or on anyone else, like the one he'd played on Astrid. So only a few days ago—on the spur of the moment—I'd snatched up a few things I thought vaguely might come in useful in case of an emergency and stuffed them into the recess. I wasn't even thinking of myself at the time, let alone Astrid. It was just a reflex action—something to help a practical joker's possible victim or victims if he sprang some juvenile surprise on them. I ought to have recognized it for what it was: an effort on the part of my unconscious to warn me that I was stepping into danger. Only, now it wasn't a silly practical joke—and I was damned glad I'd had that fragmentary gleam of foresight.

All the same, I was still desperately anxious as I inserted my hand under the step. What if the bundle wrapped in the duster wasn't there? What if that sadistic bastard or one of his cronies had removed it?

Ah!

My fingers encountered the solid bulk of the cloth. I drew it out and deposited it gently on one of the steps. My fingers were trembling. I made myself replace the panel and screw it back in position. I was so impatient I dropped one of the screws twice. It was important that Gabriel and the others shouldn't learn I was no longer utterly defenseless.

I unwrapped the bundle. My eager fingers explored the contents. Everything was there. Everything. All the objects I'd taken at random from the trunk and glove compartment of the Maserati and rolled in the duster. I could feel the outlines of the flashlight, the two screwdrivers, the hammer with the long rubber-covered handle. I wished I'd included the whole tool kit while I'd been about it. I could also feel the cold outline of the slender key. I'd slipped it into the bundle at the last moment, prompted by some obscure but inspired impulse.

Kneeling upright, I placed all these objects in my trouser pockets. In the right-hand pocket I put the duster, screwdrivers, and hammer, handle down. In the left I put the flashlight and also the key, pushing the key right down to the bottom, where I thought it would be safe. The flashlight had a ring with a length of the tape architects use to tie up their papers threaded through it. I always liked to provide my flashlights with a loop for safety. I wasn't going to use the flashlight till I had to, not only to save the batteries, but because its beam would show up on the monitor in the control room. Gabriel had done us a favor by extinguishing the lights. He could no longer keep track of our position. It gave me an odd feeling to think that he was seated less than a dozen feet away from us—on the other side of a wall as thick as a medieval castle, behind an iron door that wouldn't have been out of place at Fort Knox.

The chief thing now was to put as much distance between us as swiftly as possible. I scraped around on the carpet and picked up the bra. I gave it back to Astrid, inadvertently hitting her on the temple or cheekbone as I did so. There wasn't much point in giving her the bra, or in her putting it on again. Still, perhaps she'd feel a fraction less naked and helpless if she did so. She panted as she wrestled with the thing, an unmistakable taint of fear in the irregular heaving of her breath. But so far she was holding up well. She'd schooled herself to trust me. When she heard the soft clinking of the tools as I took them out of the duster she hadn't uttered a sound, though she must have wondered what was going on.

I got to my feet and reached down and pulled her upright. The worst part of our ordeal now lay ahead of us. We had to traverse the maze. I felt deeply contrite for having involved her in this mess. I drew her to me and started to run my hands down her body, murmuring endearments and words of encouragement. I held her hard against me and pinned her arms in a rough embrace. In the darkness her body seemed enormous, the body of a giantess, huge and indeterminate. I felt her mouth straining to meet mine. I had a silly feeling Gabriel could see us, almost stretch out and touch us, watch my hand stroking her shoulders, the curve of her buttocks, her thighs, reach around to touch the breasts and belly. Serve him bloody well right. I'd given up the luxury of feeling sorry for him. The body pressed against mine gave me a measure of the strength and re-assurance I needed.

I gave her shoulder a last gentle pat. Her body felt less chilled and had stopped trembling. I ran my right hand down her arm and grasped her left wrist. I locked my fingers firmly round it. I felt her arm grow taut, but kept my grip in place. She'd have to grow used to it. We had several miles to walk in total darkness.

I shuffled a couple of steps away from the door with my free hand in front of me. I was feeling for the wall. When I made contact, I began to walk forward into the maze with my palm brushing the cold surface of the steel. That was my plan. I'd follow the left-hand wall until it brought me to my first objective. It wasn't much of a plan —not very subtle—but it was the only one I had. By using the torch I might have been able to halve the time. Equally, I could have got lost. Of course, in previous weeks I'd been used to breezing through the maze. At first I'd used my own ground plan. Later came the era of the colored cords, and traversing the maze became a deceptively simple business. Now that the cords had been removed, I was as liable to get lost as the stupidest workman. If I'd known what was going to happen, I'd have taken the trouble to memorize the plan, difficult though it would have been. I'd even have had it tattooed on my chest in indelible ink . . .

I reckoned Gabriel would bottle up his curiosity for at least another three or four hours. Finally he wouldn't be able to resist any longer the urge to snap on the light and see what was happening to us. So we had that much of a start.

If you want to get out of a maze, nine times out of ten you can do it by keeping your hand glued to one wall or the other. You'll go down one blind alley after the other, but if you stick to the same wall, it will take you out of the blind alley and lead you forward again. You'll cover ten times the ground you need to cover. You'll grow dizzy from doubling back. But in the end you'll reach your goal. Of course, if the maze has a fancy ground plan with galleries that steer you back into the galleries you've already traversed, the system won't work. Like Gabriel's rats, you'll go round and round in small circles until you collapse from exhaustion. I'd designed the El Pardo Maze in such a way that the going would be relatively simple until the half-way mark. There were no blind alleys in the first half to channel the victim back to his starting point and make him feel as if he'd fallen down a ladder in snakes-and-ladders. Gabriel and I had jointly decided that we wouldn't start trying to break down our victim until he'd reached the half-way point. We'd encourage him to think the maze was child's play. The first thirty minutes were easy. Up till then the design was straightforward. Then, just when his mood was gay, his spirits were high, he was complimenting himself on his cleverness and looking forward to his dry martini—it was then his troubles really started . . .

I struck out purposefully. My knuckles caressed the smooth, cold surface of the wall. The corridors were wide and of uniform width. There were no obstructions. There was no difficulty in walking down them in the dark. The only snag was that when I reached the end of one corridor and turned to enter the next one I tended to do so too abruptly. Astrid, moving straight ahead, was brought up with a violent jolt that jarred us both. After a few minutes I learned to keep my left arm well extended and slow down as soon as I felt my knuckles leave the wall and encounter empty air.

I kept asking: *"Are you all right?"* And her whisper would come back to me out of the darkness a step ahead or a step behind me, *"Yes! . . . Yes! . . . I'm all right!"*

After a while I lost track of time. I plodded along like an automaton, mechanically registering the termination of one wall and the start of the next. My head seemed to be growing lighter. My brain was swelling and turning mushy. I couldn't gauge size or distance. At one moment my feet seemed six inches away and the next moment they were six yards away. The darkness was churning and boiling. Either it was expanding and rushing away from me, or else it was shrinking and smothering me. I marched along in a daze. I knew my mind was liable to slide back into its former dream state, yet was unable to do anything to stop it. How far did we walk, winding in and out, backwards and forwards, left and right, up one ramp and down another? My head was still throbbing from Gabriel's knock-out drops. My eyes were smarting and watering. My mouth was dry. My stomach was complaining. My shinbones were so sharp and sore I felt they'd cut through the skin. The maze was so large we'd planned to set up tables at intervals with drinks and food. Needless to say, they hadn't been set up for *us* . . .

My right hand was beginning to ache from gripping Astrid's wrist. I was glad Gabriel hadn't turned on that lunatic music again. He should have: it would have made a great contribution to our misery. As it was, the darkness seemed to be roaring all around me. Now it muttered, now it threatened to burst my eardrums like a tempest in a forest tearing at the leaves and snapping the tops of the boughs. Sealed in that blackness all kinds of fantastic images reared up in front of me . . . Gabriel's white bull . . . his mother's proud white face . . . Astrid's silver negligee . . . crimson jet of blood spouting from a severed neck . . . horses wheeling and winding in an intricate chain . . . locomotive falling off a high wooden trestle . . . shuffling on my knees round and round and round the pavement of a church . . . burning thatch hissing and crackling in my ears . . . black sack over my head as I drop drop drop through a trap-door . . .

What kept my feet moving in a slogging rhythm was hatred. I pushed the other images aside so I could concentrate on the image of Gabriel's bobbing, grinning, moist-lipped face as he mouthed and gesticulated his way through one of his monologues. He'd thrown us into his maze and slammed the bolt as if we'd been marionettes boxed up in one of his peep-shows. He was putting us through our paces in the way he put his toy trains through their paces upstairs. I hadn't realized what a drive he had to act God . . .

I was jolted out of this catatonic mood by what was to be the most demoralizing incident to happen so far. I don't know how to explain it, or whether any explanation is possible. I only know that at some point a kind of low rumbling had begun. I can't tell you exactly when. It was one of those sounds that seem to have started a very long way off and a very long time ago. It resembled the noise emitted by the 32-foot stop of a giant organ. The sound takes the form not so much of a noise as of a subterranean shaking. You detect it not with your ears but in the pit of your stomach. It was as if some great black pulse had started to beat in the darkness. It was like the first dim stirring of an earthquake. Some words popped into my mind. *"A terrifying sound . . . like thunder . . . and the Great Labyrinth is plunged in perpetual darkness . . ."*

The noise grew and grew. It mounted and mounted until it became a shattering roar. I thought the top of my head would come off. If I'd been able to identify what it was, I probably wouldn't have been so appalled by it. It sounded like a gigantic beast in agony. They say the word *panic* comes from the mind-bursting dread that men and women experience when they hear the unearthly bellow of the god Pan in the depths of the forest. Panic like that was what I felt. I was hearing the sound of fear itself—the elemental fear that plucks at the root of the brain. In the primeval blackness some shaggy monstrosity was clambering out of its hatch. It was the cry of the Minotaur, the cry you sometimes hear in the bullring when the bull stands on the crimson sand with its muscles shredded and lungs punctured and slavering gray tongue lolling out. An unseen shape was breathing its foul breath on me in the blackness. My spine had locked, and my legs had turned to water. The cry was magnified to freakish proportions. Was it simply an amplified screech transmitted by the loudspeakers? Was Gabriel trying an acoustical experiment on us? Or had he accidentally tripped one of the switches on the control panel and filled the maze with a mechanical scream? Or was it the voice of Gabriel himself? Whimpering with the weight of his rage and pain?

The shout had brought me to a halt. When I recovered my faculties, I found I was running. Running hard.

The unthinkable had happened. The worst thing of all.

Astrid and I had become separated. I was no longer grasping her wrist.

Black.

Somewhere in the past few distracted moments we'd lost touch.

Black.

Where was she?

Black black black.

Then I heard her screaming.

BLACK.

Screaming my name.

BLACK BLACK BLACK.

Screaming screaming.

16

"*Astrid! . . . Astrid! . . .*"

No alternative now. I had to use the flashlight.

I snatched it out of my pocket. The beam splashed a dazzling white oval against the wall ahead of me. Its outline was as sharp as if cut by scissors. When I swung it about, it gave me eerie glimpses of myself against the silvered walls. My limbs in their stark black-and-white garb were curiously angular and stick-like.

Switching on the flashlight restored my presence of mind. Rushing about was stupid. It would lead me deeper into the maze in the wrong direction.

I stopped and shone the beam on one end of the corridor, then the other. If she was in a neighboring corridor, she'd see the beam and follow it. I advanced up the corridor to the next bend and went on playing the beam on this side and that. I kept on calling her name. I didn't whisper now. I shouted.

God knows where she'd got to. A minute or two was more than enough for us to get parted irretrievably. I blamed myself for my carelessness.

Paradoxically, it was Gabriel who intervened to save us. He must have been sitting there in the control room with his glass of milk in his hand. He must have caught sight of a flicker of light on the control panel. It would have told him we had a flashlight. And if we had that, what else might we have? The position of the spark of light on the screen would also warn him that instead of zigzagging about in an aimless fashion, we were meeting the challenge of the maze in a purposeful way. He would have decided to switch on the lights again so he could check on us by means of the scanners.

The bright glow grew more rapidly, as if he was turning up the lights in a hurry. My eyes began to tingle. I blundered into walls and went on shouting her name.

I was lucky. I don't know if the maze had led her around in a circle or whether she'd retraced her steps, but all at once I heard her calling out. I started to move in what I judged was the direction of her voice. For several ghastly minutes we appeared to be stumbling down corridors that were parallel, yet inaccessible to each other. We could hear one another, but couldn't make contact. The pall of nightmare dropped over me again.

Then suddenly through the watery haze that was pricking my eyes I saw her run across the top of the corridor I was in. If Gabriel hadn't switched on the lights, I'd have missed her. Our naked feet were soundless in the pile of the carpet. I uttered a cry and broke into a run. My head was buzzing, and my thighs and shins made me feel as if I'd been put on the rack, but I managed to reach the corner with a fair turn of speed. Facing me was a dividing corridor with three branches. My heart sank.

I went to each of the branches in turn. When I shouted her name, I realized my voice was growing hoarse and feeble.

Then—eyes blazing and hair flying—she came springing out of the middle corridor and bounded into my arms.

And at practically the same instant the damned racket started up again. Not the fatuous music—the bull-roaring, or whatever it was. Once again it began as nothing more than a low-pitched reverberation and soared by degrees to an all-embracing, oceanic scream. It was enough to melt the flesh on your bones.

We clung to each other as if it were a hurricane that was going to blow us away. She lifted her shaking hands and pressed them to her ears. She was reaching the end of her tether. I didn't know where I'd find the resources to hang on much longer myself.

There is something restorative about hatred. It makes the adrenalin flow. I jerked my head like a snake this way and that in fury. If Gabriel was watching us, he'd have seen the venomous expression on my face.

I was convinced he *was* watching. He was spying on us as he'd spied on us in Los Angeles and New York. Getting a kick out of registering the mess we were in. I swung my head from side to side as if I expected him to stroll around the corner with the familiar facetious grin on his face.

We were only a yard away from one of the points on the ceiling where the thick glass of a scanner glared down at us in the pitiless light.

All right. I'd give him something to watch. I'd show him I had a couple of tricks of my own. He could sit up there puncturing our eardrums and driving us out of our skulls with that atrocious noise, but he'd find he wasn't invulnerable up there in his little box. He'd find out he wasn't God. I'd do something that was like taking a long needle and pushing it slowly right into the pupil of that damned inquisitive eye . . .

I took Astrid, gently forced her to lower her hands from her ears, and walked her three or four steps to the right. I positioned her carefully in what I calculated was the best place for her husband to get a good clear look at what we were about to do. I put my hands on her waist and slowly urged her backwards. Her hips came forward and I leaned in toward her and gradually we went down together onto the carpet. I spread her legs and lowered my body between them. I settled myself on my elbows and cradled her head in my hands and began to kiss and caress her with deliberate and ostentatious leisure. I planted long, slow kisses on her neck and breasts. I started to make love to her as if we had all the time in the world . . .

She probably throught I'd gone out of my mind. Perhaps Gabriel's madness was infectious. I could never have acted out a vengeful scene like that if I'd been quite sane. There was a submissive and uncomprehending look in her eyes. She murmured some disjointed words that could have been query or protest or endearment.

I put down my head and parted her sweat-sticky hair with my lips and whispered, "Put your arms around me . . . Kiss me . . . You want me to make love to you . . ."

Her eyes widened. She didn't understand, but she could see there was cunning in my madness. She wrapped her arms around me and reached up to fasten her mouth on mine.

I pushed aside the negligee and eased down the bra and nuzzled my lips between her damp breasts. Didn't Gabriel enjoy conducting people to ringside seats to watch Leonidas going through his paces? I slid my fingers beneath the panties. She quivered, and I felt her knees rise around me and her arms tighten. I began to work the flimsy material away from her buttocks.

The lights went out. All at once. In a rush. No long, theatrical fade-out.

I laughed. If this was a battle of nerves, at last I'd won a round. My little scheme had paid off. I'd forced him to switch off the lights again.

I jumped to my feet. I recovered my grip on the flashlight, dangling from its loop on my wrist. I switched it on and helped Astrid up. I felt I hadn't run far enough in finding her to destroy my sense of direction. I was pretty confident I only had to go back one corridor to pick up the original point where I discovered I'd lost her. I reckoned that it couldn't be far now to my first objective, which was situated at roughly the half-way mark.

As I took her hand and started to follow the left-hand wall again, I wasn't really as confident as I kept telling myself I was. What if I'd boobed? What if we were actually walking back toward the entrance? What if Gabriel had succeeded, during one of my absences from El Pardo, in doing something really cunning? Like changing the ground plan? Or altering the passages so as to open up new blind alleys? What if he'd managed to change the maze in such a way that now there wasn't any exit? If all the passages were sealed in an endless circle and there wasn't any way out at all?

We were moving along briskly, hugging the wall, when she suddenly said, "The air conditioning . . ."

I didn't slow down.

I asked, "What about it?"

"Why isn't it working?"

We came to a corner and rounded it.

She repeated, "Why isn't it working?"

"It's working. We're hot. We've been walking too fast."

"No. It's getting hotter and hotter. Can't you feel it?"

She was right. I could. The air was definitely warmer and heavier.

Another corner.

"Well?" she asked.

"Imagination. Try not to think about it."

"It's *not* imagination! It's stifling!"

Without stopping, I tried to figure out what was happening. It wasn't difficult. Gabriel had shut off the air conditioning and pushed the heating up as far as it would go. I could hear the dry hiss of the heated air pumping through the louvers above us. Soon the needle on the regulator on the wall of the control room would read over a hundred degrees.

My silk shirt was soaked through. I felt the sweat saturating the cloth on the inside of my thighs. Astrid's hand was wet and slippery.

"What are we going to do?" she asked. And then, when I didn't answer, "Darling! We just can't go on walking!"

If we stopped, we were beaten. We'd lie down like a pair of exhausted animals and die there. For the first time, I felt her offer resistance. She was ready to rebel. She wanted nothing more than to be left alone, to sink down on the floor and welcome whatever it was she'd have to endure.

I pulled her along by force, moaning and protesting. We were gasping for air as if we'd been thrust into a furnace. As we were struggling up what felt like the millionth ramp and turning the millionth corner, she collapsed and let herself fall forward without any attempt to save herself.

135

I blundered on a couple of steps and had to go back and
heave her up. As I bent, I swore at her so violently her
white face craned back at me in sheer surprise. I wrenched
her up by her arms with a bruising roughness that made
her squeal.

17

LEFT turn, right turn—right and left—left and right. I hauled her along behind me with an iron resolution. The atmosphere was rapidly becoming so sweltering that to my muddled mind the beam of the flashlight was a bar of white molten metal and the blackness around it was boiling and bubbling.

I'd almost forgotten in that hellish cauldron of a maze what it was I was looking for. Then suddenly . . . mercifully . . . I came upon it. One moment there was just the frightening sameness of one corridor after another. The next—and there was the vivid scarlet bulkhead jutting out of the right-hand wall ahead of me in one of the most interminable-looking of the corridors.

We were on the right track. I'd achieved my first goal. We'd reached the dead center of the maze. And my harshness with Astrid in making her hurry was justified: another few minutes (or however time was reckoned down here under the ground) and we'd have been scorched and scalded into oblivion . . .

I released her and let her drop to her knees, then crumple forward on her face. I fumbled the hammer out of my pocket and crossed to the bulkhead. It was five feet across, stretching the whole length of the wall from ceiling to carpet. I started to pound blindly at its scarlet panels, but they didn't splinter fast enough, and I knew I was losing energy. I had enough sense to reverse the hammer and use the claw-head to tear at the edge of the bulkhead, where the joints were. I needed more strength than I had left, but actually the panels yielded easily, the screws snapping out of their holes like miniature gunshots. It was lucky the bulkhead casing was only a temporary one, of wood, painted to look like steel for the purpose of the opening party. In a few days' time it was scheduled to be replaced with a proper metal one.

When I'd stripped off enough of the covering, I was confronted with a tangle of wires beneath. This was the place where all the wiring of the maze ran through a central core and was available for inspection and repair. Essentially it was a big junction-box. I wasn't an electrical expert, and I didn't know what those thickets of wires signified—fat wires like snakes or thin ones like worms, distinguished from each other by plastic sheathing in all the colors of the rainbow. I played the flashlight at random, then took the hammer and used the claws to rip at the wires indiscriminately. I'd destroy them all. It was like breaking up the action of a huge piano or a gigantic harp. The treble strings parted easily, while the bass strings offered more resistance. When Astrid came crawling up on her hands and knees to watch me, I slapped the flashlight into her hand and ordered her to hold it on the bulkhead as I worked. I needed both of my hands for some of the thicker wires. There were streams and cascades of blue and white sparks like a flurry of Chinese fire. I could feel the furry electrical kick in my wrists in spite of the solid insulation of the handle. I had to get the job done somehow, kicks or no kicks. It was our only chance to cut off the heating, which otherwise was going to kill us. I'd also be cutting off the air supply—but I had to take a chance on that. I hoped there'd be enough air to last our remaining time in the maze. And by stopping the fans and the air from circulating I could prevent Gabriel's blowing any kind of toxic material through the air vents and getting us that way. I'd dealt with the lights and the television screen, as well. When the wires were smashed, he couldn't see us or keep track of us. I'd have gained us a certain amount of new room to maneuver.

Naturally, when he discovered I'd smashed the electrical system he wasn't going to simply go on sitting still up there. It would madden him even more. I was stoking up his fury. He'd hit back. How, I didn't know. But he'd slash back at us, we could be sure of that.

I'd face that when it came. Meanwhile, I had to work out a plan for threading our way through the second half of the El Pardo Maze.

Think. Think. Think. Think. Think. Think. Think.

I was deadly tired, and needed a rest.

The time had come for what orchestral conductors call a *Ruhepunkt*, a breathing space. God knows what hurdles lay ahead. It was dangerous to loiter—but equally dangerous for us to plod on without enough strength to lift our arms over our heads.

I lowered my body to the floor beside Astrid and relieved her of the torch. My limbs felt as clumsy as if they were encased in an old-fashioned diving suit. I could feel small muscles quivering in my calves, in the upper part of my arms, and inside my thighs. Astrid, still on her hands and knees, came close to me where I lay sprawled with my legs out against the wall and laid her head on my knee. I switched off the flashlight. The sudden tremendous darkness was soothing and healing. The air didn't seem so baking hot. Already it seemed to be a few degrees cooler. I closed my eyes and let my limbs go slack—and immediately started to float off into sleep . . . brown leaves drifting outside the white lace curtains . . . red sports car with skis strapped on the roof . . . sapphire sapphire sapphire sapphire . . .

I had to expend a colossal amount of will-power before I could force myself to open my eyes. I compelled myself to switch on the flashlight. My eyelids seemed to be gummed together and lead weights were attached to them. To keep myself from dozing off I started to check in a bleary way through my pockets. Screwdrivers . . . duster . . . key . . .

A chill sliced through me.

Key?

No key.

No key! . . .

My weariness ebbed in a flash. I leaped to my feet. Astrid's head dropped on the floor. She came awake with a little moan. In a fever I took everything from my pockets and let them clatter to the ground. I thrust my fingers into every crevice in search of that key.

NO KEY!

Oh, my God, I must have dropped the bloody thing. A mile back? Two miles? Three miles? Four miles? At the entrance? How could I face trudging back to where I'd started from, this time keeping my hand on the right-hand wall, sweeping every foot of the floor with the flashlight?

Up till now I'd been trying hard to keep any hint of my inner terror and despair from communicating itself to Astrid. Now I groaned aloud.

The beam of the flashlight, circling idly, struck the red side of the wrecked bulkhead. I took a step toward it and savagely scuffed at the bits of torn wood with my bare foot. It was nothing more than a baffled reflex. The beam happened to tilt downwards and as I kicked at a shattered plank of plywood something bright gleamed up at me.

The key!

You can imagine how avidly I pounced on it and the care with which I put it back in my pocket. It must have fallen out when I was battering at the bulkhead.

As I stood there with relief washing through me I heard a little whimpering sound. I thought it was me—then realized it was Astrid. I went back, got down beside her, and spent the next few minutes comforting her as one comforts a child.

She grew calmer, but I realized we simply had to rest a little while longer, no matter what fiend was at our heels. We had to. And I wanted to try and work out what to do if we got as far as having a chance to use the key. Gabriel wasn't just going to let us stroll calmly out of the maze and walk away . . .

18

WHAT I did next couldn't have been much more reassuring to Astrid than any of the things I'd done before.

As I sat there, with her crouching against me, I unbuttoned my shirt and pulled it off. I propped the flashlight against the upper part of my leg and started to tear the damp silk into strips. As I worked, my brain was furiously shaping the next part of my campaign.

She lifted her head and stared at what I was doing. The beam of light struck up under her chin, throwing a shadow across her face so it seemed to be cut in half. Her tired eyes glittered at me out of deep pools of darkness. I tore off a piece of the shirt and handed it to her, indicating that she should copy me. Giving her something to do might take her mind off her troubles. Fortunately, the shirt tore easily.

I shredded the silk into strips about an inch and a half wide. Then I took each strip and tore it into individual pieces about three inches long. You can get a surprisingly large number of pieces of that size from an evening shirt, size forty—and we were going to need every single one of them. We put the pieces on the floor between us, and the pile grew to quite respectable proportions. We ripped up even the cuffs and the collar, and I saved the buttons and put them carefully in my pocket. This was a situation in which anything, however trivial, might sooner or later come in useful. It was almost pleasant, sitting there performing that bizarre little ritual. I could feel the air on my naked torso. The temperature was definitely dropping. The only things that spoiled our little interlude were certain small matters such as hunger, thirst, and fear.

"Astrid—"

"Yes?"

"We'll have finished this job in a moment. We'll have to be moving on . . ."

"Oh . . . yes!"

"I'll be using the flashlight, so there's not much danger we'll get separated . . ."

She uttered a small anxious sigh. I patted her hand.

"If it happens, though, we've got to handle it differently from last time . . ."

Another nervous sigh.

"If you find you're lost, stop where you are and sit down and don't do anything. Understand? Don't move. Wait where you are. Let *me* find *you*. Understand?"

I was stuffing the mound of rags in my left-hand pocket, with the hammer and the other tools. There wasn't room for more than a quarter of them, but I wasn't going to clutter up the pocket where I'd put the key. I wouldn't make *that* mistake again . . .

I told her, "Take the rest of the rags and carry them carefully. Don't drop any. Dropping them could confuse us—lead us the wrong way."

"What are we going to do with them?"

"You'll see."

She got to her feet and made a container of her arms. I loaded the rest of the rags into them.

"Listen," I said. "We've got the most complicated section of the maze ahead of us. It's going to be pretty wearing—but if we could tackle the first part, we can steer our way through the rest of it. We're going to use these rags as markers. We couldn't do that before, as we wouldn't have had enough for the whole maze, and anyway, it wasn't strictly necessary in the first half."

"I don't see—"

"Trust me."

"But Gabriel—"

"Don't think about him. Just concentrate on the job in hand. Take every minute as it comes. Don't think further ahead than that."

"I—I'll try . . ."

"Good girl. Ready?"

"I—think so . . ."

"Right—here we go!"

The fact that we were on the last lap—even if it was likely to be a long one—added a certain amount of spring to our step. It was also encouraging to be acting according to a definite plan, even if I hadn't any idea how well the plan was going to work out.

What I did was this. We walked down the middle of each passage following the circle made on the floor by the flashlight. Whenever we came to the end of a corridor, where it split into two or three branches, we took the left-hand branch. In the original plan the point where a corridor branched off into other corridors was called a *node*—a technical word derived from the French *noeud*, a knot. It was a term used by Gabriel's rat-fancier from the University of New Mexico, so we borrowed it. At each node I placed at the entrance of our chosen branch three of our little strips of rag. We went on, and I made certain we kept up a businesslike pace. I wanted to work up a purposeful rhythm for this final act of the drama. Nonetheless, it seemed an age before I once more encountered one of the nodes where I'd previously put three of my rags. There were moments when I had a sickening feeling we'd somehow got out of the second half of the maze and regressed into the first half. That would have been our death sentence.

When I saw those three strips shining again in the beam, I shook with joy. Literally shook. I took a single piece of rag out of my pocket and put it at the end of the passage we'd just left. This was a node with three branches, so I selected one of the two other passages, unmarked by the sign, and we entered it.

That was my strategy. We'd keep on walking until we came to a two- or three-branched node, and if there were no unmarked paths at that point it meant we'd already explored this particular branch system. In that case, we'd turn around and retire down the corridor by which we'd arrived. However, if we reached a node with one or more unmarked paths leading from it, we chose one of them and as we entered I stooped and marked it with two strips of rag.

In this way we could be certain we were visiting every part of what remained of the maze. We made it a rule when we reached a node never to take a three-marked path unless there were no paths unmarked or with one mark only. And when we entered a one-mark path, we added the two marks we always left on leaving a node. Thus it became a three-mark path at that node.

Astrid didn't understand what was going on, and I hadn't got time or breath to explain it to her. But as we began to run across more and more of the silk strips, she realized I was fathoming out the right way to go. Her attitude became intent, and her steps grew alert. She was ready with a handful of rags the instant I needed them. Of course, this was a tedious method of solving the problem, but at least it was sure and bound to be shorter than the primitive hand-against-the-wall method I'd used before. But my supply of rags was limited, and I began to worry about running out. I'd long ago emptied my pockets, and Astrid's pile was getting low. Still, there were always my trousers and Astrid's negligee.

However, on the whole I felt better than I had for several hours. Cautiously, tentatively, I allowed myself a tiny glow of optimism. There was no doubt the air was cooler —even slightly chilly? But the new atmosphere made me feel fresher and more vigorous. I don't want to give the impression we'd somehow got used to the maze, or that the horror and creepiness were in any way wearing off. But I was certainly feeling a good deal more confident.

I was just telling myself that those ramps, leading unendingly up and down, were the worst part of it—and cursing myself for my own ingenuity in putting them there—when—

"*Listen!*"

Astrid stopped. I stopped, too.

"What?"

"Can't you hear it?"

"Hear what?"

"That noise?"

I listened. I shook my head. "No."

"You can't?"

I tried again. Nothing. "Come on," I said, "we've got to—"

"*Wait!*"

To humor her, I listened one last time.

She asked, "Hear it?"

Yes. Now I heard it. Voices. She shrank back against the wall, clutching what was left of the rags. I gave her shoulder a squeeze, took the rags, and pushed as many as I could in my pocket, keeping the rest in my free hand.

"Come on!"

We set off again. I didn't want to loiter, brooding about the presence of other people in the maze. Why would they be there, if they weren't stalking us?

Gabriel must have known we hadn't collapsed. He'd decided to track us down. Perhaps I'd set him off by the way I'd made love to Astrid. Perhaps he wanted to cut the comedy short. Short and sharp.

We couldn't be far away from the exit. The El Pardo Maze was big—who knew that better than I?—but it had to come to an end somewhere. The rear entrance was formidable. It had a door almost as solid as the door of the vault. But I had the key. I'd ordered that rear door myself and driven down to inspect it at the foundry at Texarkana. It was shipped to El Pardo provided with four sets of keys. I'd handed Gabriel three and kept back one for myself. It had been useful to have it while I was still working on the maze. It was this one that I'd slipped off my key-ring— acting on the merest hunch—and put in my emergency bundle under the step.

I knew that getting through that rear door was going to take more than just a twist of a key. I thrust the thought away from me. At the moment, I wasn't going to set myself a bigger goal than just reaching the exit.

Actually, if Gabriel and his companion (the faithful Larry?) were in the maze, why shouldn't we stand a fairly good chance of getting out ahead of them? Why shouldn't we leave them floundering about in the corridors, miles behind us?

I put on a spurt. Practically all the branches at the nodes had marks on them now. Another few turns—another few minutes—*had* to bring us to the exit.

I kept listening for voices. Why had someone called out in the first place? Did they break silence because they were having the same difficulty as we did in trekking through the maze? Encouraging. Gabriel couldn't be using my original sketch-plan. It was too big. Of course, he'd had time to make a photographic reduction or trace a route from the master panel in the control room. All the same, without light, traversing the maze was bound to be confusing.

It was cold. The temperature had dropped further and quicker than I'd expected. We'd started to shiver: but at the same time the silly idea got stuck in my mind that the cold air was coming in from the outside and we must be close to the exit.

I don't know what it was that revealed the fact that we were really and truly approaching the end of the maze. It could have been just animal instinct—the nocturnal creature sensing the dawn before the stain of light appears on the horizon. I recall that for some time I'd been haunted by a dread that my flashlight batteries were running down and the beam was getting weaker. I had the same sensation you sometimes get on those endless Texas highways when you glance at the gas gauge and see your tank is nearly empty. You can almost feel the gas draining away and wonder if you're going to make it to the next gas station. I had that same feeling about the flickering beam ahead of me. I was sure it was growing feebler and paler by the second. It became an obsession. I strained my eyes at the yellow circle and tried desperately to persuade myself it was as bright as ever . . .

And then a possible, a marvelous explanation crept into my tired brain. Perhaps the beam of the flashlight *was* growing weaker . . . because the surrounding darkness *was growing lighter!* . . . *Light was seeping in from the world above!*

I started to run, even though we were at the bottom of a ramp and had to run uphill. I could hear Astrid panting behind me.

We had only to keep running toward the light. We must be in the last corridor.

I was sprinting now, desperate to reach the end of the long steel alleyway, when—

BLAM! . . . BLAM!

19

TWO objects struck the wall at shoulder-level like blows on an anvil and went shrilling away down the corridor ahead of us. I knew immediately what they were, but the shock was so intense I couldn't help freezing in my tracks and looking round.

A mistake.

Another explosion set the air in the corridor vibrating, and there was an almost simultaneous clang as the bullet hit the wall at the far end.

I fled. I could hear Astrid's breath whistling in her throat as she fled at my side. There wasn't another shot, and we managed to scramble into the mouth of the corridor on our left, the side nearest us.

It was a miracle I hadn't fallen and smashed the flashlight. I didn't even remember how between the first and second shots I'd somehow had the presence of mind to switch it off. All I'd seen reflected in the steel walls was a wide flare of light like the light from a powerful electric lantern. Somewhere in that pool of light stood Gabriel, a hunting rifle hugged into his shoulder, Larry beside him.

I switched on the flashlight for a second, keeping the beam turned away from the corridor we'd just left. I saw

Astrid jammed back against the steel wall as if she wanted to melt through the metal, her breath bursting out of her as if she'd never be able to get it back.

"You all right?"

A stupid question, but she still had enough courage and presence of mind to give me a little wobbly nod. I took her hand and pressed it hard, then raised it to my lips and kissed it. I swung the beam of the flashlight around carefully and shone it on the floor. We'd taken refuge in the left-hand corridor of a node. There were two strips at the entrance, a yard from my bare foot. The strips told me we'd already traversed this particular corridor. Another flick of the torch told me that the corridor directly across the way from this one was unmarked by rags, and that that was the one we should have taken—*would* have taken, if it hadn't been for the shots. To reach it, we had to cross the corridor we'd just left—the corridor where Gabriel was installed with his rifle, as if this was the deer-hunting season and he was after more heads for his trophy room, or operating one of the shooting games in his penny arcade or practicing in his private shooting gallery . . .

I had to act quickly. He'd come stealing silently down that corridor at any moment. He'd flush us out where we stood cringing together and blow off our heads without further ado. He must have gone crazy to throw all his former plans out of the window like this. He'd arranged for us to die of terror, exhaustion, thirst, starvation—deaths he could have brought about simply by closing an iron door and getting in his car and driving away. Our deaths could never have been traced back to him. Now, when he shot us, there'd be personal involvement, a big mess to clean up, bodies to be disposed of. I suppose he now thought a gradual death was too good for us and wanted the satisfaction of finishing us off with his own hand.

Why the delay? What was keeping him? Why wasn't he already standing there facing us, gun in hand? Perhaps even in his madness he still retained a spark of prudence. If I'd managed to wreck the central nerve center of the maze I could still be dangerous. He might have figured that since I had a flashlight and other implements, there was more than a logical chance I had a gun, as well. In Texas, that was a reasonable inference.

I reckoned he'd either try to intercept us or get ahead of us. Since he'd come this far so quickly he certainly had a map. But I was sure there was a definite glimmer of light in the square outline of the corridor we had to enter. We were near the exit. We had to move before Gabriel stepped in to block us off.

I judged the angle of the path we'd have to take and switched off the flashlight.

I took Astrid's hand again and whispered, "We're going to run across this next corridor into the corridor beyond. He can't shoot in the dark . . . Ready?"

Without waiting for a reply, I darted across the corridor, pulling her after me. I'd taken three steps when there was a savage detonation. Astrid screamed. Her knees buckled. My forearm slammed against a wall in the blackness as I hauled her to safety.

Gabriel *could* shoot in the dark. He had an infrared gunsight.

He'd hit Astrid. So much for the assumption that whatever he'd got in mind for me, he'd only put her in the maze to teach her a lesson. He was going to kill her. My forearm was almost numb. I switched on the flashlight and examined her as she kneeled leaning forward against my knees. The bullet had creased her back, ripping the negligee and nicking the strap of her bra. There was a shallow runnel in the flesh from which the blood was oozing.

I picked her up in my arms and carried her farther along the corridor in the dark, her legs bumping against the wall. She was unconscious or paralyzed with fear. She couldn't have started feeling the effect of the bullet yet.

At the end of the corridor I felt the cold wall come to an end. I used the flashlight again. Same situation. The unmarked branch of the node was ahead and could only be reached by crossing another corridor. I floundered forward, expecting a bullet in the ear or the side of my neck.

A shot screamed past. I dodged back. Where had it come from—behind me, or from the corridor on the right? If he was behind me, I was a dead duck. There was no avoiding it: I had to make certain.

I took one of the two screwdrivers out of my pocket and awkwardly, hampered by Astrid's dead weight, tossed it out across the lateral corridor. It hit the wall on the far side with a sharp clatter. Instantly a shot scraped sparks from the steel wall as if the screwdriver had been a clay pigeon sprung from a trap.

I gasped at the brutal smack of the bullet, but at least I knew for sure where Gabriel was. Mercifully, he hadn't gotten behind us. He was tracking us along a parallel corridor and moving ahead to station himself for each shot as we emerged from each of the lateral passageways. He was evidently taking care not to expose himself, in case I had that gun. Or perhaps he was merely enjoying himself. I judged he was between twenty-five and thirty-five yards away.

I didn't know how many more lateral corridors we had

to cross before we reached the exit. I didn't know how many more ramps we had to climb and descend. There was no doubt now I could detect light in this part of the maze, but it wasn't yet strong enough for Gabriel to see us with the naked eye or for Astrid and me to give up using the torch.

I waited. Gabriel waited. He was probably steadier now, fighting down his rage, settling himself comfortably for the next shot. His hand would be firmer, and his eye keener. He'd certainly hit on an excellent way of narrowing the margin between us. A hunting rifle is a great reducer of the odds . . .

I leaned against the wall to lessen Astrid's weight. I couldn't carry her far in my present state. Her flesh was cold as a corpse's. To my surprise, I wasn't afraid. I wasn't afraid, because I'd used up all my fear. I was filled with a weary, sulky anger that we'd come so far only to be cut down within sight of the finish line. I tried to think what to do next, but the thoughts were fused together in my head like frozen ice cubes.

Have you ever heard of *Kukushka*, or *Little Cuckoo*? It's a game the officers of the old Russian Army used to play to while away the winter nights in Siberia. The candles in the mess would be extinguished, the curtains drawn tight, the room plunged in darkness. An officer would place himself on a chair against the far wall, facing the door, pistol in hand. The other officers would leave the room and take turns entering it. The man who entered could enter however he liked—upright, crouching, on his hands and knees, crawling on his belly. He could walk, or he could run. He could leap to the right, or to the left. The only requirement was that at the moment he crossed the threshold he had to shout, "Kukushka!" And as he shouted it, the man with the pistol fired. He fired at where he thought the voice was coming from. So it paid to be quick and to be crafty and to be a ventriloquist.

If I'd been on my own, I'd have made a dash for it, or gone on my hands and knees, or run across stooping like someone playing Kukushka. But I had Astrid to take care of. I lowered her to the carpet and crept back as silently as I could to the corridor I'd just left. I calculated Gabriel would have gone on ahead to his next position. He wouldn't expect me to retrace my steps. I didn't switch on the flashlight. I crawled out into the lateral corridor and groped around gently at the base of the near wall until my hand closed on the screwdriver I'd thrown a couple of minutes before. I thought Gabriel might just fall for the same trick twice.

I returned to Astrid, picked her up, and balanced her on my shoulder as well as I could. I lobbed the screwdriver far down the corridor against the opposite wall. I waited a tenth of a second after the shot went screeching past my hiding place and made a rush for the opposite corridor. A second shot hit the carpet with a dull smack at what seemed an inch from my heel.

This time I didn't need to use the torch to check the marks in the branches of the nodes. The slight radiance in one of the entrances was unmistakable. I wondered whether it was daybreak outside, and whether I hadn't noticed the light sooner because it had been night during our time in the maze. All I had to do was keep going straight ahead. I didn't bother to retrieve the screwdriver. I'd pitched it too close to where Gabriel might be standing, and anyway, it was useless to try the trick a third time. I considered using the hammer: it would make a more impressive clang as it struck the steel wall. But Gabriel mightn't fall for it, and I'd also be wasting one of my precious bits of hardware. It was only the knowledge that I had something to defend myself with that dissuaded Gabriel and whoever was with him from making a direct frontal assault. They knew I'd fight like a cornered animal, because I had nothing to lose.

I was still fingering the hammer when I remembered the buttons of the silk shirt I'd sacrificed. Awkwardly, shifting Astrid's unconscious body about, hearing some part of her anatomy thump against the wall, I fished the six tiny buttons out of my pocket.

I threw them across the lateral corridor. No answering sound—or none that I could catch. Perhaps they were too light to carry to the far wall. I'd failed to provoke Gabriel into firing prematurely. And I'd run out of objects to throw. It was stalemate—with the odds on Gabriel. I had to move—but when I moved, he'd shoot me. Then I thought of the sapphire ring. It took me what seemed an age to locate Astrid's hand, then her finger. It seemed to take even longer to slide the ring off the finger, even though the sweat on the skin helped me. I gripped it tight and threw it as hard as I could. This time there was a distinct sharp click. It was faint, but I knew that if I heard it, then Gabriel would catch it, too. Like mine, his nerves were stretched and keyed up to register the slightest noise.

I waited.

He didn't fire.

What was he up to?

I caught a snatch of subdued conversation. Just a few words, but enough to identify Gabriel's quick, light voice.

A glow rippled along the steel walls of the lateral corridor ahead. He must have told Larry to switch the lantern on. The glow lasted only six or seven seconds, then disappeared as abruptly as it appeared. Probably Gabriel thought he might catch me in the open, tiptoeing across the top of the corridor, a perfect target. Or perhaps he discovered the light was too garish and problematical and thought it was better to rely on the infrared sight. He must have motioned Larry to turn it off again.

I acted with commendable speed and presence of mind. At almost the same second as the light went out, I hobbled, rather than ran, across the lateral passage. The shot Gabriel loosed off plowed harmlessly into the carpet and was so late and inaccurate he must have pulled the trigger at random.

Once more I was in a position of temporary safety. My strength was definitely on the ebb. He'd also be starting to guess that, whatever else I had, I didn't have a gun. I couldn't carry Astrid much farther, and she showed no sign of returning to consciousness. Here I was, staggering along the corridor and up a steep ramp with Astrid, while my adversary was padding along the parallel corridor encumbered with nothing more burdensome than a rifle and a pocketful of cartridges.

I advanced to the mouth of the next lateral corridor. There I put Astrid down. I knelt painfully and deposited her as gently as I could on the carpeted floor. She was breathing lightly and irregularly. I stayed kneeling for a few moments, dead beat, seeking to recover a little strength. I didn't dare pause too long, haunted as I was by the mental picture of Gabriel appearing in front of us, sighting down his gun-barrel. I was also afraid that if I waited too long I'd never manage to whip my stiff limbs into action again.

I floundered to my feet and wallowed along to the end of the corridor. The slope of the ramp felt as cruel as if I were climbing a mountain. I had enough presence of mind to keep well back from the lip of the tunnel when I reached it, so as not to expose myself to the sharpshooter down the corridor to my right. I had a definite idea he was shortening the distance each time by walking a few feet farther forward. I tried to clear the rising mists from my brain as I peered across the intervening corridor at the next step of the obstacle course. How far did I still have to go? . . . How far?

When I raised my eyes, a colossal surge of excitement raced through me. It was as if I'd put my hand on one of the naked wires in the wrecked bulkhead. Opposite me, as I looked up the ramp, there was only one entrance. And beyond it, vaguely emerging in the cold, pearly light of day, was the dark glitter of a flight of steel stairs leading up to the rear exit of the maze. These were steps, not a ramp. They rose steeply and majestically—a final sadistic twist in my design. If Gabriel couldn't put a bullet through me in the shadows of the maze, he'd be able to pick me off at leisure as I toiled up that gleaming staircase . . .

All the same, I felt a flash of irrational hope. I was someone trapped in the depths of a cavern who sees the brightness of the cave-mouth looming ahead of him. The fog in my head evaporated. I was seized by a lunatic impulse to storm straight ahead. I choked it down. Thoughts were rushing without logic and sequence through my mind.

I went back to Astrid, took hold of her by the ankles, and dragged her as gently as I could manage a dozen yards back down the corridor. I'd decided to leave her where she was. I could act more freely without her, and she'd be less open to danger. It would be easier for me to do whatever I had to do and come back and fetch her when it was over—if I was still alive. I knelt down and nudged her body close to the wall until she was actually touching it. I wanted her to be far enough back for there to be a good chance of Gabriel's lantern missing her as he passed by in the other corridor.

Moved by a sudden impulse, I bent forward and kissed her cold mouth. Then I got to my feet and went back to the end of the corridor. I looked at the distant staircase, divided from me by the deadly No Man's Land of the lateral corridor. Fifteen feet under fire.

What was I to do?

I was cleaned out of ideas. I couldn't think of anything remotely original, let alone brilliant.

I suppose I actually loitered there for less than twenty seconds. Then I did the first thing that came into my head.

I ran the gantlet.

20

I can't say I burst out of my hiding-place like a quarter-miler kicking off from the blocks. I was stiff with cold and half lame. I had to run uphill. But I came out faster than I ever thought I could. The prospect of being sniped at concentrates a man's mind wonderfully.

I hurled myself forward with my head crushed down into my shoulders and my arms swinging.

The gun seemed to go off a yard from my right ear. It sounded like a cannon. I thought I'd be lifted clean off my feet by the blast and the impact of the bullet. There was a crash. I spun around, tottering. Something stung my cheek and mouth and the top of my chest. I felt a tearing pain. Another explosion, and something hit the back of my skull like a brick. The impetus of the double blow and my initial momentum sent me reeling forward, and I went sprawling into the mouth of the tunnel opposite. In the same movement I picked myself up and propelled myself forward like a football player after a tackle. I rolled and scrambled toward the towering staircase like a cat thrown over a high wall.

Gabriel would be close behind me. He'd come hurrying in for the kill. I got to the bottom of the staircase. It was sharp and sheer as the staircase of an Aztec temple. As I prepared to climb, I expected the crack of the next bullet in my spine. I thought I'd already been fatally shot.

With my bare foot on the first icy step I happened to turn my head. There was a recess in the wall at the foot of the stairs. I remembered that there was one on each side. They were mere slots in the wall, three feet wide and four feet deep. They weren't intended for any special purpose, though Gabriel thought he might buy a couple of classical statues to stand in them. They were part of the structure. The design had just worked out that way. Instead of making myself an open target on the stairs, I might as well postpone my death for a moment. I might as well get my breath back and die with dignity, on my feet, instead of banging and bumping down a flight of stairs like a sack of potatoes.

With a bound I reached the recess, turned, and fell back into it. My legs scarcely supported me. I was like a corpse propped in an upright metal coffin. Shivering, I realized that Gabriel's first shot had hit the torch as it swung loose on my wrist, showering me with splinters of glass and cutting my face and chest. The second shot had creased the back of my scalp. I fingered the hair and there seemed to be a flap of wet flesh hanging loose.

From the corner of my left eye as I stood rammed against the wall I could see the topmost stair and part of the square door with its panes of reinforced glass. I stared at the strengthening daylight like a condemned man. The light splashed down the steps and slashed their rigid geometry with gay and sparkling lines.

A few yards away, there came a genteel click as if someone was cocking a gun. The sound of a soft shoefall. I slipped the screwdriver into my left hand.

The barrel that came poking past my hiding-place

wasn't, as I'd expected, the barrel of a rifle, but the barrel of a pistol. I didn't give myself time to philosophize about it. I jackknifed out of my iron slot and whacked the extended forearm with my broken flashlight. At the same time I brought the screwdriver upwards with a sharp hard jab.

Larry stepped backwards with a gasp. He held his hands upwards and outwards away from him as if they'd been attached to wires. He'd taken off the black blazer, but was still wearing the red turtleneck sweater. The sweater was even redder now in the area of the abdomen where the handle of the screwdriver was sticking out just under the breastbone. The blood was spreading over the woolen cloth as if I'd driven a nail into a bag of ink. His black-rimmed spectacles fell off, and the gun went up over his shoulder in a blue arc and bounced along the carpet. His knees bent, and he went over backwards. He hit the floor with his shoulders and the back of his head like an acrobat doing a back flip. His legs straightened and his arms came up jerkily and his hands folded themselves in a curiously tender way round the haft of the screwdriver without being able to pull it out.

The last thing he saw was the shadowed figure of a man with a bloodied face and savage eyes, barefooted, naked to the waist, neck and body seamed with welts and scratches. I don't know whether his eyes were still open as I swung away from him and made for the stairs. I started to mount them, using my hands and feet with the agility of a monkey. I hadn't felt any twinge of guilt or disgust at what I'd done—my time in the maze had reduced me pretty much to the condition of an animal at bay, or one of Gabriel's rats. My aching head was craned backwards, and my eyes were fastened on the metal door above me. I could already make out the thin slit of the keyhole with the corona of daylight streaming through it.

I hadn't climbed more than four or five steps when there was the rip and kick of a bullet. It struck the metal step immediately ahead of me and tore a jagged white sliver from it that missed my head by a centimeter as it whanged away. I flopped forward on my face and stayed motionless.

A few more steps and I'd have—have— Well . . . No matter . . . Not now . . .

I rolled over on my elbows, and Gabriel was below me. He was wearing a red turtleneck sweater like Larry's. He was lowering the gun. It was a bulky weapon with a sling. Clamped to the top was a telescopic sight that looked too large for it. He let his arms drop and held the gun loosely at his hips. In the gloom behind, I could make out Larry's body, lying in the same position as it had fallen.

He wanted me to sweat before he pulled the trigger.

I didn't care much. It was only like putting an exhausted creature out of its misery. My will to live was guttering down. I watched the neatly clad executioner raising the rifle to his shoulder again in a way that was almost detached. His movements were measured and precise, as they were when he photographed one of his railroad accidents. He was going to extract the last ounce of satisfaction out of killing me. I could almost hear him deliberating with himself where to put the bullet.

I started to rise to my feet, for no particular reason except that it seemed the only act of minor defiance left to me. The snout of the gun tilted with me. It crossed my sluggish brain that he was going to shoot me right in the face. Then the tip of the barrel was depressed again, and I

saw that he was going to let me have it in the belly . . .
No . . . Lower down . . .

If he'd simply gone ahead and loosed off at my face I
don't think I'd have stirred a muscle. I'd have accepted it
fatalistically like the bull in the slaughterhouse waiting for
the lethal spike behind its ear. But that other thing! . . .
He was stupid there. I remember I'd already begun to move
when the voice came out of the black corridor behind him.

"*Gabriel!*"

The muzzle was swinging to follow me. My attempt to
skip to one side would only have delayed the shot by two
seconds. The end would have been the same. The shout
altered that.

"*GABRIEL!*"

Astrid. She came running forward. The shot that had
wounded her had ripped her bra, and it was hanging loose.
Her breasts jutted from the open negligee. With her sweat-
plastered blonde hair standing up and streaming behind her
she looked like some distracted Fury or goddess of the
Underworld. He should have been prepared for it. He
should have noticed I was alone on the staircase and must
have left her behind. But he was taken by surprise. He
whirled around confused, staring, gun sagging. As soon as
he saw who it was, he lifted the barrel immediately and
squeezed the trigger from a position down around the
level of his stomach.

She was only a few feet away. He couldn't have missed
—except that at the moment when he spun around I was
already catapulting down the four or five steps that divided
us. I came down on him an instant before the gun went
off. I hit him in the back and the gun sprang into the air to
his left and he went diving in the other direction. He col-

lided with the wall as he fell, and as he tried to get up I was on him again. I got the hammer in my hand and clouted him twice behind the left ear, once as he was rising and once as he was falling.

I tripped over him and nearly went flailing into the wall myself. I took a heavy dive onto the carpet and just lay there. I remember trying to get up, but couldn't make it. I think I blacked out . . .

It didn't seem a second before Astrid was kneeling above me and crying and stroking my face. I woke instantaneously to what seemed exactly the same situation.

She had to help me up. I clung to her as I gazed down briefly at Gabriel, then lurched over to take another look at Larry. I kept hold of her while I pointed down at the pistol. She had to keep me from falling as she saw I wanted her to stoop down and pick it up for me. She put it in my hand with a tremor of revulsion. My fingers were so palsied they were hardly able to grasp it.

She had to help me up the stairs. My legs were bars of water. It took an age to reach the top and several light-years longer before I could dig the key out of my pocket and put it in the lock.

It needed several efforts to turn the key, even though the mechanism was freshly oiled, and several more to turn the ornate bronze handle and open the door an inch . . .

I shuffled off to the right of the door and motioned her to walk through it. She hesitated. I motioned again. She was so used to obeying me by this time that she slowly dragged back the heavy door and stepped around it into the world outside.

The draft of fresh air that curled around the door was so intoxicating it made me dizzy. I'd meant to stand behind the door, but the air got to me and I slid down the wall and sat in a nerveless heap in the corner.

I'd guessed from the outset that Gabriel wouldn't leave the rear exit unguarded. Whoever was on duty there had probably been given orders to shoot. But after all these hours, and maybe as much as a day and a night in the open, he'd probably be sleepy and sluggish. He'd have been expecting to see me—not Astrid—and her appearance was bound to puzzle him . . .

I seem to recall voices and a car door slamming. At length there were slow and careful footsteps on the broad gravel apron that had been laid only a couple of days earlier outside the door. They stopped for a measured moment, then came on again. I'd been on the verge of dozing off, probably as a result of that anesthetizing gush of air. I thumped my kneecap with the barrel of the gun to wake myself up.

He came through the door with a pistol held in front of him, just like Larry a few minutes before. I lifted my head and saw his shadow on the frosted panes above me. I tried to raise my legs a little to brace myself. He entered cautiously and stopped at the top of the staircase, weaving his head about.

I shot him four times, twice at the top of the steps and twice as he started to pitch forward into the empty air. I think I hit him all four times, though the last bullet might have missed.

Somehow I hoisted myself up off the floor. Somehow I reached the outside. Somehow I pushed the iron door closed again, locked it, and put the key back in my pocket.

The birds were singing. My eyes hurt. Was it morning, or afternoon? Away in the far distance, across the grassless brown meadow that covered the maze, I could make out as a vague blur the white spread of the house, behind its screen of pine trees.

I stood outside the rear exit with its classical pediment and Corinthian columns—a replica of the pediment and columns on the great house to which it was joined by that tortuous and terrible network of underground passages. I rocked backwards and forwards, out on my feet.

I jerked my scattered wits back to the present at the sound of a car starting up. Dimly I registered that there were two cars parked one behind the other on the new service road connecting the maze with the distant house. One was biscuit-colored and the other royal blue. The blue car pulled out and drove away past the car ahead of it with a scur and swish of its wheels. We heard it humming away down the drive in the direction of the main gates. Then the noise of its engine died away, and the empty shining day was silent again.

We drove back to the house at ten miles an hour. I was fighting against a great wave of blackness. Astrid sat with her head on the back of her seat. Her face was streaked with grime and her hair matted and tangled. My right hand was smeared with blood where I'd wiped it against the wound on the back of my head. The caked black blood was moistened by the sweat that ran down my bare arm. It came off in a sticky smear on the rim of the steering wheel.

21

THERE was no one in the house. Gabriel had arranged it that way. He'd sent away all the household servants and gardeners and the last remaining workmen on the site.

We took a shower to remove the blood and dirt. We didn't talk. We were too numb and weary. What was there to say? I cleaned and dressed Astrid's hurt back as well as I could with materials from Gabriel's medicine cabinet, and she put a temporary dressing on the back of my head. Then we changed into fresh clothes.

Upstairs, in the rooms in the empty mansion, the hands of the clocks circled the vacant dials. The locomotives and freight cars stood idle on the tracks of the model railway. The miniature racing cars waited silently on the starting grid. The model soldiers were drawn up regiment by regiment, waiting to be summoned into battle. The bombers and interceptors were suspended motionless in the air.

In the penny arcade the rows of pinball machines gathered dust. The player pianos and mechanical organs were dumb. The sticks of the ice-hockey teams were raised in frozen attitudes. The batter's bat was lifted as he waited for a ball that was never pitched. The racehorses galloped down the course without gaining a millimeter. The cats on the rooftops snoozed peacefully without anyone to pot at them. The condemned men waited patiently for their executioners to pull the levers.

The kinetic sculpture in the darkened gallery whirred and clicked, with nobody to heed them.

Nobody peered through the pinholes to stare at the peep-shows.

The man and the woman in their white robes ran through the mysterious landscape pursued by the cloud of insects and with the volcano spouting flames behind them.

The steel ball ran endlessly across the tilting plate. The fluted glass rod twirled endlessly round and round and round and round and round and round in the make-believe fountain.

the garden game

'I repeat again,' said Svidrigaïlov:
'There would never have been any unpleasantness
except for what happened in the garden. . .'

DOSTOIEVSKY: *Crime and Punishment*

'I forsee that man will resign himself each day to new
abominations, that soon only soldiers and bandits
will be left.'

BORGES: *The Garden of Forking Paths*

IT was inevitable, considering how brutalizing my trade had become in these last few years, that sooner or later I should have found myself involved in something as strange as the Garden Game.

There had been an increasing grimness about my recent undertakings. My cousin, Harrison Hopwood, whom you will meet shortly, has no doubt been secretly cataloguing them with disapproving relish.

The joke, of course, is that I have embarked on them from the purest, the most patriotic of motives: and what have they brought me, except the prospect of a miserable old age and the mistrust of all those good citizens on whose behalf I have engaged in such desperate enterprises?

I suppose Harrison and our faceless masters can't altogether be blamed where the Garden Game was concerned. It was really a by-product of my normal activities—if you can call them normal. I brought down the whole business, which took me before it finished to Central Europe and America, largely on my own head. I was betrayed into it by something dangerous to possess in my line of work: a sense of obligation, or personal responsibility, or whatever you want to call it.

I assure you, at forty-seven I am growing too old and fragile to cope with sinister larks like the Garden Game. It would frighten men half my age who are just launching out, at Harrison's instigation, on this thankless profession. The cottage I dream about, nestling beside a trout stream among the dales of Cumberland or Westmorland, is starting to seem wonderfully inviting to me now.

This most recent instalment of the Rickman saga began

six hours after an ungrateful government had grudgingly released me from prison.

The authorities finally decided to let me loose on a cold rainy night in mid-December. They had kept me locked up in Leigh Central Prison for nearly eight months: and you have to remember that for nine months before that they had let me rot in a barbed-wire compound in West Africa. In that stinking camp in Nigeria I was practically fried to death; then I was hauled back to England and pushed into a freezing white-washed rabbit-hutch with walls ten feet thick. You can imagine what sort of shape I was in— hardly the condition to cope with the strenuous events ahead of me.

Of course, I enjoyed special privileges at Leigh Central. I was treated as a kind of political prisoner. The governor was under Home Office instructions to deal with me lightly. Although I was kept in isolation, the door of my room, which was in the hospital wing, was locked late at night and unlocked early in the morning. I received as many visitors and as much mail as I liked; I sent out for books to the local library; on occasion I was allowed to purchase my own wines and delicacies at a nearby delicatessen. It was like being a well-to-do prisoner in Newgate or the Fleet Prison in the eighteenth century. The governor didn't like it, but he had to comply. Like everyone else, he had read the long accounts of the capture and court-martial of my group of so-called 'mercenaries' in the English papers, and accepted what he read at its face value. Journalists know a juicy bone when they see one, and they had certainly made us look bad. All the same, when I was in solitary confinement in that filthy compound there was a trio of journalists who managed to keep me alive by smuggling in food to me and persuading the guards to beat me up only two or three times a week instead of every day.

Because of my special position at Leigh Central, I was able to regain a good deal of strength by running and doing exercises. Every day when it was fine I trotted for an hour round the prison yard; on days when it was wet—and I had been out of England so long I hadn't remembered how much it rains in Yorkshire—I worked out in my cell with a set of weights. I was still hampered by my broken ankle, where the bits of bone refused to mend in spite of the skill of the prison doctor, who treated me with tender care while making it plain that he disapproved of me. There was usually a copy of *The New Statesman* lying around in his surgery, so there was no point in trying to convince a man of his kidney that there was more in my case than met the eye.

I had been hearing rumours for some weeks that Whitehall was trying to reach a secret agreement with the Nigerian government, and that I might soon be discreetly released. Harrison himself, in one of his cautious and infrequent messages, had hinted that my day of liberation might be at hand. I suppose he expected me to weep tears of gratitude. Anyway, the door of my cell was opened at ten-fifteen at night, when I was settling down to the last chapters of *The Adventures of Roderick Random*, and I was told to pack my belongings and be ready to leave in an hour. I was handed a heavy leather suitcase containing a raincoat and some clothes that I didn't immediately recognize as mine, as it had been seventeen months since I last wore them, or had seen that suitcase. I was so used to my tattered mud-stained denims, then to the grey prison uniform, that my fingers were clumsy as I put them on. I was pleased to notice that I hadn't put on any weight, and that the band of the trousers seemed to be slightly looser.

I think they decided to push me out into the rainy night at that hour because they were afraid a flock of journalists might learn the news and descend on the gaol. I doubt if they need have worried: with all the violent events that fill the news these days, who would remember the misadventures of an obscure soldier-of-fortune in Africa over two years before?

Carrying the suitcase, to which I had now transferred my few books and the box of water-colours I had been amusing myself with, I was taken through silent, darkened, sour-smelling concrete corridors to the governor's office. He was seated behind his Victorian desk, his heavy arms inert on the blotter in front of him. Behind him stood his deputy. I put down the suitcase and stepped up in front of the desk. In the dead but ever watchful silence of the prison I could hear the rain beating against the blinded walls and streaming through the gutters.

The governor stared at me with his bulging blue eyes, the deputy with his ratty black ones. I stared back at them, saying nothing. In the governor's expression there was the same curiosity mixed with resentment that had been there for the past eight months and seventeen days. I had been a model prisoner, nursing my wounds, exhaustion and bitterness with the patience that still came hard to me, but which I had learned to master in the past fifteen unrelenting years. They regarded me as a mysterious master-criminal whom they would have liked, had they been allowed, to commit to the maximum-security block. It is often believed that one English gentleman will temper the wind to another English gentleman in distress; but that isn't true, either in the professions, the Stock Exchange, or in prison. The governor, sitting there lumpishly in the shadow of the lamp on the filing-cabinet behind him, would have crucified me as cheerfully as dear Colonel Hamid, who used to enjoy kicking me in the groin in Lagos.

I had been in similar situations before, and didn't feel called on to plunge into conversation. If they had anything to say, now the farce was ending, let them get on with it. Were they waiting for me to fall on my knees and apologize? Maybe they were cross at having to leave their private quarters on such a night to attend to my release.

It may have been my appearance in an expensive suit and a smart white raincoat that made the governor lumber to his feet and wave his hand at the chair beside me. I could sense a certain respect in the attitude of the warders behind me, standing a few paces further back than they would have done if I had been in prison drab. I shook my head. I didn't want to accept any favours, and I didn't want to sit down and chat: I wanted to finish the comedy as soon as possible. He took a packet of cigarettes out of his pocket and held it out to me. Again I shook my head. Even if I had been a smoker, I wouldn't have taken one. You may gather that the events of the past two years—savage fighting, the deaths of six men for whom I was responsible, a scandalous trial, an ankle smashed by a mortar-shell, a year and a half's imprisonment —hadn't improved the sunniness of my disposition.

The governor put the packet back in his pocket and cleared phlegm from his throat. His voice was ponderous, with a marked Yorkshire accent.

'Well, Mr Rickman.' He deliberately emphasized the 'Mister'. I ignored that. 'I have had a communication from my superior concerning you.' His deputy picked up a letter from the desk and placed it in his hand. 'It is brief and to the point.'

The cuff of the silk shirt slid over my wrist with unaccustomed smoothness as I held out my hand. He hesitated, then reached forward over the desk. I took the letter and glanced at it. The heading of the Home Office; four lines of instructions; the scrawled signature of an assistant undersecretary; the cheap buff-coloured stationery reserved for second-class correspondence. I didn't even rate the cream-laid paper. Three sentences ordering my release under the most discreet circumstances possible.

I handed the letter back. He seemed to be searching for something to say. I wondered if he was going to treat me to a homily about having paid my debt to society, and the rest of it. He saw the expression in my eyes and thought better of it. For the first time it began to strike me that I was about to become a free man again. I felt the dryness in the mouth, the tightening under the ribs you feel before going into action. For me, I suppose, the two things were always much the same.

The governor cleared his throat again and extended a meaty hand. I ignored it. I never shake hands with policemen, at any time, anywhere; I know too much about them. I picked up the suitcase and turned to the door.

Escorted by the deputy-governor and one of the warders I walked through more of those misery-saturated corridors to the main gate. The last fifty yards lay along a kind of cloister or covered way, the rain slopping down in sheets on either side of it. The tall gatehouse with its Victorian battlements lay ahead, outlined in the watery yellow glare of the battery of powerful lamps that ringed the inner courtyard. I shouldered my way past the warder and took the lead, quickening the pace until I was almost running.

I was left standing with the warder beneath the black vault of the gatehouse while the deputy went into the reception lodge. I sat on my suitcase, my heart thumping like a schoolboy going home for the holidays. I felt strangely weak. I could see the deputy talking to the gatekeeper, then he went over to one of the windows and peered out. I suppose he was looking to see if there was a reception committee waiting for me. It was extremely cold and I tightened the belt of the raincoat. A sergeant with a ring of keys clipped to his belt sauntered out of the lodge and gave me a flat, suspicious policeman's stare. I stared back at him.

It occurred to me that if no one was waiting for me I was actually in something of a hole. I seemed to remember vaguely that when a man left prison he was given a five-pound note by a benevolent government. I had been handed no such gratuity. So here I was, a hundred and fifty miles from London, at twenty-five to eleven on a wet winter night, without a penny in my pocket. I considered going into the lodge and speaking to the deputy; perhaps he could arrange a loan to pay my train fare, or at least let me use the phone to try and ring Sam Teague in Hackney. I could wait in the lodge until he arrived to pick me up, probably sometime in the small hours. I dismissed the thought. Rather than put myself under an obligation to them I would rather walk to London, every step of the way, suitcase or no suitcase, damaged ankle or no damaged ankle.

The deputy emerged from the lodge. I rose. The pudding-faced sergeant opened the iron-studded wicket set in the double doors. The deputy wisely made no attempt to shake hands with me, but said in a way which I have to admit was quite decent:

'Goodbye, Major. Will you let me wish you good luck? . . .'

I gave him a nod and bent my head to step through the wicket.

The door crashed shut behind me.

I WAS standing, stranded, in a dismal, dim-lit provincial street. I didn't know which way to walk, whether left, right or straight ahead. Yet the rain on my face was good; my first rain for over a year. I felt light-headed.

I tossed up mentally, hefted my suitcase, swung to the left and started walking down the worn pavement between the shabby little terraced houses. There wasn't a soul in sight. A hundred yards away, at the far end of the street, I could make out the bow window of a public-house. The coloured lights and the blare and beat of music came to me through the curtain of rain.

I was turning up the collar of my raincoat when some instinct, obviously not blunted by my spell in prison, prompted me to turn my head. A car that I had vaguely noticed higher up the street behind me, on the same side of the road, which I assumed was parked and empty, had its headlights on. I could hear the cough as the starter was pressed. It started to roll forward. The lights probed down the street towards me, refracted by the rain.

The excitement I felt on my release drained away. Why the hell hadn't I realized that some sort of reception committee would be waiting for me? I should have swallowed my pride and asked the governor to let me slip out by a side door. Or I could have insisted on remaining till morning, when it was light and the streets were busy.

The car was gaining, though very gradually, as if the murk made the driver uncertain. The events of the past hour had scrambled my wits. I tried to think. I stepped to the edge of the pavement and set down the suitcase squarely in the road. It couldn't stop the car itself but it might make the driver pull up or hesitate—or the noise of the case hitting the fender might scare or unsettle him.

I glanced at the windows of the houses nearest me. The curtains were drawn and the lights were burning cheerfully. The tinny boom of the T.V. set threatened to burst the walls. I could knock on one of the doors. I could push my way inside when it opened. But what if the family's eardrums were so blasted by television they were slow to hear my knock, and slower still to rouse themselves and shuffle into the dark passage to answer it? Whoever was in the car could run me down and finish me off before Dad had got the door half-open and was blinking into the sodden street . . .

I'd run for the pub. There'd be light and sanctuary there. Or there might be an alleyway between the pub and where I was now, an opening down which I could sprint and gain the next street, or lose myself on a railway-cutting or among allotments . . .

I broke into a run. Almost at the same second I heard a thump as the car smashed against the suitcase. I ran harder. There was the sound of a car door banging open. A string of curses. Feet pounding the pavement. A voice shouting.

. . . 'Sir! . . . Major! . . .'

I slowed down. I stopped. I recognized the voice.

I turned and started to walk back in the direction of the car.

The bitter relief that washed into me was spiced with disgust for my makeshift performance. I was rusty. I'd have to get back to basics. I'd have to perk myself up.

Teague's bulky shoulders and brown pockmarked face were outlined by the headlights against the tracery of the rain. He was groping around in the road for the suitcase. If it hadn't been for the rain, I would have recognized right away that the car was my own royal-blue Jensen. I would have saved myself a lot of fright and trouble.

Teague was stooping down in the road on the other side of the flooding gutter as I came level with him. He was wiping the worst of the wet from the leather case. He wore his old army trenchcoat. I saw an expression of concern on his blunt features, blurred by the downpour, as he looked down at my dragging right ankle. He had known I'd been wounded, but obviously didn't realize that it had left me with such a limp.

He came forward, pitched the suitcase behind the front seat, then helped me as I struggled to take off my raincoat. He held the door as I settled myself in the passenger seat, taking care not to knock my ankle. He closed the door, walked smartly round to the other side of the car, removed his own soaked raincoat and climbed behind the wheel.

'Sorry about that, Major.' We started to weave our way through the depressing maze of working-class streets. 'I could have waited directly outside the gates, but I'd been asked not to make myself conspicuous.'

'Who asked you?' I leaned forward to fiddle with the controls of the heater. In almost a year in England I'd never felt really warm. I'd forgotten how to work the heater control.

'Mr Hopwood.' He took an eye off the road and adjusted the heater for me. 'It'll start coming hotter in a minute.'

'So he called you?'

'Last night. He told me the time of your release. I drove up this morning with your suitcase. The governor said you'd be out soon enough; he made me wait.'

Soon enough . . . Policemen . . . Still, it explained why I hadn't been handed any money. They knew I was being met, though they hadn't seen fit to tell me . . .

'Mr Hopwood wants to see you tomorrow, Major.'

'Tomorrow?'

'He'll call you in the morning.'

'He doesn't waste time, does he?'

'Do you think he's got another job for us?'

His steady voice, with its West Country burr, came out of the darkness. He didn't sound enthusiastic. Probably he was thinking the same thing I was. After being so long out of circulation, and with a cracked ankle, didn't I need a long lay-off before plunging into another of Harrison's little capers? You could scarcely blame him. After all, our last outing hadn't been exactly a blazing success. And, as usual, his would be one of the necks we'd be putting on the chopping-block. I glanced at his square profile. The beams of light from the street lamps ran over it like water over a squat boulder. He was frowning. I nearly told him that during the long days in gaol I'd almost made up my mind to tell Harrison to go to hell. And it was true that I had been studying the advertisements in the property columns of the paper for that cottage in the Lake District, with access to a good trout-stream . . .

Something made me hold my tongue. Out of policy I seldom confided in the people who worked for me, on the principle that what they didn't know couldn't hurt them. And there was no point in being premature. My interview with Harrison would be ticklish. I wish he'd given me more time to unwind and prepare for it. But that was always his way: to keep us all off-balance, keep us on the wrong foot . . .

Teague, bending forward, was running the tips of his fingers along the underside of the dashboard. I heard a click as he pressed the stud that released the hidden compartment. His hand came up with a fat silver flask. I took it gratefully. He was a resourceful man. Before he became my second-in-command he was a highly regarded adjutant and quarter-master of an R.E. regiment.

The flask contained cherry brandy—just the ticket for a tedious drive on a rainy night. I drank a third of the flask and held it out. I saw him shake his head and give a grin in the glow from a passing store-front.

'No thanks, Major. We've got enough on our plate tonight without the police stopping us and making me breathe into a little bag . . .'

The warmth from the heater was beginning to register. I adjusted the catch of my seat and stretched out my legs. It was fine to relax and feel the chill in my bones begin to dissolve. I took sips from the flask and savoured the sensation of speed and freedom after the tomb-like stillness of the cell. I watched the lighted buildings wheel past and saw the rain and sensed the wind and clouds. I felt the car rock and the springs jog beneath me . . . I was beginning to live again . . .

'I hope you don't mind me bringing the Jensen, Major? As soon as they flew me back from Lagos I brought it into the garage and laid it up. I didn't know how long you'd— well—be away . . . Then when Mr Hopwood called ten days ago and told me to stand by in case you were released, I brought it out and checked it through. It's really in very good nick . . .'

And that, I reflected drowsily, was a damned sight more than I was . . .

I took another pull at the flask. My ankle wasn't hurting, in spite of my exertions fifteen minutes ago. It was holding up well. That at least was an encouraging sign . . .

Teague was negotiating the city streets cautiously. We didn't want to draw attention to ourselves. It was when we were driving through a residential quarter on the other side of town, and had been silent for some time, that he suddenly said in the quiet way I was familiar with, and which made me sit up:

'Major, I don't want to worry you, but there's a car following us.'

I sat up further. 'Oh? How long has it been there?'

'Since we left Leigh Central. I've been waiting for it to sheer off, but it hasn't.'

I brought my seat upright. I craned my head to look through the rear window but wasn't surprised that all I could see was a hazy pair of lights about fifty yards behind.

'Police car?'

'No.'

'What make?'

'Can't tell. It's not a sports car, though, so unless it's some sort of a special job we've got the legs of it . . . Point is, in a couple of minutes we'll reach the ramp of the motorway . . . and we'll never shake them then—not if I have to observe the speed-limit and drive as if my boots were made of paper . . . unless you'd like us to get picked up for speeding, that is? . . . I mean, it would give us protection, wouldn't it? . . . But I don't suppose you are exactly keen on that, tonight, are you? . . .'

'Not exactly, no.'

'Then what say I lose them right away, before we get to the motorway?'

He kept watching the other car in the mirror, maintaining an even distance: but his big brown hands shifted from the bottom of the wheel to a purposeful ten-to-two, and I saw the stiffening of his powerful body. I said:

'You haven't got the gun down there, have you, under the dash?'

'Afraid not, Major. I took it out when I sent the car to the garage.'

'Did you bring one yourself?'

'No. I thought that since I was visiting a prison I'd better be clean . . .' His solid jaw tilted forward. 'We're coming to some traffic-lights, Major. And we're not going to run them —we're going to slow down and come to a stop, like gentlemen and Christians. The fellow behind will shut down and stay fifty yards behind us. He's been doing that all night. Maybe he's already got the spot picked out when he's going to spring his surprise on us . . . The second I stop, fasten your safety-belt . . .'

I screwed the top on the flask and slipped it in my pocket. He drew up with deceptive smoothness at the lights. The instant the car stopped he slid his arms into the harness, snapped the buckle and tightened the straps.

Seconds before the red clicked off he let in the clutch and

the Jensen rammed forward with the Pirellis howling on the wet black tarmac. It was what in his racing days he used to call 'laying a patch'. I had been through such moments with him before, and was braced for it, but even so my body was thrust back savagely into my seat.

Thank God, the roads were empty at this time of night. Teague threw the car round corners, picking them at random, doubling back. Parks, churches, cinemas, public buildings and supermarkets flashed past. In general he tried to keep away from main streets, but every now and again one of them loomed up and several times he took a chance and ran the lights. I sat tight and kept silent and let him get on with it. If it came to a choice, I'd prefer to try and explain to the police rather than tangle with the people in the car behind . . .

Teague was enjoying himself. He was a transport specialist. He always liked to drive our trucks and cars—drive them fast—what he referred to as 'wringing it out.' His brother owned the garage in Hackney where the Jensen had just been serviced, and when he first joined me he was still taking part in drag-races and stock-car races. During my recent seclusion he had occupied himself by lending his brother a hand: and I'm quite sure when he said he'd 'laid up' my Jensen FF he'd actually been joy-riding around in it. As soon as I bought it four years ago he'd badgered me into letting him modify it— changing the gears in the differential for greater acceleration, putting on wide-oval tyres and special light wheels—'mags', he called them. In several other respects he wasn't particularly skilful, and some of the grimier aspects of our work he could be made to carry out only with reluctance. Like me, he sometimes had too nice a conscience; he suffered from the disadvantage of being altogether a decent man. But the driving gave him infinite pleasure.

In what was probably less than ten minutes, though it seemed a hundred years, he cruised to a stop on a dark and deserted street and cut the engine.

'That ought to do it, Major. He knew his business, who-ever he was—but we knew where we were going to turn, and he didn't . . .'

He got out a flashlight and produced a map. Without turning on the roof-light, holding the map well below the level of his knee (I was pleased he remembered some of the lessons I'd taught him), he scrutinized it.

'Well, Major, there'll be no motorway for us tonight. We'll have to use byroads . . .'

I took the flask out of my pocket and treated myself to another mouthful.

AFTER a while I settled back in my seat and sank into a light doze. In spite of the external warmth of the heater and the internal warmth of the cherry brandy I was too keyed up to sleep soundly. I was beginning to feel warm for the first time for eight months, like a carcase taken out of the deep-freeze. There had been a few odd days in the frugal Yorkshire summer when I basked in the sun in the high-walled yard, but even in August my cell had been a grey and chilly place. I half-expected to be lulled into slumber by the rocking motion of the Jensen and the steady thrumming of the engine, blended with the click of the wipers and the swish of the rain: but the mildest noise and movement was unsettling after the measureless, deadly stillness of my isolated quarters in the hospital block.

For an hour I lay back drowsily, not wanting to move, disinclined to talk. Teague, understanding my mood, drove silently and at a steady pace. From time to time unbidden images came into my mind—the fiasco in Africa, the meeting with Harrison, the beefy face of the governor, my bleak now-empty cell with the iron bedstead, Maggie's thin humorous face and gleaming red hair. Then I would turn my head and open my eyes for a minute and see Teague's stolid features illuminated in the greenish light of the dash. Now and again he cast a wary eye in the mirror: but there was never any hint of pursuit now, scarcely any other cars at all on the empty country roads by which we were wheeling southwards towards the capital.

Even with my eyes closed it gave me a sense of peace and returning strength to be driving through the rainy heart of England. On either side of us the soaked winter fields stretched away into the soft thick blackness towards the matted lines of the groves that crowned the crests. The animals lay quiet in their byres or under the sheltering lea of the sturdy hedgerows. The farmers and their wives and children were asleep at the centre of their little kingdoms. This was the real, the ancient, the undying England, the England I had thought of in Malaya, in Kinshasa and Indo-China—and in Lagos and Leigh Central. This was the England all my work, such as it was, had been for—and for which, I suppose, it had all been worth while. It was in this England that that magic cottage of mine would be situated— soon, soon, let it be soon ... I had a feeling, as the dripping boughs and muddy ploughlands whirled past in the deep darkness, that Teague and I were keeping a lonely, loyal vigil, that in our secret way we were helping to keep guard, two men on watch in a landscape where only the fox, the weasel and the stoat were otherwise alert and stirring.

We drove through small towns with arcaded corn-markets built in the reign of William and Mary, or Queen Anne, at their centre . . . yes, the real, honest England, surviving all the slights and insults, the pettiness and the dishonest rhetoric. A few miles beyond one of them, when we were again enveloped in the cloudy night and smothering rain, Teague stopped the car to top up the tank from the spare cans he carried in the boot. I wandered down the road in the fine drizzle and stamped up and down to stretch my cramped limbs. I stood by a farm gate and made water on the ground. It is a strange little sensation to relieve yourself in the country at night: your urine splashes on the ground, you feel the connection between your insides and the naked earth, united by the long leisurely stream of liquid. I remembered the crusted bowls and smelly tin pots of Leigh Central. Standing with the rain on my face I felt again how the journey was beginning to restore me after the months in gaol.

When we started off again I was wide awake and began to

talk. There was a lot I wanted to ask Teague, a lot I needed to catch up on. We skirted the subject of the African disaster —that could wait till later, when we could dissect it and decide where and why the whole thing came apart. I questioned him first of all about his own activities in recent months; I knew from his monthly visits to Leigh Central how, by some miracle neither of us could yet explain, he and the other four survivors had been abruptly released from the compound at Lagos and flown back on an Italian jet to London. I knew, too, how Harrison had debriefed him: but he hadn't said much about how he'd been living since then. He hadn't been starving, but he'd been having a fairly rough time, even though he hadn't complained. Helping to run a small garage wasn't quite the style for a trained and experienced man like him. It was his own fault, of course: on his visit to Leigh I offered to let him go, urged him to take a sensible job, but he insisted on hanging on.

Well, at least I knew where Teague was now, and what he'd been doing: it was the other four, the juniors, who concerned me. I was disturbed by the little that Teague had been able to tell me about them in prison.

'So Harrison didn't debrief them, at the time he debriefed you?'

'No, he didn't bother. I was the number two, after all. What did the rest know?'

'And he didn't pay them off?—he didn't come across with the balance of the money we owed them?'

'He couldn't have done, could he? And they must have been as mad as hell. Otherwise why would they have taken off like that?'

'I told them over and over again they'd got to stay in touch with you. I drummed it into them. You heard me. Harrison might have finished with them, but I hadn't. I've got responsibilities towards them.'

'Responsibilities?'

I handed him the flask with the last of the cherry brandy.

'Here, drink up. It can't do any harm, out here.' He took it and drank. 'Yes,' I said. 'Responsibilities. I've got to return them where I got them from. Nice and bright and shiny. In the same condition I got them.'

'You really feel like that?' He sounded surprised.

'Of course I do. Don't you? I mean, these men are rather special types, aren't they—like you and me? All that time in gaol, I wasn't easy in my mind about them.' I stared out of the bleared window at the lights in the upper storey of a farmhouse, far out across a watery pasture . . . (what were they doing up at half-past two in the morning? . . . making love, quarrelling, dying, bringing a baby into our mad world, watching an old movie on TV?) . . . I went on: 'No, I'm not easy in my mind about them . . . Haven't you got any idea where they disappeared to when they reached London?'

'They scattered the minute the wheels hit the runway. All four of them. If I hadn't been shipped back on a later plane—in handcuffs, mind you—maybe I could have kept an eye on them.' His bulky shoulders rose and fell in the gloom. 'As it was—!'

'Damn it, they can't have simply vanished into thin air, can they? They were still technically on assignment.'

'The only one I ever heard from was Grady Bailey. I told you about the phone call I had, six weeks after I was released. Not that he said much—only that he was passing through London, that he'd got a fine job, that I was to tell you he was sorry you'd had to carry the can back for the whole operation, that he hoped you'd be out soon . . . When I asked where he was speaking from, he rang off. Somehow I felt he'd been warned not to get in touch with us—that he felt he'd already said too much . . .'

Grady Bailey. Twenty-six. Born Durham. Educated Pelham Grammar and Heidelberg, where his father was R.S.M. in the Green Howards. Lieutenant in the Rifle Brigade. Detached for special duty—which meant, of course, *my* ill-fated little lot . . . The youngest of the twelve of us, one of the toughest and most aggressive, certainly the most cheerful and agreeable. And the biggest daredevil. And the only one of us who was married—I felt at the time I was wrong to take him on. Still, he certainly knew a lot about explosives.

Where was he now? What was he up to? I wished to hell I knew.

I remembered telling Teague, at Leigh, that Thea Bailey had turned up unexpectedly at the gaol to visit me. Grady's wife turned out to be a tiny, fragile girl who couldn't have been more than twenty. She'd been crying, and acted during the twenty minutes we were together as if she didn't believe they'd let her out of the gaol again. She was a sweet girl, though a bit silly, poorly educated, and not very bright. She was worried sick. She'd made the long trip from London to Leigh specially to ask me why her husband had disappeared and when she could expect him back. She sat dabbing her eyes and squirming on the hard chair in that bare and icy visiting-room reeking of carbolic. What could I tell her? She'd gone to the H.Q. of the Rifle Brigade. Naturally, they couldn't tell her anything—only that he'd been seconded at War Office orders for an unspecified purpose, and for an indefinite time. They probably thought he'd run out on her.

Then I saw her stuff her damp handkerchief in her pocket and take out three registered envelopes and a much-fingered and folded letter. The first registered envelope, posted in London, had reached her a week after her husband's return to England on the Italian airliner; it had contained fifteen hundred pounds—a sizeable sum for a humble subaltern in an infantry regiment. It was a great deal more than any of my own payments to him had been.

The letter had accompanied the first envelope. It had been posted in Colchester, a town neither of them had been to in their lives. It told her in stilted but sincere phrases how much he loved her, urged her not to worry about him, and closed by saying that he'd got a chance to make more money quickly than he'd probably ever earn in the rest of his life; he'd try to get in touch with her again, if he could. The other registered envelopes came at monthly intervals and contained five hundred pounds apiece. Again, not bad pay for a second lieutenant. No letter each time.

I stared into the night and decided that as soon as I reached London I'd contact her. I'd find out if she'd heard from him again, whether the cheques were still coming—or had stopped . . .

'Teague,' I said, 'it sounds as if our Grady has found himself another employer . . .'

'Lucky, lucky man . . .'

'The question is, have the others found the same employer as Grady?'

'You mean, such a damned good employer they didn't even need to drop in to collect their pay?'

'Exactly—but what kind of employer would want to hire an odd bunch like that? And what on earth would he hire them for? . . .'

Teague laughed. 'What indeed, Major? . . .'

'And God only knows what kind of trouble the four of them could get into in eleven months! . . .' There was a slight pause, then Teague said soberly:

'May I say something?'

'What?'

'Well, then, Major—I wouldn't trouble yourself too much about them if I were you.'

'Oh?'

'No, if you'll forgive me for saying so, once we've both thrashed out the pros and cons of what happened in Africa, for our own sakes, we ought to forget Kano and Sokoto and everything that happened on the Niger. We took the licking of our lives, and what's the point of dwelling on it? . . .' He kept his eyes rigidly on the road ahead, but the Cornish voice was determined: he meant to have his say. 'What's more, Major, you know that I was dead against our taking on that business in the first place—and definitely not with such an expanded unit. And tell me, Major, except for Bailey, did any of the others bother to ask what happened to either of us, to you or me? Why should we worry about them, when they didn't worry about us? The pair of us got beaten half to death. You were tried for your life and nearly shot. You were locked up for almost a year and a half. Tell me, where was Bailey then? Where were Asher, and Douglass, and Lurtsema? They got away with little more than four months —then Mr Hopwood, or whoever else it was, bailed them out. They were free and clear. No phone calls from *them*, Major. No good wishes *there*. Believe me, you don't owe them anything. Nothing at all. So why be sentimental about them? Why not let it all go?'

'My dear Teague, you ought to know better than any one that I'm hardly a sentimentalist . . .

'I'd always thought so, Major, and you've always impressed on me that sentimentality is dangerous—isn't that so?'

I sighed. The night seemed darker all of a sudden.

'. . . That is so, Teague . . . That is so . . .'

THE rain was easing to a thin mist by the time we reached London. The sky was lightening over Hendon and Hampstead. On this grey morning the city was numb and sorry for itself; the clouds pressed down on the slate roofs like a dirty bandage.

Hardly the hero's return, or roses, roses all the way . . .

We drove through a torpid West End into Mayfair. My ankle had been aching for the past hour; my spirits grew dull and heavy as morning approached.

We reached Brecon Crescent, behind Curzon Street. Teague switched off the engine and slumped in his seat yawning, dark hair rumpled. Wearily he hauled himself from behind the wheel and collected the suitcase and the coats. However, neither of us were too exhausted to cast a wary eye at the deserted streets around us.

I felt the tenderness in my ankle as I put my foot to the ground. I limped up the curving flight of steps to the front door, fumbling for the keys Teague had handed to me on the way down. The keys and a few other trinkets were all the personal possessions the Nigerians had left me; they had pinched all my other personal effects: two watches, a wrist-compass, my big Vorholz field-glasses, my father's honey-carnelian seal-ring, my wallet with the snapshots of Maggie.

It needed two separate keys to unlock the door of my mews flat, another two to open the garage below, another two to open the back door. A lot of keys: but I didn't fancy any one sneaking into the flat from the garage below, or planting explosives there: and like a sensible general I liked to make sure I had a clear escape route to the rear. When I stayed in hotels I asked for a room on the ground floor, or on the first floor with a balcony and a flowerbed underneath, preferably with a fire-escape handy. It pays to spend a few extra minutes choosing your accommodation with care.

In Brecon Crescent I had installed expensive Miles and Durrant Five-H locks on both doors, in addition to Robarco bars and steel mesh on the windows. The doors were smooth surfaced, cut flush with the jamb to prevent jemmying, and backed with a plate of steel. You will gather that I am not a trustful type. If I had lost the keys Teague and I would have had to wait another four hours until my bank in Piccadilly opened and I could fetch a spare set from the vaults. It was a few minutes past six.

I opened the garage for Teague to put the Jensen away, then let myself into my small two-storey house. A depressing odour of damp and mustiness trickled out to welcome me; I pushed the door wide open to admit some fresh air. I didn't unfasten the solid metal mail-box inside the door (no open slit through which an enterprising gunman could pot you as you stood in the hall.) There wouldn't be many letters, because I didn't often give out my address and phone number, and my name didn't figure in street directories and in the phone book. I didn't subscribe to newspapers and magazines; no point, when I spent most of my life outside England.

I felt a distinct sense of pleasure at stepping into my own house (sentiment can be dangerous, Major), even though it was as bleak and bare as a barracks. Maggie always said the place reminded her of a transit camp: but it was the only spot on earth I could call my own. Not even Harrison could take that away. I paused and looked round the hallway, with the fine old Farrendon prints of Wellington's campaigns. I felt my throat constrict as I saw them; I remembered how when I was a very little boy at Whinyates—gone now, gone, like so much else—my father would show me the print where General Barton Rickman was conferring with the Duke at Badajoz. 'Who commands here?' 'I do, my Lord.'

'Desire your men to form a column of companies and move on immediately.' 'In what direction, my Lord?' 'Straight ahead, to be sure.'

I don't know why, but standing there in the ice-cold hall I had the feeling something was wrong. I took two steps down the tiny hallway and flung open the door of the drawing-room. I saw at once what was amiss: the place had been searched—thoroughly. I stepped over to the curtains and drew them back. It was a pretty, white-painted room, of modest dimensions; in the forlorn rainy light it looked as if a hurricane—an orderly hurricane—had passed through it. The furniture had been pushed back against the walls and every movable object had been piled in the centre of the once polished but now dull parquet. The Turkey carpet had been rolled up and lay on top of the window seat. Later I found that the boards had been taken up, then meticulously replaced. The pictures had been taken off the walls and put in the middle of the room with the other things; even the fire-irons were stacked there. Evidently the walls had been tapped and the chimney-place probed. My books, including my eighteenth-century first editions—the only valuable things I possessed, and the only ones I cherished—were piled neatly with the rest of the objects.

I knew what they'd been after—but for God's sake, hadn't I assured them over and over again that I hadn't got what they were looking for? I felt weak all of a sudden as I surveyed the disciplined ruin of my household; I went and sat on the window-seat on top of the carpet. I didn't so much resent the searching—that had happened before, and after all they hadn't smashed or damaged anything. No, it was simply that after I'd given them my word they'd taken advantage of my absence to ransack my home and my meagre stock of goods. Bastards.

Teague came along the hallway and found me sitting there, head lowered, hands on knees. He inspected the scene in front of him.

'Same thing in the garage, Major, They even took down the benches, unscrewed the toolracks from the walls, emptied the spare cans of fuel . . . How the hell did they get in?'

I knew how they'd got in, just as I knew what they were hunting for. I only shrugged. I hadn't told Teague and the others, even when we were in Africa, what we'd been sent there for, or for what six of us had died. I'd have to swallow this, as I'd had to swallow all the rest during the last fifteen years. But it was hard . . .

It was then, at that low point, almost as low as the mockery of a court-martial and the months in prison, that Teague showed his class. Tired as he was, he brisked up, started lighting fires with damp wood and damp coal, switched the heating and hot water on, brewed up a strong pot of tea, and put the upstairs bedrooms to rights so we could go and get some sleep. An awful bone-deep chill enveloped the whole house; the search must have taken place weeks, even months ago. The searchers had carefully closed the doors behind them. Very considerate.

We drank several cups of black, sweet tea, waiting for a little heat to creep through the pipes and the fire on the hearth to burn less smokily. Then I dragged myself upstairs, shed my clothes and ran a bath; steam and rusty brown water came out of the taps for a minute or two but were followed, to my relief, by scalding hot water. I lowered myself gratefully into the tub and started the process of soaking the stink of prison out of my skin.

I spent an hour in the bath, occasionally turning the tap with my toes to replenish the blissful hot water. The knot of resentment in my stomach began to dissolve; nothing could change the great fact of my liberation. I climbed out of the bath and rubbed myself down vigorously with a big rough clean towel—every action was a luxury. I went into the icy bedroom (searched too), wrapped myself in three blankets and stretched out on the low, wide bed; it was unbelievably soft after Her Majesty's mattresses at Leigh Central. I told myself I had spent too many years sleeping on hard beds, and benches, on floors and on the ground; I was beginning to need my comforts; I was getting old. Teague said the sheets in the airing-cupboard felt damp, so we didn't use them. I didn't bother to draw back the curtains over the windows.

I could hear Teague moving about below, putting the house in order. I turned on my side, secure in the knowledge that I could rely on him to lock up tightly before he came up to turn in. Then I lifted my head as I caught the gleam of the silver frame on the photograph standing on top of the night-table. The frame was long tarnished, and there wasn't enough light to make out the photograph itself. I didn't need to look at it: it showed Maggie and me in my thirty-foot ketch in the Orkneys, that first radiant summer six years ago when she came to Scotland with me. I sat up, took the photograph, opened the drawer of the night-table and placed it face down inside. The glass grated on something hard. I took out the photograph and felt inside the drawer. My hand emerged grasping, by its stubby ice-cold four-inch barrel, one of my pair of PPK Walthers. I had forgotten how I used to keep it handy, on the floor beside my bed, ready for emergencies. I slid out the clip and checked it. Full. My visitors had obligingly replaced it when they found it. A brief image of Teague glancing in his rear-view mirror at the car behind flickered across my mind; I placed the Walther on the floor, within reach of my fingers.

And then, though I hadn't slept for over twenty-four hours and was relaxed from the opulent wallow in the bath, I couldn't sink into the deep sleep I needed. My brain churned; my limbs thrashed and twitched. I would bob down from time to time beneath the surface of consciousness; but mostly I hovered on the threshold of waking, where I was haunted by distressing pictures from the past. Maggie's white, blazing face and the stinging words she spoke, here in this bedroom . . . the raid on the refinery at

Karazaki . . . the empty safe in the manager's office . . . Nolan bleeding to death with the futile tourniquet round the bleeding stump of his thigh . . . the raid on Wakoja . . . another technical success—but nothing except the same routine papers in the safe . . . Parasopulous with the side of his head blown away . . . Liddell-Jackson dumped across the wire . . . the holocaust at Kabassa—flames and smoke shooting up into the night sky a mile high—the whole plain lit up as far as the Bight of Benin . . . Fox, Burton and Hearne crumpled and done for outside the main gate . . . can't reach the office . . . can't reach it . . . Frazer gut-shot at the door . . . can't . . . drag him back . . . night alive with fire . . . oil-tank explodes . . . Rupert Douglass's eardrums burst and bleeding . . . can't . . .

God knows how many times I'd played this nightly news-reel over and over to myself: now it was more vivid and brutal than ever. Eventually I swung my legs to the carpet and sat for a long time on the side of the bed. All the same, I must have slept longer than I imagined, because I could hear Teague snoring loudly and healthily next door.

I got up and crossed to the windows. It was mid-after-noon. The sky seemed greyer than ever. I parted the curtains on one side and looked out.

A light weak snow was falling; fat wet flakes drifted sloppily along the curve of the crescent. It was still not cold enough to be a full-fledged snow-storm, and the flakes weren't settling. They didn't seem to be hampering the pedestrians who were moving up and down the crescent in a thick stream.

The crescent was busy. It was a short-cut between Curzon Street on one side and Shepherd Market on the other. I like to live in busy places. In lonely ones it may be easier to spot ill-intentioned characters, but it's harder to lose them when necessity arises; and people hesitate to stick a knife into you or shoot you if you can mingle with a crowd.

THE GARDEN GAME

I was about to leave the window when my eye fell on one of the cars parked in a continuous line on the other side of the road. A short squat-looking man in a white trenchcoat was leaving it on the pavement side. As he did so he turned as an afterthought and tapped on the window. The man inside leaned across and wound it down. They talked; then the man on the pavement pointed diagonally across at the house. It was his bad luck that I happened to be looking out of the window at exactly that moment. He must have seen the curtain stir; his head went back as he stared up at the first floor. I registered a broad, sallow face with straight, short blonde hair; his almost colourless eyes were set very widely apart. For a few seconds he stood there with his mouth open, then recovered his self-possession and ducked back into the car.

I went back to the bed and draped a blanket around me. I picked up my PPK. I'd fancied I was a forgotten man, and within twelve hours of leaving prison I'd been chased, found that my house had been searched, and discovered that I was under surveillance.

I left the bedroom and wandered downstairs, holding the blanket with one hand, carrying the gun in the other. Teague's snores rang through the house. I padded down the hall and checked the locks. I poked my head into the drawing-room. Teague had put the carpet down and replaced the furniture; the room looked civilized again.

I moved back down the hall towards the kitchen. I was going to brew more tea.

As I passed the table with the telephone, it rang. I paused. The sound was daunting, unexpected. It couldn't have rung for months, and only a handful of people knew the number. The noise of snoring stopped abruptly. At the third ring I came to life and picked up the receiver. It was dusty, like everything else in the house.

Teague's sturdy form appeared at the top of the stairs, clad only in underpants.

I held the phone to my ear, listening, saying nothing, then the familiar suave, buttery voice began to speak at the other end.

Neither of us, nor Teague, knew it at that moment, but the Garden Game had begun.

We never spoke more than a few words to each other on the phone. We never mentioned names or places.

'Is that you?'

'Yes.'

'Welcome back.'

'Thanks . . .'

'Any difficulties?'

'A few.'

'Can you cope?'

'I think so.'

'Ready to meet?'

'Yes.'

'Same place? Same time?'

'Right.'

We hung up.

Teague came downstairs.

'Well, Major? Are you seeing him tonight?'

'Yes.'

He frowned. 'Do you think he's got something lined up for us?'

'He might. Still, I've got to have a serious talk with him before we arrange anything definite.'

Harrison and I always met after dark. This made it easier to shake off pursuers if we had to. At six-thirty Teague and I went down to the garage by the inside staircase. He started the Jensen and warmed up the engine. I stood by the door. When he gave me the sign I threw up the shutter on its counterbalanced hinges. He drove out and braked, leaning over to open the door on my side. I brought the shutter down and slid into the car and slammed the door in one continuous movement. He jammed the Jensen between two cars, ignoring a chorus of motor horns. We swung in the direction of the car watching the house, so if it chased us it would have to make a U-turn against the flow of traffic. Unless there was a second car parked on the other side, we must have lost them by the time we reached the top of the crescent.

Teague continued to take evasive action all the way to Soho. I could have been wrong, but I didn't think any driver in the world, even a London cabby, could have kept track of us. A few minutes before seven he set me down in Old Compton Street, and to make doubly sure I wasn't being followed I walked the last half-mile to the rendezvous through the web of alleys between Old Compton Street and Frith Street.

I told Teague to park in Poland Street and go into the Blue Griffon and wait for me. I borrowed his watch. It was important not to arrive at the Coquille d'Argent before ten past. When Harrison and I agreed to meet at seven he arrived ten minutes before the hour and I followed at ten minutes after. If he thought anything was wrong he would leave straight away and we would meet the next evening at our next rendezvous. We had a list of places we could use, taking each in rotation.

The Coquille d'Argent is a small restaurant at the top end of Frith Street. Its owner is a man called Felix Salomon. From his flat-footed walk and his pot-belly you wouldn't think he had been a leader of the Resistance years ago, an associate of Jean Moulin. It was then he had first worked with Harrison, for whom I was fairly certain he had continued to perform little services ever since. He put on a delicious and inexpensive lunch, so at midday the restaurant was packed; but his prices rose steeply at dinner-time, and the first floor was then closed. It was there that Harrison, who liked to combine his passion for secret diplomacy and his passion for good food, chose to conduct our business. The staircase was a pace or two to the left of the door, and was unlighted, so it was easy to slip upstairs unseen.

He was seated at the far end of the long room, at a table with a small rose-shaded lamp, which was the only illumination. It was the only table with a cloth and cutlery. He had already ordered himself a Punt e Mes and looked up sharply as I reached the top of the stairs. He rose and walked a few steps down the room and took both my hands in his soft, well-manicured fingers. His impressive head was like the head of a late Roman emperor, with its high broad forehead and big curved beak of a nose.

He leaned forward to scrutinize me as I stood there, the snow dissolving on my dampened shoulders.

He gazed at me with concern. Even in the rosy light he could see the gauntness of my features and the prison-pallor beneath my normally sun-browned skin. I had received a shock myself, studying my face in the big mirror in the bathroom at Brecon Crescent, which reflected my face more mercilessly than my scrap of shaving-mirror at Leigh Central.

He led me to the chair opposite his own and fussed over me, rapping on the table with the handle of a knife until Felix emerged from an inner door to wait on us. I ordered a glass of his Chambéry *fraise*. The air in the room was chilly.

To give the devil his due, I believe that in his own way Harrison did care a little about me. I was, after all, a relative. On the other hand, our relationship didn't prevent him from feeling a certain contempt for me. I was the member of the family who had gone wrong, after an excellent start, and it didn't matter that he was the one who had tempted me from the path of virtue. As he settled his dapper, portly figure in his chair, methodically unfolding his napkin, I could see the old resentment in his bland bureaucratic face, its impressive bald dome framed by wings of grey-flecked hair. He bore a curious grudge not only against me but against all the men who worked for him. It was as if it was somehow our fault, not his own taste for intrigue, that had side-tracked him from his respectable career at the Treasury, where he might have become an under-secretary. As it was, he supervised an odd little department in the Home Office, a department which was considered disreputable, when it was known at all, by his colleagues in Whitehall.

'My dear chap,' he said, putting on his glasses and opening the menu, 'you don't look well . . . no, really—you don't look well at all . . .'

'Does that mean,' I asked with a smile, 'that you're going to stake me to a few weeks of well-earned vacation? . . . In the Bahamas, say? . . .'

He coughed. 'Well, as to that, we shall have to see, won't we? . . .'

He looked at me over the top of his spectacles, with their heavy frames and thick lenses.

'You know,' he went on, 'in spite of the little chat we had when we last saw each other'—he meant the half-hour we spent together when I was on a stretcher at London airport, while I was being handed over by the Nigerians to the British—'I never quite understood what went wrong out there? . . .'

'Everything.' I chafed my cold hands together.

'Oh, not quite everything, surely? You prevented the other side from sabotaging several of our major interests, after all . . .'

'I told you before I went out what would happen,' I said bluntly. 'What else could you expect, with a full-scale civil war in progress?'

'Of course,' he said softly, 'you *did* fail to find the Dunsterville papers . . .'

I said bitterly: 'Yes, I failed, didn't I? And I wonder if you also noticed that I lost six men? . . .'

'I suppose you haven't had—well—any second thoughts about them—the papers, that is? . . .'

'Second thoughts?'

'I mean, as to where they might be? . . .'

I sat up straight and slapped down the menu. 'Look, Harrison, I know you think I've got your blasted papers—that I'm holding out on you—'

'My dear chap!—'

I held up my hand. Our voices sounded curiously dead and muffled in this upstairs room. 'You didn't even trust me enough to tell me what they were all about in the first place. And then you send Special Branch to tear my house apart to see if I've hidden them there.'

'My dear Morven, do you mean to tell me your house has been searched?'

'Oh, come off it, Harrison. All you had to do was to obtain a warrant to open the safe-deposit in my bank. You know I keep my spare keys there. Tell me, are those men who are watching the house yours too?'

'What? Have you got men watching you? They're not mine, I assure you.'

He shook his wattles like a ruffled turkey. He moved his chair back until his eyes became two pink pools in the rosy light. He took the handkerchief out of his breast pocket and wiped his palms. He was a great palm-polisher.

I said: 'So you people are still sweating about those papers, whatever they are? After more than a year?'

'We certainly are, my dear fellow. A great many purveyors of matériel, if I may put it like that, still feel they're sitting on a time-bomb. The man who possesses the originals of the Dunsterville correspondence can set off that time-bomb at any time . . .'

The glasses turned as he held up a warning hand. Felix came in to take our order. We ordered his *poulet de grain à la Wantzenau*, with a bottle of Quincy.

Harrison waited until Felix had closed the door behind him, then he said:

'I gather that your companion, Mrs Mallison, has left London, and that she didn't go to see you in prison?'

Again the little touch of malice. He didn't like women, disliking them most of all when they interfered with the lives of his operatives. He asked:

'Has she gone back to her husband, perhaps?'

'I'm sure she hasn't.' I hesitated, but had to ask: 'Tell me, Harrison, do *you* know where she is?'

He spread his hands. 'Me? My dear boy, I haven't the faintest idea.'

I hated to do it, but again I had to go on: 'Do you know if she's got her divorce yet? Have you heard?'

'My dear fellow, why didn't you mention it before? If I'd known, I'd gladly have made all the enquiries you wanted. You know that, of course?'

I shook my head. I didn't want him sniffing around more than I could help. Maggie was outside all that. It was because she wanted *me* to move outside it that we'd quarrelled.

It was when Felix had served us our roast chicken and drawn the cork of the Quincy that Harrison brought up the matter which was weighing on his mind. I knew it was important because he mentioned it so casually. But first he brought his long nose down to his plate and snuffed at it appreciatively, then dipped it into his glass to savour the first mouthful of wine. He set the glass down and looked thoughtfully for a moment down the darkened room with its shrouded rows of tables and chairs. The soggy splodges of snow, suffused by the neon lights of the strip-clubs and restaurants, could be seen plopping down on Frith Street through the distant window.

'Tell me,' he asked, with elaborate indifference, 'have you ever heard of a man called Martagon?'

'Who?'

'Martagon? Carl-Conrad Martagon?'

His glasses tilted as he studied me with a covert sideways glance to see how the sound of the name affected me. I sliced deliberately into my chicken. In spite of the occasional delicacies I was permitted to purchase at Leigh Central, I

36

would have to be careful to eat moderately during these first days of freedom.

'Carl-Conrad who?'

'Martagon'. He passed a plump hand over his naked skull. 'A very intriguing fellow.'

'What does he do?'

'A little of everything . . . a lot of everything . . .'

'A strange name. What nationality is he?'

'Swiss. An extremely influential and wealthy Swiss.'

'And why are you asking me about him? What does he do for a living?'

'He is president of O. G. Sarzens.'

'The firm that makes the sound-ranging equipment and echo-sounding gear?'

'Among other things.'

'Then he must be very wealthy indeed.'

'Very.'

'Still, I would have thought Sarzens was harmless enough, from your point of view? The Swiss government is pretty strict, isn't it, about letting arms firms sell only to neutrals?'

This made him smile.

'And where does this Herr Martagon live?' I said. '—Is it Herr Martagon, or Monsieur, or Signor Martagon?—'

'Herr. He was born in Rheinfelden. Oh, he has a number of establishments.' He paused and looked at me keenly. 'Morven, are you sure you've never heard of him?'

'Never.'

I should have known that he was leading up to something important; but I was out of practice in this sort of Byzantine discourse, bored with talking about a man I didn't know. If I'd been patient and heard him out I might have saved myself a lot of trouble. However, Harrison saw that I was preoccupied, picking at my chicken without concentrating, and after hesitating a moment he poured us both another glass of wine and changed the subject.

'Morven,' he said carefully, 'I hope you realize that I did

absolutely everything I could to rescue you from Nigeria and lighten your lot when I'd got you home?'

He was clearly worried by my silence and constrained manner.

'I assure you,' he went on in his plummy voice, 'that we moved heaven and earth to get you reprieved, then to have you transferred to England. We were forced to leave you at Leigh for so long because the Nigerians were adamant. Hang it all, Morven, they originally demanded you serve the entire fifteen years. Fifteen years—think of that. We had to keep you locked up until the fuss had died down, long enough to save their faces.'

I laid down my knife and toyed with the cold stem of my glass, frowning down at the ruby-tinted tablecloth.

'I always do my best for my people when they get into trouble,' he continued. 'Even when it's their own fault, or when they've exceeded their orders, or even when—well—' he paused delicately '—when they fail . . . You'll agree with me there, won't you?'

I said nothing. Perhaps I was too full of gratitude to speak.

'Did they treat you well at Leigh? I laid down special requirements; repeated them at frequent intervals. Did the governor deal with you properly?'

The mention of that lard-faced governor made me raise my head. I pushed forward my glass.

'Your governor,' I said, 'was a horse's ass. One thing he did disturbed me, though—'

'Oh? What?'

'He insisted on calling me "Mister" the whole time.' I leaned forward until his eyes were visible behind the glasses; he was compelled to look me straight in the eyes. 'Tell me—about my rank. Am I still Major Rickman, or am I not?'

In prison I had lain awake at night, nagged by a half-memory that a soldier who was found guilty of a criminal offence automatically forfeited not only his rank but also such little considerations as his pension, pitiful though it might be, and his medals. I had a D.S.O. from Brunei, among other things, that I was childishly and unfashionably proud of. Silly, of course—but hadn't Teague warned me that I could be sentimental?

I had written twice to Harrison to enquire about this specific point. No reply. However, he must have been checking, because he raised his glass and waved it in a grand circle. His eyes beamed with crafty good nature.

'My dear Morven!' He was the very picture of the *faux bonhomme*. He was always seigneurial when giving away something that cost the Department nothing. 'My dear chap, if only I'd realized how anxious you were—oh, how very careless of me!' He reached out his sticky palm and patted the back of my hand. 'My dear boy, there was never any question of your giving up your rank, no question at all. I don't know what could have put such an idea in your head? Not only that, but I can assure you that your usefulness to the Department, and the esteem in which it holds you, haven't been in the slightest degree impaired by the *débâcle* in Africa.'

Typical of him to reassure me and rub in my failure at the same time. I knew that he'd have stripped me of all my poor privileges in a minute if the Nigerians had wanted it, or if it had been politic to do so. Nevertheless I was unspeakably relieved. At Leigh I often pretended to myself, in my darker moments, that I didn't care about my humble rank and modest decorations; but what else had I to cling to? . . .

There was a chinking noise behind my chair. It made me jump and turn, gripping the back of the seat. I saw Harrison look at me curiously.

It was only Felix . . . Gone was the peace and quiet of prison . . . I was learning how to be nervous again . . .

Felix, who had seen men duck before, calmly set down our dessert in front of us. Harrison's mouth twitched with distaste as my jacket fell partly open and he glimpsed the PPK tucked under my shoulder. He never liked to be reminded of what the work of his neat and smoothly run office finally came down to. He asked Felix to bring us a second bottle of Quincy.

Having received a reassuring answer to my last question, I decided to risk asking the next one. I said:

'While we're about it, Harrison, perhaps it's time we mentioned the matter of money?'

He stopped chewing, as if he felt an unexpected twinge of indigestion. It was always in bad taste to ask him about something as vulgar as money. He said cautiously:

'What about it?'

'To start with, there's the terminal payment on the African trip. It was another one of the things I wrote to you about from Leigh, remember?'

'I do wish I'd been able to visit you personally, Morven'; his rich voice dripped with regret; 'but it wouldn't have been—well—you know—diplomatic . . .'

I said firmly:

'What about the final payment? It's due.'

'Well, Morven, I'm aware of the delay—'

'Delay? Some delay!—Well over a year—'

'I was expecting to have the whole matter settled by the time you were released—'

'Why hasn't it been, then? I thought I'd find the credit slip in my mail-box, as usual. Where is it?'

He become unctuous. 'Morven, you'll appreciate that there were several complications in this case. In view of the—er—losses' (—another distasteful reminder of the terminal activities of his Department—) 'drawing up accounts has been rather difficult. And I don't like to repeat it—but the excursion wasn't a success, after all . . .'

I said tartly: 'Look, we've never worked on the principle of payment by results—otherwise you'd never have found anyone who'd be stupid enough to go into the field for you. Surely you realize that?'

I was becoming angry, but struggled to appear cool. A

show of temper never intimidated Harrison, though he sometimes pretended it did. I guessed what had happened: he had minimized the mission's lack of success by reducing the amount allotted to it in his books. In that way he had been able to represent it to his superiors as a side-show, instead of the major, bloody, no-holds-barred effort it actually was.

I might have been amused by his little ruse if I hadn't been in a bind. I needed the money. This isn't a business in which you become rich; Secret Funds aren't famous as a generous paymaster. I wanted money to be able to marry Maggie; the mortgage payments on the house hadn't stopped because I'd been out of commission; I'd been responsible for the small but regular retainer for Teague, whom I didn't yet want to let go. I reckoned that I had about three thousand pounds in the bank, and that my collection of first editions was worth somewhere around the same figure. You can't buy much of a dream-cottage for six thousand pounds.

I pushed my dessert away and jerked my chair back. The room seemed colder than when I entered it. I felt shivery. With a delicate motion Harrison laid down his spoon and fork, took out his handkerchief and dabbed his palms. He smiled at me, a peculiarly false and brilliant smile.

'Morven, I assure you, you needn't worry about your—ah—emoluments.' He made them sound like the wages of sin. 'There is a purely temporary hitch. I'd expected to have everything settled before you left Leigh, but thanks to some rather good staff-work'—here he coughed modestly—'you were released earlier than we expected. So I must ask you to be patient for a little while longer. However, I must admit that the amount of money you will receive is bound to be affected by the fact that you failed to lay hands on those papers. I must be frank about it: my superiors were disappointed...' He sighed and shook his head; he switched on a smile even more potently insincere than the first. 'But I give you my word—I'll do everything I can for you. There, does that satisfy you?' He pointed at my plate. 'Why aren't you eating?'

I looked away. The snow was still floating down in the same spiritless way. So it all depended on those damned papers—whatever they were? . . . I asked myself why he was playing with me. He always had a purpose.

The explanation came when Felix returned with the new bottle of Quincy. He took away my uneaten compôte without even a reproachful glance at it. He had seen men lose their appetites, too.

'We're talking about money, are we?'

Harrison leaned back, lacing his hands on his stomach. He looked like a jovial devil with the roseate light caressing his bald head.

'Tell me, would you be willing to make another try at it?'

'At what?'

'Finding the papers?'

I stared at him. Again he produced the handkerchief and dabbed his palms like a well-bred animal patting its paws.

'So you want those papers that badly?'

'We do. And we still think you're the best man to get them for us.'

'You want me to sneak back into Nigeria?'

'Wherever it takes you. Nigeria—Europe—across the Channel, even.' He always spoke of Europe as a remote and mysterious place. 'Perhaps even to Kirghizia? . . .'

He smiled. Kirghizia had been our most daring *coup*, renowned in the esoteric circles where Harrison moved. He could never resist referring to it.

'This time we'll let you go about it in your own way. Last time we made a mistake—sending you out with a big unit was foolish. But we must have those papers. Our stance in the Nigerian war was bad enough to begin with. If those papers fall into the wrong hands . . . well . . . they show certain— . . .' He wiped his mouth. 'Nigeria, my dear fellow, means oil, after all . . . lots of oil . . .'

I picked up the bottle, poured myself a glass, drank it and poured another. He moved his own plate away from him with a fastidious thumb; he hadn't finished his fruit-salad; he must be anxious.

Of course, he was blackmailing me—withholding my pay for the previous job to induce me to accept this one.

He sipped his wine.

'I'm sure I don't have to remind you of your duty, Morven?'

'Oh, no, you do that regularly. Last time you did it, it took me to within six hours of execution.'

The handkerchief described scrubbing motions.

'Well, Morven?'

I threw my napkin on the table.

'No, Harrison.'

'What?'

'I'm not ready yet.'

'My dear boy, if you want to take some time off—a couple of weeks—even three—'

'Very generous of you, I'm sure . . . But it's not that—though I can obviously do with the break—'

'The Department might be able to arrange a loan—an advance . . .'

'No, no—you've got it wrong—'

'Wrong? In what way?'

'You won't understand—but I've got a job of my own to do first—'

'What sort of job?'

We were interrupted by Felix bringing us a plate of cheese and a pot of coffee. I got up and limped over to the peg and put my overcoat back on; apart from a certain glow from the wine I was cold, and the talk of a return to Africa was making me colder. I sat down again and helped myself to a wedge of Brie.

'Harrison, what do you know about Grady Bailey, Gavin Asher, and the other two?'

'Rupert Douglass and Hans Lurtsema?' He had a memory like an elephant.

'Do you know where they went, after you'd persuaded the Nigerians to let them go?'

'Us? It wasn't us who persuaded the Nigerians to release them . . .'

'It wasn't? Then who was it?'

'I don't know.' He saw the look in my eyes and spread his hands. 'I don't. Honestly.'

'Is it true they didn't report to you to collect their severance pay?'

'Quite true.' He didn't look as if their act of self-denial exactly broke his heart. No doubt he wished his other operatives were as public-spirited. He cut off a sliver of *reblochon* and sampled it. 'But, Morven'—he waved the cheese-knife—'why are you asking about your former associates? Didn't I just point out that next time we don't want you to take a team with you?'

'I intend to find them, Harrison.'

'Find them—?'

'Right.'

'But why? Did they do something discreditable in Nigeria? Something you want to punish them for?'

'On the contrary—they all behaved admirably. Those who lived—and those who died . . .'

'Why, then?'

'Didn't I say you wouldn't understand?'

'They're no longer of use, are they? No threat to you—or to the Department?'

'No, Harrison—'

'Well?'

'They happen to be a threat to themselves.'

The dewlaps wobbled. 'You're right, Morven. I don't understand.'

I swallowed a piece of Brie. 'I recruited those men. With your assistance, of course—access to War Office and NATO files, and so on—but I recruited them. I took them out of their units; I spent eight weeks showing them a lot of tricks their mothers didn't teach them; then I took them to the Niger. And there was always the very clear understanding that when I'd finished with them I'd return them personally to the units they came from.'

'My dear fellow, don't you see that they relieved you of that obligation themselves, when they returned to England and failed to report to me?'

'No, Harrison, I don't see that.'

'It's quite true, none the less.'

I said: 'Haven't you any idea where they went after they left Nigeria?'

'Does it matter?'

'Do you know where they went?'

He was genuinely puzzled. 'Well, I've had the odd report on my desk, from time to time—'

'Well?'

'Oh, just the odd hint or two—'

'What kind of hint?'

'Believe me, dear fellow, they aren't at all important now—'

'What kind of hints?'

'Well then, if you must know—from time to time there have been scraps of information that one or the other has slipped into some country or other—usually singly, often in pairs, and sometimes three or four together. France, Germany, Italy, Austria, Portugal, Iran, Morocco, America, Japan, Brazil . . .' He saw something in my face that made him bend forward, his eyes enlarged behind the thick glasses. 'You aren't going to be stubborn about this, are you?' Stubborness in his employees was reprehensible, if they weren't exercising it on behalf of the Department. 'Why, tracing those men could take months—I mean, you haven't got the time or the money—and the Department has this urgent task for you . . .'

'What do you think they're up to? Why do you think they're travelling from one place to another?'

'I haven't the slightest idea.'

'Harrison—?'

'I haven't the slightest idea, Morven.'

'Are you sure?'

'My dear chap, would I lie to you?'

I drained my coffee and rose to my feet buttoning my overcoat.

He looked at me, his eyes glinting redly behind the spectacles. 'I know', he said, 'that when you were in the army you were a highly conscientious officer—though I admit that was why I approached you and asked you to take on special duties. But you know, I can't allow you to let your private scruples obstruct a public call to service—'

After a few glasses of good wine he liked to hold forth in mellow tones on the subject of service. His own service was undertaken in his office, or in the restaurants and clubs within a mile of it.

I thrust my hands in the pockets of my overcoat. I hadn't intended to make a speech, but now I heard myself explaining to him why I was taking on the self-imposed task of running four capable and grown-up men to earth. At that time I honestly didn't believe it was going to require too much time and effort; I just wanted to locate them, talk to them like a Dutch uncle, assure myself they were all right.

I told Harrison I felt a genuine and acute sense of responsibility for them; it had plagued me from the moment that I was hit in the leg at Kabassa, crawling down the irrigation ditch, and became finally separated from them. I tried to explain that they seemed to me to be so much like myself—or myself as I had been at that time, before I knew better. They liked to fight; they loved trouble; in some ways they were very childish and immature. I just couldn't let them wander off into the blue without tying up the loose ends. It offended my sense of order, of the proprieties. I knew what, in their wilful way, they were capable of—what a whole mass of unnecessary complications they could get themselves into—just as I had. I reminded him that when he'd winkled me out of the Hussars it was on the same understanding as I'd offered the Nigerian job to Bailey and the rest . . . And I'd never gone back to the Regulars . . . I'd been artfully conned from one job to the next . . . and I'd been a fool . . . oh, yes—I waved Harrison's objections down—I'd enjoyed the excitement, and he'd flattered me about the importance of the work, and he'd seen to it that regular promotions were put through—but I ought to have returned to the sane and sensible life he'd separated me from . . . Well, now I was too old; superannuated; past it; fit for the knacker's yard . . . However, I could still make sure those four young men—and I'd killed their six companions, remember—didn't wreck their lives and careers as I'd wrecked mine . . . I was going to make certain they were put firmly back on the rails, on the straight and narrow . . . They were fundamentally good boys, and clever, but they were also violence-prone—which admittedly was why I had picked them . . . They had records of brawling and wounding . . . I was going to see to it that they weren't seduced into the kind of immoral existence men of their skills and temperament could easily fall into if they weren't discouraged . . . They were a peculiar crowd in many ways—not like the men I could have commanded in the Hussars . . . still, for what it was worth, damn it all, they were the only men I had, and until they were properly mustered out I was still their commanding officer . . .

I'm not given to long speeches, so both Harrison and I were very much surprised at my unexpected eloquence. The speech was all the more piquant because it was punctuated by the audible chattering of my teeth. I hoped I wasn't coming down with 'flu or pneumonia: I'd had a bad case of pleurisy four years ago, after the business in Kirghizia. All I wanted was to go back to Brecon Crescent, turn the heating up full blast, and crawl beneath a pile of blankets . . .

Harrison's eyes were more opaque than ever. The handkerchief was working overtime. But he heard me out in silence, the Roman head tilted to one side. He knew better than to oppose me when I was in such a pig-headed mood. It was better to give up for the moment and let me go. He could always phone me again in a day or two, when I'd calmed down.

I buttoned my coat tightly round my neck, shook his soft hand, then padded away between the ranks of empty tables. I went downstairs and out into chilly, sleazy Frith Street.

Holding my collar against my mouth, I battled my way back against wind and sleet to Poland Street.

Teague was alone in the private bar of the Blue Griffon. He rose from the bar as he saw me enter. His square face seemed gloomier than ever, and I put it down to the bleak weather. The inside of the Blue Griffon didn't feel any warmer than the inside of the Coquille d'Argent.

With a little shiver I walked up to the bar and rapped on it with a coin. When the barmaid came I ordered a double brandy and indicated Teague's half-empty pint.

He held out an envelope. An ordinary white envelope, blank on both sides. I took off my glove and slit it open with my thumb. Teague said:

'A fellow came in—short fellow—thirty minutes ago . . . white raincoat . . . yellow hair . . . had a drink at the bar . . . handed me that . . . 'For Major Rickman' . . . foreign accent . . . I ran after him . . . —there was someone waiting for him with a car . . .'

I took out a pale blue slip of paper. On the top was embossed, in dark blue, the graceful emblem of a peacock displaying its tail. Three sentences were typed on an electric typewriter:

'It occurs to me that you may be the sort of man who would like to become involved in an unusual and lucrative

GAME. Four friends of yours have already decided to become players, and they speak very highly of your capabilities. If you will pack a suitcase and stand by, you will be contacted.'

Fastened to the paper was a visiting-card on which a name was printed in neat italics:

CARL-CONRAD MARTAGON

THE call came at six-fifteen next morning, before it was light. I struggled out of a long and refreshing sleep to the sound of the phone ringing in the hall. I switched on the bedside lamp. I was enmeshed like a cocoon in my three blankets. The room was like a furnace. I was sweating freely, which I took to be a good sign.

I sat up and was about to throw off the blankets when I heard the voice of Teague down in the hall, answering the phone. I lay back drowsily, trying to catch the tail-end of my dream. It was something about water, sailing off Yarmouth —or could it have been Belize?—on a burning blue day . . . something clean and simple and gay . . .

Teague appeared in the doorway. He was dressed in sweater and slacks. He had been up for an hour tinkering with the Jensen.

'Are you awake, Major? That was someone on the phone —could be the chap in the Blue Griffon. He said, can you be at the B.E.A. counter at London Airport at nine-fifteen? Somebody will meet you there. Then he rang off.'

Teague sounded peevish and unenthusiastic, as he had when we had mulled over the matter some hours earlier. He had expected a few days in which we could do some stock-taking and catch our breath, and like Harrison he thought my intention of clearing up the tag-end of the African episode was quixotic. He went off with a face like thunder when I told him we'd have breakfast and be ready to leave in an hour.

I dozed off for another ten luxurious minutes, then had a leisurely shower and shave and spent fifteen minutes wrapping a crêpe bandage round my ankle. It would be the only leisurely portion of an extraordinary day . . .

The snow had stopped, though the sky was still a sullen pewter. As we drove through the slush to the airport Teague was tight-lipped. Over our toast and coffee he had suggested that the least I could do was to alert Harrison: all it needed was a phone call. I refused, forbidding him to get in touch with Harrison when I was gone. I didn't tell Teague that Harrison had talked about Martagon at the Coquille d'Argent. Obviously that wasn't a coincidence—though I couldn't see the connection. Anyway, if I alerted Harrison he'd only think I'd been lying when I said I didn't know Martagon. Of course, he never hesitated to lie himself, but he thought it *lèse-majesté* for other people to lie to him. What was the link, then?—Harrison—Martagon—Bailey and the rest?— . . . yet as we drove past London's dreary western suburbs and the tower blocks standing sentinel over the raised spine of the M4 motorway I was less worried about Harrison and Martagon than pleased that I was apparently going to see my former charges again, and soon. It seemed that discharging my obligation was going to be less troublesome and time-consuming than I'd imagined . . .

It was true, I reflected, as we drove through the tunnel towards the European terminal, that the message sounded innocuous enough, though the business of asking me to stand by was strange, then summoning me at an ungodly hour. However, it didn't appear to warrant putting Harrison on the *qui vive*. It seemed quite friendly. I'd prefer to investigate on my own. Besides, if these people were capable of running me to earth in the West End, on a wet winter evening, they could easily elude any of Harrison's watchdogs.

As expected, the man who met us at the ticket-counter wore a white trenchcoat. He had straw-coloured hair and his amethyst eyes were widely spaced. He was much shorter than I had previously noticed, dwarfish, almost, and was older than I'd supposed, about thirty-five. I can't tell you why I found him repellent.

Today he wore a neat suede trilby which he took off as he approached, carrying his tartan suitcase. He came up to us without subterfuge, shook our hands in the formal Continental manner, and introduced himself simply as Jenbach. He pronounced it clearly twice, to make sure we got it correctly. He ushered me straight to immigration, where I said a brief goodbye to a scowling Teague. Within five minutes my new companion and I were in the transit-lounge. The ticket he handed me was a first-class return to Vienna. So far so good, I thought in my innocence, tucking it in my pocket. I'd had some pleasant times in years past, on the Kärntnerstrasse and the Kärntnerring . . .

After the brisk beginning came a hitch. Our plane, due to leave at eleven, was grounded: snow-flurries over Central Europe: Frankfort, Munich and Vienna socked in. That, I supposed, was the explanation of the 'stand by' part of the invitation: no dark significance, merely that my hosts had anticipated the uncertain weather. And so for four hours we waited easily, Jenbach and I, until the front should lift. We had a drink, then another drink, and shared a ham sandwich; I bought *The Times* and *The Economist*, Jenbach bought *Paris Match* and *Der Spiegel*. We smiled and nodded as we raised our glasses and politely exchanged magazines. We didn't bother to strike up an elaborate conversation, since we both knew that he was only a courier and go-between and that my business was with Carl-Conrad Martagon. I noticed that he read and spoke English without any trouble, with an unexpectedly soft high voice and a lisping accent. I noticed too that his nose had been impressively broken once or twice, and that he was huskily built and moved quickly and with precision. He wasn't in the least impatient and the interlude passed painlessly. As for me, I'd had enough practice in time-wasting in the past two years not to mind reclining on a comfortable sofa in a warm lounge, a whisky in my hand and my ankle propped on a well-padded chair.

It was the same during the flight. We sat amiably side by

side, drinking whisky-sours from miniature bottles and eating plastic food from plastic trays. Afterwards I leaned back and shut my eyes and made love to Maggie, at impossible length and in several improbable positions, as I'd done a thousand times in gaol. When I opened my eyes, the plane was taxiing, Jenbach was shaking my shoulder and reaching down our coats from the overhead rack, and outside the curved round windows it was pitch black and the snow was fairly thudding down.

If I'd hoped to be transported to a snug room at the Astoria or the Imperial, I was disappointed. A chocolate-coloured Mercedes 280 SE with a chauffeur in a plum-coloured uniform was waiting for us on the brightly lit concourse. We were whisked away immediately through the blizzard in what I judged was a southerly direction, towards Graz and into Styria. At least, I *hoped* it was south—after half an hour I had a nasty jolt when it suddenly occurred to me that the Hungarian border, after all, was only a few miles away. It was a grim thought. Long before the Kirghizia caper, Harrison had shown me a copy of the East German dossier on me, with notations from Poland, Bulgaria and Hungary. He thought it was a great joke. I was described as a desirable catch, highly suitable for exchange purposes. I glanced at Jenbach; he looked back in the darkness of the car and smiled, his face shadowed by the suede hat, his gloved hands pressed on his stomach. I was glad I had taken five minutes in the bathroom that morning, before I put on my shirt, to make a sling out of a length of crêpe bandage, insert one end through the trigger-guard of the slim little Walther, and fasten it round my neck so it lay in the small of my back, a spare magazine fixed to the grip with a strip of adhesive plaster. It wouldn't be noticeable, wasn't uncomfortable when sitting down, and would escape the attention of any one conducting the usual routine search for a concealed weapon. Still, I now wished I hadn't drunk that extra couple of whiskies on the plane.

The headlights could barely penetrate the swirling snow, but the chauffeur drove swiftly and confidently, not turning his head; obviously he had driven this road many times before. The metal studs on the tyres made a monotonous sound on the icy road, like a continuous ripping of silk. Now and again we would run through a village and I would catch a glimpse of the exotic onion-dome of a church looming through the veiled whiteness, looking ominously like the churches I had seen in Kirghizia, on the trek before the pick-up, when I got the frost-bite. In the main squares the stations were boarded up for the winter; they stood like blank grey obelisks in a painting by Chirico. Soon we left the Marchen-land and were running steadily uphill through the pine trees of the Wienerwald; their densely packed trunks whirred past behind the curtain of snow as if we were driving through a snowbound valley whose sides were lined with corrugated cardboard.

Again the monotony of the snowy journey made me dream. I leaned back on the soft cushions of the warm interior and indulged once more in my Maggie fantasy—then in my fishing-cottage fantasy—then both together—which meant that Maggie and I were making love in front of the log-fire in the little parlour—or on the stairs—or in the bathroom—or in the snug little bedroom—anywhere—everywhere—summer and winter—night or day . . . And then I pulled my mind back and forced myself to think about reality, about the four young men I would be meeting soon, about their individual characters. It seemed a lifetime since I'd last seen them, on that misty and mosquito-ridden dawn in a tumble-down thatched hut in a deserted village. It was hard to visualize them. I remembered the Dutchman from Friesland, Hans Lurtsema, because of his ox-like physique and his strange mixture of the boisterous and sardonic, now bellowing with laughter, now tight-lipped with suspicion clouding his little black eyes. Rupert Douglass I remembered because of his Scots accent, his brilliant and deceptively innocent smile, his soft catlike walk, his Jacobite courtesy, and the bonnet with the streamers and silver badges of the Highland Division that he'd insisted on wearing. It almost broke his heart when he lost it the night of the skirmish at Sabalayah. Grady Bailey, of course, was the most vivid of the lot, his thin nervous appearance belied by his infectious high spirits expressed in hair-raising practical jokes (a knife suspended over the lavatory, dropping when you yanked the chain; a garter-snake under the chafing dish; a scorpion in the sleeping-bag; and his terrible and almost as deadly puns and spoonerisms). Gavin Asher, on the other hand, was practically a blur. After Teague he was the most earnest and dedicated of the party, our electronics and communications specialist. I seemed to recall that he was scruffy, wore his hair long, often didn't shave, and kept his kit and his weapons in a careless condition, which constantly made the regimentally minded Teague tick him off. Yet he was already a captain and had been decorated for service in the Arabian Peninsula and mentioned in despatches in Cyprus. His brigadier in Signals had raised hell before Harrison could get him sprung for special duty. He was superb with his bits of apparatus, and it was due to him that we weren't all wiped out at Mongalla. What's more, he fought like a lion. Strange that I couldn't remember what he looked like, or even hear the echo of his voice, though he came from near Preston and spoke broad Lancashire; we had yelled at each other down a whistling wire enough times. On the other hand I could clearly recollect the way he raised his arm and cocked his head back when he drank bottled beer. He had an immoderate and superhuman thirst— another characteristic that raised Teague's hackles. He had been our non-conformist, and was technically the best of the bunch.

I was mulling over these scraps of memory when, without what seemed to be any warning, the Mercedes suddenly slowed, ran on for a few minutes, then braked and came to a halt. Had we arrived? I pushed my nose against the glass. The snow was thicker than ever—not the anaemic snow of London but great thick ropes forming deep drifts at the sides of the road and under the pines. I could just make out a dull yellow glare away to the left. The chauffeur turned round and muttered something my limited knowledge of German wasn't good enough to catch, then left the car, admitting sharp arrows of freezing air.

Now, in a flickering orange light, I could make out the outline of a small building. Classical, light-painted, with tall windows, it was like an old summerhouse; behind it were high black gates. The scene was like a theatre-set with flares or lanterns. The chauffeur, his peaked cap pulled down, shoulders hunched, trudged forward towards a group of men—three? four?—who stood watching the car. They huddled together, clad in woollen caps and long cloaks or oilskins, with some sort of long wrapped bundle at their feet. One of them was very short and squat, and when he removed his oilskin hood for some reason I saw the lamps gleaming on his big round bald head. The men were leaning on long-handled implements of some kind . . . spades, were they? . . . could they be spades? . . .

I put my hand on the door-handle, meaning to step out and relieve the tedium of the drive. Jenbach's fingers, light and authoritative, rested on my arm. His teeth gleamed in the dull sulphurous light as he shook his head. I don't take well to contradiction, and was tempted to press my point: but Jenbach might press his, and could call on reinforcements; so I leaned back against the dark-brown cushions, feeling the warm pressure of the PPK . . . Save your energy for the big moment . . . stupid to tangle with the hired hands . . .

In any case, the chauffeur's conference with the men in the oilskins lasted only a couple of minutes. Had he lost his way, and was asking for directions? He climbed back in the car and slammed the door. Again he turned round to talk to Jenbach, laughing in a deep cracked voice and waving something in his hand. It looked like a bundle of banknotes. He stuffed them away in his pocket and spoke in a thick local accent, so rapidly that again I couldn't understand him. I caught only the word, repeated several times over, '*Pfauhahn!* *Pfauhahn!*' I didn't know then what it meant, except that it was some sort of a bird: a *Hahn* is a cockerel, and I wondered idly, as the car started up again, whether illegal cock-fighting went on in the villages of the Weinerwald, and the chauffeur was collecting a bet. And my guess, for that matter, wasn't all that far wrong, at that.

Later on, when I looked *Pfauhahn* up in a dictionary, I discovered that it meant *Peacock*.

WE reached our destination twenty minutes later. There was no missing or mistaking it. We came around a bend with our tyres hissing, and there in front of us, straddling the road, was a towering battlemented entrance-gate that reminded me immediately of Leigh Central. Martagon's place in Austria was a *schloss* or castle.

The gates swung open as we approached and another car drove out. It was impossible to see it clearly against the yellow oblong of light with the kaleidoscope of snow billowing around it. Its headlights were blinding, and we felt our way past it slowly, each machine juggling to stay close to the crown of the road. As it edged past on my side I saw that it was an ambulance, red crosses painted on its doors and its pleated white curtains drawn. Our chauffeur raised his hand to the other driver, then we were in the courtyard.

A figure muffled in the same garb as the men down the road at the summerhouse stood by the gates as we entered. The chauffeur saluted him too. There was a row of cars in the courtyard, their snowy tops and hoods glistening in the lights from the rows of windows around three sides of the square. The Mercedes manœuvred its way carefully round them until we stopped opposite a small entrance, dimly lit, with bare wooden stairs. I didn't see the main entrance. Evidently the side entrance was good enough for me.

I don't know what I had expected . . . a smiling host, flanked by spaniels, hurrying forward to greet me down a noble flight of steps? I sat where I was until Jenbach tapped my arm. We got out, the chauffeur took my suitcase from the boot, and we entered the castle by the small entrance. As our shoes squeaked across the hard-packed snow, I had time for a quick glance at the courtyard. Its dimensions were compact, like a courtyard in a middle-sized Oxford or Cambridge college. In spite of its mediaeval-looking battlements, with conical turrets at the corners, something about the building told me, even at night and in a snowstorm, that this was not an ancient stronghold but a copy of a Gothic castle, in the style of Wyatt or Viollet le Duc.

At the top of the weather-worn stairs, sounding hollow under our feet, we emerged into an exterior cloister, running along the outside of the walls at the level of the first floor. Beyond it I could glimpse the gloomy mass of pines patiently accumulating their burden of snow. The columns supporting the stone roof of the cloister were embellished with fantastic animals, the snow drifting into their gaping and snarling jaws. We walked along it heads down, the chauffeur first with my suitcase, myself sandwiched in the middle, and Jenbach bringing up the rear.

We turned the corner at right-angles, then descended another flight of steps and marched in procession down a repulsively dark and gloomy stone corridor, empty and lit with naked light-bulbs. Gloomy or not, at least we were out of the cold and the snow. It seemed to slope downwards into the bowels of the earth. Eventually we came to a tall, forbidding-looking door, painted black. Jenbach advanced with a key in his hand and unlocked it. Then, quite civilly, in his light voice, he asked me to wait a few minutes, opened the door and went through, locking it behind him.

I was left in the dismal passageway with the chauffeur. He leaned against the wall, keeping an eye on me. He had placed my suitcase beside the door, and I sat down on it, nursing my ankle, smarting dully with stiffness and cold. My surroundings were disagreeably reminiscent of the mournful corridors of Leigh Central.

It was ten minutes before Jenbach came back. He must

have concluded his business satisfactorily; his movements were brisk and certain. He gestured to the chauffeur to pick up the cases and held the door wide.

We ascended a short, gently sloping ramp. Then we came out under an archway into an utterly new and breath-taking world. It was all suddenly so different and unexpected I stopped short in amazement.

I was standing in an enormous inner courtyard, about a hundred and fifty yards square. It had been transformed into a gigantic hot-house or conservatory, crammed with tropical plants and trees. After the unrelieved whiteness which had occupied my eyes all day, my senses were confused by the vivid jumble of greens and the brilliant hues of their fruits and flowers. For a few moments I felt actually dizzy. My senses spun. I had walked into a secret, magic garden, totally enclosed by the dark red granite inner walls of the castle, broken at the top only by a sort of latticed gallery. The entire top of the courtyard was roofed over with great sheets of glass, suspended on a gleaming framework of polished steel, raked and cantilevered at such an angle that the snow slid off it instead of settling in a dead weight. Tilting my head back, I saw a big grey scad detach itself from the mass clinging to the crown of the roof and slither downwards into space.

Jenbach poked me on the shoulder. Dazed, I walked forward again, obediently following the chauffeur as he threaded his way through a maze of twisting, sandy paths between the towering growths. It was hot and humid, and I was carried back in time to Nigeria or Kinshasa, or the stifling rain-forests of Chiapas on the borders of Mexico and Guatemala. A heavy, scented, oily, oozy odour hung in the air. Between the royal palms with their coppery fronds were trees that resembled the strange trees of Mexico, pointed out to me during the course of a painful journey by my Lacandón guides: the Tree of the Little Hands, the Poor Man's Raincoat, the Tree which Weeps Blood, the Fire-

Eating Tree, the Lipstick Tree, the Cannon-Ball Tree, the Strangler Tree . . .

Branches bent over me, flaunting their fat and monstrous blooms, scarlet and ivory, crimson and gold. Beneath the trees flourished a hundred varieties of tree-ferns and gunneras. They formed a thick hedge, screening out the other winding paths that I sensed lay on the other side. Tree-orchids and vines were twined around boughs and tree-trunks, bringing back even more strongly the weird waxen blossoms of the rain-forests—flaring blue Mantle of the Virgin, cascading silver-barred Zebrina, rose-violet Flower of the Dead, gaudy yellow Horns of the Devil, or the rich creamy Vanilla Orchid. I crossed the courtyard in a trance. I felt I had stumbled into one of the nightmare landscapes of Max Ernst, or into one of the lunar jungles of the Douanier Rousseau, haunted by the plants and trees he had seen in the swamps of Veracruz when he landed there as a boy with the armies of France. I felt crushed and stifled beneath the mass of this striped and mottled foliage.

And so we threaded our way, circuitously, through this silent, torpid, vegetable maze towards another archway looming high on the other side of the quadrangle. Constantly twisting, turning back on ourselves, it seemed to take us an age to get there. Two or three times we passed men who were workmen or gardeners, dressed in smart-looking shiny blue coveralls or jump-suits. They eyed us as we squeezed past them on the narrow paths without pausing in their work. Some of them were wetting down the gravelled track with sprinklers, while others raked the sand behind them. For no good reason, an image from the *corrida de toros* leaped into my mind—the *monosabios* smoothing the cruelly trampled arena. On a wider area, somewhere near the centre, like a clearing in the forest, one man was sweeping up a mass of fallen leaves and petals around the bulbous roots of a banyan-like tree, and two of his companions were tying up one of its lower branches with wire. The branch had fallen or been torn away; I saw the hanging strips of bark and the dry, white, fibrous interior.

The crossing must have taken between five and ten minutes, though it had the timeless quality of a dream. I was interested to see, as we approached the archway, that the stonework around it was deeply chipped and flaked. The surface was seamed with scars and pockmarks. Only as we were passing under it, and descending the ramp beneath, did it occur to me that the marks, showing up dark pink on the liver-coloured granite, were made by bullets and steel-splinters. Obviously in the last war, before the garden was constructed, the courtyard had been the scene of a battle between the Wehrmacht and the partisans, or the advancing Russians. I think it was that realization that confirmed my sense of vague horror and dismay, the feeling of encountering a slimy, and intangible evil. What was the purpose of this sinister courtyard, with its secret garden? . . .

We went through another black-painted door, a counter-part to the one on the other side. At once we were back again in a wintry, monochrome world, as if the lush greenery and flamboyant flora through which we had passed was a hallucination or fleeting vision. Then we were suddenly ascending another staircase and entering the residential part of the *schloss*.

Here the corridors were softly and expertly lit and decorated in a quiet shade of peach. At intervals there were stained-glass windows painted with knightly scenes of love and combat. A deep orange carpet lay thick underfoot. The draughts and gnawing cold of the other side of the *schloss* were replaced by the grateful warmth of central heating. Central heating . . . what would the tough old warriors in the painted windows have thought about that? . . .

Turning sharply round a corner, after traversing what seemed miles of empty corridors, all at once we almost ran into a man and a woman emerging from a room on the right. They were more startled to see us than we were to see them, though the chauffeur pressed himself back against the wall, pulling the suitcase out of their way. The woman glanced at us as she went by—wide dark eyes outlined in black, hair piled high and fastened with silver combs. She was tall, dressed in flame-coloured silk cut low to reveal the opulent white-powdered breasts; pungent scent, like civet. Her expression was sly and sated; it wasn't difficult to guess what they had been doing inside the room. The man was coatless, wearing gym-shoes and a plain white shirt that looked none too clean. As he turned and closed the door I saw that a tiger or panther or some big cat was embroidered in purple on the left side of the shirt, over his heart. He was young, lean and vigorous, and looked flushed. He gave us a direct, arrogant stare as he passed us, taking the woman's arm and hurrying her away from the door and down the corridor.

Jenbach's face remained expressionless. He opened the white-painted door two doors further along and ushered me inside. On it was the number *17* in big German numerals—and it was a very good thing, at that, that I happened by chance to notice and remember it.

The chauffeur placed my suitcase on the wooden rack at the foot of the wide bed.

I UNPACKED, took a piping hot shower, re-wrapped my ankle, put on a clean shirt, and hid the PPK before I discovered that Jenbach had locked me in. I intended to leave the room and make a careful little *tour d' horizon* around Herr Martagon's domain—and found I couldn't.

Why? Why the furtive introduction to the *schloss*? Why hadn't Martagon been there to meet me?

I looked at the watch lent me by Teague. Seven-thirty. How long would they leave me here? Martagon must be in the castle, surely, otherwise he wouldn't have brought me here, would he?

I took stock of my surroundings. The room was furnished in a simple and elegant style, with *Bauernstil* furniture; light, airy, comfortable. The cushions, bedspread and curtains were of a bright flower-patterned cretonne. There was that very faint, cold, damp, whitewashed odour that you often get in rooms in rural Germany and Austria. I went to the window, meaning to look at the view into the courtyard, for I judged that the room was on the inner and not the outer side of the building. I drew the curtains and found myself staring blankly at a narrow ogival window, featuring another of the castle's stained-glass paintings. A dull glow came through it from the other side, just sufficient to light up the dim shapes rendered in subdued blues, winey purples and deep purple greens. An armed knight on foot was thrusting a broad-bladed Roman-type sword into the shaggy throat of some grotesque heraldic monster, its outline too dark to see clearly. I wondered why it had been necessary to bar the window with four steel rods, disguised as reinforcements for the stained-glass but obviously serving another and less aesthetic purpose.

There was nothing else in the room of any interest. On the walls were steel engravings of soldiers displaying the fanciful uniforms of the Pomeranian grenadiers at the time of Frederick the Great. These were the giant-like and expensive soldiery with whom, on a board marked out on the floor of the great hall at Sans Souci, Frederick would play at living chess against his generals or other royal opponents. The room was bright and impersonal, like a room in a leading hotel in the Tyrol or the Salzkammergut. On top of a painted cassone was a tray holding a generous selection of drinks. Refreshed by my shower, though puzzled by my reception, or lack of a reception, I went over and poured myself a couple of fingers of Canadian Club.

It was just as well I did. All at once, faint and far-off but horribly distinct, came the sound of the most ghastly shriek I have ever heard. I thought at the time that it couldn't have come from the throat of a human being. It was a raucous, prolonged, metallic scream. It lingered on the air, then slowly died away. I gulped at my drink.

I suppose I was expected to wait patiently, like a good boy, until Jenbach came to fetch me. And I imagine I would have done, if I hadn't been unsettled by that inhuman cry and hadn't pulled the curtains apart and left them open. I had settled back on the bed in stockinged feet, with my glass in my hand and *Der Spiegel* propped on my knees, when suddenly an immensely powerful light clicked on from the outside, beyond the window. All at once the dull colours in the stained-glass became living and jewel-like hues— sparkling rubies, amethysts, sapphires and emeralds. The figure of the knight was brilliant in his steel-blue armour, as with a sulphur-coloured panache trailing like a meteor from his coiffed helmet, he delivered the death-blow to the rearing beast cutting at him with its curved talons. Above their heads was a black inscription in menacing-looking Gothic letters. The colours in the glass overpowered the anaemic light of my bedside-lamp and splashed the whole room with weird blotches of grass-green, ocean-blue, and reds as rich as blood. It was like the lights going up in a theatre whose stage I couldn't see. And at the same time I seemed to hear all kinds of surreptitious clicks and whisperings, like the stage-hands getting ready for a performance and the orchestra warming up . . . What was going on out there, down in the garden? . . . What was happening? . . . I started to feel restless and curious—and in no time at all the feeling became intolerable.

My prison was a well-furnished one, but I'd had enough of prison in this past year. I finished my drink, retrieved my PPK from beneath the mattress, my pocket-flashlight and spare pair of field-glasses from my suitcase—mere opera-glasses, really—put on my shoes, and fetched the little holdall containing useful tools from the bottom of my toilet-bag. It was a simple kit, made in Japan and bought at Selfridges, and contained nothing more lethal-looking than a nail-file, an icepick, a bottle-opener and similar sundries; but the steel was first-grade, and it took me just about twenty-five seconds to locate the tumblers of the big old-fashioned lock, force them back by making a lever of the ice-pick and bottle-opener, switch out the lights, and let myself into the corridor.

I closed the door quietly, slipped the glasses and tool-kit in my pocket, and walked swiftly back the way Jenbach and the chauffeur had brought me. I remembered passing a small staircase two corridors back. I wanted to get up high, to the upper floors.

The corridors were empty. I reached the staircase, carpeted with the same deep pile as the corridors. My steps were soundless as I ran upstairs.

Well—this had already been a day of surprises. How could I know that the surprises and scarcely begun? I couldn't imagine the *schloss* containing anything that could give me a greater shock than the exotic garden—a piece of Africa transferred to Austria . . . But I was wrong . . .

On the next floor, to the left of the stairway, was a door covered with a black material, heavily studded with bronze nails. It looked interesting.

There was no handle. I gave it a push and it budged slightly. It was closed by a spring. Another, more vigorous push, a glance over my shoulder at the empty corridor, and I ducked inside.

Jenbach ought to have locked this door too . . . I soon understood one of the reasons why the inhabitants of *Festung Martagon* weren't anxious to let their guests wander around . . .

I found myself standing in a small box-like vestibule, like an office waiting-room, complete with a chair, a table, a couch along one wall. It was painted a pastel green; a lamp shed a subdued light in one corner. It was empty, impersonal, and I had almost made up my mind to leave when I heard a groan—a long, low, rending sound from somewhere deep in a man's chest. I moved back against the wall and stood still. Now I could see that at the far end of the room there was a partition with an opening at one side. Again there came the liquid, bubbling groan, incredibly prolonged.

I trod softly to the screen and put my head round it. The lighting in the other room, which was narrow but two or three times longer than the vestibule, was so dim that it took me a minute to adjust my eyes to it. Then I realized that I was looking into a miniature hospital-ward; it had eight beds, four on one side and four on the other. The lamps at the heads of only three of the beds were lit, though the bulbs were very weak.

I took a step into the room, encouraged by the fact that I could make out a door at the far end. I went on tiptoe down the ward and tried the other door; it too operated on a spring. Passing through the room enabled me to register that there were five patients, all men, and that three of the beds were empty. I came back into the room to study their occupants more closely. What had happened? Were they victims of a road accident? A flying accident? An accident inside the castle, a fire or an explosion? Or a mass accident while skiing or climbing in the mountains? . . .

But why should the *schloss* run its own hospital, instead of driving the casualties to the nearest town? And what had that ambulance been doing—bringing in the wounded? . . .

And these men had been badly hurt, no doubt about that. They had also been skilfully and professionally cared for. The man whose groaning I had heard was in the bed nearest to me, one of those that were lighted, and his head and naked torso were swathed in bandages and a drip had been inserted in his forearm. His eyes were closed, his breathing tortured. Next to him, propped high on pillows, was another man whose bare body was wrapped in miles of bandage, with huge pads on the right shoulder and upper arm. His eyes were open and glittered in the semi-darkness, vaguely following me but not fully conscious.

The other patients were all recumbent and motionless, probably sedated. Beside one of them was an enamel trolley with instruments, medicaments, and stainless-steel kidney-shaped bowls. The sheet was drawn up to his neck and he kept turning his head from side to side on the pillow. Beside him lay a man with blood-soaked wadding on his abdomen, the bedclothes down around his knees, a spatter of blood on his shirt looking black in the meagre light. His eyes were screwed tight in pain, and a rasping sound forced itself from between his lips. On the left side of his shirt, above the heart, was some kind of an emblem. I bent forward to try to make it out. I reached up and pressed the button beneath the strip-light. The emblem was a stylized phoenix, stitched in red, a bird rising between billowing flames. I switched off the light.

These men were young men; none of them over thirty-two or thirty-three. They were strong, athletic, well-muscled. Whatever the accident was, it must have been related to some sporting activity.

I turned and leaned over the last bed, the one closest to the screen. The man lay on his back, stretched out very still. I couldn't see the rise and fall of his chest. He lay on the top of the made-up bed, his limbs neatly composed. Again I clicked on the light.

The man was dead.

On his white open-neck shirt, over the heart, was a dark-blue embroidered insignia—a peacock, like the one on Martagon's card, shown in profile, the tail sweeping behind it, the crowned head erect, one claw delicately poised.

The man was Grady Bailey. His thin, clever face looked reckless and carefree even in death. There was a dark, clotted, gaping wound with raw edges in his right side. It was so big I could have put my fist into it.

I heard the door from the staircase creak. Voices. Horribly shaken as I was, I still had the presence of mind to run down the room and let myself out through the far door.

I kept it open a crack and put my eye to it. Two men in white hospital coats came round the screen, one of them holding a bottle of plasma; the other carried a small oblong case and a clipboard.

I let the door close gently on its spring. I was in another corridor, indistinguishable from the others, complete with stained-glass and hunting prints.

I was searching for another staircase. More urgently than ever, I wanted to reach the top floor.

I HAD a lot of luck, that first part of the night. Either because the *schloss* was bigger than I thought, or because the guests and staff were concentrated on the courtyard, I found the staircase and crept upstairs unobserved.

The top floor was reached by an old-fashioned circular staircase, its iron handrail flaking beneath my fingers. It brought me to a sloping trapdoor under the eaves. I had to put my flashlight in my pocket and employ both hands in the darkness before I could shift the stiff bolts.

As soon as I began to open the trap, I was bathed in a glare of light. It was so brilliant that it almost made me lose my footing on the iron stairs. Quickly I lowered the trap, debating whether or not I had been spotted. After a moment I raised the trap an inch or two and tried to peer out, shielding my eyes with my hand. It was clear that I was close up beneath the roof under one of the powerful lamps that floodlit the garden, and that had now been switched full on. The question was, would my shadow give me away as I moved past it, momentarily blocking it?

The trap was heavy, but I let it rest on my body as I crawled out from under it like a snail creeping from its shell. I inched my way flat on my belly along the level space outside. I didn't know rightly where I was or what to expect —shouts or shots. I clenched my teeth and hauled myself out of the trap and past the beam of light as speedily as possible.

I then found I was in a very odd situation. I was crawling along a level area about twice the width of my body. It was paved with sheets of rough, wrinkled lead, laid so as to overlap and caulked at the seams with age-old crumbling solder. It only took me a few seconds to realize that I was on what had originally been the roof of the castle; on my right was a balustrade of herring-bone brickwork, beyond which was a sheer drop to the courtyard; on my left rose a steeply pitched roof covered with cracked and ancient slates held in place at the lower edges by rust-red iron tingles. At intervals there were depressions leading to what were once the conduits for rainwater, now removed, with the laps of lead bent downwards for the sake of neatness. There were black cobwebbed holes where the drainpipes had entered the top of the balustrade.

Twelve feet above my head, where the roof flattened out, the glass dome of the tropical garden was suspended on its steel struts like a canopy. I dragged myself over to the shelter of the balustrade, rolled over on my back, and found myself looking up at the night sky through the thick glass. The snow was smashing softly down at me, crashing into the sloping panes, seeking to grip, then slithering down and away towards the invisible pines.

I lay motionless, praying I hadn't been noticed. It was a curious sensation; I was half-frozen by my closeness to the icy glass and half-fried by the spotlights. I forced myself to wait a full minute, then wriggled like a worm out of range of the lights towards a broad patch of shadow. Again I cowered close to the bottom of the balustrade, where there was an unbroken bulwark of brick, listening intently, hardly daring to breathe.

Apart from the ceaseless hissing of the snow, a profound silence seemed to brood over the garden. The earlier clicks and whisperings had ceased. Cautiously, I rolled over on my stomach and raised my head until I could peer through the lower courses of the open brickwork. I was on a level with the tops of the trees, the snaky, shiny tops of the palms, the feathery tops of the towering ferns. I could see something I hadn't seen when I walked through the garden at ground-level. The tops of many of the trees had been trimmed to prevent them scraping against the glass, while the taller ones had been braced with wires and skilfully bent in a previously determined direction. It was both a wild garden and a garden that had been deliberately controlled.

I worked the field-glasses out of my pocket, lifted my head a little, and took a look down into the courtyard. From this angle the middle and lower branches obscured my view and I could only make out small disconnected sections of the sandy paths. At first I thought the place was deserted. It was only when I was shifting the glasses to another place that I caught sight out of the corner of my eye a very slight movement. The figure of a man, apparently crouched double, trailing something behind him, flickered for a moment past one of the gaps in the foliage and was gone before I could register it clearly. I waited, watching the same spot for at least five minutes; nothing else happened.

Swivelling around with the glasses, I happened to make a sweep with them across the distant side of the courtyard, below the balustrade, on a level with what would have been the top floor of the *schloss*. There was an area there that was shining brightly, a wide expanse about thirty feet across that I had taken to be a trick reflection off the roof. I was hurrying the glasses across it because the glare hurt my eyes when I thought I detected something moving behind it. I shifted on my elbows a few yards further along the roof, into deeper darkness, and adjusted the glasses.

I'd been partly right: the glare was caused by the reflection from the roof: but it was also caused by a reflection from a long single sheet of glass stretching out below me. A kind of double reflection, in fact. I now found myself staring through my glasses into a spacious upper room. It was evidently designed as an observation-post from which the occupants could look down into the garden below. It occurred to me that they probably enjoyed a magnificent and uninterrupted view, and I realized that it must be for their benefit that the trees had been wired back, giving them a clear sight of the meandering pathways and the central clearing. The garden had been laid out with those god-like spectators in mind. It was like the royal box at the theatre.

But what were they watching? Pushing the glasses forward into one of the V-shaped gaps in the balustrade I found I could shade the lenses from the lights and obtain a steady support. Slowly I panned the glasses across the whole length of the window. I could now see the occupants fairly clearly. There were both men and women packed tightly together, some sitting, some standing, all posed as stiff and still as figures in a waxworks or dummies in a lighted shop window. They watched whatever was going on below in a state of suspended animation.

Seated almost in the centre was the woman in the flame-coloured silk. She held a pair of gold pearl-inlaid opera-glasses, her white-gloved fingers poised elegantly in the air. Her ivory breasts bulged juicily as she leaned forward. I didn't see the man who had been her escort in the corridor, but close to her was a woman who must have been twice her age yet who was in her way even more striking. She sat in a gilded chair, a plump-faced, middle-aged woman in black. She tapped with a lorgnette on the shelf that ran the length of the window and the huge diamonds on her fingers winked chromatically at me. I counted eighteen spectators, all of them in evening dress, most of them in their fifties and sixties. At least one of them, a cadaverous, palsied-looking man with thick silver hair, propped on an ebony cane, must have been in his late seventies. From the differences in their physical appearance I judged they were of several assorted nationalities. One splendid, spreading and matronly lady dressed in burgundy-coloured satin, with eyes as black as obsidian and a *café au lait* complexion, reminded me of some stately Mayan idol. Wherever they came from, they were clearly a prosperous and well-nourished group, well satisfied with themselves. They all had an expression on their faces that I found very striking: they were watching the garden in a way I can only describe as predatory, like sleek birds of prey on a housetop.

Precisely in the middle was a slight, yet commanding, figure in a mulberry-coloured dinner-jacket. He stood erect amid a semicircle of watchers like a captain on the bridge of a liner, watching the courtyard through giant binoculars clamped to a black metal tripod. I was surprised to notice, when he put up a hand to adjust the focus, that alone among the men he was wearing a pair of white gloves. He was trim and slender, and when he tilted back his head I could see the shrewd glitter of his eyes under the straight eyebrows. At the same time he gave off an unmistakable aura of illness; his face was the colour of the inside of the torn branch I saw as I crossed the courtyard. Directly I set eyes on him, that first time, I thought there was an air about him of—how can I describe it?—something diseased . . .

There was the loud and unexpected sound of a shot from down below. The glasses jerked in my hand, clattering against the bricks and almost falling to the courtyard. Four seconds later came the sound of a second shot. By then I was already swivelling the glasses downwards and traversing as much as I could of the garden from left to right and back again. The crack of the shots had been muffled by the vegetation, but I identified them as rifle-shots, not shots from a pistol or automatic, which make a higher, lighter noise. After the first shot my ears caught the *whingg* of the bullet as it missed its target and rattled against the granite wall away to my left. The crack of the second bullet terminated in a thump, as if the bullet had entered the sand or a tree trunk or some other soft object.

I craned forward, trying to keep down and stay concealed behind one of the buttresses of the balustrade. For at least two to three eternal-seeming minutes nothing at all happened. Not a leaf trembled; not a spiked frond swayed. Then a pair of blurred figures in white, like drifting pocket-handkerchiefs, seemed to trickle down two of the broken segments of path, crossing several yards apart in opposite directions. All I could really see was the patchwork of varicoloured greenery.

Then I made an abrupt shift of the glasses. The foliage of a bluish-green bush at the side of one of the patches of pathway had started to quiver in a mysterious way. It looked like an enormous bird fluttering its feathers. There was a third rifle-shot, ending in another muted slapping sound. I kneeled up on the leaded roof, struggling to focus on the mysterious rustling. I was posed at an awkward forty-five degree angle and the lights from the arc-lamps cast strange slanting shadows.

What happened next was so unexpected I almost gave myself away by leaping to my feet. My hand shook and I could hardly keep the glasses to my eyes.

The bush bulged outwards and a man fell out of it backwards. To me, he seemed to be falling infinitely slowly, a figure in slow motion. His body straightened as it neared the ground and he gave a little kick with his heels. Then he lay level on the mustard-coloured sand, flat on his back. His mouth gaped and his eyes were open and he stared up at the snow-brushed canopy far above him.

I could see his face clearly, I could see the peacock emblem on his white shirt. I could see the spreading stain on the right side of his chest. And more than that, I could make out beyond any possibility of a mistake who he was.

Rupert Douglass.

I felt terribly angry and impotent. God knows what I would have done if the action below hadn't continued: I was already on my knees: I might have jumped up and started raving and shouting.

The bushes shook again, three or four yards further along the path. A man stepped out on to the pathway, peering carefully in each direction, his body taut and wary. He kept turning his head from side to side, an animal alert for the scent of danger. He carried a hunting-rifle with a sling and a scope, muzzle down.

Satisfied, he moved stealthily towards the prostrate Douglass, approaching cautiously, wanting to make sure his antagonist was dead. Another glance around, and he bent over Douglass, keeping a clear couple of feet away from him.

He was stooping forward, looking at Douglass, when there was a sudden whirl of activity that left me bewildered. It happened so fast I could hardly follow it even with the help of the glasses.

The bushes at almost the same spot where the huntsman had emerged literally seemed to burst apart. A third man, a negro, hurled himself on to the path, leaping sideways, legs apart, landing like a cat. His left arm hung uselessly straight down at his side. In his right hand he hefted a shotgun by the barrel—already raised high—already making a brutal glittering arc as it came smashing down. Again everything seemed to reach me in agonizing slow motion.

The butt of the shotgun descended with blunt and paralyzing force and took the huntsman smack on the back of the head. He must have felt his skull crumple in a devastating black flash. The rifle spurted out of his hand and he went down like a log across the body of Douglass, his head macerated and spraying blood like a crushed plum.

And then another fantastic thing happened. Douglass's body started to wriggle: he began to crawl free from under the weight pinning him down. He bounded to his feet—and —my God—he was *laughing—laughing*! He'd been faking— well, not quite faking—he held the right-hand side of his chest—though the excited way he moved his arm as he talked to the man with the shotgun indicated that the wound was superficial, probably on the inner muscle of the arm.

The man with the shotgun was laughing too, all over his black face. He tucked the butt under his good·arm, ignoring the bloody mess that smeared it, opened the breech and slid out the two shells. The pair of them danced about in their glee, congratulating themselves on the success of what had obviously been a risky though successful tactic.

A man in a blue jump-suit, trailing a rake behind him, followed by another carrying a watering-can, came briskly along the path from the right; half a minute later two more appeared at the left, bearing a stretcher. On the stretcher, face down, one arm trailing on the sand, was another white-shirted man. I couldn't see any blood, but he looked dead, very dead, no play-acting there . . .

Then the overhead lights suddenly made a loud fizzing noise and promptly faded to a quarter of their full intensity. The garden below was plunged into the steamy semi-darkness in which I had originally seen it.

THE next three hours, culminating in the sharp explosion outside the turret-room, were very confused. This was when I had finally scrambled back to Number 17, after getting lost a couple of times. Then I drank most of the rest of the bottle of Canadian Club.

Technically, the ability to be cool under fire has always been rated one of the chief requisites of my trade; I had recruited my people for the Niger River on that principle. Now, because I had become personally involved—'sentimental', as Teague would have put it—I had broken my own rule and was bewildered and disturbed.

Grady Bailey . . . Rupert Douglass . . . Then where was Hans Lurtsema? . . . Where was Gavin Asher? . . . in the *schloss*? . . . or in the ambulance with the red crosses on the doors? . . . an arm flopping off a stretcher? . . . a hole in the side? . . . blood on the shirt? . . . or pulping skulls with a rifle-butt? . . . or lying out in a grave in the woods with men shovelling frozen earth on them? . . .

By my third tumbler of Canadian Club I was disorientated. I felt full of guilt. I kept seeing Harrison's sly face in the pink glow of the empty restaurant. At least the two of us had carried out our acts, legal or illegal, in the name of what we had taken to be morality. We had been trying to create or preserve some sort of decent order in a world where order was crumbling, even though it had been our sad fate to have to resort to force and violence in order to achieve it. I was used to the spectacle of physical anarchy; but now I was confronted with a moral anarchy that was too close to me. What I had just seen, which was obviously a kind of institutionalized violence, was a grim parody of all my efforts over the past fifteen years. It brought into question the whole rationale of action by which I had lived. I had lived by the concept of justified force and sanctioned violence: and to see civilized men, men with whom I had associated and with whom I had fought, indulging in a kind of vehement savagery was peculiarly shocking to me. It also had the effect of making me question the causes and consequences of my own activities. To what extent had Harrison's lectures about country and duty been a cover for a desire to indulge in fraud and deceit? To what extent had I been killing for the thrill and pleasure of the thing, as Douglass had half an hour ago? . . .

I sat on the bed in the darkness, the glass in my hand, the PPK stuck under the mattress beneath me. The only light in the room filtered through the stained-glass from the horrible and now-dimmed courtyard, where the knight in his blue armour was still hacking at the ravening beast in a welter of dark glowing greens and reds . . .

. . . What to do? . . . How to get in touch with the three survivors? . . . (—*Were* there still three? . . .) . . . What to say to them, when I did? . . . Whether to be angry—or coaxing—or conciliatory? . . . What?— . . .

I got up and crossed to the cassone and poured more neat whisky in my glass.

I'm not squeamish, but now I felt actually sick; I almost went into the bathroom to vomit. It's one thing to commit violent acts yourself, for a purpose, in the heat of the moment; it's another to watch them done in cold blood, by someone you know. I could still see the glint of the negro's teeth and hear the thud as his thick arm swung the shotgun . . .

I'd been sitting in the darkness for an hour by Teague's watch, trying to sort the situation out, cursing myself for having stumbled into it in the first place, when Jenbach finally condescended to reappear. He knocked, got no answer, tried the handle, and stood there in the entrance disconcerted when he found that the door swung freely open and the lights were turned off.

His head turned sharply, his eyes searching for me. Then he saw me in the glow from the corridor. He relaxed. Without betraying any agitation (I had to admire that) he asked in his husky, lisping voice whether I would care to come along and see Herr Martagon now? If I would accompany him, Herr Martagon was waiting.

I got off the bed without saying a word, drained my glass, and went out into the corridor. Again the long trek began. He set a brisk pace and I had trouble trying to keep up with him. I was light-headed, partially drunk. I've really no excuse for such unprecedented stupidity—however, you have to remember that it was now almost nine o'clock, that except for an airline lunch my diet since dawn had been largely a liquid one, and that it was still less than forty-eight hours since I'd been catapulted out of one of Her Majesty's compulsory rest-houses. And, what's more, in all my other capers, even in the ones like Kirghizia, where there'd been no chance to reconnoitre, I'd been able to prepare myself beforehand with maps, photographs, intelligence reports, every sort of special material. And now here I was, bolted without warning into a foreign country, trying to deal with a totally unknown antagonist who evidently had a very peculiar taste in murder . . .

Ploughing along behind Jenbach's squat figure, I resolved in a hazy sort of way to say as little as possible to Martagon tonight. The coming encounter could only be in the nature of a preliminary skirmish. I'd keep my mouth shut, get back to my room as soon as I could, wedge a chair under the door-handle, and catch up on my sleep. Tomorrow the churning sensation inside me would have died down, and I could sort things out more rationally. I didn't feel any immediate sense of danger. After all, what Martagon wanted from me, didn't he, was only some sort of discussion about his '*unusual and lucrative GAME*' (I still had his note in my pocket)?

THE GARDEN GAME

It came as no surprise to me, even in my unsteady state, when Jenbach finally ushered me into the room with the wide glass window from which the spectators had watched the proceedings below. We went through a vestibule and up a short flight of carpeted stairs, all of a warm wine-colour, and entered the room through a pair of wide double-doors covered in red felt.

The room was enormous, but because it held so many people, and because the ceiling was low and painted the same claret colour as the walls, it seemed smaller than it was. It actually extended almost the entire width of the third floor of the *schloss*. The tall red velvet curtains on either side weren't drawn, and on one hand I could see the cold blanched snow, driving through the pine-tops and pelting the windows, while on the other the single sheet of clear glass presented a calm view of the tropical trees of the garden, dark green and motionless like monstrous weeds at the bottom of a gigantic pond.

A buffet supper was in progress; the candle-lit room echoed with the tinkle of plates, glass and cutlery, the shouts and laughter of men, the shrieks and giggles of women. It was hot. Cigarette and cigar smoke, perfume, and the smell of food hung in the air. In front of me were the people I had watched through my binoculars. The pale-skinned woman in the flame silk was spearing pieces of cold fowl on to a plate at one of the heaped tables, surrounded by an admiring male court; the coffee-coloured Mayan deity in the burgundy satin was seated on a straight-backed chair on a kind of dais, accepting the homage of an older group of men, including the tottering old ruin with the ebony cane. Throughout the room knots of people huddled together or milled about, food and drink in hand. I noticed that they helped themselves with boundless appetite from the piled-up dishes, or splashed drink into their glasses from the array of bottles on the smaller tables or from the gleaming silver ice-buckets.

It was a scene of extraordinary gusto and animation. Everyone was eating as if they had just been released from a long fast. There was something enormously greedy about them, like vultures feasting. Their eyes were unnaturally bright, their cheeks were flushed. The breasts of the women rose and fell as if they had just emerged from a hot dishevelled bed; the necks of the men bulged against the collars of their ruffled shirtfronts and the sweat beaded their congested faces. As I stood at the top of the steps inside the door, watching Jenbach weave his way through the throng towards the far side, I wondered where I had seen a crowd like this before. It wasn't after a bull-fight, or after a motor-race, where the spectators come away in a thoughtful, somewhat melancholy mood; these were like the people emerging from a boxing-match, or after the cock-fights I had seen in Central America, the sort of people who love to see blood shed vicariously and are made restless and excited by it.

The atmosphere was too hectic for anybody to pay attention to me, even though I was the only person, apart from Jenbach, not in evening dress. However, I wasn't left alone for long. Jenbach soon returned, bringing with him the slender man in the mulberry-coloured dinner-jacket whom I had seen in the observation window and had mentally compared with the captain of the ship. Somehow I wasn't surprised when Jenbach introduced him—deferentially, raising his light voice to make himself heard above the uproar—as Herr Carl-Conrad Martagon.

Standing two steps below me, he smiled at me, taking stock. He, Jenbach and I were the only really calm people in that feverish company. There was something impressively self-contained about him. His face was even whiter than I had realized, a sick, terminal whiteness: but his smile was friendly, if tinged with irony, and extremely attractive; he was the possessor of an immense, dangerous charm.

'Major Rickman,' he said, 'I'm delighted to see you and

to welcome you to Blühnbach. It's exceedingly kind of you to have come at such short notice—and in such beastly weather.'

There was a slight emphasis on the English idiom, but the pronunciation was smooth, the voice well-modulated. Every now and again he had a trick of letting his voice taper off into a kind of polite sigh, a deprecating fall that made the ends of many of his sentences difficult to catch. Apart from this one habit, he spoke it perfectly.

He wasn't in the least put out by the frankly hostile way in which I was staring down at him. He mounted the steps and took me by the arm, gently drawing me into the room.

He didn't offer to shake hands, probably because he sensed I might refuse, but more probably because of the condition of his hands. What I had originally thought were white gloves, when I saw him adjusting the field-glasses, were actually fine linen bandages; the fingers had been left free and the bandages were drawn tightly between each finger, webbed to cover the whole of the palm, the back of the hand and the wrist. They were as neatly and profession-ally bound as those of an Egyptian mummy, and seemed to extend far up his sleeve, perhaps as high as the elbow. He moved his forearms in a stiff, deliberate way, and the appear-ance of the fingers, sticking out of their coverings, was curiously feline and claw-like. At first I assumed that he had had an accident, or that as frail-looking as he looked he might have been indulging in some of the bloody capers in the garden; but after a few minutes it became obvious that he was actually suffering from some kind of erysipelas or eczema, and that his hands had been bound up because of his furious and almost uncontrollable urge to scratch. Now and again he would frequently forget himself and knead his wrap-ped wrists together, or grind and scrape the back of one hand with the back of the other. Whatever the trouble was, it evidently kept him in continual torment.

He drew me towards one of the tables, inviting me to eat, remarking that I must be hungry. The food looked tempting, but I declined. I was past eating. I also tried to refuse a drink, since there was a half-plan stirring at the back of my fuddled mind for which I knew I would need a clear head; but he wouldn't hear of this and pressed a glass of champagne on me, and when I had half-finished it motioned me to drink up and poured me another.

We walked across the room in the direction of the picture-window. The guests parted for us, hardly bothering to glance at me but treating him with respect, not venturing to speak until spoken to; obviously he was very much the king of his own castle. For me, the occasion had an unreal air, like a party in Hitchcock or Buñuel, the participants seeming to take on more and more the characters of birds and animals. The heat, the smoke-laden air and the swirl of bodies in the red, candle-lit room were beginning to affect me. I wondered whether the Canadian Club had been drugged: but it was out of the question, since I drank some of it before my expedition to the roof, and heaven knows I was sober enough then . . . No, I was only tired, out of my depth; it was a long time since I'd last been present at this kind of festivity . . .

If Martagon, bandaged hand beneath my elbow, felt any hesitation in my step, he gave no sign of it. On the way to the window I recollect that he introduced me to some of the random merrymakers who happened to cross our path. He used christian names, either from a desire to be informal or to make it harder or even impossible for me to identify them afterwards. Close up, their diversity was unmistakable; some were European, but there was a small man of delicate bone-structure whom I took to be from Ceylon or Singapore; a woman whose accent was almost certainly French-Canadian; an Australian; an Irishman; and one youngish man, so tall and thin as to be almost emaciated, who struck me as Syrian or Lebanese. Martagon exchanged only a few words with each of them. When the elderly man with the ebony stick showed signs of bearing down on us, he took my elbow again and steered me forward purposefully.

I remember we passed the statuesque lady on the dais, who inclined her massive torso towards us with becoming gravity; Martagon greeted her briefly, calling her Marta. More clearly, I remember a girl in a gold and white dress, with a fresh face and fair skin and striking auburn hair, who immediately struck me as far too innocent to be a member of this particular crew; she looked definitely out of place. I didn't catch the name Martagon gave her, but I gathered she was his secretary. She shook my hand, and when she spoke it was obvious she was English. I don't know why I should have been surprised or a little shocked by this, but I think we both looked a little ashamed at meeting a fellow-country-man in this particular place. What's more, without either of us being able to put a finger on it, we both seemed to recognize each other—I'm sure of that. Where had we met? She was only twenty-three or twenty-four—must have been just a girl when—? . . .

Martagon gave me no time to speculate; he guided me on. We were almost at the window, where there was an embrasure where we could speak in private. However, just before we reached it we passed a curious group whom I didn't register closely at the time (the Canadian Club was still in my bloodstream), but among whom was a man who was destined to play an important part in the story later. If I'd realized it then, I would have looked at him more closely.

There were six or seven of them, all men. They were clustered round a huge piano, a concert-grand. They were using it as a desk, and they all had cheque-books in their hands and were scribbling and tearing out cheques and thrusting them at each other. It was like settling-time at the races, or the ring concluding its accounts after an auction. They did in fact look like bookies or dealers, as they were mostly beefy, jaunty men, chomping on their cigars in high good humour and with the air of big winners. One of them, however, was morose, and the others were laughing at him; I suppose that's why I remembered him—that, and the fact that he seemed to be wearing an inordinate amount of gold. He was flicking a cheque across the polished surface of the piano to one of his cronies, his fingers glistening with gold rings, his cuffs with chunky gold links, his wrists with hefty gold bracelets and watchbands. As he straightened up I caught sight of the jewelled studs in his shirt-front. He stepped back, almost into me, fastening the cap on his fat gold pen, and when he turned I saw a distinctive pin or badge in his button-hole: a golden phoenix, rising between flames.

Bad temper allied to drink had made his square face a ripe plum-colour, contrasting with the slick silver of his hair. When I heard him speak, his flat American accent made me think of Texas or Kansas; he was a Southerner or Westerner of some kind. The others were teasing him, calling him *'Olly'* or *'Uley'*, or something of the sort, and he was retaliating by saying something about *'GETTING HIS OWN BACK, ON HIS OWN TURF, IN TEN DAYS' TIME . . .'* It was all very vague then, though it became clear later . . .

At any rate, when he mentioned the ten days, Martagon put a hand on his shoulder and looked at him warningly. *'Careful'*, he said, as if he only meant to warn the American about stepping back into me. *'Uley'* or *'Yewley'* mumbled an ungracious apology, his red-veined eyes glowering like a surly boar's as he swung back to the grand-piano.

'Yewley' . . . odd name . . . —yet Martagon's English—precise to the point of pedantry—made the syllables stick in my mind . . .

In the embrasure Martagon sat on the red velvet banquette, took out his cigarette-case and offered it to me. I shook my head. He selected one, put the case away, produced a lighter, and lit his cigarette with deliberate movements hampered by the thick wrappings on his hands.

'Well, Major', he began, putting the lighter clumsily back in his pocket, 'I know you must be tired, after your journey, so I certainly don't intend to keep you very long tonight...'

I said nothing. We were ensconced in reasonable privacy at the top end of the huge sheet of glass that ran the whole length of one wall. On the ledge beside him were strewn opera-glasses and binoculars, and it was littered with screwed-up wads of paper like discarded betting-tickets. The party threshed on behind us.

I looked down into the courtyard, under its high glass roof. I had been right: from this point there was a clear view of all the sandy paths. They seemed to converge on a spot under the centre of the window, and the trees had been tied back in such a way that every path was visible.

The thought of those green depths made me shudder. Now it was shadowed and deserted, more than ever like the bottom of some sinister lake or pond. I could fancy strange primitive creatures swimming down there—blind, bleached, bony monsters with bristling jaws, like the dragon in the stained-glass window in my room . . .

He saw my expression, drew on his cigarette, and said slowly:

'You know, I hadn't intended you to see our little Game tonight—not straight away . . . —that was supposed to come later—when I'd explained it a little, and you'd grown more used to it . . . However, I wonder what you made of it, exactly, up there on the roof? . . .'

I stared at him, controlling my surprise. He gave a half-smile.

'Oh, yes'—he gestured out of the window with his cigarette—'We saw you up there, during the last contest. The reflection from the lenses of your field-glasses gave you away.' He smiled again. 'I'm pleased to note that you're a very resourceful man, Major. We never dreamed you'd reach the roof. Poor Jenbach was very—what is the expression?—*put out* . . .'

As usual, the English idiom was faintly underlined. He shook his head, not at all upset, but evidently approving my initiative. I finished the last mouthful of my champagne and set the glass down on the sill. I felt a tingle down my spine at the thought that they'd known I was up there all the time.

'No,' he continued, 'I hadn't intended that at all . . . I only brought you to Blühnbach today because I'm leaving on a business-trip tomorrow afternoon that might last more than a month . . . —And as soon as I heard you were being released from prison, Major, I knew I'd have to act quickly, as I very much wanted to talk to you about several things . . .'

(How had he known I was being released from gaol? . . . I hadn't even known that, myself . . .)

'Well, Major, you're not being exactly talkative, are you? But never mind, that's all to the good; I didn't fancy you would be. Isn't there anything you want to ask?'

I turned my back to the window. He must have seen the anger in my eyes. He was a small man; he must have known I could have picked him up and thrown him through the glass window seventy feet to the ferns and gunneras below. He continued to regard me calmly, dapper in his dark-red dinner-jacket, half-smiling still.

'Yes,' I said, 'there is something I want to ask very much.'

He blew out smoke, then said almost casually: 'I suppose you've seen Bailey, as well, then?'

'Yes,' I said, 'I've seen Bailey. And the first thing I'm going to ask you is, where are the others?'

'Others?'

'Rupert Douglass. Gavin Asher. Hans Lurtsema.'

He sighed.

'Where are they, Herr Martagon? I want to know.'

'Now, Major—'

I moved closer. 'Where are they?'

He shook his head. 'No, Major, you mustn't be impatient. I think it will be better if we talk about this tomorrow, calmly. After all, it's only one of the things I've asked you here to discuss . . .'

He saw me half-lift my hand. He must have known that for all my calm I must be close to an outburst. He stood his ground.

'Tomorrow,' he said. 'I promise you, we'll talk in the morning. Tonight it will simply be enough for me to welcome you to Blühnbach.'

Jenbach was at my elbow. The burly bunch around the piano had stopped horse-trading and were regarding me silently.

I should have left it there; at least until I'd had a night's sleep and could think straight . . .

Since leaving Leigh Central, I'd done everything badly. I seemed to have forgotten almost everything I'd ever learned over the years.

I made no preparations: took no precautions: I lowered my head and went boring in blindly.

I'm almost ashamed to tell you what happened.

Briefly, after being escorted back to my bedroom by Jenbach, I put my head under the cold tap, cleaned my teeth, changed into slacks and a black jersey, waited twenty minutes, then sallied forth like the knight in the window to locate Rupert Douglass and the others—only *he* wouldn't have been so stupid . . .

I wanted to act while Martagon and his guests were still busy in the observation room.

I'd got it firmly in my mind that the three men were situated somewhere in one of the towers.

I was prowling around the spiral stairs in the tower closest to my room . . . peeling paint . . . musty smell like toadstools . . . flashlight in one hand and PPK in the other . . .

It was then that they jumped me—the chauffeur in the plum-coloured livery and two men in the blue nylon coveralls, one of them with a bald head . . .

And as I went down, and the blackness rippled over me, I thought I heard again that strange, distant scream I'd heard earlier, in my room . . .

DEEP, deep, deep in Martagon's garden with a scummy light seeping through the branches . . .

I was sunk in an eerie dream. I was wandering beneath the twisted boughs, asking myself if I was the hunter or the hunted. Through my brain, over and over again, ran the words: *And here were forests ancient as the hills . . . ancient as the hills . . .*

I couldn't tell whether the aqueous light was daylight or moonlight. Beneath my bare feet was a rotting carpet of slimy black leaves; they squelched between my toes as I prowled forward; they gave off a mouldy reek that grew more nauseating with every step. The trunks of the trees glistened wetly and I took care not to touch them because they were coated with a kind of reddish ichor, like mingled water and blood . . .

. . . *Forests . . . ancient as the hills . . .*

The trees were like no trees I had ever seen before. In one place there was a clump of squat growths that seemed to possess overlapping scales instead of leaves; in another, there was a stand of plants like pampas-grass which, when I looked closely, were covered with symmetrical rows of feathers. At intervals I skirted stinking pools of water with boggy margins. Waterlogged tree-trunks wallowed in the dark depths, their drowned roots spread like hair, their lower limbs crystallizing into some black and shiny substance . . .

It was like no forest I had seen in Africa, Asia, Guatemala or Mexico. It was a place without time—no day, no night, no winter, no summer. Yet I had an impression that the forest, with its trees and creepers, was immeasurably old. For a stretch of time that I couldn't calculate I was utterly alone, walking in an empty world. Then, little by little, I became aware of small sounds . . . the buzz of insects . . . sucking and plopping at the margins of the ponds . . . dry clicking in the undergrowth . . . monotonous humming from somewhere high above like the sighing of a distant Aeolian harp . . . hint of something like a tune, a broken pattern of notes, modal, like Pan-pipes . . .

Impossible to pin down the moment when I realized the forest was alive. A light cloud of insects settled round me and began to sting my arms and neck; I flapped my hands in vain. A twig crashed like a pistol-shot; something shaggy flickered between the trees; my ears caught the sound of a soft snarl or growl. Suddenly the branches above my head creaked and swayed and a grey shape with lantern-jaws and leathery wings swooped down close to my head, making me duck. Its wings clapped together clumsily as it veered round and swept back towards me. I glimpsed a burning orange eye, a row of yellow teeth like a crocodile's . . .

I started to run down the glades with their uncanny light. At first I loped along without any great sense of panic. Then, rounding a bend in the track, I came face to face with an animal fashioned in the drifts of a nightmare. It stood square, its claws planted on the path, its horned head lowered. A bony ruff or crest rose from its neck; a spiked tail lashed angrily behind its squamous sides. It was only my fleetness of foot that carried me past the razor-like horn slashing at my legs . . .

And then the dream became a continuous pursuit, backed by a barrage of weird and deafening noises. I clapped my hands over my ears and ran . . . ran . . . ran . . . bumped into the sticky trees . . . leaped over fallen logs, scraping my shins . . . splashed madly through the gummy pools . . . chased by demons . . . creatures out of Hieronymus Bosch . . . eaten by swarms of flies . . . semi-humans in skins with clubs and slings and spears and grinning snouts and slack mouths

smeared with crimson . . . stab . . . chop . . . flail . . . running
. . . staggering . . . feet slipping, sliding, slithering on the
stinking slimy leaves . . .
    ancient . . . ancient . . . forests ancient . . .

A hand shook my shoulder.
    I sat up in bed.
    A man in a white jacket stood beside me, holding a tray
with a pot of coffee.
    '*Frühstuck, mein Herr.*'
    Oh, all very civilized.
    He put the tray on the bedside table. Beside the coffee-pot
lay my PPK.
    A sense of humour, too.
    God, how my ribs ached.
    As he promised, Martagon met me at ten.
    We walked together outside the *schloss*. The snow had
stopped during the night, and a snow-plough had scraped the
paths, its blade cutting the edges as clean as a knife. The
packed snow squeaked under our feet as we walked together
in silence towards the pine trees fringing the slate-grey
expanses of an ornamental lake. At a discreet interval behind
us loitered Jenbach and the chauffeur.
    The *schloss* seemed smaller by day than it had the previous
night, though even a small *schloss* is a large establishment.
According to Harrison, Martagon owned more than one
habitation, but Blühnbach was surely the loneliest and most
isolated of them. It seemed to huddle in the snow, its dark
maroon walls encrusted by patches of snow like the skin of
a leper, with lumps and weals where the drifts clung to
clumps of ivy. Above it the clouds pressed low, grey and
seamless and swollen with more snow. The wind was bitter.
I clenched my fists in the pockets of my raincoat and felt the
cold bite at my wounded ankle.

Martagon wore a camel-hair or vicuña overcoat and a scarf of pale blue silk. On his head was a Russian-style cap of brown astrakhan. By daylight his features seemed pinched and pallid, the sense of sickness more pronounced. It was impossible to judge his age with any accuracy; he could have been anywhere between forty and sixty. In his ungloved hands—he couldn't wear gloves over those thick, pleated bandages—he carried a plastic bag filled with birdseed, the top fastened with a rubber band.

He waited until he had negotiated the slope, placing his feet in their over-shoes in the softer places on the paths, before he spoke.

'I'm truly sorry about last night, Major. Won't you please accept my apologies? I did ask you to be patient, you know . . .'

'What happened to me was unimportant.' I was determined to be neutral and cautious—no more mistakes; but I couldn't help a note of bitterness creeping into my voice. 'What I'm concerned about is what happened to Grady Bailey—and what could soon happen, if I don't stop it, to Rupert Douglass and Hans Lurtsema . . .'

We were approaching the margin of the lake, the snow-drifts thick on the coarse tussocky grass that bordered it. Where the grass showed through it was a sickly winter-yellow. The snow-plough had gouged out a smooth, broad circle at the edge.

'Douglass is clever,' said Martagon. 'I don't think you need worry about Douglass for a while . . .'

'I want to collect my people without delay and take them back to London.'

'Yes'—the sigh could be heard in his voice—'I was always told that you'd be after them, one of these days . . .'

We stopped in the icy circle, separated from the mournful stretch of water by spiky grasses. In the distance, on the far side, I could see an obelisk silhouetted against the pines like a carved grey bone. Now we had left the upper slope we seemed to be sheltered slightly from the wind.

'I'm sorry to have to inform you, Major,' said Martagon in his precise voice, 'that your people, as you call them, have already packed up and left Blühnbach. All except poor Bailey, of course . . .' He was fumbling with the rubber band on top of the plastic sack. 'They return to training-camp at once—to get ready for the next encounter, you know . . .'

'Oh? And where is the training-camp?'

Another smile. 'Oh, I don't think I can tell you that, Major. After all, I don't want to lose them, do I? Anyway, I'm hoping that when you've heard my proposition, you'll be quite contented to leave them where they are . . .'

He saw me staring at his fingers, poking through the elaborate bandages. The cold grey light made them repulsive. The sides of the fingers were covered with lines of small blisters; the knuckles were cracked and exuded a yellowish liquid.

He smiled again. 'My doctors tell me it's something called dyshidrotic eczema. There's some hope that one of the new steroids can bring it under control. Still, one gets used to it . . .'

We were both studying his hands in a detached way when, without warning, behind me, I heard the same shrill, unearthly scream I had heard in my room the previous evening. Martagon's smile deepened as he saw the startled expression on my face.

From a cluster of pines, fifty yards away to the left, a number of pale blobs were moving towards us across the snow. After a second I saw what they were—birds—peacocks. Looking drab and discouraged, they picked their way haughtily towards us through the snow-powdered grasses, lifting high their spindly legs and huge flat feet. The tails of the males were folded, and they looked anything but gorgeous; in fact they were faintly ridiculous, and Martagon watched them with a satirical glint in his eye, his fingers crisping the seed inside the bag.

There were eight or ten of them. They approached us delicately and surrounded Martagon in a dignified circle, their heads with their beady black eyes swaying backwards and forwards at the sound of the seed.

He began to feed them, scattering the seed at his feet, though two or three of the birds condescended to eat a few grains from his hand, which he held in such a way that the pointed beaks could not peck the sore fingers. He nodded at me as he saw my enquiring look.

'Yes,' he said: 'The peacock. Those of us who play the Game take our badges from where we live, or our pets, or our hobbies . . .'

Some of the males were young and without tails to boast of, while some of the fully grown males had shed their tail-feathers and sported only a mouldy stump; this did not prevent them from giving themselves immense airs. The females were grey-backed and dowdy and paid no attention whatever to their consorts or their offspring. Martagon went down on one knee. He coaxed them close to him with a curious wistfulness or tenderness in his pale face. I hoped they would concentrate on their feeding and not give vent to that nerve-scraping yell.

Dipping into the bag with his oozy fingers, surrounded by his clucking brood, he launched at last into an account of the curious activity of which it turned out he was both inventor and director.

'I think the time has come,' he said, 'since you've actually seen it, and since your former colleagues are so intimately concerned with it, that I ought to tell you about the Garden Game . . . Besides, as I said last night, it's one of the chief things—perhaps *the* chief thing—I wanted to talk to you about . . .'

I waited, watching the sharp beaks retrieve the rustling seed. He'd been right when he'd said I wasn't a very talkative man, and a year in gaol had deepened this habit of silence. Anyway, I'd decided that my role today was to watch—and listen—and to be careful . . .

He sighed his mild, soft sigh, rose, and brushed at his knee with a bandaged hand. At last he said:

'You know, believe it or not, the whole thing started with a wretched little fist-fight—a common dockside brawl, of all things—in Singapore . . .'

I let him tell his story without interruption. He spoke quite frankly and naturally, with a lack of concealment that I wondered at at the time but was to understand fully an hour later. Somehow the story seemed more hideous because of this very simplicity, though I don't think it struck him in that way.

Apparently it all began at a conference in Malaysia, four years before. He didn't say what sort of conference it was, but given O. G. Sarzens' main field of activity it wasn't very difficult to guess. The delegates had been housed in the Golden Lotus, a brand-new high-rise hotel on the water-front. Late one night he was in the room of an old business-friend of his, a Swede whom he identified only as Pär. They were going over the schedule for a joint presentation next morning. Pär's room was on the fourth floor, directly overlooking the wharves. Suddenly they heard a disturbance outside. At first they took no notice; such squabbles and outbursts were common in that busy port, even at two in the morning; but eventually they got up, stretched, and wandered over to the window with their drinks in their hands. There, under the glaring blue arc-lights on the quay below, two men in white shirts were squaring up to each other with long knives. They looked as though they meant business. The men around them were making no attempt to restrain them.

Idly, without really caring, Martagon remarked that he thought the smaller of the two men would win. Pär immediately pulled a crumpled fistful of Malaysian money out of his pocket and offered to bet on the other man. Martagon laughed and took him on. The small man lost. They went back to their schedule.

That was the time when Malaysia was having trouble with the Chinese community, and south-east Asia generally was disturbed; the Indonesians were busy chopping up several millions of their fellow-countrymen and throwing the pieces into wells and rivers. Two or three nights later there was another brawl on the quay, practically in the same spot. Again Martagon lost.

The second bet had been more substantial; Martagon's pride and judgement were becoming involved; he wasn't a natural loser. He told his local representative to hire a couple of Malaysians and arrange for a third fight under Pär's window—thus making sure he would be backing the winner next time. Well, I didn't grasp all the details of what happened next, but apparently the Swede, who was no fool, guessed or found what his trusty Swiss comrade might be up to; he hired one of the goriest of the local goons, and inserted him in the ensuing fracas. Martagon's man got knifed, poor devil, and Martagon lost for the third time running.

Naturally, he couldn't leave the matter there. He and the Swede—(was the latter, I wonder, one of the well-fed crew round the grand-piano?)—put their cards on the table . . . 'I've got a man who can beat your man' . . . They were leaving Singapore next day, but were due to meet in a month's time in Washington. They agreed to bring their respective champions with them and find a suitable venue. Martagon sent Jenbach to the States with instructions to recruit a first-class street-brawler in a hurry . . . —not such a tall order, after all, in that part of America. Jenbach came up with a negro who was reputed to have killed at least two policemen. He fought the Swede's man, another Malaysian whom the Swede had smuggled in, at 3 a.m. one May morning in Franklin Square, under the rear windows of the Seward

Hotel. Promptly at three, Martagon and the Swede took their places in the window of the former's room and watched the duel by the light of the park lamps. Franklin Square is three blocks from the White House; but of course stabbings and beatings are nightly events in that part of Washington, and people have been mugged in broad daylight outside the railings of the White House itself. Martagon's negro won. The dead man was left lying in the park, and the negro was whisked away in a waiting car.

'Actually, he was the older brother of the negro you saw last night,' Martagon explained, as calmly as if he was describing a vicarage tea-party. 'He lasted over a year— twelve or thirteen fights—until a few weeks ago. His mother now lives in one of the biggest houses in Harlem...'

From that night the Game started to snowball, to take on a definite form and shape. Martagon delicately blew a piece of chaff from one of his blistered fingers as he told me how other colleagues whose discretion he could trust had been gradually brought into the Game. I gathered that in one way or the other they were all connected with the armaments business. He and the Swede had noticed how much more dramatic the fourth fight had been, amid the trees and bushes of Franklin Place, with each man being put in by pre-arrangement through a gate on the opposite sides of the park. An enclosed park or garden, with a vantage-point above, seemed an ideal location; better still, it lent itself to privacy. Recruiting to the club had therefore been largely on the basis of whether or not the invitee owned a patio or similar feature that could be converted into a private cockpit. At Blühnbach, his estate in Austria, Martagon already possessed a fine courtyard that he had quickly converted into an out-standing site for the new cult; but he hinted that there were at least a dozen other places that were almost as spectacular.

It was at about this point in his story that one of the older male peacocks, after a lot of ducking and shuffling, decided to favour us with a display of his tail. He unfurled it, standing with his back to us. Fascinated though I was with Martagon's recital, I couldn't resist trying to edge round so that I could view the splendour of the tail from the front; but as I turned the bird turned with me, lazily presenting me with a view of his imperial backside.

Martagon laid a white-bound hand on my arm.

'Wait. Be patient. He'll face us in his own good time . . .'

So we waited, and in half a minute or thereabouts the creature swung indolently round and presented us with the full glory of his feathers. It was dazzling. The tail was in a state of winter replacement, like an antique fan of silk and lace that had sustained damage: but even so the arc of bronze-green suns that the bird lifted above his back seemed to burn and fizz against the snow, shimmering chromatically as he shook them languidly. Martagon gave me an approving glance as he heard me suck in my breath with admiration. Then the tail was lowered, the amazing show disappeared, and the bird once more looked as drab as its mates.

Martagon scattered another handful of seed, the blackish grains bouncing and pattering on the scraped white surface.

'Of course,' he went on, 'the Game has changed a good deal since those prehistoric days in Malaysia. Among other things, by this time we've gradually evolved a proper set of rules . . .'

For one thing, he told me—(and I still couldn't understand why he was taking me so much into his confidence)—the contestants, or 'Players' as he called them, were no longer confined to simple knives. They could use chopping or cutting tools of any size and variety—whatever came most natural to them. As for other weapons, a regular tariff had been established, although the regulation was strictly one weapon per man. Thus you could use a rifle with a scope, but were permitted only one shot; a rifle without a scope was allowed two shots; a hand-gun, three shots. The weapons and bullets were checked by independent judges before the contestants entered the courtyard. There was a man who was an archer, owned by a Belgian, and after much wrangling by the steering-committee he was awarded three arrows; he was presumably still active, though recovering from a serious wound. Any amount of body-armour or protective covering was in order, provided you wore a white shirt—the same colour for all—and provided the armour was worn on the body and not carried separately in the shape of a shield or a similar device. One man came in with a huge steel riot-shield, behind which he proceeded to wedge himself into a corner with a shotgun sticking out through a slot; they had been compelled to call off the match. But you could wear a steel waistcoat, or even a tin-hat if you liked—except that experience had shown that such items slowed a man up. Speed and fleetness of foot were naturally all-important. One of the best chaps they'd had was a man from Bolivia or Paraguay, a little bit of a fellow, who employed nothing larger than a kind of glorified old-fashioned cut-throat razor. He was devastating with it. You could also carry brass-knuckles, spiked-knuckles and gadgets like that, though here again they could prove a greater hindrance than a help, and you had to get a special ruling on them first. Hand-grenades, of course, and similar explosive devices, were taboo, for obvious reasons.

He spoke of these lethal activities in a cool and collected way which I thought extraordinary. Then he emptied out the last of the seed, carefully folded the plastic bag, and put it away in the pocket of his camel-hair coat.

I had heard him out without offering any comment; but now I couldn't resist asking him what it all signified—why he and his friends would want to indulge in such an insane and criminal activity? . . .

Those were the words I used—speaking very carefully and unemotionally . . . *Insane . . . Criminal . . .* I spoke the words tactfully, judiciously—but I spoke them just the same . . .

I could see the cold curlicues of my breath spiralling into

the sombre sky. I didn't feel anger, particularly, only a sense of repulsion. The words didn't offend him. He stood without speaking, inserting the tips of his fingers tenderly into his coat pockets, frowning at the icy black waters of the lake, considering before he spoke. The peacocks, sensing there would be no more food, stalked away towards their shelter beneath the pines.

'I was hoping that you, at least, would understand the appeal of the thing,' he said at length. 'However . . .' He paused again. 'To be honest,' he went on slowly, 'I'm not sure I wholly understand—myself—the deep attraction of the Game . . . Obviously it must be connected with my profession in some way . . . My friends and I manufacture armaments, you see—we make planes and ships, tanks and artillery, high-explosives and automatic weapons—yet we never get to witness the application of these interesting contrivances at first-hand—we never get to see the end-result, as it were . . . Oh, sometimes we walk or fly over a battlefield, when the fun is over—but we never actually see men using the tools we have placed in their hands—we never see the heat and sweat, the tension of the fight . . . and that can be very frustrating, don't you see? . . . After all, where's the point in being in the business of dealing out death if you never see death actually dealt out? . . . I suppose the Game gives us a feeling of getting close to the roots of our profession . . . getting down to the fundamentals . . .'

His gaze left the icy lake and found mine. He had been speaking quite seriously, as if exploring his own sensations; now he smiled.

'Of course,' he said, 'it's all doubly thrilling to a Swiss like me, or to a Swede like Pär. You'd be surprised how many people from neutral countries you saw up there in the Red Room last night. After all, we neutrals missed the experience of two world wars, and naturally we feel deprived . . .'

A lone black bird, a rook or crow, swung into view above the trees on the far side of the lake and flapped towards the *schloss.* Martagon took his hands from his pockets, raised them as if holding a shotgun, and swivelled daintily to follow it. The bandaged forefinger pulled on an imaginary trigger.

He dropped his arms, turned and took one of mine, and we started to walk back up the slope, the way we had come. Jenbach and his companion waited for us, blowing on their hands and stamping their feet.

'Really, Major, I'm not going to apologize for my friends or myself. After all, where the arms business is concerned we're performing a service; we're catering to popular demand. Humanity pretends it wants peace, but deep down it craves for bloodshed. I'm sure I don't have to list for you the wars that are going on now. You're a soldier, after all— you know almost as much about them as we do. The world has never known a single and entire day of peace since the dawn of creation. There is no good reason why it ever should. It may be a cliché, but it is nevertheless true, that man is a fighting animal. Moreover, psychologists will tell you that his aggressive and acquisitive instincts are not at all the scourge that liberal politicians declare them to be; they happen to be the most valuable instincts of all, the source of all our energy, our ambitions, our creativity, the pledge of our survival as a species . . .' The voice flowed on in the accentless English; he clung tighter to my arm as we negotiated a slick spot. 'You, Major Rickman, are British. May I tell you that for one year in this century, and for one year only—1969—there were no formations of British troops engaged in active warfare anywhere in the globe? However, twenty thousand of them are now engaged in Northern Ireland . . .' He slipped a little and recovered himself. 'May I quote you a few figures? I quote from memory, from data supplied by my research department, but I think I'm right in saying that in the past ten years the annual expenditure throughout the world on armaments has risen from 120 billion American dollars annually to 200 billion dollars. The

United Nations, I believe, has reported that during the 1960s the governments of 130 nations took 2000 billion dollars from the pockets of 3500 billion people and spent it all on armaments . . . ah, that lovely United Nations! . . . more power to it! . . . the wonderful tensions it creates and keeps alive! . . . the splendid wars it has given us! . . . where would O. G. Sarzens be without the United Nations? . . .' He laughed. 'And in the 1970s, my people tell me, the cost of armaments will rise to almost 3000 billion. Think of that! So when I tell you that at the present time only 4 billion dollars are being spent throughout the world on medical research, while 25 billion are being spent on research into weapons, doesn't it indicate that Thanatos, my friend, is several times stronger than Eros? . . . Oh no, Major—I'm certainly not going to apologize for a little sideshow like the Garden Game . . . The marvel is that, unlike the governments whom we service, our taste for bloodshed is so orderly and so moderate—even if we do sanction two-a-side encounters from time to time, or even three-a-side . . .'

He had begun to breathe rather heavily, his mouth open; there were pink patches on his cheekbones and round his lips. As he toiled up the slope, seeking firm spots for his rubber-shod feet, he started to tell me how enthusiastically many of his associates had welcomed the new 'sport'. Several of them were already connected in some way with conventional sports or blood-sports. One of the Americans was part-owner of the NFL team that won last year's Superbowl; another American owned a slice of two of the leading heavyweight contenders; a third, a Puerto Rican, ran the biggest cock-fighting cartel in the Caribbean; a fourth, who was French, had provided the stake for a string of young *fenómenos* in the bull-ring.

He was about to elaborate further when we crested the causeway-like embankment of the road and turned towards the *schloss*, a hundred yards distant. Around the gateway I could see clearly the pits and pock-marks made by tank- and mortar-shells. As we did so, the double-doors of the entrance opened and a chocolate-coloured Mercedes drove out (—the one I was in last night?—) and slowly approached us. The chains on its tyres made a slapping noise on the icy surface. I caught a glimpse of the man in the back seat as he leaned forward to tap the driver on the shoulder. The car drew up as it came abreast of us.

The rear window slid down. The red face of the man whom they had called '*Uley*' or '*Yewley*' peered out of the window, eyeing me suspiciously. On his head he wore a dark green Western hat with a fancy brown feather band round it; he put it on the seat beside him, mopping at his face with an outsize handkerchief. The gold pin in the shape of a phoenix which was in his lapel the night before now did duty as a tie-tack. He stuck his hand out of the window and said quickly and guardedly, in his flat voice:

'Ten days, then, huh?. . . And make sure you bring your cheque-book, O.K.?. . .'

Martagon, unable to shake hands, touched the American's square, thick palm lightly with his fingers. The window closed and the car drove off down the road through the forest.

Martagon looked after it with an expression of private amusement. I didn't bother to ask who the American was; anyway, he wouldn't have told me.

'What time is it?' he asked.

He couldn't wear a watch with his wrist swollen to twice its size by the bandages.

'Ten forty-five,' I told him.

We started walking towards the *schloss*.

'Time to talk seriously,' he said.

Down by the lake a peacock uttered its rasping cry. I winced and turned my head. My companion looked too.

A number of the peacocks were performing a dance on the open snow. They pranced like folk-dancers, beaks parted, wings brushing the ground. They leaped and skipped in a

soft explosion of feathers. Then one of them gave a tremendous somersault, hurtled backwards out of the ring, and
strutted arrogantly away.

Martagon chuckled.

'This sharp air makes them lively,' he said. 'They look
absolutely marvellous, don't they? Actually though, they're
terribly, terribly stupid, poor things . . .'

WHEN we reached his study, we took a few moments to thaw ourselves out in front of the crackling logs in the huge stone fireplace. I held the soles of my shoes to the flames while he flexed and unflexed his weeping fingers, smiling down into the heart of the blaze.

He pressed a bell and in a moment the girl whom he had referred to last night as his secretary entered through a side door. She carried a decanter and a plate of dry biscuits. She gave me a sideways glance as she set the tray down, friendly and somehow apologetic, then went quickly out without looking back. She looked as fresh as she did the night before, and again I wondered who she was and what she was doing here. While she was in the study I was able to glimpse, through the side door, the functional character of the room beyond—impersonal, neon-lit, furnished with steel filing-cabinets, typewriters and a Xerox machine, a strong contrast to the dark brown wainscotting of the study itself.

Martagon poured from the decanter and brought me a glass. A rich and warming madeira.

'So it was you,' I said, 'who pulled the strings to get my fellows out of Africa? . . .'

I still spoke cautiously. I was anxious to extract as much information as I could—but I was also anxious to get out of Blühnbach alive . . .

'Ah—Africa . . .' He was still smiling into the waving red centre of the flames. 'Eighty-five *coups d'état* since independence . . . a very promising continent . . .'

'Tell me, why didn't you spring Teague when you sprung the others? Why didn't you spring *me*?'

'Teague? Well, Teague is very much your own man, isn't

he? Therefore he's hardly such promising material as the others. And you, Major—well, you were rather a special case at the time; my friends in Nigeria were very angry with you. All the same, I did put in a good word for you—which is more than your own people could—or even *would*, maybe . . . Besides, to be quite frank, although you performed magnificently last time, don't you think you might be getting a little *long in the tooth*?'—a faint foreign emphasis on the idiom—'I mean, for something as strenuous as the little Game we've been talking about? . . .'

I ran a mouthful of madeira round my teeth and looked at him in silence. What do you say to a man who claims to have saved you from daily beatings and from the firing-squad—especially if you hate his guts? . . .

'All the same,' I asked him, 'I suppose it was useful to know that I was safe in gaol when you were putting your proposition to the younger men?'

I went over to the enormous walnut desk, poured myself another glass of madeira and helped myself to a plain biscuit.

'I shall still want to talk to them. Nothing has changed that. I still want to try and reason with the ones that you and your friends may still have left alive . . .'

'Oh, good heavens, Major, I understand that. If I may say so, your feelings do you a great deal of credit. You'll forgive me if I say that I find the remains of your British feudalism extremely touching—yet not unimpressive. You come of that generation that still crawls out to collect the bodies of its own dead and to retrieve the wounded under fire; the generation where the officers don't go to bed until they've seen to the welfare of the troops . . .'

'Why did you have me followed when I left prison? Was it because you felt that my first thought would be to get in touch with them?'

'Followed? I didn't have you followed, Major.'

'Oh, come along—'

'No. It wasn't my people, I assure you. I imagine it was

your cousin, Mr Hopwood. He seems to trust you much less than I do.'

'Then how did Jenbach get in touch with me?'

'He only had to watch your house in Brecon Crescent; we knew when you were leaving prison.'

(And how did he know that? . . . And why did he follow me when I went to meet Harrison in Soho, instead of putting the slip of blue paper through the letter-box? . . .)

He went over to replenish his own glass. 'Please don't take these things too personally, Major . . .'

'Did you have anything to do with searching my house?'

'Was your house searched?'

'Thoroughly.'

'I'm so sorry. You mustn't blame me. I had nothing to do with it.'

'I wonder if I can believe that?'

'It was your esteemed cousin, again, who must have searched your house.' He broke a biscuit tenderly between his fingers. 'I didn't need to search it, you see. I already knew what your searchers were looking for. And I knew where it was.'

I stared at him. He placed half a biscuit in his mouth, munched it, washed it down with a sip of madeira. There was something oddly spiderlike about the restricted movements of the fingers in the bulky wrappings. He gave me his most charming smile.

'Stay here a moment, will you, Major? There is something I've brought you all this way to show you. I'll fetch it. It won't take a minute.'

He moved around the desk and walked in the direction of the door of the office. As he opened it I heard the sound of a typewriter, which stopped. The door closed and I distinctly heard a key being turned. I was alone in the study.

There was no point in doing something crass, like rifling through the papers on the desk. There would be nothing there, otherwise he wouldn't have left the room. Anyway, I didn't want to take any more false steps. I moved behind the desk to the window and looked out. Nothing but the snow-laden ranks of pine trees . . . *And here were forests ancient as the hills* . . .

Idly, I examined my surroundings. The study was a pleasant, lived-in, informal kind of room, low-ceilinged, in which the predominant notes were leather and burnished wood. The smell of polish mingled with the smoky scent of burning logs. The bookshelves, on all four walls, ran to the ceiling, and were packed. I noticed editions of Proust, Hardy, Mann, James. The tokens and testimonials of the occupant's trade were everywhere. On the desk, on side tables, in spaces between the books, were models and statuettes of several generations of tanks and artillery. A trapezoid monster of Battle of Cambrai vintage made a contrast with a sleek low machine of a type that might have rattled through the paddy-fields of East Bengal. An ancient howitzer that could have seen action at Tannenberg or along the Isonza stood on the same shelf as a graduated family of modern ballistic missiles, their Brancusi-like shapes cast in gleaming aluminium. I was particularly interested by a bronze group of statuary depicting a team of horses dragging a 12-pounder and its caisson into action, the drivers in their dolmans and pill-box hats vigorously wielding their whips. It reminded me of the reproduction of a picture by Caton Woodville, showing the guns being brought up to the front at the Marne, that used to hang on an upstairs landing at Whinyates. I wondered what had happened to it. Probably knocked down for five bob at the final auction, or pitched out to rot in the rain . . .

I was stroking the smooth flank of a nuclear submarine when the door of the inner room opened and Martagon returned. Under his arm was a thick manila folder. He smiled and nodded at the model.

'A beauty, isn't she?'

What portion of her lovely hide or lovely innards did she owe to O. G. Sarzens? . . .

He was awkwardly holding out to me the heavy folder, indicating I should look at it. I took it and carried it over to a chair beside the fireplace. He went back to his desk, picked up the other half of his biscuit, and seated himself in the deep leather chair behind it, tilting it back and watching me quizzically as I read.

He had nibbled his way through several more biscuits by the time I looked up and laid the folder on my knee. He was amused by the puzzled expression on my face. I rubbed my hand across my mouth. My lips felt rather stiff.

He nodded.

'That's right, Major. That's the Dunsterville file . . . A copy, of course . . .'

The sheets I'd been studying were in fact Xeroxed.

I said quietly: 'You've got the original?'

He smiled. 'I have—but I wouldn't want you to sit too near the fire with it . . .'

I opened the file and leafed once more through the top documents. Some were single sheets, some several sheets stapled together. There were letters and memoranda alternating with sketches, drawings, and closely typed schedules and specifications; all were meticulously dated, signed or initialed. J. M. F. Dunsterville, his son P. J. F. Dunsterville and their senior partner Frederick A. Galley-Thompson must have been among the most orderly minded of industrialists—and also among the most indiscreet and careless, considering that this whole correspondence, infinitely damaging from a diplomatic and technical point of view, had been allowed to fall into the hands of the competition. And Carl-Conrad Martagon, as I realized, was no tender-minded competitor. The papers could play havoc with the British position in West Africa, or throughout Muslim Africa in general.

I looked up again. 'Where did you get it?'

'Kabassa.'

I should have known. A feeling of bitterness went through

me, like acid on my tongue. *Kabassa*. So it had all been useless. The oil-tank bursting in a storm of flames . . . Frazer with his bowels spilling out . . . Button pitching forward on his face . . . Hearne and Fox down at the wire . . . *Useless* . . . Martagon's men had got there first and were already gone . . .

He came over and lifted the file from my lap and took it over to the desk.

I rose and stood with my back to the fire.

'Why did you show me that?'

'I asked you to come to Austria so that you could see it with your own eyes. I want you to go back to London and tell Hopwood that it's in my possession. I'd like you to carry that message for me. There's no other man whose word he trusts so fully.'

'I haven't seen the originals.'

'You don't need to. Could I have made that complete duplicate if I hadn't got the originals in my hands? You can assure Hopwood that I haven't traded them off—at least not yet . . .'

I moved from the fire. It was getting too hot. I felt hopelessly confused, enmeshed in circumstances I didn't understand. What part was Harrison playing in all this? . . . To mention just one thing, how had Martagon and Jenbach got my home phone number, which was kept strictly confidential? . . . Had Harrison given it to them? . . . Why? . . . Had he connived at this trip to Blühnbach? . . . Was I expendable, was he selling me out? . . . I felt the helplessness of the man-in-the-middle . . . It had all happened too soon . . . I wasn't mentally prepared . . . nor physically either . . .

Martagon was watching me. He wasn't smiling now. He was rubbing the backs of his bandaged hands slowly together, the ineradicable itch again afflicting him.

I said, 'Don't you feel reluctant to let me into the secret? Aren't you afraid of what I could do with the information?'

He opened the folder and began to thumb through the papers.

'Oh, no, Major, not in the least. In fact, this file is my little bit of insurance with you as well as with Hopwood. Don't you see that? I don't think you're likely to breathe a word about my little pastime, are you, or about what you saw down there in my garden last night, while I've got the Dunsterville papers? As I said before, you're a man of somewhat old-fashioned ideas . . .'

He had extracted three or four documents from the file. He picked up a pencil and made a note of their serial numbers on the inside cover. Then he brought them across to me.

'Here. A specimen of the contents. Give these to Hopwood. Ask him to check them with Joe Dunsterville, at Sheffield.' He laughed. 'I'd love to see old Joe's face, when he hears I've got them. It'll help him to understand why the British Government is going to award some of its contracts in future to subsidiaries of O. G. Sarzens, instead of to Dunsterville . . .'

He went back to the desk, closed the file, and placed on top of it a paperweight in the shape of a sharp-nosed armour-piercing shell. Some more chafing of the bandages on the wrists and the backs of the hands. Then he said:

'Tell me, Major—what do you want from life—I mean, *now*? . . . What are you looking forward to?'

'Looking forward to?'

'. . . Let me see, how can I put it tactfully? . . . Would I be too far *wide of the mark*—' (leaning on the English phrase a little)'—if I said that as far as your superiors were concerned you might very well be—let's say—*washed up*?' (leaning on it again) . . .

I said nothing. His manner had become exceedingly bland, as if he wouldn't dream of offending me for the world. I took another step away from the blaze behind me.

'Your cousin owes you nearly four thousand pounds,' he went on. 'You've got a little more than three thousand in the bank. And you must be very concerned . . . oh, I *must* put this delicately . . . about—what's her name?—Margaret? . . . . . . Mrs Frank Mallison? . . .'

It wasn't surprising that his people had got in and out of Kabassa before we did . . . He knew more about us than we knew about ourselves . . .

He said, 'How would you like to earn, say, twenty thousand pounds a year?'

'Twenty thousand—?—'

'That's right.'

I folded the papers he had given me very deliberately and put them away in my inside pocket.

'And what would I have to do to earn such a princely salary? Oh, I know you're very generous, Mr Martagon. After all, you were paying Grady Bailey between five and fifteen hundred pounds for each—how shall we describe it? —each exhibition. Isn't that so? Are you going to pay his widow a pension, or a lump sum as a death grant? She's a nice girl, a pretty little thing. I know—I've seen her . . . But I suppose you know about that, too? . . .'

His pale, neat features remained impassive. He wasn't a man to be disturbed by sarcasm.

'I am perfectly serious, Major Rickman. I will pay you a yearly fee of twenty thousand English pounds to act as my *lanista*.'

'As your what?'

'A Roman term, meaning a manager or trainer.'

'Trainer of what?'

'Why, of my troupe of Games-players, of course.'

Well—honestly—I was struck dumb by the man's effrontery . . . He saw me gape and heard me gasp, then continued before I could protest, speaking more quickly:

'No, before you become indignant, won't you at least hear me out? After all, this is a proposition that could be very important to you—solve all your problems—bring you together with Mrs Mallison, perhaps? . . .'

THE GARDEN GAME

'We'll leave Mrs Mallison out of this, Mr Martagon.'

'Oh, yes, of course, Major—please, *please* forgive me. But at least this proposition ought to interest you. And it's a job that would suit you, at this time of your life, and which you could very easily perform . . .'

I winced. Had the word reached even this far that Morven Rickman was near the end of the road? . . .

He opened a cigar-box with a trophy of arms on the lid and offered it to me. I took one.

'What's the proposition?' I said.

He handed me a cigar-cutter and we made a grave little ceremony out of preparing and lighting our cigars. They were Partagas, and merited careful attention. I moved the chair a little further away from the molten glow of the logs and sat down facing the desk, leaning back and crossing my legs.

'I used the Latin word,' he said, 'because our analogy is with ancient Rome—with the ancient and honoured profession of the gladiator . . .'

He saw me smile slightly and held up a reproving finger.

'No, no, Major, I am not exaggerating. The comparison is not a trivial one.' He seated himself comfortably in his deep leather chair and drew his glass towards him, the picture of a man at ease. 'Maybe what we're discussing here are the first steps in the eventual restoration of a great institution, one of the foundation stones of a once-splendid Empire . . .'

He reached down and opened a drawer. From it he took a number of sheets of paper, each enclosed in a separate plastic sheath. He shuffled them with his hobbled fingers.

'I had a spot of research carried out. The results are very interesting. Did you know, for instance'—he consulted the sheets—'that most of the greatest Roman writers appear to have been in favour of gladiators? Let me see . . . some names at random . . . Horace, Cicero, Tacitus, Juvenal, Martial,

Petronius, Pliny the Younger . . . And the Emperors who
staged gladiatorial displays were by no means only the
degenerate ones, like Domitian, Caligula or Nero . . .' He
put his finger on a place on the page. 'Here, for example, is
Julius Caesar himself, in 46 B.C., staging a real-life battle in
the Circus at Rome, with over 500 men a side . . . And here
is the great Augustus, with displays involving 10,000 fighters
. . . And Claudius, fighting miniature campaigns in the
Campus Martius . . . And Trojan, in A.D. 107, entertaining
the Romans with four months of festivals in which 10,000
gladiators and 10,000 wild animals were engaged . . .' He
turned a page. 'I see that my researcher—one of the most
reputable scholars in Switzerland—estimates that in the eight
years after A.D. 106 the number of gladiators fighting at the
imperial command was in excess of 23,000 . . .'

He laid down the page. Behind his head the tops of the
pine trees looked like the bristling tips of an army of spears;
the dark grey sky was bleak.

'Of course, Major, we can't re-establish this extraordinary
activity—which was so essential for keeping up the martial
spirit of the Empire—all at once. We have to be realistic.
What we now have in the Garden Game is the world of the
gladiators on a tiny scale; we are running a kind of pilot
project. The climate of opinion is still not favourable—
though I must admit that it's steadily improving. What,
after all, are the deaths of 23,000 men in the context of the
twentieth century? Why, they're a flea-bite. Twenty-three
thousand men died in two hours at the Somme, or during
the March offensive, or in two days at Stalingrad. Death on a
large scale is something the world is learning to harden its
mind to. Of course, there is a dwindling residue of religious
feeling, and of good old nineteenth-century liberalism—
the sort of thing that makes your English politicians go
on huffing and puffing about the *"moral leadership of the
world"* . . .' (Here he tilted back his padded chair, blew out a
cloud of smoke, and laughed loudly.) 'Oh, yes, for a few

years more the Garden Game will have to remain a private pursuit—until public opinion decides to stop pretending and puts itself in line with public practice . . . And after all, with the acceleration of the world population—doubling and redoubling every fifty years—war is becoming a necessary instrument of population-control. We're entering the era of the Great Death. Professional killers will be in demand. You never know, Major, in a few generations men might rise up and call us blessed. After all, extermination by skilled killers, in a stylish and entertaining way, might be preferable to extermination by famine, or plague, or by mechanical means, don't you think?—by which I mean the use of nuclear devices, for instance? . . .'

Thrusting his body far back in the soft chair, the dark eyes in the dead white face were an inky black, like pebbles in the snow. If the vigorous scraping at the wrappings on his hands was an indication, his thoughts seemed to excite and exhilarate him. I didn't break the flow but sat silent, studying the tip of my cigar.

'Also, Major, you must do us the justice of agreeing with me that we're not barbarians. We're not totally bloodthirsty. What we're running isn't a slaughterhouse; it's something more like the old trial by combat, or the mediaeval tourney, over which kings and queens were proud to preside . . . Oh, I agree that the possibility—even the probability—of the death of one of the contestants is absolutely essential to the whole business—it's what makes the Game serious, don't you see—it's what gives it the feeling of *playing for keeps* . . .' (the slang phrase was delicately underlined). 'But you've seen for yourself, Major, that every participant in the Game isn't killed off. You've visited our little infirmary upstairs—a compulsory feature by the way, of all our meeting-places . . .' (His tone implied that the people who had watched and gambled on the Game in his Red Room last night were in the category of high-minded humanitarians.)

'We don't always turn our thumbs down, Major. Many of our players are granted the *indulto*. In the world of the gladiators it used to be called the *missus*—permission for the loser to live to fight another day. And sometimes—more often than you'd suppose—we have a contest in which neither or none of the men is injured at all—a stand-off, or *stans missus*, as the old Romans used to put it . . .'

He beamed at me. The Garden Game was a jolly romp, a slightly more serious version of basketball, or billiards . . .

'Now, Major, this position of trainer, or manager—'

He waited until I looked at him. He lifted the decanter; I shook my head. He looked very pleased with himself; we were fast becoming comrades. He made it sound as if he was offering me the vice-presidency of an old-established and respectable company.

'I think I told you that your former companions had already left Blühnbach for their training-camp. As you can imagine, this is a very necessary establishment, and all of us with a stake in the Game have paid a great deal of attention to it.' He picked up one of the plasticized sheets and glanced at it. 'The Romans did too, of course. There were three imperial schools for gladiators in Rome alone, and dozens more scattered throughout the Empire. Naturally, if we want our own men to acquit themselves well, my friends and I have got to adopt the same system.' He laid down the paper. 'Now, I've got to admit that my own particular team has been performing rather poorly in recent months. Frankly, there's a lot of money to be made, and I can do a great deal better than I have been. What I need is an experienced man to run the whole show, to take charge of my fighters, their athletic trainers, their armourers, their doctors, and all the rest of it. Naturally, after the tremendous show you put up at Kabassa, I thought of you—who else?'

I threw the rest of my cigar into the fire and stood up.

'Having you in my employ would give me a tremendous advantage. After all, Major, you're already an expert in this business. You know how to pick the right men and how to work them up to the proper pitch. You've got an eye for a sound prospect. And they trust you. They work for you. You know how to bring them on. You know what their specialties are, or ought to be—whether they ought to fight '*light*' or '*heavy*', as the Romans used to say—whether they should be '*Thracians*' or '*Gauls*' . . .'

He drew his chair closer to the desk and leaned forward, looking at me with bright dark eyes. The tip of the index finger of his right hand, inside the aureole of bandage, pressed down hard on the sharp tip of the model shell on top of the Dunsterville file. It was really very curious to listen to the mild and cultured voice of the fragile, white-faced man talking so easily about the blood, death, pain and wounds of a group of silly, greedy, misguided, courageous young men.

'Twenty thousand English pounds, Major—*with* a share of the winnings on each individual contest . . .'

He rose to his feet, the desk between us.

'You don't have to make up your mind at once. In the meantime, in any case, you have to return to London, to consult with Hopwood and tell him about these.' He tapped the file. 'You'll have an opportunity to talk to him about your personal position. However, it's time that you took stock, Major—and I think you'll find that it's time for a change. I'm sure you'll see that you can do very much better with me than you could ever hope to do by continuing to work for Harrison Hopwood . . .'

He slid open a drawer of his desk. Using his thumb and forefinger as pincers, he extracted a single beautiful blue-and-gold peacock's feather, with its shining devil's eye. He dropped it on the desk in front of me.

'Don't be in a hurry to make up your mind,' he said. 'I realize that it's a big step, especially for a man like you. You have scruples. But don't you think it's time you shed a few of those old ideas of yours? After all, in the world we live in today, they don't really make much sense any more, do they?

And don't you think you ought to stop letting Hopwood take advantage of you—of your special skills and abilities? Why don't you do what everyone else does now—cash in on them? . . . So why don't I contact you again in—say—three weeks, and you can give me your answer then? . . . Think about it, Major, think about it . . .'

TEN days later, on December 8th, I was lying concealed with Teague on the broad flat roof of a mansion on the outskirts of Phoenix, Arizona. My situation was virtually the same as the one I had occupied ten days earlier in Austria; but this time I was in much better physical shape and infinitely better prepared. I had come to collect Douglass, Asher and Lurtsema, and I didn't intend to return home without them.

We had been on the roof for nearly four hours. However, the sky sparkled with big warm stars, so close in the wide Arizona night we could almost reach up and touch them, and the temperature was a delicious fifty—a change from the muck, slush and cold which the inhabitants of England were enduring at that moment.

The mansion had not been easy to track down; it was only by a miracle that we had stumbled on it. If we'd failed it would have been a serious setback; we'd have completely lost touch with Martagon and his repulsive activities and have been blundering around in the dark. Ironically, I believed I had solved the minor problem of the identity of Martagon's secretary without any difficulty at all. The very next morning, an hour after taking off from Vienna, somewhere over the Black Forest, it flashed into my mind that the auburn-haired apple-cheeked girl was probably the daughter of John Verrinder. Ten years ago Verrinder was commercial counsellor at our Oslo embassy—still was, for all I knew. I was fairly sure I had met the girl there when she was no more than a flat-chested little schoolgirl. Verrinder had been instructed to take me under his wing for a couple of months, to give me cover; and although he hadn't liked it very much,

I'd lived more or less amiably at weekends in the bosom of his family. He wasn't a bad chap, though dry, and his wife was rather a bird-brain: but I'd adored tobogganing and larking around on the skating-rink with their brood of children. The girl was the only daughter, a skinny, lively kid with great big eyes and carroty pigtails, and that's probably why I remembered her. I didn't recall her name, apart from wondering how she came to be working for Martagon. I dismissed her from my mind. Later, if I had time, I might look into it.

Finding and identifying the man called 'Yewley' was the urgent and immediate matter. I started racking my brains about it in the hotel outside London Airport where I holed up as soon as I landed. I went there and took a room and phoned Teague and lay on the bed and thought hard about that damned 'Yewley'. All I had was that odd first name. How the hell could I track him down, inside two weeks, with so little to go on? . . .

I told Teague I'd call him at five, at another number. This was because Harrison maintained a permanent tap on my home phone. All Teague had to do was to go to the local post office, making sure he wasn't being followed, and at five o'clock enter a booth whose number was noted in my pocketbook. At five I went down the foyer, contacted him after a couple of tries—someone at his end must have made him wait—and gave him a number of instructions. First he was to go to my bank and withdraw fifteen-hundred pounds out of my current account; I'd call the manager to authorize it first thing in the morning. Then he was to take our regular passports—*regular* passports—to Bill Kanavy at the American Embassy in Grosvenor Square and get us fixed up with a couple of American tourist visas; that, too, I'd arrange with Bill early next day. Finally he was to pack a pair of suitcases with light clothing and stand by to take another call at four o'clock.

Harrison, of course, would know where I was. He would

have received word from passport control when I returned through London Airport. Probably one of the C.I.D. men on duty would have tailed me to the hotel. Later he would receive a call from my bank manager, who had standing instructions to call him whenever I did anything interesting. On the other hand, I thought that Bill Kanavy might—might—keep his mouth shut. He owed me a large favour from the last time we'd worked together, before they'd retired him to a nice soft job behind a desk. However, even if Bill did call up Harrison, he'd certainly give me the visas first, and America is a very big place . . .

I then went to bed, put a no-disturb sign on the door, and slept till nine next morning. When I got up it was raining heavily. I had breakfast, made my calls, and skulked around the hotel. It was surprising that Harrison made no attempt to get in touch with me; for some reason, he was letting me play my own hand. It made me even more certain that something fishy was going on, and even more determined to go it alone. When I'd read the papers, and given the chambermaid a chance to tidy my room, I went back to bed and slept once more, with the rain swishing against the windows.

At four I phoned Teague, learned everything had gone smoothly, and told him to drive down and fetch me, stopping only in Hounslow to make sure the tank of the Jensen was filled. I was on the steps waiting for him, my chin huddled in my raincoat collar against the cold, stinging rain. He swung into the forecourt. I threw in my bag, jumped in, and we were off.

I was thankful for the rain. Rain makes it a hundred-per-cent easier to shake off pursuit. The lack of visibility, steamed-up windshields and loss of speed help the fox and not the hounds. I told Teague to drive straight into Reading and spend twenty minutes driving round the back streets. Then I set him on the A4 to Newbury, where we turned abruptly on to A343 and drove south to Andover. There we made a few more off-putting manœuvres before taking the

A354, which carried us in little more than one hour from Salisbury via Blandford Forum straight to Weymouth. We didn't talk; I let him concentrate on the road. These weren't the dirt-roads of Asia and Africa on which he loved to blind along at 120, but with me holding the map like the co-driver in the old Mille Miglia we covered the 200-odd miles at a very brisk clip for staid old England. Since these were, for England, good, straight roads, with a fair amount of room for passing, we reached Weymouth just before midnight. At Weymouth we parked the car in a big commerical garage near the docks, took a cab for the last half-mile, and ran up the gangplank of the *Pandora* just as she was weighing anchor.

Of course, in modern conditions you can drive round for hours and a wide-awake policeman or immigration officer can put an end to your little game with one phone call. Still, I knew they'd be watching London and the nearby airports, and probably the ports; but I'd never been out through Weymouth before. It was then that Teague and I used our false passports. I'd picked these up on the Continent three years earlier, and they were items in our professional equipment which I didn't think it was Harrison's or anyone else's business to know about. On them we were described as 'salesmen and business executives'. Anyway, if the cross-channel route could work for Burgess and Maclean, years ago, it might work again for us too, with luck, and if we timed it right . . .

My God, that was a miserable crossing. It was rough, and I'm a rotten sailor. The waves and rain lashed the windows of the lounge, where I lay prostrate on the benches drinking brandy-and-milk and wondering all over again what in the hell I thought I was up to. I wasn't a policeman, or a guardian of morals; Douglass and the others weren't children. What was I doing? All I could tell myself was that it was unfinished business . . . I couldn't be put out to grass or retreat to my fishing-cottage (if I lived that long) with that shadow from the past over me . . . Martagon was right: my ideas were hopelessly feudal and old-fashioned . . . Fifteen years ago, ten years ago, I might have shrugged my shoulders and let it pass, though I doubt it . . . but now, in middle age, I'd developed a conscience, for God's sake . . . I couldn't ignore it, I couldn't let it go . . . —that would have been to brutalize myself, to betray my past . . .

If the crossing to Guernsey was bad, the crossing to Normandy on the French ferry was worse. Teague bore it better than I did; but after I had summoned enough strength to explain to him in detail what we were doing, and where we were going, he felt justified in ordering a few brandies himself. He took to staring at me reproachfully whenever he made the circuit of the deck and returned to where I lay slumped in a deck-chair.

We both perked up a bit in the train to Paris. At Orly we drank a bottle of Lynch-Bages and ate a splendid gigot of lamb—my first food for thirty-six hours—while we were waiting for the New York plane. Teague became quite cheerful. The trip across the Atlantic by Air France was agreeable, even though we had to travel coach-class because I needed to save money. Before we left Orly I found a copying machine in the main concourse and made a copy of the three extracts from the Dunsterville file. I marked them Copy Number Three and mailed them to Harrison. The other copy I mailed to a hotel in Brussels where I had an accommodation address.

From Kennedy we flew on to O'Hare in Chicago. There we hung around for several hours, trying to make sure we weren't followed. We had used our genuine passports with the American visa on landing in America; I didn't want to get Bill into trouble or make unnecessary complications with the American authorities, in case I needed help later on. From O'Hare, after dodging in and out of the gigantic airport complex, we slipped aboard a small Western Airlines plane for the hop to Phoenix.

Phoenix . . . Phoenix . . . It had been easy enough to figure out that our destination ought to be Phoenix . . . There was the gold pin in 'Yewley's' lapel, the gold tie-tack he wore next morning . . . *'We take our badges from where we live, or our pets, or our hobbies'* . . . Martagon had inadvertently given me the clue himself . . . I'd have gambled anything that I was right—and I'd already gambled a chunk of my money on a flock of ferry and plane tickets . . .

Phoenix, yes—but beyond Phoenix—what? . . . A garbled first name . . . *'Yewley'* . . . *'Yewley'* . . . almost meaningless . . .

There are 510,000 people in Phoenix. It is a vast and teeming city, one of the fastest-growing in the world. It sprawls over a vast area of the Sonoran desert. When our plane started to let down over the citrus orchards and the cotton fields, and I saw the gigantic gridiron with the central avenues lined with broad date-palms rolling out beneath us, I had a feeling of the enormity of my task. Our first glance at the Phoenix phone book, the obvious line of attack, wasn't reassuring either. It was six inches thick, with four hundred names to the page. When we'd settled into our motel room near Sky Harbor Airport we stole a second copy from a phone booth and both went to work on it.

Our first job was to make sure *'Yewley'* or *'Uhley'* or *'Ooley'* wasn't some sort of nickname, a contraction of a last name. We landed at six, and by midnight we had compiled a list of over a hundred names, ranging all the way from *Yewell* and *Yoal*, through *Ulander, Ulery, Ullan, Ullman, Uhlig, Uhlundahl* and *Uhlmann*, to *Olay, Olayo, O'Lea, O'Leary* (scores of these), *O'Leal, Olivo, Olivas* and *Olimski*. We wrote them out with their addresses on long slips of paper and fell into bed, exhausted.

Next day we meant to rise bright and early. We intended to hire a car from one of those coast-to-coast rental companies, so we could leave it later in any city we liked; then we'd start checking out the addresses to see which of them needed closer investigation. However, we were so tired after a five-thousand-mile flight and a drastic time-change that we slept till noon. Almost another day lost. Believe it or not, with all the delays and travelling, nearly seven of my ten days had slipped by. Today was Thursday, and the Garden Game at 'Yewley's' place was due to be played, if what I'd heard at Blühnbach was correct, on Sunday night.

At first, however, we assumed that three days would be plenty. We consolidated our names and addresses into districts—Chandler, San Marcos, Mesa, Tempe, South Phoenix, Scottsdale, Glendale, Peoria. Then we started quartering the city in our rented Torino, its colour an unobtrusive beige. We were in a fairly confident mood. After all, we knew what we were looking for: a ranch-sized establishment, the home of an enormously wealthy man. Whenever we found that one of our names belonged to a man in humble circumstances, we could eliminate him. Whole districts could be eliminated in this way. We were searching for an imposing, four-square, fortress-like residence, which could have a garden hidden at its heart.

Such a building would have to be the home of a millionaire; but the trouble, as we soon learned, was that Phoenix swarmed with millionaires and near-millionaires. The city was a fast-growing industrial centre. General Electric, Sperry Rand, Reynolds Metal, Goodyear Aerospace, Western Electric, Kaiser Reynolds, and other firms all had plants there. Our man could easily be president of such a concern, and if he was—the horrid thought nagged at me—he might have an unlisted address and phone number. Of course, I did have one clue: like all the patrons of the Game my man was engaged in or intimately connected with the armaments business. However, I couldn't identify one particular concern that dealt exclusively with armaments, though practically all of them must have been in receipt of government arms contracts in one form or another. So that was another lead that petered out. Another thing: Phoenix is a city where the

Mafia is well entrenched; its booming real-estate, building and service industries are ready-made havens for 'laundering' the extortion and gambling money from Nevada and California. The Mafia chieftains like the Arizona climate, and the surrounding desert makes a splendid natural graveyard when there are bodies to be disposed of. If our quarry was a *capo mafioso*, we could hardly expect him to advertise his name and address in the local phone book.

It was on the third night, when we'd been driving around all day and Teague was visibly starting to lose heart, that I hit on the significance of the word 'Yewley.' It was a sheer fluke. We had turned in early and Teague, exhausted by the unaccustomed warmth and the dry light desert climate, had already switched off his light. I reached out and picked up one of the two books I'd brought with me. When I had told Teague to pack, I asked him to put in something for me to read—of American interest. To be on the safe side, he chose military history. The book was a biography of Stonewall Jackson, with my father's book-plate inside the cover. I stared at it for a long time, tracing the florid design with my finger. Then, in the introduction, there was a reference to Grant's river campaign at Vicksburg. I sat upright in bed.

'*Teague—!*'

In the bed across the room a single eye opened and regarded me with a notable lack of enthusiasm. I said:

'*Grant* . . . Ulysses L. *Grant* . . . *ULY*sses—*YEW*ley! . . .'

This earth-shattering revelation caused him to raise his head at least half-an-inch.

'Don't you *see*, Teague? All we've got to do is to search the phone book for the people whose first name is *Ulysses* . . . There can't be many, even in America! . . .'

The prospect of hunting through half-a-million names for this odd appellation did not appear to thrill him.

'And we'll make enquiries—we'll ask around—it's a name that will stick in people's minds! . . .'

I swear he was staring at me with pity. He reached out and

turned on his bedside lamp. Then he heaved himself upright, threw back the covers, and swung his pyjama-clad legs to the floor.

'Sir, I've been thinking . . .' He spoke accusingly, as if it wasn't his province to do the thinking in our association and only my ineptitude was forcing him to do so. 'I mean, wouldn't it be a lot easier if we simply went down to the airport and kept watch? If as many people are involved as you say, and they're coming from all over the world, most of them are bound to use the main airport, aren't they, even if some of them come in private planes?'

It was such a blindingly simple suggestion I should have had my head examined for not having thought of it.

Poor old Rickman . . . Certainly time to retire . . .

Teague stared at me in complete silence for a moment, then once more switched off his light, lay down, turned over, and while I was still gazing in his direction, hypnotized by his brilliance and my own stupidity, emitted his first grinding snore.

THE next afternoon—Thursday—we embarked on our round-the-clock vigil at Sky Harbor.

In the morning, however, heartened by Teague's brain-wave, I took a couple of hours off to buy us some weapons, the logical step at this stage. I had told Teague to leave his gun in Brecon Place and left my PPK behind the facia of the Jensen, which no doubt Harrison and his boys had discovered days ago. Passengers on transatlantic flights were being systematically searched and I didn't want us to be arrested as highjackers: and as I said before, I didn't want complications in the U.S.A. I could have asked Bill Kanavy to take steps to fix us up, but that would have been unfair to him—and anyway, procuring weapons in America isn't the most difficult thing in the world. We merely drove to the nearest discount-store—called Square-T—where literally hundreds of hand-guns were laid out in neat rows between the counter selling women's lingerie and the one selling automobile accessories. I would have liked to have gone to a decent sporting-goods store, but here again economy was a factor. It was, of course, an elementary error to economize on such vital equipment, and we duly paid the price for it; but at the time we were pleased enough with our purchases. I chose a Merkel ·22 automatic, which only weighs 25 ounces, has a 4-inch barrel, and is a copy of my favourite Walther; Teague, who did better, bought a ·32 ACP Prinz 300. I paid $78 for one and $84 for the other. We reckoned we wouldn't need anything larger than belly-guns—and hoped we wouldn't need those. Then we bought four boxes of ammo to go with them and we were in business—just like that. No nonsense about gun-control in these Western states. We

walked out with our toys in our pockets, climbed into the
Torino, and drove four miles west to Estrella State Park, where
there are 2000 acres of wilderness. We located a likely spot
where a dirt trail came to an end at the foot of a sandstone
crag. In the face of the crag was the entrance of an old mine-
shaft, boarded up. The boards were scarred and splintered
with hundreds of bullet-holes, showing that the youth and
chivalry of Phoenix drove out here for the same purpose we
did. Among the mess of tin cans and rubbish in the area we
found an old chewed-up car-mat. We wedged it in the
boards, retired a few yards, and popped off twenty or so
rounds apiece. Teague was always a good marksman, and
although I hadn't practised for well over a year, and my gun
was a shiftless little brute, I hit the target several times with a
satisfying dull thwack.

Ninety minutes later Teague was situated at a strategic
point in the central lounge at Sky Harbor, while I ate a bowl
of chile in the airport restaurant. Twenty minutes later I
relieved him and settled down in a distant corner behind a
newspaper for a long wait. I didn't like this gum-shoe stuff,
but I'd endured long waits before, in far less comfortable
places.

I must have been there about eight or nine minutes when a
flood of passengers began to fan out from one of the arrival
bays. From my vantage spot beside a tall flowering shrub I
looked across and ran a casual eye over them. I jerked to
attention. Rupert Douglass and Hans Lurtsema were walking
in the middle of the crowd. They walked quickly and looked
hot and flustered in their heavy European clothing, raincoats
draped across their arms. They were escorted by four men
who had obviously travelled with them, and who were
carrying all the hand-luggage. The whole small tightly knit
group, in their dark suits, stood out in strong contrast to the
surrounding crowd dressed in shirtsleeves, slacks, Western
hats and Western boots. Three of the escorts were young and
forceful-looking, but the fourth was an extraordinary little

man, stubby and with immensely broad shoulders, his round skull bald as an egg, built like a wrestler. I seemed to have seen him somewhere before, though I couldn't remember where, and I was much too excited to bother about it now. But I did have time to notice that while Douglass and Lurtsema both looked fit and in first-class condition there was a difference in their bearing. Douglass, self-contained and cat-like as ever, seemed alert and confident, while the giant Dutchman, a head taller than the others, looked pale and anxious; when his little eyes weren't fixed on the ground he kept glancing around almost furtively, like a prisoner casting about for a way of escape. And where, I wondered, was Gavin Asher . . .?

My impulse was to jump up and confront them, escort or no escort: then what I took to be common sense prevailed and I hunched behind my newspaper until they passed. I trailed them down the long red-carpeted exit corridor to the lower level, shielded by the last stragglers from the plane. I had plenty of time to call Teague away from his *huevos rancheros* so that we could collect our Torino and position it where we could watch the airport entrance; it would take our quarry fifteen minutes to collect their baggage.

When they emerged a saffron-coloured Ford LTD was waiting for them. They got in rapidly and the car drove off. I somehow got the impression, from their grouping as they left the terminal, from the way they handled the baggage, and the casual yet authoritative way they laid their hands on Douglass' and Lurtsema's arms as they entered the car, that two of the escort had been assigned to Lurtsema and two, including the bald-headed man, to Douglass. Douglass sat in the middle at the front, Lurtsema in the same position at the back.

I huddled down as Teague started to follow the LTD. There was no need to expose ourselves unnecessarily. However, Teague was skilful at this exercise, and the LTD seemed to have no inkling that the neutral-coloured saloon that kept three or four cars behind it was on its tail. In any case, they must have been packed in too tightly to be able to turn their heads. Their car swung immediately on to the interstate and drove north in a leisurely manner before turning right on Shea Boulevard. Teague and I knew the plan of the city only too well by now. We crossed the Scottsdale Road at the Country Club and headed east into the desert, with the raw sandstone crests of the McDowells on the left and the Indian reservation on the right. Away up on a bluff we could see faintly gleaming the long low windows of Frank Lloyd Wright's private palace at Taliesin West.

About four miles further on, just before the road reached the Granite Reef Dam, the LTD turned sharp left and disappeared. By this time, because the road was dead straight and there was now no other traffic, we were forced to fall back until the other car was hardly more than a dull yellow dot. We drove along very slowly and saw that a paved private road led to a huge two-storey ranch-type house set back half a mile from the road, on the foothills of what on the map I was holding was called the Mesa Encantada.

As we cruised innocently past, I caught sight of a painted sign on the open chain-link gates.

I gave Teague a nudge.

It read: *ULYSSES G. UNDERWOOD.*

U P there on the roof, I asked myself a series of anxious questions. Teague and I lay prone behind the white-washed adobe parapet, shielded—we hoped—from detection by a cluster of gently humming air-conditioners that sprouted at this corner of the huge quadrangular building, covering a triangular segment of the roof. They were bulky grey metal boxes, slatted and cowled, standing five feet high, like extra-terrestrial creatures engaged in a conference. We remained motionless, trying with our black slacks and sweaters to blend into the shadows, thankful for the warmth of the evening and for the fact that there would be no moon tonight to rise behind the ragged crests of the McDowells and flood the landscape—and the roof—with a bright clear light.

I had plenty of time, in the two hours between our stealthy arrival and the start of the proceedings in the court-yard below, to examine our situation. It hadn't been possible to make any concrete plans before we had identified and reconnoitred the Underwood mansion. We'd been compel-led to improvise and make our initial preparations in a rush, which I always hated. Yesterday morning we'd driven along Bell Road, the road that delimits the northern boundary of Phoenix and runs through the citrus groves on the far side of the mountains. We'd sweated up to the ridge in a temperature of nearly 80 (two weeks before Christmas! . . .) and crept along the ridge for more than a mile until we came to a point where we could examine the Underwood ranch through our field-glasses.

Passing the glasses to each other, we were relieved to see that the flat downward-sloping foothills on which the ranch was set were not so denuded of cover as we feared. It was

sown thickly with the inevitable sagebrush, interspersed
with spiky globular Spanish bayonets with their shrivelled
brown plumes. At night, an approach to the north-western
corner from the nearer of the flanking arroyos oughtn't to be
too difficult. We had already picked out the convenient
stand of air-conditioners situated at that very corner. We
then drove back to the motel and stayed indoors till dark, so
as to minimize any chance of being spotted, and only later on
risked a relaxing swim in the motel pool, with the coloured
lights strung between the palm trees.

My intention in flying to Phoenix was to confront
Douglass and my other truants personally, to come face to
face with them and convince them of the madness of their
present actions, and make plans to extricate them from the
Garden Game. I suppose it sounds thin—but what else could
I do? How else could I gain access to them, guarded as they
were, incarcerated in Martagon's private prison? I didn't
know whether I'd be successful: all I knew was that I owed
it to myself, and to them, to make an honest effort. I would
appeal to their common sense, their loyalty, whatever rags of
pride and decency Martagon had left to them. I kept seeing
Douglass's sly, cocky face and springy step, as I had seen him
at Sky Harbor, and Lurtsema's white sweaty cheeks and
forehead, as if he'd been ill on the plane. As I cautiously
shifted my limbs and flexed my ankle I couldn't help thinking, as Teague must also be thinking, stretched out in the
darkness a dozen feet from me, that I was handling the whole
expedition ineptly. That's what happens when you dash into
these things: you treble the risks and treble your inability
to deal with them. I couldn't blame Teague being restive,
though I wasn't particularly conscience-striken about dragging him into the mess with me—that was his job and, as
second-in-command of the Niger river fiasco, he too bore a
responsibility towards his former subordinates, whether he
liked it or not.

Tenderly massaging the butt of the Merkel, I reflected

that, if Teague had been with me in the lounge instead of in the restaurant, we might have confronted Douglass and Lurtsema there and then. Their escort mightn't have started any rough stuff in a public place; I might have had an opportunity to put my case to them on the spot. On the other hand, we could have been grabbed or shot, and Douglass and Lurtsema smartly hustled away; we would have tipped our hand, and Underwood's goons would have been combing the city for us. This way we were at least close to our prey, without our presence being detected, and I could seize any chance that might soon offer to locate the rooms of my former lieutenants and argue them into returning to London with us.

We parked in a side-road close to Shea Boulevard and waited for the spectacular Western sunset to die out of the sky and the soft night to flood the land. Then we coasted towards the Underwood ranch at an unobtrusive speed. When we had travelled a few feet past the mouth of the arroyo, Teague, making sure the road ahead and behind was empty, stopped, snapped off his sidelights, shifted into reverse, and rapidly gunned the car backwards on to the shallow bed of the arroyo. There was a horrible grinding and clanking under the car as Teague urged it over the rocks, and I did mental arithmetic about the bill for a new muffler. The arroyo ran straight back towards the mountain, but we couldn't get more than thirty yards from the road without risking getting stuck. The car would be easy to spot if any one came poking around, so we quickly covered it with the blankets we had bought in a supermarket. They would conceal the reflective surfaces of metal and glass. When we had finished, the humped shape blended in fairly well with the surrounding boulders. We had settled up our bill at the motel and our bags were packed in the boot. We climbed up the side of the arroyo and headed for the house.

God knows what I expected to encounter on the short journey to the house. Most of the time we were squirming over the shaly surface of the desert on our bellies, like scorpions or rattlesnakes. These people were wealthy and mean enough for anything—dogs, wire, mantraps, anti-personnel mines, even searchlights and sensor-devices, for all we knew. As I hauled myself forward, I was haunted by the memory of Martagon knowing I was up on the roof at Blühnbach, when I imagined I was quite invisible. Away on our right, a whole succession of cars began to stream along the main road and follow each other up the side-road to the Underwood house. Activity was beginning. We had been wise to make our move so soon after dark, otherwise the business in the arroyo might have been detected.

I suppose it took us twenty minutes to reach the wall of the house, moving with exquisite care. God, how that blasted desert bristled with thorns. Our hands, knees, elbows and faces were scraped and torn, our clothing was riddled and ripped. We began to appreciate why cowboys wear chaps and tie strips of cloth round their horses' legs. We were bloodied and exhausted by the time we reached the corner of the mansion, thankful that our long crawl was made briefer and a little less painful by the guidance provided by the lights burning on both floors of the house. On the other hand, the whole way across Teague had to hold on to the rope tied round my waist, which couldn't have made the trip easier for him. But we couldn't risk becoming separated, either going or coming, on a moonless night. We didn't know if guards were watching us, or if our movements had been accidentally noticed by some guest looking casually out of a window; we trusted that the twilit interval between sunset and the full onset of the night would confuse the eyes of any would-be observer.

We made it in apparent safety to our first rendezvous. We untied our ropes, knotted them together, and threw them around the upper set of beams protruding from the adobe wall just below the parapet. We climbed quickly in our canvas shoes up the wall and on to the roof.

Then, for the first half-hour, while we got our breath back in the lee of the air-conditioners, I brushed and picked the thorns and spines of those miserable desert plants out of my flesh and clothing; I could hear Teague doing the same, cursing me, cursing Arizona, and cursing his former companions under his breath. From time to time the air-conditioner gave out a disconcerting groan and rattle as the mechanism came into periodic operation. Cars continued to arrive, their headlights bouncing blindly off the white walls below. The young fresh night was filled with the slamming of car doors and with voices and laughter, both male and female. We kept our heads down. We knew what was going on; the audience was arriving for the next instalment of the Game, the next session at the Colosseum with the gladiators. They would be wearing evening dress, the women with their breasts half-bare, drenched in perfume, the men patting the cheque-books in the pockets of their dinner-jackets. They would all be there: the woman with the dark melting eyes ringed with black, the silver combs in the thick coils of her hair; the woman in red silk, carrying her pearl-and-gold opera-glasses; the woman with the chocolate skin and the beaked nose of a Mexican idol; the silver-haired, paralyzed man with the ebony walking-stick; the starved-looking youngster; the well-fed, plump-bodied, elderly men with their apoplectic complexions. At the thought of them an angry lump formed in my throat. I pressed my head on my arms and clenched my teeth. I felt a curious tingle when I reflected that Martagon, too, was somewhere down there, a few yards away, adjusting the big binoculars on the stand in front of him, smoothing down the front of the dark mulberry jacket. I wondered where he fancied I was, where he fancied I'd gone after leaving his snow-bound *schloss*? . . . He probably imagined that at this moment I was catching trout in the Lake District, or holed up in some hotel with Maggie, agonizing over his proposition and slowly coming to the conclusion that I ought to take it . . .

THE GARDEN GAME

We had a nasty moment a few minutes after I'd glanced at the luminous dial of my watch and saw that it was nine-thirty. We heard a trap-door opening at the far end of the roof. We'd carefully noted the position of the entrances on the roof when we studied the house the previous day, which was why we'd decided to station ourselves behind the air-conditioners. I'd guessed that the grounds and the house, including the roof, would be searched for intruders before the Game began. We had worked out a technique, and were ready. Immediately we had reached the roof we had tied our ropes round the middle of the two air-conditioners that were nearest the outer edge of the parapet. Now, softly, as the voices approached and the beams of flashlights began to flicker across the roof, we slipped over the parapet and lowered ourselves on to the beams jutting from the outer wall. There we squatted, hoping the guards wouldn't notice the ropes. If they did, and looked over the parapet, we would drop to the ground and beat a retreat to the arroyo. I felt the smooth round surface of the beam under my rubber soles, slid the safety-catch off the Merkel, and craned my head back. I could get a shot in before hitting the desert.

The voices grew loud . . . were overhead . . . then retired . . .

We relaxed, waited till we heard the trap-door shut, and pulled ourselves back on to the roof. We unwound our ropes and tied them round our waists.

I was sweating. Teague seemed to be reacting more calmly than I was. The ankle felt good, though, and was standing up well.

I was wiping my scratched palms on my sweater when all of a sudden the arc lights clamped to angle-irons on all four sides of the courtyard were switched on. They came alive with what seemed a frightening hiss and a roar. Instinctively I flattened myself on the roof.

Teague gasped at the suddenness of it. This, too, I had

139

warned him about, and told him at all times to keep his head down.

If Martagon was right, and the Game had evolved a hard-and-fast routine, the meeting at Phoenix would follow the same pattern as the one at Blühnbach.

Footlights . . . Overture and beginners . . . I almost expected to hear a band strike up *El Gato Montés,* or *Gallito*—or *The March of the Gladiators . . .*

TONIGHT I'd left the glasses behind; they were an encumbrance, and I didn't want a repeat of last time, when they'd betrayed my presence to Martagon. So when, after five minutes, finally we thought it was safe to raise our heads, the courtyard of the Underwood mansion under the brutal glare of the lights appeared to be absolutely enormous, to stretch away to infinity. The people who participated in the Garden Game were certainly wealthy.

There was no need, out here in the South-West with its perfect climate, to enclose the courtyard. Many of the trees and plants, their outlines weird-looking to our English eyes, soared higher than the level of the parapet. I only recognized them because of the tour-book of the American Automobile Association which someone had left in our motel room, and which had a section on how to identify desert plants. Now I recognized, among other things, several sorts of yucca, with their round spiked base from which white papery plumes shot up, sheathed in the blazing lights, as high as thirty feet. Similar in appearance, so that I confused them with the yuccas, were the sotols and lechuguillas, also furnished with cruel blade-like leaves as sharp as swords. I pitied any of the players in the coming Game who tripped and fell into one of these unforgiving growths; his flesh would be sliced to ribbons. The graceful agaves, growing even taller, with their yellow tufts and smaller mats of prickles at their root, seemed almost gentle in comparison. Interspersed with these rigid, rectilinear plants, like a soft net spread on stiff uprights, was a variety of trees and bushes, some in flower, some not. I could make out, without being able to name them precisely, types of acacia, mesquite, palo verde, and the spectacular bird-of-paradise tree with its blood-and-honey blossoms. What flowers there were on these delicate, feathery trees were mostly of subtle pastel shades—lavenders and pinks, shimmery blues and lemons—that struck me as an utterly incongruous background for the savage encounters about to take place. The gravelly soil in which the plants stood had recently been doused with water, and although this garden was uncovered it possessed the same rank vegetable smell as the garden in Europe. The manner in which the paths that wound their way through it had been laid out was also the same, and they appeared to converge on a spot almost directly beneath us. There, I imagined, was the great glass window through which Martagon and his companions would follow the intricate convolutions of their deadly pastime . . .

I was even more aware of the sick lump in my throat when I thought that Douglass, Lurtsema and Asher were at this very moment preparing to earn another instalment of their pay, or bribe, or blood-money, or whatever they liked to call it. More than ever I wished that I'd been able to intervene and talk to them earlier . . . Now, I could only cross my fingers and pray . . .

The intensity of the lights drained the last mild glow out of the sky; we seemed to be crushed beneath a dense black weight. Waiting for the Game to begin, I can't tell you what an oppressive sense of dark and brooding evil clutched at my heart. Teague and I seemed so feeble, our actions so puny, our opponents so strong and well-organized. And this was only what they did in private, for their amusement, to while away a few idle hours . . . I had a vision of a whole world involved in their professional activities, whole continents and nations being forced to dance to their satanic tune, to participate in a universal version of the Garden Game . . .

I was pulled back to reality by the realization that something significant was happening down in the courtyard. Unfortunately, as at Blühnbach, although we were only a few yards away from the point where the paths converged on the glass box, it was sufficient to distort our whole view of things; we were screened off from much of the action by the trees and plants. I dared not move directly over the box, as there were powerful lights set up there, and we might conceivably have been heard in the room below. Therefore we were only able to witness the contests in a very hazy and restricted manner, which only increased my anxiety on behalf of my own men.

The first contest was waged with weapons that made no sound except for a curious swishing noise. It was fought mainly on the far side of the courtyard; and apart from a number of grunts, and a good deal of rustling among the foliage as though animals were passing through a forest, and a final staccato yelp that was suddenly cut off, we saw nothing. At the sound of that final cry I sensed that Teague's body stiffened in shock. I had tried to prepare him by describing, as well as I could, what would happen: but when it finally came the real thing was bound to be atrocious. Perhaps it would have been better, at that, to see what was happening instead of having to guess at it. Once in Thailand I was in an office at police headquarters when a man was being beaten to death in the yard outside; it was an experience that haunted me for an unusually long time.

The first fight, like the ones that followed, took about twenty-five minutes. That seemed to be about the average time. Sometimes a fight would be over in ten minutes, or stretch out to forty-five, but mostly they lasted just under half an hour—which is a very long time, when you come to think about it. Whatever the weapons that were being used, the fights followed more or less the same pattern. At the given signal, the contestants were introduced through doors on opposite sides of the courtyard; their first task was to seek each other out, in such a way as to come on the other man by stealth and have the advantage in attack. Thus the opening part of the contest was devoted to the subtle and silent skills of tracking, skills as old as mankind itself. The two men crept and circled in the bright garden like prehistoric hunters, Mousterians or Magdalenians, or like the Apaches or Comanches who had terrorized Arizona less than a century ago, or the crafty trackers of the modern Congo or the Amazon. Every nerve was alert, eyes and ears straining for the tiniest hint of the enemy, all the faculties concentrated in a supreme effort to catch the faint whisper or murmur which, undetected, meant maiming or death. Twenty minutes of such concentration represents an illimitable stretch of ordinary time, a lifetime, an eternity. And then, when the quarry is sighted, caught sideways-on or with his back to you, he is killed swiftly, by a single blow. Our aboriginal forefathers, hunting the mammoth or sabre-tooth tiger, knew that with such dangerous prey one blow was all you had. For all these men in the courtyard were killers— selected for their murderous activities in Singapore, or New York, or along the Niger—then tautened and trained to a hair in the special camps that Martagon had mentioned . . .

The next fight took place somewhat nearer the centre of the courtyard. This time we distinctly heard the two doors into the garden open at almost the same instant, no doubt on a phone call or a visual signal from the viewing room, then closing again. I could picture the two antagonists slipping through them, with a parting pat of encouragement from their seconds or handlers. The neutral referee or representative of the other side would be there too, to check that the players wore the right equipment and carried the right weapons.

This second fight was long drawn out. The manoeuvring for position went on for an interminable time. At intervals we caught what might have been a glimpse of a body creeping along one of the paths—and once one of the men came right out into the open where we—though not his opponent—could see him quite clearly. He was a small and wiry man with reddish hair, wearing the regulation white shirt with some sort of animal emblazoned on it above the heart. He was rounding the end of the garden, between the foliage and the white adobe wall, trying to out-circle his enemy. He carried something black in his hand, holding it loosely at his side, but I couldn't see what it was at such a distance and in the few seconds he was visible. Whatever it was, it worked for him, because no more than three or four minutes later, without any of the gruesome sounds that usually accompanied the ending, the stretcher-bearers in their blue jump-suits panted past beneath us carrying a stretcher on which lay a man almost too tall for it and too heavy for his bearers. His eyes were open and appeared to be staring straight up at us, making us draw back behind the parapet. Actually they were already sightless. I could see no wound on the front of the body. The smaller man followed the stretcher a pace or two behind, tucking something away in his waist. His attitude was regretful, less like an enemy than a man accompanying a comrade from the stricken field. I could just make out that the animal on his shirt was a rampant lion, lashing out with its claws . . . *Lion?* . . . —could be a score of places . . . the lion of England, or the three lions of Scotland? . . . *León?* . . . *Lyons?* . . . Finding the Phoenix had been a good deal easier, thank heaven . . .

Teague kept his head lowered while the stretcher went past. When he lifted it I saw he was looking rather green . . . Who can blame him? . . . I'd tried to prepare him; he wasn't normally blood-shy; but this was bloodshed of an unnatural sort, like being compelled to witness an execution . . . I was glad the rule tonight seemed to be single combat only . . .

At least the directors of the spectacle kept the wretched thing going. No sooner was one victim carted off than, after a swift raking and scattering of fresh sand, the next fight began.

I remember I was reflecting that the sand wasn't laid down purely to cover the bloodstains, or give a footing on the slick spots, but was also intended to help the noiseless skill of the tracker. And then I saw Rupert Douglass step carefully, moving as smoothly as a snake, through the screen of trees that divided one path from another. He scarcely disturbed a single leaf. Something thin and blackish dangled from his right wrist. He waited for three full minutes, absolutely motionless, head thrust forward, watching the alley from which he had come; then, equally slowly, he stepped delicately back again and out of sight. My heart started to thump in my chest; I heard Teague stir and clear his throat nervously.

I wish I could say we were privileged—privileged is not the word—to watch the whole of this fight. I hadn't been able to see what weapon Douglass was carrying, but it obviously wasn't a rifle: so when I heard a rifle-shot I was startled and immediately imagined the worst. The image of Grady Bailey's narrow face, smiling in death, flashed into my mind; I gave a little groan. But then another man, a stranger, padded round the end of the alley below us and traversed the neutral area between the garden and the courtyard wall. I realized that the fight wasn't over. The man had a hunting-rifle with a scope attached to it. He was holding it across his chest at the angle which in my old army days used to be called the high-port. I recalled Martagon's description of 'the tariff'—*'rifle with scope: one shot'*—and understood why the newcomer, a loosely-knit man with fair crinkly hair, was sweating and looking anxious and moving fast . . .

And then, right under us, the fight reached its savage peak.

I had always known that Douglass was quick on his feet. All my men had to be proficient in unarmed combat, but the Scotsman was outstanding, and more or less took charge of that department when we were training for Africa. If he was agile eighteen months ago, the speed of his movements now was supernatural. He had put his sessions in Martagon's camps to good use. The man with the rifle was halfway down the alley when Douglass emerged like a cat between the sword-like leaves of the yuccas behind him. His opponent had good ears and quick reactions. He also had guts. He wheeled and threw the rifle with a jerk at Douglass and came in behind it fast. Douglass stooped and the gun whirled over his head and he was flying at the other man before the other was properly in balance. They crashed together in the manner of *sumo* wrestlers. I knew Douglass was good at *judo*, almost in the red-and-white belt class, but he now felled his opponent by getting his right hand outside and on top of the other's and bringing him down with a throw that was more like the *uwate-nage* in *sumo* than anything in judo. It was so quick I couldn't follow it. There was a spurt of sand as Douglass dragged his enemy round—then he was suddenly kneeling upright behind the other with his hands crossed round his neck. This was pure *judo*, the *sode guruma* or *slave-wheel*, precisely executed. The slave-wheel is a stranglehold, and at first I thought he was choking his man by pulling the neck of his shirt across his windpipe. I could hear the man gagging as his heels and hands dug into the ground. Then I realized that Douglass was throttling him with a wire loop—that was what had been dangling from his wrist— a double thickness of wire with cloth- or leather-bound ends . . .

And he was laughing . . . Douglass was laughing . . . as he had laughed at Blühnbach, after he'd pretended to be dead . . . tugging on that damned wire and laughing . . .

I can't describe the revulsion I felt at that moment. If I'd had a rifle instead of a miserable pop-gun, I swear I'd have stood up and shot him through the head. I can't describe, either, the hate and rage I felt against Martagon . . .

My body went slack. I sank back on my heels and subsided on to the roof. I didn't want to watch the grisly aftermath a second time; I didn't want to see Douglass strutting out of the arena in the same cocky way he had in Austria. I lay on my back staring up at the sky. At least the stars looked sane. I can't convey the depth of my bitterness as I asked myself why I was risking two more lives and ruining myself on this stupid and quixotic mission . . . Bailey dead . . . Douglass corrupted . . . and what about Asher and Lurtsema? . . . were they dead too, or degenerate? . . .

I didn't have long to wait for an answer where one of the last two was concerned.

The next fight I sat out—or lay out. I stayed where I was, communing with the stars, trying not to hear the noises floating up from the garden. Teague, on the other hand, had become fascinated and began to lean so far over the parapet that I had to sit up and grab him by the belt and pull him back. It must have been during the fight after that, when I had decided to take an interest again, that Teague reached over and punched my shoulder. I rolled on to my knees and looked down into the courtyard and was in time to watch Lurtsema going into action against a man as thin as a bean-pole with the emblem of a bear embroidered on his shirt . . . (*Berlin? . . . Berne?*).

It wasn't really a fight; it was more like a tragic farce. Till my dying day I shall never understand Lurtsema's tactics, or lack of them. I'd noticed at Sky Harbor that he wore a curiously strained and hang-dog look, like a man under sentence of death. I think now he must have had some presentiment of what was to come. He simply threw all cover to the winds and came plodding straight down the centre of the path on our side of the courtyard, making no attempt to stalk his man, casting about for the enemy with a strange, bewildered look on his face. It wasn't a look of fear; he was a brave man, as he had shown at Wakoja and Kabassa. It was a look of despair, of a man hurling himself blindly at his fate. This wasn't the man I knew in Africa. He had the body of an ox, but I'd seen him move crisply and purposefully. Now he shambled along like an animal being led to the slaughter, or the defeated bull at the moment when the *descabello* hits it on the base of the neck. He blundered into boughs and bushes and left a wash of waving greenery behind him. He carried a big awkward-looking hand-gun, like a ·44 Magnum. He rounded the line of trees into the neutral area and stumbled on, facing us, the same blank look on his face.

I could have called out to him. I could have shouted. God knows where it would have got us, or him—but I could have done it—I should have done it—created a diversion—made him stop sleep-walking . . .

Then Bean-Pole jumped out of the trees almost on top of him. Lurtsema got off a single wild shot. Bean-Pole closed with him and his left hand pumped twice . . . *in* . . . out . . .

Bean-Pole stepped back and the handle of a knife was sticking out of Lurtsema's belly above the belt-buckle. He still had the lost look on his face. The blood began to spread around the knife-handle and he half-raised the gun and didn't fire it and dropped to his knees and slammed forward on his face on the gravel.

I moved back from the parapet and stood up.

THE trapdoor brought us down to the upper corridor. It was empty. Everyone was downstairs, enjoying the fun. The corridor was handsome. The walls were whitewashed in simple, South-Western style; the skirtings, cornices and outer sharp angles were rounded; plain rough-hewn columns were set at intervals in the centre of the polished parquet flooring.

The lights were Mexican lanterns. We were grateful for their subdued quality, glad that there were pools of shadow behind the line of columns. The smell of smouldering piñon-wood hung on the air, an oddly sweet and soothing odour for such a sombre background.

I crept along close to the left-hand wall; Teague hugged the right one. With every step we took from the trapdoor we were more deeply committed.

As we came to the right-angled bend at the end of the corridor we heard voices. Teague stepped over to join me, and after hesitating a moment I took a peek round the corner. A quick glance told me that there were six or eight men in the other corridor, most of them in blue denims, a couple in white shirts; they were talking in groups. Then I heard a rattling, like a rubber-tyred hotel-trolley being wheeled towards us. I looked at Teague, without being able to see his face clearly. Should we run for it? The noise seemed to be coming towards us; another few seconds and whatever it was would round the corner. Then, as I raised the Merkel and held it against my chest, the strange clattering stopped. Knuckles tapped against a door. A pause. The knuckles rapped again.

I had to risk another look. We couldn't loiter there for

ever: at any second someone could come along the corridor behind us. Again I put my head around the rounded edge of the wall and took a hurried peep. I was surprised to see that the clattering had indeed been caused by a hotel-trolley or dinner-wagon. The stubby, dwarfish man with the bald head whom I saw escorting Douglass and Lurtsema at Sky Harbor had pushed the trolley down the corridor and was knocking at a door ten feet away from us. He was wearing a dark blue sweater with a high collar that made his bulging neck look as thick as a tree-trunk. Luckily he wasn't facing in our direction, but I could see him shaking his jowls as he knocked on the door with a half-irritated, half-indulgent smile on his face. On the trolley was a silver ice-bucket with two bottles of champagne in it and a number of plates under silver covers. After a moment he gave a shrug, scratched his shaven skull, and ambled back along the corridor.

It seemed to me that most of the men were beginning to drift away in the direction of the staircase at the far end of the passage. I gave them a half-minute, put my gun away, and walked around the corner in as leisurely a manner as I could muster. We couldn't wait any longer. I stopped opposite the door and drummed on it with my fingers, softly but in-sistently. I turned my back to the distant end of the corridor, hoping that in the half-light and in my dark clothes the bald man and his friends would take me for one of themselves, if they glanced round at all. Douglass or Asher could be behind that door. I had to take a chance on it—it was the only one we had.

I kept up the subdued knocking with my right hand, agitating the doorhandle with my left. I felt horribly exposed, out there in the open. Then suddenly the door was wrenched open from the inside: and the instant it started to move I pushed myself violently at it, my hip hitting the edge of the trolley and jarring it noisily. Teague came round the corner in a rush and piled in behind me. The door slammed behind us with a bang that must have attracted the group at the stairhead.

Rupert Douglass was flung back from the door. He recoiled towards the middle of the room, staring at us in astonishment. My gun was still in my hand and Teague leaned against the door, listening.

I looked down. At my feet, where Douglass had previously let them fall, lay a tangle of dirty clothes—trousers, pants, socks, soiled shirt with the peacock emblem. Douglass had stripped them off after the fight and dropped them anywhere. Now he was standing naked except for a crimson towel round his waist and a white towel in his hand. His slender body was lithe and alert; it had the energy and tension of a spring. On the inside of his upper right arm there was a strip of adhesive plaster, covering the superficial wound he had received at Blühnbach. He had just stepped out of a boiling shower and his face and flesh were a fiery red. There was a wet trail on the floor where he had come out of the bathroom to answer my knock. Now he calmly perched himself on the edge of a chair and began to rub vigorously at his damp black hair.

'Hello, Major.' The soft Scots voice was amused, defiant. When he smiled there was a recklessness about it, a sly brilliance. His eyes had that slanting, almost Mongoloid appearance often seen in Scotsmen. He looked at our desert-torn clothes and scratched faces, our dark clothes and rubber-soled shoes, the ropes round our waists. 'Are you on another of your famous expeditions, Major? . . .' Then his expression changed, became less flippant, as he saw the look in my eyes. He stood up. 'You saw . . .?'

I nodded. 'Yes. I saw.'

The defiance came back into his dark, lean face. The smile was the smile of a crafty child. He started to towel at his back and arms. Teague, relaxing now, quickly opened the door, stepped into the corridor and smoothly drew the trolley inside the room, closing the door again.

I surveyed Douglass' room, relaxing in my turn, feeling a tremor in my slackening calves and forearms. (*God, God . . . forty-seven . . . too old for these capers . . .*) The living-room was divided from the bedroom beyond by a low open archway, Western fashion. Dark beams. No windows. Subdued lighting, throwing heavy shadows. White walls hung with Navajo blankets, Ganado and Klagetoh rugs. Pueblo pots and Papago baskets. Bright, basic Indian materials and colours.

'They do you well, here, Douglass.'

He gave me a wicked smile.

'To the victor the spoils, Major . . .'

Teague made an exclamation that sounded like disgust. Abruptly he took one of the bottles of champagne out of the cooler and began to tear off the foil. He and Douglass had never much liked each other, though in Africa they had co-operated and respected each other's work. Teague was fundamentally an open and straightforward character, Douglass a devious and secretive one. As I looked at Douglass now, I decided that I didn't like him either. When I'd recruited him, I'd seen him in the light of a young MacDuff; now I could sense the Macbeth in him.

He had recovered from his first surprise. Perched on the arm of the chair, he draped the towel round his shoulders, put his hands on his knees and stared at me.

'If you've got anything to say, Major, you'd better say it quickly.' He gestured towards the wide, low bed, covered with a sand-coloured blanket patterned with a design of flying birds. The sheets were turned back invitingly. 'As you can see, I'm expecting someone . . .'

'Evidently.'

The cork came out of the champagne bottle with a sharp explosion. Teague set the bottle down and went into the bathroom.

Douglass said, sounding indifferent: 'So you've found out about the Game?'

'Yes, I've found out about you, and Bailey, and Lurtsema
—but where's Asher?'

'Asher?' He shrugged. 'God knows.'

'You really don't know?'

'No, I don't.'

'Hasn't he been with you, all along? At your so-called
training-camp?'

He said negligently: 'He disappeared, five or six weeks
ago.'

'Disappeared?' I felt a small, cold sensation.

Douglass shrugged, smiled, let his body drop back over
the arm of the chair and said coolly:

'Perhaps he's been traded.'

'Traded?'

'It happens all the time. It's like big-time football—all
sorts of complicated deals and swaps. Still, if he's traded he'll
get a whopping great transfer-fee. These people aren't
cheap-skates—as you said, they do us proud.' Again the
brilliant, slanting smile. 'If Carl-Conrad's traded Gavin, he'll
have made it worth his while.'

Teague had come out of the bathroom with a tooth-glass.
He now splashed champagne into it and into the two wine-
glasses on the trolley. Then he brought them over to me and
Douglass. The expression on his face as he handed one to
Douglass was puzzled and filled with unconcealed distaste.
Douglass's display of gleeful barbarity in the courtyard was
still clear in his mind.

He glanced at his watch and looked at me questioningly.
I consulted my own watch, calculating. Twenty-five to
twelve. I knew from Blühnbach that the fights would
continue till about one-thirty or two o'clock. All the same,
the sooner Douglass got dressed and the three of us left, the
better. I didn't want Baldy and the others to break in on us.
But I couldn't resist, as I took a first sip of champagne—
(*ugh, sweet*)—from studying Douglass thoughtfully for a
moment, then asking:

'Tell me, what would you do if Asher turned up at the next meeting, wearing someone else's colours—and you had to fight him?'

He shook his head. 'What's Gavin to me? Just because we made one trip to Nigeria, were shot up together a few times, does that mean we've got to swear blood-brotherhood to one another for the rest of our lives? Forgive me, Major, but even when I was working for you, or under your command, or whatever you want to call it, I couldn't help finding some of your ideas rather quaint . . .' He propped himself on one elbow in the chair and stuck out his glass towards Teague, waggling it for more. 'Come on, Sam . . . it's my own champagne, damn it . . .' And as Teague filled his glass: 'Listen, Major. I don't know why you've come here, or what you're after, but I just want you to leave me alone . . . I'm happy here . . . and I'm a big boy now . . .'

'Not big enough, apparently.'

'Look, I've been looking out for myself ever since I was a kid in Glasgow. And I can tell you, working for Carl-Conrad is a hell of an improvement on the Gorbals . . .'

'You call what you've been doing work?'

'Is it all that much different from what I was doing for *you*? Didn't I kill people for you in Africa, plenty of them—and not get a quarter as well paid for it?'

'Oh yes, of course—there's the question of the pay . . .'

'And don't *you* work for pay too, Major?'

His words hit me, though they shouldn't have done; really, the champagne was abominable. I felt tired. Had I really had some hand in turning this promising young officer into the brassy, vulgar young killer lolling in that chair? . . .

'Plenty of pay, Major, and plenty of perks. Everything's going to be first-class from now on—everything's going to be *POSH*, as they used to say in your day, didn't they?—'Port Out Starboard Home'? . . . Oh yes, nothing but the best for little Rupert from here on out . . . As much money as I want . . .' He waved his glass at the waiting bed. 'And as much of *that* besides . . .' He laughed. 'Not bad, is it, for a lad whose father sold papers in Sauchiehall Street? . . . Funny thing, though—I always find I need plenty of—*that*—these days . . . especially *afterwards* . . . and you'd be surprised how much *they* want it, too . . .'

He grinned again, finishing the sickly champagne.

No, I couldn't bear to look at him . . . Again I thought of Macbeth . . . '*We but teach bloody instructions, which being taught return to plague the inventor*' . . . I turned away, strangely disturbed, staring in the dim light at a wall-hanging depicting a pounding herd of hump-shouldered bison.

'I tell you, Major, we people who've been picked to play the Game have got it made . . . we're living the life of Reilly. How could I have done any better for myself if I'd stuck it out in the poor old British Army, or even stayed with *your* peculiar little lot? . . .'

It was the ambivalence that perplexed me. The boldness, the resource, the rare cold courage with which I'd seen him bring down his man—for God's sake, was that contemptible? Was I to despise a man's willingness to lay his life on the line? . . . *Me*? . . . He still possessed many of the qualities I'd searched for in the man I'd recruited. '*A short life and a merry one*'—an unfashionable philosophy, but was it really such a bad one? . . . '*Dogs, would you live for ever!*' . . . Was it Murat who had shouted that, or was it Ney, or Kellermann, or Davoust? . . . What had made these characteristics turn sour and ugly in Douglass? . . . Again I felt a surge of hatred for Martagon . . .

I turned from the bison.

'And how long do you think you'll be able to take it? Did you hear what happened down there to poor Hans Lurtsema half an hour ago? You ought to have watched it. If you had, you wouldn't sound quite so cocky.'

'Poor old Hans. He hadn't got the stomach for it. Hated it. Couldn't live with himself. Heart got in the way of the head. Always fatal, Major—you taught us that.'

'Tell me, how much longer do you think you've got?'

'Long enough.'

'You think so?'

'Certainly.'

'And how long is long enough?'

'Long enough to make my packet and retire.'

'How many shows like tonight do you think you can do?'

He hoisted himself easily out of the deep chair. His body was very hard and compact; there was no fat or softness; it was a precise instrument or weapon.

'The more often you fight,' I told him, 'the shorter the odds. How old are you? Twenty-four? Twenty-five?'

He put his hands on his hips, the red towel tight across the flat belly. God, the confidence of young men; their insane conviction of immortality. Had *I* really felt like that, once? . . . He laughed his dry, Scotch laugh.

'Oh, we don't fight all the time. We're not compelled to fight at all, when we don't want to. But—*no fight, no money*! . . . I don't fight every time, myself, even though I feel in great shape. And after all, even people like Carl-Conrad can't afford to stage these jamborees more than eight or ten times a year. They're busy people. They've got their businesses to run. The fights are planned in a regular way, like a regular season.'

'And you think you can take part in these stupid things as many as eight or ten times a year?'

'Major, you've no idea how much I've improved; how much progress I've made. If you think I was good in England, you ought to see what I can do now. Oh, when I was with the Army, in Borneo and Radfan, or when I was in Africa with you, I got shot at plenty of times, often came close to being killed. Honestly, I don't believe that in this particular job I risk my life many more times a year than I did before, or than I'd do if I'd stayed with you, or in the Army . . .'

I put my glass down on the trolley.

'I'm amused that you talk so familiarly of Martagon—'

'He treats me well.'

'You sincerely believe that a man like that is ever going to let you retire?'

'I know he will. He told me so.'

'Can you tell me the name of any man who has actually been allowed to retire?'

'Well, no—but the Game has only been going two or three years. But the lads talk about it all the time.'

'I'm sure they do.'

For the first time a shadow of something like uncertainty passed over his face. I sensed an advantage.

'I've only met your employer once, but I doubt very much if he lets anyone go once he gets his hooks into them. I don't think he'd enjoy the spectacle of a crowd of his ex-pugs lounging around the world, entertaining people with accounts of their various scraps and dust-ups; I imagine he's got enough trouble with the security side of the business as it is—else why would he provide such a close bodyguard for you, when you landed at the Phoenix airport yesterday?' He looked startled at that. 'No, his best plan is to keep appealing to your simple sense of greed; neither you nor any of the others were originally rich boys, I imagine. He'll make as much money out of you as he can, use you up, then throw you away. He'll wring you dry—but as long as you're good enough to win more fights than you lose—and you've only got to lose one—he'll make a profit out of you, won't he? You're a commodity, Douglass. What's more, if you don't oblige him by eventually getting killed, when your usefulness is over, he might even attend to it for you. As I said, he doesn't want a lot of gossip and loose talk. He seems to be clever at choosing places to get rid of the dead bodies . . . there was plenty of room in the forest at Blühnbach . . . there's plenty of room in the desert around this house . . .'

He pressed himself back in the chair, one leg over the arm, the sulky defiance back in his face. But he was troubled.

Probably I'd hit on the truth: he and the others were watched, segregated, confined to training-camp when they weren't fighting, kept on a tight leash. Grady Bailey probably had a hard time finding a way of sending that letter to his wife. Martagon's gladiators were the prisoners of his own praetorian guard. The fellows who knocked me on the head in Austria and hustled Douglass and Lurtsema into the car at Sky Harbor were professionals. Jenbach was no amateur, either.

Douglass was frowning. He got up and threw the white towel on the floor. His lower lip stuck out with juvenile petulance.

I could see from the expression on Teague's broad face that he didn't care whether I persuaded Douglass to leave the Underwood mansion with us or not; in his opinion the whole expedition was quixotic. He didn't think Douglass was worth saving. I'm not sure that I did, any longer; but it was my duty to try.

'You haven't figured the odds—or you've figured them wrongly . . . like Bailey . . . like Lurtsema . . . like Asher, for all we know . . .'

Suddenly Teague, setting down his glass, moved over to the door. He stood beside it, bending his head, listening.

I said quickly to Douglass:

'Hurry—get dressed—we've got to get out of here—'

He stared at me, incredulous.

'Leave here?'

'Before your Carl-Conrad chews you up and spits you out—as he did with my other men.'

Teague looked at me warningly. Douglass laughed.

'Major, we're living high on the hog . . . on the fat of the land . . .'

'Don't be a fool. Leave while you still can. While we can get you out. You won't get another chance.'

He waved a hand at the elegant room, at the bed.

'Give up this?'

'Look,' I said, 'I've come a long way—taken a lot of risks
—to haul you out of this—'

He was recovering his self-possession.

'Now, Major—'

'Get it through your head—I'm not leaving Arizona—'

'Major, please—would you drag a poor Scots boy away
from the fleshpots?'

I stepped towards him.

'Don't argue. You're coming with us.'

He put out a hand mockingly, as though to ward me off,
still laughing.

There was a low knock on the door.

Teague flattened himself in the shadows against the wall
behind. I moved round behind Douglass.

I prodded him towards the door, stepping close behind
him. We couldn't leave whoever it was out in the corridor
pounding on the door.

Douglass turned the doorknob, the door opened, a woman
came swiftly into the room.

She was smiling, eager. She was the woman I saw in the
upstairs corridor at Blühnbach, the one in the flame-coloured
silk. She wore the same heavy black make-up round the eyes,
the same heavy scent.

'Rupert—'

The accent wasn't English. It was thick—Slav or German
—though it may have been the passion and excitement in her
voice.

Then she saw me. She didn't know me. Teague leaned
with his back against the door.

She looked at us, arrogant, surprised. The wet, ripe lips
parted. Her arms were folded over in front of the yellow silk
robe. When she dropped her arms to her sides, the robe
opened. She was naked beneath. Douglass cupped his hand
under one of the heavy breasts, with its broad dark nipple.
He looked round, grinning.

'See what I mean, Major—*fleshpots*? . . .'

I jammed my gun in his back. All of a sudden I was in a cold rage, in a mad hurry. I wanted to get out of this place, where while we were talking murder was going on on the floor below. I reached down, groped around on the floor, and picked up the trousers and the shirt with the peacock emblem. I slapped them against his chest.

'Grab them—you can put them on when we reach the roof.'

'What—*now?*' He was still trying to joke, though the smile was brittle round the edges. He sensed my rage.

The woman swung towards the door and took two quick steps towards it. Before she took a third step Teague scooped up the white towel from the floor with one hand and wrapped a big arm round her from behind. He passed the towel over her mouth with one hand, pressed the Prinz into her side with the other. She tried to hack his shins. He slapped her once very hard on the side of the head and tightened the towel over her mouth. She stood still and stared at me with huge, angry, dark-ringed eyes.

I said: 'Better take her up to the roof.'

She started to struggle again, outraged, furious. Teague gripped her tighter, hurting her. Douglass put out a hand and placed it on the sleeve of the yellow robe.

'No—do what they tell you—exactly what they tell you . . .'

My gun was puncturing his ribs. He spoke urgently. He knew I wasn't fooling. He'd been too close to me at Kubassa, Wakoja, Sabalayah . . .

I pushed him towards the door. He said quietly:

'You'll never get away with this, Major. I don't know how the hell you ever got in here in the first place. Your only hope is to let me put in a good word for you . . .'

Teague opened the door noiselessly. He put his head into the corridor, gave me a nod, and went out, wrestling the woman ahead of him. Douglass hesitated.

I said: 'Go ahead. We're taking you with us. But if you do

anything stupid—rather than leave you here—I'll kill you . . .'

He shrugged and raised an arm in mock surrender. He sauntered into the corridor, hugging his clothes, the legs of the trousers trailing on the ground.

As before, I was glad the corridor was dimly lit by the Mexican wall-lamps. Teague had a few yards start and was hustling the woman towards the distant stairs to the roof. He thrust her along as if he was manhandling a sack.

Douglass swaggered in front of me, not exactly dawdling but managing to take his time, too proud to be hurried, too fond of playing with danger.

We made good time. I don't know what betrayed us. Teague and I wore rubber-soled shoes, Douglass was barefoot—it may have been the low heels of the woman's shoes scraping on the polished parquet.

Maybe we should have left her in the room, ripped the phone out, gagged her. We only meant to take her as far as the roof.

There were steps behind us. I shot a glance over my shoulder. Obscure figures at the far end of the dark passage. A shout.

Douglass slowed down and tried to stop. I slammed the gun-barrel into his back almost hard enough to break his spine. He jerked forward.

The steps were closer, running. I can't give you the exact sequence of what happened. These things are always confused, especially in semi-darkness.

It may have been Teague who fired first. I heard his shot go past my ear and whang down the corridor. Then the air was humming with bullets.

Teague was on the lower steps. He had turned round and was trying to pull the woman after him. Unless he went up first he couldn't push the trap-door open. The men attacking us couldn't have made out much more than a confused mass milling around the foot of the stairs.

I think the woman broke loose, stumbled downstairs and tried to run down the corridor. Douglass attempted to stop her. Whether he was being heroic, because he felt affection for her, or whether he acted from impulse, I can't say. Her heavy body bumped against him. I saw him fling out an arm. He wrenched round in front of me and seemed to be trying to block her, shield her. At the same moment I heard a sharp grunt as a shot hit him, I should judge in the lower part of the chest. It must have been a high-velocity bullet as it lifted him off his feet and he went backwards and his head cracked against the lowest step. The woman gave a cry, twisted around, and dropped on her knees beside him.

Teague, near the top of the staircase, fired four shots in succession down the corridor.

I hadn't even fired my gun. I bent over Douglass, hauling at the woman's arm to get her out of the way. I could smell her ripe perfume. She shook my hand off, fell across Douglass, her hair streaming over him.

Teague ran down the stairs and grabbed me. He was trying to drag me up the stairs.

I couldn't see Douglass clearly. Even if the woman hadn't been in the way the light was too dim. He was still clutching the clothes against him. The black mass of the woman's hair covered his throat and chest like a clotted cobweb, but his eyes were open and glittered with a crazy unfocused stare.

Teague was pulling me up the stairs. I didn't want to leave Douglass . . . *retrieve your wounded under fire* . . . I still hate myself for leaving him, even though I was certain—well, almost certain—he was dying . . .

I lashed out at Teague, but he'd got a grip on my collar and was lugging me towards the trap-door. He punched it open and it crashed back against the roof. I thrashed around, but he wasn't going to leave either of us down there with Douglass, and in the back of my mind I knew he was right . . .

A vague shape of a man appeared at the bottom of the stairs. Wriggling backwards on to the roof, I stuck out the Merkel and pulled the trigger. The damned thing jammed. I hurled it at him, saw him duck at the downward curve of my arm against the sky, heard the gun bounce off his bald skull.

Teague threw the trap door back down and we were sprinting along the roof under the stars for the shelter of the air-conditioners. Teague flung his gun away and started unwinding the rope from his waist as he ran. The arc-lights were still on in the courtyard. *Hunt below, and hunt above . . .*

Teague flicked a loop round one of the cowled boxes. He went first, hand over hand, down the single rope. The rope was snapping about like a rattlesnake, but I caught it and swung myself over the adobe parapet and kicked my way down behind him.

The roof above seemed swarming with men. Shots. They were firing only by the dim glow of the arc-lamps in the courtyard behind them. Even so some of the shots passed close.

I couldn't say whether I hurt my ankle by smacking it on the parapet, or against one of the protruding beams, or when I let the rope slide through my hands and dropped the last fifteen feet. I hit the stony surface of the ground with tremendous force. When I picked myself up I can remember the waves of pain as I limped back across the colossal pin-cushion of the desert towards the arroyo and the hidden Torino.

M Y first reaction, as Harrison moved the cheque across the tablecloth with a polished nail, was of shame and confusion.

Don't you work for pay too, Major? . . . Furious, gleaming eyes as I left him, crumpled and defenceless, at the base of the stairs . . .

I pushed my chair back until I was beyond the pink circle of light. My eyes were tired. I was weary and discouraged from the journey. Even two days' rest hadn't revived me. *Bailey, Douglass, Lurtsema.* Three of the four of them dead. Two in one night.

So much for the great mission of rescue.

The silver light and suede darkness of Arizona were a million miles away . . . A week ago I was swimming at midnight beneath the palm trees in the motel pool . . .

I tilted the legs of my chair forward and picked up my glass of Sancerre. I asked myself what was the best way to break the news to Harrison that I'd made up my mind to pack it in . . .

Delicately, he manoeuvred the cheque to a point in front of me where the lamplight was brightest. Now I could see the figures.

The amount on the cheque was ten thousand pounds. In spite of myself, the size of it gave me a shock.

Harrison leaned back, studying the inch of ash on his Macanudo, running a fleshy hand over the smooth grey wing of hair.

'Four thousand of that, of course, represents your arrears of salary for the Niger enterprise.' With a perfectly straight face, he added: 'My masters have now authorized me to pay it to you—and they want to apologize sincerely, Morven, for any inconvenience they've caused you . . .'

I didn't touch the cheque.

'I expect you're wondering what the balance is for?'

I neither nodded nor shook my head.

'The balance represents the advance on your next assignment. I'm sure you will consider it generous?'

I sat silent. Usually I argued with him; laughed at him; became indignant. Now I said nothing. There was nothing to say. My silence troubled him. The handkerchief came out; palm-polishing began.

'Aren't you going to ask me about the assignment?'

'No.'

'You aren't?'

'No.'

'Why not?'

'I'm not interested.'

More polishing. The eyes blinked owlishly behind the heavy glasses.

'I don't understand.'

'Harrison, I've decided to quit.'

'Quit?'

'To retire gracefully—while I'm still able to.'

'Retire? You? Oh, some, my dear fellow, this business has been your whole life. And how can you retire when you're at your peak? I mean, when you're indispensable?'

'Did you say—*indispensable*?'

'Absolutely.'

'I wonder why you're bothering to flatter me?'

'Flatter you, my dear fellow?'

'Oh, for God's sake. You knew perfectly well I'm getting past it. These past few days have shown me that. And I'd have thought after the African fiasco you'd have been only too glad to pension me off.'

He put the handkerchief away and poured more of the straw-coloured wine.

'You're depressed, my dear fellow. I can see that. But please—ask what that additional six thousand is for—'

'Harrison, I don't want to know. During the past forty-eight hours I've thought it all over carefully. Please take that cheque and rewrite it for the exact amount you owe me. Nothing more. Then find yourself another man.'

'There *isn't* another man. There is only *you*.'

'Flattery again?'

'My superiors would like me to state that there is another six thousand pounds to follow, when you have finished the job in question.'

I sighed, tilted my chair back again, was silent for a moment.

'Harrison, I wish you wouldn't be quite so bloody pompous, for Christ's sake. Can't you see, really, that I've come to the end of it? That I'm sick to death of it?'

I leaned forward and slid the cheque back at him.

More blinking, the spectacles filmed with pink from the shade of the lamp.

'Sick to death of it,' I said.

I turned my head and looked towards the window at the end of the empty restaurant. The chairs were stacked up on every table but ours; their upthrust legs were a stick-like version of the courtyards of Blühnbach and Phoenix, a miniature forest of menacing growths. Outside the window I could see the rain still weeping down on darkened Soho.

Rain, rain, rain. Nothing but rain since landing at London Airport. My clothes and my body felt continually damp. The sheets on the beds felt damp. The napkins and tablecloths in the restaurant felt damp. The whole damned world felt damp.

Felix came in with a new bottle of Sancerre. Harrison was silent, pressing the spectacles on the bridge of the decadent-imperial nose, solemn now, calculating the next step. Felix withdrew, impassive, saying nothing.

Harrison wiped his mouth with his napkin and put it beside the empty dessert-plate.

'Morven, you don't seem to appreciate that I'm offering you twelve thousand pounds. Pardon me for saying so, but doesn't your present bank-balance stand at a little more than thirteen hundred, after you took out that fifteen hundred the morning you left for America?' He raised a plump hand as I looked at him. Did everyone in the world know how much I had in the damned bank? 'Oh, don't worry,' he went on. 'Whatever you were doing in America was your own affair. My man lost you at O'Hare.' His expression was the usual bland mockery of truthfulness. 'But you know, you'll need that money more than ever, if you've really made up your mind to retire—which of course I can't accept. And what about Mrs Mallison? . . .'

I closed my eyes.

. . . *Maggie* . . . *Maggie* . . . Frazer hugging his bleeding bowels at Kabassa . . . Hearne kneeling with his hands crossed on his shattered chest . . . Nolan with a leg missing at the thigh . . . Parasopulous screaming somewhere in the darkness . . . Liddell-Johnson cartwheeling off the water-tank and falling forty feet to the barbed wire . . . Button, crawling through the gate leaving a trail of blood shining stickily in the moonlight . . . Bailey with the black hole where his abdomen had been . . . Lurtsema reaching out for death, the blank look on his face . . . Douglass with his head lolling against the lowest step . . .

Cold. I felt cold.

'Of course,' said Harrison, 'you'll already have guessed what the assignment is that I'm talking about? . . .'

I struggled to sit upright.

'Harrison, I sent you those Xerox copies from Orly for one reason—because I thought it might help you. I didn't want you to interfere with my trip to America—but I didn't want you to be left without a clue about the papers if things went wrong out there . . .'

'I take it you've seen the originals?'

'Martagon has got them—as if you didn't know. Tell me, did you somehow arrange to get me sent out there?'

'Morven, how can you say that?'

'I say that because I don't know what the hell is going on —which is another reason for getting out.'

'Morven, listen to me. All right—I knew Martagon had the Dunsterville and Galley-Thompson papers. I'd realized that was why you couldn't locate them in Africa. That wasn't your fault; God knows, you tried hard enough. But you know now exactly where they're located—'

'Not necessarily. He showed them to me at Blühnbach, but he could have taken them anywhere by now. Or perhaps the originals weren't even there in the first place—'

'Wherever they are, you're the logical man to get them for us—'

'*Martagon.* I've had a bellyfull of Martagon.'

'Yes, yes, but you've met him—you know the situation.'

'I can't take on Martagon. Nor can you—unless you're planning to use the Army?'

'You'd have help—the sort of help you had in Africa—'

'And a hell of a lot of good that did me, didn't it?'

'You can do it for us, Morven. You can.'

'You want to get me killed? Get poor old Teague killed? Haven't we done enough for you, this past fifteen years?' I pulled out the gilt chair beside me and propped up my leg on it. Even in the crimson lamplight he must be able to see the thick layer of bandage under the sock. 'And what about that? Have you seen *that?*'

He stared at it dubiously. Then he extinguished his half-smoked cigar and took off his spectacles. He leaned forward with his elbows on the table, rubbing his eyes.

'You know, Morven, I'm getting old, too . . .' He sighed. This change of mood—which was probably play-acting— immediately put me on my guard. 'You know, my dear chap, for some reason I've never been able to fathom, you've always tended to underrate yourself. And why? Because more often than not you've been successful in whatever we've asked you to do, haven't you? And what's more, you've always survived, haven't you? Of course, I've realized that the African business upset you. All that time you spent in gaol started you brooding. I knew such a long period of inactivity would be bad for you. Believe me, I moved heaven and earth to get you out at the earliest possible moment—*the earliest possible*—believe me!' He continued to rub his eyes as he spoke; they looked pouched and watery. 'You survived Honduras, you survived Equatoria and Kirghizia. You survived your recent visit to Austria. You survived whatever it was you were doing in the United States. You've got a talent for survival. And you're the only one who possesses the key to the Dunsterville affair. Tell me, then—wouldn't it be nice to retrieve something from what you regard as the shambles of the African business?—and survive *that* too?—and come back to whatever it is you want to do with the twelve thousand pounds the Department is offering you? . . .'

I studied him for a moment: then I asked him something I'd been wanting to ask him since our last session in this place.

'Harrison, did you know about the Garden Game? I mean, right from the beginning?'

He stopped massaging his eyelids.

'*The Garden Game*? Martagon calls it that, does he? Oh yes, I knew about *that*.'

It took me a moment to digest.

'You mean, you knew my men were being exploited by Martagon—yet you didn't encourage me to find them—you didn't help me to extricate them?'

'Morven, be reasonable. I wanted you to find Martagon, yes. I wanted you to locate the Dunsterville papers. Apart from that, your four men were extraneous, don't you see that? Compared with that, those men—*any* men—were irrelevant and disposable.'

For once in his life, if late in our professional relationship, my cousin had given me a perfectly honest answer.

'And you didn't consider that we owed them anything,' I said, 'that we had a responsibility towards them?'

He picked up his glasses and put them on very slowly. Immediately his look became purposeful again.

'Morven, your friends did their job. The hazards were explained to them. They were paid for it—except for the instalment they didn't see fit to collect. I don't want to sound brutal: but they took their wages, and are dead . . .'

'And it still doesn't bother you that my friends, as you call them, were our own countrymen, our own flesh and blood?'

He sighed again.

'Sometimes, my dear chap, I can't help seeing a great deal of your late father in you.' I was surprised by the wistfulness in his voice. 'I loved your father. I used to love staying with you, when I was a boy, after my own parents died. I didn't even mind when you and your brothers used to bully me, though you were all younger than I was. It made me feel *accepted*, somehow. At school I wasn't popular; I was left to myself. Ah yes, I was happy at Whinyates . . . All the same, I wish I *didn't* see so much of your dear father in you . . . Already, when we were boys, the old General seemed too romantic, too chivalrous . . . You know, those aren't words we've been able to use for a long while now—yet you've always got them in the back of your mind whenever I send you out in the field . . . They interfered in Africa . . . and now they're interfering with the Dunsterville assignment . . .'

'There *is* no Dunsterville assignment.' I stood up. 'I had some personal business with Martagon. It's over. I've failed.'

I limped over to the coat-rack and took down my rain-coat. I glanced distastefully towards the distant downpour. The sleeves and shoulders of the raincoat were still damp.

'I'd like to help you—but I can't. You shouldn't have asked too much of me.'

He pushed back his chair. He came across to me, shaking his head reproachfully.

'*Morven—Morven* . . .'

The cheque dangled between his fingers. He folded it and creased the fold with thumb and forefinger, then tucked it in my top pocket.

'Put it in the bank. Think about it. I'll call you again.'

The red lamplight gave him more than ever the appearance of a jovial Mephistopheles.

I felt very tired. I hated going out in the rain.

I SAT silent in the Jensen as Teague drove back to Brecon Crescent. The previous day he had gone down to Weymouth to collect the car. He found it in the garage near the docks exactly as we left it almost two weeks earlier. It wasn't difficult to tell that it had been thoroughly searched, but the PPK had been clipped back under the dash.

Teague and I had scarcely spoken to each other on the five-hour drive along Insterstate 10 from Phoenix to Los Angeles. Partly it was because I was as usual letting him get on with a piece of fast driving; partly because of the pain in my swelling ankle. But partly it was because we were both nauseated and embarrassed by the event we had just lived through. I have said before that it gave rise to conflicting emotions inside me about the nature of my trade. Teague felt that too. He wanted to convince himself that what we had seen lay completely above and beyond our normal activities, and resented having been brought into an action that he had previously called futile and unnecessary. As for me, I bore a vague, general, unfair resentment towards him because I wanted to blame someone else, at least partly, for my own failure and humiliation, and he happened to be the only one available. It was with the same feelings of reserve that we paid off the Torino and flew back over the Pole to England. I spent much of the trip at the rear of the plane, with a stewardess packing ice from the galley round my foot. It was much the same in London; there was a constraint between us; we couldn't adjust our emotions to this alien chapter in our long association.

We drove down Regent Street and Oxford Street to Marble Arch. It was a week away from Christmas, and since our last visit to Soho the rest of the Christmas decorations had been put up. In the solid column of sight-seeing traffic, undeterred by rain, we crawled beneath plastic sleds and plastic reindeer, plastic Santas and plastic Stars of Jerusalem. The shop windows cast a tinsel glare on the wet crowds. The garish reds and greens, the bogus glitter on the fake holly and mistletoe, were hollow and meretricious, and I felt depressed as I touched the pocket with Harrison's cheque. In the old days action was the anodyne for any doubts I felt about who or what I was defending. No longer.

I tried to think of Maggie. I tried to think of what the Germans would call my long-in-silence-wished-for cottage in the North Country. I tried to think of them both together, projecting the twin vision on to the steaming mass of humanity on the swarming pavements. *Maggie's white skin flecked with amber spots . . . streaming auburn hair . . . a dappled boulder above a shadowed emerald pool . . .*

Twelve thousand. With the other three or four it was enough for a tenuous retirement. I'd never bothered about money much; the task itself sustained me. Now they wanted to pay me three or four times what they'd ever paid me before. Could I turn them down, even after they'd abandoned me in Lagos, let me rot in Leigh Central? Even when they'd done nothing to recall my men and return them to their proper duty? Was I really the only man? Did I owe them a final risk, a final effort?

I was feeling distinctly sore and sorry for myself when the Jensen drew up outside the house in Brecon Crescent. As I climbed out into the rain, after a glance up and down the street, I was wondering whether I should have tried to find Maggie as soon as I was released from Leigh. It was time to start getting my life back on the rails . . .

I was standing at the top of the steps, fiddling with the twin keys of the front door. Teague had unlocked the garage below and was putting the car away; the engine reverberated beneath my feet. The man must have been waiting in a neighbouring doorway. He came up the five steps behind me without making a sound.

'*Major—*'

The voice was close to my ear. I turned at once and moved away sideways at the same time. Part of my brain reproached me, as so often this past three weeks, with my slackness and carelessness. Then I saw, braced back against the rain-slick railing, that the man in front of me was standing unaggressively, almost humbly. The garage door went down with a crash and Teague was at the foot of the steps, staring up at the man, big shoulders hunched.

Teague recognized him before I did.

'*Asher?*' he said. '*My God, is it *Asher?'·

I stepped forward to look more closely. Now, beneath the shapeless brim of the rain-soaked hat, above the turned-up collar of the raincoat, I saw the hard narrow face of the man whom I'd assumed had gone the same way as Bailey and the others. He was unshaven. The hat and raincoat were dirty and nondescript, and I remembered how in Africa he'd been the sloppiest man in the unit. His hair, wet with the rain, was still shaggy and needed a trim. I remembered, too, how he'd got us all out of the ambush at Mongalla.

I grabbed him by the sleeves of the raincoat and shook him till the raindrops flew off his hatbrim. I have never been so glad to see anyone in the whole of my life. I thumped his shoulders and punched his chest.

'It *is!*—it *is!*—*Asher!* . . .'

He looked around and said in a low quick voice, in the Lancashire accent I was beginning to recall:

'Major, can't we go inside?'

He sounded anxious. I lost no time in opening the door. The three of us moved rapidly into the hall. I closed the door and slipped the catch.

Asher took off his hat, shook it, and stood dripping on the hall carpet. He had evidently been waiting for us for a long time.

'I got away from them,' he said. 'I've been dodging around for a couple of weeks on the Continent, the last week in Denmark. I slipped across two nights ago—landed at Harwich—had to jump ship . . . one of the first things they do is take your passport away—only give it back when you travel to a meeting. I didn't have any money left—they put most of it away in a deposit account. I had to hitch-hike to London . . . remembered coming here with the radio-equipment . . . came straight to you . . .'

The words poured out in a rush, thick and indignant.

'No need to stand around here,' I said. 'Take those wet things off and we'll go in the drawing-room. What would you like? Tea? Coffee?'

'Have you got any beer, Major? And something to eat?'

It so happened that Teague had stocked up with a dozen cans, the day we first got back. Asher drank them all, and ate his way through a mound of sandwiches, between the time when he started to tell me his story and the time, three hours later, when we went to bed and he dossed down in a sleeping-bag on the kitchen floor.

He had a habit, which came back to me, of holding the can up high and tilting his head back and letting the liquor run in a stream down his throat. His hands were large and clumsy-looking, with swollen veins; but I remembered how confidently they had handled the electronic gear which the rest of us couldn't understand in the slightest. He sat awkwardly on the edge of one of my four Hepplewhite chairs, a tall, stringy young man of not more than twenty-three or twenty-four, one hand on a damp knee-cap, the other wrapped around a beer-can, a mass of tangled brown hair falling round his ears and on his unspeakably filthy collar. He had been sleeping in his clothes, and smelt like it. From time to time Teague, who hated slovenly soldiers, would frown and wrinkle up his nose; but even Teague, I saw, was pleased to see him, and considered him, as I did, in the light of something at least that was saved from the wreck . . .

Both of us warmed increasingly to him as the evening went on. In Africa he had been monosyllabic, wrapped up entirely in his gadgets. Now, as the rain poured down outside and the tale of the past months burst out of him, he showed himself, in spite of his weakness in getting involved with the Game, as a man of shrewdness and intelligence. It was certainly strange to listen to him pouring out his tale of violence in my neat bright room, with the curtains drawn against the foul weather, the fire on the hearth, and the orderly rows of books behind his tousled head. He wasn't a man who'd been born with many advantages; he'd acquired his technical skills painfully, at trade-schools and night-schools; but when it came to the crunch he'd been saved by a streak of rough common sense that would have saved Grady Bailey and Rupert Douglass, too, if they'd been more stable and hadn't been so greedy.

Like Douglass, Asher had been a working-class boy who'd loved to fight; and when all was said and done, I hadn't recruited him just for his technical abilities but also because he'd got a consistent record of disciplined pugnacity in Cyprus and the Arabian Peninsula, two of the clasps on his General Service medal. It was therefore not altogether surprising that he'd fallen for Martagon's blandishments, conveyed to him by Jenbach, and become a recruit for the Garden Game. Being young, he and the others had been fretting themselves to death in the compound in Nigeria: and then Jenbach had turned up and sprung them loose on behalf of a mysterious Swiss benefactor. They were half-sold already. They'd just had a strong dose of action along the Niger, and in spite of the losses they were emotionally keyed up and eager for more of the same. Young men are resilient; it's middle-aged men like me, who are also burdened with the cares of command, who have lost the habit of snapping back quickly. Nor can Asher be blamed, really, given his background, for wanting to take advantage of what seemed like a sudden chance to earn a great deal of money.

Apparently none of them was told, before the first meeting, that the whole purpose of the Garden Game was to stage an atavistic duel to the death. Of course, they knew it was a serious business, and that given the lethal nature of the weapons employed no holds were barred, and fatal accidents were bound to occur. But they certainly didn't know that they were intended to do more than gain a clear edge over their opponent, at which point they expected to be able to reach down and help him, however bloody, to his feet.

They soon learned. In their first fights they were pitted against seasoned performers from the earlier generation of the Game, and it was a miracle—and perhaps a melancholy tribute to the training abilities of Teague and me—that they all squeaked through. Asher got a smashed knee-cap, a smashed elbow and almost, as he lay on the sand, a smashed skull, before Grady Bailey came to the rescue and killed his assailant. They all crept back to their quarters in a shaken mood—yet only a few hours later, flushed with the sense of victory and pleased by the prompt arrival of their first pay-checks, their natural high spirits began to reassert themselves. It hadn't been so bad; certainly no worse than what they had recently been through at Kabassa; and if they buckled down to work, stuck together, and trained hard, they could take on any opposition brought against them . . .

And, to begin with, they *did* stick together. They worked out joint exercises and manoeuvres; they bolstered each other's morale. When the members of the small British group fought as allies, they were unbeatable, and hardly ever sustained any significant injury. Oh yes, I had chosen them well . . .

Asher couldn't tell me, sitting there in his rumpled clothes, with his Adam's apple working as he guzzled his light ale, at what precise moment the honeymoon ended and the night-mare began. It was probably after the first long series of fights. Douglass, he said, was the toughest of the lot, which was why he'd lasted the longest; he'd enjoyed the lush living, he'd enjoyed the fights, and he'd earned a lot of extra money betting on himself. In various ways, however, the pressure was gradually beginning to get to the rest of them. Bailey kept up a good front, laughing and playing practical jokes to the end; he was convinced he'd be able to retire early and return to his wife with a pile of money; they'd buy a hotel and live happily ever after. Oddly enough, like Douglass, Bailey didn't mind the killing, which was strange in such a charming and otherwise kindly and generous young fellow.

It was the ultimate necessity to kill that unsettled the two other members of the quartet. Playing rough they wouldn't have minded; it was playing for keeps, in these unnatural circumstances, that they couldn't adjust to. Like Bailey and Douglass, Asher and Lurtsema had enjoyed busy careers as subalterns in the Army, where they'd been shunted from one brushfire campaign to the next. They'd done their share of public killing—and yet the *private* killing of the Garden Game had got them down. You would have thought the former would have hardened them to the latter—but it didn't. It was the difference between being a self-respecting soldier and being a hired assassin. Curious, really—Asher said he'd killed more men with me, in Nigeria, than he'd killed in the whole course of the Garden Game; but the former deaths didn't trouble his conscience at all, while the latter drove him half-crazy. And what he said convinced me that this was the whole root of the matter: the distinction between bloodshed legitimized and sanctioned by society, and bloodshed that was regarded simply as individual crime and murder . . . It was a distinction, if any, that none of us properly understood . . . And here was I, an experienced soldier, after all—and hadn't the sight of those men, hacking and clapper-clawing one another in the green hell of those courtyards, played havoc with all my own notions and assumptions? . . .

Something of the same sort had happened to Asher and Lurtsema. Lurtsema should have tried to get out sooner. He and Asher were close friends, shared the same quarters, trained together, fought together. As he spoke, punctuating his discourse with a frequent tilting back of the head and lubrication of the throat, I could tell that Asher had grown attached to Lurtsema, and was unaware that he was dead. I wondered how I was going to break the bad news? . . .

It was certainly an odd combination, the ox-like Dutchman and the lanky Lancastrian, but in many ways they complemented one another. And unfortunately, when things began to go sour, they also began undermining each other's morale. Lurtsema started to develop a horror of every facet of the business, but steeled himself to continue at least a few months longer because he wanted to accumulate a stake for the future; he was supporting a mother, two grown sisters and a teenage brother in Eindhoven. Asher, equally disillusioned, equally loathing himself, decided to make the break and begged the Dutchman to do the same. The Dutchman said he'd do so after the next fight—which was, I supposed, the one that had taken place at Blühnbach. He said he'd go to Martagon, ask for his money, and demand to be released. When that time came, Asher had already slipped away; but I guessed that Lurtsema had in fact challenged Martagon on the night I was at Blühnbach. He must have received a dusty answer. No doubt he was told in blunt terms that there was no retirement, no withdrawal, that he was trapped and must continue to the end. So he staggered on, appalled, his will to live destroyed . . . to the tragic débâcle at Phoenix . . . where Martagon probably bet heavily against his own man and cleaned up a packet . . .

Asher was smarter. He'd been wondering for months why, after the first two or three big cheques, he and the others had received advances and expenses but never again the complete payment. This was retained, doubtless for their own good, by their kindly patron. It was a way of keeping them in line, like working for the company store. He'd also learned, from one of Martagon's original gladiators, a veteran who had since died of wounds, that the idea of formal retirement was a mirage. His native good sense, buried for so long by youthful excitement and excess, began to assert itself. He decided to desert. However, Martagon must have noticed that one of the hired hands was showing signs of restlessness—and a surprising development occurred.

Asher leaned forward, waving a half-empty can.

'Know what he did?'

'What?'

'He *sold* me.'

'He *what*—?'

'Major—that bastard *sold* me! . . .'

And that was what had happened. He was traded, in exchange for a cash sum and a pair of untried novices. Martagon was right: the Garden Game was a kind of crazy extension of prize-fighting, or ice-hockey, or professional football.

'And do you know who they sold me to?'

'Who?'

'A woman.'

'Oh?'

'That's right—a *woman*.'

'What woman?'

'Some big fat bitch from Bolivia or somewhere. She came round to my room prodding and poking me as if I was a prize bull. Can you imagine it? *Without even consulting me!*'

His narrow face was so crimson with outrage I was tempted to laugh. But I didn't. I remembered the squat, unbending, slit-eyed, obese, ochre-faced Indian idol at the post-Game party . . .

Asher stood up. He shuffled his dirty shoes on the carpet, looking scruffier than ever. He put down his beer-can on my Adam mantelpiece. He was worried about something.

'Major, I came to you because . . . *well* . . . I'm not sure where I stand . . . legally, I mean . . .'

'Legally?'

He was afraid there might be criminal consequences for having taken part in the Garden Game.

A nice point.

I tried to reassure him—yet he was dreadfully uneasy. His awareness of what he'd actually been involved in had awoken late, but now it refused to let him rest.

It was at this point that I told him about Hans Lurtsema. I could have left it till morning, but I decided to get the whole thing over now.

The small white room was extremely quiet. When I finished, the pattering of the rain on the windows seemed very loud. To my surprise, he asked me a great many questions about the Dutchman's last moments—how he'd looked, how he'd moved and behaved, how he'd been struck, how he'd fallen.

He turned and stared into the sinking fire. He picked up the beer-can and crumpled it in his large hand.

'You know, Major—we weren't *afraid* of dying, none of us—but damn them— . . . *Hans!* . . .' He looked up, the stubbled face filled with anger. 'If we could only have done it . . . died . . . I mean . . . *FOR* something? . . .'

My gaze travelled from Asher to where Teague's bulk was crammed in the elegant white chair.

I got up and went into the hall. I found the number and dialed Whitehall. When I was put through to the Home Office I asked to be connected to the Night Duty Officer.

I ignored his protests about the lateness of the hour.

HIRING the two cars was expensive. However, I took Harrison at his word when, in his fruitiest tones and during the course of the longest phone call we ever exchanged, he promised me solemnly that the Department would foot the bill for all expenses—without arguing.

A car in reserve was a definite part of the plan—if anything improvised so speedily can be dignified by the name of a plan. The ability to improvise is a military virtue; but for some time past—another sign of advancing age?—I'd always liked to make my preparations with a feeling of taking plenty of time and trying to cover every foreseeable contingency. Of course, once the action begins it's impossible to anticipate everything; but the sense of having laid the groundwork is what gives you confidence to modify your arrangements quickly and coolly.

Now, driving up through the pine woods again, I had the suspicion that at best the three of us were only going to scramble through the ordeal ahead of us. I sat beside Asher in carefully concealed gloom as the dark blue Mercedes ran uphill into the Wienerwald; occasionally the dancing dots of the headlights of the Mercedes following behind would slide across the mirror as we negotiated a bend. Teague was taking the icy road cautiously; we wanted no mishaps before we reached the jumping-off point.

A full moon was shining high above the pines. The tall trees stood as straight and sharp as steel girders; there was an inhuman stiffness and stillness about the vast forest; not a fox or rabbit, no small creature or living thing moved or left a track in all these glittering blank spaces or all those empty rides between the ghostly groves. The wide, white night seemed to be waiting.

When we reached snow-blanketed Vienna, six hours ago, our first destination was the obscure garage on the Amalienstrasse at which one of Harrison's local contacts, an experienced Iron Curtain operator, had hired the 280 SEs for us. He had been unable to procure cars of a dark chocolate colour, but beneath the bleached light of the winter moon the royal blue would probably pass. I noticed, and probably Teague did too, that the contact was not present at the car-showroom to ask if there was any other way in which he could make things easier for us. Still, considering the other arrangements I'd instructed him to make, via Harrison, he was wise not to hang about and advertise himself. As for the car-hire people, they were obviously experienced in transactions of this type. A representative of the firm emerged briefly from his office, handed us three sets of keys and told us the cars had been paid for for forty-eight hours. He was back in his office by the time we drove into the street, with the yellow trams clanging past and the solemn burghers in their galoshes trudging along with their briefcases and Christmas packages tied with ribbon. Despite Harrison's midnight assurances, we were once more strictly on our own. At any rate, the inside of an Austrian gaol would be a palace after the squalor of Lagos...

There was no alternative to quick action. Where Martagon was concerned we had to make the best of our small advantage of surprise. In two more days the three weeks he gave me to think over his offer would be up. My plan rested on the initial pretence that I was seeking him out at Blühnbach to give him his answer. Moreover, he had been quite specific about the three weeks, which suggested that his business travels would be over and he would be back at Blühnbach. If we left it till later, it mightn't be so easy to track him down.

The three of us seemed a puny force to attempt an attack

on Blühnbach. Staring out at the gleaming forest, no one was more aware of that than I was. However, three men were more likely to gain admittance than thirteen or three hundred; and we could hardly launch an all-out assault, could we, with tanks, artillery and flame-throwers? Anyway, the pits and pockmarks in its walls showed that such salvoes had been fired before, and had proved costly.

No, we had to rely on swiftness, secrecy and surprise. It was for reasons of secrecy that we'd sneaked out of London, without alerting Martagon, without even calling him from Vienna when we'd landed. We wanted to drop on him without warning, like parachutists. Our only chance was to swagger across his drawbridge, hammer on his gates, and trust to our colossal triple bluff.

There was a fearful number of *ifs* about it. The pines wheeling past, rank upon rank, were like an army of bayonets. There was the question of our private raid on the Underwood mansion. We hadn't left any traces; our opponents hadn't come close enough to see us during the skirmish; but we hadn't exactly been wearing stockings over our faces, and Douglass' woman-friend had got a good look at us. Anyway, Martagon would easily put two and two together; it was unlikely that he and Underwood would write off the incident to the activities of business rivals; in any event, I'd warned him that one way or another I still meant to reach and talk to my men—that is, any of them who were left—sooner or later.

What attitude would he take? Had he got wind in London of our movements and intentions? We knew from the Blue Griffon business how effective his intelligence system was. Was I leading my companions into a trap?

Almost as soon as I'd put the phone down, and started to plan strategy, I'd offered to release Teague from the assignment. Of course, he grumbled and shifted his weight around and made objections—but he accepted straight away, offended by my clumsy suggestion. Teague and I would go on to the end, whenever and wherever that might be.

It was Gavin Asher, driving steadily beside me, who was showing exceptional courage here. He, after all, was the defector, the traitor to the Garden Game. I imagined the people who ran the Game would devise brave punishments for a deserter. I wouldn't care to be in his shoes if Martagon's men caught him. I was impressed by the quiet and unwavering determination he showed as we came minute by minute nearer to Blühnbach. His face, clean-shaven now, caught the flickering shine off the snow. The long jaw was determined; he stared directly in front of him. After the rainy midnight when he learned that Lurtsema was dead, he hadn't mentioned the Dutchman again; but I knew that all the time he was helping us make our meagre preparations he was thinking of him—and probably of Bailey too.

We were travelling down a straight stretch of the road, the chains rippling in a steady rhythm on the glassy surface, when I caught sight of a familiar landmark. I put a hand on Asher's arm and motioned him to pull up.

We slowed and stopped. Teague saw our brake-lights glow and alertly came to a smooth halt behind us.

I opened the door and swung myself out of the car. The sudden cold was biting. I told Asher to stay where he was and keep the engine running. Teague stuck his head out of the window, and I walked back to him, treading carefully on the icy road, and gave him the same instructions.

The summerhouse was set back thirty yards from the road, to the left. I ploughed through the snow towards it. The drifts were deep and frosted to a crust on top; the rubber soles of my suede boots made a crisp snapping sound as they penetrated to the cottony snow beneath. In the diamond light I saw that the summerhouse was actually an ornamental gatehouse set at the end of a carriageway that probably ran towards the *schloss*. The gates behind it soared up towards the broad blank moon, the ironwork slender yet strong.

I didn't want to waste time, but I had to satisfy my curiosity. I waded through the snowbank piled beneath the lintel of one of the tall windows and looked inside. The floor was a mass of shadows. I took my flashlight out of the pocket of my anorak and played the beam through the ice-encrusted panes. Now I could make out what looked like a pile of dilapidated basket-chairs, rotted floorboards, and a heap of long straight objects like tangled spillikins. Shining the flashlight obliquely, rubbing away my breath where it fogged the glass, I could identify these objects as digging tools, spades and forks and mattocks, with lumps of frozen blackish earth still clinging to their blades and tines.

I switched off the flashlight and crunched across to the gates. At the height of my waist I could see the massive square lock. Around the lock a rusty chain as thick as a man's wrist had been fastened in place with a black heart-shaped padlock. Beyond the gates a sloping snowfield ran uphill towards the razor-sharp line of the crest, where the spangled earth met the star-powdered sky.

The tendrils and curlicues of the baroque ironwork writhed against the snow like the leaves and branches of the courtyard at Blühnbach or Phoenix. Without thinking, as I came up to the gates I grasped the bars with my bare hands. The shock of the freezing metal ran through me like a current and made me step back.

I could see nothing in either direction on the far side of the gates. There was no churning or puddling of the snow to show where the earth had been disturbed. Yet below that white snowsheet, bland beneath the moon, lay the gashed bodies of the losers in the Garden Game—*gladiatori non missi*—Grady Bailey among them . . . I stood there for a moment, thinking about him . . .

As I trudged back to the car I felt a crushing weight on my shoulders. When . . . or *if* . . . we returned to England, I wouldn't be able to put off any longer breaking the news to poor little Thea . . .

We were drumming down the highway, and I was still brooding about my errors and omissions, when Teague started flashing his main beam on and off behind. I sat up. He was warning us that, by dead reckoning, we were within four or five kilometres of the *schloss*.

I murmured to Asher to slow down. I leaned forward, straining my eyes for the rise in the road that led to the low causeway which ran the last mile or so to the entrance. I had taken note of the causeway when I climbed up on to it with Martagon, the day he was feeding his peacocks.

As soon as I saw the dark hump in front of us, I rolled down the window and signalled back to Teague with my flashlight. Asher pulled over as close as he could to the side and stopped, keeping the car below the level of the hump.

There was a swishing sound as Teague drove his Mercedes as far as he dared on to the snow-packed verge. I stuck my head out of the window and watched him make a neat hard 180-degree turn and run the car off the road on to the verge on the other side, pointing back the way we had come. He wasn't able to park it far off the road, for fear of getting bogged down; and although the line of the forest made it reasonably inconspicuous, any one using the road would be bound to spot it. We just had to hope that none of Martagon's people would be roaming around at ten-thirty at night, and that his guards and watchmen would confine their activities to the immediate surroundings of the *schloss*.

The door of Teague's car closed softly. A moment later he slid into the seat behind me and tapped Asher on the shoulder.

We moved forward and breasted the rise and saw the wide bulk of the *schloss* spreading out ahead of us.

I don't know how the others felt. I imagine it was the same as I did—heart pumping, lump of lead behind the ribs. I took a couple of slow, deep breaths.

We didn't look at each other as we drew up at the iron-studded gates. We sat tensely, the purr of the engine sounding unnaturally loud. No sign of life from the building in front of us. We couldn't sit there all night. One way or another, the matter had to be pressed to a conclusion. I leaned across, put my hand on the horn-ring, pushed it down and held it there. The noise sounded shattering in the frosty night.

It produced results. In no time at all a wicket-gate opened in one of the double-doors. In a moment of split vision I was transported backwards to Leigh Central and the fat sergeant with the ring of keys on his belt. Two men came out. They were dressed in dark jackets and black sweaters. I got out of the car.

After that events moved in a curious fashion, neither fast nor slowly. It was like reporting an accident in a police station, or clearing customs. Things happened in slow-motion. Ironically, I even felt a twinge of exasperation, a touch of boredom.

One man came forward, the other stayed by the wicket-gate. In my rudimentary German I started to explain who I was and what I wanted, then found to my relief that we got on better if I switched to French.

The man spoke little. Finally he made a sign and a third man stepped out through the gate, at which the first man disappeared inside. I waited at least fifteen minutes, blowing on my fingers and stamping my feet. Asher and Teague sat motionless.

At length the first man returned. The gates opened. I leaned down and gestured to Asher, and he drove into the semi-circular courtyard. I followed on foot and the three men walked briskly in the rear, keeping their distance as Asher parked the car in the spot we had decided on when we were laying our plans in London, opposite the open stone doorway with the yellow hanging light which I recognized from my first visit.

So far, so good. We'd been scared we'd be told to leave the car outside the gates.

As I went through the gates I walked slowly, turning my head to inspect what I could of the bolts and fastenings. With a sense of dismay, I saw that they looked elaborate. No quick exit.

The first man kept close behind me. One of the other men paused to shut the gates. They reckoned, rightly, it was wiser to lock our transport in the courtyard.

Teague and Asher got out of the car. They locked the doors as they closed them. The three men approached the car warily, in a wide circle. We kept our hands by our sides, in full view.

Then the first man did something we'd half-expected and were prepared for, but which we'd hoped wouldn't happen.

He went up to Asher and held out his hand for the key.

Those fellows were well-trained. They were making the moves we would have made ourselves.

Asher, as we'd rehearsed, dropped the key on his palm with just the right amount of hesitation to make it look natural.

We now had to pray that when they searched the car they'd content themselves with taking the crowbars and wrenches we'd put in the boot as a decoy. They wouldn't reckon we'd be stupid enough to bring weapons with us. When they searched the interior, we hoped they'd sift through the meaningless junk we'd piled on the floor behind the back-seats and dump it back again without disturbing the panels beneath the carpet below. It was dark. They mightn't notice the floor had been raised two or three inches ... they mightn't ... *mightn't*. ... but there again, they *might* ...

I turned my head.

Jenbach was standing beneath the yellow light, the pale hair gleaming, the amethyst eyes expressionless.

He gestured with his head. I nodded to Teague and Asher and we walked towards him.

But it wasn't to be as easy as that.

They searched us, in the entrance. They ran their hands under our arms, sides, thighs, legs and around our waistbands. Fingers prodded the padded quilting at the front of my anorak and pulled and patted none too gently at the surgical bandage round my ankle.

We passed.

Jenbach turned and we fell in behind him. We walked upstairs with two of the others behind us, while the first man went back across the courtyard towards the gates.

Another pair of men had appeared from the gatehouse, and the tall gates were already closing. They shut with a well-oiled, well-cushioned sound that hung ominously on the crystalline air behind us as we climbed the stairs.

WE were taken along the same route I had followed on my first visit to Blühnbach. First came the cloister with the fantastic animals snarling from the tops of their columns, then the cold drab corridor with the naked lightbulbs. We marched in regular order, Jenbach ahead, his two janissaries at the rear. No one spoke. This wasn't a night for talking.

As we were turning out of the cloister into the corridor, without warning the grating cry of a peacock, somewhere out under the lee of the dark pines, rang out in the hushed night. Teague, who hadn't heard it before, broke stride with an exclamation of surprise and alarm. The mad-sounding noise seemed to fracture the clear glassy dark around us. It put us even further on edge.

Tonight Jenbach produced his key and passed us through the black-painted door without delay. I heard Teague, stepping through behind me, give a gasp of amazement as he walked into the inner courtyard. He stopped, gazing up at the distant roof with its steel supports. The glass panes were clear of snow now, except for a filigree of frost around the edges; beyond them we could see the limitless dead blackness of the sky. He needed, as I had, a touch on the shoulder before he advanced towards the sand-strewn paths into the fantastic garden ahead.

. . . *Tree of the Little Hands . . . Fire-Eating Tree . . . Tree Which Weeps Blood* . . . again I wandered between the swollen, waxy, exotic plants with their fiery, musky blossoms. In the courtyard it was an eternal and overpowering summer. Each growth coiled up from the purulescence of its predecessor . . . *Lipstick Tree . . . Cannon-Ball Tree . . .*

gorged orchids . . . glutted vines . . . every shade and contrast . . . every tone and blend . . .

The first time I saw the hidden garden was on the evening of a Game, when it was lighted and men were hosing and raking its serpentine alleyways. Now it was deserted, inhabited only by shadows. The flowers that studded the branches and hung from the creepers shimmered in a phosphorescent mist, lit only by moon and stars. The garden wrapped itself around us as we wound through its pulpy interior, our shoes whispering on the sand. The shadows were carnivorous, swaying and palpitating like an octopus. The lianas that brushed our faces as we trod at Jenbach's heels were pythons with luminous scales . . . *Flower of the Dead* . . . *Horns of the Devil* . . .

Even Jenbach turned his head from side to side, as if the mephitic genius of the place was lurking beyond the ferns and gunneras, its rotting vegetable features a mask that no sane man should set eyes on. He walked quickly, apprehensive of losing his way, wanting to escape from the garden rapidly.

I was sweating, partly from the quick pace, partly from nervousness at the action ahead, partly because even in mid-December, in Central Europe, at eleven at night, it was sticky in the courtyard. Those infernal growths throve on a high temperature. Their rancid perfume seemed to grow more potent at every step, clinging to our clothes and skin.

I turned round to sneak a look at my companions. Teague shambled along, shoulders hunched, head swinging this way and that. Asher walked bolt upright, hands stiff by his sides, face white as plaster and head held high. There was something in his bearing of a man marching in defiance of his executioners, or stalking towards a stony vengeance. The cold light was concentrated on the surface of his eyes in twin bright points. He strode forward without hesitation. I remembered that he had trodden these twisting lanes before.

I think everyone was pleased to reach the other end of the

courtyard and go through the other black door on the far side. As this was an unexpected visit, and we weren't invited guests, we were taken directly to our destination and not to the guest wing. Jenbach and his men seemed anxious to get us there rapidly, where we would be immobilized and it would be easier to watch us; they were uneasily aware that even though they had weapons it was still a case of three against three. Our unheralded arrival was producing its unsettling effect.

I don't know what kind of reception I'd been expecting. I'd been keeping an open mind, avoiding preconceptions, remaining flexible. As it turned out, our entry into the dimly-lit, dark-panelled study, lined with books, was uneventful. Martagon's greeting was agreeable; his eyes flickered over the the three of us, and as he looked at me I saw what I took to be a gleam of amusement in his eyes. He was going to enjoy the coming interview. Three chairs had been set out facing the big walnut desk. We sat down, Asher on the left, Teague in the middle, me on the right. Jenbach and his two henchmen took up their places at the back, standing between the chairs and the door. They were more relaxed, now they had the tactical advantage. The meeting had the air of a trial before a judge in chambers, or a secret court-martial.

I looked briefly at Teague. He was naturally uneasy in his unfamiliar surroundings, and had been shaken by the cry of the peacock and the bizarre appearance of the courtyard. Now he was further startled by the sight of Martagon's hands. I should have warned him. Martagon, in his shirt-sleeves, stood behind the desk on the right-hand side; on the short side, between him and Asher, stood a young man, a doctor, whom I hadn't seen before. On the desk in front of him was a white-covered tray with an array of bottles, dressings, and surgical instruments. A large enamel bowl was filled with a steaming liquid, and a smaller one contained lysol or carbolic, giving out an incongruous smell in this sophisticated room. He was a dark, slender, square-faced man in a black suit, and while we were taking our seats and making desultory remarks he went on uninterruptedly with his work. Martagon didn't introduce him.

He was engaged in changing the bandages on Martagon's hands. The powerful desk-lamp had been angled to provide him with a spotlight. The sleeves of Martagon's silk shirt were rolled back to the elbows, and he stood with his arms out while the doctor snipped carefully along the backs of the thick bandages with long-bladed scissors. The bandages extended almost halfway up the forearms. When he had cut them through, the doctor carried the soiled and discarded casings in the blades of the scissors over to the blazing logs in the fireplace and dropped them into the flames, where they sent up a hissing cloud of sparks.

Martagon's hands, wrists and the lower part of his arms were a disgusting sight. No wonder he was tortured by the urge to rub and scratch. The flesh looked like decaying lumps of meat, disfigured with bluish-red sores and blotches and running with a pinkish-yellow pus. As he held them out towards the doctor, in the harsh circle of the lamp, they looked like bleeding stumps. He noted our reaction to them with sardonic humour.

In a casual voice, looking now at the doctor and now at us, he began to talk. His voice, coming out of the semi-shadow, was as polite as ever, but nevertheless held a note of triumph and superiority. From the beginning he assumed that Asher and I had come crawling back to Blühnbach as supplicants, acknowledging his ascendancy over us. I suppose one couldn't blame him; this was what I'd deliberately hinted at when I was talking to the man at the gate. Our posture as supplicants was part of the plan.

He referred to the Phoenix episode: but after the first nasty moment I realized with surprise that he regarded it only as a minor irritation. True, he had lost one of his star performers by the death of Rupert Douglass; nevertheless he implied that Douglass's luck, by the law of averages, had been running out. The incident had caused no bad blood among the other members of the syndicate, although a certain lady—and here he smiled—had suffered a certain amount of grief and embarrassment. However, no doubt I now wanted to compensate, in my own way, for Douglass' loss. And the Phoenix escapade might prove a very good thing if it finally rid my system, once and for all, of all that nonsense about rescuing and rehabilitating my former colleagues. As usual, he enunciated the English idioms precisely, with a slight self-satisfied emphasis. I got the impression that he actually applauded my Arizona foray, as if it was a token of my ability to take the initiative and argued well for the future.

I sat upright on my straight-backed wooden chair, making my face as expressionless as possible, forcing myself to sit still. We didn't want any unguarded movement to give us away too soon; but it was hot in here, after the frosty night outside. I opened my anorak. There was a real danger we might get drowsy.

The doctor had unscrewed one of the jars and was smearing a brown unguent on strips of lint with a spatula from a sterilized packet. This gave Martagon an opportunity to lower his hands. I said nothing; I wasn't required to make replies. I made myself look passive. Inwardly I felt hatred for this white-faced, delicate-looking, smooth-tongued man whom I regarded as a murderer, a blackmailer, the originator of a monstrous enterprise. The curtains behind his head were drawn tight, but I never let myself forget for a moment the garden that man had planted and how he had watered it with blood . . .

While the doctor was laying the lint on his hands and trimming it, he said that presumably I was bringing some sort of message from Harrison. He enquired if we'd had a pleasant dinner two nights ago at the Coquille d'Argent, smiling when I started slightly. Where was the leak? Someone in

Harrison's office? Someone at the Coquille d'Argent? . . .
Salomon himself, perhaps? . . . When—or if—I got back to
London, I'd have to tell Harrison to check Salomon out . . .

As the supercilious, accentless voice flowed on, I kept
asking myself the question that would make or mar the
entire operation. Were the Dunsterville papers in Martagon's
study, or the office next door, or were they somewhere else?
I was compelled to gamble that they were here at Blühnbach.
He had brought the copy out of the inner office when we
had talked in his study before. No doubt he'd had the three
sheets Xeroxed before he handed them over: and I'd
glimpsed a Xerox machine with other business machines
through the open door of the inner office. So it seemed
probable the papers were kept in a filing-cabinet next door.
With some dismay, I saw that tonight the door of the inner
office was shut tight. The secretary, of course, would have
left hours ago: but the door looked solid, and I was sure it
would have an up-to-date lock—two serious disadvantages
when we made our move . . .

Martagon extended his right hand and held it stiff while
the doctor's blunt fingers wound a thick bandage around it.
The doctor bound a pad on his patient's palm, then pleated
the bandage over the wrist and up the arm. He never spoke
or acknowledged our presence, concentrating on his work
and ignoring the conversation around him, as if he believed
that too much interest might be dangerous. Martagon
regarded the crisp new bandage with approval, flexing the
fingers that poked out at the end. His white face turned
towards me. I tried to clear my mind of my churning
thoughts and listen to what he was saying, maintaining the
same neutral expression.

'. . . *Or maybe you've come to Blühnbach on another errand,
Major, a more personal one? . . . Maybe you've come to tell me
that you've thought over my proposition, and decided to accept? . . .*'

His eyes slid across to Teague, studying him in the same
patronizing manner. He winced slightly as the doctor pulled

the bandages tighter with one hand and kneaded them with the other, but his eyes didn't leave Teague's face.

'... *And Captain Teague* ... *how nice of you to bring him* ... *how pleasant to meet him* . . . *I take it you want to ask me whether you can take him on as your assistant?* ... *I know how accustomed you are to working together* ...'

Teague's body shifted on the hard chair. I looked at him out of the corner of my eye. He was flushed. He was moving his weight forward, while trying not to betray the tenseness of his broad shoulders. Asher was mainly concealed from me by Teague, but his posture appeared perfectly natural and relaxed. At that moment there was something deceptively tranquil about the entire room. The three of us sat still. Martagon watched the doctor complete the bandaging of his left hand. The doctor snipped the ends of the knot and dropped the scissors on the tray. A log fell softly in the warm ash on the hearth. Jenbach and his companions in the shadows behind us seemed to be more at ease. We were careful not to turn and look at them.

Martagon stifled a yawn. We had descended on him at a late hour; there would be plenty of time for discussion in the morning. However, he couldn't resist a little dig at Asher before he wished us goodnight. He didn't want him to sleep tonight thinking that all was well, that he was going to escape the consequences of his misconduct. He wanted to start him sweating.

'... *And Asher here* ... *one of our most promising performers* ... *Yes, Major, I rather fancied you'd persuade him to return to us* ... *ask us to be lenient* ...'

He was smiling at Asher, a sorrowful, paternal smile. The doctor picked up a fresh roll of bandage and broke it out of its sterile package. Martagon went on:

'*However, I regret to say that it might not be quite as easy as you'd hoped, Major* ... *You see, in our friend Asher's case—*'

And that was as far as he got.

We'd agreed among ourselves. The one who felt the time

was ripe would make the first move. The others would back him up.

I don't know if Asher was needled by Martagon's remarks, or sensed the opposition had dropped its guard. He was sitting forward on his chair as if he was drinking in every word that Martagon was speaking about him. He had imperceptibly closed the gap between himself and the desk to no more than four feet.

Without warning he pitched himself forward and cannoned into the doctor. The doctor went sprawling into the corner, the roll of bandages streaming towards the ceiling. Asher's arm hit the lamp and sent it cartwheeling off the desk and crashing to the carpet. His fingers slid under the rim of the tray and tipped it viciously straight upwards and away from him. The light from the falling lamp lit the cascade of boiling liquid from the enamel bowl as it shot towards Martagon. The liquid struck the unbandaged hand Martagon was still holding out, hitting the raw flesh. Martagon staggered back with a horrible cry of pain.

The man behind Asher hurled himself in Asher's direction. He forgot that Asher was a graduate of the Garden Game. Off-balance, his back to his attacker, Asher spun like an ice-skater, his arm flashing in a circle. The edge of his palm curved up as hard as a discus and cracked the man across the windpipe.

Jenbach, behind Teague's chair, shot off the mark as fast as his own man. His gun was out and he threw himself between the two chairs to obliterate Asher. Teague stuck out his left leg without rising and tripped him. His momentum carried him forward and his skull hit the edge of the desk with a ripe smack. Teague was already dropping off his chair to pin him and finish him in one smooth action.

I wasn't wasting any time, myself. The instant I saw the forward motion of Asher's body I started to move. I flung myself backwards into the man behind, chair and all. We went down together in a heap. He slammed against the book-shelves on the back wall and there was a shower of leather-bound volumes and something hit me a glancing blow on the side of the head. As it met the carpet it bounced against my hand and instinctively I grabbed it and realized it wasn't a book but something square and chunky and I hefted it and flailed at my antagonist. The flames of the fire shone on it as I raised it and brought it down and I saw it was a bronze model of a breech-block and the man's breath was whistling and he went limp and I hammered him twice more and went crawling on hands and knees towards the inner door.

Martagon was screaming. He had collapsed in the leather chair thrusting the raw scalded hand high in the air above his head. Teague was holding Jenbach face down by the hair and swinging his head repeatedly against the front of the massive desk. Asher's knee was jammed across the doctor's chest and he was settling with him in a way I couldn't see because the desk was between us.

I was at the inner door. I gripped the handle and pulled myself up, my fingers slithering because they were sticky. I gripped it harder, not expecting it to turn, wondering how I was going to get the door open. It swung wide as if someone was pulling at it from the far side. I was jerked forward and stumbled headlong into the blackness of the inner office.

THE door slammed behind me. Total darkness. I should have realized Martagon would put men in the inner office.

I stumbled and fell, thrusting out my hands in front of me. My shoulder collided with smooth cold metal.

I rolled sideways, unzipping the anorak, fumbling for the PPK on the string under my shirt. I tore it loose.

There was a fizzing sound and the neon lights came on with blazing intensity. I blinked, levelling the PPK. I was crouched in an awkward position at the foot of a Xerox machine and couldn't focus my eyes. Anyone could have shot me a dozen times before I could regain my feet.

The first thing I saw was the secretary, the girl with the red hair and the fair skin. She was beside the door of the windowless room, her hand on the switch. I looked around, my mind still stupid. The office was empty. She wore a plain dark-blue dress, black pumps, no stockings or make-up. Her face was shocked and frightened.

Behind her was a bank of grey metal filing-cabinets. My wits began to clear. *How was I to get into them—find the papers—and quickly?* We only had a few minutes before the alarm was raised.

I looked wildly at the cabinets. They were full-sized; strong-looking; four drawers apiece. They were secured by an iron safety-bar running through the handles, fastened into a slot at the bottom and padlocked at the top. There was a combination-dial on the top drawer.

My mind started to race . . . throbbing in my shoulder, my ankle . . . Could I use the bar as a lever to wrench open the drawers? . . . Could the three of us pull them over and lay them front down and rip off the plate on the back like stripping a safe? ... I tried to force myself to think coherently ... My heart was beating fast ... the girl was staring in horror at the streaks on the hand that was holding the gun ...

Then I saw that she was holding, tight against her chest, a thick, square, white object.

She suddenly held it out in front of her and walked towards me. She thrust it at me. I raised my hands to take it, almost dropping the gun.

It was a used white envelope, with a block of stamps in one corner, an address-label cancelled with two strokes of a blue pencil. It was a foot long and nine inches wide and packed fat with material and swathed with strips of Scotch tape.

'*Here!* ...' ... breathlessly.

I understood. She nodded.

'I was contacted ... told you were coming ...'

She put out her hand—I could feel it trembling—and pushed my arm, indicating the door.

I smiled, feeling immense gratitude, immense relief, clear-headed again.

I took a pace towards the door, then stopped.

'Laura? ... Laura Verrinder? ...'

She smiled too, in spite of the fear in her eyes.

'Yes—though here I'm Dora Venning ...'

I moved back to her, slid the PPK into the pocket of the anorak, and took her by the shoulder.

'Come on—we'll take you with us.'

She stepped back, shaking her head.

'I'll be all right.'

'Listen—'

'I can still be useful here.'

I hesitated.

'*Please*!' She came forward and touched the envelope.

I was tempted to take her by force. I cursed Harrison for getting a girl like this into this mess ... '*do I have to appeal to your sense of duty, Miss Verrinder?*' ... then realized that if

she'd landed here she'd be well-trained, properly covered . . .
you had to say that for Harrison, damn him . . .

She did an unexpected thing. She stood on tiptoes and
kissed my cheek.

Absurd thoughts . . . skinny schoolgirl with carroty pigtails holding tight to my hand as we circled on the frozen
lake . . . her father emerging from his bedroom as she clung
shrieking to the tea-tray on which I was dragging her down
the corridor . . .

She moved around me to the door, opened it, and
switched off the office lights. In the glow of the room
beyond I could see her auburn head motion me on.

I entered the study. The first thing that struck me was the
silence. Martagon had stopped screaming.

He was sitting in his chair, bandaged hand trailing on the
polished floor. I stepped over to look at him.

The handle of the surgical scissors, the steel bright in the
flames of the fire, protruded from the silk shirt beneath the
breast-bone. His eyes, quite dead, were fixed on the scissors
in surprise. '. . . . *Who could do such a thing to Carl-Conrad
Martagon? . . . as if he'd been nothing more than another vulgar
brawler in the Garden Game? . . .*'

I glanced up at Asher. He leaned against the wall, arms
folded. The light of the fallen desk-lamp struck upwards at
his narrow face, obstinate and severe.

The girl was standing in the doorway, the back of one
hand pressed to her mouth. Her eyes brimmed with fear and
horror.

I straightened, my hand on the arm of Martagon's chair,
glad its back was towards her. I looked at her interrogatively
. . . Surely, with her employer dead, she shouldn't stay at
Blühnbach? . . .

She saw what I meant, flapping with her arm to tell me to
go away. I considered a moment—could I really leave her
there? . . . Then I realized that with Martagon and the others
dead there was no one to connect her with what had

happened. Martagon's colleagues would assume she'd been working late and had hidden in the office while the struggle was going on. They'd probably think it wise to keep her in the organization, make her the secretary of someone like Underwood . . . She was right—she could still be useful.

The arm was flapping more impatiently. She was a very brave and remarkable girl.

I moved towards the door. Asher followed me. Teague opened it, peered out, nodded that the corridor was clear.

I moved out first, fastening my anorak, thrusting the thick envelope down the front of it, zipping it firmly in place.

Oh God, fifteen years, fifteen full years of it . . . and only ten minutes to go . . .

All was quiet as we moved down the corridor and headed for the tunnel. Teague handed me one of the pistols they'd taken from the men we'd left behind—nice solid jobs. He also held up the key he'd removed from Jenbach's pocket.

We went down the ramp and Teague opened the black door. We went through into the courtyard and Teague locked it behind us.

We were conscious of the crunching of our shoes on the coarse sand of the paths. Even with our rubber soles it sounded loud. I realized what a good tracker a man would have to be to take part in the Garden Game. Asher, in fact, seemed to be making no noise at all, compared with Teague and me; he padded along silently, leading the way. He moved without hesitation, weaving left or right, taking this fork or that. We followed behind him, keeping an interval of a dozen feet between us. It was easy to see he had walked the course before—had successfully fought over it.

Now we were glad there was nothing but moonlight in the courtyard. The fatty scents of the plants were overpowering in the thin beams that trickled through the splayed and swollen leaves. We kept to the path to avoid the knotted roots and knife-edged leaves that in places stuck out over the border.

It seemed to take an eternity to traverse this gravid forest . . . Chiapas . . . Gautemala . . . Zaïre . . . *and here were forests ancient as the hills . . .*

My flesh beneath the quilted anorak was coated with sweat. A flabby blossom brushed my face, its petals the colour of a corpse, releasing a fungoid and powdery perfume.

205

I was in the middle, hugging the envelope. I don't know how much of the garden we had crossed when we heard voices behind us. There was a snapping, rending sound, as if the black door was being forced, then a babel of shouts and orders. I don't know what the others felt, but I was seized with a sudden horror of being trapped in this courtyard, in these grotesque surroundings. The sense of being enclosed by the jungle intensified. I felt a taste of vomit in the back of the throat. This must have been the feeling that crept over the players in the Garden Game when the full realization of their situation swept over them and they knew there was no turning back: they must strike and kill in this place, or else die in it.

Our twistings and turnings became more rapid. We exchanged our first shots as we were emerging from the fringe of trees and bushes and saw the second black door ahead of us. Asher and I loosed off a couple of rounds at the shadows loping through the quivering fronds while Teague thrust Jenbach's key in the lock. A few random bullets hummed like wasps out of the shrouded foliage and struck the pock-marked granite above our heads.

Again Teague locked the door behind us, slamming it. We scuttled along the ascending ramp towards the cloister. My shoulder still felt sore after the fall in the office, and my ankle was so weak I tottered rather than ran. All the same, whenever we reached one of the naked bulbs that lit the corridor I pushed up off my good leg and jumped high to smash the bulb with the butt of my pistol, holding the envelope firm against my body with the other hand. I actually felt a lightening of the heart at the thought that at least we weren't going to be hunted down and killed in that hideous Garden.

I'd gone leap-frogging almost the whole length of the corridor before there was another crash as the locked door burst open. Again random bullets sang along the corridor as our antagonists fired at the retreating circle of light.

The cold struck us as we emerged into the open cloister. It brought water to our eyes and seared our lungs. Then we were running beneath the snapping jaws and bulging eyes of the heraldic beasts. On our right stretched the pine trees, motionless under the moon as if the whole forest landscape was caught in a spell. Their stark lines were a clean contrast with the tropical turmoil in the courtyard below.

In spite of my ankle I raced along step for step with the other two, the air rasping my throat. Our faces in the moonlight were chalk-white.

We must have been gaining on our pursuers. As I put my hand on the iron bannister leading down to the outer courtyard and the Mercedes, I felt a swell of hope. A hundred yards to go.

Asher ran down the stairs ahead of me. I was close on his heels, bounding down behind him, praying no one was lying in wait for us in the courtyard because we were so bunched together. We had got halfway when Asher glanced around for a second, missed his footing, and went crashing down the remainder of the flight. His body whirled over and over, striking the stone balustrade and inner wall with sickening thuds.

I saw the dark bulk thrashing at my feet but couldn't stop because of my own speed and because Teague was right behind me. Asher was only a few steps from the bottom and I jumped the remaining distance over his tumbling body. I cleared him and came down hard, and some part of him hit me on the back of the legs and knocked me flying. I tried to get up and found my ankle had gone and set myself to crawl the remaining distance to the Mercedes.

I left Asher to Teague. I hoped to God he hadn't broken his neck. There were echoing shouts in the cloister above and answering cries from the direction of the main gate.

I reached the car on hands and knees. Teague was dragging Asher towards me. I could see Asher's arms and legs moving in the moonlight, bright as day, and realized he was conscious. I had already torn off my right shoe and was rummaging for the car-keys, of which Teague and I carried the hidden spares. My fingers were stiff and mutinous from the abrupt exposure to the cold. For a second I couldn't find the key. Then it was in my hand. Kneeling upright, I tried to thrust it into the lock. It was frozen. I put my lips on the handle and breathed on it. Teague crashed down beside me in the shelter of the car, pulling Asher after him. He leaned out beyond the rear wheels, gripping his right wrist with his left hand, and fired at the top of the staircase. He must have found a target. There were sounds of hurried withdrawal.

The key went into the lock. I opened the lee-side door of the car and dived at the floor of the back seat. I tore up the carpet and the thin sheet of metal beneath it. Shots hit the window above me and showered me with glass, and others were hitting the body of the car with a deep socking sound. The interior of the car was dark, and I had to work by touch, but it was easy to find what I was looking for. While Teague aimed more shots at the starlit square at the top of the stairway, I threw aside the junk on top of the carpet and snatched the Lambdas out of their hiding-place. I pitched them on the ice-slick cobblestones behind me, where they rattled and sent up sparks, and went on groping for the grenades and spare magazines.

Teague had to stop watching the stairs while we slung the guns round our necks and rammed grenades and magazines in our pockets. Asher was only half-conscious, so Teague slung a second gun round his neck too. There was a vicious burst of fire from the top of the stairs as our pursuers took advantage of the lull and started crowding down. At the same time someone began to fire at us from the direction of the main gate, thirty yards behind and at an angle to our left.

The men at the gate and the men on the stairs were firing blind at the car, trying for a lucky shot. We couldn't stay where we were. Teague poked his Lambda out behind the rear of the car and I poked mine out beyond the radiator and we each squeezed off a long burst. Teague evidently found the spot, as there were cries from men who were hit and the thumps of bodies hitting the ground and as others dived for cover. The fact that we now had Lambdas must have come as a nasty shock. I squirmed round and sent a spray of bullets in the direction of the main gate and the gatehouse, and was answered for my pains by a stream of revolver or rifle shots that shattered the headlights and what was left of the windshield. There was a rubbery smell as air spewed out of the near-side tyre. My right hand and arm were suddenly soaked with warm liquid, and I thought I was wounded before I realized water was pouring out of the punctured radiator. I hastily crawled back a couple of feet. The men in the gatehouse were well protected and well armed.

I really wasn't enjoying this. I wondered if I ever had.

I could feel the cold cobbles through my anorak. I banged in a fresh magazine. Teague was holding off the men around the stairs; they wouldn't rush us till we made our move for the gate. We could hear them groaning and bellowing. The men at the gate were waiting for us to come to them: which we would have to do. Any plans we had previously worked out about using the car to crash the gate, or give us cover till we got it open, had to be abandoned. At any moment a shot would hit the gas tank and we'd be burned alive, or picked off as we ran like rabbits in the resulting glare.

We'd got to make a dash for it, in the open. After a couple of gruff words to Teague, I stood up and left the shelter of the car and pelted towards the main gate, bending double, sweeping bullets at the gate and gatehouse. After six paces I went down and thought I'd been shot, then knew it was my ankle that had given way. It was just as well it did: a bullet went past my head in the spot where my skull had been an instant before, and another corkscrewed through the padding of my anorak at my hip.

I kept firing, somehow managed to get up, limping on slowly.

When you're in a battle, you never know if you're winning or losing. One moment you think you're on top—the next you're sure you're beaten. The thing changes from second to second. It was like that now—when we opened up with the Lambdas I felt we were home and free—a couple of minutes later I thought it was all up . . .

Teague . . . Asher . . . I had a curious leap in time to a year and a half ago, and was suddenly doubling towards the gate at Kabassa in the African night . . . —stupidly charging into the jaws of disaster . . .

Last assignment . . . and I was making another hopeless mess of it . . . *Maggie . . . time to retire . . .*

And like most battles, in the end the outcome hinges on something insignificant in itself, but which has colossal consequences . . . something no one involved in can possibly foresee. In our case it happened that someone in the gate-house had left the wicket-gate in the main gate open—either because it hadn't been closed after we first entered, or because somebody opened it to let in guards who were outside when the hullaballoo in the courtyard broke out.

Anyway, all at once the lights in the courtyard were switched on and the whole place was bathed in a sudden high shadowless light. But that worked both ways—the instant the men in the gatehouse started potting at me I swivelled and gave their door and windows a longer and more accurate burst than I was able to do by moonlight. The windows crashed around their ears, and at the same time I saw I was close enough to use a grenade, fished one out of my pocket, blew on my fingers, pulled the pin and lobbed it through the doorway, plunging forward on my face in the same moment. I heard a hoarse yell inside and there was a pause that stretched like a stubborn piece of elastic and then it snapped and there was a wave of sound and light that billowed out like an earthquake.

A second later there was another detonation behind me. Hugging the cobblestones, I craned around to see that

Teague had treated the men round the staircase to a dose of the same medicine. Debris was streaming up in black fragments against a screen of flames. Teague himself stumbled forward in the glare. He was halfway between the wrecked Mercedes and where I lay, a few yards from the gate. He had an arm round Asher, who flopped along like a drunken man. Where Asher's nose should have been was a stain as if someone had hit him smack in the face with a plate of strawberries. The fall downstairs had splattered his lips and teeth and nose.

Now. I twisted my head back towards the gate. *Now.* I saw the small square glimmering in one of the great studded double-doors. *Now.* I shouted to Teague as he came down in a heap beside me, Lambdas grating on the stones beneath the big body, dragging Asher down with him. *Now.* In the smoke and glare and confusion I propelled myself at the wicket-gate. *Now.* I reached it, saw there was a two-foot strip of wood across the foot of it, tried to lift my leg to clear it, felt my ankle collapse, and went crashing backwards over it on to the roadway beyond. *Now.* Lying there with the wind knocked out of me, Teague and Asher came crunching down in a bundle on top of me.

We were in a helpless condition. We lay there stunned. If our enemies had been in a state to follow us to the gate, they'd have found us lying like a bunch of boobies at their feet. They could have finished us off with three shots. As it was, they were in a worse state than we were, and it took them several stunned minutes to get their bearings.

By that time we were on our feet and reeling down the causeway towards the spot where Teague had parked the second Mercedes.

Asher kept slipping and falling on the rutted ice. It was all we could do to haul him up. We were like punch-drunk fighters. We wrapped our arms around each other's shoulders and lurched along like boozers careening home from the pub along a moonlit country road.

It was only when we reached the car, and Teague was

groping behind the fender for the place where he'd taped a spare key, that I realized I'd only got one shoe on. And it was only then that I remembered the envelope zipped inside my anorak. With a sense of panic I fumbled for it.

It was still there.

As I was lowering my bruised body on to the cushions beside Teague, I paused and looked back. We'd stretched Asher across the rear seat. From the distant courtyard a spiral of fire curled upwards towards the stars. The open wicket-gate was a crimson oblong against the black square of the gate.

I was slamming the door, and Teague was pressing the starter, when from close at hand, among the pines, rang the scream of a peacock. Exhausted as we were, we stiffened. Asher lifted himself on his elbow.

I was tempted to climb out of the car and throw a hand-grenade at the damned thing.

Then I let my body go limp. Thank God, I was past all that.